YO-DBR-248

To Norma and Ken,

I have no doubt God made you our most appreciated neighbors. May He bless you two as you've blessed us.

Rob Mc Creery

(AKA - Joseph Scot)

Flight of the Caroline

Flight of the Caroline

Joseph Scot

Quartz Hill Publishing House
Publishing arm of Quartz Hill School of Theology
Quartz Hill, California

Copyright © 2017 by Joseph Scot
All Rights Reserved
Printed in the United States of America
Cover design by R.P. Nettelhorst

ISBN: 978-1-365-29151-7

Quartz Hill Publishing House
43543 51st Street West · Quartz Hill, CA 93536
www.theology.edu
info@theology.edu

Chapter One

Marner Bay, southern California coast
8:30 PM, June 20th, 1923

" "There goes Zelda!"

Carrie MacGregor heard the distant male voice and looked up just in time to see a woman in an Egyptian headband Charleston off the end of the high dive and into the pool. But the eldest heir to the Van Burean estate just sighed and diverted her attention more inward. This party held very little interest for her. Tonight, she had more serious subjects with which to grapple.

For the last hour, the twenty-eight-year-old had sat, hidden in the evening shadow of a well-manicured oak tree, trying to decide who and what she was—Christian or not, wife or not. But the questions had proved themselves too big, too complex and overwhelmed her again as they had every day for the last month. So she gave up the struggle, for the moment, and leaned back against the cool, cast iron bench that had adorned that same small portion of her family's property for the last two decades. *Might as well just watch this insane circus for a while,* she confessed to herself. *Anything's better than simply going round and round in my mind. I'll try to think it all through again later.*

Carrie shifted for a better view through a break in the honeysuckle, and shook her head at the soggy high diving flapper who now dogpaddled to the pool's far edge. *Another drunk!* It seemed almost all the guests were intoxicated or soon would be. She could not comprehend why most of her old friends were drinking like sailors on liberty. *They didn't do that before the war. Why now?* On the tail of these thoughts, her conscience reached out and gave her a thump. *There you go again, being judgmental! Nine years a believer and you still can't get that right!*

1

Carrie had retreated after dinner to the little alcove she now occupied. The Robbers' Roost. That's what she had called it for as far back as she could remember. Hidden from the rest of her father's estate behind a vine-choked trellis, it had often proven itself the perfect refuge. As a child, she would escape to its sanctum whenever she wished to go unnoticed. That's the way she felt right now—wishing to escape this particular celebration…and go unnoticed. That's why she had returned to indulge the roost's invisibility for the first time in fourteen years.

Out at the party, the high-diving Charleston woman, not sober enough to negotiate the pool's chrome ladder, remained in the water. She squealed twice for male assistance, and, as a reward, soon found herself lifted up onto the relative dryness of the patio tiles. Soon after, as if making an effort to top the last act, a fully-dressed hand-holding couple climbed up the high dive tower and took the same daredevil plunge, sending a chlorine spray over a poolside group that had been bouncing in their deck chairs to the hot jazz band's syncopated rhythm. Carrie emitted a small gasped and waited for the victims' inevitable outcry of indignation. But none came. Most of the soaked bystanders simply chose to applaud the mad divers rather than appear as spoiled-sports.

Carrie let go a tiny laugh. *Lunacy!* This was the kindest thought she could muster. *Sheer lunacy!*

"Here she is, Albert." Carrie's mother swept through the trellis archway with the sleeves of her vaguely Chinese gown waving like butterfly wings. "Hiding in her little rabbit hole, just as I said." She wore a straight black, China Doll theatrical wig and drew smoke from a foot-long, silver cigarette holder. After a moment's pause, she expelled the smoke with an exaggerated exhale and negotiated a generous sip of contraband champagne from a long-stemmed crystal glass.

2

Carrie sighed and said. "I was not hiding." She crossed her arms and seated herself more squarely on the bench. Carrie had long ago grown used to her mother's dramatics. *How else would an ex-stage performer behave?* she thought. But she said, "I'm simply not yet ready to become part of all this." Her last words were as much sighed as spoken, and she waved a careless hand in the general direction of the party.

"Am I to understand that you do not approve of this celebration?" Carrie's father, Albert, stepped into the alcove, careful not to rub his tuxedo against the vines or spill his brandy.

Carrie shook her head. "I don't approve when so many of the guests are drunk."

"You're opposed to drinking?" Albert feigned astonishment. "Candice, my dear, did you hear your daughter?"

Candice responded after exhibiting a tolerant smirk. "Caroline, don't lecture your father."

"I am not lecturing, Mother. I am simply responding, and when will you begin calling me Carrie? Almost no one calls me Caroline anymore."

"It's the more dignified form of your name; I prefer it." Candice made an unpleasant face. "Carrie sounds so much like what one would call a maid." She increased the sourness of her expression. "Carrie indeed."

"I like it." Carrie kept her tone even. "It's simple and has an honest sound." She paused. "And it's what my friends call me."

Candice returned the even tone and added a patient smile. "Do you mean your farm-friends at that little church?"

"Some of them, yes."

"Well, I'm not your friend. I'm your mother." Candice's pleasant expression sagged a bit. "*Caroline* you were born, and *Caroline* you'll stay as far as I'm

3

concerned. If you want to be called Carrie, you'll have to go find a farmer to do the honors."

Carrie decided to sidestep the unwinable argument. Instead she turned back to her father and continued the previous conversation undaunted. "I'm *opposed* to *drunkenness*, especially on a scale like this." She indicated the party again. "I don't understand, Father."

Albert settled down onto the bench next to his daughter. "And what exactly is it you don't understand, my dear?" He gave his well-barbered, reddish-brown hair a two-fingered smoothing, his pencil mustache twitching as he worked. "Go ahead," he said, his voice sporting its usual timber, balancing somewhere between boredom and a subdued expression of superiority. "I'm listening."

Carrie felt the cool sarcasm of her father's demeanor, but ignored it. "I don't understand why you permit such behavior. Before prohibition, you would have simply shown the door to people who could not control themselves."

Albert attached an expensive cigarette to his own small silver holder and lit the well-packed tobacco at the end. After playing the gentleman and exhaling smoke well away from his daughter's face, he leaned back as much as dignity would allow and cleared his throat. "I suspect you see public drunkenness as a sign of moral disintegration." He raised his snifter and took a small sip of brandy. "Well, from a certain point of view, that may be an accurate assessment." He paused to flick a tiny newborn ash to the ground. "However, even though we are the official party hosts, your mother and I do not consider ourselves people of low character."

Carrie opened her mouth to protest, but Albert raised a preemptive hand for silence.

"Neither, as you know," he said, "are we particularly religious or temperate. Like many of our class since the end of the Great War, we've merely become people of the times."

"People of the times?" Carrie shrugged. "What do you mean?"

Albert turned to his wife. "What do I mean, Candice?"

Tearing her attention from the distant party, Carrie's mother took another sip of bubbly. "Oh. Well, let me see. How to put this." She extracted the cigarette butt from its long holder and pressed it into a sand-filled, Greek urn. "Ever since liquor's become illegal, simply everyone seems to have decided they desperately wish to drink. Sadly, some of them do not seem to know their limit." She flung her hand up in a pantomime of surrender.

Albert leaned forward with just the hint of a small groan escaping from deep within. "To distance ourselves from all this, to hold ourselves aloof from the present turn of events would mean we would have to reject most of our friends." He rose from the bench and faced his daughter. "In other words, we would have to reject everyone who is anyone."

"Social suicide." Candice shook her head. "As I've always told you, a happy life comes from the friends one cultivates. To be happy, one must keep friends happy. The rest will take care of itself." She punctuated her statement with a nod.

Carrie did not respond but felt a pang of pity. Once she had believed much the same thing. *You are indeed trapped, Mother, but you don't even know it.* She almost wanted to argue with them, but understood it would be futile. One thing was certain, however. Carrie had changed much since the days when she lived here. Things like social standing were not so important to her anymore. Her parents knew of her change in attitude and had pronounced it foolish at best.

Albert finished his brandy and went to the alcove's entrance where he hailed one of the servants. He handed the man his empty snifter and engaged him in conversation.

After a few seconds, he turned to Carrie's mother. "Candice, we need your expertise. We seem to be on the verge of a shrimp crisis." He motioned her over, and she complied with a stately glide.

"Indeed not," Carrie heard her say. "Tell Rodrigo, if they're not fresh as can be, send them back and order more elsewhere. That is absolutely my final word on the subject."

The servant nodded but spoke again in a subdued tone. Albert's eyebrows shot up as he listened. "Well, by jingo!" He pounded a fist into his palm. "Why in thunder didn't he deliver the full twelve cases?"

Carrie changed her position on the bench and crossed her legs, not yet feeling inclined to leave her childhood hideout. In those younger days, she'd fled there mostly because she'd felt awkward amongst the hoards of handsome, imposing guests that continually passed through the estate. She feared they would laugh at her gawky feet and spindly legs, or, even worse, ignore her.

But that gangly child was gone now. And the woman who had taken her place soon became one of the most sought after debutantes on the South Coast. Carrie smoothed her exclusively designed shimmy dress down over a very attractive adult figure and primped a lock of brunette hair back into place. She smiled at the memory of formal balls and cotillions that had occupied her teen years, and she let that mood linger a moment before allowing it to drift away.

Albert's voice rose again. "Good, then. That's an end to it. But I want him to see to it personally." The servant nodded again, and Carrie's father dismissed him with a half-wave. "Very well, tell him now." He returned to the alcove and spoke to his wife over his shoulder. "I think that should settle things in the kitchen for the night."

Candice followed and answered without enthusiasm. "I certainly hope so. It was all becoming quite tedious."

"So, my dear," Albert again addressed his daughter. "I take it from your dark expression that, all in all, you do not approve of your little party."

Carrie felt a fleck of indignation. "It's not *my* party, Father."

Candice chimed in with a wounded tone. "Why, how can you say that? You *know* we're giving it for you. Of course it's your party! If you're going to resume your rightful place in Marner Bay's social circle, you must, of course, be properly welcomed back."

Carrie's indignant spark, fanned by her mother's words, now blossomed into a small flame. "Mother, I am still a married woman!"

Candice's face tightened. "Only in the most technical sense of the term."

Albert removed a bit of lint from his lapel. "Yes, and I was under the distinct impression that your moving back home more or less spelled the death knell of that most unfortunate union." He took a pull from his cigarette.

Carrie stood. "That may or may not be. But either way, at this time, I do not yet look upon myself as *single!*"

"Caroline, dear." Candice finished the last of her champagne and set the glass down onto the paving stones. "You cannot be serious. Why, we've already announced your return to the social calendar. It's being run in all the society columns."

Carrie's response came out a little louder than a whisper. "You should have asked me first."

"Why?" Albert removed the smoldering cigarette butt from its holder and shoved the dying tobacco into the sand urn. "You would have merely made the same emotional protest we're listening to now." He blew through the holder and placed it back into his inside coat pocket. "Sometimes, Caroline, a parent must act in a child's best interest, even if that child does not understand."

"I'm not a child!"

"That's debatable at best," Albert said. But, after a moment's hesitation, he sighed and put his hands into his pants pockets. "I'm sorry. That was unfair. However, you must admit this sojourn amongst the common people has not been one of your better ideas." He raised his eyebrows and almost smiled.

Carrie remained silent.

Albert cleared his throat. "I see. You think you still love this gypsy husband of yours."

Carrie maintained her silence a little longer. There it was, the most important question in her life right now. Did she still love Jack? Even though he'd abandoned her, even though he'd abandoned his sons, did she still love him? Carrie thought she might know the answer. *Yes. Maybe. Possibly.* But it made her angry even to confess this state of semi-confusion to herself. It made her feel weak, victim-like, and she wasn't raised to be a victim.

"I really can't say right now," she replied and plucked a honeysuckle blossom from its stem.

"You'll cheer up once you've mingled a little." Candice patted Carrie's arm with a light hand. "We've invited *all* the truly interesting people and the *most* promising bachelors. I have no doubt you'll have a good time, if you'll just come out of hiding for a little while."

Carrie pulled the blossom apart and was tempted to taste its nectar. Instead, she tossed the flower off into the shadows. "All these things are for an emerging debutante, not a mother of two young boys." Impatience tugged at the corners of her polite resolve. Her parents had been trying to steer her toward divorce from the moment she arrived. All it had accomplished, though, was to make her more defensive of her married status.

Carrie had no intentions of acting the available woman tonight, but there would be no peace if she spoke the truth on that subject now. So she said, "Look, if you'll just give me a little time to gather my thoughts, I promise I will come out and mingle." She turned her palms upward. "Is that acceptable?"

Candice returned the gesture. "Well, I suppose it will simply have to do. But, don't take too long gathering those thoughts. Your father's been trying to do that for years without much success." She sent a half-smile Albert's way and started to leave, but stopped. "I know you may not think so, but I *am* attempting to do what's best for you. It's the way I show love, Caroline." Candice glanced down for an instant. "It's all I can do." Then she passed through the trellis arch and out into the party.

"Why, thank you, My Heart," Albert called after her before she could cruise beyond earshot. Then he turned back to his daughter. "Gather my thoughts, indeed." He produced what appeared to be a genuine smile, and his face took on a more relaxed expression. "I think that's adequate grounds for divorce or some such thing. Drat though, there's never an attorney around when you need one." Albert straightened the sleeves of his tux. "Your mother's absolutely correct, you know. She and I both," Albert paused and the smile left him, "are thinking only of your ultimate welfare in whatever we do for you. You are still my only daughter, and I am quite fond of you." He allowed himself another brief smile and sighed a tired sigh. "Don't stay here too long now," he said, then he too disappeared out into the celebration.

Carrie sat back down on the iron bench. Then she leaned forward and pulled aside a cluster of leaves to get a better view of what was happening outside the alcove. Still not ready to join the party, she discovered, however, that she was, in fact, just a little curious about its goings-on. It had been a long time since she'd attended any such event, and it seemed obvious now that much had changed, in a social sense, since the war.

Beyond Robbers' Roost, the party proper looked to be a crowded affair that stretched from the glass-walled ballroom of her family's Georgian-style mansion past the pool and patio area, and out to the stone-railed walk near the cliffs that hung above the Pacific. The busy scene reminded Carrie of ants – the way they cover a picnic sandwich dropped on the ground, each little creature concentrating on its own business, yet still remaining a part of the swarm.

At the deep end of the huge Roman pool, the high-diving couple that had earlier made the big splash, refused all offers to help them from the water, preferring to swim around in their formal wear. Carrie watched but remained loyal to her vow to curb her judgments.

After a while, a betuxed young man, with an overly rouged woman attached to his arm, wandered up the path away from the electric patio lights and sat on the polished marble bench just in front of Robbers' Roost. Less than four feet away from the unseen Carrie, the man gazed at the crowd while his partner adjusted the hem of her pink sack-dress and pulled up her turned down hose. Recognizing *him* as the youngest son of one of the poorer rich families of Marner Bay, Carrie placed the *girl* as someone who worked for an exclusive local florist.

"So who was that going into the water before?" The young man reached into an inside coat pocket and produced a cigarette case.

The woman looked off toward the soggy couple finally being assisted from the pool. "I don't know the girl, but the boy is Rolland Gladstone. He buys a lot of orchids. I think his family owns oil or ships or something." She sighed then laced her fingers together. "He's such a *sheik*!"

Carrie rolled her eyes in the darkness. *Not the brightest penny in the purse, are you, my dear.*

The young man shook the mooning female off his arm. "Say, maybe you'd just better decide whose sheba you are. You know, there are lots of other shop girls that would like very much to be at this shindig." He tapped a Gasper on the lid of its silver case before he put the tailor-made cigarette between his lips and ignited it with the case's matching lighter. "I don't have to put up with any banana oil from you."

Why you obnoxious little rat! Carrie held a carefully muffled breath and concentrated hard on all the Christian reasons why she should not grab this man-boy from behind and pull him backward off the bench.

He took a stylish drag and let the smoke go with an upturned face. "You know, I think old Dr. Freud would love you."

"What?" The shop girl sounded confused.

"You've got a complex. Don't know how to take care of a man—all closed off."

Carrie put her hands over her mouth and tried to keep herself from setting the rat straight. *Well, one of you has a complex, anyway!*

"I'm sorry." Now, the shop girl sounded both confused *and* dejected. She was silent for a moment, then gingerly draped herself onto the rat's arm again. "You're the only sheik for me, Donny. You're all I want."

He blew some more smoke before he patted her hand. "That's good. Just don't forget it."

"I won't." The girl punctuated her answer with a snuggle. "We're not gate-crashing, are we, Donny? I mean, you were invited, weren't you?"

He chuckled his condescension. "Of course, I was invited."

And it will be the last time, if I have anything to do with it! Squirming on her bench, Carrie could feel her tolerance for this rodent dwindle.

"Well," the shop girl said, "who's this party for? I mean, you said it was some kind of a coming back party. I don't even know what that is. Is it like a coming-out party or what?"

The band finished its Charleston with the usual flourish and, after a brief silence, started up with the Shimmy. But they played louder than before, making Carrie's eavesdropping a little more difficult.

The mostly-pink shop girl on the marble bench began to bounce and writhe with the rhythm of the music. Donny flicked his cigarette off into the Van Bureans' honeysuckle. "What did you say?" He only now seemed to realize pink girl had spoken.

She appeared little more than slightly hurt as if she were used to being ignored. "I said, who's the party for?"

He folded his arms and sighed the sigh of one explaining something unimportant to a child. "It's for Caroline Van Burean. This is her father's estate."

"This place is a palace." Pinkie squeezed Donny's arm and giggled. "He must be very rich!"

A small but familiar pang of sadness settled on Carrie's heart. She wanted to tell this girl the money caused as many problems as it solved, but she knew that would do no good. The wealth was probably all Pinkie could see.

After another long, rude delay, Donny turned toward his date. "Is he rich, you say?" For an instant, his cream-oiled, patent leather hair caught the lights of the party. "Very rich, indeed." He produced a flask, the color of his cigarette case, took a drink, and replaced the vessel back into his inside jacket pocket without offering any to his companion. "He's the youngest of four brothers from a New York Dutch, diamond brokerage family. They've been busy compounding one fortune upon another since the seventeenth century. Albert—"

"Who?" Pinkie interrupted.

Donny's exasperated sigh erupted again. "The father, my dim little flower. He's been placed in charge of the family's West Coast Jewelry stores. I'm sure you know the ones. Caroline's Jewelers?"

Pinkie's voice indicated a light switching on somewhere. "Ooooooh! Caroline's."

"Yes." Donny raised a thin index finger to his face and smoothed the faint upper lip caterpillar that remotely resembled a mustache. "Albert named the stores after his daughter." He raised his eyebrows in an expression of mock sympathy. "Doesn't that just pull at the old heartstrings?" He doubled up a diminutive fist and lightly pounded it over the general area of his heart.

Pinkie took a defensive tone. "Yeah, Donny. I think that's swell. She must be a real sweet kid for her daddy to do that for her."

Donny shook his head. "If you knew Carrie the way I do, you wouldn't say that." He stole some cream oil from his hair and stroked it onto the struggling mustache. "She's an over-aged, spoiled brat."

"Who's Carrie?" Pinkie stretched with a yawn.

Donny smirked. "Carrie is Caroline. She only allows—"

"My friends!" Carrie could take no more. She stepped out of the dark, through the trellis arch, and placed herself in front of the speechless boy before he had time to regain his breath. She glanced back to a shocked Pinkie. "I only allow *my friends* to call me Carrie." She focused her attention back on Donny. "And that doesn't seem to include you tonight, does it, Donny Dimples?" Carrie smiled a little wicked smile after speaking the rat's childhood nickname. Then she pinched his cheek and withdrew her hand like a cobra pulling back from a strike.

Donny swiped a tardy defensive fist through empty air, then sucked in a fast breath. "Don't call me that!" His impotent response dissipated into the darkness.

Having saved up her frustration for several minutes, Carrie was not inclined to break off the attack just yet, even though she already felt the subtle gnaw at her conscience. "You think yourself quite a ladies' man, don't you,

Dimples?" She reached for his cheek again, but he shied away.

He sniffed once and tried to set a trembling jaw. "You can't talk to me like that; I'm not six years old anymore!" Then he slumped, glanced at Pinkie then turned quickly back to Carrie.

"That's right." Carrie crossed her arms and stepped back so she could see both their faces at the same time. "You're *not* six anymore." She felt a sly smile creep across her lips. "You're eleven years older now, aren't you?" Carrie focused her gaze upon the pink lady to drive in the meaning of her words.

As if on cue, Pinkie's mouth dropped open. "He's only seventeen?" She swung around to Donny. "You're only seventeen? You said you were –" She did a quick, silent, lip-moving calculation. "Oh, my gosh! You're five years younger than me! I'm out with somebody's kid!" She shot up from the bench, as if it were a hot grill, and whirled off toward the patio. "Seventeen! I'm so *stupid*!"

Donny stood up. "Genie, wait!"

Pink Genie never slowed, but turned about, walking backward with a daredevil stride, to deliver a final salvo into jailbait Donny's ego. "And if you think I'm gonna' carry a torch for you... you... you little drugstore cowboy, you got another thing coming!" She swiveled back around just in time to avoid a waiter with a tray full of champagne. "Oh! Excuse me, I'm sure." Then, she too disappeared into the bowels of the party.

That's when livid Donny turned to face the cause of his humiliation. "Caroline...I'll make you sorry for this!"

Carrie was calm but firm. "Run home, Donald. You need some time to grow up."

"We'll see, Carrie!" Donny sputtered as he turned away and quick-stepped down the garden walkway.

"Mrs. MacGregor to you," she said more to herself than to the boy who had already moved almost beyond hearing.

She watched him evaporate into the greater mass of guests, then she turned toward the bandstand. The all-white band still dispensed hot jazz, but now the *Black Bottom* had replaced the *Shimmy*, picking up the tempo. Carrie took a deep breath and walked toward the sound. *Well, I'm out of the roost now.* She smiled. *Might as well join the ants.*

She walked down the flagstone path that led to the raised patio near the pool. Then Carrie thought she heard someone call her name. She stopped at the edge of the mob and strained to filter out the background of trumpet and trombone. *Nothing.* The *Black Bottom* drowned out everything. Then, when Carrie was about to head for the house to rest her feet and check on her children, she heard it again. "Miss Caroline." Carrie half spun around, but could not even identify the gender of the voice amidst the party cacophony, let alone spot its owner.

"Was that you?" she asked a thin, red headed young man in a yacht club blazer. She had known him from college a thousand years before, but the blazer looked newer than that.

"What?" he answered, but kept his gaze on a sleek, undulating flapper whose very short dress got even shorter every time she waved her hands in the air. "What was that you said?" He raised one eyebrow.

"Nothing." Carrie searched the pool area for a familiar face as the jazz seemed to grow even louder. "I simply thought I'd heard someone calling me."

The man leaned a little more her direction, but never looked away from the dancer. "What?"

She placed her mouth near his ear and spoke a little softer than a yell. "Nothing! Never mind!"

He nodded with athletic zeal, but Carrie wasn't sure if he was responding to her or merely keeping time with the

15

music. The tempo of the nod and the *Black Bottom* appeared to be one in the same.

Making her way around the open-air dance floor to the house, she stopped for a moment and gazed inward through one of the ballroom's twenty beveled glass doors. As usual, a small crowd milled about within. South Coast summer etiquette dictated that dancing be done under the stars, but many preferred to mingle indoors, safe from the evening's Pacific breeze. As a result, the indoor party was almost as populous as the one outside. *The older, richer guests always gravitate to the ballroom.* Carrie smiled. These were mostly her *parents'* friends, people she had known all her life, but on a more distant basis than her own crowd.

"Champagne, Miss?" A tall caterer's waiter suddenly stood behind her with a hovering silver tray of illegal giggle water.

Answering with a polite shake of the head, she once again brought her attention back to the ballroom where no one would actually dance until October when fall would bring its onshore storms. Shoulder-to-shoulder classical mirrors lined three sides of the great entertainment hall, giving the illusion of endlessness, as if an infinite number of connecting ballrooms stretched out in two directions to their vanishing point. This optical trick used to fascinate Carrie when she was seven or so. Now, she thought of it as a metaphor for the upper class life she had lived before her marriage. *That life* had *also* been, for the most part, a deception just like that of the never-ending ballroom, full of tricks and false images, meant to hide numerous realities that almost always lay just beneath the surface of the illusion. *My life then was a lie,* she thought, *just like these mirrors.* But, liars or not, the mirrors were still beautiful, and the fantasy image they portrayed, addicting.

The bandleader's voice pushed a rendition of "Ain't We Got Fun" through a megaphone and roused Carrie from her musings. She smiled at her weakness for the mirrors' spell. *Women are always going to be drawn to pretty things. Being saved doesn't seem to change that very much.*

The lyrics of the song now being sung were well known and catchy. Soon almost everyone within earshot of the band was singing along—that is everyone but Carrie. On the contrary, the words of this song with its inferences that love trumps money always reminded her of the early years of her marriage. And she soon found her attention slipping away from the here-and-now and back into old memories of that time. Like the image of a handsome windblown husband-to-be, Jack, at Newport Beach before the war. Young and handsome, in a rugged fashion, with an expression that seemed to dare life to throw danger his way. That picture flickered in her mind's eye for an instant, then evaporated.

In the middle of this musing, Carrie's confession about the temptation of pretty things drifted back into her consciousness and demanded attention. *That's nothing of consequence. Why are you thinking about that? Stop it!* But something about it bothered her. How much did she like the trappings of luxury? Had she liked them enough to affect her marriage? Had it influenced her decision to return to her father's estate? She shook her head as the accusations rose to the surface. *No! I'm here because my husband abandoned his family. He left me no choice!*

The band singer aimed the megaphone back and forth across the crowd with practiced skill, making sure that every portion of the patio received an equal dose of his muffled, honey-sweet tones. As she listened, Carrie's fleeting-memory-cinema began to flicker again. And this time, it included herself and a grime-faced Jack sharing a sandwich on the running-board of his dirt-track racecar—someplace in Indiana—again, before the war. Jack's goggles sat perched on the top of his head, revealing clean whitish circles around his eyes. They had pretended to fight over their ham-and-cheese feast and between bites had laughed about some now long forgotten shared secret.

Then all at once something in the real world caught Carrie's attention from across the ballroom, short-circuiting her revelry in the past and pulling her back to the present. This intruding distraction took the form of a dark haired, statuesque – at least five foot seven – woman in an expensive looking fringe-hemmed frock that cut her just above the knees. Her hair had been bobbed in a boyish Garconne cut with as many spit curls plastered around her face as fashion would allow—an austere haughty expression dominated her face, just the kind of person one would expect to see among the Jazz Age elite of Marner Bay. The woman raised a delicate finger in an aristocratic wave, and the natural patrician grace of the motion gave Carrie the impression that the creature she saw exemplified the upper class as much as anyone else she had seen tonight.

Then one of the older Vanderbilt cousins noticed Albert Van Burean's daughter studying her own reflection in the mirrored east wall. He lifted his glass to her and broke the trance. Carrie quickly dropped her gaze and tingled with humiliation. The stylish woman she'd seen was, of course, herself, but at the moment, that confession was not a pleasant one.

She whirled away from the glass wall and sought some solace in observing the guests. Swimmers—most *not* in formal eveningwear—occupied all parts of the pool, while other guests—most fully dressed—preferred to sit at nearby tables, drinking and exchanging small-talk. The polished granite dance floor fairly bulged with princes and pretenders in various stages of inebriation. A few adventurous souls meandered about the manicured garden walks, but many simply stood near the bandstand and sang along. Carrie recognized some of these people, but most were not true friends, or, at least, not for years now.

Then, as a fresh Pacific breeze rose up to blow against a sheltering line of eucalyptus, Carrie, all at once, felt hemmed in by all that swirled around her. She craved peace and quiet again, and the urge to get away was almost overpowering. Finally, she turned her back to the band and hurried off toward Robbers' Roost again. *I'm not part of this anymore! I'm not!* She plowed through the patio assemblage like a fast ship through low swells, almost knocking over one giggling woman and bathing the jacket of the man next to her in spilled champagne. *I'm only staying here long enough to decide my next move!*

Carrie picked up her pace and was just short of running when she finally heard the mystery voice clearly.

"Miss Caroline!"

A hand touched her shoulder, and she spun around to see Adel, one of the family maids, wearing an expression that said, *Something's wrong*. She was out of breath as if she too had been running, and unfortunately, her chronic nervous stammer had also kicked in.

"Miss Caroline...your...your...."

"Relax, Adel!" Carrie put a calming hand on the woman's forearm. She knew she would have to settle her agitation or never hear the anticipated message. So she encouraged her with a low soothing tone. "Take a breath and slow down." She waited a few seconds while Adel regained control and stopped hyperventilating. Then, when the maid's chest ceased its heaving, Carrie said, "Better now?"

The girl nodded.

"All right, what is it?"

Adel simply stood there, making unsuccessful attempts to speak. Then, before she could find her voice again, a large bald man in a tuxedo at least one size too small came trotting up beside her and stopped.

"Oh," he said in the hoarsest voice Carrie thought she'd ever heard. "I see you have located the lady in question, Miss Adel." His grammar qualified as correct and his tone sounded politely formal, but there still existed something about the deliberately measured speech that gave the impression this was not the way this mass of walking muscle was used to conversing in unguarded moments. The same went for his general carriage. He stood with his arms slightly out from his side, his back ramrod straight. Carrie couldn't decide whether the suit merely pinched him or the raw animal mass of his physique was simply on the verge of overpowering his clothes. Either way, she found herself quite intimidated by the sheer menace of his size, which had to be at least a head taller and twice the bulk of any man in sight. He appeared uncomfortable as he tried to conform to a social environment that seemed not to be his natural habitat. Carrie pictured a broomstick up the back of his jacket and had to stifle an undignified snicker.

"Adel, I don't think I've had the pleasure of meeting this gentleman." Carrie managed to keep a serious expression *and* modulate her tone, no small feat at the moment.

Adel glanced back at the bovine giant and blushed, but soon regained her composure along with the power of speech. "Uh, this is Francis...I mean, Mr. Polinsky. He –" She cleared her throat and swallowed.

The man, sensing the maid's difficulty, stepped around her, and, with a formal air, presented himself to Carrie as if he were making a recitation before his grammar school teacher. "Miss Caroline, I have been employed by the Van Burean Diamond Exchange to be your father's personal torpedo."

Adel nudged him from behind and half whispered the word, "Bodyguard."

"Oh, yes," the torpedo continued, unperturbed. "Personal bodyguard."

The strains of *Has Anybody Seen My Gal?* found its way from the megaphone on the patio stage out to where the trio stood, momentarily interrupting the conversation.

Carrie led Francis and Adel back to the bench in front of the Roost, farther away from the bandstand noise. "I don't understand, Francis. Uh, I hope you don't mind if I call you by your first name."

The monster smiled and flexed knuckles that hung half way down his thighs. "Not at all, Miss. It would be an honor." He briefly bowed his head, causing a momentary reflection off his shiny pate.

"Very well." Carrie met his bow with a nod of her own. "Please, tell me then why my father feels he needs a personal bodyguard."

Francis clasped two massive paws in front of a more than amply filled vest and took a deep breath. "Well, Miss, it's like this." He tugged at his collar and hesitated, as if trying to decide what he should say. Then he ended the pause with a shrug and began. "You see, there's these hard boiled mugs what owns gin mills off the main drag. And they likes to muscle in on every pushover they can find."

Not quite sure she understood what had just been said, Carrie turned to Adel with a look that said, *Can you translate?*

The maid took the hint and stepped forward. "There are gangsters who own speak-easies in seedy areas who like to intimidate unprotected businessmen."

"I see," said Carrie, noticing the complete and mysterious absence of Adel's characteristic stammer in Francis' presence.

The man gave her an enthusiastic nod. "I most heartily concur with that, Miss!" He screwed his eyes up to the top of his head, as if he were reading a prepared statement printed on the inside of his skull. Finally, he held up his index finger. "To continue…Said mugs took notice of the advantageous locations of Mr. Van Burean's ice shops and decided they'd persuade your father to let them peddle hooch out the back."

Adel said, "The gangsters wanted to intimidate Mr. Van Burean into letting them sell illegal alcohol from the back rooms of his jewelry stores."

There came more nodding from the torpedo. "When your father said 'nix' to that, these gentlemen pointed out that maybe someone might get it into their head to toss a pineapple into some of Mr. Van Burean's high class joints or …." He hesitated again. "Or even bump off your father personally."

Clearing her throat again, Adel glanced at her shoes. "They threatened to bomb the stores or kill Mr. Van Burean if he did not agree to their terms."

"The local flatfeet won't pinch these bums cuz they themselves are on the take."

"Many of the local police are corrupt, so they won't arrest these men."

Francis raised his thumbs and stuck them deep into his chest. "That's where I come in, Miss. Your uncles back in New York have hired me to come out here and make sure everything stays Jake with all yuz good folks."

Adel inspected her hands and smiled. "Mr. Polinsky is here to protect us from harm." The two exchanged a cryptic look, and Adel's smile grew a little. "It's been several weeks now, and there's been no sign of mischief on the part of the gangsters. Apparently, Francis'…Mr. Polinsky's reputation has preceded him." She sneaked another side-glance.

"And what *is* this reputation?" Summing up the man's effect on Adel, Carrie found it even more difficult to maintain neutral composure.

"Suffice it to say, Miss, that I have had experience with both sides of the bootlegging situation in New York, having been a duly appointed officer of the law and, at a later date, a—shall we say—*representative* of shadier interests." He raised his eyebrows. "I found both professions not to my liking, so I have recently begun a career as a ...uh...." He stopped to search for the right word again. Soon a small spark flickered in his eyes. "Bodyguard. That's it. A bodyguard to more deserving folks than I have been associated with in the past." His recitation complete, Francis refolded his hands and relaxed his face to its previous, noncommittal composure, something halfway between that of a butler and a mortician. He looked around with the contented air of a man who appreciated peace wherever he could catch some.

"That's very interesting." Carrie smiled. "I'd not heard any of this. Most likely my father didn't want me to worry." Truth be told, now being better informed of the dangers at hand, she wished her father had hired two torpedo/bodyguards. "Why is it I haven't seen you around the estate until now?"

"I mostly stays out of sight, Miss. I can watch the joint better that way."

Carrie nodded. She *would* sleep easier knowing Francis was out on night patrol.

Suddenly, there came a rustling in the nearby foliage, and a much drunker Donny stumbled out of the Robbers' Roost. "You owe me an apology, Carrie!" A greasy shock of hair dangled over one eye, and a half-smoked Gaspar hung, smoldering, from wet lips. He struggled for balance as he stood in front of her.

Carrie re-hoisted her wall of authority. "I thought I told you to go home."

With wobbling fingers the youth snatched the smoldering cigarette from his mouth and waved it at his nemesis. "You had no right!" He took a half step toward her. "You had no rieee—!"

In the blur of an instant, the surprised Donny found himself hanging suspended by his collar and pants from the powerful grip of one Francis Polinsky, who now easily held the jerking, flailing boy at arm's length about three feet off the ground. Carrie had not noticed her father's torpedo coming to her rescue. He had been silent in the performance of his duty and very, *very* quick.

"What do you want I should do with this cake-eater, Miss Caroline?" Francis' arms vibrated with Donny's frantic attempts to swim in midair.

"Get your hands off me, you screwy goon!" The boy arched like a swordfish on a hook, but to no avail.

Francis twisted him around so that they were nose to nose. "I suggest you stifle this unseemly behavior forthwith, or I might be forced to massage your teeth on one of Mr. Van Burean's ritzy lamp posts." He punctuated his statement with one violent shake. The boy went as limp as if he were drugged, but kept fear-widened eyes fixed on Francis. Glancing at Carrie, then back to Donny, the bodyguard said, "I think he'll be good for a while. You want I should show him out now?"

That was it; Carrie could not maintain a serious demeanor any longer. She let out a torrent of laughter and could not speak until she caught her breath several seconds later. During that time, Francis did not alter his sober countenance.

"Yes, you may escort the gentleman out." She laughed a little more.

"I'll put him out one of the side gates, so as not to disturb anyone," Francis said and bowed slightly with Donny still in hand. "It has been a pleasure to meet with you, Miss."

"Thank you ever so much for your help, Francis," she said, appreciating the services of this monster-man tonight. Although Donny was indeed young, Carrie knew him to be no physical weakling—no telling how things might have turned out had she been alone.

"Any time, Miss." Francis nodded first to Carrie, then to the maid. "Miss Adel." After that, with Donny tucked neatly under his arm, Francis strode off toward the side path that ran along the house, where he soon became lost in the shadows.

All at once, Carrie's original question resurfaced. "Adel, what was it you first wanted to tell me?"

"Oh, my... goodness!" Her face returned to the same troubled expression it had first held, with a little added frustration. "It... just flew... right... out of my head! I'm... so sorry!" She took a breath. "There's sort of an emergency... at the front gate!"

Chapter Two

The anti-aircraft shell detonated much too close, and the concussion hit Jack MacGregor like two giant hands clapping a mosquito between them. His ears rang, his nerves numbed, and all subsequent outside noise became muffled long enough for him to fear he'd gone deaf. Pain had not yet arrived, but he expected it soon, prompted by the slow red tide that had begun to soak the legs of his flying suit. That made it clear he'd been hit, but at this point he didn't know how bad. Truth be told, at the moment, he didn't *want* to know—too many other things to think about. He'd get around to fear and pain soon enough. *Just not right now.*

Despite some unexplained smoke that flowed from under the cowling, the 400 horsepower Liberty engine still drove the open-cockpit De Havilland's big wooden prop, and the controls continued to respond as they should, even though Jack, for some reason, found it a little hard to move his feet on the pedals. The combat-scarred bomber, like its pilot, had been hurt but, also, like Jack, remained flyable …it seemed. That meant he had a decision to make. Should he and his gunner turn back or try to press on to the target? As if on cue, not wanting to be ignored any longer, his legs finally began to sting, and he noticed a new moist, red blossom enlarging out from under his safety-belt, the almost certain indication of an abdominal wound. He took a quick inventory. *The pain's not bad. So far.* And he did not feel dizzy or faint. But that could change at any second, and he had Dutch to consider. Even if the gunner could fly a little, he couldn't do it from his backseat perch, separated from the flight controls of the front cockpit by almost three feet. *So, whatever happens to me happens to him.* This was the part of his job Jack hated most—making life-and-death decisions for the both of them. So much rested upon his judgment right now. He could not afford to be wrong.

So he took time enough to consider the options. Not much time—but just a little slice—a piece, no more than a moment. But in that moment, something small happened that would, as small things sometimes do, bring about a large and very immediate change to the current time and place. A wayward drop of hot oil sailed out from the neighborhood of the valve covers, into the slipstream and stuck to Jack's cheek, burning a little and jerking him completely out of the skies over 1918 France. He took a deep, spasmodic breath like he always did when his mind returned to the present. Then he released his gaze from the past and refocused his consciousness back onto the reality in front of him.

He still saw an airplane engine and prop, both doing their respective jobs as before...with as much noise as possible. Only now *no* threatening smoke wafted tail-ward. The fabric of the wings and fuselage had *not* been torn by hot shell fragments, and—he took a quick glance downward—his legs and side appeared undamaged and un-bloodied.

What's more, he now sat in the rearmost of the plane's two open cockpits. *And there's someone else up front. Not even Dutch—some stranger.* Jack twisted his neck from side to side, trying to prime his memory. *Oh yeah. It's Bob Arbid, the grower's kid from Indio.* Jack paused for more recollection while he clenched the rear-cockpit's controls for reassurance as to who was actually flying. Then he finished his thought out loud. "He's going to buy the plane!"

The brown-headed kid in front twisted around in his seat as the wind back-lashed his hair. He scrunched his face and lifted his goggles as if it would help him hear better. "What's that Mr. MacGregor?" he yelled over a universe of noise.

Jack hollered back, "I said, you're going to buy my plane!" *Why'd I say that? Not too bright.*

The younger man in front pulled his goggles back down and grinned. "Yes, Sir! Yes, Sir, I am!" An eyebrow went up. "You haven't changed your mind, have you? I mean, we still got a deal, don't we?"

Good. He's not smart enough to think I'm crazy. Jack nodded and patted his customer-to-be on the shoulder, then motioned for him to turn back around. When the young man was once more consumed with the passing scenery below, Jack nodded again. But this time, it had nothing to do with his passenger. It was merely the pilot's admission to himself that he knew his mind had once again been more or less absent from his body but had now returned.

While waiting for his breathing to slow, Jack had another talk with himself. Flying alone much of the time, he had gotten into the habit of having one-man discussions aloud in which the wind carried his words aft into oblivion, far from anyone else's hearing. But the boy up front had the ears of a bat, so Jack kept his conversation internal this time.

Okay, MacGregor. Get a hold of yourself, boy! He made a rapid, 360 degree survey. *We're in our own little Curtiss Jenny, not a De Havilland bomber. Check? This is the pass at Banning, California, not the Western Front. And it's 1923. We've been back for almost a full five years now.* Silly as it felt, these self-inflicted Dutch-uncle sessions seemed to help after the occasional short disembodied visits back to the war. They gave him a few simple things to concentrate on until his complete awareness of the present returned. Gradually, Jack felt his tension subside. *Okay. This is good.* He loosened his grip on the joystick. *This is better.*

The sun had just settled behind the western hills, leaving twilight to await the coming night. Jack inhaled another slow gulp of exhaust-tainted air and took as long a time letting it out as he could. Realizing his shoulders still remained arched with tension from his short-lived trip to the immortal past, he purposely slumped down into the cockpit in an attempt to loosen the muscles. *I'm back.* It was more of a declaration than an observation, full of determination to stay back—here in the present where he belonged. Jack hoped he could *do* that this time.

He looked up at one stubborn star—the only one visible this early—Mars or Venus—he wasn't sure. It hung like a dim lamp, just sputtering to life in the dying afterglow of sunset. Then he scanned the pass below. Everything remained bathed in the dull post-mortem luminescence of early evening, so he could still make out the thin, gray strip of the new highway.

"That goes all the way from Indio to Riverside now!" Bob hollered back over the resonance of the little liberty engine as he pointed to the paved ribbon below. The pair had long since gotten used to the background noise and shouting at each other. Bob kept pointing repeatedly like he was afraid his host was going to miss the landmark.

Jack nodded in the exaggerated, almost stage-actor manner he'd learned flying in the Army. Then he yelled back into the prop-wash, "I know. I flew this way last week. When I left California a few months ago, it was still mostly logs and railroad ties. It's a lot prettier now."

Now it was the boy's turn to nod. "She's smooth as silk," he said over his shoulder. "Nothin' but level asphalt from one end to the other."

Jack checked his airspeed indicator, then leaned out of the cockpit. Looking straight down, he spotted the lights of what he thought was some kind of roadster. He shook his head and chuckled while he adjusted his leather helmet. The car was gradually catching up to the plane's fast-fading shadow on the ground.

Bob noticed too. He twisted sideways and pointed like a madman as he peered down at the road. "Hey!" He rubbed his goggles with a checkered shirtsleeve. "That there car's goin' faster than us!" He shot Jack a look of amazement, mixed with a touch of disappointment.

"It's just a headwind!" Jack responded with his confident instructor's tone. "Don't you remember when I told you about headwinds?"

The rancher's son shook his head, so the instructor continued. "The wind in the pass is going about forty miles per hour toward the East. We're doing seventy to the West! But that's just our airspeed! To find out how fast we're moving over the ground, you have to subtract the speed of the headwind from our airspeed! You understand?"

The boy nodded slowly.

"Okay then!" Jack hollered and, out of a long-engrained habit, thumped the fuel gauge with his finger. "So, forty from seventy is thirty! Right?"

There came another slow nod from the Jenny's future owner.

"Our groundspeed is thirty miles per hour!" Now, it remained the instructor's turn to point down at the roadster, the headlight beams of which were progressively pulling out from under the plane. "The car's probably doing almost fifty, so that gives him a twenty mile per hour jump on us!" Jack raised a palm in resignation. "That's the way it goes with headwinds!" His eyes passed over the broken altimeter—another instrument cross-check habit—and he reminded himself that a new one waited on prepaid order in Bob's name at the Seal Beach Airfield. Jack glanced over the side and, for an instant, focused his attention on the aircraft's eyeball altitude. *Looks to be about five hundred feet above ground level. That's all we need.* "Now, if this was a tailwind," he prompted Bob, "we'd be doing right around a hundred and ten. Depends on the wind direction." Jack smiled his best salesman's smile. "You understand?"

"I got it now, Mr. MacGregor."

Jack leaned over the lip of the cockpit and watched as the car pulled ahead of his Curtiss biplane. Then the lights of a ranch house crept by with almost agonizing sloth, and he laughed again. *Yep, looks like we're doing about thirty. If this breeze were any stiffer, we'd be going backwards.* Jack looked at his wristwatch. Eight-thirty. *We're going to have to do better than this, or I'm not going to make it. Of all the nights for a headwind!*

Another ranch slipped past; then there was only the highway and the railroad tracks running through the pass's short, dry grass and brush. A small creek cut deep into the earth as it snaked its way west. Small clumps of cattle, seemingly content with their lot, meandered and drank at the bottom of its steep banks. In contrast, on the high, hilly north side of the pavement, a large flock of sheep dominated the scene.

Bob gestured downward again. "Look at all those big round rocks in that field! They're mostly all the same size!"

Jack shook his head. "They're sheep!"

"How can you tell?"

"Rocks don't move!" Jack drew the boy's attention to a dog, bullying some of the flock out of a small grove of trees.

"Are those sheep too?" Bob pointed to the far western end of the pasture.

Seeing the line of boulders near a dry-wash, Jack rolled his eyes. "No, those *are* rocks!

"How do you know?"

"Sheep don't pile up one on top of the other!"

After surveying the sky for other planes, Jack noticed the shepherd's shack and a utility shed a little farther up the hill beside some wire-fence pens. He wondered what it would be like to live a life that uncomplicated. The notion seemed almost biblical in its simplicity. *A shepherd. Just get up in the morning and watch the sheep. No splintered props, no rusted turnbuckles, no fabric peeling off the wings at the bottom of a loop you're performing above some county fair crowd.* He sighed. *You just sell your sheep and bank your money. Nothing trying to come apart and kill you.*

Jack felt lazy now. He didn't even want to fly. At least not right at this particular moment. It had been a long, tedious leg from Indio, and fatigue had staked its claim. He wanted to take a rest and think about pastures and shepherds and sitting under shade trees. Not airplanes. *Stupid crates are nothing but headaches! They've ruined my life!* Jack knew, even as this thought rampaged through his mind, he didn't mean half of it. But the *other* half he *did.* He wished tomorrow had already come, and that Bob had already paid for the Jenny and flown off with it.

So what's the problem? You've got a co-pilot this trip. Use him. Jack decided that was the best advice he'd ever given himself, so he tapped Bob on the shoulder. "You want to fly it a little while?"

Bob's grin grew so wide Jack thought the boy's face would split. "Can I?"

"Why not?" Jack couldn't help but smile too. "You're a pilot now. She's going to be yours after tomorrow, anyway!"

Bob snatched the controls with so much enthusiasm Jack had to keep a tight grip on the stick to maintain the Jenny's stability. Finally, after a couple of half banks and an *almost* roll, he felt his former student calm down enough to safely fly the plane by himself. That's when he shouted the magic words. "You have the aircraft!"

Bob hollered back on the prop wash, "I got it!"

Then Jack let go of the joystick and took his knee-high, lace-up boots off the pedals. Now he could relax for a while—*not go to sleep, mind you*—but just rest his arms and head on the edge of the open cockpit a few minutes or maybe take in some scenery. After all, the boy had soloed several times, and survived every flight. Jack loosened his safety belt a notch, leaned back against his wicker seat, and began to daydream about issuing orders to his sheep dog while reclining in the shade beneath some ancient oak. Eventually though, his eyelids betrayed him, and he became more a part of the dream meadow than the reality of the plane. He had almost gotten to the point where he could feel the soft grass beneath the seat of his pants when something pulled him back to reality.

The clatter of the Jenny's OX-5 engine broke its rhythm. It wasn't much of a change, almost imperceptible, but it was enough to catch Jack's trouble-honed attention. In an instant, he brought his consciousness to heel, focused his attention on the wooden instrument panel, and restarted his neglected crosscheck from one gauge to the other with more than a little apprehension. Nothing looked threatening so far though—at least nothing major. But five thousand hours of experience told him to wait and stay alert. Jack peered back over the side of the cockpit again and surveyed the area below for a place to put the plane down, should his suspicions of trouble bear fruit. But he couldn't find a clear stretch of ground that was not cut with gullies or strewn with river-rock. Not one place anywhere in sight gave him the five hundred feet he wanted for a problem-free landing roll. And the telephone-polls stood much too close to the highway to consider its very inviting smooth pavement as a safe option.

Jack twisted around in his seat to search back toward the meadow that hosted the grazing sheep. The Jenny hadn't made much progress against the muscle of the headwind, and he could still see the pasture not too far behind. But, *it* didn't look like a full five hundred feet either—more like three hundred. But then again, with this same headwind slowing the approach, he just might be able to land short enough. *Might even get this thing stopped before we bite into a boulder sandwich.* Still, he hoped he'd misread the engine, and that he had done all this worrying for nothing. That would be nice—to simply continue on without a sudden emergency ...for once.

Bob flashed a wind-whipped, open-cockpit smile over his shoulder. He seemed to be having a good time playing with the controls—doing shallow climbs and lazy S-turns—getting the feel of the biplane. Jack, on the other hand, paid little attention to the revelry in the front seat. He merely uttered an oath into the air that rushed past his mouth, then he continued to contemplate his premonition of impending disaster. A forced landing was not what he needed tonight, especially after promising his grandmother he'd be at the ranch in time for supper. Jack rolled his eyes behind his goggles. *I just get this flying herd of parts sold to the kid, and now I'm not even sure it'll make it the five miles to Beaumont, let alone all the way to the coast! This could* only *happen to me!*

The feeling that something unpleasant was about to occur wouldn't leave, even though there didn't seem to be much evidence of anything actually going wrong. So, choosing to remain loyal to that nagging itch that had proven itself an unsung prophet so often before, Jack kept right on looking for a clear place to land. He did this for almost another five minutes but continued to find only more boulders for his efforts.

"Now, those are some *big rocks*!" Bob was looking at the same spot as his mentor.

Jack pictured himself, Bob, and the Jenny broken and twisted among the huge granite slabs. He swallowed hard and answered, "Yep, big rocks."

Bob went back to concentrating on his flying. Jack sighed and decided to put off any decision to turn back to the safer meadow for another few seconds. With as little headway as the poor biplane had been making against the wind's onslaught, he knew they wouldn't get far in that time anyway and could probably still make it back to where he saw the sheep. *Back to safe pasture.* He smiled at the

34

spiritual metaphor. Then he did something he hadn't done in months. *God, if you're still listening to me, please let me finish this one last flight before this motorized kite falls apart.*

Jack was about to follow his prayer with an *Amen* when the partially crystallized oil line he had been meaning to replace for weeks finally rebelled against its neglect and disintegrated, sending a steady supply of wear-blackened forty-weight out into the slipstream. The oil soon covered the engine's exhaust manifold, all of Bob's face, and part of Jack's. It caused the super-heated exhaust stacks to smoke and Jack's goggles to glaze into near opaqueness. He automatically pulled the goggles up off his eyes and seized the controls.

"I've got it!" Jack yelled to an agitated but well lubricated Bob. The boy immediately pulled his goggles up too and began wiping his face with a blue bandana. Jack leaned as best he could out of the stream of oil and smoke. He groaned at the drill. It was not the first time this had happened. *But why tonight?*

The right wings dipped abruptly down as Jack swung the Jenny back around into a steep one-eighty toward the sheep meadow. Immediately, the plane's ground speed picked up as the headwind now became a tailwind, adding its forty miles per hour to the Jenny's seventy indicated airspeed, resulting in Jack's previously calculated and more hurried one hundred-ten. *Well, that helps a little. Might even get there in time.*

"Wha...what happened?" Bob twisted around in his seat. He had most of the oil off now, but was still smeared with a mixture of confusion and fear. "What'd I do?"

Jack shook his head. "You didn't do anything!" He suddenly remembered to put his airplane salesman demeanor back on. "It's just a little oil line!" He peered around Bob to look at the exhaust stacks. *Anything catch fire yet? No? Okay. We're okay.* Jack forced a Cheshire cat grin. "Oil lines aren't a problem. Messy, but not a real problem!" he said, but he thought, *as long as the engine doesn't seize, and we don't burn up before we get down.* "Everything's fine!" Jack continued the sales pitch. "We'll just have to make a little stop! That's all!" Bob nodded and turned back around. Jack squinted eastward toward the advancing night, looking for the last-chance pasture.

Poor, oil-coated Bob gripped the sides of his cockpit like a vice on a pipe. Jack, however, was relatively calm as the sheep and pasture came into view. Things were irritating but simple now. He knew the sale of the Jenny might be in question, but the issue of the pair's survival was cut and dry. No deliberation on that. The oil line had made the most important decision. From this point on, Jack knew the questions would be uncomplicated. Could they get back to the meadow before they had to land? Could Jack land without plowing into the scores of sheep that now occupied most of his intended landing area? But what was uppermost in Jack's mind as he flew over a row of smooth granite boulders at the upwind end of the field was how long it would take the brakeless, use-worn biplane to roll to a stop.

Chapter Three

"Emergency? What's happened?" Carrie's patience waivered a bit as the maid struggled to get her next word out.

"It's...It's...It's your husband's grandmother!" Adel blurted at last.

"Hannah?"

"Yes, miss!"

Visions of her treasured in-law suffering some injury or illness filled Carrie's imagination. In the last several years, she had grown to love the woman more than she did her own parents. Thoughts of her being in harm's way ignited protective instincts and anger with Adel for not coming to the point quicker. "Well, say it, girl! What's happened to her?"

Adel's stammer worsened. "Uh...she –"

"Hey, everybody!" One of the young party sheiks leaped onto the bandstand and solved the maid's mystery in a voice that proved loud enough to be heard by all without a megaphone. "Some old hag's chained herself to the front gate and won't let anyone pass!"

"Oh, no!" Carrie moaned and turned back to Adel. "Tell me it's not Hannah!"

"Come on!" The young man yelled. "You've *got* to see this!"

The crowd poured off the patio and through the ballroom, heading like a tidal surge, through the house, toward the front gate of the Van Burean estate. Adel shook her head. "She said ... she said she wants to see you... right now!"

Within moments, Carrie found herself hurrying down the gardener's path that ran beside the mansion toward the gatehouse. How she got there, however, was a little bit of a blur in her short-term memory. She had told the maid to go back into the house. "And don't say a word about Hannah!"

Or something to that effect. She couldn't recall the exact words. She only remembered bolting down the deserted gravel trail as soon as Adel had left her.

After a few seconds of running between the junipers and oleanders, Carrie soon kicked off high-heeled dancing shoes that would have paid Adel's salary for a month. Still accustomed to a recent middle-class existence, she groaned at the waste, but knew, at least now, there was a better chance of not breaking her neck in the faint twilight. The fine crushed rock on the path proved cold and bit into her feet, not to mention what it did to her silk stockings. Carrie was not used to running much, and she was not used to going unshod under any circumstances except when bathing. It had only been a minute or two since she'd started her race to the gate, but already the soles of her feet stung and breathing had become a chore. At this point, Carrie officially christened the little five hundred yard jaunt a labor of love.

She caught a glimpse of the big circle driveway in a space between two pines. No crowd there as yet. She pictured the semi-intoxicated upper crust mob, everyone joking and bumping into one another as they wandered through her family's home on their way to the main entry door, and for the first time tonight, she was glad of their drunkenness. It would slow them up and buy her time. Then Carrie did something she had not done for well over a month. *Lord, let me get to Hannah before anyone else!*

For a moment, Carrie started to question herself as to why she'd broken her fast and actually spoken to the Almighty. Then she realized the effort of such complicated thought used up desperately needed oxygen.

You're trying to run a quarter of a mile, you goof! Better stop this introspection and just concentrate on getting to the gatehouse before you run out of time and breath!

She fixed her concentration on the tiny stone building that had just come within sight. The path ended there in front of a closed door, but Carrie could already feel herself nearing the end of her energy. So she doubled the rhythm of her breathing and broke into a pant. Soon, strength seeped back into her legs, and she began to believe she might make it to her destination without losing consciousness. *I just hope the doors are unlatched!*

Fortunately they were. Carrie burst through one doorway and out the other. Then her knees gave out, and she collapsed into a gasping, heaving mass on the grass just outside the east wall. Kneeling there while the burning in her lungs dissipated, she waited for her eyes to regain focus. When they did, she put them to use and looked around.

Several roadsters and limousines sat motionless by the side of the entry road. Their drivers leaned against the vehicles sulking and muttering. An empty sheriff's car squatted in the center of the lane with nightshift deputy, Bill Hawn, standing in the headlights' glare. He was talking to an old woman, who sat on the pea-gravel driveway, leaning against the front gate. Bill's side of the conversation included numerous arm gestures. But he sounded more frustrated than angry.

"Hannah, please!" The man spread his hands in supplication. "You can't *stay* here. The Van Bureans are going to file an official complaint if you don't unlock that chain!"

Carrie mentally groaned. *Oh, good grief, it's true. She's shut the gate and chained herself to it! Again!* Carrie knew the story well of how decades before, when Hannah was a Bloomer Girl, she had chained herself to the Governor's carriage wheels in the name of women's suffrage. The poor man had merely stopped off in Marner Bay for lunch on his way south to San Diego, but Hannah found out he was in town and made sure his departure endured a long delay. *And the rest is history.* Carrie sighed softly.

Hannah pushed a hairpin a little tighter into her gray bun, then folded her arms across her chest. "As I've already told you, I am not concerned whether the Van Bureans file a complaint or not. I'm surprised to hear they haven't done so already."

Carrie snickered and, since she'd almost regained her wind, rose to her feet.

"Not yet." Bill pushed his tan broad-brimmed hat back on his head. "They phoned, and I talked them into waiting, but you're going to have to leave. You're holding up their party, Hannah. People got to go in and out. You know?"

Still a little lightheaded from her run, Carrie walked toward the scene. Her approach went undetected since both main characters were bathed in headlight beams.

"You talked 'em into waiting, did you?" The old woman reset her folded arms and stuck out a defiant chin. "Well then, you can just untalk 'em! 'Cause I'm not moving 'til Carrie gets here!"

Bill snatched the hat off his thinning scalp and bounced it off the ground. "Hannah, you're wearing my patience down! Now, you unlock that chain like I said! I don't want to have to arrest you!"

Carrie stopped at the edge of the shadows. Although she'd been in an extreme hurry to intervene just moments before, strangely, now all she wanted was to listen to Hannah tie Bill into knots just a little longer. Carrie knew the party crowd was already on its way. *The access road from here to the house is almost a quarter mile long. Is there time?* She decided there was and leaned carefully against a car fender as she watched a few more seconds of the show.

"Well, you go right ahead and do your arresting!" Hannah unraveled her arms and took a firm grip on the iron gate. "And don't think I'm afraid of your little jail, Billy

Hawn! It will not be the first time a member of your family has dragged me to it!"

"Yes, I know." Bill shook his head, rolled his eyes, and spoke in an almost sing-song chant. "You chained yourself to the governor's carriage in '02' for the cause of women's votes, and my father arrested you. I know. I was there too. I saw him do it."

"He most certainly did." She released the gate long enough to smooth her dress around her legs. Then she resumed her vise-grip upon its bars.

"Yes, but you and I both know," Bill continued, "that you *refused* to budge, just like now. He had no choice. Furthermore, there was no dragging about it. He *carried* you to the Paddy Wagon. Didn't he."

Carrie quietly snickered as Hannah turned her face away from her assailant. *Poor Bill. She's not going to let him save her.*

"Didn't he!" Bill repeated.

"I don't remember," Hannah said to the sky.

"How'd you get here, anyway? I don't see Floyd's truck anywhere."

"I took a taxicab."

"You hauled that chain into a cab?"

"The driver was very helpful."

Bill sucked in a deep, controlled breath and let it out slowly. "All right, then. That's it. Are you going to unchain yourself, or do I get out my lock-pick?"

"I'm not leaving until I see my granddaughter!"

Bill picked up his hat and dusted it off. "I see. Well then—"

"Wait, Bill." Carrie came out of the darkness. *This seems to be my night for eavesdropping,* she thought, but she said, "Let me talk to her."

"Miss Van Burean! I mean, Mrs. MacGregor." Bill re-creased the crown of his hat, placed it back on his head and squared it. "I didn't see you." He looked back and forth between the two women. "Sure thing. Go ahead. Maybe *you* can reason with her."

Carrie walked toward the criminal chained to the gate. Hannah frowned at Bill as he returned to his car, but the old woman's tone and expression changed as winter to spring when her grandson's wife knelt beside her. "Carrie, honey. It's so good to see you."

Carrie had to concentrate hard to avoid smiling at the way Hannah had dealt with Bill Hawn. It took maximum effort to come up with an ominous, rebuking voice, but she managed it. "Hannah, what do you think you're doing?"

"Waiting for you, dear," she said in a matter-of-fact tone as she fussed with her wedding band.

Carrie's amusement began to drain as she felt herself becoming the object of Hannah's strategy. "Hannah, I'm not Bill. I won't play that game. So why don't you just tell me what you're up to."

"Why, I don't know what you mean." Hannah sat up straight and smiled into Carrie's face.

Feeling herself being pulled toward impatience, Carrie scooted closer until she was face to face with the other woman. Then she spoke in a manner that let Hannah know the dance was over. "Hannah?" She paused for effect. "I'm here now. What do you want?"

Hannah sighed, and her body relaxed. She seemed to welcome the end of the pretense. "They wouldn't let Floyd or I see you."

"Mother and Father wouldn't?" Carrie smiled faintly and shook her head. "That's ridiculous. I only told them I didn't want to see *Jack* just now, but you and Floyd," she paused, "are always welcome. Father and Mother know that. There must have been some misunderstanding."

Now, it was Hannah's turn to shake her head. "Albert came to the gatehouse *personally* when we arrived." She indicated the little building with a tilt of her head. "He told us we weren't welcome and were not to return."

42

"Father said that?" It was no secret to Carrie that her father did not approve of Floyd and Hannah in general, but this was the first she'd heard of Albert being overtly rude. Had he really gone that far?

Hannah gave Carrie the calm gaze of truth. "He did just that very thing."

Carrie stroked her chin. "Did you try calling me on the phone?"

Hannah nodded.

Carrie frowned. "I see. I wondered why you hadn't been by to see the boys."

"Then why didn't you call us?" The old woman's voice turned a bit stern.

Struck with a small shard of guilt, Carrie glanced down at the gravel. "I was just about to. Do you believe me?"

Hannah softened. "Of course, Carrie. My granddaughter wouldn't lie."

Carrie's discipline broke, and she hugged the woman as best the chain would allow. "You know I'm a sucker for elderly bloomer girls who call me granddaughter."

"Yes, dear. I know." Hannah stood up and gave her chains a shake. "But I do still need to talk to you."

Carrie rose and straightened her shimmy dress. "Well, then you're going to have to make Bill happy and unlock that chain." She could hear the distant noise of the party mob now, but remained determined to maintain composure. The last thing the situation needed was a dose of panic.

"Chain?" Hannah glanced back in the direction of the faint clamor, but said nothing about it. Then a mischievous little laugh escaped her lips, and she returned all attention to the steal links in her hands. "Oh, this old thing?" She pulled a large, tarnished key out from behind an undone button near the top of her dress and opened the ancient padlock. "It's served its purpose." She untangled the chain from the gate and cradled it in her arms as if it were a child. "I'm going to keep it a while longer though." She raised her eyebrows. "You never know when you're going to need one."

Laughing out loud, Carrie wrapped an arm around her grandmother-in-law. "Come on. We have to get out of here if we're going to talk." She led Hannah to where Bill stood unconsciously thumping his fingers on the back of his spotlight. "Could you take this dangerous gate-chainer to the Texaco station on the Coast Highway…and wait with her until I arrive?"

"Sure thing, Miss Van …uh, ma'am, but we'd better move fast if we're going to avoid that crowd." He pointed up the Van Burean private road where at least forty members of California's social upper echelon laughed, stumbled, and staggered their way toward the estate's front gate. They had made the distance from the house a little quicker than expected.

"Oh, no!" *The deuce with composure!* Carrie turned quickly to Hannah. "All right. Go with Bill, old dear. And don't give him any grief. Promise me?"

"Word of honor." Hannah smiled a closed lip smile. She held up her left hand, put it back down, then raised her right. "I promise." The suspicious smile continued. Bill shook his head.

"I mean it, Hannah!" Carrie started to run as she spoke. "Bill, I'm going to leave by the back gate in about ten minutes, so get her out of here!"

The deputy took a second glance at the babbling herd that had almost reached the now unlocked gate. "Yes, ma'am! Right now!" Then he opened the right patrol-car door for his new passenger.

Carrie trotted through the gatehouse and up the hidden gardener's path just as the inebriated throng arrived. She could hear Bill's engine start over the grumble of voices, so she knew Hannah and Bill would make good their getaway. However, after a few yards of jogging uphill, she found herself praying again. *Lord, give me the strength to get up to the garage!*

The path's gravel not only shredded her stockings and dug painfully into her feet as before, but, as she was now headed uphill, also gave way under her steps, causing her to slip. *I can do this,* Carrie told herself and kept her legs moving. She began her cross country runner's pant again and waited for the increased strength she hoped would follow. By and by, it came, and she found herself able to continue at a descent pace.

Soon the gabled silhouette of the garage rose in the glow of the back property's lights, and Carrie slowed to a walk. Her breathing remained heavy, but she found she was not exhausted—another small miracle. *Thank you, Lord.* The building that used to be known as the carriage house before automobiles had replaced horses sat obediently off to the right of the Van Burean mansion. The second story chauffeur's quarters still showed illumination within, which meant Addams had not gone to sleep yet. Carrie decided not to bother him. This time, she'd swing open the big firehouse-sized doors herself. *One simply has to remember to throw all of one's hundred and twenty-five pounds into it. Not an easy chore after running a quarter mile uphill, but it can be done.*

She smiled as she opened the latch on one heavy pine door and leaned back to tug against its weight. This was not a thing she would have done before her marriage – refrain from bothering a servant with a difficult task. She could not deny, despite her persistent weakness for luxury, that God and her husband's middle class family had indeed made permanent changes in the way she saw things. She could never be totally uncaring to working people again, no matter what.

Finally after coercing both doors open, Carrie stepped in and took a precious extra second to give her new Stutz Bearcat an admiring gaze before feeling along the row of wooden pegs, just under the garage's side window, for her extra keys. Those found, she seated herself behind the wheel of the shiny yellow convertible and put on the sensible shoes she'd stowed behind the seat for rainy days, another habit wrought from her middle class sojourn.

The Stutz roadster, however, had nothing to do with the middle class. It had been a *coming home* gift from her father, meant to celebrate not only her return, but the new life to come. He did not seem to hear when she told him divorce was not yet certain, but that was no surprise. *None of the Van Burean patriarchs, least of all Father, hear anything that does not align with their plans for the universe.* She had to admit, though, she did *like* the sleek car – not only for the freedom it gave, but for its beauty and comfort as well. All the same though, something felt different now from the days before her marriage. Carrie no longer viewed the car nor anything else that Van Burean wealth could buy as a reason for living. Her years away from the family's money had changed her. Now she saw the Stutz as a mere ornament to be enjoyed—not worshipped as before.

However, as she turned the key and flicked on the ignition switch that fed life-giving power to the shiny chrome button on the dashboard, she still appreciated her father's decision to order her Bearcat with one of the new electric starters. Were it one of the numerous crank-start cars that could be seen everywhere, she would probably have had to bother Addams for help whether she was in a hurry or not.

But the magic technology of the starter button freed her from the humiliation of asking for masculine muscular assistance. So she pushed the button, and, in an instant, the engine caught and growled itself into readiness. Carrie smiled at the way the Stutz purred. She *did* love this car! *That's not a sin, is it?* Carefully slipping it into gear and releasing the hand-brake, she eased out of the garage and drove down the little dirt side road that lead to the back gate where the cliffs subsided into low hills that eventually descended down to the beach. With this back access being so seldom used, except by delivery trucks, Albert Van Burean's daughter anticipated little chance of discovery. *Neither by the* Gin and Tonic Brigade *nor Father.*

Carrie sighed and accelerated away from the garage. The so-called road to the back gate was more or less a sparsely maintained wide dirt path. Crisscrossed with ruts and rain gullies, it gave the Bearcat's springs a chance to show if they were worth their exorbitant price tag or not. Great hulking pine and cypress trees blocked the artificial light coming from behind the house, making the road inkwell-dark, except where the headlights swept. This absence of illumination and a haste-distracted state of mind, helped Carrie find the road's roughest side as well as causing her to almost run over the family chef as the Stutz gained speed coming off the first downhill switchback.

She screamed too late as she swerved and skidded to a stop. "Rodrigo! I didn't see you!" Carrie shifted into neutral and set the big hand brake. "Are you all right? What are you doing out here?"

The tall, dark mustachioed Spaniard dusted off the foxtails he'd collected when he'd jumped from the road into the weeds to avoid Stutz's hungry bumper. He snatched his toque from the ground and seated the traditional, white mushroom-shaped hat more securely onto his head than it had been before his daredevil leap. Then he approached the car with a haughty expression. "The fish market she sends the wrong shrimp. So, your papa he say to Rodrigo call another fish market and see to the delivery personally." He adjusted his hat again pulling it more firmly down upon his head. "So here I am. Rodrigo will go to the delivery gate and see to everything himself while pots boil over and my idiot assistants burn my heavenly rolls." He punctuated his last sentence with an energetic nod that shifted his top-heavy hat, so he straightened it yet a third time.

"You were going to walk all the way down to the gate?"

"*Si.*"

Carrie swung open the passenger door. "Come on. I'll drive you."

Rodrigo leaped from the ground to the running board with amazing agility, then settled himself into the seat after a bow worthy of a matador. "*Gracias*, Carita." He snapped the door shut with a flourish. "Maybe now, I will get back to the kitchen in time to give the hors d'oeuvre rolls and crab puffs a decent burial." He put his hat in his lap and shook his head.

She started the car moving again and drove on in silence for several seconds before she heard Rodrigo's big sigh. Carrie knew what it meant. The man beside her had guessed from her uncharacteristic quiet that there was something on her mind and he was waiting to hear it.

She tried to distract him. "Dinner was simply wonderful. I'd meant to come to the kitchen to tell you earlier, but Mother insisted I be ready before the first guests arrived."

"Why do you play with Rodrigo so?" He kept his eyes straight ahead. "Why do you tell me silly things about the dinner?" He sighed again. "Why do you not say what you want to say?"

Carrie tried to offer a denial, but only tripped on her thoughts and sputtered, "I'm not... I...I was only—"

"Do you think Rodrigo a fool? Have you not been in my kitchen since you were no bigger than a rabbit? Say what you wish to say!"

She down shifted for another switchback and eased into the curve. "I didn't want to burden you when you have so much to see to tonight."

His tone softened. "I have taught you everything I know as a chef." He glanced at his driver and performed a small, seated swagger. "With the exception of a few very secret things that will come to you when Rodrigo leaves this life." He toyed with one end of his handlebar mustache. "You have told me all your secrets a man is fit to hear since you were little. All the things you couldn't tell Mama and Papa." He gave her a long look this time. "Do you think I think these things are a burden?" He straightened as if bracing himself. "Come. Tell Rodrigo the worst and be done."

Carrie hesitated for just a moment before she spoke. "I prayed tonight. I didn't mean to. I just slipped into it."

Rodrigo cocked his head. "And you think this is bad?"

"I haven't addressed God in prayer since the boys and I came here." She cleared her throat as she felt the lump starting to fill it.

"Why?" He laid his arm along the door.

"That's right after I realized that my husband really *had* abandoned me, and...I decided then that *God* had abandoned me also." *There! I've actually said it to someone!* "Too many simply horrid things had happened to me for so very long. I just couldn't see how God could love me and allow all of it." She took a breath. "So about a month ago, I stopped praying."

"I see." Rodrigo rubbed his chin. "So you have been thinking that prayer is nothing more than wasted words."

She nodded in the darkness, then realized she needed to answer. "Yes, until tonight." She paused. "I was trying to get to Hannah before the crowd did. She—"

"Ah, yes." He ran his fingers along the fold in his hat. "I heard about the front gate." He chuckled softly. "Hannah. *¡Que muchacha!*"

"I just started praying." Carrie shook her head. "It must have been desperation or something. Or maybe I simply did it out of old habit. Just some kind of emotional reaction."

49

Rodrigo stretched out in the seat. "You believe that?" He waited for a response, but when he got none, he went on. "No matter what you say, one thing is true. You prayed." He paused again. "I think God, He grabbed you and pulled you back to Him, and He says, 'Talk to me, Carita! It was not I who sent Jack away from you!' *¿Que no?*"

He patted her shoulder gently. Carrie *thought* she had felt the Lord's pull like Rodrigo said, but hearing her proxy parent say it out loud made the thing easier to believe.

"You know, Jack didn't actually *leave* us." Carrie shocked herself as she spoke. She didn't know where *those words* had come from or why she was voicing that particular truth now. "He simply didn't come home for six months, and there wasn't enough money for the boys and I to live on, so we went to stay with Floyd and Hannah." And so at that moment she had done it—finally said it all. The words she'd been holding back too long had begun to spill out, and Carrie felt powerless to stop them. "Then it was months again without seeing him. Jack, I mean…with his grandparents supporting us! I felt like such a burden on them." Her throat began to close once more, causing her voice to squeak. "That's why we came back here." She paused. "But it doesn't feel like home here anymore." She slowed for a ditch and laughed a sad laugh. "Rodrigo, I would have *stayed* with *Hannah* had Jack not seemed to forget about us so completely. He sent almost no money. He very seldom wrote." On the edge of tears, Carrie summoned her Van Burean upbringing to help dampen her feelings. "It *did* feel like he left us."

"Pride!" Rodrigo said.

"What?"

"This Jack, he has too much pride. He does not want to come home until he is a hero in your eyes. Things have not gone good for him, so he stays away and tries to make it right. His pride blinds him to what he does to his family."

50

Carrie felt as though someone had lit a small candle at the far end of a long, dark cavern. "Do you really think so?"

"*¡Seguramente!*" He turned slightly toward her. "My papa he was a fisherman *en Espana*, and sometimes when the catch was bad, he would do the same, stay out trying to catch more fish....*¡Estupido!* While his family starved. He could have worked the grape harvest to make up the difference, but 'no' not him. He was a fisherman, he say. He own his own boat. He would not stoop to pick another man's grapes! Not him! Pride. Your Jack too has this pride. *¿Si?*"

Tears hovered nearby, but for a different, better reason than sorrow. Maybe Rodrigo was right. Maybe Jack really *hadn't* wanted to abandon them. "I think you're a wise man, Rodrigo."

The Spaniard waved the compliment away. "Hey, maybe God, he wants to whisper a little to you through Rodrigo's mouth. Maybe, eh?" He snickered.

Carrie laughed away some of the sadness. "Did they teach you to be so understanding at *Le Cordon Bleu*?"

"No." He undid his top shirt button and looked around, as if embarrassed by the mention of his Parisian cooking alma mater. "They teach Rodrigo that men of *Espana* always stand in line behind Frenchmen for the finer jobs, no matter how much better chef they are!" Then he laughed too. "Unless you leave France and come to America. Here people only care how your food tastes, not what accent you speak with." He paused. "And sometimes these people have curious little girls who want to make friends with their papa's chef. Such things are the chocolate sauce of this life. *¿Que no?*"

She slid the clutch to the floorboard and shifted into another gear. It felt like hope lurked nearby, though Carrie wasn't sure why. Maybe it was because driving always made her feel better or because the night was cooler at twenty miles per hour. Or maybe because, for the first time in almost a month, she was talking to someone who *wasn't* trying to get her divorced. She glanced at her friend. "You think I've changed."

Suddenly they were out of the shadows and entered the realm of a distant high-intensity lamp that had been secured to a tall pine which stood like a sentinel at the edge of a cliff that hung above the estate's lonely back gate. Carrie could see Rodrigo's smile now, and she felt an old familiar warmth inside.

"Eight years ago," he said, "you would not have worried yourself for Hannah or anybody else. You were too pampered then, spoiled."

"A little princess?" A rush of shame made her cheeks and ears tingle.

"*Si*...princess. That's right." He made the statement matter-of-fact with neither malice nor sarcasm as if he were merely confirming a linguistic translation. Then he hesitated. "*Pero*, you were only half a princess. The silly half. There was a good half, *tambien*. A half that knew what was real and good. Even when you were little. That's why you come to play with your father's servants, when your brother would not. And that's why these servants they all love you so much." He feigned a stern demeanor. "*I* do not love you, but the *rest* of them do."

Carrie tried to stifle the smile that peeked from the corners of her mouth when she heard the old game the two of them had played forever. A small snort escaped through her nose and stole the last of her adult dignity. "And I don't love you too." She forced an exaggerated frown that went wasted in the passing shadow of a lone oak tree.

Rodrigo nodded. "Good. That is good that we do not love each other." He briefly wagged a finger in her direction. "Because you know, if you did love me, you might kiss me, and we could never have that."

She rolled her eyes, but dutifully played her part in the ancient ceremony by taking her gaze from the road for an instant and planting a peck on the chef's olive-hued cheek. "Take that!" Carrie said and giggled like a little girl. It was the first time she'd done it— both the peck to the chef and the giggle—in longer than she could remember.

He mimed the face of having tasted something bitter. "*¡Ai!* That was terrible! Do not do that awful thing again!" There was the required two seconds of silence, then he quickly patted her shoulder.

That was the moment she finally felt it – like she *was* home. The feeling had been absent ever since she'd returned to the Van Burean estate, but now it came to her in the Stutz Bearcat while playing a childhood game with a haughty chef. Carrie sighed as she remembered that it was *truly* the household staff that had been her real family all her life. *Without them, I would never have known love of any kind.* She smiled. They *were my home!* She relaxed for the first time since the start of the party, feeling comfortably warm despite the cool, coastal air rushing around the open car. Then a darker memory returned. "There still was the half of me that was the princess, though."

Rodrigo nodded. "*Si.* That is true. *Pero*, you were never that way to us."

"No, not to any of *you.*"

Carrie didn't see the little creek until the last minute. It flowed down from the hills and cut across the road, directly in the path of the Stutz. She slowed for it, but too late, and ended up bathing the car, herself, and the chef with a gallon or so of fresh runoff from the cliff-top estate's irrigation system. *She* thought it felt good, but Rodrigo said nothing. She decided not to comment on the experience.

Carrie waited a moment, figuring Rodrigo would be a better audience if he'd had a chance to dry out as they drove. Finally she said, "It's called Economic Darwinism."

"What is?" Rodrigo's tone indicated that he wasn't quite dry yet.

She pushed some curls from her eyes. "The way my brother and I were raised. Survival of the fittest. We were taught if someone was poor or if they were in any kind of physical distress, it was probably their own fault or, at least, the fault of their physiological evolution." Carrie noticed her passenger's blank look. "That means, if you help someone who's less fortunate than you out of their mess, they'll probably just get right back into that mess again because they're basically inferior to you to begin with. Which means they're stupider —which is why they're in that mess in the first place."

Rodrigo gave his head a shake and grunted. "I know that is what your father thinks," he said. "I have heard him say things like this many times."

"Snobbery." She nodded slowly as the passing headlights of Coast Highway came into view between two ethereal junipers. "That's the milk I was weaned on." She forced a weak smile. "I guess it soaked in about halfway." She felt a grabbing in her stomach as she thought of people she'd wronged through the years when she was the Van Burean princess. Carrie held her breath, and the tightness eased. Then she thought of being with Jack at college so many years past, and a quick running parade of their courtship sprinted through her memory. The day they met in the writing class. How he'd seemed so different from every other boy she'd ever met. The excitement he brought into her life. And the love. Yes, he brought love to her. First, his own romantic style of it. Then, later, the love they shared for the Lord. She knew she had loved Jack when they had courted, and, just now as she drove to the highway, she realized that she *did,* in fact, *still* love him now, if only—.

"I still love my husband, you know," she blurted to her friend; then she slowed the car as they neared the gate where not one, but two fish market trucks, patiently awaited the chef's inspection and approval.

"Oh, we all knew that." He waved her off as if what she'd revealed was yesterday's news.

She stopped the Stutz at the gate. "How could you know when *I* wasn't sure until just now?"

Rodrigo raised his eyebrows and snapped his fingers. "We can tell." He smirked. "Tonight the Mulhollands' chauffeur offered three to one that you'd divorce this Jack MacGregor, and nobody would take him up on it. We all knew it was …how you say…a sucker bet. We knew you'd go back."

Carrie tensed. She wasn't quite ready to consider going back yet. "I don't know." She paused. "If I could just be sure I could trust him again." Carrie pursed her lips. "But I don't know."

The Spaniard put his hand on the driver's arm. "You'll go back. You just need time. *No te preocupes*…Don't worry. It is in God's hand." He patted her, then got out of the Bearcat. "And so are you." He closed the door. "*Vaya con Dios*, Carita." He opened the gate. "And give Hannah my best." Rodrigo waved her through. Carrie responded with a thrown kiss and accelerated out onto the highway toward the Texaco station where she hoped the old woman waited.

All right, Hannah, Carrie mused as she rounded the curve and caught sight of the sheriff's car in the gas station lights. *Let's find out what you're up to because you surely did not pull a stunt like this just to see your great-grandsons.*

Chapter Four

"Whoa!" Bob yelled as Jack turned the Jenny upside down and dove in a half loop toward the earth.

Jack's first instinct was to apologize to the boy for not warning him of the impending aerobatic maneuver, but upon second thought, he changed his mind. If Bob was truly going to be a pilot in his own right, he'd have to get used to unexpected things happening in the air. Jack mentally nodded satisfaction at this last thought. He knew it to be total hogwash, but it sounded profound and relieved him of the need to feel guilty for a thoughtless act.

He pulled out of the dive a comfortable distance from the ground and discovered that he was just a little too far right for a normal approach to the sheep pasture. Jack corrected the error with a slight swing to the left then pulled back on the joystick in an attempt to kill off excess airspeed. He cut his engine, so it wouldn't seize for want of oil. Next he crabbed the biplane into side-slip to lose more altitude quickly, while, at the same time, keeping the oil smoke, that billowed rearward from the manifold, streaming on the other side of the aircraft and out of his face. The maneuver worked, and the craft came out of the sky as if it were cast from lead. But as Jack straightened out his angle for landing, it became apparent that he was going to have to aim for one narrow, clear rift of grass between two large carpets of sheep.

Bob emitted a strange, little noise—something halfway between a moan and a cry—and threw his arms up in front of his face. Jack touched the plane's large main wheels down, missing the sheep—barely. But then kinetic energy took a hand, causing the Jenny to crow-hop back into the air—still going too fast and using up more of the precious yards remaining to the boulders at the end of the pasture. At this point, even though the Jenny was temporarily airborne again, only eight or ten feet separated it from the top of a woolen sea. But now there were no more clear areas in the pasture. Sheep milled everywhere, including directly in the path of the plane.

We're going to chew up some sheep. Jack grimaced and groaned into the slipstream. Then, before he realized it, he did the unthinkable again. *Lord, give us a place to go.*

He glanced at his airspeed indicator, saw the needle drop well below stall speed, and felt the plane sink beneath the seat of his pants. Jack craned his head around the rising nose of the Jenny. The sheep were still there—running everywhere! *Here we go!*

"Brace your feet on the firewall, Son," he yelled to Bob in the front cockpit, but the boy didn't move. He just sat like a post, arms crossed in front of his face. Jack pictured the plane flipping over after digging into the flock before him. He gave the sky a quick glance. "Lord, please!" Jack prayed again, his low tone inaudible in the wind. He resisted the urge to lift his feet off the pedals as the biplane dropped closer to the confused, running creatures.

Then a comet of black and white fur slashed through the panicked flock just ahead of the Jenny's wind-milling propeller. *The shepherd's dog. Thank you, Jesus!* The little canine raced back and forth and around in circles, cutting off wooly deserters and bullying the rest out of danger. A series of intricate complicated maneuvers, done lightning quick, it was over in less than two seconds, just as Jack's wheels touched down upon a stretch of dry grass and desert sage...now devoid of sheep. The plane rolled to a wing-rumbling stop a little less than a hundred feet farther—safe, undamaged, and a respectable twelve feet short of the first line of boulders. As forward motion ceased, the veteran pilot let out a sigh and unbuckled his safety belt. He looked at the first big rock. *I guess three hundred feet was enough.* He chuckled and raised himself up in the cockpit. *Alive and well again. What more could a young boy ask?*

Jack slapped Bob hard on the shoulder and watched him jump. The boy dropped his arms and whirled around. Jack manufactured a confident, *nothing to it* smile. "We're down, Bob." He pulled off his leather helmet and stuffed it into the pocket of his flying suit. "Everything's all right now." Jack swung his legs over the side of the cockpit. "You might as well get out. The flying part of trip is over for a little while." He leaned forward and slid the rest of the way to the ground.

Bob just stared open-mouthed for a moment then followed his mentor to solid earth. "I thought we was gonna die for sure, Mr. MacGregor!" He pulled his goggles down over his head so they hung loose around his generous Adam's apple. He pointed to the speeding, black and white bullet as it corralled the flock into the far junction of two tree-lines. "That there dog saved our lives!"

Jack kept his calm, confident smile nailed firmly in place, taking care to restrain all he really knew of the danger that had just past. *Never let the customer see you're worried. He might have second thoughts about being a pilot ...or buying the plane.* The Jenny's present owner yawned and performed an exaggerated stretch. "Naw. Those sheep would have cleared as we got closer. I've done this before." He inwardly winced at the lie. "But I have to admit. That bright pup did make things a lot easier."

"Well, we're glad to have been of service, *Senor*."

Both Jack and Bob turned toward the source of the voice. It came from a short, stocky man dressed in rough canvas trousers and a plaid shirt. His hair looked as thick and black as his beard, which, although trimmed short at the bottom, spread over most of his face. A dark, drooping, unlit pipe hung from his mouth.

"To save the sheep is good for both of us. Wouldn't you agree?" he said between semi-clenched teeth as the unlit pipe bobbed with his words. "I am Bernardo Santana Domingo De Catalan. But you can call me Bernie." He thrust out a leathered palm.

Jack took the hand and shook it. "Pleased to meet you. I'm Jack MacGregor, and this is Bob Arbid." He gestured toward the oily youth.

"I'm buyin' the plane," Bob blurted.

Bernie smiled. "New pilot, eh?"

Bob shook his head. "Naw, I got almost forty hours."

Bernie held his smile. "*Bueno. Que hombre.*" He made a fist and flexed his bicep. The shepherd's accent sounded vaguely Hispanic, but still strange and unfamiliar.

"Thanks a bunch for your help. You and the dog, I mean." Jack hesitated. "Excuse me for asking, but you don't sound Mexican."

Bernie whistled to the dog. "*Ola*, Black Jack! *Venga se!*" The dog quickly finished his task and raced to his master's side as if he were shot from a gun. The shepherd smiled at the two pilots. "I do not sound Mexican because I am not." He said no more but continued to smile.

Jack saw that he was expected to guess, so he obliged the game. "Uh, you're from Spain?"

Bernie looked pleased but shook his head. "No." He shrugged. "You are close though. My family lived there more than one hundred years ago, but we've been Californios since then. I am Basque." He patted his chest. "This is my sheep camp." He waved to the shed and wire pens. "And you are my guests." He spread his bear-like arms. "Welcome." The Basque gave oily Bob the once-over. "Looks like you boys have a little oil leaking from somewhere." He reached down and ruffled the fur on his dog's head then smoothed his own beard with the same hand.

At the mention of the oil leak, Jack held his breath for a moment to soothe the remainder of his nerves while he rebuilt his confident smile. "Just an oil line. Nothing vital." He swallowed away the dryness that half-lies always left in his throat and gave thanks that he was talking to a man whose knowledge extended only to sheep. It made it easier to bluff Bob through this little hitch in the sale.

Bernie continued stroking his whiskers. "Nothing vital. Yes." He scanned the two pilots for a moment as if making some sort of decision. Then he gave his dog one last pat and leaned down to give him loving orders in a soft but firm tone. "Black Jack, *ve te a su trabajo.*" The little canine shot off again toward the distant flock, and the shepherd, sporting a strange half-smile, turned his attention back to Jack. "Well, then. An oil line." He walked a few steps toward his shack. Jack instinctively followed, and Bob followed Jack. Bernie turned his head and spoke over his shoulder. "You know, my friends. I think perhaps I have something to help you."

Jack unbuttoned his flying suit. "Really? What's that?"

Bernie continued toward the small plank building. "An oil line," he said, keeping his tone even and matter-of-fact.

Jack hurried a step to catch up. "You have aircraft oil line hose?"

Bernie shook his head. "No. It's for my truck. But it will fit an OX5 engine, if your clamps are still good. That's the beauty of those little Curtis power plants. They will happily accept a small list of automotive parts without complaint."

Jack stopped suddenly, causing poor greasy Bob to collide with him as they passed under the vague twilight shadow of a big oak. "You know about aircraft engines?"

Bernie turned around. "Oh, I see what you're saying." He spread his arms and waved them around at the flock and sheep pens. "How could a man who herds sheep know of airplane engines? Where could he have gotten such knowledge?" He took a step toward Jack. "Or do you mean how could a Basque be smart enough to understand such complicated matters?"

Holding up his palms in surrender, Jack shook his head. "I didn't mean either of those things." He paused to consider the wisdom of his next statement and decided to take the chance. "But you have to admit," he said. "It is a little unusual to find someone who knows engine repair in a sheep camp. We've been blessed."

Bernie didn't answer for a moment, then he nodded. "Blessed. Yes. We are blessed." He looked at Bob as if truly seeing him for the first time. "Boy, why don't you go into my shack there...." He pointed to the small board structure. "And use my wash pan to clean your face. You look like you just hugged a greased pig. There's an old gray towel on the stand that used to be white back last September, so you won't hurt it much."

The boy bobbed his head. "Much obliged." Then he trotted off.

Bernie strode to a row of high wooden shelves nailed to the shack wall and began rummaging through the assortment of tools and random materials that lay there. In the almost nonexistent light, Jack could just make out a few familiar shapes like pliers or screwdrivers. The mild after-sunset glow, however, seemed to be sufficient for the shepherd as he ran his practiced fingers over the eclectic piles like a man reading Braille. "No, no, no. Uh? No," he muttered as he half looked, half felt for what he wanted. "No, not there. Where are you, *mi gato pequeno*?" He went to the next shelf and began the search again. "No, no." Suddenly, he stopped and smiled. "Ah! *Esta aqui*! Here she is!" Holding up a small coil of black neoprene hose, he released his smile to become a fully matured grin. "Just what the doctor ordered. *Que no*?" He wiggled the hose's end so it looked like a snake. Then he laughed. "Such a little worm to bring down a big bird." He laughed again and elbowed Jack, who decided it was a good time to let go some of the tension of the landing with a more subdued snicker. "Come," said Bernie. "Let's fix your airplane." He clapped his guest on the back, grabbed a pair of pliers, and led the way out to the Jenny.

As they walked, Jack felt his curiosity overcome caution, and he ventured the obvious question. "All right. I have to ask. Where *did* you learn about Liberty engines?"

"*Bueno*! A man of action. I like it." Bernie revealed a satisfied smile as he glanced at Jack. "At the Glenn Curtiss Aeroplane Factory during the war when I was in training for the Army. I ended up as a mechanic...first at a flight school—got a lot of experience with Jenny engines there—then with a bomber squadron in France. De Havilland DH4's. Those were the big Liberty engines though—four hundred horsepower." He made another flexing pantomime with his bicep. "They had the power of a bear." He looked off into the night as if seeing something invisible to anyone else, then he shook the expression off. "I liked working on them very much."

Jack tripped on a shadow-hidden squirrel mound and had to catch up as Bernie hiked on. "But you like sheep better now?"

They reached the front of the biplane, and Bernie quickly began unfastening the engine cowling with the easy grace of a man completely familiar with the work at hand. "I like both the sheep and the airplanes, but, after the war, I had little choice. Mechanic jobs were for the Anglo doughboys. A Basque? Well, he can go tend the sheep." He paused. "These are my family's sheep, though. There is no shame for me to be here." He swung the metal cover off the engine and peered up at the remains of the old, offending oil line. "But make no mistake. I do love to work on these engines."

The Basque soon removed the line's metal clamps and cleaned all crystallized remnants from the oil system's two metal nipples. Then he held up the new rubber line to eyeball the length he would need. Jack walked around to the front of the engine to get a better view of the work. He would have made this small repair himself, but this unusual man seemed to be having a good time. And who was Jack to spoil it?

"You're in my twilight," Bernie said matter-of-factly.

"Sorry." Jack took a giant step to one side and squatted down to better see where the mechanic/shepherd was working. "You work fast."

Bernie pulled a long knife from a sheath that hung from his belt and cut off the excess hose. "Army always wanted 'em done in a hurry."

"Yeah, I remember." Jack pulled up a blade of grass and rolled it between his fingers. He had begun to like this shepherd. "At least, I always wanted my ship ready as soon as it could be."

Bernie pushed one end of the new line onto its steel nipple. "Army pilot?" He spared his guest a squinty-eyed glance.

"Yeah." Throwing down the grass blade, Jack sighed. "Matter of fact, I was in a DH-4 squadron, myself."

Bernie grunted softly, then tightened the clamp back onto one end of the new line. "Where *was* this squadron?"

"St. Jean du Loc." Jack managed a tentative smile.

After securing the final clamp, Bernie stretched his arms and duck-walked out from under the Jenny. He milked an upper body stretch and groaned mildly. Then he swiveled his head and made his neck crack. "I was at Voisin, just to the south. Didn't care much for France though. Too soggy for me." He leaned down under the engine again to give his work a final inspection.

Bob half yelled, half yodeled from the shack. "Hey, Mister! You got a privy around here?"

"Sure!" Raising up to answer, Bernie banged his head on the underside of the engine mount. This immediately stopped his upward progress and caused him not only to grab his scalp but also to back out from under the plane to keep from repeating the move.

Jack could almost feel the man's pain as he listened to the oaths hissed around the man's pipe, still secured between clenched teeth. He decided to help.

"Where's the outhouse?" he asked his hurting host.

"Far end of the west tree line."

Jack cupped his hands around his mouth. "Go to the end of those west-most trees there, Bob!"

"Okay!" Bob answered then disappeared.

Bernie groaned as he shook his head. "*Gracias*." He blinked his eyes then opened them wide as he continued rubbing his crown. "That bit hard." He took a deep breath and let it out all at once. "So why you selling this lady?" He lifted the cowling over one side of the engine.

Jack stalled on answering for a few seconds. He helped Bernie position the engine's sheet-metal covering and secured the thing with the screwdriver. Should he spill everything to this stranger?

He chuckled, then rolled his eyes. "I'm selling her for love."

"*Valgome, Dios!*" Bernie joined in on the laughter. "*Pobresito.* Tell me about this. Is she a flapper, this lover of yours?"

Jack pulled a red rag from a leg pocket in his flying suit then wiped his hands and face. "It's even worse than that." He paused. "She's my wife." He handed the rag to Bernie and immediately felt a twinge of embarrassment for letting the conversation turn personal.

"Then you are a fool." Bernie used the rag and tossed it back.

A surprised Jack caught the thing, stared at it a moment as if *it* had spoken the insult, then re-pocketed it. He knew he'd made a mistake—not in regard to the oil rag...but in navigating the conversation. *Never open up to people you don't know!* He was a fool indeed! "Now wait just a—"

One leathered palm went up as Bernie broke into a yellow-toothed grin. "My friend, I too am such a fool." His hands indicated the plane he had just repaired. "I searched for a mechanic job from coast to coast after I returned from the Great War." His lip curled as he shook his head. "Nada. But I too had a wife and she says for me to come back and take care of the sheep." He smiled again and shrugged. "Here I am." He sighed. "Love is a terrible thing. *Que no?* It makes a man endure things that should not happen to his mother-in-law."

The two shared another laugh, then Jack's mirth suddenly died. "Ya know, I just remembered. I don't have any more oil for this thing. I was basically just hitching a last ride to the coast before turning it over to young Bob."

Bernie's left eyebrow raised almost to his hairline. "*Mi casa es su casa.*"

Jack scratched his head. "What'd you say?"

"My house is your house." Bernie looked a little smug. "And so is my oil."

"You have oil?" Jack almost choked on the sentence . What else did this mechanic in shepherd's clothing have stashed in his pasture – a hanger and fuel truck?

Bernie spread his hands. "Yes. I have oil."

"Enough to fill this old girl?" Jack thumbed back toward the Jenny.

"You bet your life. Come with me." Bernie started off toward his shack again and motioned for Jack to follow.

"How much oil do you have?" Twilight continuing to succumb to the growing darkness, and Jack stumbled again over the same squirrel hole.

Bernie cleared his throat. "Oh, right around ten cases here and maybe another ninety or so back at the main house. I'm not really sure. Never counted it all, but it's a big stack, you betchya."

They were not ten miles from the desert's edge, and, despite the fact that the sun had been down for a while now, the temperature still stood at a good eighty degrees. Jack unbuttoned his flying suit down passed the belt on his jodhpurs inside and flapped its open seams for ventilation.

"Holy smokes, Bernie! Where'd you *get* a hundred cases of oil?"

"I was at the Presidio in San Francisco just before I got my discharge. They was gonna burn all that oil and hundreds of cases more. So I got permission from the disposal officer to come back with my truck and load up as much as I could carry. One load only. That's all he give me 'cause he was ordered to burn whatever was still left the next day. So I load my truck up high so she'll just make it under the streetcar wires and I creep the seventy mile back to Monterey mostly in second gear. That's where my family has the hacienda ... the house ...just east of Monterey as you go to Salinas."

Jack closed his mouth. "A hundred cases of motor oil!" He gave Bernie a tentative back-slap. "Brother, you were blessed!"

Bernie eyed his companion. "Hmm. That's the second time you have said that. Are you a man of God, or do you just like to play with holy words?"

The Basque's candor once again caught Jack off guard. But he also found it refreshing. "Say, you don't waste any time getting to the point. Do you."

"Like I said, I like men of action...even if it is me." He waved an expressive hand in the air. "What is the *point* of not coming to the point?"

Jack's forehead furrowed as he tried not to lose the line of conversation. "Right. Uh...what was the question?"

"Are you a man of God?"

"Well." Jack paused. Not because he did not want to answer but because it was the first time anyone had asked that question in such a direct and challenging manner. His admiration for this shepherd increased again. "Yes. As a matter of fact, I am. Or at least I try to be. That's part of why I'm selling the plane."

They reached the back of the shack, and Bernie pulled a black, time-eaten tarp off a tall stack of wooden crates.

There were wide spaces between the crate's thin slats through which peaked a profusion of olive-drab metal cans proudly bearing *US Army* in black-stenciled letters.

"Don't see your friend." Bernie hefted a case of oil onto what looked like a child's wooden wagon then grabbed another.

Jack loaded a third crate. "I don't see him either." He searched the shadows toward the nearby tree line. "Hey, Bob!" he hollered. "You fall in or something?"

A disembodied reply soon drifted back from behind the oaks. "No sir, Mr. MacGregor. Looking for the …the, uh…."

Bernie interceded. "Oh, there's a Sears catalog on the shelf just over your head! But watch out for black widows!"

"Thank you, Sir!" was Bob's answer, but a muffled oath was heard shortly after.

Bernie went into the shack and came out a minute later with a large metal funnel. He tossed it on top of the oil cases. "So why does this wife of yours want you to sell your plane?" Picking up its handle, he pulled the wagon out toward the Jenny.

"Well, she didn't actually say that. But I know as well as I'm standing here that she'll be happier once it's gone." This time Jack saw the squirrel hole coming and sidestepped it. The act gave him a momentary feeling of triumph.

Bernie stopped when he got to the Jenny and dropped the wagon handle to the ground. "*Bueno*. So why does your wife want the plane gone?" There was a hint of impatience in his voice.

"She thinks it's kept me away from her and the kids." Jack ran a grimy hand over the blond stubble on his face, immediately darkening the day-old whiskers. "She's right, of course. In order to make any money at all I've had to fly around the country either selling rides in places where planes are rare or sign on with a flying circus." He turned the soles of his boots up for inspection then shuffled them into the sod to remove a smear of sheep dropping. "Didn't make much money though, but I thought if I could just stay at it long enough I'd find a way to make my name known and bring home a feed sack full of cash." As he spoke, Jack began to feel hot, too hot even for a warm summer night like this. This was no mystery, however; nor was it a first-time occurrence. Jack often ran minor fevers when he felt he was being scrutinized with reference to uncomfortable subjects. And he felt very uncomfortable, at the moment, sharing so much about his failures. However, strange as it seemed, at the same time it also felt good to tell someone— like lifting a great weight from his chest—like he could breathe easy for the first time in a long time.

Bernie slid some oil cans out of their case and set them on the plane's lower wing. "How many kids you got?"

"Two. Both boys." Jack handed Bernie more cans. "They're four and seven." He discarded an empty case and opened the last one. Then he lowered himself down onto one knee and leaned sideways against the little wagon. "I didn't mean to stay away from them so long. I just wanted to...." He sniffed and fought back the empty feeling that rose up inside. "I just wanted to...."

"You just wanted to show your wife and your sons that you were not just some bum that had left his better days behind him." Bernie climbed up onto the plane and unscrewed the oil filler cap. "Am I right?"

Jack sighed as he nodded. Then he cleared his throat. "Yeah. That's about it."

"And the longer you stayed out without success the more you knew you couldn't go home without having made your fortune. You want to hand me that funnel there, Jack?" Bernie held out his hand.

"Yeah," the kneeling pilot answered, but instead of complying, he merely continued to stare off into space. For that moment, a parade of lost opportunities raced past the eye of Jack's mind, each one progressively more painful than the one before it—each one adding its measure of shame to an already heavy load. Then he reeled his consciousness back to his body and stood up. "Oh, yeah!" He grabbed the neglected funnel and passed it on to the mechanic. "Sorry."

Opening the oil can with a pocket can opener, Bernie began replenishing the biplane's supply. "I did the same... stayed away too long chasing a dream. You're not the only *hombre* that did not strike it rich after the war. You know?" He tossed an empty can onto the grass and caught the next one Jack threw to him. "I think you are doing the right thing...going back and all."

"I have to. Along with how lonesome I feel when the sun's up—at night, I haven't been able to dream about anything but my family...for months. And lately, I've even started seeing their faces in daydreams. It's been driving me screwy." Jack flapped some more relatively cooler air into his flying suit. *Boy, is it getting hot!* "I know when I'm beaten," he said. "I need to get home and take care of my family, and the three hundred dollars from the Jenny will help get things rolling again. I know it's not much, but at least I won't show up empty-handed."

"I'm sure they'll greet you with open arms no matter how many dollars you have." Bernie suddenly spit out into the grass. "Ugh! Gnat! I hate those little devils!"

"It's not going to be that easy." Jack kept the supply of oil-cans and confessions moving. "They've already gone to live with my in-laws."

"That's bad." Bernie spit again. "Ai! You little son of a maggot's tail!" He shook his head side to side in an effort to avoid another gnat.

"Bad. Yeah. That's for sure." Jack paused. He knew Bernie was right...both about in-laws and gnats. Carrie moving back to the Van Burean estate was a bad sign, something he'd been trying not to think about for the last few days. It did not bode well for his chances of reuniting with his family. His in-laws would try to prevent that. This was a sure bet. So he decided not to think about all this for just a while longer. "Well, the money from the plane should do the trick," he said and tried to believe it.

Bernie stayed hunched over the oil intake for a while. Jack could still hear him spitting out gnats. "You do not seem too sad about losing your airplane," he said and spit again. "Who is your other lover?"

"What?" Another lover? Jack didn't follow. But he did wonder why the gnats were only hanging around Bernie at the moment.

Bernie didn't turn around. "You're not sad over your loss. There must be something else you love to do just as much as flying...or maybe more. Another lover. *Si?*"

Surprising himself, Jack quickly answered, "Yes, there is."

"Well, who is she?"

Another quick answer. "Writing fiction." There it was, and it made Jack feel good to be honest on that subject, too.

"Friction?"

"No. Fiction. Telling made up stories in books."

"Ah. Parables."

"Yes. Sort of."

"Just like Jesus."

Jack considered this a moment. "Well, yes. I suppose so, although I've never thought of it that way."

Bernie glanced back over his shoulder. "I think that is a good love to have."

Jack nodded semiconsciously. "I think so, too."

Bernie turned around, caught another oil can from Jack, then gave him a long look. "Looks like this Jenny's a little past her prime. *Que no?*" He raised an indicating hand and gave the biplane a symbolic once-over with it.

Jack produced a little of his salesman tone. "Young

Bob's going to be attending college in Los Angeles. This old girl will serve him well enough. He just wants to impress coeds and fly home to Indio once or twice a month."

The last of the oil went into the reservoir and Bernie tightened the filler cap. He slid down to the ground and tossed the empty can into the growing pile with the rest. "That's good." He paused. "It's good that is all he's going to do with her." He sighed and paused again, staring into Jack's eyes. "Because you and I both know this machine would not last long doing much else." He cracked his knuckles. "It needs, at least, an engine rebuild, if not a whole new engine. That little ninety-horse Liberty's on its last legs. I could tell that much when I heard you fly over the first time." He bent down and started throwing empty cans back into the open cases. "And it'll take at least another hundred dollars to fix the other things that'll make this kite safe to fly again. *I* have just seen this tonight. *You've* been *flying* her. I *know* you know this old girl's in sad shape." The shepherd threw the last of the cans into the boxes, and the boxes back onto the wagon. "Does this boy know these things?"

The weight of guilt dropped squarely onto Jack's shoulders. He'd tried not to think of this either, not telling Bob the true condition of the airplane he was buying. He'd tried to pretend for the sake of the sale that all was well. But now someone else had spoken the truth out loud, and Jack could not keep the deception going any longer. Especially not with Bernie, whose opinion he had strangely come to value over the last hour or so.

He turned away. "No. He doesn't know yet." Jack picked up a wayward oil can and turned it around in his hands. "Do *you* intend to tell him?"

Bernie gave the emerging stars a long look. "Nope." He paused and gazed off in the direction of his shack. "That's your decision."

71

Jack hated Bernie's words the minute he heard them. His *conscience* had been nagging him ever since Bob expressed interest in buying the plane. *Tell the boy the truth. God will provide.* That's what he kept hearing in his innermost ear. But how could he do that? Bob would walk away, like anyone with an ounce of common sense. The boy wasn't quite as dumb as he sometimes sounded. That being the case, Jack would most certainly return to his family empty-handed.

Over the last few months, all his dreams of making it as a flyer had been blown away like ashes in a cyclone. Where had God been all *that* time? How could Jack trust Him now?

Still, the voice of conscience persisted. *God will provide.*

Then Jack remembered how he had prayed to make it back to the sheep pasture for a safe landing when the oil line had broken. And now, here he stood...safe and whole. He paused in his thinking for a moment and gazed up into the brightening stars. Then he took a resupplying breath and began to consider things once more. Perhaps he *could* trust God again. Perhaps, if he did, and he told Bob the truth about the Jenny, things would turn out all right...somehow.

From a distance, the sound of someone whistling *Turkey in the Straw* echoed across the pasture. Then the two veterans heard Bob curse as he tripped over Jack's squirrel hole.

"Well," Bernie said, "You say you are a godly man." He gestured to the approaching Bob. "Now is a good time to find out for sure. *Que crees?* What do you think?"

Tell Bob the truth. Jack ran a hand through his hair. Feeling something pressing on his chest, he closed his eyes. *God, if this is you speaking through this man, please back me up and provide. Don't make me go home poor again!*

He opened his eyes just as his young student got within

conversational range. Jack nodded to Bernie. "Right." He rubbed his hands together and sighed. "Time to pay up."

"Yep." The shepherd pulled the wagon off toward the shed. "And as for me, I am going to check on my sheep."

"Oh, they're okay, Mister." Bob stumbled to a halt in front of his instructor. "That little dog's still got 'em all bunched up." Bob looked after Bernie for a moment, then turned back to Jack. "That pup's a smart one. Isn't he?"

Jack cleared his throat. "Listen Bob, there's something I need to talk to you about, and I don't know as to whether you're going to like it or not."

"What's that, Mr. MacGregor?"

"It's about the plane. Some things you need to know."

Chapter Five

The Bearcat's tires yelped their protest as they struggled for traction through Caroline's too-fast left turn. Bits of old asphalt broke loose as a consequence of the assault and flew off into a drainage ditch, flushing a cottontail from the reeds. Carrie accelerated back up through the gears, then remembered, almost as an afterthought, that she had a passenger. She glanced sideways and touched the old woman on the shoulder.

"You all right, Hannah," she said against the wind blowing through the open car.

"Sure I am, Honey." Hannah flashed a wide smile at her driver then pulled a blade of dried grass from her front teeth. "That was a wonderful four-wheel slide. Are you going do any more like that tonight?" Her eyes danced in the faint reflected light of the dashboard instruments, showing off a spark of pure excitement.

"No, I'm not, and where'd you learn about four-wheel slides?" Carrie feigned a stern tone and fought the temptation to laugh.

Hannah relaxed back into the seat. "Oh, I picked it up from—" She seemed to catch the last unspoken word and pull it back down her throat like stuffing the cat back into the bag. Then, finishing with a matter-of-factness that sounded a bit too cagey, she said, "From somewhere. I don't remember exactly."

"It's okay to say Jack's name." Carrie shook her head slowly as she spoke. "I won't go into a fit."

Hannah didn't respond, so Carrie just kept driving.

The Stutz hit a small pothole that started the back wheels fishtailing. Carrie stabilized the car then gave the speedometer a glance. They were doing well over eighty. She let off the accelerator and scanned the rearview mirror. No headlights in sight. They were alone on the road.

She'd gotten away from the gas station as fast as she could, keeping her speed up all the way down the Coast Highway. She didn't think anyone would want to follow, but, just in case, she'd put distance between the car and the general area of the family estate as quick as possible. *So now,* Carrie thought, *here we are motoring serenely down Foxtail road and my grandmother-in-law's not volunteering any information. What are you up to, old woman?* She looked over at Hannah again and tried to glean something from her manner, but nothing came. After a few seconds, she gave up and just asked. "Hannah, what's going on?"

"Oh, I told you that, Honey. They wouldn't let us talk to you."

"Okay. Well, here I am then." Carrie waved her hand to indicate a physical reference to the car. "I'm a captive audience. What do you want to talk about?"

Hannah leaned forward toward the windscreen and peered out beyond the headlights. "Oh, I'll talk to you soon enough, but right now, since there's not a streetlight for ten miles, I want to make sure you don't miss our driveway in the dark."

Carrie shook her head. "I'm not going to miss the driveway, Hannah. Now please, what is it you wanted to tell me."

"There it is, Dear." The older woman pointed through the almost total absence of light before them.

"What?' Carrie squinted in the same direction.

"Our driveway," Hannah answered. "You'd better turn now!"

It was true. Carrie had been so distracted by Hannah's persistent avoidance that she'd not seen the familiar white wagon wheel that marked the entrance to the MacGregor ranch. Irritated, more with her own mistake than with the old woman's game, she turned sharply into the short gravel drive and again had to fight to keep the car under control.

She managed to slide to a stop in the gravel without hitting the house—but just barely. Then, as the dust drifted away, she leaned back against the seat, and took a few seconds to catch her breath and get her nerves back on a leash. The night had just given birth to a fresh-rising moon. So Carrie simply sat there for a couple of non-thinking seconds, waiting for the appearance of the man in the big silver disc who always seemed to be looking back—at least out of one eye. After that, she released a calming breath and surveyed her surroundings. The place hadn't changed one little bit since she'd left the month before. The planks on the sprawling one-story ranch house still begged for a much overdue coat of whitewash. Clay flower pots, dripping with geraniums, still dangled from hemp cords strung from the porch rafters, and the barn gave shelter to at least one owl, now taking wing from the upper loft...all just as before. For an instant, she felt like she *was,* in truth, home again. But then she banished that thought as an unwanted intruder.

"That one wasn't quite as exciting, but it was still good." Hannah grabbed a side-glance and gave Carrie a wink. "You've really got the knack for steering this...what do you call it?"

"It's a Stutz Bearcat." Carrie rolled her eyes and prayed for patience.

"Bearcat," Hannah mused. "Now that's a name I like." She turned to Carrie. "It's a strong sort of name. Very much like you, I think."

Carrie turned to face her passenger. "You're stalling." She paused. "Aren't you."

Hannah glanced at the floorboards then back to Carrie. "Well, maybe just a little."

This is getting tiresome, Carrie thought. *If I didn't love this woman so much, I'd throw her out of the car.* But she said, "Why, Hannah?"

"Why what?"

Carrie's sigh sounded almost like a growl. "Why are you stalling?"

Hannah got out of the car and rummaged behind the seat for her chain. "Maybe I'm waiting for the Lord to give me my words." She coiled the steel links around her arm and smiled at Carrie. "Would you help me carry this thing into the house? It's mighty heavy."

Carrie grimaced and shook her head. "You didn't have any trouble hefting it earlier this evening." She killed the engine and the headlights, then got out of the car, taking the chain from Hannah.

"That was earlier and I was much younger then." The older woman started up the porch steps, looking back for Carrie to follow. "It's late now, and I'm old again." With that, they entered the house.

The legendary chain was unceremoniously deposited into a closet, then Hannah led Carrie through the kitchen and out, via the back door and a swinging gate, into the grass field that lay beyond the back yard's picket fence. "This is where I go to do my serious thinking," Hannah said, looking up at the starlit sky. "Leastwise, I do when it's warm outside."

Carrie took a deep breath. "Well, how about this time you do some *talking*, instead."

" Hannah?" The voice of a young woman came from behind the two and startled them both. Carrie turned and recognized Hannah's eighteen-year-old adopted daughter. The girl had just moved out a few weeks before to get married.

"Oh, Dorothy! You startled me." Hannah put her hand on her chest and caught her breath. "What do you want, dear?"

"Sorry," Dorothy said. "Didn't mean to scare you. I just wanted to...uh. Can I talk to you for a minute?'

The old woman smiled a sympathetic smile. "Is this about you and Barney?"

Dorothy glanced around and shuffled her feet. "Uh, yes, Ma'am."

"Well, that'll take more than a minute." Hannah put a hand on Dorothy's shoulder. "You remember Caroline, of course.

"Oh, yes." The child-woman nodded to Carrie. "Nice to see you again."

"Hello." Carrie felt genuine concern for Dorothy. She had sympathy for any woman in her first year of marriage.

"Carrie and I were just about to do some really serious talking ourselves. It's the kind of talk that really can't wait." Hannah stroked a stray hair back off of Dorothy's forehead. "Can I talk to you in the morning, or is it something that can't wait either?"

Dorothy pursed her lips and sighed. "It'll keep 'til mornin'."

"You're sure?" Hannah leaned over to peer into Dorothy's downturned face.

The girl looked up and nodded. "Yeah, I'm sure."

Hannah patted her arm. "All right, then. I'll see ya for breakfast. Seven sharp. Floyd'll be done eating by that time."

Dorothy nodded again and quietly moved off toward the front drive. Hannah turned back to Carrie. "Wait just a sec." She closed her eyes and put one hand to her forehead.

This surprised and concerned Carrie a little. "Hannah, are you all right?"

The old woman kept her eyes closed but answered quickly, "Hush now. I'm praying."

Carrie nodded respectfully, but her patience continued to wear. "Okay." She looked up at the stars, dimed by fresh moonbeams, and, while she waited, tried to soak up some of their serenity. She closed her eyes and let the soft coastal breeze that rustled the grass whisper peace into her ears. The nearby field's aroma teased her nose until finally she surrendered and breathed in all of the grass, clover, and eucalyptus she could, holding their essence captive for just an instant longer than normal before allowing it all to escape. *I love this old ranch*, Carrie thought. *I'm not sure why, but I do.* She also loved the old woman who stood beside her praying, even if Hannah *was* at that moment driving her crazy. And she loved Hannah's weather-beaten, Lincolnesque husband, who was right then walking along a seemingly endless row of metal drums, setting ablaze whatever was within them with an oil-rag torch. *All Floyd needs are chin-whiskers and a stovepipe hat*, she mused and then remembered she'd never seen him do that particular chore, with burning oil drums, before. It held her attention for a while.

"Amen," Hanna said. "Okay, I've got it."

Carrie came back out of her thoughts. "Got what?"

"What I'm to say to you."

Carrie smirked a little. "Hannah, are you trying to tell me that God's telling you what—"

"Don't make fun now." Hannah's response sounded serious with a slight edge. "I'm not joking about *this*."

Carrie felt a little ashamed at that point; she hadn't meant to ridicule. She just couldn't remember ever having heard Hannah talk like that before. "I'm sorry." She looked out at the field where her grandfather-in-law had just lit the last of the drums. Their flaming presence seemed to form a ribbon of fiery light down the center of the pasture and tugged at her memory. She felt like she'd seen something like it before but couldn't recall where. "What's Floyd doing?" she asked.

Hannah glanced quickly at her husband then looked up at the sky again. "Oh, he's ...he's just lighting smudge pots to keep the grasshoppers off the pasture."

"Those are pretty big smudge pots. Aren't they?" Something bothered her about Hannah's answer. "And they're not making much smoke. They're just burning."

"Caroline, that's not what I brought you here to talk about," Hannah snapped.

Carrie was caught short and properly impressed by Hannah's reaction. She'd never heard her even raise her voice much before. *Whatever this is about,* she thought, *it must be really important to her.* She turned to face her grandmother-in-law and gave her her full attention. "I'm listening, Hannah," she said softly.

Hannah touched Carrie's hand. "I'm sorry, Carrie. I guess I just let my feelings get the better of me for a sec." She looked down at the ground and took a deep breath before starting. "Caroline…Do you still love my grandson?"

Carrie skipped a breath, and a small, electric pain ran from her head to her heart then back again. That was the last question she wanted to hear at that moment, and Hannah was the last person she wanted to hear ask it. She had more than one answer for it, though. Some she wanted to share; some she didn't. She tried to find a safe one to give Hannah. "He left us."

Hannah's answer was quick. "From what I saw, you left each other."

Carrie's tone became cool. "He went off barnstorming for weeks at a time, leaving us in that rented shack. And when he'd finally come home, he wouldn't even have enough money to feed the boys, let alone pay the bills." She looked into Hannah's eyes, and her tone softened. "I wanted to go to my father for a little help or even get a job, but Jack wouldn't have any of it. That's why I came to you then." She paused to wipe her eyes, then she let the strain of the last few years came out in her voice. "Most of what he made selling rides and doing stunts he poured into that stupid old aeroplane! I can't tell you how much I hate that piece of war surplus junk!" She sniffed and tried to dam the coming tear tide with a petite finger. "Oh, I don't have my purse!"

Hannah pulled a fresh pressed handkerchief from a small breast pocket. " Here, dear." She handed it to Carrie. "It's clean."

"Some tomato I am." She blotted and blew. "Acting like someone's kid sister."

Hannah took a deep breath. "He should have quit barnstorming when it didn't work out."

Carrie looked up, red-eyed. "I thought you said he could be a great flyer."

"I did right after the war." Hannah shook her head. "But not at the expense of his family." She looked away for a moment. "That's not even being a man. 'Take care of your family first.' That's what Floyd and even Jack's father taught him. It looks to me like my grandson forgot that."

Carrie's tears came faster now, and she gave up trying to capture them. "Why did he do that, Hannah? He said he loved us." She shook the betraying drops from her face. "Why did he leave us alone like that?"

Hannah answered with a thoughtful, sympathetic tone. "He just chose his desires over you and the boys." She closed her eyes a moment as if she were lost in thought or more prayer. " I believe he's trying to be a success in his own way, so he can prove he's just a good as...." She hesitated.

"My family," Carrie finished.

"Maybe," Hannah said. "Or he might be trying to show his *own* father a thing or two." She brushed a horsefly away from her face. "It's still no excuse, though. If he's your husband, he's also your provider and protector. That's what the Lord says, and Jack knows it. He has no excuse, and I am ashamed of him!" Hannah turned away from Carrie and scanned the distant hills.

Carrie found herself genuinely taken aback. "Hannah, I've never seen you like this! I thought Jack was the apple of your eye."

The old woman turned back around. "Well, the apple of my eye seems to have gone rotten ... hasn't he?" She sighed and searched the horizon. "And, like the good book says, 'If the apple of your eye offend thee, pluck it out.'"

"The good book doesn't say that." Now Carrie was puzzled. Hannah knew the Bible, chapter and verse, from front to back. Many times, when Carrie and the boys were visiting, the old saint would recite entire sections from memory without cracking the book itself. *Something's wrong,* she thought. *She sounds like she means to disown him.* Out loud she said, "You wouldn't refuse to see Jack. Would you, Hannah?"

"I might," Hannah kept her back partly to Carrie, and switched her attention from the pale horizon to some small clouds that were crossing in front of the moon's bright disk. "Yep, I just might, if he doesn't straighten up real soon."

Carrie heard a persistent, rhythmic squeak coming from behind her, and turned to see Floyd striding from the barn, balancing what looked like a red-painted milk can on the back of an old wooden pull-wagon. Again, something seemed strange to her. Familiar, yet somehow out of place. But she still couldn't put her finger on exactly what it was. Curious, she called out to the old man as he came near, "Floyd, what are you doing?"

Floyd looked almost confused for an instant, but he answered, "Oh, this is just gas fer the...uh...."

"*Smudge pots,*" Hannah finished her husband's sentence.

"Yeah," he confirmed. "*The smudge pots.*" He spoke over his shoulder as he wheeled the wagon past the women and toward the flaming line of drums. "Don't want 'em to run out."

Once again, something about the *smudge pot* subject nagged at Carrie's subconscious, but she couldn't really think much about it just yet; there was still the matter of Hannah and Jack. "Hannah, you can't disown Jack!"

Hannah kept her eyes on Floyd as she answered. "Why not, Dear. He left my great-grandchildren to starve."

"We weren't exactly starving." Then another distraction reached Carrie's ears, the very distant sound of an approaching airplane engine, barely audible over the noise of the night insects. Now *she* looked up as she spoke. "And I know for a fact that Jack really believed he was building a future for us. He thought he *was* providing for his family." She paused. "He used to tell me how you and Floyd had to sacrifice in the beginning to get your dreams going. That's what he thought we...both of us...were doing. Sacrificing for our family's future."

The sound of the plane's engine had grown louder now, but Hannah only gave the sky a cursory glance. "Must be the night mail plane from San Diego...on his way to Los Angeles. Seems like about time for him."

"Right, the mail plane." Carrie was getting frustrated again. "Hannah, we're talking about you and Jack!"

Hannah took a step closer to Carrie so they were almost face-to-face. "I heard you, Carrie. So, do you really believe that Jack was actually trying to be responsible in his own way?" Her words came out fast as if she were in a hurry to get through them.

Carrie took a moment to think. "Yes."

Hannah looked her directly in the eye again. "Do you think he'd listen if someone reasoned with him?"

Carrie paused once more. "If they could make him see what his sky gypsy act has caused. Yes, I think he'd listen now. You can't cut yourself off from him now, Hannah. It'd just kill him!"

"All right then, Honey. I won't." Hannah smiled a very small smile just for a split second. "But do me a favor will you?" The sound of the plane's circling back to overfly the pasture again provoked Hannah into one more quick upward glance.

Carrie did the same, then answered Hannah with divided attention. Something was annoying her. Something was gnawing at her consciousness trying to break through. "Of course. What do you want me to do?"

Hannah's expression turned more serious, but appeared oddly forced to Carrie.

"If you see Jack before I do," the old woman said. "Will you tell him everything you just told me?"

" There's no chance of that, Hannah. I'm going back home tonight, and Jack won't be allowed on the estate. You know that."

"But if you *do* see him first," Hannah insisted.

"Hannah, that can't—"

"Please...if you do."

Carrie sighed. "All right. If I see him first, I'll tell him."

"Promise?" Hannah pushed.

"Yes!"

Hannah's little smile returned. "Good."

It was at that moment that Carrie heard the plane's engine cut out, causing her to instinctively look skyward again. "Sounded like it stopped," she said as she watched the pale blue flames of the plane's exhaust stacks slowly descend in the darkness.

Hannah turned her back on the field, walked a little past Carrie, then came to a halt with her face toward the house. "Oh my," she said calmly. "I hope he's not in trouble."

Then it all hit Carrie at once. The mysteries melted away, and all the little, vague familiarities suddenly came together into one clear stream of realization. *Those aren't smudge pots,* she thought. *They're just gasoline drums cut in half, and I have seen them lit like that before...at an airfield Jack flew from in the Army. They were bringing in an overdue plane after dark, and they lit drums full of gas so the pilot could see where to land.*

She heard the engine rev up for a second, then wind down to idle. She could see the far drum's firelight reflected off the craft's fuselage. It was an oily orange with more repair patches than a farm-boy's britches. Carrie shook her head and took a deep breath of control before she spoke. "Well, Hannah, I think he'll stay out of trouble as long as his grandpa's *smudge pots*," she overemphasized the words, "don't blind him and he doesn't run over his grandma's picket fence!"

The plane touched down well before mid-field and rolled to a stop a safe distance from the burning drums.

Hannah kept her back to Carrie and the scene. "What do you mean, dear?"

"You know it's Jack, Hannah! You set this whole thing up! How could you?"

Hannah did not turn around. "Are you sure that's Jack, Honey?"

"What do you mean 'am I sure it's Jack'?" Carrie watched through the ghostly glow of the gasoline drums as the pilot jumped from the wing of his well-weathered Curtiss Jenny. The wooden propeller swung its last revolution and the engine died. Then the man pulled his leather helmet off and gave Floyd a masculine hug. "Unless Floyd has a very close friendship with the San Diego mail pilot," Carrie said, "that's Jack."

Hannah finally turned toward the field and looked at her six-foot tall, blond grandson in his faded tan flying suit. He was clean-shaven but slightly coated with oil that had blown off the engine in flight. "Why, I think you're absolutely right, Carrie. That is my grandson. And, since I was looking the other direction when he arrived, *you* saw him before I did... didn't you?"

"Yes, so?"

"So Carrie, you can tell him what we were just talking about and what you said to me about how you believe he was *trying* to do the right thing."

Carrie suddenly found it a little hard to breath as the prospect of talking to Jack became real. Talking or even thinking about seeing him face-to-face was one thing, but now he was here in the flesh! "Hannah, I can't!"

"You promised."

"Hannah, you don't understand!"

"You promised."

Carrie watched the two men at the plane. Jack stood in the front cockpit now, inserting one end of a large wire-framed funnel into the fuel tank. "He's not ready to listen," she said. "Look, he's ignoring me!"

Floyd handed the red can to Jack and helped him tilt the bottom end up to pour the gas into the funnel. Hannah said, "I think Floyd wishes *that* was *his* plane." She shook her head. "Jack's not ignoring you, dear. We're beyond the firelight; he can't see you here."

The men finished fueling the weather-worn biplane, and Jack hopped to the ground to follow his grandfather and the hand-wagon back to the barn. They were headed directly for the women, but, as yet, the younger man hadn't seen them.

In an instant, Carrie's nerves wound themselves into electrified barbed wire cables that caused her body to tingle with an inaudible buzz. "Hannah, I don't know what to do!" She sniffed and wiped her nose with the handkerchief. "I *do* want us to be together but not the way it was! And I'm afraid if I just come to him right now, all ready to patch things up, he'll just think I'm a pushover, and we'll be off to the same old races again!"

"Carrie, what does the Lord tell you?" Hannah locked eyes and traded winks with Floyd as he passed.

"Hey, hold up a little, Grandpa!" Jack called from a distance to the old man who seemed to be deliberately outpacing him. "Where's the fire?" He had started to catch up but still lagged a few yards behind Floyd.

"He's saying something about praying, I think, But…" Carrie blinked soggy eyes and shook her head with a violent snap. "Does He mean pray right here…now?" She looked back and forth between Hannah and the rapidly approaching Jack.

"You'd better hurry, Honey." Hannah's tone held both urgency and a touch of amusement.

Carrie turned her back on Jack and closed her eyes again with one hand to her forehead as she'd seen Hannah do, but adapting a more intense face scrunch. She tried to think of a fast, appropriate prayer, but all that would come was *Lord, guide me now!* She waited a split second, in hopes of an immediate answer, but when that did not arrive, she opened her eyes and turned around just in time to meet a shocked, opened-mouthed Jack.

He had the look of someone who had been jumped by a man-eating tiger and sounded as if he'd just learned how to use of his tongue. "Carrie… what are you doing here?"

Carrie looked briefly to Hannah, who answered the unspoken question. "No, he *didn't* know you were going to be here."

Carrie turned back to her husband. "Is that true, Jack?"

"Sure, it is!" He looked confused. "If I'd known you were here, I wouldn't have come."

Hannah winced at her grandson's unfortunate response and waited for the inevitable reaction from Caroline.

It came in less than a second. "Oh, you wouldn't, would you?" Carrie found herself at full throttle by the end of her third word. "Well, let me tell you something, Buster Brown!'

"No, No! Hold on, Carrie! That's not what I meant!" Jack was in the middle of the whirlpool now with no idea how he'd gotten there. All he could do at that point was fight to keep from drowning. In desperation he looked to Hannah. "Grandma, tell her I didn't mean it that way!"

Hannah stepped forward for just a moment. "Jack, take the goggles off your helmet."

"What?" Jack said, even *more* confused now.

Carrie's lungs heaved with aggressive energy, but for just this moment she kept herself close-lipped and silent.

Hannah remained matter-of-fact and merely repeated, "Take the goggles off your helmet."

"But why—"

"Jackie?" Hannah asserted the grandmother privilege of evoking his childhood moniker.

And Jack surrendered, defenseless against such a tactic. "Yes, Ma'am." He said and complied with her instructions.

Hannah pressed on. "Now, unzip your flying suit and give them both to me."

"Grandma, what—"

"Hurry up, Jack." She kept her tone even, and he complied again, leaving himself clad in his usual faded, gray shirt, black tie, and jodhpurs. "Now, talk to your wife, and don't forget what we said last week."

Jack reflected for half a moment while he checked the laces on his knee-high boots, then he seemed to remember something. "Yes, Ma'am."

"Hannah?" It was Carrie's turn to break in now, her anger supernaturally in suspension. "Why'd you want those things?"

The old woman clutched the bundle to her body and answered over her shoulder as she walked toward the house, "The goggles are expensive, and pretty soon he's going to be too warm for the overalls." She walked that grandmother walk of carrying a burden with dignity all the way to the kitchen door, then she made one final announcement before going inside. "When you kids get through with your chat, there'll be supper on the table for you. It's been in the warming oven a good part of the night.

I doubt if either one of you has eaten yet." Then she was gone.

Carrie thought about protesting that she had already dined. But, for some unknown reason, she found herself strangely hungry again, so she let it go and turned to Jack immediately after the door closed behind Hannah. "So what did she tell you last week?" She perceived a strange calm buoying her at the moment. But, along with this newfound placidity, an awareness of the potential for renewed hostility lurked just beneath the surface.

Jack looked around and shuffled his feet. "She said that, whenever I saw you again, I had to agree with whatever you said for the first five minutes." He knelt down to retie a rebellious boot-lace. "She said you'd probably be absolutely right for at least that long."

"She say anything else?" Carrie's manner remained unseasonably calm thus far, but her tone betrayed something more ominous.

"Yeah." Jack hoisted himself up. "She said that, even if you weren't right, you're entitled to say anything you want for five minutes anyway."

"So, what's supposed to happen after five minutes?" Carrie gave her nose and face one last general wipe, then sequestered Hanna's handkerchief into her topmost undergarment for safe-keeping.

"Uh, you're supposed to calm down so I can talk to you." Jack pulled a red bandana from his back pocket and mopped beaded sweat from his forehead.

"And what if I don't get reasonable after five minutes?" Carrie cocked her head and glared directly into Jack's eyes.

Jack looked down at his other boot, tug-tested the lace, then returned his attention to Carrie. "Oh, in that case, I'm supposed to keep my mouth shut and just keep on listening until you're done."

Carrie folded her arms, pursed her lips, and tapped her foot on the ground. She did this for several seconds, the kind of seconds that feel like years. *What am I supposed to do with this dope*, she thought. *Just when you want to cut him out of your life, he goes boy scout on you. So now, if I give him what he deserves,* I'm *the witch.* She took a deep breath and tried to exhale as much anger as she could before she decided anything. She closed her eyes and put her hand to her forehead again. It seemed this was becoming *her* official prayer posture too, or at least she felt more comfortable when she prayed that way. *All right, Lord,* she began. *Tell me what you want me to do.*

Carrie felt Jack touch her arm.

"Carrie?"

She jerked away. "Leave me alone! I'm thinking!" she snapped. Then in a calmer tone she added, "And praying."

"Okay," Jack said in an almost inaudible voice, then stepped back a little.

She waited for some sort of divine communication, but again none came that she could distinguish from her own thoughts. *I'm waiting, Lord.* But still no response. "Well, I guess I'm on my own," she said out loud.

"What?" Jack raised his head as if he'd been praying too.

Carrie began to pace and made two complete oval circuits in front of jack before she spoke. "Well, you don't have to worry about me yelling or going whacky on you. I'm not going to do that, see? I'm going to remain a lady; I'm going to be mature and understanding." Her words came out fast and breathy, as if she'd just run a mile or she was trying to get it all out before she lost consciousness. "I do *not* think everything was your fault. I know I had a part in it." The course of her pacing became more confined until finally she was navigating a tight circle, hugging herself as if she were cold or lonely. "I think I even understand what you were trying to...I think I... I.... Aw, hooey!" She whirled around as she screamed the last two words and snatched Jacks leather flying helmet from his pants pocket. "You big dope!" She began beating Jack about the face and chest with the leather helmet. "You big...." She hit him in tempo with each word she yelled. "Stupid...Dope!" Then she went back to random blows. "You left us alone! You just left us alone!" She threw the helmet at him and he instinctively caught it, so she just began raining fists on him as if he were a giant hunk of dough that had to be kneaded. "What's the matter with you! Are you stupid or just so selfish you don't care about us!"

Carrie paused almost a second, so Jack waited. She just stood there hyperventilating while he eyed her as if he were peering around a corner. She sank to her knees and began toying with a dirt clod that the wheelbarrow had churned up.

Jack ran a hand through his thick yellow hair and edged a little closer. "Has it been five minutes yet?" he asked, speaking slow in a voice that was almost too calm and too careful.

Then all at once she sprang up and threw the clod, hitting him in the forehead. "No, it hasn't!" Carrie felt her face flush. "I'll let you know when it's your turn to speak, if ever! Got it, mister?"

"Yes." Jack wiped the dirt from his face and backed up again.

"Do you have any idea how hard it is for me to trust or respect you now?" Carrie had regained her breath and could feel still more banked up anger waiting its turn to flow in her husband's direction. She decided not to break off her attack just yet. This had been a long time coming and the man *had* to hear it all. "Well, do you?" Jack opened his mouth to answer, but the endeavor became stillborn as Carrie responded *for* him. "No, of course you don't! How could you? You're Mr. Stupid! Aren't you?"

She let him answer that one, but allowed him one word only.

"Yes," he said.

"You bet you are!" Carrie picked up another couple of dirt clods. "You're spoiled and selfish! You only think of *you*rself!" She threw another clod at Jack, but her anger caused her to throw too hard, and it missed him, even though he didn't move.

"You and that stupid *airplane*!" On the word "airplane" she hurled her remaining missile at Jack's Jenny. She listened in the dark for evidence of a successful attack and was rewarded with a plunk as the dried mud bounced off the craft's stretched fabric. Then, she yelled at the sound. "Stupid airplane! Stupid, stupid airplane!" She walked toward it, and Jack followed. "I hate you!" she told the resting Jenny. She reached the first of the burning drums and stopped. "Do you hear me, *stupid airplane?*" She kicked the flaming drum then stepped back from the flames. "I hate you!" She kicked the drum again, causing some of the still burning gasoline to slosh onto the ground .

Jack spoke up. "Carrie, be careful."

But Carrie continued kicking. "I hate you! I hate you!" The drum was rocking now, more gas spilling onto the grass. Fortunately Floyd had been irrigating and mowing this particular field to rent out as horse pasture to neighbors. This kept its verge a vibrant green, making it almost impossible to ignite. The only thing that would burn here was the gasoline itself. "I hate you!" Carrie screamed and gave the drum one last spiteful kick. That's when it tipped over, sending several gallons of burning fuel coursing in the direction of the plane.

Jack moaned, "Oh, no!" as he sprang to outrace the creeping fire.

"Sure, go ahead!" Carrie shrieked. "Hurry up, and save your little *aeroplane!*" She ran after him, continuing to yell. "I wish you'd have worried as much about your

92

children as you do about that thing!" Jack reached into the front cockpit, pulled out a small camp shovel, and began throwing dirt onto the advancing stream of flaming liquid disaster. Carrie just paced behind him and continued the assault. "Did you hear me, Jack? This flying machine is just a *thing*! Your family is more important than a *thing*! Do you understand that?"

"I understand." Jack answered between labored breaths as he continued to combat the fire.

"What?" Carrie shrieked. She wanted him to repeat what he'd said. Just answering once would not be enough this time.

"I said I understand." He dug a smile-shaped ditch—with the open portion facing the fire—that caught the gasoline flowing toward the Jenny. Then once the burning liquid filled the smile, he covered it over with soil, and the flames began to die out. Jack breathed a sigh of relief, then hyperventilated the rest of his answer. "I know now what I did to you and the boys. I understand what I did wrong."

"You keep quiet!" Carrie lashed again. "It hasn't been five minutes yet!"

"Yes it has."

"I don't care! I'm not ready yet!" Her words were still angry, but her tone had subsided somewhat. "I'm not reasonable yet."

Jack took a last deep breath and grabbed Carrie by the shoulders. She struggled, but his firm grip held her still. "I'm going to tell you some things anyway because you need to hear them right now before you say anything else." He paused for an instant. "Any insult you could throw at me would be right, along with any name you could think up. It's all true. But there's one thing that's also true. I love you and my sons more than my own life, and, if you will give me another chance, Carrie, I'll prove that to you." He let go of her and stepped back a little. "I will," he added and gave her a sad-eyed half smile.

"Don't you give me that puppy-dog face, Jack. I see you coming a mile down the road. You weren't worried about losing me a few minutes ago. You were scared that precious Jenny was going to burn up. That's what was foremost in your pointed little head."

"I couldn't let it burn, Carrie. I'm—"

"Yes, I know," she interrupted. "That's what I'm saying. You don't—"

"Hold on!" Jack cut *her* off this time. "I couldn't let her burn because I'm selling her!"

Carrie continued as if he hadn't spoken. "You know, Jack, it wouldn't matter what you told me right—" Then her last word froze in her mouth as *his* last words sunk in. "Sell her!" she gasped. "You're going to sell your plane! To who?"

"Some kid who just learned to fly," he answered. "He has no wife or kids." He paused. "But he does have $300.00." Jack shrugged. "I didn't think the guy was going to go through with the deal when I finally told him how bad a shape that old Jenny's really in." He wiped sweat off his forehead with the back of his hand. "But he said he wants her anyway, and he thinks 300 is a fair price. He's coming here with cash tomorrow.

"You're really selling her! You really are!"

"Yes." His voice sounded soft, almost a whisper. He stood looking at her for a moment, then he said it. "I love you, Baby. I mean, you're really the cat's meow."

She let him come closer. "I ought to just leave right now."

Jack put his hand gently on his wife's shoulder. "I wouldn't blame you if you *did* scram out of here. But before you go, I want you to know one thing." He took hold of both shoulders again and pulled her just a little closer to him. "There's never been any other dolls in my life but you since we met. You're the only one and always will be. Like I said, I love you."

She looked up into his face, then pushed him back a little. "I hate you." She groaned out the words. "You know that?"

"Yeah." He handed her his helmet again.

She sobbed, beat him several more times with the helmet, then handed it back. "I've missed you." She grabbed him and pressed her cheek to his chest. "And I love you too." She knew she meant that. The angry, hurt part of her hated that fact, but it was true enough. She did, after all, miss and love the man, and believed in her innermost heart that there could be no one else *for* her. Other men seemed shallow compared to Jack, and, whenever he was gone, she felt unprotected. Her husband would protect her from harm if it came to that. Of this she had no doubt. Other men she'd known were too selfish and would never take any personal risks on her behalf. But that kind of protective instinct did exist in Jack. He'd just gotten his priorities confused somewhere along the way. *He might begin to straighten out now, but I'll have to keep an eye on him*, she thought. *He does tend to stray from responsibility.*

Jack put his arms completely around his wife and spoke softly into her ear. "I want us to be back together. I want my wife and my sons back."

"We'll have to discuss that," Caroline murmured.

Hannah's old dinner bell rang in the distance, and the younger couple looked toward the kitchen where Floyd and Hannah peered out through the open door. The last of the gasoline drums were flickering out in the night breeze now, leaving only a bright moon and pale stars to compete with the darkness. "I *want* to discuss it." Jack said. "Besides, I think that's what *they* have in mind." He nodded toward his grandparents' house.

"That's fine with me." She relaxed for the first time that night and even smiled a little. "I've come to appreciate their help...even their interference."

"What do you mean?" Jack asked.

Carrie cuddled closer and chuckled "Wait until I tell you how they got me here."

"How's that?"

"After supper."

"You hungry?"

"I don't know why, but I'm starved."

Jack kept one protecting arm around her as they walked toward the farm house. "Good," he said. "Let's eat." He was silent for a moment, then turned toward her. "By the way, how *are* the boys?"

"I was wondering when you were going to get around to asking," she said with a slight edge.

Jack stepped over a stray chunk of granite. "I never had a chance."

Carrie considered that statement for a moment, then said, "I know." But she thought, *You have no idea how true that is, poor man...in more ways than one.* Somehow, as they walked, she kept from smiling.

Just then, the glimmer of the evening's moonlight seemed brighter than it had just a few seconds before. It appeared to wash over the field like a floodlight almost bringing a kind of supernatural life to fence posts and eucalyptus saplings, bullying away the darkness that had ruled earlier in the evening.

Jack sighed a closed-mouth sigh and cleared his throat. "That full moon's supposed to be up 'til morning . Or, at least, that's what some sheep-herder told me."

"What sheep-herder?"

"Just someone I met on my way here. He keeps a close watch on the Farmers' Almanac. Said it helps with the sheep somehow. Kind of an interesting fella. I'll tell you about him sometime."

Carrie clasped her hands in front of her. "So he said the full moon would stay up the rest of the night."

Jack nodded. "Yeah. Supposed to stay big like that, too. All night."

"Your grandma calls that a harvest moon."

"In France they called it a bomber's moon."

Carrie walked silently for several seconds.

Jack sighed again. "Sorry. Didn't mean to talk about the war again. I've probably already told you that." He paused. "About bomber's moons, I mean."

Carrie gave him a quick side-glance. "That's all right," she said. "I don't mind hearing it again...about the moon, that is. I just don't want to hear about the bombing and ...so on."

"I know. The thing about the moon was all I was going to say."

She put her hands behind her back now and clasped them again. "That's all right then."

Chapter Six

Amuffler-less, war surplus, Indian motorcycle, proud possession of a local bootlegger, growled across the back of Floyd's property like a crazed wildcat trying to shake the rider from its back. Jack could picture that particular man and cycle without seeing them because he *had* seen them so many times before, doing the exact same thing. The beast's mechanical snarl registered so loud that it penetrated the walls of Hannah's dining room, creating the illusion that the machine circled, ready to pounce, just outside the back door.

Floyd looked up from cutting his roast beef and listened for a second. "Sounds like Farley's got a snoot full of his own merchandise again."

Hannah waited for the racket to diminish into the distance, then she answered. "I don't like it one little bit when he roars around drunk like that. I'm always afraid he's going to crash into the hen house or maybe run someone over in the dark."

Floyd stretched and went back to his supper. "I don't care for it much neither. I'll talk to him again as soon as he sobers up."

Hannah released a cynical snicker. "Whenever that is."

Opposite Floyd and Hannah at the big pine dinner table, Jack and Carrie sat side-by-side but a little too far apart. Jack knew the physical separation meant something. He just wasn't sure what. Could Carrie be uneasy about the evening's whirlwind reconciliation? Maybe she hadn't used up all her anger yet. He decided it didn't really matter. He was going to—somehow—rebuild his family, regardless of what that entailed. And if it meant enduring more cold distance and tongue-lashing for a while, then so be it. At the moment, though, he wished he could figure out what to say to get their conversational train back on the rails. Carrie didn't seem inclined to help. She just sat stone-still, staring at the dining-room's flowered wall paper. Jack used his fork to move his peas from one side of the plate to the other, trying to think of an opening line. But, in the end, all he could do was sigh. Carrie sighed too, but hers sounded more dramatic. Jack suspected *that* probably meant something too, but once again, he came up short as to what. So he reasoned that the best course of action was to just not think about it…for now.

Floyd cleared his throat and raised his eyebrows in Hannah's direction. The old woman shook her head. "You two don't have to play nice for us, you know. Say what needs to be said between you and be done with it."

Carrie looked up from her plate to Jack, then sighed and said, "The boys and I lived here with your grandparents for six months, and you only came to see us twice. Why?"

Jack put his fork down and looked at his grandma. She gave him an encouraging nod, so he answered. "I sent money home."

Carrie pushed her plate away and folded her hands on the table. "Not much money. Besides, money's not you. We needed you. Your sons needed you."

Jack rested his chin on his hand. "How about you?"

Carrie twisted around in her chair to face Jack. "Yes, I needed you too. So why didn't you come home?"

Jack didn't answer right away. He just looked off into nothing and tried to think of how he was going to speak the truth but still make Carrie understand. This sort of deduction proved difficult for him and he took a very long time to go through it. He would probably have taken even longer had it not been for Floyd asking him to pass the potatoes. He was still half lost in his deliberations and didn't respond to his grandpa's request right away.

Consequently, the next thing he heard was Carrie snapping, "Would you pass the potatoes to your grandpa, or is that too much of a commitment?" Hannah gave her a sharp glance, and Carrie winced. "Sorry," she said. "I didn't mean to say that."

Jack swallowed hard. "I was ashamed to come home."

Carrie's face softened. "Because you weren't making much money?"

"Yes!" Jack slapped his palm on the table, making Carrie jump a little. "I was a flop. Everyplace I went, someone else had already been there with a better plane, a better stunt, or a better sales pitch. I'm a pilot, not a circus performer." He grimaced at the memory of the wing-walking clown act someone had almost talked him into. "I tried that twice, ya know. Joining a flying circus. They both kept wanting me to commit suicide six times a week, so I quit each time." He exhaled long while looking at his hands, then turned to his wife. "Carrie, all the bumming around, all the barnstorming is over for me. The only thing I want now is to get my family back."

Hannah seemed distracted through the last part of Jack's speech. First, she just sort of looked around the room with a random gaze and a puzzled expression on her face, then she began to sniff in almost every direction. "Floyd?" she said, her voice laced with concern. "Is it me, or do you smell smoke."

Floyd scraped his chair away from the table and went to the kitchen window.

"Yep," he yelled back through the doorway. "Dry grass is afire back by where Farley rode through."

Hannah was already beside him, holding onto his arm. "Sparks from that Satanic contraption of his! I'll just betcha'!"

Floyd moved rapidly toward the front door. "Probably so. Thing's got no dern muffler." He looked to Jack. "Come on, son. Wind's movin' in our direction. We got us a little fire to put out."

Hannah started for the wall phone in the front hall. "And quick, too. It's headed right for my hens! I'll call the firehouse."

Jack sprang from his chair, but glanced back at Carrie. "Please, stay. I'll be back as soon as I can." Then both men were out the door.

They trotted into the barn where Jack snatched up a shovel and a Maddox. Floyd shouldered two lengths of hose and turned to Jack. "I'll get these screwed together, Son, then I'll be right out. You go on ahead and start cuttin' some firebreak."

Jack nodded, then ran out the back of the building toward the fire, dropping the shovel just the other side of the southernmost structure in a long row of hen houses. With the Maddox, he started tearing up the sod from under the waist-high, dry field grass about ten yards away from the old wooden building. He did this as fast as he could, forming a shallow half-moon ditch in the fire's path. That done, he began to dig up the sod behind his original firebreak line, trying to make the barrier too deep for the fire to jump. But the burn began to lengthen out and pick up speed as the evening breeze stiffened. Jack wasn't sure he was cutting the break wide enough to keep the flames from running around him, but knew a long thin trough would be too easy for the fire to cross, so he just kept working on what he'd started, enlarging it and praying for the best to happen.

Floyd came around the corner with the last ten feet of his joined hoses, water gushing from the end. He started soaking down the walls and roof of the long narrow chicken house. The wooden walls of the structure, being ancient and dry, drank up the shower like an enormous sponge, leaving little evidence of its bath in the end. This forced Floyd to continue dousing the old boards over and over again. Finally, he turned around to check the fire's progress against Jack's. He didn't like what he saw.

"Son, that's gettin' mighty close. You better get the scythes."

"We've got them right here!" Hannah and Carrie

rounded the corner, both in overalls and work shirts, each with a long wooden-handled scythe on her shoulder.

"Thank you, ladies!" Floyd threw down the hose and grabbed both tools. He tossed one to his grandson as he got near the fire line. "Here ya go. Now let's each take an end of the break and stretch it out. We gotta knock down the high grass or the fire'll run around us." The wind had picked up, and the thick tide of smoke finally reached them, momentarily engulfing Floyd. He stopped to cough, then tied a red bandana around his nose and mouth, bandit style.

Jack did the same and, keeping an eye on the flames, began cutting down large swaths of dry, wild grass with a furious stroke. As he did this, he also kept watch over the women to make sure they remained safe. Floyd mowed his end a little slower than Jack, but with a determination of equal ferocity. Hannah took over the abandoned hose and kept the henhouse and the surrounding area drenched while Carrie evacuated great double handfuls of smoke-stunned fowl from their nests to the relative safety of the barn. Then the wind's intensity increased again, so Jack had to double his efforts to clear grass ahead of the fire, which seemed to be trying to race around the firebreak with a conscious intent to get to the ranch's combustible structures. Jack glanced back at Floyd. The old man held his own but could just barely keep ahead of the burn and was not staying as far in front of it as he should have for his own safety.

A few seconds later, on the next glance, Jack saw Floyd down on one knee, heaving as if trying to catch his breath. He decided to run to the old man's aid, but, before he could move, he saw Carrie charge out and grab Floyd's blade. She tore into the tall grass with a maniacal swing and extended the clearing well past the oncoming threat. Then she just kept mowing down more grass at the same determined pace. Jack knew he should be worried about her being so close to danger, but, strange as it seemed, he felt only a sense of rightness. *Carrie's here with me and we're doing this together.* The realization of that gave him an odd peace; it was the way things were supposed to be.

Soon, however, a rogue wind picked up dozens of sparks and carried them over the firebreak to within a few feet of the threatened hen house. The tinder dry verge there ignited in an instant. Floyd, having caught his breath, ran back, took the hose from Hannah, and attacked the fresh outbreak. When the situation near him got worse, Hannah appeared beside her husband with a shovel and, in a series of smooth steady motions, began throwing dirt onto the flames. The old couple worked that way together for almost a quarter hour, slowly pushing the enemy back.

As Jack worked and watched his grandparents, he once again felt a sort of confirmation in his heart that this was the way things should be for him and Carrie—working together to hold life's threats at bay. He couldn't shake this thought, no matter how busy he got, almost as if someone were continually whispering it into his ear.

Jack didn't hear the siren or notice the presence of the county fire truck until a high-pressure stream of water shot over his shoulder. The blaze was well over half contained by that time. And the final result—the MacGregors had succeeded in saving their out buildings, not to mention *all* the poultry.

Still, Floyd wasn't completely happy. "Hannah, I wish you two would've stuck to gettin' the chickens out of harm's way. Most of 'em were still in the hen house. We might've lost a big chunk of our meal ticket if that fire had spread a little faster." He coiled the last of the three hoses up in the barn. Jack wiped off the shovel while Carrie helped her grandmother-in-law put the chickens back in their nests.

Hannah straightened with indignation. "Why, you old fool!" She stopped in mid-trip with the last of the brooder hens in her arms. " Carrie and I were too busy saving your ungrateful skin to worry about the poultry." She put a squawky Rhode Island back into its straw-lined box, then picked up both scythes and took them to their respective wall pegs.

"Saving my skin! You did no such a thing! I was just catching my wind. And I'd have got it back in a second or two, you can just bet, and I'd have done just fine. You should have just stuck to putting them hens in the barn and let me be."

"Floyd, that's the most foolish thing I've ever heard you say!" She hung both tools up and steadied them. "Matter of fact, this conversation is so silly I'm not even going to grace it with my participation." She beat some ash off her overalls, then took a long sigh, and looked back up again. "Except to say this." she said, a little less agitated. She put her arms around her husband. "I don't care if you can't do everything like the old days. I am amazed that you can do all you do." She gave him a hug, and he seemed to relax a little. "You know, most men your age *aren't* your age because they're already dead." She got him to smile that time. "So, if you need my help once in a while, like when you're fightin' grass fires, I just want you to know it's all right with me." Then she extended a hand toward Jack and Carrie. "And I'm sure it's all right with them too." She squeezed the old man hard.

He grinned at her, squeezed back, then started toward the hen house. But after a couple of steps, he commented over his shoulder. "Still think you should've saved the chickens first."

At that point, Hannah gave chase and swatted him three good whacks on the back, which raised a medium sized cloud of ash dust. Then he put his arm around her again as they went to check the hens.

Carrie watched the old couple intently but remained silent. Then she turned to walk back to the main house with her husband. All Jack could think of was how heroically beautiful she seemed at that moment with smoke stains on her face and ashes on her cloths. The county fire truck rumbled past them by the hog pen. Having extinguished the last of the fire, they waived, and Jack returned the gesture while mouthing a grateful *thank you*. Carrie, still silent, kept her gaze upon the ground in front of her. Jack drew closer, put his arm around her and administered a small hug. "I love you, Carrie," he said, then kissed her sooty hair. "I want you with me again."

She stopped in the driveway beside the Stutz and looked up at him. Tear tracks drew pink lines down her gray dusted cheeks, and her eyes were brimmed with more. "Jack, I can't—" the words caught.

Jack seized the opportunity. "Not like it's been, Carrie. I promise!"

She wiped and smeared her face with the sleeve of Floyd's old work shirt. "I love you too." She got into the Stutz, appearing to Jack like a moving statue in the moonlight. "But I have to think," she said and hesitated an instant. "And I have to pray." She shut the door and started the engine. "I want to be with you, too. And I know the boys do. But I still have to pray." She took hold of his hand. "Okay?"

Jack nodded. "Okay." This was not as good as he had hoped for, but not as bad as he had feared. "I'll be here for a while." He smiled. "Got to sell the plane, ya know." He squeezed her hand, then let it go.

"I got to go," she said then turned the car around in the driveway, but stopped short beside him. "I do love you, Jack." She spoke with an insistent tone.

Jack shook his head slowly. "That's the best thing I've heard all month, Hon'!"

"Okay!" She said with a strange determined looking little nod, then drove out onto the highway, not remembering to turn on her lights until she was a good ways away.

It wasn't until that moment that Jack realized she'd

forgotten to clean up and change back into her dress. *I wonder what they're going to think of that at the old Van Burean estate. I'd like to be a fly on that wall.* Then he walked to the house, wiped his feet on the front door mat, and went in to wash.

Chapter Seven

"Oh, no!"

Carrie swerved hard right to miss squashing the ground squirrel, headlight-frozen in the middle of the road. She aimed to place the creature dead-center between the tires as the electric tingle of adrenalin raced up her spine. It was a sensation she at once loved and hated, but a thrill just the same. That is, she thrilled to the tingle, not the killing of small blinded animals. She swiveled in her seat, craning her head back over her shoulder, trying to see if the self-destructive critter possessed enough intelligence to stay still and survive. But the red illumination of her tail-lights proved inadequate at this pre-dawn hour on the Coast Highway, and the outcome of the maneuver would forever remain a mystery. Carrie made an arbitrary decision that the animal had escaped injury (since she had neither heard nor felt a telltale thump), and she vowed to remember the incident that way. Just the same, her heart still raced a bit now, and her palms sweated on the steering wheel enough to prompt her to wipe them on the car seat.

She glanced at the speedometer and caught herself doing almost eighty again. *This is getting to be a habit.* She eased her foot off the accelerator. *The estate's not far ahead.* She pressed her top teeth down onto her bottom lip. *I need a little more time to think; better slow down a little more.* She watched the meter's needle as it descended along its prescribed arc, then she nudged a little pressure back onto the pedal as the car slowed to forty—a good speed for thinking. She'd have time now, and there remained much to consider and decide before the end of the drive.

Earlier that evening, Carrie had thought she'd have days, if not weeks to ponder whether or not to trust Jack again. *One can love without wanting someone back, and one can want someone without trusting.* But now, after seeing him, she knew one thing for sure. *God help me, I still want him!. But no halfway measures. We'll either be together as man and wife*—she paused to let the rest of the thought form—*or we'll have to somehow stay apart. I couldn't be satisfied with just a taste of him now and then in some bizarre getting-to-know-each-other-again dance.* Carrie thought about that a moment and asked herself once more if she wanted to try life *without* Jack. "What should I do, Lord?" she asked the night sky and waited a second. No audibl*e* answer. *Can I trust him this time?* Again – silence.

He did leave us, after all. She wiped away a single droplet of liquid fear that had just now escaped from the corner of her eye. *Will he run away again?* Only the sound of the night air that rushed around her ears replied as the Stutz rolled up the highway.

But as time passed, the rhythm of the tires on warm asphalt lulled Carrie into a continuous stream of memories. Childhood summers at the estate, combing the tidal pools for starfish below the cliffs where her parents property merged with the Pacific—spring trips to New York, watching a Broadway musical, sitting next to her mother, who could always memorize the words to the songs by the second chorus. But, in the end, one very strong memory pushed out all others and felt as real as the car in which she sat.

Carrie saw herself years before in a Creative Writing class at Howard College, not far from home. She had forgotten her textbook and had to share with a young man she'd paid little attention to prior to that day. He had sand colored hair and seemed a little on the awkward side, but something happened that afternoon that would change the way Carrie saw *him* and everything else from that time on. The professor had read the boy's story. She could still remember much of it, full of flying airships and empires a century into the future. It struck her as exciting, romantic, and written with such skill that it seemed more like fact than fantasy.

She decided to sneak a peek at this young would-be author sitting beside her and discovered that he was already looking at *her*. She wanted to look away but couldn't, caught in the spell of their linked attention. And there was something in his eyes, some gleam or inner light, something different from every boy she'd ever met— something she could not explain but saw there just the same.

After that encounter Carrie felt a strange attraction for this young man and would talk to him after class each day. Over time, she discovered that this fledgling writer actually embodied much of the courageous spirit of his fictional characters, and the more she knew about him the more she liked. Jack had a bravery that lacked the ego she'd seen in too many college-age males. He possessed wisdom but without the arrogance most undergrads shared. He wanted to be a professional writer, but intended first to experience some of life's adventures. "The more you experience the better you write," he said the day they went to the bullfights in Tijuana. That day, Carrie lost her lunch in an alley outside the bullring—too much blood-letting on too-hot a day, or so Jack said. That day also, she had decided that this fellow was something she had been looking for most of her young life. Or at least, she began to feel that way after he apologized for taking her to the bullfights in the first place. She liked him even more after he helped her clean up. *Chivalrous,* she thought. *Almost to a fault.* And by the next weekend, in her mind, he'd become the man she must have. Within a month, their relationship had turned to what they both finally admitted to as love, and, by semester's end, Carrie broke off her engagement with Arthur, her well-to-do fiancée.

Carrie felt the memories nestle into her heart as she procrastinated up the highway. And soon after, a calm, secure feeling seemed to settle around her like some sort of invisible cloud. After a few seconds of experiencing this *everything's-wonderful* phenomenon, she surrendered to it and gave her answer into the onrushing wind, "Very well. I understand, Lord. I *will* go back to my husband."

A cat raced out from the tall grass on the seaward side of the road and stopped stupidly in front of the Stutz. Carrie mashed on the breaks, skidding to a stop inches from the feckless feline. The animal stood there for a long moment, blinking into the high-beams. Then it shook itself with regal indignation and marched off into the darkness.

"Well, I'm glad you finally made up your mind, Your Majesty!" Carrie called after the creature with some impatience. Then she laughed. "Is this how you feel with me, Father? Now that I've finally decided what side of the road *I'm* to be on?" Carrie felt joy replace her amusement as she started the car moving once more. Now…finally…she knew without a doubt what she was going to do from here on.

The Stutz soon rounded a small knoll and came upon the lights of the Van Burean estate's front gate. A month before, those lights had signified security and safe haven. Now they simply illuminated the entrance to the inner driveway. Carrie turned off the main road and headed up the gravel lane to the house.

On her way, she glanced up at the full, descending moon and started *da-da-ing* some old song from the turn of the century about a *silvery* one. She didn't know why she was singing it, but, for some reason, it made her giggle. Happiness seemed to permeate her, more at the moment than it had in a long time. The feelings surprised her, and that made her feel even better. She giggled again and slowed her speed as the Stutz approached the big carriage house door. But something was out of order there. True, the doors still stood open, and the lights burned bright inside, just as she had left them. That all remained as it should be. But now, Addams, the massive chauffeur, stood in his shirtsleeves, leaning against the door jam. And as the Stutz muttered in and stopped, he moved toward the driver's side of the car. Then, when the well-exercised engine had been shut off, Addams opened the car door.

"Have a pleasant drive, Miss Caroline?"

Carrie, still under the influence of inspired happiness, swung her legs out with an almost dreamlike movement. "Yes, Addams. I've had a very pleasant drive." She stood up as if just arising from a night's sleep, and stretched.

"I trust you deposited the elder Mrs. MacGregor safely at her home." He continued his door-holding pose with practiced skill.

Stepping toward the rear of the car and leaning back against the fender, Carrie folded her arms and relaxed, awash in a romantic mood she had not indulged since college—not since she and Jack were courting. "Who?" She looked casually over at Addams and realized she wasn't sure what he'd asked.

"Hannah, Miss Caroline. The woman you left with. Remember?" The chauffeur added a pinch of mild rebuke without sarcasm. "I assume you were able to drive her home without incident."

"Oh, yes. Hannah." Carrie shook her head as if to clear it. "Yes, I took her home."

He closed the door with skillful nonchalance. "And did you have a nice fire?"

This last question did finally catch her off guard. She thought, *how did he know about the fire?* But she said, "What do you mean?"

Addams, leaned over, and flicked some stubborn, wind-resistant ash from her blue, cotton sleeve. "Well," he said, "either you've taken a nap in someone's fireplace or you've been helping the MacGregor family fight the grass fire that could easily be seen for miles in any direction."

At that moment, Carrie realized she still wore Hannah's bib overalls and work shirt. "Oh!" A sheepish smile spread across her face as she surveyed herself and tried to slap off some of the fire's debris. "I forgot!" She shook the front of the overalls and stamped her borrowed boots discharging black singed grass onto the garage floor. "I must look awful!" She leaned to one side and attempted to look around Addams and into the car's side-view mirror.

He smiled and stepped back. "No, Miss. You don't look bad at all." The corners of his mouth neutralized once more and he cleared his throat. "Your father instructed me to keep the lights on and wait here for you. He was quite worried."

"How long have you been out here?"

"Since right after you left. As I said, he's been quite worried."

"Oh, my!" Carrie stopped brushing her overalls as a slight pang of guilt washed through her. She touched Addams' bare forearm with her soot-stained hand. "I'm sorry, Addams. I seem to be causing a lot of trouble tonight."

"No, miss. No trouble. I just thought you might like a weather report before you sail into the storm. So you can batten down the hatches, as it were."

She slumped back against the car again. "Thank you, old friend, but I'm just not worried about that tonight."

Addams nodded. "You *do* seem quite cheerful."

"Very."

"Then you're reuniting with the young Mister MacGregor."

"Yes." Another smile emerged and broadened. "In a few days, I think."

Addams nodded again – but with more enthusiasm. "That's grand. Just grand."

"Yes, I think so, too." Carrie pushed away from the car and started for the open carriage house doors. She cinched up a loose overall strap and wiped the tip of her soot stained nose with the back of an equally pigmented hand.

112

"Hatches battened. I'm off to stormy seas." Carrie turned at the threshold. "Thanks for waiting up for me. I'm sure you had other things you'd have rather been doing."

He walked to the left door and took hold of its handle. "Not at all. I'd not have missed your arrival tonight for a king's ransom." He pulled it shut and walked to the other as Carrie stepped out onto the driveway. "By the way, Miss."

She turned around again.

Addams took a deep breath, "You at no time looked awful or foolish tonight." He glanced briefly at his shoes then back to meet her gaze. "In my humble opinion, you did, and do, look ... heroic. I think you are a very brave young woman."

She stood, stunned, for an instant. The chauffeur had not voiced an observation that personal in twenty years. This was an historic occasion. Two full seconds of silence passed to mark it before an appropriate response could materialize. "Thank you, Addams. That means a lot to me."

"My pleasure, miss." And the second door closed between them.

Carrie stepped past the white Greek pillars of the great house's front entrance, through the Venetian entry hall, and across the ballroom's polished Florentine marble floor. She emerged out onto the expansive back patio where she knew somewhere within its confines her parents would be recovering from the night's festivities. As the salt laced gusts of the pre-dawn coastal breeze caressed her face, she leaned on the stone balustrade that overlooked the Roman fountain and mused upon the difference between the two worlds she now straddled. Beyond the patio terrace, used earlier tonight as the open-air dance floor, lay the Olympic swimming pool with pennant-topped changing tents lined up along its south side like the medieval pavilions of jousting knights. Farther out and surrounding that area was the croquet lawn and, finally, the cliff walk, trimmed with another classical granite balustrade.

Carrie pictured a weather-beaten chicken coop between the pool and the cliffs. She amused herself with the fantasy of having one secretly built there while her parents were away in Europe.

That would be a trip to the hospital for Mother. Then she spotted them, still in evening clothes lounging at the big glass table on the dining veranda where the light from the nearest electric pole-lamp illuminated the late edition of Albert's evening paper. Carrie meandered toward them and struggled to suppress the smile that fought to escape and spread across her face.

The two sat on opposite sides of the table, her father buried in his reading, her mother watching the moon reflect off the Pacific. Servants and caterers, bathed in the lunar half-light, called to mind ghosts cursed forever to clean up the debris left by drunken Roman gods. Carrie strolled over near the seated duo and raised herself up to sit on the balustrade with a casual air, deliberately blocking her mother's view of the gardener raking paper flowers and small articles of clothing from the lawn.

No ignoring little Caroline because she's been bad. This time, they'll have to deal with me face to face. Might as well get this out of the way first crack out of the box. "Hello, Father...Mother." She folded her arms and sighed. "Excellent party, didn't you think?"

Her mother stared at her as if she'd seen a nightmare manifest itself into reality. "Good God, Caroline! You look like a charwoman! What's happened to you?"

Albert gave his daughter a quick glance of moderate disapproval, went back to his paper, and spoke to his wife without looking up. "Now, Candice. I see no need for drama. Caroline is a grown woman and, as such, is certain to have ample explanation for her appearance." He turned to the next page and scanned it. "I'm as sure of that as I'm sure she's going to explain her *disappearance* earlier this evening."

114

Upon finishing the last word of his sentence, Albert shot Carrie a dagger-like glance over the top of his glasses before returning his attention to the evening news. He read another two seconds then turned the page once more – this time almost tearing the paper – and muttered in a low angry tone, "How the devil does our government expect United Fruit to produce bananas if the Marines can't keep the local bandits under control!" Albert snapped the paper closed with an impatient rasp and tossed it onto the table beside him. He cleared his throat, stretched his arms, and folded them over his chest much the same way as his daughter had done. "So, young lady, what exactly *did* happen tonight and why are you covered in coal dust?" His voice raised half a strained octave. "We were quite concerned as to your whereabouts and condition tonight! Quite!"

"Sorry. I didn't mean to worry anyone." Carrie slid down from the railing and gave Hannah's clothes another slap, which produced a small, gray, localized cloud. "It's not really coal dust, you know, Father. It's ashes." She leaned back against the railing and swatted her overalls again. Her mother emitted a small cough, although the tiny ash puff never came closer than five feet from the woman's face.

"Really, Caroline!" Candice produced a small, delicate handkerchief from somewhere within her dress and positioned it in the general vicinity of her nose and mouth. Then she expelled another delicate cough.

There go the theatrics, right on cue. "Yes, Mother. *Really.*" Carrie folded her arms again. "Ashes from a real fire. A grass fire, as a matter of fact."

Albert lit a Gaspar with the large, gold table lighter and exhaled with deliberate control. "Yes, Addams said there was a fire out in the direction of the MacGregor ranch; I suppose that's where you picked up your new fashion look." He examined the end of the cigarette for an instant, then returned his attention to his daughter. "Early firehouse, isn't it? Or is it chicken house?"

"Hey, look at this!" The voice of the handyman calling to the butler echoed off the walls bordering the yard. It provided a timely distraction for the trio near the table. The man had fished an expensive glass urn from the pool and now held it up for view. The thing was relatively small but was stuffed with what appeared to be an entire woman's wardrobe, complete with shoes.

"My word," the butler replied. "Wonder how she got all that *in* there."

"Beats me." The handyman shook his head, then aimed his long-polled boathook at a straw skimmer hat that floated near the low diving board. "I wonder what she's wearing *now*," he said, but the butler didn't answer.

Carrie, unshaken by her father's barbs, sauntered over to the table, eased into the remaining chair, and turned it so that she faced him directly. "The fire broke out shortly after Hannah and I arrived."

"Oh, that dreadful old woman!" Candice fanned her face with her hankie, then tucked it back into an invisible lodging, somewhere below the neckline of her dress.

Carrie frowned in her mother's direction. "So naturally, I stayed to lend what assistance I could."

Albert ticked off an ash into a silver tray. "Naturally."

"We should have gone ahead and had her arrested." Candice finished the last of her martini and set her long-stemmed glass down a little too hard. "Chained to our front gate, indeed. Why didn't you call the police, Albert?"

"Sheriffs, my dear." Albert seized a nearby decanter of brandy and poured until his snifter was half full.

"What?" One martini past her comfortable limit, Candice fumbled a scented cigarette from a jade box on the table and struggled with the large table-lighter.

Albert's tone took an impatient turn. "We don't have police here, my dear; we have sheriffs. And I did call them. But that's all academic when our daughter drives the getaway car."

Carrie shifted in her chair but held her annoyance in check. "You must have known that I wouldn't allow her to be arrested. She's my grandmother-in-law."

"Not for long." Candice finally got her cigarette lit only to accidentally flip it into a small bucket of melting ice. It went out with a hiss, and she frowned.

Carrie pushed her chair back from the table. "Well." She cleared her throat. "That actually brings up another issue."

Albert took a sip from his glass. "And what, pray tell, might that be?" He leaned back and crossed an ankle over his knee, exposing black silk socks.

Carrie stood up and circled around behind her chair. "Actually, Hannah will remain my in-law for quite some time because I intend to reconcile with Jack."

Candice gasped. Albert took two large swallows of brandy.

Carrie continued. "As a matter of fact, the boys and I will probably leave before the end of the week."

"You're not serious, Caroline!" Candice grasped the arms of her chair as her face flushed a darker red than Carrie could remember ever seeing on anyone before. "My God, you just left the man a month ago! And now you're running back to him. Are you intoxicated?" Candice waved her left arm to emphasize the statement and in the process batted her martini glass several feet behind her where it shattered on the stone floor. A servant girl, who had already been sweeping nearby, rushed over to the scene of the crash with her dustpan and, displaying the efficiency of a vaudeville magician, made the debris disappear. Then *she* vanished as well.

"No, Mother, I'm not drunk." Carrie suppressed a laugh. "I am in full possession of my faculties."

"Well, that's debatable, I must say." Albert pulled sparingly at his Gaspar and chased the smoke with brandy.

"I think otherwise, young lady." He flicked a stubborn ash into the tray. "I think you are indeed drunk, but with spirits of girlish, romantic emotion rather than alcohol. In a word, you are being immature. You are riding on the whim of the moment, rather than considering the unpleasant reality that brought you back here last month. This so-called husband of yours simply cannot support you. That's the truth of the matter, and that's what you're choosing to ignore."

"I don't need all this, Father." Carrie raised her hands to indicate the surrounding estate. "I'd rather have Jack's love."

"Yes," Albert crushed out his smoke. "That's what you told me just before you got married. But it's not the tune you sang when the fellow abandoned you— when he ran off to become a circus performer. Was it!"

"He was a barnstormer, a stunt pilot," she protested.

"No difference." He pushed his snifter aside. "He left both you and his sons to follow some childish pipedream. Probably thought he'd be the next Lincoln Beachey, no less. But he didn't send you enough money to support a canary. You had to move in with his grandparents. Even his own father wouldn't agree to take you in, and that man has a pleasant little house with ample room right on the bay."

Carrie leaned forward onto the back of the chair. "Probably because you threatened him. What did you tell him, Father? That you would fire him as your attorney and use your influence to totally ruin his law firm as well?"

Albert attempted a chuckle. "Oh, nonsense, my dear. George MacGregor is his own man. He simply agreed that his son's marriage to you had been an unfortunate mistake, owing to Jack's apparent irresponsibility."

Carrie knew Albert well enough to be certain he'd pressured Jack's father in some irresistible way. And she was likewise familiar with George MacGregor's social climbing tendencies. He *would* refuse to support his son's marriage *if* he thought that marriage could somehow damage his financial standing. She was certain of that now, and she'd suspected it when the man had refused her and his grandsons shelter seven months before. He had proclaimed his wife's acute and highly contagious illness at the time as an excuse but added that he thought the Van Burean estate was a much more appropriate place for her and the boys, with advantages he could not provide. Carrie had remained unconvinced, however, by that thin rationalization. She'd seen the signs of her father's bullying too many times not to recognize them. She didn't know what threats Albert had made, but she had seen the fear in George's manner. That was proof enough for her.

Carrie returned to the edge of the veranda and resumed her original stance, arms folded in front, back against the stone railing. "Father, you and I both know you did something to cause George to slam the door in my face. But that's a moot point, isn't it? Because we went next to Floyd and Hannah's. And you knew *they* could not be intimidated."

Albert finished his brandy in one gulp. "The point is, Caroline, that you didn't stay there a day longer than six months. You still came home." He leaned forward in his chair. "You still came home because you knew then, as you know now, that you don't really belong in that kind of squalor and neither do my grandsons. You'll always choose the better life, and, when the boys are old enough to understand, so will they."

"We did choose the better life." Carrie remained still and met her father's gaze. "We went to the ranch."

"Oh, Caroline! Stop this!" Candice once more pulled the hanky from its hidden place and waved it in the air. "You're just being stubborn again. You just want your way. Whatever that may be at the moment. You're just like your father." She used the hanky to dab moist makeup from beneath her eyes.

"No, mother. I'm not being your spoiled little girl. I'm

being a wife." Carrie stepped away from the railing and started for the house. "I'm going back to my husband and we're going to be a family."

"Poppycock!" Candice said as she threw the handkerchief onto the table and attempted to light another cigarette.

Carrie kept walking toward the ballroom doors.

"You'll be back, Caroline." Her father twisted around in his chair as she walked away.

"Only to visit, Father," she said. Then she opened one of the glass doors and passed through the ballroom. The night had begun to catch up with her by the time she reached the staircase, and she climbed to the second floor with a weary pace.

At the room where her sons slept, she opened the door and peered in, throwing a shaft of light into the darkness. Kenny, her seven-year-old, lay facing her, his open eyes catching and reflecting the intrusive illumination.

"Mom?" he moaned.

"Yes." Carrie knelt between her sons' twin beds and stroked Kenny's mop of light brown hair. "Party keep you awake?"

"Yeah." He sat up and rubbed his eyes. "It was kinda' noisy for a while."

"It was?" She feigned surprise.

Kenny yawned. "Yeah, some of the people were really funny, too. Me and Eddie was watching from the window."

Carrie leaned on her elbow. "Tell me about it."

"Well, some guy climbs to the top of the high-dive, only he wasn't wearing no bathing suit."

"Any bathing suit."

"Yeah," Kenny said. "He was wearing one of them penguin suits instead."

"A tuxedo." Carrie added.

"Right. So he goes up there and he jumps off, but he jumps off the wrong side and lands on the grass... and I mean hard. Splat!"

"Splat!" Eddie's four-year-old head poked up from under his covers, revealing a toddler's grin and short hair almost as dark as his mother's. "He goes splat, Mama!" The boy pantomimed the pancake-style landing with his little open palm and giggled as only small children can.

Carrie grimaced. "Did you learn that word from your big brother?"

"Uh-huh." Eddie scooted up onto his knees and repeated the word again proudly. "Splat!" He giggled again.

"He just sort of laid there and he didn't move for a long time, Mom." Kenny regained the floor. "Then some ambulance guys came and put him on one of those little beds that's got handles on 'em."

Carrie fought a smile. "A stretcher," she said.

"Yeah, and you know what?"

"What?" Carrie enhanced her enthusiasm.

"As they took him away, he wakes up and grabs a bottle of something off a table and starts drinking it."

This one even surprised Mama. "Really?'

"Yeah!" Kenny nodded athletically.

"Splat!" Eddie interjected, not yet bored with his new word.

All three of them laughed this time. Finally Carrie shushed them down. "All right, listen to me now. How would you both like to go back to Grandma Hannah's and live with your father again?"

The boys looked stunned for an instant, then Kenny ventured a question in a cautious tone. "Will you live there too?"

Carrie's eyes began to water. "Yes, I will."

Both boys cheered and bounced out of bed to hug their mother. Carrie's control ebbed. She began by laughing with the boys but ended up sobbing. She managed to pull herself together, however, within a few seconds, and hoped her sons hadn't noticed her tears in the semi-darkness. She kissed them both and tucked them in again. "Now, go to sleep. We'll probably start packing tomorrow. We'll be leaving this week, and there's a lot to pack."

Carrie left their room, then went to her own and peeled off her fire clothes. She marveled how the boys weren't even interested in why she was dressed that way. *Children just accept what adults do.* Then she shook her head and fell onto the bedspread. There would be no bath tonight. Too exhausted. Carrie noticed a gray smudge her forearm left on the stark white bedding. Her mind shrugged. She knew at some other time she might be horrified, but tonight she simply did not care. *I'll let the laundry maid deal with it. And if it turns out to be ruined, Father can replace it. He'll hardly miss the money.*

Then a disconcerting notion crept into her thoughts. *I wonder why father gave up the argument so quickly. That's not like him at all.* Suddenly, the fatigue she'd felt left her and she sat straight up on the bed. Carrie knew Albert never withdrew from a fight unless he had some sort of flanking maneuver in mind. She went to the seaward window at the end of the upper hall alcove and looked down at the little tuxedo-clad man still seated out on the patio, smoking another cigarette. He was instructing Addams about something. Carrie leaned on the windowsill and sighed. *What are you planning, Father? What trap are you going to set for me now?*

Chapter Eight

"Father, you car thief!" Carrie's yell echoed off the walls and marble floors of the foyer like a wild animal's cry in a box canyon. "Come out from wherever you're hiding!" She stopped directly under the chandelier and did a half turn to scan all the connecting rooms for any sign of her prey. "Where are you?" She walked to the edge of the sunken living room. "Where *are* you?" Then she swooped up the south hallway, her robe-tails lifting off the ground like a flag in a low, morning breeze. "You might as well crawl out right now! I'm going to find you sooner or later!"

"I'm in here, my dear," came the voice from the library.

Carrie backtracked to the door she'd already passed and flung it open with such force that the hinges cried out and the inside knob dented the wood paneled wall behind it. "You had my car stolen!" she shrieked as she stomped across the Persian rug that covered the polished hardwood floor.

"Nonsense." His reply was characteristic of his usual demeanor—placid and controlled. "I merely had it shipped to San Francisco aboard the S.S. Walter Beatty. She left at six this morning. A very tight little ship with excellent passenger accommodations, or so our shipping agent tells me." He took a sip of coffee, then replaced his cup onto the side table, all the while careful not to spill on his morning paper.

She stood directly in front of him now, challenging the newspaper for his attention. "And who, may I ask, gave you permission to ship my car *anywhere*?"

He looked up from the page he was reading. "Why, you did, my dear." He dropped his eyes again and calmly turned to the next page. "Last night. Don't you remember?" He raised his face briefly for emphasis, then turned to another page and submerged himself into the news again. "You said that you wouldn't be needing it for a while, so I was to have it sent up to your brother. You thought he'd enjoy driving it through the wine country." He finally folded the paper and faced his daughter with an expression of mock innocence. "I'm surprised you don't recall. You were very specific."

She sat down on the chair opposite him and closed her robe. "And this is the lie you told Addams to get him to drive it down to the docks?"

He leaned forward and fixed her with a granite gaze. "Lie or no, Addams would have driven the car anywhere I said simply because I said it. *He* is *my* servant, not yours." He carefully placed the paper on the table and finished his coffee. Then after two choreographed blots with a linen napkin, he focused on Carrie again. "I merely told him that little story so he would not feel that he'd somehow betrayed you. I'm not unaware of the affection the staff feels for you.

"But you had no right to take my car!" She wasn't yelling anymore, but her words still rang with anger.

"I have the right of a father." His voice stayed even, but took on a much more serious demeanor. "A father who will do whatever it takes to keep his daughter from making another disastrous mistake."

Carrie rose to her feet. "Do you really think this will stop me from leaving? I'll simply call a cab."

"Yes, you may." He withdrew a gold cigarette case from his smoking jacket and selected a Gaspar from within. "But that cab will not be allowed past the front gate." He removed the short holder from his pocket, then fitted the cigarette into the tip and lit it. He inhaled deeply but was careful not to blow the smoke toward Carrie. "You and the boys may leave only by the gardener's gate, taking nothing more than what you can carry." He took another drag, blowing it out a bit more indiscriminately. "If I am to be defied by you, I will at least have the satisfaction of not subsidizing your rebellion with a cab load of possessions that have been purchased with *my* money."

Carrie shook her head. "Father, none of this will prevent me or the boys from being with Jack."

"Perhaps not." He tapped an ash off into a small crystal tray. "But here's something that may prevent Jack from wanting to be with you." He paused for more smoke. "If you leave here against my wishes, know that you will receive no further financial support from me...ever. You will have only what remains in your purse. You will no longer be entitled to anything from my estate as my heir." He leaned forward and pointed at her with the cigarette. "In other words, Caroline, I shall remove you from my will and from my life as if you'd never existed."

Carrie said nothing for several seconds. She merely stood opposite her father looking into his face. Then, finally, she cleared her throat and spoke, but in a voice barely above a whisper. "Do you really mean that?"

He put the holder-perched cigarette into the ashtray and curtly nodded once. "It's my final word on the subject."

Carrie nodded too, then sniffed. "Then good-bye, Father." She walked briskly across the library floor, but stopped and turned back around at the doorway. "I feel very sorry for you, you know. Very sorry indeed." Then she left the room and climbed the stairs to gather her sons and pack.

Chapter Nine

Juan, the Mexican gardener growled like a crazed grizzly. He hammered his fist three times in rapid-fire succession on the thick oak door of the front gatehouse and bellowed, *"Valgome, Dios!* This is not right!" He stood, still facing the door as if addressing his words to it. In fact, they were meant for the ears of the other Van Burean servants who had gathered behind him near the gardener's gate. "Children are a gift from God! This Mr. Van Burean, he wastes his gift!" Then he took a breath and turned around. It was only then that he saw Carrie and her sons standing with bags in hand waiting to leave. He took in a quick breath, blinked, and bobbed his head. "I am sorry, Miss Caroline. I did not see you coming. I meant no disrespect to your father."

Carrie set down her alligator grips. Kenny and Eddie followed suit. She told herself she was not going to cry. "You don't offend me, *mi oso.*" She went to the bear-like man and hugged him. "I only wish my father felt the same." She released him, and he just stood there looking at her for a second. Then he sniffed and went to unlock the little iron gate that was hidden behind a juniper bush near the side of the gatehouse farthest from the main gate. *I am not going to cry,* she reminded, but this became more difficult as she remembered her childhood and rides atop Juan's shoulders through the estate's pine groves.

Addams stepped forward like a general surrendering a gallant but defeated army. His back, rifle-straight, and his uniform, perfectly pressed. He doffed his chauffeur's cap, cradled it in one arm, and stood with his heals properly together. "Miss Caroline, the staff wishes me to express our...." He paused for a moment, seeming to search for a word. "Our regret over your departure." He cleared his throat. "And furthermore, they... uh, we, that is, want you to know that we wish you all the best in your endeavor to bring your family back together again. In short, we applaud you."

Adel pushed forward clasping a handkerchief in front of her. "Mr. Masters ... wanted to ... see you off too, but his ... duties kept him at the house. He said to apologize for his ... absence, but a butler's work is never done. Mr. Van Burean's having ... luncheon guests today, you know." She took two deep breaths, visibly nervous from fighting her stammer.

"Yes, I know," Carrie said and felt a pang going through her chest as she was once more reminded that her father would not be wishing her well today. He would not concern himself with her actions in any way. He would, however, make sure that his luncheon guests were comfortable and well fed. Masters, the butler, would see to that.

"Yes." Adel blushed, then seemed to remember something else. "Oh, and Mr. Masters also ... said, 'God speed'. Yes, that's right. God speed."

Juan came back from the gate, wiping his cheek on a khaki sleeve. "Rodrigo is stuck in the kitchen. But he says—"

"Rodrigo is here!" The wiry, white clad chef with a dark mustache bigger than Juan's slid to a lung-heaving stop in the center of the gathering. He bent over and held his knees for a couple of heartbeats, then spoke in a hoarse, breathy voice. "Mr. Masters is minding the stroganoff for a moment."

"Lord knows then what that'll turn out like," Addams quipped.

Rodrigo chuckled only once. "I said *only* for a moment. A man does not rise to a position such as mine by being foolish." He placed his hands on Carrie's shoulders. "I am glad you are becoming a wife again," he said. "Then all my teaching has not been *por nada*. You will cook wonderful dishes for your family once more like Rodrigo showed you. Yes?" Carrie bit her lip and nodded. Rodrigo embraced her and kissed her in the manner of a French general.

"You know," Carrie began, "some people have said they felt sorry for me because my parents left me alone so much. Some have said because of what Father and Mother are like I don't know how it feels to have a real family. But they were wrong." Carrie looked around at the little group and felt the tide of emotion within herself surging. "I've known for a long time, despite what my parents did or didn't do, that I've always been part of one of the best families anyone could have... all of *you*." Then she embraced Adel, and it happened. She felt her resolve to remain in control dissolve. *Oh, I give up,* she thought, and let the quiet tears drizzle down her cheeks.

Then, she noticed Addams drifting away from the group, so she went to him and took hold of his hand. He half turned away. "Oh please, Miss," he said, failing to meet her eyes. "I don't deserve your affection. Were it not for me, you'd be driving your very own car out that gate!" He pointed to the large double main gate that had been locked shut to prevent any unauthorized taxis from entering the grounds. "I would drive you to the MacGregor home myself," he continued, "but your father has ordered everyone to remain on the property until you've been gone an hour. I should do it just the same." He shook his head. "I am such a coward!"

Carrie took his other hand as well. "No. You are a man with a family to care for, and the fact that you are thinking of their welfare before your own feelings in the matter gives me nothing but admiration for you." She stretched up on tiptoe and gave him a quick peck on the cheek. "Besides, it won't kill us to take a cab. I've already called one," she said, and as if on command, as soon as she spoke her last word, the taxi materialized, turning into the drive from the coast highway. "See," she teased. "Abra cadabra!"

Addams nodded, but did not speak. He just sniffed and picked up her bags.

Rodrigo and Adel seized the boys' cases while the beefy Juan scooped up a knickers-clad lad in each arm. "I am sorry we did not have more time together my fine boys. I would have shown you how to cut down a big tree." He gave them each a squeeze. "Make you strong for your papa!" He squeezed them again and Eddie giggled.

Carrie looked back at her sons as the group flowed toward the gardener's gate. They both bore the healthy, sun-blushed look of rural children. Not even a month at the Van Burean estate had robbed them of that. They both wore broad smiles, and the sight of them in the arms of the Mexican gardener warmed Carrie's heart and reassured her that she indeed had chosen the right course, despite the cost. She had no doubt why the boys were so happy. They both knew they would soon see their father.

Carrie took a final look at her old home. The thick, white trunks of the Georgian pillars appeared even more impressive from outside the gate (the only way most people ever saw them). They seemed to embody a certain stubborn determination in the way they struggled against the forces of gravity to hold up the massive east balcony. *Much like Father,* she thought. They'll *never give in either.* Shaking her head, she turned her attention, possibly for the last time, to the more soothing vista of the grounds. She knew she'd miss that more than the house. It was far more beautiful than any park in the area, with its eclectic mixture of perfectly spaced eucalyptus, maple, and pine that dotted the immaculately groomed lawns. And it had been her world when she was little, an easy place to be happy.

Almost every material thing a child could want had been provided there, with tall oleander bushes standing guard inside the spike-topped brick wall, giving the illusion that there was no outside world beyond the estate's boundaries. Caroline sighed with a final memory, one that reminded her that despite all the parties, ponies, and pretenses that had made up most of her childhood, there still remained one thing she had lacked—something most less-privileged children took for granted—genuine loving parents. She had never had that as a child, and she did not have it now. *Nothing's changed.* She smiled a familiar sad little smile, indicating the acceptance of realities beyond her control.

Soon all the suitcases were loaded into the cab, but, before it could pull away, Francis came jogging out to the pavement like a gorilla at a track meet. Adel took a few steps toward him, but stopped a discrete distance. The torpedo reached the rear of the hack and just leaned on the door for a couple of seconds, catching his breath. Carrie guessed he'd probably run all the way from the house like Rodrigo. He hung onto the open window edge until he'd regained most of his wind, then handed a dog-eared copy of Shakespeare's *Romeo and Juliet* back to Adel. For a reason she did not fully understand, that little scene made Carrie's faltering smile bloom into maturity. She couldn't help it and almost laughed despite all reasons to the contrary.

Francis took one more giant breath and straightened up to his usual pallbearer's stance. He swallowed, cleared his throat, and folded his massive hands in front of his belly. Carrie knew what this meant; a recitation of something the bodyguard had been turning over in his mind. He took another moment then glanced up to his unseen crib notes. "Miss Caroline. Uh, I mean, Mrs. MacGregor, Adel, she says you're aces. And, even if I hadn't had the extreme pleasure of making your acquaintance, that would be enough for me." He hesitated a second to glance again at his ethereal script. "If there ever comes a time…well, that is…" He cleared his throat again. "If you ever find yourself in the lurch, as it were, and need some muscle—" He jabbed his thumbs into his pectorals. "You just call for

Francis Polinsky. And everything'll be jake." He stuck one paw in through the window to seal the pact. "Put her there."

Carrie daintily placed four slender fingers into the torpedo's grip and felt them slightly pressed with a gentleness that put her more in mind of a surgeon than a bodyguard. She made an attempt to say, "Thank you, Francis", but the lump that had just formed in her throat would only allow her to whisper it.

"My pleasure, miss," he said and stepped back to stand beside Adel.

Soon, the last waves goodbye were traded, and one small portion of the MacGregor clan pulled out onto the highway and into an uncertain future. Carrie set Eddie on her lap and tussled Kenny's hair, but he was too absorbed in looking over the front seat and out the windshield to notice. She glanced back through the rear window just in time to see her childhood home disappear behind a small rise. She sighed, then put one hand to her forehead and closed her eyes. "Oh, God, please, make it work this time! I'm scared. Help me to be what you want me to be."

"What's that, lady?" The gravel-voiced cabby cocked his head half sideways.

The question caught Carrie off guard. "Oh, nothing." She shook her head automatically, even though the man wasn't really looking at her. "I was just praying."

"Yeah, I do that sometimes myself," he said. "'Specially last week before they fixed the brakes on this thing."

He said no more, so Carrie settled back and tried to calm her fears while she waited for the cab to carry her to the next chapter of her life.

Chapter Ten

At ten in the morning, Floyd slapped his old, leathery hand down on the truck fender hard enough to make the metal clang in C sharp. "A pickup is the most useful kind of truck there is," he said. "And, for my money, Ford's got the best one on the road!"

Jack let go of Carrie's hand and walked out to where Floyd stood. "You'll get no argument from me on that, Grandpa. How long you had this one?"

Floyd put his foot on the front bumper. "Oh, just a year."

"Really!" Jack was amazed. True, he could detect no rust, but the entire body appeared to be a mass of small dings and scratches. "She looks older," he said, but he thought, *like maybe a century.*

Floyd nodded. "Yeah well, she's been rode hard and put away wet many a night. I work my trucks; that's true. But it's got a good engine. Good gears. You treat her right, an' she'll do the same by you."

Jack glanced back at Carrie and Hannah. His wife shrugged. His grandma nodded.

Just then, Kenny raced out from around the corner of the house. He laughed and waved a small, red ball over his head. "Come on Ruff! Get the ball!" The boy looked back at his brother and a big, tan, flap-eared mongrel Floyd and Hannah's had bought from a neighbor a few days before. The latter two scrambled around the corner of the house and pursued Kenny in a torrent of barks and laughter, cutting straight through the middle of the adult conversation in progress.

Carrie intervened. "Kenny, Eddie, you two just take Ruff out to the pasture and play there! Your father and I are talking to Grandma and Grandpa!"

The red ball chase never even slowed after the maternal rebuke. The brothers simply responded with "Yes, ma'am" in duet and veered, with Ruff in tow, between the barn and the clothes line, then stampeded off into the quarter section of grass that stretched out beyond the buildings.

Jack turned his attention back to Floyd. "What did you mean 'Do the same by me'?"

Floyd waved his hand over the truck. "I mean, boy, my new truck should arrive sometime this week. I'm giving this one to you. I'll even throw in the stake sides."

Jack went almost speechless. He didn't know why Floyd wanted to give him the truck, and he didn't know what to say without seeming ungrateful. In the end, all he could think of was, "Why?"

"Why?" Floyd sounded irritated. "Why! Because you're gonna' need her. Thought *you'd* understand *that*!"

"Floyd," Hannah broke in. "You didn't tell them the other part yet."

The old man looked confused for an instant. "I didn't?" Then a light seemed to go on somewhere. "Oh...no, I didn't, did I." He took his foot off the bumper and stepped closer to Jack. "Well, it's this way, son." He nodded to Caroline. "You need to hear this too, Carrie." Floyd paused. "Hannah and me, we don't want you kids staying here at the ranch and working for *us*, anymore."

Jack's heart sank. He'd been counting on staying with his grandparents as a leg up for a new life, a chance to gather resources for another assault on the outside world. They'd always said their home was open to him and his family. He didn't understand their sudden change of mind. "But I've already sold the plane," he sputtered.

"Have we done something wrong? Is it the boys?" Carrie sounded nervous too. She had told Jack she'd also been grateful for this time of renewal and regrouping at the MacGregor ranch.

"Oh, heavens no!" Hannah gave Carrie a side squeeze. "You two being here with us together is an answer to our prayers. And the boys are our special gift from the Lord."

Jack saw Carrie smile and kiss his grandma on the cheek.

Hannah went on. "It's just that we think the Lord's blessed you with something better. Tell 'em, Floyd."

The old rancher pulled the brown Fedora off his head, scratched his scalp, then rehatted himself. He gave the barnyard a good once-over-look and leaned back against a corral plank. "Your grandma an' me figured you'd have a better chance at everything if'n you two had a place of your own." Jack opened his mouth to protest that he couldn't buy a house with the three hundred dollars he'd gotten for the plane, but Floyd cut him off with and upraised hand. "Now, just hold your horses 'til you've heard it all."

Jack subsided into silence out of respect.

Floyd continued. "I'll make it short."

Carrie moved in beside her husband and pulled his arm around her.

"Your grandma," Floyd said, "reminded me of something that I think is true." Floyd shifted into a more sympathetic tone. "It's hard to become a family again when you're still livin' in someone else's house. Your family needs time and privacy to work out the kinks. And how could you do that when you're worried about other people listening in?"

Hannah joined in now. "He means you have to be alone to fight and be intimate, and that means you need your own place." She gave one exaggerated nod, as if all matters on that subject were settled. Then she turned to her husband. "Floyd, tell them the rest."

The old man took a breath. "We're gonna stake you to a little ranch up in the mountains north of the San Fernando Valley near a town called Sweet Springs. Some old friends of ours live right next to it and told us about the place. It's got a house, a good well, and 160 acres. It was going great guns sellin' chickens and eggs until eight years ago when the owner died. Then his wife left the place to go live with her son, and that was that." The old man looked up and searched through his memory in the sky. "It's got an electric-powered cold-house, five really big coops that you'll probably have to fix up along with everything else. Each has a thousand bird capacity. So, as soon as you're ready for 'em, we'll ship you six hundred Rhode Island and Leghorn hens with a few roosters thrown in to get you rollin'."

Jack broke in. "But who would we sell to?"

Floyd allowed himself a small half-smile. "There's a hotel there in town called the Hunter's Inn. There's also a good-sized fishing and rowing lake less than a half a mile away from the main street. And the Southern Pacific's got a yard and a passenger station somewhere betwixt the two, so there should be enough spring and summer business to hold you 'til you can drum up sales elsewhere." Jack's Grandpa took out a red and white, polka dot bandana and bullied a flattened, dried wasp off the truck's windshield. "Oh, and it's got a good size airfield, too. Somewhere's out by the lake. I spoke to the hotel's owner and he says he'll order from ya just as soon as you're ready. His old supplier lost all their stock in a fire and threw in the towel. So, like I said, that should get you started. That's how *we* did it, your grandma and me." He smiled at Hannah and winked, then turned back to the truck and rubbed away at a bee squashed against the headlamp. "Town's got a store, a butcher, a café, and a speak-easy." He cleared his throat and glanced at his wife. "So you should be able to sell some more birds or eggs to *them*. I've had you helping here ever since you could walk, and Carrie's got more than six months of chicken ranchin' under her belt. I think the two of you can pull it off, if you give it everything you've got." Floyd snapped his bandana like a bullwhip, sending its two deceased bug-occupants flying. Then he mopped his forehead with it. "So what do you think? You want to give it a try?"

When Jack didn't answer right away; Hannah stepped into the pause. "Your neighbors up there would be long-time friends of ours. Their names are Ben and Ruth Smith. They've done about everything there is to do on a farm or a ranch." Hannah raised an encouraging eyebrow. "They said they'd be glad to get you settled in."

A wave of fear and doubt washed over Jack and automatically spilled out of his mouth. "But *you* buy up local beef and supply that to hotels along with chickens and eggs. Wouldn't this hotel expect us to do all that too?"

Floyd shook his head. "Naw. There's a cattle spread already handling that. All this place needs is a poultry and egg supplier. The only reason we supply beef around here is because this used to be a cattle ranch. *Our* cattle ranch, as a matter of fact. We used to run White-face Herefords here."

Hannah watched a wave of mild surprise wrinkle her grandson's forehead. Then she said, "Before you were born, Jackie."

"Oh." Jack nodded.

"Yeah," Floyd continued. "So we already had the contacts and the experience to broker other people's stock. You won't need to bother with that."

Jack could not believe what he'd been hearing. Had Grandpa gone crazy? *I'm not ready to take on something like this by myself, and God only knows what Carrie's thinking!* He felt his fears beginning to overpower him, so, before he made a fool of himself in front of his wife he reverted to pure logic. "Grandpa, you can't afford to just buy us a ranch!"

"We're not going to." Floyd sat down on the truck's bumper. "The widow that owns it will hold paper on it, instead of the bank. She'll accept a two-thousand dollar down payment. That's what we'll supply. The monthly payments'll be up to you to make." Floyd leaned down and snapped the stalk from a wayward alfalfa plant. He stuck it between his teeth and spoke as he began to grind away on it. "Well, that's our offer, son, your grandma an' me. What'd ya think?"

To say Jack felt overwhelmed would be a gross understatement. He couldn't really tell for sure what he thought about any of this. The offer was not something he was ready for. True, he had no better prospects at the moment. But a ranch was a much bigger commitment than an airplane. Perhaps one that would last for a lifetime. Could he handle something this big...something this involved? And then, what about Carrie? What does she think about it? Looking down at her face, which was already looking back up into his, Jack tried hard to decipher the code displayed there. But he couldn't, so he simply turned to his grandpa and attempted to say something intelligent. All that came out, however, was, "I, uh...I mean we...."

Jack felt a hand on his shoulder and heard Hannah's voice from behind him. "D'ya need more time, Jackie?"

The nickname immediately calmed him. She was the only one who ever used it. Possibly because she was the only one in the family who had that degree of tenderness for him. Funny how sometimes when she did that it would raise his hackles, and other times it would be as a soothing balm. How she brought about the differing results had always been Hannah's secret. Must have been something to do with her tone...or maybe her expression...or the humidity...or maybe it was sunspots. He sighed and turned to look at his wife. She nodded vigorously. "Yes, ma'am," Jack replied. "I think we do need a little time to talk."

"All right, then," the old woman said. "Take all you need. You may even want to sleep and pray on it a few days."

As soon as his grandma's last word was spoken, Jack saw a rapid eyebrow wrinkling exchange take place between the old couple. Floyd's eyebrows shot up almost to his hat, and Hannah's dropped down into a deep, dark "V", which sloped toward the bridge of her nose. This brought about an immediate change in Floyd's brows, which descended back to their former "at rest" position.

"I think," Carrie said, "all we need is a few of minutes in your flower garden. Would that be okay?"

Hannah waved a hand at the brick walkway that lead under the vine-covered trellis and into the area of the flowerbeds. "Carrie honey, you be my guest."

Carrie nodded and took hold of Jack's hand. He responded with a single nod of his own and led his wife into the garden. The latticed wall stood six feet high there and the honeysuckle that grew on it added almost another foot. It surrounded the little yard on three sides and was broken only by the two large opposing trellis gates. The house itself formed the north boundary.

Hannah's flowerbeds exploded like popcorn with profusions of petals in every hue of the imagination's palette. Evidence of the old woman's faith and obedience in preparing and tending the place, not to mention the Lord's obvious blessing, emanated from every bed and corner. As the couple entered this serene, set-aside world, the thought suddenly came to Jack that this was the way God had meant the earth to be. Mankind obeys; the Lord blesses. It seemed an elementary lesson for life. This would be a good place to talk with Carrie about *their* life-to-come.

A low octagonal bench ringed the willow tree that reigned over the center of the yard. Carrie sat down there and smoothed out her blue, cotton summer dress. Jack preferred to stand with his hands in the pockets of his Jodhpurs, rocking his lace-up boots back and forth upon the brick walk. "So what do you think?" he asked.

She extracted a broken stemmed daisy from the ground and began a slow harvesting of its petals. "You know, if you'd have asked me that question yesterday, I'd have laughed and said we should go look for an apartment somewhere." She had spoken this to the daisy, but now she raised her eyes to her husband. "However, just a minute ago as Floyd was talking—and this is really going to make you think I've gone entirely crazy—the whole thing sounded right somehow." Jack started to speak, but Carrie shrugged and spoke first. "I know! I know! This doesn't sound like me. But maybe that's what makes it right. Maybe it comes from someone a lot wiser than I am."

Jack wasn't sure he followed her. "You mean Grandpa?"

Carrie giggled. "No, silly! God."

Jack nodded. At least he knew who she was talking about now. "Oh, yeah. God." He did think she was starting to sound a little strange, but he kept a respectful tone. "You think a chicken ranch is God's idea?"

Carrie shrugged. "I don't know." She pulled a petal off the daisy. "It's just so strong, this feeling." Carrie performed another amputation on the little yellow flower. "I think we should do it, Jack! I might change my mind later." She shook her head. "I probably will. But right now, I think we should start a ranch." She paused and took a deep breath. "Look, you sold your plane for me and the boys. That was your proof of love for us." She swallowed and gulped more air. "Now, I think God has shown us the best path for you...and us. This is where you're supposed to lead us, and my proof of love for you is to follow you and help all I can."

Jack had not seen her this excited since the night she accepted his proposal of marriage. Still, for him it seemed like too much too fast. "Wait a minute, Carrie!"

"Please, Jack! Let me finish!" Carrie already had the flower half denuded. "You've been doing ranch work for years, and Hannah said I was learning fast the six months I was here. I know quite a bit about chickens now, and what I don't know I can learn!"

Jack stopped rocking on his boot-heels and shook his head. "Carrie, all I've ever done here was help work the place. I've never tried the business end of it. I don't know if I'd be any good at that. Selling chickens and eggs, I mean."

"Well, how do you know," Carrie snapped, "if you don't at least try!" Her eyes were flashing in the late morning sun and she seemed to be right on the edge of delivering a second stinging rebuke when suddenly something changed in her expression. She emitted a small gasp and put a hand to her mouth. "I'm sorry, Jack." Her tone sounded apologetic as she dropped her hand. "I didn't mean to do that." She got up and walked to the west trellis that looked out onto the grass field where Ruff and her sons still cavorted in competition for the coveted red ball. The pasture there was green and irrigated, unlike the dry, whitish-yellow quarter section to the south that now wore the black scar of the grass fire.

Jack thought about how Carrie had kicked the burning gasoline drum over in the more verdant area three nights past and how grateful he had been that Floyd had decided to keep the field where the Jenny had landed well watered. Otherwise, as a result of his wife's fit of anger, it would have ended up fire blackened as well.

Carrie sighed. "Look, I know that I get impulsive sometimes. I know that occasionally I jump into things without thinking them through. You're going to have to keep an eye on me in that area. It's true." She paused. "There, I've said it. I can't get any more honest than that." Carrie turned around, still picking at the daisy. "But this is different."

"How is it different?" Jack took a couple steps toward her.

"Something we learned at our little church down the road here when we were still in college."

"Yes?" Jack walked up beside her and leaned against the trellis.

"It was the day after we got saved, our first real Sunday service." She glanced at her flower and pulled off another petal then turned back toward the open spaces beyond the garden. "I was talking to one of the older ladies there. She was telling me how she was always happier when she let the Lord make the more important decisions in her life."

A warm wind blew up out of the east and caused the taller grass beyond the pasture to wave. Carrie nodded as she recalled the old woman's words. "She told me that sometimes after much prayer, the Lord would actually put things onto her heart so strongly and inexplicably correct that she could not deny that it was divine guidance. She called it the Holy Spirit screaming in her ear. I asked her how I would know if that was happening to me, and she said that if it ever happened, it would be so strong that I'd have no doubt."

Carrie sighed and half-turned back toward her husband. "Jack, I've been praying for two days and nights for God to show us what to do. When I left Father's house, I asked God to guide us and speak to our hearts...to give us signs. And then, a little while ago, when Floyd told us of their plan, I think I actually *did* hear the Holy Spirit screaming in my ear. He said, 'This is it! This is where God wants you to go!' I know I sound like a loon, but I'm telling you the absolute truth." Carrie looked down at the daisy, stroked the next petal then tore it off.

She turned away from the garden again and watched the wind play with the tops of the distant eucalyptus trees that marked the ranch's boundary. Ruff had Kenny on the ground, attempting to steal the ball from his hand. Eddie climbed atop the huge canine and the pair rolled over with

Ruff turning around and licking the smaller child from toes to nose. Carrie said, "You think I'm crazy. Don't you?"

Jack put his arms around her. "Absolutely not." He gave her a loving squeeze and laid his cheek against her hair. Then he spoke softly beside her ear. "I've been praying the same thing. I just didn't feel what you felt when Grandpa was talking." He let his arm drop and walked a few paces before turning around. He gave a short massage to the back of his neck. Something didn't seem quite right. Carrie had made plain what she thought God wanted and what she thought the two of them could or should do. But not once had she said that living on a chicken ranch is what she *wanted*. Jack folded his arms across his chest. "Tell me the truth."

Carrie faced him head-on. "Always."

"Does the idea of raising chickens make you happy, or is it what you think you *should* do?"

Carrie looked out at the pasture again. "Jack I…." She hesitated.

"Tell me the truth."

She sighed and fussed with her wedding band. "You're right." She took a long breath. "It's not what I dream about, and it scares me." She fixed her gaze upon his eyes. "But neither do I hate the idea. And what I said about God's leading I believe to be true. I think he has shown us our road." She walked toward him a bit. "Now." She stopped. "You tell *me* the truth."

"Yes?" Jack shifted his weight.

"Are you really so set against this…I seem to remember you telling me that next to flying and writing you enjoyed working on your grandparents' ranch more than anything." Now, *she* crossed her arms.

Jack put his hands in his pockets again and just stood there a second, then shuffled one boot toe in the dirt. "Yes, I do like ranch work." He rolled his tongue around inside his mouth as he considered his answer. "But, like I said, I don't know how good a businessman I'll make. I'm not Grandpa." He shook his head. "I mean, I just got through going bust in the flying game, ya know. Maybe I just need to work for somebody else to keep from losing my shirt." He looked up at some cotton-ball clouds. "But still—I think part of me *does*...really want to try this." Jack gave out a low groan. "I just hope I don't put my foot in it again." He looked straight into her eyes. "And I hope you don't change your mind."

She returned his gaze. "I hope not either." She glided closer and touched his shoulder.

And the touch had a strange, soothing effect on Jack. He smiled at how something that doesn't necessarily mean that much *can* mean so much.

"Truthfully, part of me doesn't like the notion at all," she said. "Part of me wants the latest fashion, my breakfasts served to me, and a charge account in every store I go to. *That* Carrie would never move to this ranch, not even at gunpoint. The other me loves God, you, and the boys more than anything in the world." She fidgeted with her nails. "There's nothing she wouldn't do for you." She clasped her hands in front of her. "That girl wants to go...*because* of that love." She put a hand on her husband's arm. "As of right now, if you decide to go up to this place, I'll follow you and be the best ranch wife I can."

He remained silent for a moment. "I just don't know. It's not what I had in mind for us. I was just thinking about getting a job. That's all."

"That's good," said a deep, masculine voice from the garden entrance. "Because I think I might just be able to help with that very thing." It came from a mustachioed man in a dark gray, pinstriped suit. Slightly overweight for his height, which was about the same as Jack's, he wore a Hamburg which seemed to work together with his gold watch chain to complete the picture of a man who was more used to carpeted offices and hotel lobbies than the grass and cut stones of a country garden. "I hope I haven't interrupted a private moment." He thrust his hands into his pockets and rocked back and forth on his black leather high-tops in much the same manner as Jack had done a few minutes before. He looked toward Jack. "Your grandmother told me you two would be out here. Good to see you, Jack." He nodded to Carrie. "Miss Caroline."

Carrie returned the cool nod. "George, you can call me Carrie, you know. I know you're my father's attorney, but you're also my father-in-law. That gives you certain privileges."

George MacGregor pulled in his chin and emitted a small moan. "I've never been comfortable with that privilege."

Jack shook his head. His father sounded the same as he always had—distant and businesslike. He even demonstrated this demeanor on the rare occasions when he attempted tenderness with Jack's mother . Or at least, that's how it seemed. Jack accredited the manner to a life spent being the legal representative of one of the state's most powerful men.

Carrie glanced at Jack then back to George. "You're Father's lawyer, not his servant. You have the right to be familiar with your own daughter-in-law."

George shifted his weight nervously. "I'm not comfortable with being your father-in-law just yet, either."

"Is that the reason you refused your grandsons and I lodging at your home?" Carrie folded her arms and widened her stance. "Or was it because Father ordered you to?"

George did not meet her eyes. "As I said at the time, Blanch was not well." He cleared his throat. "I didn't want you or the boys catching anything."

"Oh yes." Carrie turned away and spoke to the field. "That *is* what you said."

"What is it you want, Pop?" Jack asked. "Why are you here?"

George took his watch out of its pocket and checked the time. "Mr. Van Burean is called Father by his family, but I'm just Pop." With a sigh, he snapped the watch shut and slid it back into its pinstriped hiding place.

Jack went to his wife and put his arm around her. She turned around to embrace him.

"Pop's what *I'm* comfortable with," the younger man said and raised his eyebrows. He fully meant the sarcasm. And even though it did give him a small pang of regret that it had always been this way between them, Jack still felt his attitude justified.

They'd never really had a good relationship for as long as he could remember. George had always pushed his son to embrace the advantages of the upper-middle class. He made no secret of the fact that he expected the boy to follow him into the legal profession. But Jack never shared his father's love for a life lived amongst leather-trimmed offices and yacht club social functions. He had always, with the exception of his precious fiction writing, gravitated more toward the outdoors and his grandparents' ranch. Eventually, despite having earned a bachelor degrees in both English Literature and pre-law, Jack had actually refused to go to law school altogether, choosing first auto racing and then aviation in its place. He knew that he had wounded his father with these decisions. And he also knew it had placed a wide chasm between them. But he did not believe either of these things could have been avoided. The life his father had planned for him seemed like a very small cage, and Jack could not allow himself to be locked into it. As a result, George had always acted as if his son had personally rejected *him* instead of merely choosing not to become an attorney.

And then there were the consequences of more recent occurrences. Concerning those, Carrie had hit the nail square on the head. Even though this was Jack's father, he was also the man who had refused Carrie and the boys shelter when they had run out money less than a year before. Carrie had said she was sure this action had been meant to force her to go home to her father. However, all it had actually accomplished was to push her toward staying with Floyd and Hannah instead. Jack had already argued with George over the incident via long distance telephone, with the older man maintaining that the only blame to be had should be placed squarely on his son's shoulders for not seeing to his family's needs. Jack had felt the sting of this truth and ended up simply agreeing before he replaced the phone's earpiece back onto its cradle. Yet, despite his own feelings of guilt, the bitter taste of what his father had said and done lingered. No matter what else could be said about it all, George MacGregor had refused to allow Carrie and the boys to stay in his home—however temporary that stay might have been.

So now, months later at his parents' ranch, George faced his estranged son. He straightened his own shoulders as he looked into the young man's eyes and seemed to gird himself for something. "Jack," he said, "whether you believe it or not, I have always acted in what I have thought were your best interests." He paused as if to consider something. "As a matter of fact, I am here to do that very thing once again. There is a job as apprentice legal clerk waiting for you at my law firm if and when you choose to accept it. Of course, it would be at starting wages, but that would improve in time."

Jack shook his head. "Pop, I have no experience."

George began to perspire in the late morning, summer heat. "One of your bachelor degrees is in pre-law."

"That was years ago."

George unbuttoned his coat. "No matter. The experience you gain there will sharpen you up."

Jack ran a hand through his hair. "Grandpa has another plan." He hated it when his father tried to pressure him. It never intimidated but often left no alternative but to deal with the situation in a curt, sometimes rude manner.

George pulled out a monogrammed, white linen handkerchief and mopped the burgeoning beads from his forehead. Then he carefully refolded the prissy thing and put it expertly back in its place. "Yes. He's told me about it." He chuckled and took a step toward his son. Jack stood his ground. "Jack, don't you think it's long past time to take a realistic look at yourself?" He waited with his usual penetrating stare, the one used so often in the courtroom, and the one his son had learned to despise. "Think about this a moment. I know you've been helping your grandfather for a long time, but now you're talking about running an entire poultry operation by yourself."

"He wouldn't be by himself!" Carrie's voice rose to a point just below where she would have lost her dignity.

George ignored her. "Where have your impulsive decisions gotten you in the past? Are you a champion racecar driver?" His eyebrows arched and he waited a moment. Then in the absence of his son's response he answered for him. "No." George paused again and locked his hands firmly behind his back. "Are you the successful owner of a fleet of commercial aircraft?" He rocked a bit on his heals again. "No." he said. Then he spread his hands toward the couple. "Why, you're almost destitute."

Jack knew he should say something in his own defense, but the desire died before he could even form it into words. The sad truth here was that his father was expressing things Jack himself had already considered. He had even come to share his father's point of view concerning his financial management abilities. This attitude had materialized on more than one occasion, especially on cold nights when he lacked enough money to send even a small portion home to Carrie and the boys. But this time, something felt different. Instead of the usual despairing acceptance of the notion that he was worthless as a provider, a new idea entered his mind.

God is with you. Fear not. It echoed through his being, pushing out the usual darkness. *Fear not and follow me. I have plans to prosper you, not to harm you.* Suddenly, Jack felt no need to respond to George. He just stood calmly and waited for his father's next words.

George let out a slow sigh. "The sad truth here is that you're simply not a businessman. You may be a good racecar driver or even an expert pilot, but, Son, you just don't seem to have a head for business." He turned away and began to pace, speaking as much to the air as to Jack. "Now, don't you think you owe it to yourself – to your family – to put your efforts where they can do the most good rather than waste more time on another foolhardy adventure?" He waited for a word from Jack, but none came. George gave his head a slight shake and continued. "I'm not trying to hurt you, you know. I am trying to help."

More silence.

"I see." The older MacGregor nodded. "Well then. In view of the circumstances, I will leave you both to discuss things between yourselves. But I will say this before I go." He took a very deep breath. "Taking this job in place of, once again, setting sail for disaster would be the best thing for both of you. Please, do not dismiss the opportunity out of hand. Promise me you will at least consider it."

Finally Jack spoke. "I will." He remained stiff.

"Very well, Jack. Thank you for hearing me out. I hope to see you at the office within the week." He nodded to his son and then to his daughter-in-law. "Miss Caroline."

Carrie's return nod proved almost as brief as her expression was cold. She reproduced her husband's frozen posture until George MacGregor had disappeared around the corner. Then she whirled to Jack. "Father sent him! I know it!"

"Probably." Jack exhaled a mixed bag of tension, old anger, and long-held sadness. "He could lose half his clients before supper if Albert passed the word." He shook his head. "It doesn't matter."

"No?" Carrie leaned a little closer, then seemed to rediscover the daisy in her hand.

"No, because it's just what I needed to hear." He took a deep breath and held it an extra heartbeat to clear the lump that had suddenly grown in his throat. "He doesn't think I'm up to the monumental task of supporting my family—at least not without his supervision." Jack ran a hand over the back of his neck again. "Okay," he said while staring at a tiny cumulus cloud that happened to be passing over the ranch house. He had noticed it just a second before and discovered that, for some reason, it seemed to calm him to look at it. He didn't know why it did, but he was glad just the same.

"Okay, what?" Carrie discarded another petal.

Combing his hair with his fingers, Jack continued to watch the cloud and discovered it also helped him to focus his thoughts. "Just now," he said, "while Pop was letting me know I was still worthless…"

She grimaced at the remark but answered tentatively, "Yes?"

"I thought I heard the Holy Ghost yell in *my* ear, too." He allowed one chuckle to escape.

"That so?"

"Yeah." Jack lowered his gaze to Carrie's upturned face. He winked and permitted a very small smile to spread from the corners of his mouth. "I think we should start a chicken ranch in Sweet Potato."

Carrie giggled, "Sweet Springs."

"That's what I said."

She plucked the last petal off the daisy. "See, I love you. The daisy says so."

He hugged her hard. "Glad to hear that, Hon'."

After that both of them just stood silent, looking into each other's face, letting their embrace linger in the silence that followed the tense verbal exchanges of the last few minutes. Only the warm east wind bullied the garden's stillness. But after few seconds, bits and pieces of distant conversation began to blow over the top of the honeysuckle and settle down into the garden. Jack recognized the voices as those of his grandparents, but only part of their exchange made it over the blossoming folage.

First came Hannah's voice. "Floyd...can't just blurt...and expect...time to think...."

Floyd's answer, though, was easily discernible. "Oh, hogwash!"

Carrie turned around in Jack's arms. "You think we'd better tell them before they change their minds?"

Jack chuckled. "Or Grandpa moves up to Sweet Springs by himself and leaves us stuck here."

With that, they walked back through the garden and out the east trellis gate to tell Floyd and Hannah about the screaming of the Holy Ghost, their decision, and how blessed they felt to have family like them.

Chapter Eleven

Bang!
The right wheel of the trailer slammed hard into a cavernous pothole, sending a shockwave forward from its wooden spokes all the way to the ears of the towing vehicle's passengers. Jack had managed to avoid this minor abyss with the Model-T truck, but the trailer's tire swung out a little wider and blundered right into it. Then came the inevitable jolt on the drive-train as the engine struggled to pull the load out of the hole, which it did after a neck-stretching deceleration, an awkward jerk, and almost a full half-second of arm-wrestle-like struggle.

"Oh, that was the worst one yet!" Carrie adjusted her neck and resettled Eddie on her lap.

Jack wiped his forehead with an already sweat-soaked sleeve. "Sorry. I thought I was going to miss that one for sure. Model-T's aren't as easy to drive as your Stutz. You don't really steer; you just sort of herd them." He leaned his head out of the cab and yelled to his older son, who sat back in the cargo bed with the family's goods. "Kenny, you all right back there?"

The boy leaned around a box and answered in a voice of equal volume, "Y-e-s, sir. I'm okay. 'Cept, every time you slow down the dust catches up with us."

"Well, there's not much we can do about that! Just tie your bandana around your mouth like Jessie James." Jack coughed as he pulled his head back inside. "He's all right. Now, what were you saying?"

Carrie shifted a little to get comfortable. "I said, 'Why was Dorothy living with Floyd and Hannah, if she's not really related?'"

Jack looked uneasy. "Well, It's not generally known."

"I'm your wife, silly! I'm not going to say anything!" His caution irritated her a little, but she decided to let it pass.

Jack nodded. "All right." He paused for a moment, as if trying to think of something, then began. "Cover Eddie's ears."

Carrie did so over Eddie's squirming protests, then returned her attention to her husband. "Yes?"

"In short," Jack said, "she's Carlyle Hilliard's illegitimate daughter, and my grandparents took her in when her mother killed herself."

Carrie's mouth dropped open. "No! Hilliard, the hotel owner? Oh, my Lord, Jack! Does she know?"

Jack cleared his throat and navigated around another hole. "She knows about Carlyle. He's always paid for her needs. He didn't exactly try to bribe my grandparents to keep quiet, but he suddenly started treating them with more respect than the rest of the Marner Bay crowd ever did." Jack was quiet for a moment. "But Dorothy thinks her mother died in an auto accident." He gave his wife a peripheral glance. "I suppose, in a way, that's partly true. She did go off a cliff where the highway bends out toward the beach. But the sheriffs said there were no skid marks. She never even tried to apply the brakes. She just drove off the edge."

"But why did your grandparents take Dorothy in?" Eddie tried to squirm free, but Carrie tightened her grip around his ears. Then he applied his young masculine skills toward twisting out of this new wrestler's hold; however, his efforts availed him nothing. He remained trapped within the grasp of his mother's palms and her determination that her youngest son should hear no evil just now.

"The girl's mother sometimes worked for them. They had grown to love Dorothy long before she was orphaned."

"I see," Carrie said and removed her hands from her son's now crimson ears. The boy rubbed them immediately and gave his mom an annoyed look. "My Lord. Poor Dorothy," she muttered, then settled back into the car-seat. After a few seconds Eddie started squirming again, so

Carrie leaned forward, adapting a firmer grip on his hips. Then she contented herself with looking around at the countryside. Mostly dry wild grass and chaparral, with occasional clumps of tall evergreen trees surrounding ranch houses of all description, from squat adobe/wooden mixes to elaborate multi-storied framed Cape Cods. "I thought this was supposed to be in the mountains."

"It is," Jack responded. "We've been climbing for hours."

"It all looks like desert to me." Carrie wrinkled her nose.

Jack shook his head. "It's both, actually. They call it high desert. Sort of dry mountains without the forests." He ground the truck down into a lower gear as the grade steepened.

Carrie had just begun to relax a little when steam started wafting from the radiator. *That's about the umpteenth time today,* she thought. *And we've already had to stop twice to let this ridiculous truck cool down.* She turned to Jack. "Is the truck going to overheat again?" she asked, honestly expecting her husband to know the answer.

Jack let out a big male sigh. "I don't know, Carrie." His voice sounded laced with irritation. "But I think we're almost there!"

The tone of his last words sounded like something a little short of a bark, so she smiled, fluttered her eyelashes, and turned her attention to the scenery again.

The road continued to wind up Saber Canyon like a river of dust and clay. It lapped at the banks of dry, high-desert grass with little mounds of fine, tan powder, instead of whitecaps. In the adobe center of its course, more ruts and bottomless potholes, baked hard by the July sun, lay in wait for the next unsuspecting tire or wagon wheel.

Then *another* bang resounded as the trailer wheel hit yet *another* hole. But this time, something else happened as well. The trailer began to swing in a maniacal fashion from one side of the narrow road to the other, causing the little truck to sway with it. Finally, despite Jack's best efforts to get things under control, the right wheel loped drunkenly into a deep ditch that ran parallel to the road. After that, it just proceeded to roll along the trench's length, unable to escape this natural trailer trap. Jack jerked the wheel hard left and shoved the gas pedal to the floorboard...but to no avail. The depth of the ditch proved too great. So the wayward wheel simply continued its confined course, forcing a frustrated driver to slow to a stop as the sound of the decomposed granite road surface grating against the undercarriage of the trailer echoed up to the model-T's cab.

"What? What is it now?" Carrie let out her *long-hard-hot-trip* frustration in one snappy sigh, while trying to keep monkey-like Eddy from hanging too far out the truck's windowless side.

"Mama, I wanta' see!"

"You keep quiet, young man. And sit still!"

"But Mama, I can't—"

"I said to keep quite!"

The Ford's jet-black fabric top hoarded the sun's heat, cooking the cab's occupants. The curls of Carrie's bobbed, brunette hair hung lazily around her face, having given up their spring many miles back, and her lip rouge was a chewed-off, licked-off memory. She caught her faint reflection in the windshield and frowned.

Jack let the engine die in gear and set the brake. He slapped some dust off his jodhpurs and tightened the laces on his boots.

He still looks like he just hopped out of an airplane, Carrie thought but kept it to herself.

"Well, I guess I'd better go find out what's happened, so I can come back and tell *you*. Then maybe...just maybe you can settle down some... you think?" The groan in Jack's voice mixed with the squeak of the door as he swung it open and slid out onto the road. He leaned onto the

154

truck's chassis and looked her directly in the eye. "It's been over four hot hours now, Carrie. I've had enough trouble with the radiator. I don't need you to start in too."

"Well, you try and keep a four-year-old occupied and out of his father's way all the way from Glendale to Sweet Springs in the middle of July." Eddy tried to stand up on Carrie's lap, so she leaned him halfway out the open window where he could look around. The child kicked his feet to push his stomach against the door, wrinkling his mother's short, floral-print dress; she sighed and smoothed it with her hand. "All *you've* had to do is drive."

Jack backed up a little. "And stop to cool the engine off...then drive some more." His volume and tone softened a little as he struggled to maintain a scowl.

"And cool off the engine and drive some more." Carrie giggled a little and smiled just a crack. Then she released half her grasp on Eddie to shoo a bothersome horsefly away from her nose.

Jack sighed, wiped the sweat from his face with his shirt sleeve, and leaned forward to kiss her...but she beat him to it with a quick peck on the lips.

"Sorry." She pulled an embroidered hankie from some hidden place and dabbed carefully at her face. "It's just so hot, Jack!"

"I know," he said and wrinkled his moist brow. "A little hotter than it is on the coast, and that's a fact." He sighed again and shook his head. "I gotta get on back there, Hon'." He indicated the trailer with a tilt of the head. Then he pecked her back, on the cheek this time, and winked. "Just another sunny, Southern California day, right?"

"Daddy, kiss me, too!" Eddy piped.

Jack smiled and ruffled his younger son's hair as he left the truck.

"I'll do more than kiss you, little man," Carrie grinned at her youngest, then lowered her eyebrows in a mock evil expression. "I'll play your belly like an old trombone, I will!"

"No, Mama, no!" Eddie giggled and hugged his belly for protection from the dreaded, tickling raspberries he knew were coming.

Eddy's squealing giggles echoed within the Flivver truck's cab and escaped out into the breeze. Carrie hoped Jack could hear it all; he always said he liked hearing Eddy laugh—as if it were some sort of tranquilizer for him. A tranquilizer. That would help just now. It'd been a *much* worse trip than she'd expected. Eddy was wound tighter than a six-day clock, and the truck's radiator had never ceased its threat to give out and leave them stranded miles from help. She felt sorry for Jack having to keep a cool head through so much turmoil. But then she felt sorry for herself, too…and for much the same reason.

Carrie opened her door and held it with her foot to get a little more ventilation. Then, after pulling up Eddy's trousers and tightening his suspenders, she sent him to play on the sparse grass of the embankment, so she could dig out her compact and affect some repairs to what sweat, wind, and nerves had done to her makeup. When she had completed that task, she snapped the compact mirror shut and slid it into her purse. She folded her legs up and turned around in the seat, bracing her back against the dashboard, dividing her attention between Eddy's play and the activities of her other two men. She heard no noise beside the occasional wind gust that rustled the grass, unless she counted the sighs and groans Jack emitted while he stood beside the truck-bed, staring at the trailer.

After several seconds of that, he turned to Kenny, who still sat, back against the cab, feet braced against a box. "Go get us a big rock," he said to the boy. "To put behind this back wheel." Jack pointed to the truck's right rear tire.

"Yes, Sir!" The boy bounded from the vehicle and scrambled up a small embankment.

"And keep an eye out for rattlers!" Jack yelled after.

156

"Yes, Sir," came the diminishing reply.

Jack shuffled back to the wheel-eating ditch and hunched over to survey the state of things. Kenny soon returned, stumbling under the weight of a more than boy-sized granite egg that he clutched against the bib of his denim overalls. He wedged it, as best he could, behind the T's wheel and looked toward his dad expectantly.

"Like that, Dad?" he asked, pointing to his handiwork.

"Yep, that's got her." Jack added an extra pump of manufactured enthusiasm to his answer. "That's how you do it!"

He crouched down in the ditch, beside the lame trailer, staring and squinting through hand shaded eyes. He bobbed his head up and down like a slow-motion version of an ostrich challenging for combat, while Kenny peered over his father's shoulder and emulated him, practicing the ritual moves, perhaps readying himself for the day when he, too, would have to assert dominance over a rebellious tow-vehicle of his own.

Carrie smiled as she watched. *That's certainly not the type of man Mother and Father had in mind,* Carrie thought. *"They'd have an absolute fit if they could see us now.*

Jack had worked his way half under the trailer now, on his back, looking up, inspecting for damage. Carrie could see only his legs from the knees down sticking out into the sun, with a smaller pair of limbs right beside—Kenny, still acting out his apprenticeship to the letter. Carrie thought this cute at first, but then she remembered the trailer had been disabled, and the whole situation suddenly made her nervous.

"Aw, I can't see...can't see if anything's broken from here. I'll have to crawl under from the other side." Jack began to wiggle out, feet first; Kenny did likewise. "Watch your head, son."

"Yes, Sir."

"Jack?" Carrie had begun to feel the heat as the breeze died down, taking longer than its usual respite between gusts.

Father and son rose up from the dust and noticed each other's backsides. "Here." Jack turned Kenny around. "Let me swipe you off a little, so your mom don't get mad." He swatted the boy's clothes, creating a small dust cloud that soon drifted away.

"Jack," Carrie persisted.

"Okay, that's good enough." He straightened up and turned toward the truck. "What?"

"I don't want Kenny under the trailer like that. It's broken...It might fall on him."

"Well, what about me?" Jack chuckled low, and Kenny snickered.

Carrie remained un-amused. "Jack, I don't want him under there!" She waited for her husband's response. But there was only the renewed shush wind and the buzzing of a muted male voice as Jack muttered something under his breath. So she pressed. "Please!"

"Okay, okay!"

"Dad!" Kenny protested against the humiliation of being babied.

"No, your mom's right. Besides, what I really need is for you to find another rock to block the other trailer wheel. I want to make sure this thing doesn't move while I'm under there. So you go find another one and take care of that wheel like you did with the truck. Go on now."

"Yes, Sir." The boy scrambled up the bank again, a little suspicious, but obedient.

"Thanks, Jack."

"Oh, don't mention it. All part of our friendly service." Jack walked around and slid under the trailer on the side farthest away from the ditch. "By the way..." His voice sounded a little muffled from beneath the axle. "You *are* going to save me if this thing falls, aren't you?"

"Well, I guess I could unhitch the truck, so Kenny and I could drive for help..." The breeze had picked up a little more—and with it her humor. "But you'd have to watch little Eddy while I'm gone. I can't drive and hold him too...Sweetheart." The last word was laced with more than an ounce of sarcasm.

He answered in kind, "Well, that's a load off my mind."

Only the wind hissing through the foxtails broke the silence of the next few minutes—that and Jack muttering incoherently under the trailer. Carrie saw that Eddy had played himself out, making small mounds in a patch of sand, so she put him on the truck seat out of the sun and let him nap. This left her free to stroll to the top of the embankment and look around a bit. Once there, she held a roadmap to her forehead to protect her eyes from the sun.

She could see they had gotten stuck on a road that traversed an ascending plateau at the head of Saber Canyon; below her spread over six miles of high desert grassland, rippling like waves on a lake in the now stiffening vagabond currents of tinder-dry air. Heat dominated the day so far, a moistureless desert kind of heat that sucks at the skin and steals the water right out of the body. But the relentless breeze remained strong and gusty, giving frequent bursts of semi-cool relief, so one only needed occasional shade and water to stay comfortable, or at least remain safe from the hazards of the temperature.

Kenny came chugging up the hill, carrying another large rock and puffing like a steam locomotive. He stumbled in a small washout but managed to throw his burden ahead before he fell. Upon rising, he slapped the dust from his clothes and picked off the burrs and foxtails before he addressed the granite chunk again, which he finally hefted to his chest with much groaning and more railroad sounds.

"Kenny, you be careful with that. It's heavy!" Carrie

had a habit of stating the obvious to express her fears and feelings. Sometimes it was more dutiful than necessary.

The boy shifted the weight of his load for better balance, looking slightly annoyed at the distraction. "Yes, ma'am. I'm being careful," he grunted, then after a moment of determined hesitation , he took off once again at a squatting run and disappeared behind the hillock.

Men are all alike...even the short ones. Carrie turned around to look up-canyon, trying to make out their new home. But they weren't close enough yet and the brow of a hill blocked her vision. Anxiety seemed to haunt her today, partly from fear and partly from anticipation. This whole venture continued to be way beyond her experience, let alone that of her parents. A chicken ranch in the high desert—and she'd given up the security of her family's support to do it! She'd actually defied them to be with her husband...to have her *own* family together...to try for that happy, content kind of life her parents had never known.

She'd been told back at their little church at Crossroads that God wanted them to have that sort of good life. She hoped with all her heart that it was true, but she wasn't sure if she really believed that yet. Sometimes she just felt alone and scared...like now. She could sense that tightness that ran from her stomach to her chest and feel the little pinch in her spine. And now, little by little, all-out fear seemed to be gaining ground again. She took a deep breath and held it. Sometimes that helped. It slowed down her racing nerves and often even bought her a few seconds of outright calm. She continued to hold the breath for as long as she could, then let the air out slowly—it worked. She knew she'd be all right for a little while.

She scanned the plateau to the north. There, a large square field of what looked like abnormally tall grass, covered most of the semi-flat area; a red-plank house and barn stood like sentinels at the far end. An open wagon pulled by two large chestnut horses traveled through the low sagebrush along the field's edge, making its way toward the road. The driver rode slumped forward with elbows resting on his knees, and a broad-brimmed straw hat shading his face. A young red-haired boy, dressed in overalls like Kenny's ran a little ahead of the wagon and a large Irish Setter trotted ahead of the boy. All seemed to be converging on her family, so she lowered her map sunshade and walked back toward the truck.

Then, at that moment, before she could even see the road, the sound of Kenny's yelling reached her.

"Eddy, No!"... Stay back!... Leave it alone!... Dad!... Eddy, no!... Dad!"

Carrie broke to a run, jumping over holes and brush, then slid along with several pounds of gravel and dirt, down the short slope to the road. The truck appeared empty. Eddy had left the cab. So she raced past it toward the trailer and came upon the scene that brought her to a dust-clouded stop. Kenny stood stiff as a tree with one hand extended toward his brother. Eddie appeared to be kicking sand in the general direction of a small greenish-gray snake coiled about a foot from the trailer. The reptile's triangular head stood erect, its eyes tracked the toddler's every move, rattles buzzing at the tip of an upright tail.

"Kenny, get your brother back." Jack's voice came calmly from under the trailer.

"Eddy, come on!" pleaded Kenny, pulling on the smaller boy's hand. But Eddy jerked away and kicked more of the road at the rattler.

"Go-way!" he squealed. "Go-way!" He took a tiny step forward. "We don't want you! Go-way!"

"Dad, he won't let me! Eddy, get back!"

Jack tried to slide out from under the trailer, but that only resulted in the snake striking at him (with near success).

"Jack, go out the other side!" Carrie found her voice.

"The frame's hung up on a dirt ridge. I can't get out

that way...Eddy, you back away from that snake right now, or I'll tan your britches! Do you hear me?"

"Yeah."

"What?"

"Yes, Sir."

"Okay, then. You take Kenny's hand and back away very slowly. Don't make a sound."

Kenny got a grip on his brother's reluctant hand, and the two retreated as ordered. Carrie clutched them, one in each arm, as soon as they were out of danger. She hugged both with desperate relief, while she held another deep breath and willed her heart to slow down.

"Ow, Mama!" Eddy squirmed, trying unsuccessfully for escape.

"You just hush, young man, and stay still! Jack, what are you going to do?"

"Carrie, try throwing some rocks at it. Maybe it'll move away."

"All right." She answered then turned to the older boy. "Kenny, bring me some small rocks—small enough to fit in my hand! Hurry!"

The boy disappeared in an instant.

"Me, too, Mama!"

Carrie picked Eddy off his feet and set him roughly down behind her. "You stay right on that spot, and don't move or I'll..."

"Here's rocks, Mom!" His semi-heroic mission accomplished in a flash, Kenny now stood next to his mother, puffing deep breaths again.

Carrie collected her weapons—three smooth golf ball-size stones—and fixed Eddy with a glare. The boy froze in place, gluing his eyes to the tips of his shoes. "Okay, Jack," she said, "I got the rocks!"

"Good. Now try to hit him on the side facing the trailer. I'm hoping that'll drive him the other way."

"Jack, I don't know if I can do that! I might miss!"

Was he crazy? I've never hit anything with a rock in my life!

"Don't be silly. It's just like pitching a baseball. Just relax and take your time."

"I've never played baseball!"

" Carrie...just throw the rocks, Hon. Okay?"

"Okay."

Carrie took another deep gulp of air and let it out like a steam valve, but it didn't relax her one bit this time. She squinted against the sun's glare, then let fly the first of her three missiles. It thunked just to the right of the snake, the opposite side from the trailer. The serpent uncoiled enough to slither a little to the left, almost touching the trailer's tire and closer to Jack.

"Not too bad, Hon. Now just aim a little more to the left....Try to hit *between* the snake and the tire."

She could hear the effort to keep calm in Jack's voice. He was worried which drove home to Carrie how critical it was to somehow drive off that snake right now before it slithered further under the trailer. So she tried again, but only nicked the creature on the wrong side...*again*, causing it to uncoil and—sure enough—seek shelter (a little closer to her husband) under the trailer.

"Oh, no!....Carrie, hit him again! Hit him again!"

Carrie threw the last rock as hard as she could, but it just whizzed over the head of her intended target. "Oh, my God!" She swung about, looking for another rock, but the sound of savage growling drew her attention back to the trailer. The Irish setter she'd seen crossing the field had, like magic, appeared beside the trailer's left wheel and now stood with the snake clamped in its mouth. Then, after a moment, making sure of his toothy grip just behind the reptile's head, the dog began shaking his prey like a rag doll.

"Copper, no!...Drop it!....No!" The boy with hair to match his dog bounded with big, clumsy shoes down onto the road and circled the ensuing combat at a safe distance, goading the Setter to obedience. "Copper, drop it now!' He was bigger than Kenny and looked quite a bit older. He had a calm confidence about him that said rattlesnakes were old hat.

Not so, however, for Carrie. She'd never witnessed any real violence or threat of danger, other than on a football field or movie screen, and certainly never anything this horrific—never anything this real. All she could do was stand there, frozen to her spot, gripping her boys as she hyperventilated and watched things unfold. However, as frightening as the scene was for her, she found herself strangely fascinated, and, try as she might, could not look away. That realization bothered her a little, as well.

Copper flung the snake into the center of the road but kept it coiled there with rapid-fire barks. The boy quickly located one perfectly palm-size stone and crept forward toward the enemy. Then he stopped and half crouched about two yards away.

Carrie held her breath as she watched.

The rattler, attention now divided between the human and the dog, kept swiveling its head to cover both. The boy, squinting one eye as if sighting a rifle, extended his rock-less left arm and pointed a flat palm. Then, after poising his projectile behind and above his head, he hurtled the thing with a loud grunt, wrought from concentrated effort. In an instant, success followed the act—the rock found its mark, crushing the snake's head against the ground and causing the creature's body to writhe as the sound of its rattles' turned spasmodic, then ceased altogether. A quick shiver ran through Carrie's body ending in her chest. But she kept watching. The boy produced a large pocketknife from his overalls and strode toward his kill, unfolding its gleaming blade as he went.

Finally, Carrie found the will to look away. She sensed what the boy intended with the knife and knew that it would be a little too much for her to watch. She tried to cover her boys' eyes, but Kenny wouldn't have it and pulled free, refusing to be deprived of the bloody exhibition. His mother did not understand this, but she let go of him, just the same.

The older boy's business proved swift. By the time Carrie looked back, the snake's severed head set skewered atop the knife's blade, which the young slayer held up out of Copper's reach. Then he kicked the reptile's still wriggling body a few feet away.

"Go get it, Copper...Go get it!"

The big, red dog reached his prize in one great leap. Then he scooped the squirming thing up into an ample mouth and bounded off into a squat juniper thicket, both his and the snake's tail still wagging.

Carrie made a face and shivered again.

"Did he bite ya, mister?" the boy asked, crouching on his haunches to peer under the trailer, but careful to hold the serpent's head away from his body as the thing's dead jaws still bit at the air.

"Jack!" Carrie suddenly remembered her husband. She'd been so horrified and mesmerized by what had taken place in front of her, she'd almost forgotten about him altogether! "Are you all right?" Her voice rasped with strain.

"Naw, I don't think he got me." Jack said, answering the boy's question first. Then he slid out from under the trailer and stood dusting himself off in the breeze. "He just bit my pride, that's all. It's embarrassing being cornered under a trailer by one little snake."

"I said," Carrie repeated with a tinge of irritation. "'Are *you* all right'!"

"What...Oh, yeah...I'm okay." Jack checked his boots and noticed a new gouge on the reinforced toe. "He just kissed my boot a little. That's all...I'm fine." He smiled. "How about you?"

"Really!" she snorted. "How do you think I'm going to be with a deadly snake attacking my husband and children!"

"Aw, he was just headin' for the shade," said the boy, turning his knife so he could admire the creature's fangs. "But he *is* a Mojave Green, and *that's* one of the worse snakes there is." The boy looked all around him as if he'd lost something. "You're lucky, Mister. Only takes one little nip from a Green to put most folks down."

As the young rescuer's words found a purchase upon Carrie's strained emotions, she momentarily forgot the boys and drew close to Jack, putting her hands against his chest and looking him up and down as if checking for wounds. *He could have been bitten; he could have been dying by now!* The thought ran like lightning through her mind. She took her usual calming breath and held it, but that did no good; her heart still pounded, so she gave up and just hugged her husband, borrowing some of his relative serenity. That *did* help. She felt better and decided to hold onto him for a little longer.

Jack wrapped his arms around Carrie in response, then turned to the boy. "My name's Jack. Jack MacGregor. And this is my wife, Carrie...

"Ma'am," the boy nodded respectfully.

"Kenny and Little Eddy." Jack indicated the boys by tilting his head in their direction.

"Hi." The boy's nod was more curt this time. Jack's sons *hi'd* him back in unison.

"Ya get yourself another snake there, Seth?" The old man driving the wagon pulled up short of the road. "Whoa, Cain."

"That's me; I'm Seth." He turned to the old teamster and answered, raising his voice a little. "Yes, Sir. Got me a Green." Seth held up the head then surveyed the immediate area again. "But I can't find me no dern can to put *this* in."

"Don't swear, son." The old man turned stiffly on his

seat and began looking in the bed of the wagon.

"Yes, Sir," Seth replied. "Sorry, Ma'am." He nodded to Carrie again.

Jack and Carrie looked at each other and stifled smiles.

"That's my Grandpa Ben." Seth pointed the snake's head toward the man climbing carefully down from the wagon. If a human being and a bear could be crossbred, Ben could have passed for the result. Appearing to be in his mid-sixties, he retained the size and shape of a professional wrestler half that age. A well-trimmed white beard clung to full sun-reddened cheeks, and, like his grandson, he sported bib-overalls and clod hopper shoes.

The man doffed his broad-brimmed straw hat and exhibited a gait a little stiff with the years as he approached the group. He ran the sleeve of his shirt over a sweat beaded forehead then replaced the hat. His back and elbows had more than a slight bend to them. But rather than making him seem decrepit, it gave him the air of an honest hard-worker.

Ben handed Seth a small camp shovel and an empty tin can labeled *Bully Beef.* "Here, Boy, bury him deep, so's it don't wash up onto the road with the rain next spring." He turned to the MacGregors, and smiled. "Hello there. I'm Benjamin Smith...Ben to them what knows me." He thumbed back toward his grandson. "Got to bury them snake heads in a can, if'n ya can." He smiled at his inadvertent humor. "Otherwise, you can step on them fangs a year from now. They go through your shoe. Ya bleed. Blood mixes with the dried venom, and you've got yourself a fresh snakebite from a year dead snake." He winked. "And who might you good folks be?"

Introductions and greetings were repeated as Seth slid the Green's head off his knife into the can, crimped the tin with his foot, and jogged off into some chaparral with the shovel. Ben walked arthritically to the trailer. "Saw you break down from the house." He eased himself down on one knee and inspected the trailer's undercarriage. "Know you got a broke axle?"

"Yeah, I saw that," Jack squatted down beside the visitor.

"Thought you might've been distracted by other more pressing matters whilst you were under there." The old man winked at Carrie and made a two-fingered snake pantomime at the boys, which made them snicker. "Well, let's see how bad it is." Ben put his hat on top of the tarp covering the trailer load, lay down on his back and gave the *come here* finger curl to Kenny and Eddy. "How about you two boys help push me under."

The boys looked to Carrie for confirmation. "It's all right." She nodded. "Go ahead." So Ben locked his knees as each boy pushed on one of his shoes.

"Just pretend like I'm an old log, boys." he said. "Now let's see here...Yep...You broke her pretty good. Matter of fact...Uh...All right, somebody pull me out now."

"We'll, do it, boys." Jack motioned Carrie to help, and each of them took a foot and pulled.

Ben struggled to his feet and turned toward the couple. "Would you give me a dustin', please?" Carrie folded her road map and lightly swept him off. "Thank you, Ma'am. I do appreciate that...Now, what was I...Oh, yeah... that axle's gonna need replacing, not just repairing. She's twisted off in the middle, and your *hub's* almost left ya. You're gonna have to unhitch and take your loads up in your tin Lizzie truck 'til you got your trailer empty. Then you'll have to drag her. You're the folks that bought the old Van Meter place, ain't you?"

Jack nodded.

"Is that very far from here?" Carrie flipped open the map again and shaded her eyes.

"No, Ma'am—"

"Please, call me Carrie."

"Okay, Carrie...Your new home is just up the plateau,

behind that rise." Ben pointed off to the east.

"I don't know if our truck can drag a broken trailer up this grade." Jack wiped more sweat off his forehead and scratched his scalp.

"Well, Mr. MacGregor—"

"You can do the same for me as you did for my wife."

"You want me to call you Carrie, too?...

"Uh..."

"Sorry...Just foolin'...Jack, it is...Well, anyway...We can hitch old Cain and Abel up to your sorrow and drag it up that road easy."

"Who?"

"Cain and Abel...my Belgians there." Ben waved toward his large, muscular two-up team, hitched to the big, plank-sided freight wagon. "They could haul an elephant to market, if they'd a mind to."

Jack twisted half around to squint up-canyon against the glaring sun, then pointed. "How about just dragging it straight across these grass fields rather than following the road? Shorter."

"Whoa, no!...That's forty acres of oats you're pointin' at, not grass...We'd tear up my bread and butter like nobody's business dragging that thing." Ben looked back at Jack and rubbed his chin. "You ain't been around farms much, have you, son?"

"Just chickens. That's what we're going to raise up here."

"Chickens...Well, that's more ranchin' than farmin'. We grow *oats* for hay and feed. Lots of horses still up here. Old Henry Sargent down at the feed store, he buys all we grow and asks for more. By the way, we might as well put some of your goods into my wagon here...so's you don't have to hall it all in that little truck." Ben shook his head as if he suddenly realized the size of the job he had just volunteered for. "Well, we ain't gonna get your trailer unhitched by standing here. Come on, Jack. Let's do 'er."

The old man cupped his hands and called off into the brush. "Seth...we need ya, boy!"

The two men disconnected the truck from its defunct companion. Seth soon returned with Copper, both parts of the snake having been dutifully disposed of, and helped the adults transfer goods from Jack's trailer to Ben's wagon. Carrie watched Seth with interest as the three toted boxes and bed-slats up the dirt embankment. He was all boy, from pocket knife to red shaggy dog, but he had a certain voluntary seriousness about him that often didn't show up for years in city children. Life out on Ben's dry-land farm had obviously had a tempering effect on this young man; he didn't dawdle or seek a means of escape as they all worked. Rather, Seth exuded a calm, serious focus on the job at hand. In truth, he moved more like a man than a boy.

Carrie had to stifle a smile as she passed him. His slightly exaggerated sternness proved both amusing and admirable at the same time. She controlled the urge to grab him and hug him, instead, settling for the hope that her boys would someday mature just like that. She did have to smile just a little though as she watched Kenny and Eddy following Seth back and forth. Apparently, *they* admired him, too.

"You little boys stay out of my way now, so's you don't get hurt," Seth warned after Eddy had wandered into his path.

Kenny responded quickly. "I'm not a little boy! I'm seven!" He indicated Eddy with a tilt of his head. "He's just four."

"This many." Eddy held up three fingers, then changed his mind and switched to five.

"I'm a lot bigger than him!" Kenny asserted.

"Then how come you ain't helping, Big Boy?"

Kenny frowned; he didn't have an immediate answer for that, so he stewed over the question for a moment. Then he noticed something born of parent-nurtured habit – his own hand holding Eddy's— and a light came on. "I have to hold onto *him*. I *always* do when Mom can't." The last words were sighed with resignation.

Carrie's heart went out to her older son. He wanted to help, and he believed he could, but there he was shackled to his little brother while the important *big boy business* passed him by.

"You know, I think Eddy's big enough to help now," Carrie said.

Kenny looked up at his mother with shock and confusion.

She took Eddy from his grasp and carried him to the trailer. "We need someone to stand right here in the trailer and hold it down so this big, old wind doesn't blow it away with all our things in it. You can do that for Mama, can't you, Big Boy!" Eddy nodded a puffed-chest affirmation.

"Yeah, you hold onto that trailer, Eddy. We need you," Jack said. Eddy nodded again and gripped the vehicle's side with steel determination.

"You going to help us, boy?" came Ben's duty call to Kenny.

"Yeah!...Uh, yes, Sir!"

Carrie watched Kenny beat everyone to the next reasonably sized box and trudged triumphantly toward the wagon with his sacred burden, while his younger brother stood his post in the trailer and defied the wind. *Kenny doesn't want to just watch others do all the work,* she thought. *He wants to get into life and do something...like his father.* She could see that her oldest son had very little of the spoiled Van Burean side of the family in him. And that pleased her.

In due time, all the work had been completed. The MacGregor belongings had been stacked together in front of their new house, and their lamed trailer had been dragged up two miles of dirt road with all the tenacity and brute force two well-trained, matched draft horses could muster. The twisted remains of the axle *had* left a six inch deep furrow the length of the trip to mark its passing. But, all the same, it had made it to MacGregor property, and that's all that mattered. Now, it could rest in peace—at least for a while.

Contrary to what one might think, the ordeal of the axle and the rattlesnake had left most of the group in relatively high spirits. Ben, a veritable safe deposit box of agrarian knowledge, seemed not merely open, but eager to share as much rural wisdom as Jack could digest. Seth, despite his austere outer affectation, betrayed a genuine friendliness toward the boys, even to the point of hefting Eddy out of the trailer and into the wagon, emitting a sort of tiger growled "There we go" and a "Come on, Eddy" for the final exit at the ranch.

"Eleven," Seth answered when Kenny had asked his age.

"*I'll* be eleven someday."

"I know," the veteran child replied. "But you do okay for seven already."

Everyone busied themselves with one task or another. All seemed in good humor—everyone, that is, except Carrie. From the moment the group arrived at what Ben called the ranch, she had not uttered a sound. Shock had robbed her of the power of speech. Only one word existed that could describe the place, in her estimation — hideous…or at least some other term far worse than the rosy verbal picture Floyd had painted. Most of the fencing, both barbed wire and wooden rail, lay on the ground. Chicken coops, small barn, and sheds were not just in need of repair. They cried out to be either rebuilt or torn down!

Wild growths of Russian Thistle, Deer Weed, and Foxtail had invaded and choked most of the ground between the buildings and the beautiful thirty-foot tall pine trees that surrounded the yard. These majestic conifers, Carrie decided, were the only semi-redeeming attributes the place possessed. In addition, an unfamiliar, eerie buzzing seemed to come from everywhere and no place in particular. Carrie fantasized that this noise came from some old ghost, living at the timeworn property, resenting these newcomers who were trespassing upon his domain. She extrapolated that this annoyed spirit didn't think they belong there at all, and she decided, in general, if there had been such a ghost, she would have to agree with him on that score.

Then she focused her full attention onto the family's new home, and her heart came up into her throat. *Oh, my goodness!* What stood before her could only be described as unbelievable, and, in fact, for a moment, she actually did have trouble even convincing herself of the scene's reality. She could not think of terms to describe this so-called house, but knew she'd never seen anything like it in her life. It was the cherry on top of the whole disappointing enterprise and, as such, dealt her endurance a final blow. With that confession, she began to hyperventilate and continued to do so until her knees gave out, then she just enthroned herself upon the nearest packing barrel, and decided to stay there until the lightheaded, queasy feeling, she now experienced, went away.

Chapter Twelve

The sun had almost set by the time Carrie, still perched on the packing barrel that contained Jack's hand tools and nails, had calmed herself enough to make a serious survey of the old ranch shack that was to be her new home. Half the windows sported either protective boards or broken panes. The front door hung askew from its top hinge, leaving a large triangle of exposed empty air. A tiny kangaroo rat tiptoed out from behind the canted door and disappeared into some nearby undergrowth. Carrie shuddered; she did not like small rodents. Cute or not, they weren't welcome in any house she would occupy.

Ben put a hand on her shoulder and made her jump. "Sorry." He pulled back a little, while she settled down. "Ya know." He pointed to the grainy, semi-shrunken boards that made up the house's exterior walls. "Them boards was salvaged from an old Civil War boxcar the Southern Pacific auctioned off back in ninety-seven when they went from narrow to standard gauge." The old man smiled as if he'd just told his new neighbor she had a strongbox full of gold doubloons hidden under her house.

Carrie's composure, at this point, had already entered its terminal phase. Why had Ben told her this. *Does he really think I want to know where the stupid boards came from? This pathetic wreck of a house is a disaster, and now he's telling me the walls are even older and closer to falling down than I thought!* But just then something else pushed itself into her consciousness—the memory of what a lifesaver Ben had been for them that day. Consequently, Carrie decided not to vent her disgust with a rude response. Instead, she glanced up at him and said, with all the feigned interest she could muster, "How interesting. And it's really that old?"

"Yep," Ben continued. "Eighteen-ninety-seven, like I said." He scratched the underside of his chin. "That's the year the government opened this area up for homestead."

Carrie's stomach tightened. *Oh, Lord! He's going to go on.* She prayed, *Please, make him stop.* "Is that a fact?" she said, with a very placid semi-smile.

"It sure is," he announced. "That's the year me and Ruth come up here to stake out *our* place. We got *our* first lumber at the railroad auction, too." He looked down the hill at his multi-story farmhouse. "'Course, we've built on a lot since then, but, when we started, our place looked a whole lot like this. 'Bout the same size, too." This time he added a nod to his smile. "But it's a fact now that this old house's been by its lonesome for quite a spell. I think there must have been three or four squatters camped here at different times in the last eight years."

Surprised at the old man's acceptance of the break-ins, Carrie said, "Why didn't anyone come up here and throw them out or at least call the police?"

Ben remained nonchalant. "Oh, tweren't really anybody's business, and the folks that stayed here were mostly those who'd just fallen on hard times."

Carrie's voice took on a little bit of an edge. "Well, what about the broken windows and the door? Why did these squatters do that?"

Ben sighed. "Most of that was done by the wind... or kids doin' mischief. That happens to old abandoned houses, you understand."

"Well I didn't, but I'm beginning to."

Jack came up at that moment and put his arm around Carrie. She couldn't conjure up much in the way of charity for the way things were turning out, so she kept her shoulders stiff and tense to his touch. Dissatisfaction was a message she did not want him to miss. Apparently, he didn't.

"What's the matter, hon?" Jack knelt down on one knee bedside her.

"There's mice in the house! I saw one!" She shivered.

"Oh," he answered in a knowing tone.

"Was it a little one, or something a bit larger with a long tail like an electric cord?" Ben held his hands apart to indicate the length of the hypothetical tail.

"What?" Carrie said, a little confused, but thinking, *Who cares? It's a mouse!*

"Well," Ben went on, "if it's the long tailed critter, it's a kangaroo rat. If you scare 'em, like if ya clap your hands at 'em, sometimes you can make 'em jump almost a foot in the air."

"Is that so." Carrie turned to her husband and gave him an I'm-not-in-the-mood-for-this-conversation look.

Jack nodded in response then addressed his new friend. "Say, Ben. Why don't you take a look at the inside of the house with me?" He put his hand on the old man's shoulder. "Maybe you can give me your guess at how much it'll cost me to fix it up."

"Sure," Ben straightened up and stretched. "Be glad to."

The two men walked off toward the dangling door. Jack looked back, and Carrie rolled her eyes at him. She'd had enough homespun local color for a while, and she wanted Jack to know it. Further, she did not feel sociable at the moment, and she wanted him to know that, too.

The door fell off the remaining hinge when Jack tried to swing it aside, and a small cottontail rabbit shot out from the shadows within the house. The creature skittered between Jack's legs and off down the hill. The man jumped back out of instinct, then laughed. He did not look back toward his wife, though, but merely leaned the damaged door against the wall and disappeared into the darkness of the house's mud-hall. Ben followed close behind.

What have I gotten myself into this time? Carrie looked around at the general dilapidation of the place, and, for the first time since leaving Marner Bay, she began to doubt that God had truly led her and Jack to this place. And she began to wonder if it wasn't just another example of her rich girl impulsiveness, another time when she'd talked others, as well as herself, into committing precious time, money, and emotions to something that might be nothing more than a momentary fancy on her part. *Would God lead anyone He loved to a trashy little place like this, let alone call it a blessing?*

More of the strange buzzing she'd heard earlier began coming from within the front hall, only louder than before. There was something familiar about it now, but she couldn't quite bring it to mind.

"Whoa!" came Jack's voice from within the shack. "Look at the *size* of that thing!"

Now, Carrie remembered where she'd heard the buzzing.

"Seth!" Ben called out. "Bring my twelve gauge and a fist full of shells from under the wagon seat!"

All of a sudden, Carrie's memory kicked into high gear, and she recognized the noise as the same one she'd heard when the rattler had cornered Jack under the trailer. *Oh, God.* She began to breath faster again. *The house is full of snakes, too!*

Seth raced past her and into the house without a word or a look. Carrie heard Ben again. "Thank you, boy." Then, after a moment's pause and the telltale click of the gun's double-barrel breach being locked into firing position, the inevitable boom of the weapon's discharge brought a final slap of reality to the situation. It also brought Carrie up off the packing barrel on which she'd been seated.

"Copper!" Seth called his dog to action.

Oh, no, thought Carrie. *Not again!* She remembered the big, red dog tearing at the rattler on the road, and her stomach rebelled. She hoped she had guessed wrong as to why Seth had called him into the house, but she had not.

Within a second, Copper bounded back out the doorway and into the brush downhill, a headless, twitching snake in his mouth. At just that moment, the sun completed its work for the day and submerged itself behind the black silhouettes of the surrounding hills, spreading the charcoal shadows of twilight into every crease and crevice of the canyon. Seth ran out next, hurrying to his grandfather's wagon. He procured a large empty coffee can and a kerosene railroad lantern, then returned into the house, both items in hand.

Carrie sighed, thankful that, at least, the boy hadn't displayed the snake's head on the end of his knife as before.

"Keep the boys out of here!" Jack yelled, unseen from within. "I hear another snake somewhere. We're going to look for it in the living room."

As if by signal, Kenny and Eddie came scrambling past Carrie and headed toward the doorway, giggling and talking about the gruesome demise of the second snake.

"Kenny! Eddie! Stop right where you are!" Carrie had hollered her emergency-toned command before she'd even realized she'd spoken. The boys froze out of habit and their mother elaborated on her order. "Just where do you two think you're going?"

Kenny turned around in a rush of excitement. His brother aped his movement. "Mom, their gonna look for more snakes! We might miss it!"

Well, this is the bow atop the basket of my day, she thought, but said, "Oh my! Wouldn't that be terrible to miss seeing them butchering another slimy snake?"

Kenny's eyebrows went up. "Well, yeah!" The boy held an open-mouthed stare of apparent disbelief, most likely induced by his mother's inability to grasp the gravity of the calls to adventure that were at that very moment

178

issuing from within *the temple (shack) of the apprentice heroes' trial.*

"Yeah!" Eddie repeated. "Slimy snake!"

"You've seen snakes before at Grandpa Floyd's ranch." Carrie tried to bring her tone down from the rafters and couldn't believe she was debating the value of snake watching.

Kenny shook his head. "But that was just little old garter snakes. These are rattlers!" He said the word like reciting the name of a storybook hero.

At that point, Carrie had had enough. "I'm not concerned with that. You're both going to stay out of that house until I say otherwise. Do you understand me?'

Kenny glanced at the ground and shuffled his feet. "Yes, ma'am."

But then she offered a consolation prize. "Now, if you both want to stay close by and listen, you can sit on this box." She patted the crate that sat next to her barrel. "And wait for your father *here* with *me*." She paused. "If not, you can go out by the truck and play there. Which will it be?" She folded her arms and raised her eyebrows. The boys filed, solemn-faced, to the designated box and hopped up onto its weathered pine surface—Eddie with a little help from his brother. Carrie nodded her satisfaction. "Very good. Now see you stay there."

Jack's voice came from within the house again. "Hey, the living room floor's all torn up, and the Franklin stove's full of ash. Looks like someone used the floor for firewood. There's a big, and I mean a big hole right in the middle of it. You can hop right down into the basement."

Carrie couldn't resist needling Ben just a little. "So much for those harmless squatters, Ben."

"Oh." His answer came slow but confident. "They probably just got caught in the snow for a while."

"It *snows* up here?" Carrie was not happy with this announcement.

"Just a few days a year." Ben hollered out. "Nothing to worry abou—*Look out* there, Jack! That critter's a crawlin' up from the cellar! Seth, bring that lantern closer in here."

"Found another one! No, another two!" Jack's tone was still a little strained. "Second one just fell down from the attic trapdoor."

"Oh, boy!" Kenny bounced on the box.

"Slimy snake!" Eddie clapped his hands.

Oh, God, Carrie prayed. *More snakes. Lord, this can't be where you want me!*

Ben's shotgun boomed twice, and Carrie jumped both times. She wanted to scream or at least cry, but she wouldn't do either in front of her sons, so she settled for holding her breath for a few seconds. She looked over at the boys. Their squeals of delight matched the rhythmic clomping of their heels against the box on which their mother had imprisoned them.

"Copper! Here, boy!" Seth sounded as amused as Kenny and Eddie.

Oh, Lord! Please, no! Carrie saw the dog gallop, tongue flailing, into the house. Knowing what was to come, she turned around on the barrel until she faced away from the shack. She did not want to see it again. A few seconds passed. She heard the dog's muffled pants and his paws breaking through the brush. Then an acrid odor assailed Carrie's nostrils. She wasn't sure, but thought she recognized the smell – snake blood. The thought assaulted her imagination, and immediately the picture of the big Irish Setter tearing at a still squirming, decapitated reptile came rushing out of her memory and into her mind's eye. She fought the image, but it would not go away. The next thing she fought was the urge to retch.

"Sure are a lot of scorpions and black widows in there." Carrie shuddered at Seth's words. Then she turned around to face the men emerging out into the diminished light of the yard. The boy set the now lighted lantern on the crate behind Eddie.

"More good news, eh?" she steamed, tension fairly leaking from her sentence.

The look on Jack's face told Carrie he could see that she was getting close to her limit on the subject of poisonous houseguests. "Don't worry, hon," he said. "We'll get them cleaned out."

"We sure will." Ben broke open the breach of his shotgun, pulled out the spent shells, and put them in the bib pocket of his overalls. "I got a spray down in the barn'd stop an elephant at full charge. It'll take care of your creepin' critters for ya." He smiled at Carrie and blew the last remnant of smoke out through the gun's twin barrels. Then he looked at Jack. "By the way, you got yourself a shotgun?"

"Yes." Jack seemed self-conscious. "But it's still packed."

Ben shook his head. "Well, you better dig her out as soon as you can. Gonna come in handy. You're liable to find another snake or two."

Jack nodded. "I'll do that."

Ben rested the gun in the crook of his arm and slapped Seth on the shoulder. "Well, me and Seth are gonna go down to my place and mix up a batch of wiz-bang bug juice so's we can serve them spiders and scorpions a little supper." He backslapped Seth again. "Sound good to you, boy?"

"Yes, sir."

"Then let's get to it." Ben started off toward the wagon, his arm around his grandson. As he passed Carrie, he tugged on the brim of his hat as a form of good-bye. "Carrie."

Seth also gave her a quick nod. "Ma'am."

Carrie waited until they had turned the team around and the wagon had gone beyond earshot before she unload on Jack. "Don't even think that the boys and I are going to spend tonight in that vermin infested pile of boards." She kept her voice low enough not to be heard more than a foot or two away.

"Aw, Mom!" Kenny hopped down from the box, Eddie close behind as usual.

Carrie turned a withering scowl upon them. "Go play out by the truck, both of you."

"But we want to look for the slimy snakes." Eddie wiped his nose with a dirty finger.

Carrie rose from her barrel. "Right now, march."

The boys retreated, hands in pockets, and shuffled to the far side of the yard where they spotted some small creature crawling across the decomposed granite. At that point, their mother's bark already forgotten, they began to follow after the new prey. By now, twilight had all but fled before the advance of actual semi-darkness, but that dampened not the young men's enthusiasm for the pursuit.

"I'm going to get it all cleaned out, Carrie." Jack words hung ripe with apology.

But fear and revulsion had already driven clemency from Carrie's thinking.

"You'd better," she said, "because I'm not going in there until you do."

Jack stroked his chin. "Well, I was hoping to quick-patch the floor and use the Franklin stove tonight."

"We're not setting foot in there until you clear all the wildlife from that house! And I most wholeheartedly mean that, Jack!"

Jack sighed. "Then, I guess we'd better make camp."

"Make camp?" Carrie had thought more of staying at a hotel and perhaps coming up to work on the place during the day, at least until the house was livable. *Now* what was Jack talking about? "Make *camp*?"

"Yes. You've camped before, haven't you?"

182

"Actually, no." Carrie didn't like this idea at all. "I've been on picnics, but not where you *cook* and *sleep outside*. Jack, I thought we could just stay at the hotel in town. What did they call it? The Hunter's Inn."

Jack shook his head. "We can't afford that, Carrie. We're going to have to camp here."

Carrie felt a tide of panic rise within her. She didn't take well to these words, *can't afford,* and where did he think she'd learned camping? At her coming out party or the yacht club regatta? What was he thinking? "Jack." She softened her tone a little but could not hide the breathy nervousness. "I don't know how to make a camp. I don't know the first thing about it."

"I do," came a mature, friendly, feminine voice from within the now almost coal-mine-dark shadow of the pine tree behind Carrie. The lightlessness of official nighttime had finally prevailed, and the voice had made her jump. It had even startled Jack a little. But soon the voice became a woman who fully materialized as she stepped from the dark out into the lantern light. "Sorry. Didn't mean to scare ya." She looked to be in her late middle years, slightly plump and wearing a plain house-dress with high-top shoes. Her nickel colored hair had been pulled back into a single braid far behind metal-rimmed glasses, all of which gave the impression of age despite her relatively smooth, youthful looking skin. "I'm Ruth Smith, Ben's wife." She paused. "I could show you how to set up a proper camp. Wouldn't take any time at all. Been doin' it most of my life. But I won't."

She paused again and smiled. "Because you're not going to need a camp. You folks are going to stay with us 'til the house here is fit for women and children." Jack looked like he was going to protest, but Ruth shushed him. "Now it's all arranged. Ben's the one that talked to Hannah and Floyd before about this property, but he'd forgot how bad the place really was. So I called Hannah back and told her we'd put you up. Got lots of room. Big old house."

The woman thrust out her hand. "You're Carrie; I know." Carrie shook it. "Would have been up sooner, but I had a sick mare that needed me more than you for a little while."

Carrie could hardly believe what she was hearing. She saw Ruth as an angel who'd come to rescue her from a hideous fate. She wanted to throw her arms around the woman and kiss her on the cheek, but all she ended up doing was shaking her hand a little too long and saying in her most polite Van Burean manner, "I'm so very glad to meet you, Ruth. You have no idea how appreciative I am. Thank you."

Ruth turned to Jack. "I know your name, too. Your grandma and I have been friends for years." She put her arm around Carrie and began to lead her toward the main road while talking over her shoulder to Jack. "Mr. MacGregor, why don't you crank up your truck and bring the boys and yourself down for supper? I talked Ben into not sprayin' your house for critters 'til tomorrow, so there's nothing more for you here 'til then. Just bring down what you'll need for tonight and that'll do it. Me and your wife are going to take a little walk."

Jack muttered "okay" and something about taking the lantern, but Ruth just kept moving and pointed up at the half lunar disc that had just appeared atop the big grass-clad hill that loomed to the east behind the homestead. "Moonlight's all we need.

Once the two women reached the main dirt track and were out of earshot, Ruth turned to Carrie and said, "It's a lot scarier up here than you thought it would be, isn't it."

"Very!" was Carrie's only reply. She'd barely been able to maintain control of her emotions since she'd arrived at this so-called *new home*, and the only reason she'd been able to demonstrate any semblance of sanity at all since

184

then was because her husband and sons were present. She didn't want to break down in front of them like a blubbering schoolgirl. But now, walking down the dimly-lit dirt road, she felt her resolve to keep her outer armor in place begin to erode. That frightened her, too. What would happen if she couldn't hold herself together? That constituted unknown territory and elicited even *more* fear.

"Yep," Ruth eyed Carrie for a moment, then sighed. "T'was scary for me as well."

"You mean you were frightened when you moved up here?" Carrie's voice quivered a little, and that made her angry at the weakness she thought it betrayed. So she cleared her throat with a little too much vigor.

Ruth appeared to stifle a smile in the growing lunar glow. "No." Her voice sounded relaxed and, at least at the moment, had an almost soothing quality to it. "Down in New Mexico, a long time ago." She patted Carrie gently on the back, then clasped her hands in front of her. "I was younger than you. Ben and me was starting a little horse ranch right after we got married."

Carrie blew on the coals of her anger again and revived a little flame. "But did you have to move into a dilapidated old shack like this one?"

Ruth smiled again. "No, we didn't."

"I thought not." Carrie began to put a little of her armor back in place.

"No." Ruth scanned the surrounding wild grass plateau. "There wasn't any house at all. Just a hundred and sixty acres of scrub-land and a year-round creek running down from the San Juan Mountains." She slowed her pace a little and looked over at Carrie. "In other words, we had to *camp* for a while."

"Oh." Carrie lost a few ounces of false pride as humility washed it off. "But, at least you knew how to do that."

"I was just a town girl. Ben was the wrangler. My pa had owned a livery stable over in Las Crucas, so I knew a little about horses. But I'd never slept a night out of my own bed, let alone in the back of a wagon like we did. No, I had to learn everything new about camp livin' till our first shack was done." Ruth stopped and turned to face Carrie. "I praise the Lord that he gave me Hannah as a neighbor and friend. She taught me much of what I needed to know. Ben took and showed me the rest."

Carrie had not heard this bit of history from Hannah. "She was your neighbor in New Mexico?"

"Neighbor, friend, and life saver." Ruth started to walk again. "I don't think I'd have made it that first year without her." She shook her head. "Seems like I was ready to pack up and run back to Las Crucas about once a month. Hannah was the one to help me see that things weren't really as bad as I thought they were. Then she'd show me what to do to fix whatever I thought was wrong."

Carrie understood Ruth was trying to make her feel better, trying to tell her there was nothing to be afraid of. It *was* having, however, a very different effect. With each word Ruth spoke about the rough start of her early life, Carrie only felt less up to the challenges that lay ahead. After all, women like Hannah and Ruth were probably brought up better able to handle the rigors of life in the rough. Wouldn't someone like Carrie be better off to simply admit a mistake had been made in taking on this ranch venture in the first place? She caught Ruth by the sleeve of her dress. "Ruth?" Her voice fairly trembled now. "I hope you don't mind me calling you by your first name."

"I'd be put off if ya didn't."

"All right." Carrie stopped and took a breath to steady herself. "Ruth, I don't think I can do this. I think I was a fool to believe I could." She began to sob a little as she spoke. "This was my idea in part, you know, starting a ranch. I can't blame it all on poor Jack. No, I can't do that."

She took a few breaths. "But I just didn't know how hard it would be. There were no snakes or falling down shacks in the picture I had."

Suddenly, an animal sprinted across the road just a few feet in front of the two women. It slowed for an instant to look at them, its eyes glowing in the reflected light of the moon.

Carrie froze in mid-step and said in a voice that sounded near panic, "What's that?"

"A coyote," Ruth gently patted the younger woman on the shoulder. "They mostly won't bother ya, if you mind your own business an' let 'em pass."

That was the final blow to Carrie's armor, the last test to her resolve to stay in control. As the little coyote disappeared into a clump of desert sage, she fell to her knees in tears, only speaking between short gasps for breath. "I can't ...do this! I'm... not like...you and Han...nah! I don't know ... what I need...to, and...I'm...scared of everything here!" She fumbled in her dress pocket and pulled out a small hanky, which she applied immediately to her face. Half straightening, she looked directly into Ruth's eyes. "This is not going to work! I'm going home!"

Ruth sounded sympathetic. "Where is that?"

Carrie continued to sob, but finished the act of straightening her posture. "I'm not sure anymore!" She sniffed. "But I know it's not here!"

Ruth put her arms around Carrie and spoke in sympathetic tones while stroking the young woman's hair. "Well, some might say you're right. I don't see it that way, though."

"I'm not strong enough," Carrie said, her words muffled by Ruth's shoulder.

"All right." Ruth pulled away a little so she could see Carrie's face. "I won't try to tell you what I think right now because I know it'll just sound like a lot of talk what with the way you're feeling."

The older woman closed her eyes and let a moment pass before opening them again. "Give God a chance to help you. He brought you here, and He says He'll never leave or forsake us. So just ask Him before you go to sleep tonight what the truth of things are and what He wants of you. I wouldn't be surprised if you didn't get your answer before breakfast. Can you do that, Carrie? Put your troubles in the Lord's hands?"

"But what if all these things – all the snakes and the scorpions and the breakdown – what if they're really God, trying to warn me that I've made a mistake?" Carrie mopped her eyes and dabbed at her nose.

"Then He'll tell you that...straight out." Ruth punctuated her statement with a nod.

Carrie shook her head. *Well, God,* she prayed, *why don't you tell me now? What should I do? Stay or go?*

Carrie gently pulled away from Ruth and waited for a silent second. But nothing came to her except the rustle of the foxtails in the night breeze and the crunch of decomposed granite as she shifted her weight.

She tried again. *Did I make the right decision in going back to Jack?*

Still there was nothing but her own breathing and a lonesome heartbeat. *Are you there?* No response—save the mental echo of her last plea. Carrie sighed.

"Ruth," she said. "I really don't know what to believe right now. I was so sure God wanted me up here, and look what has happened. I don't know if I can really hear Him or not. I think perhaps I simply wanted to believe He was guiding me."

Ruth nodded again, more to the sky than to the young woman beside her. "Well, why don't you come down to the house and have some supper. You and your family can get some sleep. Food and rest, that's what you need. Then you can see how things look in the morning.

She led Carrie down a small drive that dropped away from the road and wound lazily toward the warm lights of the nearby house. "Yonder's Smith Castle." Ruth glanced back. "We're having beef stew tonight with peach pie. Good prayer and decision food."

Carrie didn't respond but merely shuffled down the little side road, her shoulders slumped with the weight of the many hopes now lost. She could see the Smiths' farm more plainly as it grew near. The house, a standard two and a half story red frame affair, had white trim, common to farms from Maine to California. The barn and sheds were also classics of the same style.

Probably got a good price on the paint, Carrie mused. Then her problems reached out and grabbed her again. *What am I supposed to do now,* she prayed as the night seemed to settle in her heart. Again, only silence, while a feeling of total loneliness wrapped itself around her.

Finally she said, "Dinner and bed sound fine, Ruth, but I think I've *already* made my decision."

Ruth did not reply. She just walked quietly a little ahead of Carrie and guided her the rest of the way down the road to the farmhouse.

189

Chapter Thirteen

A plump, four-year-old foot swung in an unintended kick, and a toddler-wise father pulled his face back in time to avoid the blow.

"So, you had two kids," Jack said while he stuffed Eddie under the covers of the child-size bed. The small bedroom in the Smith's farmhouse had the too neat look of scant use.

"Yep." Ben ran his hand over what was left of his hair. "My boy, Sam. He lives in that house across the road." He pointed through the wall toward the east as if he could see straight through its lath and wallpaper surface. "Just down the road from your place, don't ya know. And we had Janie. She was a couple of years younger than Sam. We lost her along with her husband and two girls to the influenza about three years ago." Ben sniffed once and scrunched up his cheeks. "Took 'em all in less than a month. Along with a lot of other good folks down around Los Angeles." He paused and took on the look of a man who had let his mind drift somewhere else for a second. Then his focus seemed to return to the little room. "I made these here beds for any of the grandchildren that might show up for a visit. But Sam's kids are the only ones the Lord let us keep. They come over and sleep here every once in a while."

Jack turned down the kerosene lamp on the nightstand that stood between his two sons, then he tried to redirect the subject a little.

"Thanks for helping me get those trunks into the bedroom. Saved me a lot of work."

"Don't mention it." Ben seemed to perk up a little. "Lots easier with two doin' the carrying." He fell silent again and seemed to lose his purchase on the present.

Jack cleared his throat and spoke words he hoped would call the old man back from the land of sad memories. "I got to tell you, Ben, that was the best beef stew and peach pie we've had in ages. Wasn't it boys?" He spread his arms between the beds and patted both his sons.

Kenny responded with, "Yes, sir."

Eddie said, "Peach pie!" and rubbed his stomach while licking his lips.

"Well, that's fine, gents. That really is." Ben smiled and nodded. "I'll tell Ruth; she'll be glad you liked it." He slid his ancient Ball watch out of a top overall pocket and took a peek at its face. "Looks like I better let you all get settled, or we'll be talking all night." He gave the three an abbreviated nod as he turned and left the room. "Night."

Jack took a moment to consider how it would feel to lose one of his boys, even in adulthood. Just the suggestion hurt far worse than he had imagined, so he shut the scenario off and hoped he would not live long enough to actually experience it for real. With all this in mind, he spoke to his boys in a tone softer than was his habit. "Time to go to sleep, you two."

"We're not sleepy, Dad," Kenny pleaded while he rubbed his elbow. "Really!"

Jack looked at his watch. "It's almost nine o'clock. I think you've had too much rattlers and peach pie for today."

"Slimy snakes 'n' peach pie," Eddie grinned.

"Rattlesnake pie! Ew!" Kenny drew his finger like a knife across his throat and made a gurgling sound. They both broke into belly laughs.

Jack held up his hands to signal quiet. "All right, all right. Settle down." He thought a moment on what might subdue the two wound-up youngsters. Then it came to him. "How would you like to hear a brand new story?"

"You mean you wrote another one?" Kenny catapulted himself up onto his knees.

"Yes." Jack held up his arms in surrender. "While I was out barnstorming, I'd write a little each night before I went to sleep."

"Yea!" Eddie slipped from his covers and bounced shamelessly on his bed

Jack nodded. "All right. Stay in bed; I'll be right back."

He left and strode down a creaking floor to one of the other bedrooms where his trunk sat. The sound of his sons' whispered excitement seeped down the hallway as he opened the big steamer chest and lifted out the top tray. There, in a short stack underneath some books, lay the small personal treasure trove of the science fiction and fantasy stories he'd been writing and submitting to several magazines over the last few years. Jack lifted the top three bundles and thumbed through the fourth. That was the one he wanted, so he pulled it out and left the rest.

Jack often doubted his chances of literary success in the world of professional writers. He'd even doubted his talent at times, but his stories and novel chapters were never thrown away, no matter how much he moved around the country. Maybe he really did believe in himself somewhere deep down inside.

The new ink of the title page revealed itself feebly in the dim bedroom light. *The Travels of Bartholomew Blake* it silently announced, by Jack MacGregor, who'd written it in a new-mown Kansas alfalfa field by virtue of a flashlight tied by string to a fly wire that traversed his Jennie's two left wings. He wasn't sure if he'd seriously intended to submit this one for publication, but he had always imagined himself reading it to the boys. *If no one else ever reads it, this'll make the writing worthwhile.*

He replaced the tray and closed the trunk, then headed down the hall toward the room where the boys waited. That's when he heard the women's voices coming muffled through the kitchen door, and that's when, for no particular reason, he stopped for a moment and listened.

"All I'm saying is pray on it and wait 'til morning before you do anything." The words belonged to Ruth. "I believe He'll show you His plan for you by then."

Next came Carrie's voice. "I will; I promise." He heard her sigh. "I just don't think it's going to do any good. I feel so foolish now. I talked poor Jack into all this."

The next exchange was garbled by the sound of clanging pots and rattling kitchen utensils. At this point, Jack realized he'd been eavesdropping, so he purposed himself to move on and complete his trip to the boys' borrowed bedroom. He entered holding up the brown paper and string package. "Okay. Get ready if you want to hear it."

Both young MacGregors instantly slid back under the covers. Each propped his head in his hand and turned sideways, facing the stool in the center space where their father would sit. Eddie gave his bedclothes a final pat to signal all was ready.

Jack smiled. "All right, then." He hovered down onto the little milking stool and unwrapped the manuscript. Staring at the handwritten work a while, he promised himself he would copy the scrawl with his typewriter as soon as possible. Then, after one last glance at the two eager faces, Jack focused on the page in his hands and began to read.

"The American flyer, Captain Bartholomew Blake, lay in the twisted wreckage of his French-built fighter, on the Western Front in the Summer of 1918. He stayed motionless for several minutes after the crash before he fully accepted the fact that he'd just been shot from the sky. One quick glance at his mangled body told him he had suffered many grievous injuries, however he felt no pain as yet. As a matter of fact he felt nothing at all below the waist. His hearing remained undamaged though, and he knew this because he could plainly discern the sound of German oaths and the crack of Mauser rifles firing from a nearby enemy trench."

Jack paused and looked up to see if he still had their attention and was met by the unbroken gaze of four little mesmerized eyes. The elder MacGregor's smile grew. He'd missed this—leading his sons on short, exotic bedtime adventures. To say it felt good would be a gross understatement. It had always proven itself an elixir for both him and the boys, invigorating the sense of what could be, while restoring that which the viruses of missed opportunity had damaged. Jack would savor every second of this tonight.

He continued. "It was at that point that Blake decided his life would probably end quite soon, so he began to pray that God would take him clean and quick…before any expected suffering set in. And he intended to add more to this last prayer—something about watching over his mother and young sisters at home in California—but his efforts in that direction were cut short by sudden flash of a bright, violet light that almost blinded him. Next he felt the pressure of what seemed like some sort of formless force that gripped his broken body like an invisible giant pillow that had wrapped itself around him." Jack shifted on the little stool and momentarily wondered if Ben had put it here years ago for the same purpose—reading stories to a captive audience. The memory of the old man's dead daughter and grandchildren nibbled at the room's happy atmosphere. Jack took a short breath then pushed on through that small cloud of gloom with his story.

"It made the injured pilot tingle all over," Jack read, "like a sleeping limb when it's awakened. Then all sight and sound vanished. Gone was his damaged plane and the muddy shell-holes of no-man's land. Instead, he found himself suspended in a vast, black nothingness, with no sensation of temperature or movement—not even a heartbeat—to verify that he still lived at all. His next conscious experience was that of being cold and having his face slapped hard. This was Blake's first recollection of his arrival on the planet Garon, and it was one he would remember for the rest of his life."

Jack stopped reading to survey his audience. "Well, I don't suppose you want to hear any more of this old tale, do you?" The boys groaned their unison protest, so their father replied with a nod. "Okay. If you're sure you want to hear the rest." They were. So he smiled and said, "All right," then continued the story.

He revealed how the slap had awakened Bart Blake to full consciousness at which point he realized his body was now uninjured, and, somehow, no longer on the battlefield. However, the captain soon learned from the guard who had slapped him that he was now on another world, a prisoner in the dungeon of an evil scientist-warlord, Lord Zerach (as Jack had named him). Zerach, it turned out, was bent on kidnapping and retraining enough warriors from Earth to form an army with which he would conquer the entirety of planet Garon. He was abducting these soldiers and transporting them to his interplanetary ship by means of a high-powered manipulation ray of his own invention, and would refuse to restore the shanghaied veterans to their home planet until the war of conquest had been won.

Jack's pattern was to read for a page or so then sneak a peek over the top of the bundle to see if his listeners had nodded off yet. If not, he would read on. At the point where Blake had sworn a false oath to Zerach in order to save his own life and after doing so accepted a commission as Commander to fly the villain's sky-ships, Jack stole another look. The boys were just starting into their first yawns. By the time Bart met Aarona, the warlord's servant girl, who was, unbeknownst to her master, also the daughter of a neighboring king, they were yawning again. And when she and the hero began to plan their escape,

Eddie had drifted off to Planet Garon on his own adventure, but Kenny stubbornly held one eye open and waited for his father's next words.

However, when the princess and Blake finally made their break for freedom in a hijacked sky-ship, Eddie's older brother's stubborn eye gave way to slumber. Now, with his cheek buried deep into his pillow, his imagination sailed a mile above the distant planet's surface and assisted the boy in spiriting a noble and beautiful princess of his own to safety. Jack stopped reading for a moment and waited for the soft snores that always signified the end of the night's adventure.

When that signal finally came, he gently rewrapped his story, went to the night-stand to blow out the lamp, and turned to go. It was not until then that he saw Carrie leaning against the doorjamb, smiling a soft, dreamy smile in his direction.

Out in the hall on the way to their bedroom, Jack asked her, "How much did you hear?"

Carrie remained silent while they entered the small room and closed the door behind them. Then she offered her answer while Jack lit a match and put the flame to the wick of another kerosene lamp on top of the chest of drawers next to their adult-size bed. "Oh, I came in where Princess Aarona told Bart that she would give him anything he wanted if he'd just take her back to her father's kingdom." On the last word, she giggled a little.

"That long, huh?" Jack unlaced his boots and pulled them off. He shrugged out of his suspenders and shucked his shirt. "So, what'd you think?" he stretched his well-muscled arms.

She took off her dress and pulled on a satin nightgown, that spoke of a much more affluent environment, from their old travel-worn trunk. "Well, it certainly isn't Dickens or Kipling, but it definitely got the boys off to sleep, so I

196

suppose you've got a future in the bedtime story market."
She put her stockings and shoes on a chair and got into bed.

"You still haven't told me what you think."

"Oh, I caught myself dozing off, too, at several points."

He stepped out of his jodhpurs and laid them on the trunk over his story. "Thanks a lot," he said and plowed under the covers.

"My pleasure." She yawned and turned over, facing away from him.

He pounded his pillow once, then turned away the same as she had done. He'd been hoping for something a little closer to praise. As it was, he wasn't sure whether she was just teasing or actually showing a little mild contempt for his work. Jack decided to take a chance and show his wife a little affection anyway. He reached over and patted her shoulder. "Goodnight, Carrie."

He heard her sigh. Then, "Goodnight, my brave sky-ship commander." She giggled again and whispered low, "Thank you, Lord."

Jack wasn't sure he'd heard her right. "What?" He half raised up.

"Nothing." She paused. "I just said goodnight."

Chapter Fourteen

Jack, Ben, and Seth bludgeoned nails into the last of the chicken coops uphill from the house. It had been a week since the MacGregors' had arrival at the Saber Canyon homestead. And now, Carrie stood at her kitchen sink peeling potatoes for salad and watching the struggle of man over roofing through the open window. The days had seemed long, and more repairs had been done since they had arrived than Carrie thought possible. Not the least of which involved the restoration of the windmill and the resurrection of its pump. And when this too had been accomplished, precious water had at last begun to flow into the hilltop storage tank and from there down to the house itself. Two weeks ago, she would never have thought that simple functioning indoor plumbing could mean so much. But when she first saw a stream of clear, fresh water emerge from her very own kitchen faucet, after having been pumped from their own well, she found herself unable to keep a gratitude-driven tear from sneaking down her cheek. Water meant that things were starting to work the way they should. It meant they could cook and keep things clean—themselves included. It made her think of blood, the way it keeps animals alive. So now they had water—to bring their ranch to life.

Ben had praised their unusually high water pressure once everything was working. He said it was a result of the storage tank being so much higher than the house. He and Ruth had a gentler slope to their property and were forced to resort to a tank hoisted atop a wooden tower to get even half that much flow.

At first, Carrie didn't fully understand what the old man was talking about, and her interest remained minimal at best. But as the days passed, and she found herself able to do more cooking and cleaning, she began to understand and appreciate the blessing of their own high-pressure, running water. Carrie had helped with dishes and other kitchen chores down at Ruth's house and remembered how it took forever to fill the sink or a bucket. She thanked God for giving her a better water situation than Ruth – one less thing to worry about.

The MacGregor ranch boasted a re-born house now with electric power on, windows replaced and a new front door that hung with pride from *both* its brand new hinges. Since the floor had been patched, one could even walk from one end of the living room to the other without falling into the basement. Carrie had long since forgiven Ben for his habitual long-windedness. He'd proven to be as much a life-saving good neighbor as Ruth. Spending most of the last seven days either showing Jack the best way to do things or just doing them himself, the old farmer always refused any form of payment.

So now, as she stood in her own kitchen, a week after arrival, Carrie exercised her homeowner's privilege and simply remained still—something that had not happened much over the last few days—reveling in the fragrance of desert sage, the canyon's natural incense, carried on the breeze through the open window. It grew almost everywhere within fifty miles, and she had come to like the unfamiliar scent much as she had come to do the same with Ben, who at times seemed like he had been plucked from the last century. She watched as the elderly farmer nailed a shingle onto the roof of the last chicken coop and she decided he was much more of a dear brother in Christ than a pest. She reminded herself that, without him, the MacGrergor family would probably not still be here. *Thank you, Lord,* she prayed. *He's an unexpected gift. And thank you for Ruth.*

As if by signal, there was a knock at the door accompanied by Ruth's now familiar feminine baritone. "Ham sandwiches are here." She sang with exaggerated vibrato as she let herself in the front door. "And lemonade."

Rounding two corners between the mud-hall and the living room, she navigated her way into the kitchen with a towel covered serving plate in one arm and a huge crock in the other, dressed exactly like Carrie—bib-overalls and ruffled kitchen apron.

"Oh, thank you, Ruth!" Carrie still found it hard to get used to the woman's unselfish kindness. "Let me help you get all that onto the table." She put down the spud and peeler and wiped starchy hands on her apron.

Ruth expertly landed her load and waved her young neighbor off. "You just keep on peeling. I'll join you." She bustled over to the utensil drawer, rummaged out another peeler, and after closing the drawer with an ample hip, snatched an unsuspecting Idaho from the water-filled pail in the sink. "This for tonight's potato salad?" She finished stripping half her spud naked with a lightning hand and turned the thing over to assault the skin on the remaining side.

"Yes." Carrie fished out another potato and began skinning the tuber. "Thanks to dear Mrs. Van Meter for leaving her ice-box , not to mention all her other furnishings." Carrie elbowed her peeling partner. "And thanks to you for giving me a whole block of ice. Now the potato salad will still be fresh for supper." She gave Ruth a good natured hip-bump.

Ruth feigned a scowl. "Ben bought too much ice. What was I to do, let it melt?" She finished off her potato-victim and threw it into a wooden bowl on the sink board.

Carrie peeled the last one and began to dice the flayed tubers, throwing the chopped pieces into a large pot of boiling water atop her big cast-iron, wood-burning cook stove. Then she released a sideward glance toward her friend. "Odd, how the Van Meters spent all that money to bring in electric power and construct a fairly large cold room for chicken and eggs but still depended upon an old ice box for their kitchen." She wiped her forehead with the back of her wrist. "Why didn't they just go ahead and by an electric refrigerator, as well?"

Ruth added a handful of potato cubes to the boiling pot. "Old Pete Van Meter was a very thrifty fellow—never spent a dime he couldn't justify to his budget. And Greta was the same. To the both of them, a new refrigerator had nothing to do with the business of a chicken ranch, so, to their way of thinking, that made it a luxury…the next best thing to a sin. To hear old Pete or even Greta tell it, a body could almost go to hell for spending money on anything you didn't need." Ruth sighed. "They were married for sixty years."

Carrie's forehead furrowed. "Really? Sixty years?"

Ruth nodded. "Yep. And I think that ice box was a wedding present."

Both women shook their heads and laughed before assaulting the next two spuds.

After a while, Carrie leaned back and craned her neck to peer out the window again. The men had finished their roof job and were climbing down the ladder, tools in hand.

"They're coming in; I'd better get this done," Carrie sighed, then grabbed three skinless spuds at once and chopped them at triple speed. She tossed the aftermath into the stove pot and shanghaied three more for the same fate, which was over in less than ten seconds.

Ruth watched the blurred knife movement with awe and dread. "You'd better be careful, gal. You're going to end up with potato and finger salad."

Carrie finished off another Idaho trio, grabbed some more, and tore into them like a mill saw. "Our chef taught me to do this when I was a little girl." She winked as she chopped up the last of the batch. "You ought to see me with carrots. Now that's where you got to be sure what's a finger and what isn't." She laughed.

Ruth looked confused. "Your chef?"

Carrie flinched inwardly at having unintentionally made reference to a past life of affluence. Feeling as though she'd been caught committing a crime, she cleared her throat and cleaned the peels from the sink. "My father's chef is what I meant to say." Her face flushed with a self-conscious wave. "Father has a little money." She slopped the peels into the potato bowl and headed for the garbage can. In the future such scraps would go to the chickens. But for now, with no live poultry on hand, the garbage pail would have to do, with local quail and squirrels being the ultimate recipients of the fare.

"He has quite a *bit* of money, from what Hannah said." Ruth pulled seven plates from the cupboard and, with the skill of a Monte Carlo croupier, dealt them onto the table. "I 'spect I just never thought of anybody that didn't own a restaurant having their very own chef." Then she flashed her friend a big friendly, very sympathetic smile. "But why not," she said. "If a body can afford it, why not?"

Just then, Kenny and Eddie stormed into the kitchen carrying with them the dirt and laughter of the morning, and breaking to pieces the intimate mood of just two seconds before. Carrie stepped between them and the table, stopping their assault upon lunch. "Have you washed your hands and faces?" She scanned the boys, both of whom looked like they'd plowed a field with their noses.

"No, ma'am," Kenny confessed with the forced *I did it* honesty of a cornered bank robber. Eddie put his hands behind his back and looked at the floor.

"Go on then. Use the faucet outside; there's a towel there. And tell the men to do the same."

"Aw, mom!" Kenny's expression was that of a man persecuted. Eddie was silent but rocked back and forth on his heals, his hands still hidden.

"You heard me! Go now!"

"Yes, ma'am." The boys shuffled outside as if being marched to a gallows.

"I wonder what they were having so much fun with." Carrie watched her sons through the window until they joined the older males at the faucet outside.

"Probably Copper, seeing as Seth's busy this morning." At that moment, the women heard the breathy bark of the big setter in the driveway. "Yeah." Ruth nodded. "Copper."

Carrie poked a potato chunk with a fork and stared it down with a practiced eye. Not quite soft enough yet. She watched, shaking her head as the boys pet Copper and waited for their turn at the water. "Boys and dogs. Like iron filings to a magnet." Carrie turned back to the pot and waited to stab another innocent potato cube. A few seconds passed, and the tubers were tested again without success. Then she looked up and saw a smiling Ruth watching. "What is it?" Carrie rubbed the tip of an itchy nose on the back of her wrist.

Ruth leaned sideways against the sink and put a hand on her hip. "I was just wondering what the Lord said to you that kept you from packin' up and skedadelin'."

Carrie glanced back out at the men engaging in minor faucet horseplay with the boys. "I can't say it right now. They'll be in here any second." She looked down at her apron and unnecessarily went through the motion of drying her hands.

Ruth just stood looking at Carrie for a moment, then went to the open kitchen window, and called to Ben outside. "Ya know, Ben, that last row of shingles is crooked."

Ben squinted at the nearest chicken coop. "No, they ain't."

"Yes, they are." Ruth kept a completely straight face through the lie. "You ought to see 'em from over here."

Ben surveyed the roof a second time then turned to Jack. "Them shingles look crooked to you?" Jack shook his head, so the old man turned back his wife. "Ruth, you need to rub the sand out your eyes. Them shingles are fine!"

Ruth persisted. "Well, all I know is they look crooked from here."

Ben scrutinized the coop again, then motioned for the others to follow him. "Come on. Let's measure the spacing on that son of a gun. That's the only way to tell for sure!" The other males in the herd fell into line with the leathered old bull and trudged back to the site of their last labor. Copper and the boys all hesitated for almost a second before trotting to catch up.

Ruth went back to the table and sat. "That ought to keep 'em busy for a while. Now, what were you going to say?"

Carrie covered her mouth and laughed so hard her eyes watered and her stomach ached. Several seconds passed before she could speak, and when she did, all she could squeak out was, "That was wonderful!" She laughed some more then caught her breath. "I simply *must* remember that for future reference!"

"Yeah, it's fun once you know your old f—…" Ruth stopped herself. "Uh, your mate, that is." She rolled her eyes. "Now, before I throw something at you, what did the Lord have to say to you?"

Carrie's smile softened and she turned to gaze at the distant mountain tops. "I went to the bedroom that first night before Jack came in, and I prayed…just like you suggested. I begged God to show me what I should do, or, at least, tell me what His will was." She shook her head. "But I didn't get a thing. Nothing." She turned around and walked to the table. "Then I heard Jack talking to the boys in the room down the hall, so I leaned in through the doorway and listened." She sat across from Ruth and looked into her face. "He was reading to them from a story he'd written while he was out traveling the country…flying. You know."

Ruth straightened up, her eyes wide. "He writes stories?"

Carrie nodded. "Oh, yes. And some are quite good. He's done it ever since college." She paused and glanced away. "I first began to fall in love with Jack listening to one of his chapters."

"What kind of stories are they?"

"There fantastic tales about brave people in future times or on other worlds." Carrie glanced down at her hands. "And ever since he's been saved, he's tried to put something from the Lord's word in each one. He calls them modern parables."

"So you were leaning in the doorway..." Ruth prodded.

"Yes, and there he was reading this beautiful story, and the boys loved it. They always do." She paused and glanced down. "That's when I realized..." She took a breath. "That's when I realized that, in his own way, he was sharing his love with our sons...the way only *he* could express it, and at that moment I felt," she hesitated then swallowed, "in my heart," Carrie put a fork filled hand over her heart and spoke haltingly, "that everything was as it should be. Jack was reading to the boys just as he should be. I was back with Jack...as I should be. And we were moving up here to this old wreck of a homestead...just as we should. All of it was happening the *way* it was happening because it was the Lord's will. He *made* it all happen. So I shouldn't be afraid." She shrugged. "That's all I know. So, I stayed, and things have been getting better ever since."

Ruth smiled big and shook her head. "I knew the Lord would talk to ya! I just didn't know he was going to say such a mouthful." She leaned over the table and hugged her new, young neighbor. "You just hang on to God, Carrie. You do that, and you'll be all right."

Carrie didn't say anything more for a while. She simply got up from the table, walked over to the cook-stove and stood there, enjoying the warm feeling that came with Ruth's words. *Well, I may be out of peoples' lives at Marner Bay,* she thought, *but my family-in-Christ up here seems to be growing all the time.*

Chapter Fifteen

After lunch, both men, with all three boys in tow, came out of the house just in time to see an old horse and its young rider clop to a halt in the driveway.

"It's Walt Davies," Seth chimed and walked out to the youngster that looked to be about his age. "Hey, Walt." He hollered and raised a hand in greeting. "What'cha doin' up this end of the canyon?" Jack and the rest watched as the boys talked for a few seconds. Then the visitor handed Ben's grandson a scrap of paper. Seth waved a quick farewell, as the other lad turned his mount toward the road and trotted away. The Smith boy returned with the note in hand and gave it to Jack. "Walt said the stationmaster give him a dollar to tell ya your chickens was here."

Jack read the message. "Six-hundred crated chickens delivered to Sweet Springs station this morning." He coughed then began reading again. "Taking up all available space on freight platform. Please, pick up as soon as possible. A.C. Howard, Sweet Springs Stationmaster."

The women soon came out to join the group and Carrie read the note aloud over Jack's shoulder. "Six-hundred chickens! But why didn't Floyd tell us they were coming today?"

Jack shook his head, just as bewildered as anyone. "I don't know."

"Well, I think I do." Ben nodded toward the source of a growling, popping noise that had just become audible from down where the road started up the last leg of the steep plateau.

Jack took off his snap-brim cap, shaded his eyes and squinted against the sun at what looked like a man being dragged through the waist-high grass by some angry, snarling beast. "I recognize the grumble. Sounds like a fifty horse Harley."

"Close." Ben said as he watched the boy on the motorcycle try to outrace his own dust. "'Cept this here motorcycle's an old Army model Indian. Western Union delivery boys use 'em up here." Ben chuckled. "I think that's your telegram. Probably been sittin' under somebody's cheese sandwich down at the telegraph office for a week."

Appearing to be in his mid-teens, the delivery boy, bare-headed and dressed in knickerbockers, slowed to a stop and, out of consideration for the others nearby, shut off his machine out where the main road met the driveway. He finished his journey to the house on foot, escaping the main body of his dust funnel just before it caught up with the bike. When he arrived in front of Jack, he pulled his leather-bound glass goggles up onto his forehead.

"Are you Mr. MacGregor?" He reached into his shirt pocket and pulled out a small yellow envelope with Western Union markings.

"Yes." Out of habit, Jack wiped his hand on his pants. "That for me?" He reached out.

The boy scratched his brown mop with his left hand and handed the envelope to Jack with the other. "Yes, sir. It's a telegram."

"We know that, Andy." Ben put his hands in his pockets. "'Less you stole the telegraph company's motorcycle."

"Uh, I'm *'spose* to say that, Mr. Smith." The messenger flushed a little, then nodded to Seth. "Hey, Seth."

Seth "Hey'd" the older boy back, while unsuccessfully working to hide a look of mild admiration that had crept out of nowhere to take up residence upon his face.

Jack rummaged in his Jodhpurs for a quarter and tossed it to the begoggled Andy. "There ya go."

"Thank you, Mr. MacGregor." Andy pocketed the coin.

Jack opened the message and quietly read it. He let out a quick snicker. "It's Grandpa telling us he's sent the chickens, and it's dated almost a week ago. What gives?" He looked at Andy.

"Sorry, sir." Andy hung his head a little. "They found it under the night telegrapher ham sandwich."

"Ham, huh? Not cheese? Well, I was wrong," Ben displayed a small wry smile. "And it's only *six* days late. I just can't seem to guess anything right today."

"You want the quarter back, Mr. MacGregor?"

Jack shook his head. "Naw, you keep it. You did *your* job just fine."

"Thank you." Andy started back to the dormant Indian Motorcycle out by the road. "Bye, folks. Hope it's good news for you anyway." He pulled his mechanical mount upright and kicked it into consciousness. Then Andy and the cycle performed a quick wobble on the road's loose gravel as he urged the beast back downhill, leaving a new tunnel of dust to drift back across the brush land.

"Well, let's get to it." Ben rubbed his hands together. "If we both use our trucks, we can get all them chickens up here before supper."

This took Jack by surprise. "I thought all you had was the team and wagon. Why haven't I seen a truck?'

Ben smiled. "I got a big old Ford Double-T Stake-Side I keep under a tarp back behind the hay barn. I only use it for big loads or when I'm in a hurry to get to town. But if I have my druthers, I take the team and wagon. Reminds me of better days, and it don't frazzle my nerves as much." He trundled downhill toward his own spread and gestured to Seth. "Come on, boy. Let's unveil Beelzebub!"

In fifteen minutes, everyone but Ruth and Eddie sat in one of the two dull, black trucks, rattling down the dirt course of Saber Canyon Road. Fifteen minutes after that, both vehicles backed into the freight platform at the train station.

A typical Western mining/ranching town, Sweet Springs sported an eclectic mixture of three-story brick, two-story wood-frame, and assorted mis-designed plank buildings. An exposure-warped boardwalk connected all structures for two blocks in four directions starting from the main intersection (and center of town), Saber Canyon and Roosevelt. Beyond the reach of this sidewalk, there existed merely a two-horse-wide swath of sandy dust, bordering the pavement on both sides for as far as that pavement continued, which for Saber Canyon was six miles in either direction from the crossroads, but on Roosevelt lasted only just beyond the official limits of the town proper, less than one mile from the intersection. After that, the road and the horse trail combined themselves into one dirt thoroughfare.

Railroad tracks ran atop the lake dike north of town until those tracks turned south and separated Sweet Springs from the rail-yards. Cottonwood and pine trees grew interspersed along most of the streets and between buildings wherever the impoverished water table allowed. Also, ever since the arrival of power lines from the Palmdale dynamo station back in 1900, there had existed two genuine electric streetlights, one directly in front of the bank, with the other illuminating the passenger platform of the train station; both served citizens and travelers alike every night from five to nine, November to May, and seven to nine, June to October. After that, folks were required to fend for themselves, as per lighting their way through life. Consequently, it paid for residents of Sweet Springs to own a reliable flashlight or, at least, a railroad lantern.

Ben killed the engine of his massive flatbed. Jack glanced back at the freight platform after he had set the emergency brake and shut off the ignition system of his little Model-T pickup. Wooden grated poultry crates sat stacked there as high as a man could reach, a hot, dry Soledad Canyon wind blowing through them, carrying clucks, squawks, and feathers out toward the street. Kenny scrambled from the pickup's bed up onto the dock to inspect their new property while his father, Ben, Seth, and his mom climbed the stairs to the freight office. The stationmaster, already waiting for them, leaned against the door jam, his arms crossed and jaw sternly set. A man of Napoleonic stature, he wore a starched white shirt under a black wool, brass-buttoned vest. An enormous watch chain girded his ample middle. The little man took out the large gold watch, attached to the chain, as the group approached. He inspected its face, then leered up at them. His unpleasant expression set the conversational mood as he replaced the timepiece into its nest in his vest pocket.

"Well, it's about dern time, Ben!" He nodded toward Jack. "You MacGregor?"

Jack returned the nod. "That's me. Hope we didn't cause any trouble." He feared the vague apology would be like trying to fill in the Grand Canyon with a shovel, but it was all he could do at this point. Whatever storm lay ahead would just have to be weathered.

The old railroader grunted and half swiveled toward the squawking crates. "I'm bound to tell you, Mr. MacGregor. The Southern Pacific Railroad does not take kindly to livestock being left unattended in this manner." He waved a frustrated hand at Jack's chickens. "Such transfers should be met promptly upon arrival." The stationmaster turned fully back to Jack. "That means you should have been here to pick up your property the same time as the train's arrival." He adjusted his green eyeshade. "No sir. The railroad don't like doin' business in such a fashion. Not one little bit!" He cleared his throat and spit into a rusty cuspidor that sat chained to the freight office wall. "And *I* don't care much for it, neither!"

"Now, just calm down, brother." Ben patted the man on the back. "Old Western Union didn't get the man his notification telegram 'til today. He didn't even know these here birds were coming."

"Oh." The man's shoulders dropped as he deflated a bit. "What was it... under a turkey sandwich or something?" He turned his head to Ben and raised his eyebrows.

"Ham," Ben answered.

The stationmaster nodded. "That figures. Well, at any rate, they're mostly alive, and they're all yours," he pointed to Jack, "just as soon as you sign for 'em." He pulled a clipboard from a nearby hook and handed it to Jack, who signed and returned it.

"This here's his wife, Carrie." Ben patted her on the arm.

Good show, Ben! Jack appreciated his neighbor's attempt to rehumanize the MacGregor clan. They might be doing business with this feisty little fellow for a long time.

The stationmaster touched his green visor. "Pleasure, ma'am."

After that, it was one solid flurry of loading, driving, and unloading until the umpteenth trip had been completed just before sundown. On every trip, each truck had been loaded until the crates were stacked just above the top of the stake sides, then a rope was laced across the rear of the bed to prevent any fowl from sliding off and bouncing out onto the road. Ben's flatbed took longer to load, being much larger than Jack's little pickup. As a result, Jack had to make more trips. But everyone worked as fast as possible, and all went well right up to the last trip.

Jack, Carrie, and Kenny had just finished lashing up the back of the pickup. Ben and Seth worked to load the last few crates from the station platform onto their vehicle.

"I think we've just about got her!" The old man checked the stability of the top crate on a stack by shaking it in every direction possible. "What do ya think?"

Jack wiped sweat from his brow with the back of his hand. He hadn't worked this hard since he'd left the Army. "I think you're right."

Carrie chimed in from over her husband's shoulder. "I am simply amazed at the way Ruth has been able to uncrate these birds and get them into the hen houses. With all of us bringing up crates as fast as we can, she's always finished with the last load before we get there! And all this while watching Eddie. You've got quite a wife, Ben!"

Ben smiled but kept loading. "Yeah, she'll do."

"Well, she's a stronger woman than I." Carrie shook her head.

Jack gave his wife a side hug. "I think you'll do, too."

Ben cleared his throat as Seth handed him another crate. He placed it down onto the last unoccupied space of the truck's bed, tied it to the other crates, then straightened up. "Well, if you all are done sparkin' for a while, how 'bout we get these chicks up to your ranch afore dark. What say?"

"Okay, we'll see you up there." Jack helped his wife down from the Model-T's little bed as Kenny vaulted to the ground and clambered into the cab.

"You bet." Ben settled another crate on top of the first and gave the MacGregors a cursive waive without looking. "We'll be right behind ya."

Both adults sandwiched Kenny in and slammed the doors. The truck, like Ben's, had been left running after the first trip, so Jack simply ground it into first gear and started up the paved first half of the route.

The trip proved uneventful until they got to the three-quarters mark, about a third of the way up the dirt portion of Saber Canyon Road. Jack spotted what looked like Ben's truck in his side view mirror. It seemed to be coming up behind him fast, leaving a plume of dust behind it that fairly covered the south side of the canyon.

What are you playing at, Ben? Jack hunched over to squint into the mirror. *If you don't slow down you're going to drive right into us.*

Jack kept watch on the big stake-side, approaching like a comet, and started to fear for his chickens aboard Ben's truck. With his neighbor traveling at that speed, he expected to see feathers flying up into the slipstream, if not the crated birds themselves. But there was no sign of any of the load slipping off. As a matter of fact, there was no sign of the load at all.

Strain as he might, Jack could not make out any of the crates that should have been sticking up above Ben's cab. *Has he already lost some of the load?* Jack continued to stare at the mirror, baffled. Why was Ben driving so fast? And why was he weaving from one side of the road to the other?

Almost on them now, the big Double-T showed no sign of slowing. If Jack didn't know better, he'd have thought that Ben *meant* to hit him.

And that's when things got interesting. In a matter of seconds, both trucks came to a stretch of the road where it was so narrow that, if two opposing vehicles met, one would have to pull part way off the road for the other to squeeze by. In addition, less than a quarter mile ahead, for fifty yards the road paralleled a cliff with a twenty-foot drop. If an up-canyon driver wasn't sure whether he wanted to be polite and pull off for oncoming traffic, he didn't have long to make up his mind before the cliff decided for him. It was at this point along the route, as the road narrowed, that the big, black truck tried to pass Jack on the left.

The flatbeded monster increased its speed and swung around, at first letting his left wheels go uphill off the roadbed, smashing brush as it plowed ahead. Then it came down onto the main course, forcing the MacGregors' little Tin Lizzy half way into the bushes on the other side. Jack gripped the wheel so hard he thought he'd left fingerprints in the wood as he fought to keep from rolling over as the larger truck continued to drift closer. Jack couldn't believe it.

214

Ben, what's wrong with you? What are you doing?

The pickup was being pushed further off the road every second, with the cliff moving ever nearer. Jack wondered if Ben even saw how little separation remained between the two vehicles. Maybe he wanted to pass and misjudged the distance.

No, that can't be right. You'd have to be blind or drunk not to see a truck on a road this desolate, especially if it started out in front of you.

Then Jack saw the cliff. No more time to think, no time to consider that Ben knew this road by heart and should have waited to pass. There remained now only enough time to stand on the Ford's brakes and try to keep the rear wheels from locking up. So he did both of these things and hung on tight, with his wife and son bracing themselves as best they could.

"Oh, Jack!" Carrie's fingers tore at his shoulder. "What are you doing?"

"Hold on!"

At first the little T slid in the road's decomposed granite and sand, and at one point it looked like it was going to drift sideways over some hard baked adobe clay. But at last, the rear wheels straightened out and Jack was able to shed some speed. The big truck passed, choking all behind it in a monstrous funnel of dust, blinding the MacGregors, so they could not see the cliff's edge. *Oh, Lord! How close are we?*

"Oh, my God!" Carrie's voice was shrill. "Jack!"

But providence prevailed. The earthen cloud miraculously cleared enough just in time for Jack to spin the wheel and avoid plunging down the embankment.

After he could make out their surroundings again, all Jack's thoughts became dark, threatening ones that included an arsenal of things he intended saying to Ben. Then the dust drifted completely away, and he could see the empty bed of the truck in front of him. There were no crates of terrified chickens. Could Ben have unknowingly lost them all on his wild ride up the canyon.? Was that even possible on that short a ride? And if not, what the heck had happened all those chickens? That last one had Jack stumped as he watched the other truck bounce ahead and turn right up the plateau toward the ranch. That's when Carrie saw it.

"Jack." She was still breathing in quick gulps from their flirtation with the cliff. "I don't think that's Ben's truck!"

Jack spared her one quick glance. "You thought it was him, too?"

"Yes, I did." She took a breath. "But it's not. See…there's lettering on the door."

He focused on the area Carrie had spoken of and read aloud as he made out the lettering. "U…S…Mail. U.S. Mail?" He exhaled out the fear he'd been holding in check. "Well, I'll be. And whoever that is's still burning up the road."

They watched the truck ahead of them accelerate up the hill, while still swerving radically from side to side. "Jack, I think whoever that is might be drunk." Carrie looked down at Kenny, who hadn't made a sound through the whole incident. "You all right, little man?"

"Yeah!" Kenny sounded excited. "Let's chase him, Dad!"

Jack looked at Carrie, who rolled her eyes. "Naw," he said to his son. "We'll just follow him and see where he's going. He does seem to be having a hard time keeping that thing on the road, doesn't he?" Carrie nodded as Jack turned right and downshifted to go up the hill.

They followed the mail truck through two more turns, past the entrance to Ben's place and on toward their own. Jack couldn't guess what business this mad, mystery mail driver could have at their ranch, or why he'd tried to run them down, but it was beginning to look like they were going to find out – one way or the other.

The big truck had made it almost up to the house Ben had pointed out as his son's. And it showed no sign of slowing until all at once it turned to the right, into that house's driveway. The turn was so sharp and the speed so great that the vehicle lifted up on its left two wheels as it completed the maneuver. It hung that way for an instant. Then, as its speed diminished, the right side came crashing down with all the force its mass and weight could produce. For the next few feet, it rocked and bounced until it finally lopped to a dust engulfed stop just short of the north wall of the house.

Jack followed the mail truck to where its engine died in gear, and the mad race stopped. Whoever had been driving had possibly passed out if he was drunk as Carrie had suggested. Or if not drunk, than maybe he was sick. Either way, the near miss at the cliff had earned the MacGregors the right to find out what was going on.

Jack stopped the pickup about ten feet away and got out, leaving his engine running. The sun had gone behind the hills almost half an hour earlier, and twilight had now begun its slow journey toward actual darkness.

"Be careful," Carrie whispered.

"You bet your life." Jack pulled a flashlight from behind the seat and started off for the mail truck. He heard Carrie say, "I wish you hadn't said that", but he ignored the comment.

He walked quickly to the cab of the other truck and shined the light inside. Sitting back in the seat with his hands at his side was a stubby looking man with graying copper-colored hair and a short, dead cigar hanging from between his teeth. He looked to be about ten years older than Jack.

Headlights swept past the cab, dragging Jack's attention back to the road where he saw the real Ben driving the true and actual Beelzebub, coming to a squealing stop in the drive. Jack reached in and felt the driver's chest. Its rise and fall seemed shallow, but nonetheless continuous. *Good. He's alive.* Then the invisible cloud of vomit-laced sour whiskey breath invaded Jack's nostrils, causing his eyes to squint as he pulled his head back out of the cab. *Yeah, I'd say this guy's drunk.* He sighed and turned to meet Ben and Seth, who were just walking up.

"That's my pa." Seth shuffled by Jack, his eyes downcast. "Sometimes he drinks too much. Doesn't he, Grandpa?"

Ben pulled his eyes off his son's limp body and looked sadly at Jack. "Yes, he does, and sometimes he does foolish, dangerous things when he's like this. I'm sorry, Jack. Carrie and Kenny are all right, I hope."

"We survived it." Jack raised one eyebrow. "But your son almost didn't." He let out a long tense breath. "He almost rolled his truck over."

Ben shook his head and looked into the cab. "Aw, Sam."

It didn't take a genius to see that Ben and Seth did not need any more humiliation or grief at that moment, and Jack was not inclined to throw a harsh judgment Sam's direction, either. Driving drunk was a stupid and sometimes criminal act, but he'd been there himself once or twice during and just after the war.

Jack felt as protective of his family as any man, but, since they were safe, he decided not to make the Smiths any more miserable than they already were. He knew by all rights he should be furious, and normally he would be, but something was preventing this at the moment. He didn't know for sure what that was, but he thought the Lord might have something to do with it. At the moment, all he felt for Sam Smith was pity. Carrie would agree with his decision to show mercy to Ben's poor drunken son; he was sure of that. He didn't know *why* he thought that, either. He told himself he'd talk it over with her later and see if she agreed with his decision to be merciful.

The front door of Sam's house opened, splitting the darkened drive with a shard of light. A blond-haired, middle-aged woman in a yellow dress leaned out and called in a loud, annoyed voice, "Is he out cold again, Seth?"

Seth looked to the light and sniffed. "Yes, ma'am, he's out!"

"Then drag him in here near the couch. If he wakes up later, he can crawl up on it himself."

"Yes, ma'am!" Seth started to get his shoulder under Sam's left arm, but had trouble getting the man's feet out from around the pedals.

Jack hurried over and helped untangle Sam Smith's shoes, then took the other arm.

"Come on, Seth. No need to drag him tonight." Ben already had his son's feet.

That's when Carrie came up from behind the trio and took one of the feet from old Ben. Thus they carried Sam in and laid him on an overstuffed couch in the living room. Jack looked around for Seth's mother but could not find her.

"She's in their bedroom," the boy said. "She's ashamed." He said it in a matter-of-fact way, like reporting the weather.

Looks like this has happened too often, Jack thought, but he said, "I understand."

"Mr. MacGregor? Can I still help you unload the chickens?" There was a calm pleading in Seth's voice. Ben watched Jack as if waiting for his own answer.

"You bet your life!" Jack put his arm around the boy's shoulder. "You weren't planning on letting me do all that myself, were you?"

"No, sir."

Jack walked with Seth out the front door and led him to Ben's truck. As he turned around, he saw Carrie coming behind with her arm entwined with Ben's. She smiled in that tender way she usually reserved for those she cared for, and she whispered in the old man's ear. All of a sudden, Ben smiled too, but not quite as big as his female companion. Carrie gave him a quick hug as he wiped his eyes.

"You all set?" Jack asked when he could think of nothing else to say.

"Let's get her done," Ben groaned. But the smile remained on his face.

As they walked back to the pickup, Jack asked Carrie what she'd said to Ben.

She answered, "I told him we'd pray for Sam. For the Lord to save his son and heal him."

Jack said nothing for a while after that. Then he took hold of her hand, and thanked God for the wife he'd been given. However, as he ground the Ford into reverse, he couldn't help but wonder what other problems this Sam Smith might cause. God seemed to have ordained that he'd be Jack's across-the-road neighbor, Seth's father, and Ben's son. But the man claimed the title of dangerous drunk, as well. Too bad.

"This could make life interesting." Jack backed onto the road, then eased into first gear again. The little truck stuttered forward under its load.

"You mean Ben's son?" Carrie inspected her nails in the twilight.

Jack turned down the ranch's driveway. "Yes."

"Make life interesting," she said. "Yes, it could do that. We'll have to see what the Lord has in store for us on that subject."

Jack glanced over at his wife as he stopped downhill from the chicken coops. It was hard to tell in the darkening shadows of the cab, but he thought he detected a wry smile—more subtle than Ben's had been, but there, just the same.

Chapter Sixteen

Ben and Ruth sat at the MacGregors' kitchen table fidgeting and over-stirring their coffee. Ruth looked more strained than Carrie had seen her thus far. The old woman's eyes were *after-crying* red, and her usual *in-charge* manner had become conspicuous by its absence.

"Ben finally told me the whole truth of what Sam did last night." She paused and took a breath. "So I just come up this morning to tell you good folks how mighty sorry I am." She glanced at Ben, who put his arm around her. "How sorry *we* are."

Carrie came to the table with the coffee pot and freshened her neighbors' cups. "That's not necessary, Ruth. Ben already did that last night."

"Well, I needed to tell you for myself. It's no small thing, what Sam did. And when I think on what might've happened—" She sniffed and took a sip of her steaming brew. "When I think on what might've happened, it's almost more than a body can bear."

Jack worked a toothpick through his teeth as he leaned against the sink. When he finished, he tossed it into the trash and faced the couple at the table. "Ruth, it's all over and done as far as Carrie and I are concerned. This is something we think the Lord's put on our hearts." He folded his arms and leaned back against the sink again.

Ruth concentrated on her coffee and nodded. "Well, if it's the Lord, then I'll let it be. I just wanted you to know."

"We understand," Carrie said.

There was a silent interlude broken only by the sounds of Ben's spoon tinkling against the inside of his cup. After almost half a minute had passed in this manner, Carrie knew something had to be done to mend the bridge with their new friends. That's when she spoke. "We're going to the inn today." She turned to Jack. "What did you call it?"

"The Hunter's Inn," Jack said flatly.

"Right. The Hunter's Inn." Carrie announced with a slightly too big smile. "We're going to go down there and see about our delivery agreement. Now that we have this place ready –"

Jack looked at her and raised his eyebrows.

With a sigh and a nod Carrie acknowledged his *there's-still-a-lot-to-do-yet* expression and continued. "Well, ready more or less. I think it's time we put our little old ranch to work. Start making a living, as it were." *After all, how hard can that be? The inn is going to buy all the chickens and eggs we can produce.*

The Smiths exchanged serious looks and Ben cleared his throat. "Uh, I know the owner very well. If you like, I can make the trip with you and kind of grease the skids."

"Grease the skids?" Carrie didn't have any idea what Ben's last three words meant.

"He's going to introduce us," Jack sounded amused.

Carrie gave her smile a vitamin shot, but had doubts as to how well an oat farmer with poor grammar could know the owner of a successful hotel. Unfortunately, those doubts became subtly apparent as they flavored the tone of her next words. "Oh, that would be wonderful, Ben. And how did you come to meet him?"

Ruth apparently caught the almost imperceptible tenor that had gone right past Ben. She looked at Carrie with mild rebuke in her eyes and answered her in an icy manner that well conveyed her sentiment. "Ben *sold* him the inn."

Jack, who, like Ben, had missed the less substantial part of the conversation, now seemed curious. "You owned the Hunter's Inn, huh?"

"That's right." Ben finished his coffee, got up, and put his cup in the sink. "Wasn't such a snooty sort of place when we had it, though."

Ben winked at Ruth. Her expression sweetened from its grimace for just an instant, and she giggled a little in response to her husband. He smiled, shushed her, and went on talking as his wife's countenance returned to its former ominous state.

"I started out working there as a hunting guide when old Fuzzy Mason still owned it," he said. "That was back when Teddy Roosevelt used to come up on the Hunters' Train." Ben paused and seemed to be somewhere else for a second.

"Ben." Ruth brought him back.

"What? Oh. Uh, sorry. Just recollecting some." He smiled and shook his head. "But riding horses up those canyons and through that brush got too hard on my back after a while. So I took our savings and bought the place from Fuzzy's widow when he died. But we didn't want to change anything. No, we kept it about the same as when Fuzzy owned it, like the name says, mostly for hunters. Ruth there did most of the cookin'." He nodded toward his wife. "The hunters'd bring in their kills, and she'd cook 'em up. Sometimes, if the guests was rich, they'd have their friends and family come up for a venison supper. Then they'd all stay the night. Those were good days."

Carrie had been picturing all that Ben had said. Suddenly, he seemed a little more than just an ignorant, old farmer to her. She could actually envision a slightly younger Mr. Smith leading mounted hunting parties into the nearby mountains and Ruth roasting venison for adventurous friends. She could now see the Smiths owning such a place, and she began to feel a small pang of guilt at her earlier arrogance. "Why did you sell it?" Her tone exhibited genuine curiosity this time.

Ben went back to the table and put his hands on Ruth's shoulders from behind. "The place was working Ruth too hard. Cooking, cleaning, and what not...and we were running the farm, to boot. Too much for her. Even after we hired a few local folks to help out at both places. Too much for me, too. And we were losing time with the grandchildren. We run it for over two years. Then we decided to stick to farming oats and sold the inn to the first feller that gave us a decent offer. That was the man you're gonna meet. Name's Henry, but he wants it pronounced *On-Ree*. But spells it H-E-N-R-I."

"Sound's French." Jack's interest perked again.

"He's from New Orleans. Cajun, don't ya know. Heck of a nice feller. You'll see when ya meet him."

"Well, then why don't you men get Jack's truck cranked up?" Ruth rose abruptly from her seat, gathered the three remaining cups, and deposited them into the sink. "Carrie and me'll wash up the coffee cups, and then she'll be right out to go with ya. I'll watch the boys while you three are down in town." She gave both men little mock shoves out the door. "Go on now. Scat!"

Ben and Jack exchanged glances and laughed but cleared out of the house, leaving the women alone. Carrie sensed something strange about Ruth's demeanor, but, since she had no inkling as to it's cause, went straight to the sink and quickly began to rinse out the cups. "Ruth, thank you ever so much for offering to watch the boys again. It'll make it much easier while we're in town."

Ruth said nothing at first, but Carrie did hear her give out a long, intense sigh from the doorway. Several seconds passed in silence as Carrie finished washing the cups alone. Then she set them to drain on a kitchen towel and dried her hands on her apron before turning around. It was then that Ruth spoke in a manner that exhibited an unmistaken air of controlled calm.

"You were surprised to hear that Ben knew Henri and that he'd owned the inn, weren't ya?"

Carrie didn't speak for a moment. She found herself frozen like a burglar caught in a police spotlight. There she stood, exposed for unkind thoughts about a man who had been nothing but kind to her. She had believed those thoughts were her secret. But not so. *And the one who found me out is his wife.*

Her first instinct was to run, but that would have been unladylike. Besides, it was Carrie's own kitchen. A second option was to deny the charge, and make Ruth think she'd guessed wrong. Carrie chose denial.

"Ruth, I never meant to—"

"Oh, yes you did." Ruth wouldn't even let her finish her sentence. "You just couldn't believe that people who wrangle horses or guide hunters into the hills or farm oats can save up enough money to ever buy a classy hotel, let alone have the brains to run it. I saw it on your face, and the Lord confirmed to me that it was in your mind."

Carrie was overcome with shame. She liked these people. They had always shown her nothing but love. Carrie didn't know what to do, so she backed up to the sink and grasped the edge of the counter. Not knowing what to say, out sputtered, " Ruth, I don't know what to say."

Ruth smiled faintly. "Just say you're sorry. I'm sure you'll mean it. If the Lord can forgive you, so can I."

Carrie dropped her head. "I'm sorry, Ruth." She looked up at the other woman. "And I am so very ashamed. I don't know why I thought that."

Ruth's smile broadened. "Well, don't feel too bad. From what I gather, it's the way you were raised. Takes a while to break old habits even when you know they're wrong." She went to Carrie and gave her a sisterly hug. "Don't fret none. I think the Lord just wanted you to realize what was going on." Carrie produced a nod as Ruth continued. "We'll talk more later. Right now, you gotta' get to town."

The boys were playing with Copper and Seth uphill from the house when Ben and the MacGregors left in the pickup. Ruth stood in the driveway and waived. Carrie, having squeezed herself in between the two men, glanced back and returned the gesture over her shoulder through the rear window. She didn't feel the shame as much anymore. It had started to fade the minute Ruth hugged her. The incident reminded her of when she was first saved. Shame had disappeared with that embrace too.

The brakes squealed as the MacGregors' Tin Lizzie rolled to a stop almost twenty minutes later, and Jack and Carrie got their first close look at the Hunter's Inn, which appeared to be a strange cross between a medieval castle and a mountain chalet with river rock turrets and parapets climbing up two stories in height. An even more out of place split-log penthouse topped the structure. That sported a broad, swooping, post-supported shingle roof that extended far enough out from the third story walls to protect most of the building. Carrie fell in love with the odd edifice in about ten seconds.

How divinely inappropriate, she thought. *It doesn't fit with anything I've ever seen anywhere. It's like it's out of someone's dream...just no one I know.*

They escaped the truck like sardines pulling themselves from a can. Ben cracked his knuckles and scrutinized the old building. "Kinda funny lookin', ain't she?" He craned his neck back to get a look at the top. "Most of this bottom part was the original Spanish blockhouse. These here rock walls are almost three feet thick."

"The Spanish built it?" *This old man never ceases to surprise me,* Carrie thought.

Ben rubbed the back of his neck. "Yep. Over a hundred year ago. One of the few things they built that ain't adobe." He rubbed his elbow and worked his arm a few times as if it were sore. "The road that run through here then was kind of a route of second choice for going north and south. Spaniards'd use it when there was landslides on the Coast Road, which was just as often as not. This here little fort was supposed to protect folks a' travelin through from bandits and Indians and the like."

Jack shaded his eyes and pointed to the penthouse. "Did the Spanish build that?"

Ben shook his head. "Naw. Butterfield Stage Company did that about fifty year ago. They took the place over and used it for a stage stop. You know, changin' horses and such. Sometimes passengers had to stay the night, so they built on extra rooms and re-did the place as an inn." He waved his hand at the turrets and parapets. "All that nonsense was put on by Fuzzy Mason. He thought it might help business, being sort of a curiosity, don't ya know."

"Ben, where did you learn all this?" Carrie surveyed the old bastion.

Ben shrugged. "Oh, some from old Fuzzy and the rest from Teddy."

"Teddy?" Jack asked.

"Yep." Ben squinted at a crow flying north. "Roosevelt." He winked at Carrie. "Like I said, he used to hunt up here. I was the guide. Man sure knew a lot of history. But then I guess he'd have to, I mean him having been the president and all." He nonchalantly slapped his overalls as if they were dusty, which they weren't. "Well, come on; let's go inside."

Ben led them under a rock arch to the service entrance on the east side of the building, then up a long dark hall full of doors that led to various storage and utility rooms. Finally, the group broke out into the kitchen. Fairly large and dominated by three massive wood-fired cook stoves, the main space appeared hemmed in by a seemingly infinite number of cabinets and cupboards. A huge preparation table with a chopping block that covered almost half its surface held court in the center of the room. It reminded Carrie of the kitchen at her father's Marner Bay house, only a little more crowded and a lot busier.

One relatively ample woman with chestnut hair, bound under a white scarf, seemed to be in charge, ordering two other smaller women about the place. One of the underlings looked to be Hispanic, the other Asian. Both sported white, canvas bib aprons and kept themselves in a constant state of fetching, mixing, or measuring. The obvious straw boss/chief/cook bustled about, clanging oven doors and tasting the contents of bubbling pots. Carrie thought it all seemed appropriate for a successful hotel but for one thing. Only one of the three stoves seemed to be lit. Judging from the size of the inn, it surprised her they weren't using at least two to handle lunch, considering the present summer season and the fact that Sweet Springs boasted a small fishing and rowing lake not a half mile from the center of town. Something was wrong.

"Haddie, where's Henri?" Ben's voice brought the cook's head up from the oven door, sweat dripping off her nose and narrowly missing a pan of muffins. A look of annoyance dangled from her jowls.

"How do I know? Try his office!" She gave the oven one last menacing look, then slammed its heavy iron door and eased herself onto a tall stool near the preparation table. "Who're they?" She nodded toward Jack and Carrie as they followed Ben through the kitchen.

Ben slowed a little but did not seem keen to start a conversation with this ominous woman. "Oh, these are the MacGregors," he said but kept moving toward the hallway, that led to the owner's office. "They'll probably be supplying your chickens and eggs from now on." His voice echoed back to Haddie from the narrow hall as if he were descending into a mine. The three filed away from the kitchen as Ben accelerated to a faster walking pace, but Carrie clearly heard the woman's growl as they made their way into the bowels of the inn.

"Don't need no more dern chickens!" she piped. "What we need is cash customers!"

"Don't pay her no mind," Ben said over his shoulder. "Most of us around here are plum certain she wears cactus bloomers."

That brought stifled snickers from Jack and Carrie as Ben came to Henri's office and knocked.

"Haddie, go away!" came the very Cajun-French accented voice from the other side of the door. "I have nothing more to say on the subject!"

"It ain't Haddie." Ben pushed through the door and on into the broom closet-sized office. He waved Carrie and Jack in behind him. "But I can fetch her if you like."

"Ben! Come in, my friend!" Henri said in a thick Gallic tone and rose awkwardly from his seat as the lilliputian office filled with people.

"What's the problem with Haddie this time?" Ben reached around Carrie and closed the door as soon as Jack was snug in the room.

"Oh, her?" Henri remained standing for a moment as he shook Ben's hand. "She wants another raise." He shrugged. "I cannot afford what I pay her now. How can I give her a raise? Uh?" He looked to Jack and Carrie. "But who are your companions?"

Ben slapped Jack on the shoulder. "These good folks are the MacGregors."

"Ah, *oui*. The grandson of the man who called me long distance." He thrust his hand out to Jack who shook it.

"And this is my wife, Caroline." Jack nodded toward Carrie.

"*Enchante, mademoiselle.*" Henri gently grasped the tips of her fingers and raised them slightly.

Ben laughed. "By Golly. You ain't gonna kiss her hand. Are ya?"

Henri flushed. "No, this is something I avoid now."

The comment perked Carrie's interest as Henri released his gentle grasp. Jack looked confused. "What are you talking about?" he asked.

Henri was still red up to and including his ears. "An unfortunate incident."

Ben quickly filled the gap left by his friend's reluctance. "When Henri first came here, he made the mistake of kissing one of the local lady's hands. I think her husband must've hit him three or four times before the man understood that it was just a fancy custom."

Henri cleared his throat. "As I said. An unfortunate incident." The flush left his face, and his mood changed. He turned to Jack and Carrie. "But you are not here for a Sweet Springs history lesson. You are here for business. Are you not?"

Jack nodded.

"Yes, we are," Carrie sighed and took another breath, hoping to push out some apprehension. So much rested upon this meeting, and Jack appeared so nonchalant. Didn't he know a good part of their future was at stake here?

Henri displayed a strained smile. "Why don't we all sit down?" He motioned his guests to some small wooden chairs that were crammed around the desk.

After they'd seated themselves, Jack began. "My grandpa said you wanted to make an order as soon as we were ready. Well, we're ready now, so here we are." He smiled.

The vein on Jack's neck stood out like a stretched rope and the corner of his left eye began to twitch. Carrie cleared her throat. *Well, so much for nonchalance. My poor husband is well beyond simply being nervous; he's bordering on out-and-out fear. We'll probably hear his heart pounding in a moment or two.* Hopefully, Henri would not notice these signs of stress that were so obvious to Carrie. *Lord, please give the head of our family peace.*

And so it was that the Lord gave the MacGregors favor this day, and Jack's smile held. *Good.* With God's help, her husband seemed, after all, to be able to muster a passable business face when needs be. Carrie took an easier breath.

"*Oui.*" Henri exhaled a little too long and his voice took on a more somber tenor. "This talk of ordering is all well and good, but there is one small problem."

"What problem?" Jack and Carrie answered together, and Carrie felt the flash of apprehension.

Henri continued. "You see, business has been dropping steadily since I spoke to your grandfather. It was slow then, and perhaps I should have mentioned it to him at the time, but I thought it was something temporary. A fluke. No?" He glanced down at the desk. "But, sadly, it was not. Our profits have not stopped declining, and there seems to be no end in sight."

"But why?" Carrie needed some explanation before her mind could accept this ominous setback.

"I think it is mostly because of the lake. It has been drying up. There was a little earthquake back in May, and the county experts..." Henri made an unpleasant face. "They think it may have changed the course or level of the underground stream that feeds the lake. They may be right; they may be wrong. All I know is that the lake is drying up at the rate of several yards a month. It was always a shallow little thing, but now people have to keep moving their boat docks farther and farther out from where they used to be." He emitted a sad chuckle. "Some parts of the shore are beginning to smell of dead fish, and there are fewer tourists every week. So my inn has fewer guests and serves fewer meals." He turned his attention back to his desk and wrote something on a small piece of paper. "Here is what I need." He folded the slip and handed it to Jack.

Jack read, and his forehead quickly furrowed. "But this is half the order we need!" He passed the note to Carrie.

She read quickly, and a shock ran through her. Carrie looked up at her husband. "We can't even pay our living expenses on that small an order!"

The Cajun's countenance took on a rueful appearance, but he spoke in a sympathetic tone. "I do not know what to tell you, *mes amis*. I cannot afford to buy what I cannot sell. If and when business picks up, I can order more, but until then...." He shrugged. "Perhaps, you can sell to others. But I don't know if you could make up the other half of the order that way in a town this small. You see most of the locals have their own chickens." Henri sighed. "I am sorry to bring you such bad news." He paused as if giving Jack a moment to think. "Do you still want my order?"

Jack stood up; the others followed suit. "Uh, you know, I just don't—"

Carrie cut him off. "Yes, we want it!" She took hold of Jack's arm. "We'll just have to find additional markets for our chickens and eggs." She gave her husband's arm a squeeze.

Jack turned toward her. "Carrie, we can't –"

"We can't stay here talking any longer," she interrupted again, "if we're going to fill that order on time." She opened her eyes wide at Jack and momentarily crossed them, hoping he would catch the hint and go along with what she was saying.

Jack rolled *his* eyes and turned back to Henri. "Yeah, we'll fill your order as soon as we can."

"*Bon.*" The inn's owner seemed to brighten a little as he shook the hand of the fledgling rancher. "It is done?"

Jack nodded. "Deal."

Henri pumped his new business associate's handle some more. "*Bon, bon.*"

Carrie wasn't very conscious of what occurred between the hand shake and her ending up back out in the truck. From the minute Jack agreed to meet the inn's order, she began trying to come up with a way to make up the devastating loss of half their income. Sadly, nothing came to mind. So, by the time they'd stepped out into the sunlight, she'd given up on that and started praying.

What are we supposed to do now, Lord? She slid into the middle of the little Model-T's cab while Jack gave a quick crank to the engine. She pressed her knees together, folded her hands, and waited. The little truck shuddered as

its four cylinders fired to life. Jack and Ben sandwiched
Carrie between them again and slammed their doors.
Suddenly, Carrie's mind cleared of all thought. It
frightened her at first. She jerked slightly and sucked in a
little air through puckered lips, but just as quick felt a
strange peace spread through her, so she settled down and
waited for whatever would come next.

"You all right?" Jack looked over a hunched shoulder
at her.

"What?" Carrie knew the men in the cab would never
understand what she'd felt even if it *could* be explained,
which it couldn't, so she said, "I just felt a little odd; it's
gone now." Her husband continued to stare at her with
what looked like a combination of confusion and concern,
so she added. "It's a female feeling sort of thing, Jack."

"Oooh," Jack replied with seeming acceptance. Both
men nodded in unison. Ben smiled but remained silent.

Carrie almost laughed at the ease of her deception, but
her attention soon became diverted by the words that began
to flow through her mind—so clear they were nearly
audible.

*Be calm. Be patient. Opportunities will come to you.
Just wait and do not fear. You are where I want you to be.*

She leaned back against the seat then let out all her
breath and tension. She believed she'd heard the Lord's
voice again, and took comfort in what she believed He'd
said.

Jack ground a pound of first gear and lurched out onto
Saber Canyon Road. He made an abrupt left at Roosevelt
and headed east away from town. "I want to see this dying
lake for myself," he said and bullied the transmission on up
into second gear. In less than five minutes, they pulled to a
stop near what looked like a narrow boardwalk. The thing
extended out about thirty feet over a mosaic of sunbaked
mud and stinking, half entombed fish.

Oh, my goodness, Carrie thought. *This is the lake!*

She realized the boardwalk had to be none other than the boat dock, left stranded like the dead and dying fish by subsiding water. Long-expired, splintering reeds began further out and, beyond them, mosquitoes hovered around the edge of the new algae-choked shoreline. A few small rowboats sat silent, tied to what appeared to be fence posts people had hastily hammered into the dehydrating mud. The boats barely had enough water beneath their hulls to float them there at lake's edge, and all had the look of disuse, simply acting as markers for where the changing shoreline now truly began. Carrie could see Henri had been right. The scene could be described by no other word than pathetic, and the whole area reeked of death. It looked more like a disease-ridden, oversized pond than any sort of real lake and probably did more to repel tourists than draw them.

The trio got out of the truck under a very solemn cloud of disappointment. Jack picked up a rock and threw it out past the boats into the water. "Guess the man wasn't lyin', was he." He threw another rock and scared a crow off the bow of a neglected, wooden Chris-Craft. "This place is a bust, Carrie! We're not going to make a living here." At that moment, the distant throaty roar of a biplane, taking off from an airfield almost a mile distant broke the day's deathly silence. The craft tottered against an apparent crosswind as it fought for altitude then turned south and disappeared beyond the hills that bordered the valley on that side. Jack watched in silence as long as the machine remained visible. Then, after it had gone, he shook his head, sighed and turned back to his wife. "Why'd you want that order from the inn? He told us he didn't think we could find other customers in town!"

"He said he didn't know." Carrie wasn't angry. She understood her husband's skepticism, but there existed something inside her that made her want to fight to keep Jack from giving up on their new life. She didn't understand it, but she knew she had to keep her family on that little ranch. They had to, at least, *try* to make things work. She drew close to Jack and rested her hands on his shoulders. "I know we can find more business or, maybe, a second source of income."

"How do you know?" Jack pulled her hands off and turned around.

"I don't know how I know. I just know!" She grabbed his hand and held it.

Ben cleared his throat. "How 'bout I just take a walk down the road a piece so's you folks can discuss things with some privacy."

"There's no need, Ben. There's nothing for us to discuss." Jack walked a few steps out onto the cracked, dry mud of the lakebed and kicked the first dead fish he came to. "There isn't enough business to support us here. We can't pay our bills that way, so we're going to sell the ranch and ship the livestock back to my grandparents."

Carrie felt the desperate pang again to keep them from leaving Sweet Springs. It came from within her just as if it was her own idea. But she knew that couldn't be because her own true thoughts were fearful ones. Aside from this inner voice...aside from the Holy Spirit's voice, her fear proved to be every bit as strong and despairing as Jack's. Just a few days before, she had wanted to leave even more than he did now. Ever since the trip to the inn, however, she'd wanted nothing more than to stay, no matter what. She decided this either had to be God...or she was going insane.

Carrie turned to their neighbor. "Ben, doesn't the inn still get business from hunters? I mean, it *is* called the Hunter's Inn, after all."

Ben shook his head. "Naw, that was eight or ten years ago. Not much hunting up here now. Most of the big game—deer and bear and such—they're further north in the

Sierras. You folks sure you don't want me to take a little walk?"

Carrie swung back to Jack. "All right, let's try this." She began to pace. "Give Sweet Springs three months. See if we can collect enough customers to support us. If we can't, then we'll sell and move." She was starting to breathe faster, striding up and down the landlocked dock as she talked.

Scratching his head, Jack moved toward her. "Mrs. Van Meter'll start foreclosure in three months. I'll give it two weeks."

"Two weeks!" Carrie jumped up and down like an angry elf. "You can't get results from a *lemonade stand* in two weeks! Make it two months, and I can almost guarantee things'll be better." She gnawed on her lip and took a deep breath. "Jack, I think this is what the Lord wants."

"What?"

"I feel it." She placed a delicate hand over her middle. "I feel it inside."

"Aw, that's just a stomach ache."

Carrie stamped a booted foot. "No, Jack!" She slowed herself to gain composure. "I think God's spoken to me again."

Ben turned to leave. "Uh, I think I'll take that walk now."

"Ben, wait." Carrie grasped the old man's arm. "Jack, I'm serious."

Jack's expression and tone softened. "Really?"

"Really."

Jack looked down at a half decomposed trout and shuffled his feet. Then he peered up at his wife and stuck out a stubborn chin. "One month!"

"Sold!" Carrie shouted and felt a strange confirmation from inside. This is what they were supposed to do. It was the right thing. "One month. And I think the Lord will show us his plan!"

"Well then, he'd better give us at least one good idea by tomorrow." Jack marched back to stand directly in front of her. "Because, if he doesn't, we're going to start packing."

Carrie's mouth dropped open. "You said a month!"

Jack's tone became deep and ominous. "A month to build the income, but we'd better know how we're going to go about doing that by day after tomorrow, Carrie. I'm not going to sit around waiting for ideas for a month! Either we have a workable plan real soon, or we're leaving. I mean it!" He scraped a glob of muddy, green goo from his boots onto the boardwalk/dock. "And I'll be honest with you. I'm not as certain about this divine guidance as you are." He turned and started back toward the truck. "So you might as well get ready to pack."

"We'll see about that, Mr. MacGregor," she muttered under her breath.

Ben followed Jack, but Carrie trailed behind, walking with a slow, contemplative step. She glanced up at perfectly crafted, cotton ball clouds glued to an almost too-deep blue backdrop. *Lord, give us a way to make a living up here! Please, give us a miracle!*

Chapter Seventeen

Bang, bang, bang!
     Someone pounded on the door twice before Jack could get his pants on. And, by the time he slid the bolt back, it had happened again only much harder.

"Hey," Ben bellowed through the closed door, "you two gonna sleep all day, or ya gonna come on out here and hear my good news?" He whistled "Leaning on the Everlasting Arms" through the closed door while he waited for a response.

Jack finally fumbled the door open and squinted at Ben's sunrise silhouette. He blinked both eyes once and opened them wide in an attempt to focus. "Ben, what's wrong?"

"Not a dad-blamed thing, son. But God just solved your problem for ya!" He slapped Jack on the shoulder and almost knocked him off balance.

A still half-slumbering MacGregor tried and failed to comprehend why Ben was acting so strange. He wasn't exactly bouncing on his heels, but he was minus his usual laid-back manner and appeared obviously excited about something.

"It came to me in a dream," the old man said, "just like Ruth gets 'em. I should have thought of it myself; it was plain as day. I should have remembered, but I just didn't. So the Lord had to remind old Ben while he was sawing logs!"

"Ben, what are you talking about?" Jack leaned on the door jam and scratched his stomach.

"What is it, Jack?" Carrie shuffled into the mud-hall, tying her robe belt into a bow.

Jack answered over his shoulder, "It's Ben."

"What does he want?" She yawned as she stopped behind her husband and leaned her head on his arm.

"That's what Ben was about to tell me. Wasn't it Ben?"

All four sleepy eyes turned in the farmer's direction.

"The Lord's given me a dream," he said. "About how you're going to plug up the hole in your money bucket till your chicken ship comes in." He produced a large closed-lip smile in honor of his own mixed metaphorical cleverness.

"Yes?" the MacGregors said in two-part harmony.

Ben smiled and paused just a moment. "You're going to work for the SP...the Southern Pacific Railroad...in the Rail-yard down past town. You can work as a switchman."

Dumbstruck, Jack didn't answer right away.

"You know," Ben continued, "throwing track switches for trains and such. Mostly in the freight-yard. That's where they start most of their new switchmen off." Ben pantomimed the process of throwing a switch, as best he could.

Jack remained silent. This had come out of nowhere, and he just didn't know how to respond.

Ben seemed disappointed. "Well, why the long face? God and me just solved your worries."

Jack said the first thing that came to his mind. "But I don't know how to be a switchman. I don't know anything about trains at all." This was true enough, along with the fact that working in a rail-yard did not appeal to the young ex-pilot in the slightest. He already felt it had been a little bit of a step down for him to dive into the chicken business, but, at least, in that he had the satisfaction of knowing that he was his own boss. *He* was the rancher, not the ranch hand. But on the railroad, especially in the freight-yard, he wouldn't be anything special, just another dirt-stained laborer, beholding to a boss. No, it did not appeal to him, but, in the present situation, he didn't see that he had much choice. However, he did not voice any of these opinions. He merely added, "Don't they want experienced men?"

Ben laughed. "Well, where do ya think ya *get* that experience? Railroad college?" He shook his head. "They train you right there in the yard, boy. No, what they want is a recommendation, like from a relative that works on the road or a yardmaster." He pointed his thumb at his chest. "That's where I come in. Yardmaster's a friend of mine. Stub Mahoney. That's why I know a little about it. From what Stub's told me over the years." Ben rubbed the end of his nose. "Back before Fuzzy Mason bought the inn, me, him, and Stub was all in the Rough Riders with old Teddy Roosevelt down in Cuba, don't ya know. That's why, after T.R. became president, he came up here now and again. He knew us from the war with Spain. He'd ride one of Stub's trains up, stay at Fuzzy's inn, an' I'd take him up into the hills so's he could shoot himself a deer or a black bear or something. Yep, old Teddy knew us all right." Ben seemed to drift off for a second, then with a blink returned from his ethereal journey. "Well, any old way, I'll take ya to Stub." Ben winked as he nodded. "You'll get the job, son." He yawned, his mass expenditure of energy at such an early hour finally catching up with him. "Then you can keep this old chicken ranch we all worked so hard to put back together." He smiled.

Carrie let go of Jack, straightened up, and closed her eyes. "My miracle. Thank you, Lord!" she said softly.

Ben turned his right ear toward her. "What's that?"

"Nothing, just thanking God for this job."

"Oh, that's what you was doin'," Ben said. "I didn't catch it all."

But Jack had caught the grateful prayer spoken behind him, and now he felt a little ashamed. His wife had prayed for a miracle and considered this news to be God's answer. However, while Ben had been telling him about the miracle-job that God had provided, Jack had been praying that somehow the thing would fall through. *Oh, Lord. Please...no. Not a rail-yard. Please, not a rail-yard.* He did not want to seem reluctant to either his neighbor or his wife. He did not want to neglect his responsibilities to his family. But, in spite of all that, he still did not want to work for the railroad. He wasn't proud of these thoughts, but in reality, in his heart, he really *did* believe he was too good for this kind of manual labor. He believed...deep down...he deserved better, and knowing this about himself caused him a certain amount of shame. This then provoked a little four second, internal, Dutch Uncle talk.

So are you going to let this chance to make up for past flops just go by? You going to fail as family provider again? Just because it's not a flying job or a book publisher's contract? Poor baby! Boo hoo! Now, take your thumb out of your mouth. Act like a man and take the job! Your family needs you! Nobody asked you if you liked the idea or not!

Jack forced a smile and shook Ben's hand. "Thanks, Ben. I don't know what to say."

"Ya just said it. But wait 'til I call Stub before ya start packin' your lunch. Just shows respect for me to ask him first. Makes the little varmint feel important. I'll probably give ya a final Amen on the subject before supper." He yawned again and started off toward his house, but stopped after a couple of steps and turned around. "Ya know, this is the first time the Lord ever trusted me with an important, straight-from-his-mouth message." He smiled. "I like it," he said. Then he disappeared downhill through the pines.

"Praise God!" Carrie shouted after him.

"Praise the Lord, and Amen," came the response from beyond the trees.

Carrie hugged Jack like he'd just come home from the war. "Isn't it wonderful, Jack! A job! You've got a job! Now we can stay!" She hugged him harder.

Jack turned to face his wife and held her lightly in his arms, but he did not hug her. "Yeah," he said into her hair.

242

"Great." He hoped she wouldn't detect his lack of enthusiasm. Sometimes Carrie was too good at that.

Chapter Eighteen

The front wheels of the little pickup hit a rut, bringing everyone on the front seat at least four inches into the air. Carrie sucked breath through her front teeth and shot her husband a worried glance. "Jack, be careful!"

Jack squinted into the rising sun and navigated around the next hole. "Those chickens in the back are dead, Carrie. I don't think a bump or two's gonna bother 'em." He grinned. "What, you think I'm going to wake Ben up or something?"

Ben stirred a little at the mention of his name. He scooted himself closer to the passenger side door and pulled his broad-brimmed straw hat farther down over his nose. "I'm awake," he croaked. "I just *look* dead."

Carrie gave out an impatient sigh. "That's not what I'm concerned about, Mr. Smarty-pants, there's eggs back there. Remember?"

"Oh, yeah." He seemed to take the reminder with appropriate humility and let off the gas a little.

Now one hundred percent awake, Carrie looked over at Jack and realized he had his jodhpurs and flying jacket on yet again. "That's what you're going to wear to work in the rail-yard?" She snickered.

"It's just what I happened to grab this morning." He sounded annoyed and slightly self-conscious.

"Or maybe you just want everyone there to know you were a pilot." She only meant to tease him, but felt sorry and recognized it as a mistake as soon as she said it.

He didn't respond.

The next time Jack made an evasive swerve, it was so abrupt it threw the trio hard—first to one side then to the other. Carrie *tisked* so loud it almost echoed off the windshield.

"You know, if you didn't drive so fast," she said in her most superior tone, "the ride would be much smoother."

"You want to drive?" Jack's voice swelled with sarcasm.

Carrie's eyebrows went up, and she contemplated giving the driver a full report on how much driving skill he actually possessed. Instead, she simply said, "I can, you know."

Now, Jack's forehead furrows rose to his hairline. "Drive the truck, you mean?"

"Of course," she replied. *Better than you,* she thought. The resonant sound of Ben snoring escaped from under the hat next to her.

"Really." He gave her a very doubtful look.

"I drive the Stutz like a demon." Pride spread across her face, raising her eyebrows and one corner of her mouth.

"You can say that again." Jack chuckled while he shook his head.

"I mean I'm very good," she fenced at his face with a correcting finger. "Better than most *men* I know."

Jack's countenance straightened. "This doesn't drive like a Stutz. It's more like herding a drunken camel down the road." He glanced at her body. "Your arms aren't strong enough."

"I drove this truck a little before…when Floyd had it… while the boys and I were living at the ranch with he and Hannah." She nudged Ben; he stopped snoring.

"How much is a little?"

"Once or twice a week. Whenever they got too busy to get away from the ranch but needed something from town. I'd be the one to go and get whatever was needed."

Suddenly, the pale headlights revealed the dirt road turning into two rough-paved lanes. The truck leapt onto the blacktop with a noticeable change in the ride.

Jack relaxed his grip on the wooden steering wheel. "Ah, that's better. So, you say you can drive this truck better than I can. Right?"

"No, Jack. That's not what I said! You're putting words in my mouth."

Jack waved her off. "No, I think you should have a fair chance to prove your skill as a truck driver."

"Oh, Jack! You're making too much of this! You're being a bore!" *Now, why did I have to say that?* Carrie knew she'd just made the situation worse. But then again, at the moment, she didn't care enough to stop herself. "I do wish you would just let it go!" But Carrie knew her challenging, judgmental tone would not help him do that. She could hear his breathing become more labored, as his irritation progressed toward anger.

"Okay," he said as they neared town. "Why don't Ben and I just jump off at the train station and you can go make the delivery at the inn?" He gave her a quick, humorless glance. "I'm sure they'll give you any help you need unloading. There's not that much in back, anyway."

Now it was Carrie's turn at anger. "That's just fine, Jack. Because that's what I'm going to have to do anyway."

"What do you mean?" He slowed the Ford a little and swung around a horse pulling a hay wagon with a middle-aged man at the reins.

Carrie sat for a moment before answering and concentrated on the scenery out the windshield. She didn't do it to aggravate Jack, although right now that prospect amused her. Rather, she wanted to give herself a chance to calm a rising tide of competitive hostility within before things got out of control. She wanted Jack, for the most part, un-rattled when he met his perspective employer.

Ahead, the amber incursions of dawn swept into the confluence of Saber and Soledad Canyons, giving an almost Midas touch to trees and rocks that barely five minutes before were illuminated only by a light-starved, gray promise of day. Carrie let God's morning balm soak into her spirit. She took in a deep breath, and exhaled the Devil's handiwork.

"With you working twelve hour shifts, like Ben said, I'll have to do all the deliveries, plus bring you to and from work." She spoke in an easier tone now, with no provocation in her manner. "Were you planning to make the deliveries?"

"I was going to try."

"When were you going to do it?"

"Before or after work."

"No, that wouldn't do. You'll be too tired after a shift that long. I'd say I'd better be able to drive this little truck. Don't you think?"

Again, Jack had no argument. "Uh, yes." His voice sounded a little calmer now. "I guess you'd better at that."

"By the way, who did you figure was going to drive the truck back today?"

"Ben."

She shook her head. "Oh, Jack."

He kept his eyes straight ahead as they pulled up to the station platform and stopped. He pulled the column shifter out of gear, set the hand brake, and turned toward his victorious wife. "Well, she's all yours then." Tense neck veins standing out again betrayed Jack's still simmering emotions. "I'm not sure I like it, but she's yours."

He got out and walked around the front of the truck to Ben's side. Carrie slid over behind the wheel as Jack reached in and nudged Ben. "We're here, Ben." Jack spoke just loud enough to wake the man up, but not startle him.

Ben turned a little and rose up in the seat, blinking at the new day that had just begun to sneak into the canyons from behind the eastern hills. He pushed his hat up. "Yes, we are." His arms stretched skyward. "Yes, indeedy." The old man opened the door and rolled out onto his feet. He squinted at Jack. "I'll wait for you up there." He pointed to a cast iron and wood bench up by the ticket office. Then he turned and tipped his hat to Carrie. "Well, since you're drivin' today, I'll get this young man a' workin' and meet you in the inn's lobby."

"All right, Ben," she answered out the window.

Ben clapped Jack on the shoulder and was gone.

Jack clicked the door shut and leaned into the cab. "I know you can drive the truck, Carrie. You just made me mad when you said you could drive it better than me."

"I didn't say that, Jack."

"No?"

"No."

He rubbed the back of his neck and his expression softened. "Thought you did."

She swiveled around in the seat to face him. "No." She nibbled on her lip a little. "There *is* something I've wanted to mention, though. I think I should get my car back. Two cars would make things a lot easier."

Jack's soft expression evaporated and was replaced by a full-blown scowl. "I don't like you crawling back to your father for anything!"

This took Carrie off guard; why was Jack taking that attitude. "I *wouldn't* be, silly. *Roger* has the Stutz, not my father."

Jack's face didn't change and he sounded even angrier. "I don't want you begging to any of your family!"

Carrie could feel frustration closing in again. "I wouldn't have to beg anyone. It's *my* car. My brother will bring it down whenever I like."

Jack groaned. "I don't like it."

Carrie hoisted her voice back onto its superior high horse. "It is my car."

Jack's tone became more chilled than the high desert morning air. "*Yes*, it is." He just stayed there for a second, leaning on the door and staring at her with a look she interpreted as disappointment. Then he nodded and straightened up. "I'd better catch up with Ben. See you tonight." He turned and went up the steps to where the old man waited.

"Yes," she said out her window a little too low to be sure he heard her. "See you tonight." She watched him walk up to the station platform and turn toward where Ben sat on the bench. She puzzled for a moment over her husband's stubbornness but finally tired of the subject and backed the truck into the street. *Time to take care of the business at hand,* she thought and drove to the Hunter's Inn.

Once Carrie arrived, Henri had his busboy, Raul, unload the chickens and eggs from the truck. The Cajun handed her some cash plus the inn's too-small order for the next week and excused himself, begging the press of managerial duties.

Suddenly, Carrie found herself alone in the hallway leading out of the kitchen. That's when the fatigue gripped her, followed close by an almost bottomless feeling of empty. There had been two arguments, nearly fights, with Jack just in the time it took to drive to town. He'd almost seemed to be spoiling for it.

I don't understand.

He was on his way to a new job that could mean their financial salvation. He should be happy, but he didn't seem so. Didn't he want the job? Carrie had no answer, and found only more confusion when she attempted to contemplate the matter. In fact, that particular deliberation made her feel even more tired and empty than she did before she tried to unravel it all. In the end, she decided to put the subject of male mysteries aside for the time being. Maybe revisit it at some future date when she had more energy and interest—or maybe not.

She walked unconsciously down the hall, still wrapped in thought, until she passed through a swinging door and found herself in the lobby. There, an unexpected blessing revealed itself from the back of the room—an enormous, overstuffed chair sitting like an Asian potentate as it faced the main entrance to the inn. Within two seconds, Carrie had made her way to this beckoning siren of comfort and had sunk her slender body into its inviting depths.

She sat thus now, not moving much at all, but letting every iota of womblike comfort soak its way through her outer senses and into the most sensual, selfish portion of her mind. She had been awake, super-focused and *at 'em* since the crack of dark. All her wake-up-and-perform-perfectly juices had been flowing like a torrential river for over two hours now. And those juices would have kept flowing thus, unimpeded by personal considerations of comfort had she only not sat in this chair. But now that she had thrown her Van Burean discipline out the window and crossed the line of self-denial into a territory more suited to humans, she found that she had, without realizing it, passed beyond an invisible point of no return. She was firmly caught in the chairs clutches at this point and could not escape. The quick-forming addiction to its pampering pleasures had proved too strong. She would stay here forever, and she knew it. Or, at the very least, she would remain, like Ulysses, for years, leaving only when the world ended...or Ben showed up from the rail-yard. Whichever came first.

Soon, after giving her surroundings a visual once over, she decided she liked the *room*, too. The pine plank floor reeked of honest reality, mildly softened by the huge braided rugs under the furniture. Its walls, river rock comprising the bottom half and varnished hewn log the top, gave her a sensation of security, as if she sat inside of some great, fortified nest. That felt good, too, and she knew why. It was something for which she had longed many years. It was how she would liked to have felt when she was little, had her father ever taken her up into his arms, a thing that had never occurred. It was vaguely like the feeling she got when she thought of God surrounding her with *His* love and protection. *Yes, I like this room.* Then it hit her.

This is what you want me to know, isn't it, Lord. I'm not alone; your arms are always waiting for me. You're my father. Carrie smiled. She liked this revelation. So much so that, after settling back into the chair's over-abundant stuffing, she allowed herself to relax...for the first time in months.

She stretched her feet out onto the rug and crossed her ankles, fixing her gaze, minus any particular reason, upon a lone black bear trophy-head, mounted high on the wall above the entrance. This being the first opportunity she'd had in days to truly let go, she decided to take full and rightful advantage of it. *No serious thought while I'm in this chair. For the next twenty minutes my activities are restricted to staring at yon hapless bear and maybe attempting a tiny nap.*

Chapter Nineteen

The rolling, metallic thunder of ten freight cars, drawn taut behind an angry, straining steam locomotive, echoed like a coming storm against the ears of anyone within a quarter mile of the Sweet Springs freight-yards. The insolent hiss and determined chug of controlled steam joined together to create an industrial symphony that sang the praises of the steel age. Blackish-gray smoke carried coal soot dozens of feet into the air, where it formed a dark, translucent cloud that would shortly settle and coat everything beneath it with a dull, choking layer. This would eventually work its way toward the interior of all things, strangling off any semblance of color, giving those things that had life within them the same morbid pallor as those which did not.

In the midst of all this, Ben and Jack walked on either side of the very Irish yardmaster, Stub Mahoney, both non-railroaders trying hard not to trip on the rails as they went. Each of the yardmaster's hands lacked two fingers, the reward from a lifetime of coupling freight cars together while working with sometimes-careless engineers or conductors.

"This here's Jack MacGregor, the friend I told you about." Ben struggled to keep up with the brisk pace Stub set as he high-stepped across the yard. The gait seemed to Jack like something between a fast walk and a slow run.

"So you're the Scot, are you?" Stub asked in a County Cork brogue, not too diluted by decades spent in the States.

Taken off guard by this tact, Jack muttered, "Uh, my family is Scots, but they've been here over a hundred years, I think. Long time now."

Stub eyed the younger man peripherally. "Well, that's time enough to sober up, ain't it, lad."

Jack didn't answer while he contemplated whether he'd been insulted or not. He'd almost decided he *had been* when Stub's hard granite expression cracked into a wide grin that made Jack think of a stocky, bald leprechaun with a handlebar mustache.

Stub laughed and slapped the taller man hard on the back with a mangled, two fingered hand. "I was just playin' with ya! There's a good boyo! I'm sure your clan's as good a stock as any." He continued to chuckle. "I like Scots. Especially Highlanders. They waylay Englishmen in the night, and they make passable whiskey, two of the more admirable attributes of a race." He feigned embarrassment. "Uh, oh...sorry, Ben."

The old man shook his head. "I'm from Kansas, myself. Don't mean nothin' to me. You gonna give this man a job or you gonna keep makin' jokes where you're the only one laughin'?"

Stub ignored Ben and turned to Jack. "See. Ya let a man save your life a few times, and he thinks he can talk to you any way he likes." He glanced back to his friend. "Yes, he's got the job, ya big sweaty mule, ya! Just so long as he can get along with Crusher."

That got Jack's attention. "Who's Crusher?"

"Ain't Stub here a likable old cuss?" Ben interrupted. "That's why we let him into the Rough Riders even though he didn't have all the parts the Lord sent him down to his mama with." Ben grinned and wiggled all ten of his fingers up into the air. "He was just such a sweet, little feller we just couldn't resist takin' him in. Kept 'im around sorta' like a pet, don't ya know."

Stub stopped walking and faced his old friend, pointing one of the three digits he had left on his right hand at Ben's nose. "They let me join because I whipped every man jack of 'em at the recruiting station."

"'Cept me and Fuzzy," Ben added.

Stub subsided a little. "Right. Except you and Fuzzy."

Both old veterans were silent for a sacred moment until Jack cleared his throat and repeated his original question. "Uh, who's Crusher?"

Stub pointed toward an extremely large, clean-shaven, salt and pepper haired man in pinstriped overalls and a mangled, coal stained Fedora. "That's Crusher," he said.

The man was in the process of hoisting a much smaller fellow, who looked like a hobo, off the ground by the shirt. He spoke directly into the hobo's face, then, after a few seconds, tossed the hapless transient almost ten feet. The poor fellow landed shoulder first in a small cloud of dust and sprawled backwards over a rail. "I said get out of here," the monster bellowed and took a menacing step toward his victim, who gathered himself up onto his feet as best he could and limped off toward the riverbed east of the yards.

Ben whistled to indicate being properly impressed. "He's a big one, ain't he."

Stub nodded. "About six-eight I figure, and probably tips the scale at about two-fifty or so." He sighed. "He's a little rough on bums and switchmen on occasion, but he gets the trains put together on time and keeps the yard running smooth. That's what makes the bosses happy, and that makes me happy." The leprechaun turned to Jack. "If you can keep him at arm's length until he gets used to you, you've got yourself a job."

Jack stood with one foot on a rail, sizing up the creature that would soon be his immediate boss and was put in mind of another time at an Army airfield in France when he first saw his new gunner coming toward him across the grass before a morning flight. That man had looked every bit as intimidating as this one and had been even bigger. *Why do I always get these gorillas?* he asked himself, but he said, "I think I can deal with this man all right."

"Done, then." Stub slapped Jack on the back again, smearing some new coal soot that had already settled there.

"I'll do the honors, and we'll pray he doesn't eat ya up like a sweet tart the first day." He stuck the remains of his right hand out to his old friend. "Ben, I think it's best if you take your leave now. You'll find out how it all went in due time."

Ben shook Stub's hand. "See ya soon and thanks."

"My pleasure."

Ben bid farewell to his neighbor and set off toward town. Stub and Jack started off in Crusher's direction. The man noticed them and stood, waiting and glaring with arms akimbo.

"Where'd he get the name Crusher?" Jack caught the top of a rail with the toe of his boot and almost stumbled but kept his balance. In the distance, he saw Crusher shake his head.

Stub's hand suddenly shot out and caught the younger man's shirtsleeve, stopping him where he was in mid-step barely half a second before a lone freight car, minus locomotive, clacked by on the tracks Jack had been about to step over. The ex-pilot sucked his next breath into a chest constricted with delayed tension from the near miss. He had neither seen nor heard the car coming. Less than ten minutes into the first day on the job, and Stub had already been obliged to save his life.

"Thanks." Jack held in his next breath a little longer than usual.

Stub nodded toward the little switch engine puffing and pushing another freight car over the top of a small hill at the east end of the yard. It forced the car over the crest and let it go to coast down the tracks, unmanned and alone, toward where the yardmaster stood. An elderly man standing beside a switch a few yards away pulled up and back on the switch's lever and changed the direction of the track intersection, sending the car down the next track over, where it slowed, then lightly collided and coupled with a string of flatcars already waiting there.

"You gotta keep your wits about you when you're in the yards, lad. When they cut a car loose from the hump…" he pointed to the little hillock where the half-sized locomotive worked to force another reluctant car to the precipice. "They're not going to sound a whistle or anything. You got to watch out for it." Stub resumed his high-stepping race across the rails. "Some say it's because he uses his fists to get his way with men."

A moment of confusion settled upon Jack at the abrupt turn in the conversation. "What?"

"Crusher," Stub said. "How he got his name."

"Oh, yeah."

Stub glanced back up a row of cars as an empty gondola rocked along the track behind them. "Others say he arranged for some poor sot to get crushed between two cars while they were working together. As the story goes, the other fella owed him money and either wouldn't or couldn't pay."

"I see." Jack was now looking up and down the yard area too, not wanting to tempt disaster a second time. "Thanks again, by the way. I didn't see that car coming."

"T'was nothin'." Stub kept looking around as he walked. "That was your free one. I doubt that anyone'll keep that much of an eye out for you from here on in."

Jack didn't answer. He just followed Stub the last few feet to where Crusher waited.

As the two drew within earshot, the leprechaun swelled up his chest and began barking at the monster. "This here's a new helper for you. Put him with anyone you like, but make sure he learns the ropes. He's a friend of a friend. You understand me?"

Crusher's eyebrows went up, scrunching his forehead into furrows like a plowed field. He pointed at Jack's flying gear and sneered, "What's the funny suit for?"

Stub snapped back before Jack had a chance to answer. "He was a pilot until late, but he'll drop by the company store and get some proper railroad togs when this shift is done."

Crusher shrugged. "You're the boss." Then he turned back to the switch engine on the hump as if he'd lost interest in the yardmaster's presence.

Stub snorted and turned to Jack. "You're on your own, me boyo. Keep your eyes peeled for…for anything. You understand me?"

Jack nodded. "I will, and, like I said, thanks."

Stub swiveled and walked away, waving a hand in the air and talking over his shoulder to his new employee. "Save your thanks for later 'til you're sure you're stayin'."

Jack watched after Mahoney for a while, then waited through an eternal two or three seconds of awkward silence. Crusher watched cars being pushed down from the hump, uttering no sound but bull-like breathing. Finally, the new man decided he'd better speak or be ignored the rest of the day. "Uh …is there anything in particular you want me to do?"

Crusher's eyes never left the switching operation as he finally responded to Jack in a low, guttural growl. "You say you were a pilot, were ya?"

"Yes." Jack stuck his hands in the pockets of his jodhpurs.

Crusher spat halfway between his boots and Jack's. "You fly in the Great War?"

Jack turned a large chunk of slag over with his toe. This guy was starting to make him uncomfortable. He felt a cat-and-mouse game brewing, and he didn't like it. He wished the man would just turn hostile and get it over with. "Yes," he said, not without caution.

"I suppose you were an officer and went to college, didn't ya?"

Here it comes, Jack thought, and he said, "Guilty on both counts."

Crusher turned around quickly. "Don't you get smart with me, college man. I'll whip you so bad your mother won't recognize you." He cracked his weather-leathered knuckles.

Jack relaxed a little, now that the game was over.

"College and flying don't cut no ice with me," Crusher rumbled. "Birds fly and cats eat 'em all the time. And, if college was any help, you wouldn't be here begging a job from me, now would ya?" He took in a deep breath and sighed it out. "All right, you're the yardmaster's pet, so you can stay until I can find a way to get rid of you, but hear this. While you're in my freight-yard you're nothin' but my trained dog. You do what you're told to do when and how you're told to do it. You're nobody here. Ya understand? You're nothin'! Matter of fact, I'm even gonna give you a new name." He put his hand to his mouth as if he was contemplating some great universal question. "From now on, you're gonna be Birdie, and that's all your flying means to me or anyone else here. Just a stupid, funny name, Birdie. That's you. Ya got it? I call for Birdie, you come!"

He didn't wait for an answer, which was good because Jack had already decided not to give him one, job or no job.

Crusher pointed to the elderly man standing by a switch about fifty yards away. "That's Homer. He's the least stupid switchman I got. You go stand by him today and see how much of the job you can soak up 'till six tonight. Be here again at six tomorrow morning, and I'll decide if you learned enough to stay." His face tightened up into another sneer. "Well, go on, get out of my sight or I'll throw you off the property right now!"

Jack decided it would only make matters worse to answer the man in any way, so he simply trudged off toward Homer. *He's trying to make me quit, just like the instructors in flight school. Well, he's not getting his way. This job is a temporary thing, and* I'm *going to be the one who decides when I go.* He reminded himself that his

258

family needed the money, and that reminded him that he was trying to be the more responsible, less selfish family man now.

That helped. It helped him refrain from walking off the job, and it helped him to *keep* walking to the switch where Homer stood with a confused look on his puckered, old face. In his mind, Jack kept repeating part of a scripture his Grandpa Floyd had recited to him about how husbands were supposed to sacrifice for family. *As Christ sacrificed himself for the church...as Christ sacrificed himself for the church! That* helped and even gave him a little satisfaction in what he was doing. It also kept him from running back and giving Crusher a high speed, front tooth massage. Jack decided that to leave the yard foreman's mouth un-punched was also a good thing.

Then a notion seemed to fly in out of nowhere and hit him square in the conscience. And the still small voice that came with that notion said that the Lord must have been using this experience to grind some of the arrogance out of the new apprentice switchman. *I get it, Father. Be mature. Be humble. Trust you.*

Tension left his chest, to be replaced by a peaceful confidence. And when he got close enough to be heard, Jack gave Homer a waist-high wave of greeting. "Hello. I'm Jack. I guess I'm supposed to be your helper today." He held out his hand.

Homer shook it, but looked confused. "Crusher hired *you?"*

"No. Mr. Mahoney did."

"Is that a fact? Well, I'll be!" Homer pushed his striped cap further back on his head and scratched a sweaty scalp. Then he rubbed his short, wiry, gray beard and shrugged. "Well then, first of all, you need to know how to throw a switch." He looked up at the hump and waited until a freight car started on its down-hill coasting ride.

"Watch close now. You pull this pump-handle-sort-of-thing out of this notch and all the way up until it sticks straight out." Homer followed his own directions. "Then you swing her around to t'other side of the switch and just plop her down into this other notch." He continued to perform the actions as he spoke it. "Then ya give her a little push to make sure she's in there good an' tight. And ya see?" The old switchman pointed at the switch frog that had changed the rail intersection's directional aim from one yard-track to the other, "We just lined the next car from that track into this one."

Jack stared intently at the process, logging it into his mind. Homer beckoned for his student to come closer. "Ya better step over here, son, or that freight car's gonna leave a permanent impression on your mind."

Jack looked up and saw the car coming toward him, picking up speed as it descended the grade from the hump. He stepped off the now unsafe track and stood beside his mentor-of-the-day as said car clacked by. However, on this occasion, unlike before, he made the move in plenty of time to avoid injury. Then he gave Homer a sheepish grin.

"Well, ya passed the first test, boy," the older man said. "Ya got enough sense to step out of the way of a moving railroad car. I might just be able to make a switchman out of you at that." He snickered once and grinned. Then he pointed up to the hump. "Now here comes a flatcar, and it goes down the other track there, so why don't you turn this old switch back to where it was before." Homer stepped back and waved Jack to the switch handle.

Jack nodded. "I can do that," he said as he came forward to grab the handle and apply himself to the task. But he thought, *There's got to be something wrong here. The job can't be this simple.*

Chapter Twenty

Carrie came to wakefulness with a jerk and found herself still sunk into the overstuffed chair, facing the bear-head trophy on the wall of the Hunter's Inn lobby. How long had she been asleep? She didn't know, so she looked about the room and found a monstrous grandfather clock near the hat rack. *Five minutes? I've only been asleep five minutes?* She could hardly believe it. There existed somewhere within her mind the vague recollection of a dream that must have taken at least a couple of hours to unfold. And yet the clock declared that time-table wrong. *How can that be?* Carrie tried to reconstruct the dream, although she wasn't sure why she cared so much about it.

She couldn't remember how the thing started off, but somewhere toward the end of this other reality her dream-self had taken off her shoe to look for a pebble. Then for some reason, she handed the shoe to her brother, Roger, just to hold for a second. At that same moment, Jack came along and told her to come with him but wouldn't let her get the shoe back from Roger. So she was forced to limp along with only one shoe. This turned out to be both an embarrassing and painful journey, ending with a bloody foot and Jack screaming at her to keep up in spite of her handicap. That's when she awoke. But why be concerned with this now that she was indeed awake?

Carrie explored her mental archives for any possible meaning—her mother had always told her all dreams have meaning that relate to real life—and, almost as soon as her search began, an answer materialized. It did not quite sound or feel the same as when the Holy Spirit spoke to her. As a matter of fact, it seemed very much more like it came from her own imagination. However, it *was* an answer that made a lot of sense, none the less, and carried with it a strong emotional current, so, at the moment, that satisfied her.

Roger's got my car, and Jack doesn't want me to ask for it back! She considered the dream analogy again. *I'll be hopping around on one foot, trying to deliver chickens and eggs and still get Jack to and from work. This isn't going to do, and he's being stubborn. Not to mention prideful.* She considered the consequences of the situation and decided they were not minor inconveniences. *I have to get my car back,* she thought. *I'll deal with Jack later. Besides, I won't actually be begging for it. I'll just* tell *Roger to drive it down. That's more like an order. Jack's pride should be satisfied with that.*

It all sounded good, but still something, some little hint of a dark cloud, some ethereal objection nagged at her spirit.

"You shouldn't do this behind his back," another, more familiar internal voice said.

Carrie hesitated for a little longer than an instant, then decided to ignore this vocal intruder. With much effort and regret, she extracted herself from the over-comfortable, overstuffed chair and headed for the polished pine phone booth she'd noticed against the south wall of the lobby.

Once there, she cocooned herself behind the glass-paneled accordion door, settled onto the tiny wooden jump seat, and slid a nickel into the coin slot.

In a second, the operator came on the line. "Number please."

Carrie leaned close to the receiver, almost brushing it with her lips. "Operator, I wish to place a long distance call to Mr. Roger Van Burean in San Francisco. The number is Lombard 9-5120." She relaxed back against the phone booth wall until she remembered something else. "Oh, and reverse the charges, please."

The flat, dispassionate tone of the woman at the switchboard echoed back through the wire like a metallic imitation of a human voice. "And who shall I say is calling?"

"*Whom* shall you say is calling," Carrie corrected automatically, then sighed and rolled her eyes at the little bit of upper class arrogance that had briefly surfaced again. "Lord, please help me with that," she said out loud before she realized.

"What was that, ma'am?"

Carrie shook her head with mild embarrassment. "Uh, nothing. Just say it's Caroline."

"Thank you. One moment, please."

A mild hiss began to flow from the ear-piece, followed by a small click, then silence while the operator left the line to perform whatever black magic it took to connect two people hundreds of miles apart. Carrie took that time to rebuke herself again. *I'd better learn to keep my dialogues with God internal or someday they'll come for me with a butterfly net.*

In the middle of this musing, came the electric warning, "Your party is on the line. Go ahead, please."

But Carrie's attention was still divided, and she barely noticed the operator's intrusion into her thoughts. She continued looking at the trophy bear, still lunging, jaws agape, out of the far wall, innocent guests passing through the lounge oblivious to his threat.

"Hello," the rude earpiece interrupted.

For some unexplained reason the sight of the bear prompted Carrie to continue mulling over the subject of butterfly nets and people who were thought to be insane.

"Hello?" The earpiece became more insistent.

Perhaps those who have lost touch with sanity see things like this poor bear, and think they're real.

She snickered a little and let her next words echo against the inside of the booth. "I wonder if most of the people in asylums were just talking to God and got caught doing it out loud in public?"

"I really don't know," Roger said on the other end of the line. "I haven't had the opportunity or the inclination to visit an asylum to find out. Is this why you called me collect, old dear, to discuss the criteria for judging the deranged?"

"Oh... Roger!" She jumped and flushed at his unexpected response to her out loud musing. "Very sorry. I was off in my own little world for a moment. Not my best morning."

"You better watch out." He apparently decided not to let her off the hook. "Much more of that, and someone's liable to allow you to find out what asylum inmates think first hand." He laughed. "But never fear, dear sister. I won't turn you in. Besides, I know why you called. You've been missing your sweet little Bearcat. Haven't you?"

"When can you bring it down?"

Roger was still in the mood to tease. "Well, how much is it worth to you, Darling?"

Carrie answered quickly. "If you drive it down right away, I promise not to break your obnoxious, scrawny little neck."

There was a moment's pause. "That's fair enough. You want to pick it up at Marner Bay?"

"No, bring it here to Sweet Springs." Carrie noticed Ben through the booth's etched glass. He was looking around the lobby, most likely for her. She knocked on the pane and gave a little wave. The old man touched his hat in proxy for tipping it and settled into the soft bowels of Carrie's people-eating easy chair to take up the vigil over the bear on the wall. Carrie estimated he'd be asleep in less than a minute, considering he'd already performed that feat in a Model-T truck on a dirt road.

"Where in the devil is Sweet Springs?" Roger's voice came soaked with amusement.

"It's between Palmdale and Newhall on Sierra Highway."

"Between what and who?" More stifled laughing. "I say, Dear Sister. What sort of backwater whistle-stop have you gone off to?"

"You can find it on any California roadmap. Just bring an extra bag of water and a sandwich; you'll have to drive through the Mojave Desert to get here. And, for Heaven's sake, bring a hat. I don't want you getting sunstroke."

"Why, Caroline. I didn't know you worried so much over me."

"I don't. I just want my car to get here."

Roger paused again. "I take it then, you and Father have not yet made amends."

"The boys and I left with only what we could carry and we had to meet our cab outside the front gate." She held her anger in check only with the greatest effort. "He shipped the car to the docks while I was still sleeping."

"Yes, I found that out from Mother when I called down." He sounded sympathetic and apologetic all at once. "I'm truly sorry, old thing. Father led me to believe that you were soon to follow the car to join me on some Tour de Wine Country. I never thought for a minute I was accomplice to a car-napping. I'll bring it down quick as I can." He paused. "By the way, what the devil are you doing in…where was it?"

"Sweet Springs." Carrie caught herself feeling a little impatient with her brother's provinciality. "Jack and I bought a ranch down here." She said that and waited for the inevitable snob reaction.

"A ranch? You're joking! Whatever do you grow on it?"

Carrie responded, knowing she might as well go through the dance and get the inevitable banter over with. Otherwise, Roger would drag his sarcasm out for months, if not years. "We raise chickens, Roger. We own a chicken ranch." She sighed the last words out, knowing she had given him all the ammunition he'd need for a long time to come.

She heard the small voice inside her again, saying "Discuss the car with your husband first," but she ignored it.

"Chickens! Of course!" Roger's comment brought Carrie back to the conversation at hand. "Chickens. Just like his Grandfather, old what's-his-name."

"Floyd."

"Exactly right. Floyd." He laughed, a little too high pitched for his gender—more of a giggle, truth be known. "Well, Caroline, the chicken rancher. This just keeps getting better and better, doesn't it."

"Roger, are you really going to bring my car down?"

Ben, having just awakened from *his own* momentary trip to dreamland, now looked straight through the phone-booth's glass door and raised his hands in an unspoken question about time passing. Carrie nodded and raised her index finger to signal she was almost through on the phone.

Roger answered. "Darling, I wouldn't miss seeing your new home for all the bathtub gin in Chicago." He laughed again, more heartily this time. "I'll be there with bells on!"

"All right then," Carrie said, reining in frustration. "Come to the Hunter's Inn. That's where I'm calling from."

"Yes, of course you are."

She ignored his taunt. "When you get there, ask the owner to give you directions to our place and to get in touch with me through Ben Smith. You know." She took a calming breath. "To let me know when you're coming. Jack and I don't have a phone yet. Oh, and not a word to Jack about the Stutz. I want it to be a surprise."

Roger sounded like he could barely control his amusement. "Right-o. Mum's the word. I have it all, and I'll be down before you can say 'bumpkin'!"

Carrie gave her brother a quick, cool "Thanks and goodbye", then hurried out to Ben, whom she had to wake up from his second nap since he'd arrived in the lobby.

"Boy, this here chair'll bring out the snores in ya if you're not careful." He yawned and stood up to stretch. "You callin' for your car?"

Carrie's expression dropped. "How did you know?"

Ben shrugged. "Don't know. Just seemed to figure, I guess."

"You think I should have told Jack first, don't you?" Carrie was shocked at her own words and had no idea why she'd spoken them to Ben.

"Not my business," he said as he led the way out to the pickup. "You might want to consider praying on it, though."

She decided to change the subject. "I assume, since you're here alone, that Jack got the job."

"Yep, he did." Ben smiled a mischievous smile. "T'weren't nary any doubt. Stub and me, we go a' way back."

He went to sleep again as Carrie drove him back to his farm. This left her with time to herself which she mostly used to consider all the ways having the Stutz back would make things easier. Even so, the voice inside her continued to poke at her conscience all the way up the road. "You should have told Jack first. You should have attempted again to make him see your side." And, no matter how hard she tried, she could not shut the voice off. She knew what she did wasn't going to help their marriage, even if it did make everything else easier.

Maybe I should have taken the time to convince him it was right. She considered that a moment, then shrugged. Too late now. She certainly wasn't about to call Roger back and stop him from coming down. That, she decided *would* be too much on the weak side for her. What was done was done, and that was that! The consequences would come later. *Still, I wish I knew just how mad Jack's going to get.* Carrie considered the inevitable storm of Jack's anger for an instant and decided to let him find out what she'd done when the car and Roger finally arrived.

Chapter Twenty-One

Carrie tripped on the mash hopper and flopped, face first, into a sea of Rhode Island Reds, sending chickens flowing like water in all directions. She had been measuring out that mash when she caught sight of Roger racing his dust up the hill in her Bearcat—Ben had just left after telling her that her brother had already started up from the inn. Now, overcome with relief at seeing her wayward Stutz, Carrie had lost all sense of where she was and simply lost track of the direction in which her feet were heading. Thus, her attempt to run out of the wire enclosure and down to the driveway ended in pain and humiliation without much progress toward the goal.

"Good, Caroline," she muttered. "That's how to meet family! Bruised and covered with chicken droppings." She spat out a feather as she regained her feet, then made her way to the driveway, brushing off her overalls with an aristocratic air. It'd been over a month since she'd called her brother. But who cared! Both he and her car were here!

Roger made a sharp, fast left into the drive and found refuge there, completely clear of the road, an instant before a swirling snake of dust would have devoured him. The Bearcat downshifted and brought Caroline's brother to a safe, dustless stop almost at her feet. Roger switched off the engine and raised himself up to perch atop the backrest of the seat with his feet dangling down where he'd just been sitting. With careless ease, he peeled off a pair of driving gloves and entombed them in their allotted case with a prompt snap to the lid. Then he slid the case into an ample pants pocket and ran his fingers back through his fine, dark brown hair. "You simply must have someone sweep that road off, darling. It's all covered with dirt!" He glanced back quickly as the last of his cloud drifted uphill past the chicken houses. "I say, I hope I didn't get your turkeys dirty!"

"Chickens," Carrie said her expected line with the customary smirk.

Roger rolled his eyes and smacked his forehead in mock revelation. "Chickens! Yes! Silly me! However could I have forgotten that?" He gave his older sister a wry smile and hopped out of the car. He combed his hair in the side-view mirror and wiped some of the road off his face with a silk handkerchief, continuing to use the same kerchief to brush off his stylish white golf togs, not to mention his black and white Oxfords. Then he gave the kerchief a brisk snap in the breeze. "So where's old Jack?" He folded the silken square and stuffed it and his hands into his slack pockets. "I should think he'd be here either feeding or plucking something. Aren't farmers supposed to toil from dawn to dusk? Or has he tired of that already and decided to go out to price second-hand airplanes?"

Carrie ignored the barbs and simply answer the question. "He's working for the railroad now, and, so help me, Roger, if you break into any kind of song about that, you're going to be sorry."

He held his hands up in surrender and shook his head. "The thought never crossed my mind, Sister Dear."

"Well, I know that to be impossible, but I'll accept your answer for now." Carrie crossed her arms and readied her best defensive attitude. Roger was a wealthy man's spoiled brat, Carrie knew, the same as she had been. But *she* had found a better way to view the world. *He* still thought of himself as a higher species on the social ladder and viewed all around him from that altitude. He considered money to be the proof of his family's natural superiority, and any protests made by others to the contrary were, of course, born out of simple jealousy.

Carrie knew this about her brother not only from dealing with him, but because that was the way both of them had been raised. It was the attitude and viewpoint of their parents, and something that, once in a while, she still caught herself dealing with inside her own mind. Understanding all this, she remained determined to say her straight-lines with all the innocence she could muster, even though she knew Roger had nothing but contempt for her new life. She would not be baited into defending herself. She would not give him the upper hand.

"It's true that we're making almost fifty dollars a week now, selling chickens and eggs to the inn, the little general store, and customers in town, but that doesn't quite pay the bills yet, so Jack's earning the money we need to get by until things get better."

Roger laughed. "Fifty dollars a week! Doesn't pay the bills? Caroline, what are you talking about? You have an expense account from Father!"

"That's a savings account now. Ten thousand. I'm keeping that for the boys' college. Father stopped all deposits to me the day we left the Marner Bay compound— the same as he did when Jack and I got married. Actually, he'd only been making deposits again for a month while the boys and I stayed with he and mother."

Roger nodded, then flicked a crusty Rhode Island feather off the shoulder of Carrie's work shirt. "Well, I must say, despite your financial misfortune, you've certainly managed to maintain a stunning wardrobe." He waved a hand at her debris-coated overalls as if he were presenting her at a fashion show. "I complement you on your gown, My Dear."

Carrie made a face of mock amusement. "Would you like to see the place?"

Roger smiled with what looked to Carrie like *genuine* amusement. "I can't wait!"

She gave her head a patrician shake, then started on the uphill path toward the out buildings. She motioned for him to follow. "I'll give you the three cent tour." They climbed the embankment up from the house to the part of the ranch devoted to the chickens. The closer they got, the more they

271

could hear the crowing of the cockerels over the general din of clucking that emanated from the other buildings.

"That's the cockerel house." Carrie pointed to a smallish building to the left of the path.

"Explain, please." Roger seemed a little winded by the short climb, but remained pleasant.

"Roosters. We keep them separate from the pullets." An uncomprehending expression crossed her brother's face. "Pullets are hens," Carrie said. "We have to keep them separate so the Roosters won't wear the hens out or fertilize their eggs. Also, cockerels are the first to be used as meat, so we usually want to keep them all in one place. We only kill a hen when there's a problem, like if she stops laying for good."

Roger feigned interest. "Yes, I see, and I assume by the noise and the smell that these three long buildings here," he pointed up hill, "are where you keep most of the hens?"

"Very good, Roger." Carrie added a pinch of her own sarcasm. Not the most Christian thing to do, but she couldn't resist responding in kind just once. "I'm impressed."

"Oh, really nothing to it. I just followed my nose." He sniffed and wrinkled his face.

She led him a little further to a small shed-sized, windowless structure. "We call this one Death Row. It's where we put the birds we're going to slaughter the next day, so we don't have to chase them around the larger building at the last minute."

Roger looked over the building's recent coat of red paint and made another face of disgust. "Gruesome."

Carrie couldn't help smiling a small, short smile. She'd broken her brother's *above-it-all control* for an instant—a lapse in his discipline. She also saw in his face and manner that he knew she'd caught it, and that made her smile again as she turned toward a little building, constructed on skids. "This is our brooder house."

"Where you go when you're in one of your foul moods. Correct?" Roger tried to regain his sarcastic footing, but it was too late for that. He'd already lost the advantage.

Carrie ignored his impotent attempt with more than a little satisfaction. "It's where we keep the newly hatched chicks. Helps more of them to survive. It's cleaner, protects them from the mature pullets, and it's got a heat lamp we use during cooler weather."

"A heat lamp!" Roger rallied to the opportunity for humor. "By George, Caroline. Does that mean this peasant paradise actually has electric power?" He blinked, open-mouthed, in mock shock.

Carrie blanched as she realized she had just given him another opening. "Yes, we have electricity. What did you think the poles were, coming up the road?"

Now Roger smiled. "Why, telephone, of course." He shrugged, then lightly smacked his forehead in comic recollection. "Ye gads, that's right! You haven't *got* a telephone!" Roger kept the innocent act going to set up his next maneuver. "And why, pray tell, are you telephoneless in this wilderness?"

Carrie closed her eyes and allowed herself an internal sigh. *Here it comes.* "Because we can't afford it yet. They want a fortune to bring the phone lines up this far." She answered in a flat, calm, matter-of-fact tone that held no apology and let her brother know it was time to move on to the next subject.

Roger looked up at the power line coming down from the tall, timber pole to the glass insulators on the roof of the ranch-house. His gaze followed the half dozen lines that spider webbed out from there to vital points on the ranch, including the brooder house. Then he glanced down the canyon at the line of poles that lead to town. "You know, from your lofty perch here on the hillside, thanks to the sparseness of vegetation, I can easily see most everything in your little canyon." He paused self-importantly. "There are only two or three other farms being served by this electrical line, but I can count at least five or six others within sight. What do all the rest do?"

Carrie nodded. "They use oil or kerosene lamps. A few have gasoline generators hooked to batteries, but most just get along the way farms and ranches have for centuries, without the benefit of Edison's miracles. Some places don't have brooders at all. They just let the hens mind the chicks. But they lose a lot of them that way." She sighed. "We've got one of the more modern places in the area now. It's had electricity since before the war, and that's almost unheard of around here." Carrie pointed to a small windowless building, half imbedded into the hillside just behind the house. "We even have an electric cold-house, to keep slaughtered chickens from spoiling before we can deliver them. I guess the people who owned this ranch before did a good business. They'd have to if they could afford power this far out from town."

Roger looked down at his Oxfords then dusted their toes on the back of his pant legs. "So what did you pay for this little slice of agricultural heaven?" He panned around at the dry grass and chaparral.

"Twenty-five hundred dollars. I know that's a lot more than the rest of the places in the area are worth, but, as you've seen, aside from the hundred and sixty acres, it's got electric power. Almost everything was already here. And it not only had a well and windmill, but, farther up the draw...." She pointed toward the top of a small fold between two hills. "There's a natural spring with a pond." She waited for some reaction to her news from Roger, but when none came, she elaborated. "That's very unusual around here. We're the only ones in Saber Canyon to have surface water—a pond, in other words."

Roger was finally starting to look bored. "I'm very happy for you." He yawned. "How much did you say you paid for this again?"

"Twenty-five hundred."

"There's something familiar about that amount, but I can't quite recall." He tapped his forehead as if trying to rack his memory.

"What is it?" Carrie's curiosity had been primed.

"Oh, I've got it!" He grinned, bounced once on his heels, and thrust his index finger into the air. Then he turned to face Carrie, his expression going totally dead-pan as he spoke in an amused and slightly contemptuous tone. "That's the exact amount of pocket money I carried on my last trip over to the Continent."

"Roger, you're not going to make me angry." Carrie said in an almost too-calm tone, but feeling a little distracted, for at the same moment, she thought she heard a car engine. So she turned her gaze toward the road…just in time to see the big, green Oldsmobile touring car with Hunter's Inn painted in neat, white lettering on the door. It, like the Stutz before, ran a little ahead of its own dust. And its driver, like *Roger* before, also made a high speed, left-turn into the driveway to escape the pursuing cloud. The out buildings nearest the road received another dusting, as the Olds came to a gravel-dragging halt right next to the Stutz. Carrie started down the path toward the visitors with Roger still in tow. "I'm not ashamed of what I've done or where I live, so you might as well give up trying to insult me." She squinted at the new arrivals. She'd expected to see Henri get out of the car, but these were two women, wearing big white aprons. "Now, who is this," she said to herself but also out loud, unintentionally provoking a response from her brother.

"Perhaps the Hatfields or maybe the McCoys."

Carrie shot Roger a quick, over-the-shoulder-glare, but kept walking.

"Mrs. McGregor! Haddie needs three more chickens!" The breathy voice, ripe with urgency, came out of Sue Linn, the attractive Chinese assistant cook from the inn. "Elks' Club dinner tonight, and they got more coming than they first told us!"

Ezzie, the equally blessed Mexican second assistant, stepped around from behind her co-worker. "Haddie's so mad at 'em, she looks like a tomato about to explode! She said bring them chickens fast, so Henri he give us the train station car and tells us to get going."

Carrie smiled and nodded. "That's not a problem. We'll just take three from death row."

"Where's that?" Sue wrinkled up her face.

"That red building at the end of all the white ones." Carrie pointed uphill. "Oh, ladies this is my brother, Roger Van Burean." She slid her arm around him and pulled him to the forefront. "Roger, this is Sue Linn and Ezmeralda. They are cooks at the Hunter's Inn." The women offered their polite greetings.

Roger reciprocated with a nod and a frosty "charmed".

Carrie let the subtle slight go by and threw herself into the task at hand. She pointed in two directions at once, her kitchen and *death row*. "Ezzie, why don't you go get a big pot of water heating on my stove. Sue and I will go get the roosters. We'll meet you at the preparation table on the front porch."

Carrie started to turn back toward the hill, but the girls didn't move. They just stood looking at each other.

"I'm going to ask her," Sue said to her kitchen partner.

Ezzie protested. "No, why should she know anything?"

Sue's tone remained determined. "I'm going to ask her."

"Ask me what?" Carrie waited, hands on hips.

"No!" Ezzie pulled back from Sue.

"Her great uncle's coming to dinner day after tomorrow, but he has some kind of stomach trouble. The doctor says no spices for a while 'til he's better. And Ezzie's mom only knows how to cook spicy food. Very good, but spicy. So Ezzie's mom asked Ezzie to ask Haddie for a recipe without many spices, but our expert cook is so up in the air about the Elks' dinner that she just told Ezzie not to bother her."

"She's always up in the air!" Ezzie quipped. "She's just a little farther up there tonight!"

Carrie stroked her chin. "Does your uncle like Italian-Swiss dishes?"

Ezzie shook her head. "Don't know. He's never eaten anything but Mexican food. Just like the rest of the family."

"Her mom's really nervous about it. I think she'd be ready to try anything...except Chinese." Sue made a face.

Ezzie put her hand on Sue's arm. "I'm sorry. She said he won't eat Chinese food."

"He's never tried it."

"I know, but Mama said he won't. I'm sorry." Ezzie patted her friend. "But *I* like the Chinese food you fixed for me. I told you."

Roger interrupted. "Uh, ladies!" He pointed to Carrie. "Could we get back to the subject at hand?"

Carrie took her cue. "I think the Swiss dish I have in mind will be just the thing. It's not spicy at all. It has an Italian name, which I won't bother you with. But, translated, it's called Farmers' Soup." She pulled a small pad of notepaper and a pencil from the bib pocket of her overalls. "I usually keep chick and egg counts on this, but today it will be the recipe book that Roger copies my dictation onto." She handed her open mouthed brother the items of transcription.

"I will?" Roger took a moment to glare, then closed his mouth and pasted on a Marner Bay social smile. "Why, yes. Of course, I will. I'd be delighted." He grimaced once, but took the pad.

Ezzie blinked. "You know this recipe … just out of your head?"

Roger responded for his sister. "She knows this one…and at least a hundred more." He seemed to smile with genuine pride. "Our family's chef was trained at Le Cordon Bleu, and he's been teaching Caroline practically everything he knows." He glanced at his sister. "How old were you when you began? Six?" He didn't wait for her answer. "I've eaten dishes prepared by each of them and could not tell the difference."

Ezzie looked confused. "What is a Le Cordon Bleu?"

Sue piped up. "I've read about it. It's a famous cooking school in Paris, France. They've taught chefs for kings, queens, and very rich people." She looked at Carrie like she had just met her.

Carrie cleared her throat. "Yes, well. Ezzie, better get the water heating. Sue, come with me." She started back up the slope toward the chicken area and spoke to her brother without looking back. "Come on, Roger. I need a secretary right now." Sue and Roger glanced at each other and followed the overalled ex-debutant up the path that lead to death row.

However, as they reached their destination, Roger stepped off to the side of the path. "I think I'll just wait outside," he said, still managing a smile as Carrie unlatched the red door to the house of the condemned.

"No, just come with us." She took a firm hold on his arm. "You've done this before haven't you, Sue?"

"Too many times."

"Then let's not tarry." Carrie pulled open the door to an explosion of rooster protests and minor attempts at flight. She ushered her unhired help in and latched the door behind them. Immediately, half the incarcerated flock took to the air. They squawked and rebounded off the opposite wall in an eruption of noise, feathers, and ammonia scented dust.

278

Carrie took a deep breath and dived, swimming pool style, into the largest mass of roosterhood, surfacing with a grin and a flapping cockerel in each hand. As Sue clapped her hands in admiration, Carrie bowed. "Practice, nothing more" she said and shrugged. The cocks continued to flap for their lives as their captress walked toward the door and Roger. Tightening her grip on her prisoners' legs Carrie looked into her brother's face and said, "Heat two tablespoons of olive oil in a large sauce pan and cook a large sliced onion for five minutes under a cover."

Roger's face contorted with incomprehension. "What?"

Carrie became impatient. "Write this down! It's the recipe!"

"Oh!" He flipped the pencil over and began to scribble.

Sue raced by in a circular chase pattern, after the remainder of the roosters. Feathers, the natural byproduct of this sort of pursuit, gradually filled the atmosphere within death row, including the obligatory dusting of powdered droppings. Unfortunately, much of the room's floating debris seemed to be magnetically drawn to Roger's white linen pants and palmaded hair. He sneezed violently and rubbed his nose with the back of his hand then continued writing at a furious pace.

"And cook for five minutes under a cover." Carrie said and peered down at the notepad in Roger's hand. "Got it?"

"Got it."

Sue made another dive for the cackling mob as they all completed another circuit of the shed. But she bagged no more than a handful of tail feathers for her effort. "Give me a second! I'll get one!"

"Take your time. These fellows aren't going anywhere." Carrie gave her birds a small shake, which started them squawking afresh. She turned back to Roger. "Add two sliced carrots, two sliced turnips, and stir until the oil coats them."

Roger spat something unidentified out of his mouth. "Right you are." More scribbling. "Oil coats them." He forced a smile.

"Hey, I got one!" Sue came up from the floor waving her rooster in the air while plumage rained down around her. "He must be the stupidest one. He just turned around and ran right into my hand!" She grinned the grin of momentary triumph, then humbly opened the door for her co-abductors.

Carrie led the way down to the front porch, holding her chickens out at arm's length and dictating to her brother over her shoulder. "Stir in two cloves of minced garlic."

"Right, garlic." Trying to write and walk downhill at the same time, Roger stumbled a little but managed to stay upright.

Ezzie stood waiting on the front porch as they arrived. "Water's warm already. I stoked the stove up a little."

"Good." Carrie gave one chicken to the empty-handed Ezzie and pulled three burlap sacks from under the porch's thick pine preparation table. "Let that cook four minutes."

"What?" Ezzie looked confused.

"Nothing. I'm talking to Roger."

Ezzie shrugged. "Oh."

Carrie forced the first rooster's neck between two large side-by-side nail-heads that stuck out a couple of inches from the table's thick, double-layered planks. She secured the critter's position with a length of twine wound around the nails, then she glanced quickly back at Roger. "Stir in five cups of shredded cabbage."

"Caroline, what in heaven's name are you doing?" The young, rich man's son squinted at his sister.

"We're adding the main ingredients to the soup now. Just make sure you get it all down." A warm breeze rustled through the pines that shaded the porch, and Carrie breathed in a waft of the soothing balm. She shook out one of the burlaps with her free hand and laid it beside the rooster's feet, which she still held with iron fingers. Then she grasped a hatchet that had hung suspended between two spikes driven into one of the porch beams. "Sue, why don't you take my brother off the porch till you're both out of range?"

Roger's mouth dropped open. "Certainly, you're not intending to—"

"Come on, Mr. Van Burean.", Sue interrupted and tugged on his pencil arm. Then she passed her own struggling cockerel to Ezzie.

"What? Why?" Roger whipped his gaze back and forth between Sue and his sister.

"Roger, you'd better take your white linen togs off the porch for a second or you're going to wish you had." Carrie raised the hatchet to shoulder height and paused, locking eyes with the man. "Five crushed tomatoes."

Roger looked up as Sue led him down the porch steps "Huh?"

Carrie sighed. "We're still stirring things in. Five crushed tomatoes."

The man looked uncomprehendingly at the note pad, then up at the poised hatchet. "Uh, I...."

"Sue, write it down for him please."

The surprisingly delicate fingers of the Chinese-American cook slid the pad and pencil from Roger's limp grasp with the magical gentleness that could almost surpass that of a seasoned pickpocket. That done, she continued the transcription. "Five crushed tomatoes. Got it."

Roger remained still, save for dropping his hands to his sides. He continued to stare at the hovering hatchet. "Caroline, are you really going to –"

Carrie's hatchet hand dropped and the rooster's head popped into a blue porcelain-coated pan that lay on the porch's weathered planks. The resulting blood splatter overshot the steps and came to rest a safe six inches from

281

Roger's feet. Carrie exhaled, satisfied with that result. Her brother's Oxfords had been saved.

Roger's face went gray as he looked down at the red spots on the ground in front of him. "Oh, my God!" He stumbled backward a couple of steps and stopped. "Oh, my God! What have you done?" He looked at his sibling as if he'd never seen her before.

Carrie shook her head. "I've merely killed a chicken, Roger. Nothing more."

The young man's knees wobbled for a second, then buckled, and he ended up in a seated position on the gritty driveway. "Oh, my God!" he repeated between short, fast breaths.

"Three quarts of vegetable stock," Carrie called out as she stuffed the flopping, blood-spurting carcass into the waiting burlap bag and put it under the table. It continued to jerk and thump between her feet and the table legs. Carrie gave the cavorting sack one glance then ignored it.

"Vegetable stock," Sue repeated, peeking around the notepad.

Roger took two deep breaths, then struggled to his feet. He dusted off the back of his clothing as best he could with trembling hands and watched, wide eyed, as his sister secured another bird for slaughter.

"Three teaspoons of chopped parsley," the executioner said and looked up to see Sue Linn nod. Carrie caught her brother's horrified stare, fixed on the condemned rooster, and she did not miss the sway of his body atop untrustworthy legs. Suddenly, all need to humiliate the young man dissipated, and pity took its place. "Roger dear," Carrie cooed. "Why don't you go into the house and lie down a while. I'll come get you when I'm done here." Her voice, filled with gentle concern, seemed to rally her sibling a little.

He appeared to regain a smattering strength, at least enough to climb the steps and speak. "I think I'll do that very thing," he said and waved without turning as he entered the little house. "Ladies, I bid you adieu. It has been the high point of my week."

The three women watched Roger as he left, then breathed a communal sigh and turned back to their tasks.

"Is that all that goes in your soup, Mrs. MacGregor?" Sue waited with poised pencil.

Carrie smiled after one last glance at the doorway through which Roger had just passed. "Certainly not. Let me see. What's wanting?" She searched her memory as she lopped the head off the second rooster, bagged him, and deposited him next to the first. "All right, there's also salt and ground pepper to be added."

Sue looked up. "How much?"

Carrie took the last bird from Ezzie and prepared the unfortunate fowl for his inevitable end. "Oh, to taste, I'd say." She looked back to Ezmeralda. "How ever much pepper your mother wants to risk on your uncle." She winked. "Tell her to let her conscience be her guide. If she wants, she can leave out the pepper altogether and rely on the salt alone." Ezzie nodded, and Carrie finished off cockerel number three. She stuffed him into a bag, as well, to spasm and bleed like those who had gone before, then she wiped her hands on a clean brown towel. "She should cook all that on a low flame for right around forty-five minutes."

Sue Linn finished writing and let pencil and pad hang with her hands at her sides. The hypothetical soup was done.

The work went quickly after that. The three women soaked, plucked, and dressed the ill-fated foul and had them wrapped and atop a dishtowel on the back seat of the green Olds in less than twenty minutes. Carrie had done most of the work with a well-practiced hand. That had helped to speed things along.

Ezzie's voice betrayed her amazement. "I've never seen anyone do chickens that fast. Not even Mama, and I thought she was the fastest *en todo el mundo*, but you take the cake, Mrs. MacGregor!"

"You're the bees' knees!" Sue added.

"Not the cat's meow?" Carrie feigned disappointment.

"I think your brother is the cat's meow." Ezzie flushed slightly. Sue poked her in the ribs, making her friend giggle. "He is *muy guapo!*"

Carrie chuckled. "Well, don't get too excited over him. I know he's pretty on the outside, but that's *all* there is. Just the outer shell. There's not much beneath that, I'm afraid." She tried to think of a good analogy. "Like a chocolate Easter Rabbit. Delicious to a point but hollow."

Soon, the Hunter's Inn girls and the big green Oldsmobile were once again racing the dust demon back down to town, their mission accomplished. Carrie cleaned off the chopping block, table and porch floor, emptied the chicken heads from the porcelain pan into a large outside metal trash can, then washed her hands along with the hatchet in the kitchen sink. She realized as she disposed of the chicken trimmings that she had mixed feelings about what she'd done to Roger. Carrie snickered when she thought about how out of place and uncomfortable he'd been in the world of chicken ranching.

She knew somewhere down inside her were thoughts that Roger deserved what he'd gotten, if not more. He was, after all, an obnoxious snob. On the other hand, he was her brother and cut from the same cloth as she. They had turned out very different, she knew, but still Carrie felt painfully aware that she too still harbored a bit of the Van Burean snobbery, even at this late date. So, with that being true, how could judgment be passed upon her brother for just turning out as his parents had raised him to be.

However, I'm not that way anymore, she protested within.

But another voice said, *You were blessed. God lead you away from the darkness of your past. You, yourself, did little to bring that about.*

Carrie felt sudden shame as she recognized the truth about her conversion to Christ and the changes the Lord had brought into her life. Much of it *was*, in fact, also the result of other God-led souls who had unselfishly helped her. Her brother, however, had not yet received any such guidance. At this point in her internal debate, she shifted, with reference to Roger, from self-righteousness to pity.

Carrie heard wood creaking toward the front of the house. She looked up from her work and saw Roger, done with his respite, descending the just-cleansed porch steps. She watched from the kitchen window as her little brother paced up and down the driveway, scanning his surroundings with seeming impatience. The warm evening breeze toyed with his well-lubricated hair, and made it difficult for his sterling-silver lighter to ignite his Gasper. But his mechanical Prometheus finally prevailed, and soon, a small white plume drifted away from his nostrils. He looked to be having an internal conversation of his own. Carrie wasn't sure what it concerned, but she was fairly certain he would tell her, probably as soon as she got within earshot.

Carrie dried her hands on a dishtowel and went outside, thinking she'd better get to him before he tossed his smoldering cigarette off into the dry grass, thereby starting the "Great Sweet Springs Fire of 1923".

Roger turned around just as she reached him. "Where on earth did you learn all those chicken tricks, all this chasing, and catching, and hideous chopping?" His shoulders shivered with such severity Carrie could see it. "Where did you gather all these backwoods skills?"

"The boys and I lived with Floyd and Hannah for six months. We learned much there."

"Oh, yes." He appeared to calm himself a little now. "You did all stay with the *Bloomer Girl Granny,* didn't you." Roger looked around his feet as if checking for mice. "By the way, where are your little lords of the manor? I'd almost forgotten them."

"The boys are out playing at a neighbor's."

Carrie's brother wiped clean hands across his shirt as if they were dirty. "Pity. I was so looking forward to some good old fashion farm hugging."

Carrie chalked up the subtle insult to her children as something Roger couldn't help, like a belch or a hiccup, and pressed on trying to salvage the conversation. "So, what do you think of our little place?"

Roger half folded his arms and stroked his chin. "You're serious, aren't you? All right, Caroline. Seeing as you insist upon pursuing this, I will tell you what I think." He paused then gave his answer in a significantly raised tone. "I believe that you have lost your mind!" He stared directly into her eyes and waved his arms as he spoke. "You are the only daughter of one of the most powerful and prestigious families in the country, and what are you doing? Playing the farmer's wife with a fellow who is very probably the second most irresponsible man on the West Coast!"

Carrie smirked for an instant. "With you holding first place, of course."

"Of course." He took a deep breath and let it out all at once. "What has happened to you? I do not understand. What could possibly induce you to turn your back on our family, our class…in exchange for squalor?"

"Do you really want to know, Roger, or is this just rhetoric?"

He leaned back against the door of the Stutz and folded his arms. "No, it's not rhetoric. I really wish to understand you because I confess that, for a long time now, I have utterly failed at that task."

"All right, then. But you're not going to like it." Carrie put her hands behind her back and stepped directly in front of him. Then she straightened his collar.

Roger let out a small moan as he pushed her hands away. "I imagine you're correct in saying I won't like it much, but ...pray do continue."

Carrie took a breath. "Brother dear, I've seen the light."

He stood up straight. "Oh, that again! Caroline, you sound ridiculous when you try to be religious." He patted his chest. "This is me! Roger! I'm the one who used to sneak Father's brandy with you. I'm the one you taught how to smoke!" He took a final draw off his Gasper and loaded it between his fingers to shoot it off into the brush, but Carrie snatched it away from him and crushed it out beneath her undainty farm boot. Roger shook his head and continued. "I'm the one you told to never stop being disagreeable until I got exactly what I wanted, and this last piece of wisdom wasn't passed to me that long ago!" He paused and seemed to relax again. "The only kind of light I know of is the type that turns on at the flick of a finger. Other than that, I have no experience on the subject."

She smiled a serene smile. "It's God, Roger. He's made me start to love my husband again, no matter whether he's rich or poor. And he's made me see my old life for the loveless illusion that it was. My life now is real, and my love for Jack is real. And, until you come to see things differently, there's little else I can tell you."

Roger rubbed his hands together. "Well, that's honest. Now, *I'll* be honest. This is a phase you're passing through. A long, long phase, true, but a phase none-the-less. Reality will eventually and once more break through this happily-ever-after dream of yours, and you'll wake up to find yourself not on the blissful little rose-covered farm you imagined, but a stinking, vermin-infested cesspit covered with feathers, foul blood, and chicken droppings. The sweet smell of your love will be replaced by the stench of ammonia-laden manure!" He stopped for a moment. "Sorry, old girl. I didn't mean to be so hard on you. You're my only sober relative...and I must confess a certain affection for you."

"I love you too, Roger."

He cleared his throat. "Yes, well." He extended his index finger toward Carrie's face, but kept it at a respectful distance. "You mark my words, you will tire of this game sooner or later and become once again the real Caroline we all know and admire. The sharp tongue, quick witted, woman of the world who knows how to squeeze pleasure from a stone. That's the true Caroline. I know her too well to be fooled, even if she has temporarily fooled herself."

Carrie felt a groundswell of sadness begin within, but she heeded the small voice that told her it would be useless to argue at this moment. She pulled open her bib-overall pocket and looked at a diamond encrusted pendant watch she had pinned there—her father's last gift to her from the Marner Bay Caroline's jewelry store and an item which could more than pay off mortgage on the ranch, had she chosen to surrender the timepiece to any of the reputable auction houses in Los Angeles. So far, however, the thing remained in her possession and safe from the auction block. "What time does your train leave?"

The young man grinned and glanced at his more masculine, alligator banded wristwatch, also from the family stockpile. "Six fifteen, according to the timetable."

Carrie closed her marsupial pocket. "It's five forty-five now. I'd better take you down. I've got to pick Jack up anyway."

Roger's face registered surprise as he looked her up and down. "Uh, don't you wish to freshen up just a bit first?" Roger pulled a stubborn remaining feather from its perch under Carrie's barrette.

She gave her clothes an unconscious, unnecessary brushing and smoothed her hair. "No, it's just Sweet Springs." She smiled. "And they have all seen me like this before."

Roger nodded and walked around to the passenger door of the Stutz. "Yes. Well then, without further adieu, let's to the train station."

Carrie answered his nod with one of her own as she slid into the driver's seat. Her brother bounced in beside her without benefit of opening the door. Carrie closed *her* door, turned the key, and flicked the ignition switch to ON position. Then she pushed the starter button and rejoiced inside as the long-missed, expensive growl of the finely tuned Stutz engine came to life. She could not deny that her parents' little gift still pleased her.

Had her father not had the money, he could not have afforded this treasured electric starter. She'd been starting the Model-T using every ounce of her strength applied to the hand crank for weeks now. A man's job for certain, Carrie had almost pulled a muscle on more than one occasion. But her Stutz remained a more cooperative beast and started at the touch of a finger. No other family in the canyon had a car (or truck for that matter) with a self-starter. They simply couldn't afford it.

Oh Lord, but this is wonderful!

She turned the car around and drove off toward town, feeling a small twinge of guilt over her desire for the easy driving Bearcat. But suddenly, another voice passed through her mind. It asked her if she actually believed she had brought this blessing about by herself. She answered it in her heart. *Thank you for restoring my car to me, Father.* Then she remembered something else. *Now all you have to do is not let Jack get too angry about it...please.*

She remembered the inner voice's warning her to win Jack over first on the subject of the Stutz and not to make an arrangement with Roger behind her husband's back. She had ignored that voice when she first called her brother to bring the car down. The recollection made her cringe just a little and goaded her to admit something to herself.

I should have gotten Jack to agree before I called.

She felt an invisible nod from inside and resigned herself to whatever was to come when her husband finally saw the Stutz.

Chapter Twenty-Two

Dayshift over, Jack passed the car-knockers' tool shed and had almost made it out of the freight-yards proper when Crusher clamped a viselike hand onto his shoulder. The gorilla-size foreman turned his newest switchman around in mid-stride, then, putting his foul-breathed mouth close to Jack's face, he rumbled, "What's the hurry, Birdie?"

Jack tried to manage something like an unconcerned smile. "Quitting time." He shrugged. "You know." When dealing with Crusher, he used the same rule that he'd read about in adventure novels. *When dealing with wild beasts and hostile natives, never show fear.*

Crusher grabbed a brake club that rested against one of the sheds. "As your foreman," he said, "I gotta make sure you're learnin' things." He shook the club in Jack's face. "What's this for?"

Jack answered quickly. "You slide it through the spokes of a handbrake wheel to give you more leverage when you're setting the brake."

Crusher snickered. "Yeah, that's right. But it's called tying off the brake, not setting it." He gave his student a half second's worth of eye lock and slapped his own palm with the thick end of the club. "This makes a good melon cracker too. Kind'a like a square headed baseball bat. Good to use on bums or smart-aleck mugs." He slapped the club into his palm again.

"I've never used it that way." Jack noticed that the men leaving the yard steered their courses to avoid what looked like another one of Crusher's *friendly chats*. It reminded him of the way water flows around big rocks in a stream.

"Yeah, I know that about ya." Crusher picked up a baseball sized chunk of granite slag, tossed it up a couple of feet and batted it out into the freight-yards like a poor man's Babe Ruth. The thing ricocheted off an ore gondola and narrowly missed Homer, who was walking between the tracks.

"Hey! Who did that?" The old man looked up and around as if he were ready to argue or fight, then he saw Crusher with the break club. "Oh," he muttered, put his head down, and kept walking out of the yards.

Crusher smacked the club on the side of the nearby shed. "Whose tool shed is this?"

"The car-knockers'," Jack responded.

"What are car-knockers?" Crusher leaned on his club.

"They repair damaged freight cars."

Crusher smiled. "No, they fix any car on the railroad! Passenger or freight. They do cabooses and gons, too."

Jack risked a question. "What's a gon?"

Crusher's smile broadened. "A gondola."

Jack nodded to indicate he'd filed the instruction for future reference. "Sorry, I've only seen car-knockers working on the *freight cars*."

Crusher tossed the club to the ground. "Yeah, that's mostly what gets bashed up around here, if you don't count the dopes that get caught in between or under the cars." He locked eyes with Jack again. "Gonna do you a favor, Birdie." He stretched his massive arms and yawned. "Some of the boys and I sit in at a regular poker game down at caboose number nineteen at the end of the last northwest siding."

"The one they call your office." Jack scratched the knee of his month old striped railroad overalls and ended up smearing some of the coal soot that coated them. He mopped sweat from his forehead with the sleeve of his gray work shirt and mused on how the blackish-gray residue didn't seem to show up so badly on the coarse monochromatic cloth.

Crusher grinned and spit into the slag. "Yeah, that's the place." He looked around at the men leaving the yard as if looking for someone. "Game starts in about fifteen minutes. You're invited." He folded his arms and assumed, in Jack's opinion, a what-do-you-think-about-that posture.

Jack didn't hesitate in answering, even though he felt the unspoken *you'd better be there* in Crusher's invitation. "Mr. Miliken, thank you for the invitation, but my wife's waiting in the truck. Besides, I'm not very good at cards."

One of Crusher's eyebrows went up. "That so." He paused. "Well, we like to think of our little parties as more than just cards." He rolled his eyes up, as if trying to think of just the right phrase to fit his thoughts. "We think it's more like a business opportunity." He smirked.

Jack kept to the hostile native scenario and returned Crusher's gaze without showing fear or falter. "Well, sir. It's like I said. My wife's waiting, and I'm not interested in cards just now. Even if I were, we couldn't afford it."

Crusher nodded. "Can't afford it, huh? Okay then, Birdie. I'll let ya go for now." He turned and started off toward his caboose, but added over his shoulder. "Be careful ya don't turn me down too often, college man. That's something ya can't afford to do, either."

Jack watched after his monster foreman for another two seconds, then turned and resumed his journey toward the passenger station where Carrie always met him. He knew he'd just tickled the dragon on the chin by refusing Crusher's offer, but he didn't doubt for a minute it was the right decision. Risky as it might be not to give questionable men what they want, Jack possessed enough intelligence to know there existed even more risk in becoming involved with them. Evil men tend to spread their evil like a virus, and Jack believed Crusher to be an evil man. He'd not seen enough to prove that belief beyond a reasonable doubt as yet, but he felt it as strong as he'd ever felt anything. *Might be the Lord trying to warn me off,* he thought and decided to gear his dealings with the foreman according to that hunch.

"I heard what ya told old Crusher." Homer came out from behind a switch house to catch up with Jack. "Fearful notion to tell that man *no* about anything." He gave Jack the side-glance once-over. "But, I reckon ya did the smart thing." He nodded in agreement to his own statement. "Them poker games he was talkin' about is also where he does his bootlegger business."

This one caught Jack by surprise. He'd thought of Crusher as the possible perpetrator of many sins, but bootlegging wasn't one of them. A little skeptical, Jack said, "Crusher makes whiskey?"

"Gin." Homer made a distasteful face. "Bathtub gin. But he's not the one what makes it. He just sells it for some bigger fish elsewhere's." He made an even more grotesque face. "Awful stuff! Eat the armor-plates right off a battleship, it would, but more n' more senseless cusses seem to be buyin' it every day. Keeps old Crusher busy. So he goes and gets others to sell it for him." Homer paused and looked around with a clandestine expression. "That's most likely what he wanted you for. Tote his gut-eatin' paint thinner up to the folks in Saber Canyon where you live." He shook his head. "Can't abide that rotgut stuff myself. I'm more partial to real old-fashion moonshine. Much easier on the liver."

Homer stopped just short of the last freight-yard tracks, and Jack followed suit as a small switch engine shoved a short string of flatcars past, just in front of the two men. The noise of the steam cylinders tended to drown out all other sound, so the old man waited until the beast had passed before resuming his narrative. "Now, Snuffy Franks over at the Bull Moose, he's been makin' shine and sellin' it to folks around here for as long as I can recollect. Good moonshine, too. Smooth! Like mother's milk goin' down! And the sheriff, he knows that, too. And he don't bother Snuffy none 'cause his shine's so good. No one gettin' poisoned or goin' blind at the Bull Moose. No-siree-bob.

294

'Sides, Sheriff can legally let Snuffy's place alone 'cause ...officially it's a coffee shop...ever since prohibition, don't you know. They just puts a more invigoratin' kind of coffee in their cups now. And they lets ya take as much as you can pay for home with ya." Homer walked sideways for a few steps, facing Jack, as the two neared the passenger platform. He tilted his head back toward the freight-yard. "Now, if you drink the stuff Crusher sells," he sighed, "who knows? Ya might end up kissin' your eyesight or your life goodbye."

"Who makes Crusher's gin for him?" Jack ventured.

"Why the mob, of course. From Los Angeles. Don't know exactly who they are, but I've seen their guns when they come to deliver to Crusher's caboose at night. Bad hombres, I think. So, I ask no questions, and I mind my own business. They don't bother me 'cause I'm nobody in particular. Got no money, never saved a dime, so I got nothing anybody'd want. I ain't nobody for such as them to be concerned about." He paused from his rambling for a moment and seemed to come back into focus. "But I think you did right by staying clear of that business." Homer turned west when they got to the platform steps and headed in the direction of the Bull Moose. "Hope you can *stay* clear of it." He gave a minimal wave. "See ya tomorrow, young feller."

Jack stood still for a few seconds. The old switchman had delivered a carload of conversation in the short walk between the freight-yard and the passenger platform. Jack wanted to take the time to make sure he'd absorbed it all before he moved on to the other activities of life like talking to his wife. He knew, if he didn't file it away into his memory vault right now, he'd end up talking about what he'd just heard out loud and that wouldn't do. Rail-yard thugs and bathtub gin weren't subjects Carrie wished to hear much about. She'd probably think he was exaggerating, such matters being too upsetting and very different from her gentle Marner Bay upbringing. Jack allotted Homer, Crusher, and bootlegger poker games another second of contemplation, then went up the steps to the passenger station. Time for his other world now.

Before he noticed Carrie, he saw Roger, fidgeting with his wristwatch and talking to the man behind the station's ticket window. More than a little surprised, Jack had no idea why Roger, who thought roughing it had something to do with golf and who had never really been very close to his sister, would make a visit to Sweet Springs. The slight-built young dandy seemed nervous, and, when he walked briskly away from the window toward the benches, he seemed to exude an air of irritation.

Roger sat down on the bench next to his sibling and began an animated, barely audible conversation, to which Carrie responded by shaking her head. Then she saw Jack and offered a limp wave. Roger looked up with an expression of surprise that turned quickly to open-mouthed shock. As Jack approached, Roger stood, slowly, jaw still slack, as if being confronted by a fire-breathing hobgoblin.

"Hi." Carrie said with the breathy voice of fatigue as she remained draped over one end of the oak and cast iron bench.

"Hi, Hon. Hello, Roger." Jack offered his hand while he attempted to figure out what Carrie's foppish brother was doing there.

Roger looked at the soot-stained hand and the matching bib-overalls, then replied, keeping his own hands at his sides, "Uh, I think I'll take a rain check on handshake for now, if you don't mind, old sport."

Jack shot a glance at his palm then smiled with a furrowed brow. "Sorry," he murmured and wiped himself on the front of his bibs. This immediately smeared even more of the same blackish-gray gook on his palm, so he gave up and dropped his hand. "I don't think wiping's going to help much."

Roger looked him up and down as a sarcastic smile spread across his face. "I would guess not. It looks like you've been rubbing up against the whole railroad." He put his fingers to his lips, stared at the switchman some more, and snickered. "My God, Jack! You look like you've just won the greased, striped ape race!" His snicker turned into a short laugh as he finished enjoying his own joke.

Jack resigned himself to Roger's humor. "Good to see you too, Roger."

The more diminutive man tried to stifle his mirth. "Sorry, old man. I just couldn't help myself."

Jack could easily believe that. His brother-in-law had never exactly been a tower of consideration, seeming most often to prefer flights of self-serving sarcasm to common civility. "I understand," Jack said and looked down the tracks to the south where he heard the faint puffing of the northbound passenger train. "Your train?" he asked with more than a little hope in his voice.

Roger glanced the same direction and his smile broadened. "Yes, as your luck would have it. It is indeed my means of departure from this charming little village."

Jack watched the big Baldwin locomotive haul its six-car burden up the Soledad Canyon grade, cylinder strokes growing louder as it approached, and leaving a swath of dark gray coal smoke not too high above the tracks. He turned back to Roger and finally asked the question that had begged an answer for the last minute or so. "So, what brought you down here?" Jack took an exaggerated look around. "I doubt if our scenery compares with the wine country."

The train had almost worked its way to the station. The tracks would turn northward at Palmdale. With a short overnight stay and change of trains at Fresno, Roger could be back in San Francisco by early the next evening. Carrie stood up and jumped into the conversation. "Roger just came down to visit me. Wasn't that nice?"

"Yes, it was," Roger said. *"Darned* nice of me, *I* think." He avoided eye contact with Jack by watching his train as it pulled closer. It was nearing the platform now, and Roger's voice could barely be heard over the hissing, clanging, and chugging of the slowing black iron monster. "I also brought a little gift, but I'll let you discover that for yourself. As a matter of fact—" The rest of his words were lost in background noise.

Jack saw Carrie cast her gaze skyward for just a second, but he wasn't able to make out what Roger had said. "What?" He cupped a hand around one ear.

Roger grabbed a small satchel from under the bench and spoke with his mouth near Jack's ear. "Nothing! I'll let her tell you!" The engine passed by them, drowning out all sound but its own with a steaming hiss. The younger Van Burean smiled, waved at both Carrie and Jack, and mouthed, "I have to go now".

They returned his gesture as the lead Pullman car came to a squealing stop almost in front of the trio. Two middle-aged women got off, and Roger swung up the steps to take their place upon the seat they had just abandoned inside the car. Mailbags were traded by two garter-sleeved men at the express car and, within five minutes, the conductor called out the familiar "All aboard!" He signaled the engineer to pull out, and the huge old Baldwin's drivers slowly began their first turns.

The locomotive pulled the slack out of the train's drawbars with a thundering, metallic jerk that progressed from the engine to the observation car like a slow motion whip crack. Jack saw Roger's head loll along with those of the other passengers as his section of the great iron and wood caterpillar surged forward. But then the young man rose from his seat and raced back to the door. He leaned out from the steps, called Jack's name, and threw something to him. It was hard to see it through the steam of departure, but Jack managed to catch the object. Then he turned it

298

over in his grimy hand. It was a small, hard leather case which when opened revealed a pair of soft, expensive looking driving gloves with one small word embossed on the back: Stutz.

Jack looked up as Roger waved a Cheshire-Cat goodbye from the doorway's tiny platform. After staring at the surprise gift for a moment, he turned to Carrie. She was slowly shaking her head, keeping her eyes buried behind the fingers of her right hand. Jack could not make out her expression.

Well, so much for a pleasant evening, he thought and handed the glove case to Carrie.

She beckoned with a hand signal for him to follow, then led him down the main platform stairs to the street where her Bearcat sat. Neither of them spoke until they reached the car, then she said, "Don't be angry with Roger; I called and asked him to bring it down." She sighed and leaned back against the car's front fender, a look of resignation on her face. "Feel free to be angry with me though. You made *me* angry when you ordered me not to get my car back." She shook her head. "I don't like orders as a rule, Jack. My father used to give me orders, but, aside from him, I've always been the one giving them." A dark storm crossed her face. "Well, however you want to say it, I don't like being told, point blank, what to do!" She stood up and stuffed her hands into her overall pockets. "My trouble is that I've been feeling lousy about it ever since I made the call. Not because I got the car. I still think we need it. But because I went behind your back." She glanced up at him then looked away. "I feel like such a traitor."

Jack felt remnants of the heat from his old smoldering coals on the subject as said coals tried to reignite, but other things got in the way, pouring water on the coals. First, he could not ignore Carrie's open admission of wrongdoing. It sounded completely honest and submissive enough to de-fang a rattlesnake in mid strike. Second—and he hated

299

this—she'd been right in the beginning. They did need the second vehicle. Finally, there was that impossible-to-avoid urge that ran from his heart to his head, the thing that was almost a voice but not quite. The thing he had come to accept as the influence of God. It told him to be very reasonable now, because he hadn't been so in the beginning.

Jack walked around to the passenger's side and put his hand on the door. "Give me a ride home, and I'll tell you what I think about it."

"Wait," she said as she pulled a small work tarp out from behind the seats and spread it over his intended resting place. "Otherwise, the coal black and grease gets into the seat and later our clean clothes.

Jack thanked her. Then they got in the car, and started up Saber Canyon road toward home. Silence prevailed for a while as they drove. Jack took his railroad cap off, leaving his head crowned with a big clean spot that started mid-forehead and rose up to his hairline, making him resemble a pop bottle that had just had its top removed. He leaned back against the courtesy tarp and let the wind blow through his sweat soaked hair, which began to stiffen into a gnarled sculpture. He took a deep breath. "You know, I am a little disappointed about how you went about all this. Part of me says I can't trust you anymore." Jack paused and shook his head. "But I can't really get too tied up in knots about it because I was the one that provoked you into being unreasonable. *You* were being practical. I was being prideful. I didn't want your family to know we needed them in any way whatsoever." He paused to handle a small pang of shame. "Even though we badly needed the car." Then, a little of Jack's pride resurrected itself. "I do wish you wouldn't have kept all this from me. Knowing you'd arranged for the car and didn't say anything, that's what's still hard for me to swallow."

Carrie's contrite expression changed as if she were getting close to the bottom of her humility tank. "I said I was sorry, Jack." Her voice was calm, but the hint of an internal struggle lurked in her tone. "See here, Jack. Aside from taking orders, apologizing is also not something I've been raised to do. So, in consideration of the fact that you're most probably one of the few men alive who has ever heard me make one, I suggest you accept it with some degree of grace."

Jack's first "match-to-gasoline" thought was, *You spoiled little, never-been-spanked brat! Who in the heck do you think you are?* But, the holier voice inside said, *Let the arrogance go this time. Accept her apology as God accepts yours.* So Jack said, "All right. I accept your apology."

That appeared to hit the demeanor control switch for Carrie. Her face and shoulders relaxed simultaneously, and her next words sounded clearly non-hostile. "Thank you," she said and bounced to a halt at the Sierra Highway stop sign long enough to check both ways for traffic. Carrie crossed the intersection and carefully drove around a straw-hat shaded man in a farm wagon being pulled up the road by a chestnut, two-up team. She mused for a moment on how many such wagons—including Ben's—there still were in the area. A much more common sight here than on the coast where trucks had come to rule the road, and the only horses one commonly saw were hitched to junk collection or delivery wagons. Up here they added something to the general atmosphere—a certain sense of serenity and a pace of life more humane to both man and beast. Carrie smiled and took a breath that helped bring her a little closer to the kind of calm enjoyed by the man at the reins of the wagon. Then, once the car had gone beyond horse-scaring range, she mashed down on the accelerator and took off up the final paved stretch of Saber Canyon, the increased power giving the Bearcat a little more of its head.

In a very few seconds, they were doing almost sixty, uphill, and as the slipstream wrestled with her pin curls, Carrie glanced at her grime-darkened husband and grinned. Nothing like driving fast to make one feel much better— almost as good as the slow-wagon-calm she'd just experienced at the bottom of the hill. But the ecstasy of speed lasted only a couple of minutes, then she was forced to slow down as the road turned to dirt and dropped almost a foot in elevation.

However, they were in luck as per the wind's direction. It blew gently to the west, straight across the road away from the ranch, so dust would not be a worry this time. They didn't need to drive extremely fast or slow in deference to the usual cloud of the stuff. Their dust would only waft harmlessly off to their left on their journey up-canyon and straight back behind them as they turned east toward home.

Everything seemed to be working in their favor at the moment, so Carrie's grin stayed put. "Our chicken and egg sales are picking up, Jack." She shot another glance his way and paid for it by having to crank the steering wheel quickly away from a large yucca she almost drove into. Her eyes grew trauma-wide for a moment, but then she laughed and continued her child-on-a-swing smile in conjunction with the conversation. "I've been selling to the Sweet Springs Market every trip, and I've also been making deliveries to more and more people just outside town. The word about us seems to be spreading, and I think many of the women around here are simply getting tired of taking care of their own chickens when they'd rather be cutting out dress patterns or baking pies. I think *they* think chickens are just a bother, so they'd rather we did all that *for* them."

She turned up onto the plateau a little too fast and had to S-turn around a roadrunner the engine noise had flushed from some deer-weed beside the road. The bird made it across, but barely. Carrie geared down for the grade and let the clutch out with a tiny jerk. The racing engine growled as the gears took hold, and the Stutz's occupants felt the acceleration push them mildly back into their seats. A mama quail and her chick-train trailed away from some chaparral and narrowly missed the car's left front tire. "Our chicken business *is* growing. Slowly, but it's growing."

"Sounds more like y*our* chicken business to me." Jack twisted his neck first one way then the other, trying to force the tense, rebellious muscles to let go their iron grip. "You're the one who's been doing most of the work lately." He swiveled his head again. "You do the delivering, the selling, and you're getting to know the people around here. *You're* doing the job. *You* should get the credit." Jack tried, but could not keep envy out of his voice. He wanted to add how the only people he'd met of late were freight-yard switchmen and hobos, but he decided that sounded too much like the old *whiney boy* he no longer wanted to be.

The inner voice had been urging him to continue to sacrifice his own pleasure for his family's needs, unlike what he'd done in the past. Jack felt that God was giving him the chance to prove his sincerity on that subject by giving him the railroad job. So he determined to keep working there as long as necessary, no matter how much he hated it. And he *was* beginning to hate it…more every day.

Carrie pulled her bangs out from in front of her eyes and steered around a fresh ground-squirrel mound. "We're going to make more money, Jack. I know we will." She patted his knee with apparent sympathy, then looked at the black smudge she acquired on her palm. She wiped it onto a clean area of the tarp. "I know this job's not exactly your cup of tea." She wrinkled her nose as she glanced at her still-greased palm then wiped it on the tarp again. "But someday we'll have enough income," she continued, "to get you out of that rail-yard and back on the ranch. Not that the money you make hasn't been a godsend. And the timing couldn't have been better!" Carrie flashed a smile. "And now I have my car back just when I need it the most!"

Jack appreciated Carrie's optimism but couldn't catch hold of it himself. The thick, oppressive air of the rail-yard still lingered in his nostrils, and it felt to him as if there was still a small cloud of coal smoke hovering above his head. He found that he resented her praise of the spirit-killing job he had obligated himself to work.

Easy enough for Carrie to simply rejoice over the money he earned, she not being the one who had to wade down into the freight-yard's mind-numbing abyss of dehumanizing, meaningless repetition. *She* didn't spend twelve hours a day trying to stay safe from the all too frequent accidents and still keep a comfortable distance from Crusher and his thuggish friends.

The sound of her hopefulness only irritated him now. What Jack really wanted was for Carrie to apologize for being awarded the more pleasant part of their new life. He wanted her to stroke his head, and chant *poor baby, poor baby*, but the voice of divine reason inside his head told him this was not a time to express the worst of his more self-centered feelings. So he simply said, "Well then, I guess I'm going to have to keep this tarp over the driver's seat all the time, if I'm going to be driving this thing to work." Jack didn't like the idea of driving an expensive roadster to town every day, but at least it would keep the miles off it, just sitting most of the day. He decided it was the best way to avoid repairs they couldn't afford.

The fact that Jack had just said the wrong thing became immediately apparent when Carrie almost hit one of the electric power poles that loitered along the way home. She fish-tailed the rear wheels a bit, getting the car back under control, but finally coaxed it once again into traveling a relatively straight line more or less down the center of the road.

"What in the world would ever make you think that I'm going to let you drive *my* car to that nasty old rail-yard?" There was no mistaking her tone now. Her demeanor had switched from shocked to livid without even the courtesy of a warning shot.

Jack's eyebrows rose. He shook his head as if he were trying to get water out of his ears. *I've been ambushed!* He thought they'd been talking about their chicken business and how Carrie was making more and more deliveries into town, and how swell everything was going to be. *What just happened?* Carrie had gone from encouraging to attacking in less than one sentence. What was going on? "Carrie, you need the truck to make deliveries. There's not enough room in this little car to fit much of anything." He turned around, looked behind the seat, and gestured. "All you've got here is this little cubby hole and the rumble-seat behind it. Neither of which would hold enough chickens or eggs to even pay for the gasoline you'd have to feed this high-powered beast." He shrugged then faced the windshield. "This is a roadster, Caroline. It's built for fun, not agriculture."

"It's my car!" Carrie snapped. "*My* car! Do you understand? I didn't have Roger drive it all the way down from San Francisco to have you park it down near the freight-yard to get coated with coal soot!"

Jack shrugged. "I could park it farther away, so it wouldn't get coated."

"I said you're not taking it," she snapped. "It's *my* car!"

"All right," Jack answered. "I understand you don't want your paint damaged. But will you please tell me how you're going to make your deliveries without the truck."

Carrie was silent for nearly a minute, her only activity being that of frowning and steering around ruts and potholes. Then her face lit up, and a small, tentative smile began to grow. "Why couldn't we have Ben build me a little two-wheel, covered trailer? I hear he can make almost anything. He could insolate it like the inside of an ice-box and maybe incorporate a compartment on top where one could place a block of ice. That way the last delivery will always be as fresh as the first...even in the summertime. Perhaps, he could even use the wheels from our old broken trailer to make the new one."

"Wouldn't a whole block of ice be a little heavy for you?"

"Maybe." She paused for a moment. "But, if I pull up to the ice house's loading dock, I'm sure one of the boys there will load it into the trailer for me."

Jack *wanted* to tell her it was a bad idea. In fact, considering her selfish attitude, he *wanted* to tell her it was the most ridiculous thing he'd heard all year, but he couldn't. He couldn't because, in fact, it was an outstanding notion. He knew that the minute she voiced it. As a matter of fact, Jack thought it nothing less than brilliant. And *that,* also in view of her *my-car-*attitude, was something he absolutely did *not* want to tell her. So instead, he merely said, "It might work. Why don't we stop by Ben's and ask him."

He pictured Caroline delivering eggs to some Sweet Springs housewife in the Bearcat with a fancy painted trailer, and he laughed out loud. "You know," he said. "You'll need a name for your...I mean, *our* business, something to paint on the side of the trailer." He shrugged. "Good advertising, I think." He rubbed his temple and rested his elbow on the dirt-road-vibrating door as he considered a business title. "Now, those are going to be fairly pampered chickens to be delivered behind a Stutz Bearcat. Matter of fact, they'll be more than just pampered. They'll be downright snooty." He paused to think some more. "So they'll have to have a snooty name." Jack raised his index finger into the air. "How about 'Chickens by Caroline?'"

Carrie was quiet again as they made the final curve just before coming to the little ranch road that led to the Smiths' house. Jack thought she might have discovered the small insult buried behind what he thought was a fairly appropriate name for her business. He waited.

"Chickens by Caroline," she repeated in an indiscernible tone. Then she smiled. "I like it."

Jack relaxed; she'd missed the insinuation.

Carrie continued. "I like it very much." She turned off the main road and up toward their neighbors' house. "I can't wait to tell the Smiths." She turned toward her husband. "That was good, Jack. That was really good."

Jack smiled with as innocent an expression as he could muster. "Thanks."

When Carrie told Ben and Ruth Smith her idea and the name that was to be painted on the side of the trailer, they just stood there staring at each other, without comment.

Finally, Ben said, "Why don't ya just use your truck and paint yer name on that?"

Jack suppressed a smile as his wife simultaneously slapped his arm and shook her head. "It's just the way I've decided to do it, Ben," she said. "Can you build it and match the paint to the car?"

The old farmer looked off—somewhere in his imagination, Jack figured, where a picture of the trailer was probably starting to form. Ben held his stare for a moment then nodded. "Yep, I think I can do her. 'Course, the color might look a little different on wood than it does on your car, but I can get her pretty close for ya."

A look of satisfaction passed between the women.

Then Ben pulled Jack off toward the roadster, saying, "Let me take a look at this little yeller wiz-bang of hers. I saw it racing up and down the road earlier, but it was going so fast, I couldn't get a proper peek." The two men walked back to the car in the fading light of sunset, and Ben squatted to inspect the back bumper. "I'll have to weld a trailer hitch back here." He leaned down a little, keeping a double grip on his bad knees. "Yep, I could attach it to the frame right there." Then he stood up and leaned close to Jack. "So why does your misses want me to do this?"

The younger man shrugged. "Like she said, it's *her* car."

Ben shook his legs out and took a moment to massage his knees. "Yeah, that's what I figured." He chuckled. "Ruth, she had herself a little mustang pony once. Little mare, and she did love it dearly." Ben stopped his joint massage and straightened up. "This was back before we come here. And she wouldn't hear of anyone but *her* a' ridin' the critter. Fly into a regular tizzy if anybody tried. And she wouldn't ride no other horse for love nor money neither for the longest time. Rode it everywhere, she did." He paused to take a breath. "Then finally the thing broke its leg. Just got tired from so much ridin' and stumbled in a chuckhole. Well, there was nothin' to be done about it. I had to shoot the horse. And Ruth figured she was to blame for that little mustang's demise. So the next horse she rode, she called it *our* horse...no more *my* horse, and it's been that way ever since." He walked to the side of the car and took a long, studying look. "Don't suppose that would work in this situation though."

Jack laughed and stared at the Stutz with Ben. "Naw," he finally answered. "I doubt if shooting this thing would help."

Chapter Twenty-Three

R uth and Carrie stood on the west end of the Smith's porch and watched the sunset wash over the nearby hills as their husbands crunched across granite sand toward the tail end of the Stutz. Soon, after the pink and blue sky had faded to the more subtle hues of twilight, Carrie looked around and took a quick inventory of her neighbors' barnyard. "I'd nearly forgotten all about the boys. They said they'd be playing down here with Seth, but I don't see them anywhere."

Ruth walked over to the berm that encircled a young, struggling pine. She leaned down and coerced a weed out by its roots then looked up. "I sent them both to your house with Seth when I saw you start up the road. That was about ten minutes before you got here. I told 'em to get started on their evening chores, so they'd be done before supper. Seth'll help out as well while he's watching over them."

"You are a darling, Ruth. An absolute darling!"

Ruth stuck out her chin and nodded. "Well, that's true enough. And modest too." She winked, but then switched to a more serious demeanor. "I'll tell ya something though." She tossed the weed onto the driveway. "I happen to like your fast little yellow car. Reminds me of a scooty little mustang I had once." She paused, then looked Carrie straight in the eyes. "Some of the women around here won't like your Bearcat one bit though. Not one little bit."

"But why?"

Ruth put an arm around her neighbor and led her uphill toward the main road. The moon shown full bright, and that made the walk easy—all wildlife burrows and rain-carved ditches now visible. It also made it easy for Carrie to see Ruth's still serious expression, a signal to pay attention.

"Why? Oh, lots of reasons," the older woman said. "Mostly jealousy, I think. Some may be thinking that it's sinful for a woman to do what's always been a man's privilege." She gave Carrie a little sarcastic smile. "For instance, like driving a little yellow roadster."

Carrie kicked a pebble as they walked. "What do *you* think of all this? My idea I mean."

"What, a little yellow trailer with "Chickens by Caroline" on it, being pulled around by a skyrocket?" She giggled, then the giggle turned into a cackle. "I think it's a hoot! Menfolk'll most likely reckon you're crazy, but I think it's the best idea I've heard in years. Why, women'll buy from you at least once just to see the contraption you make your deliveries in." She shook her head. "They'll buy from you, I think. But you may not be able to make friends quite as easy. And not just because of your car."

Carrie took another step and snapped a small twig under foot. A kangaroo rat popped straight up out of a clump of desert sage and landed on the human trespasser's foot, causing both creatures to squeal. Carrie froze, but the rodent scurried up the road at flank speed. When it had gone about ten yards, it stopped and sat up on its hind legs.

"That's a very stupid critter," Ruth said matter-of-factly.

Carrie had been concentrating on regaining her breath. "Why?" She scanned the ground around her, looking for more nocturnal fauna.

"Because he shouldn't be in the middle of the road with a bright moon, and he shouldn't be sitting up like that." She pointed at the "stupid critter." "Watch."

The creature held his position on the crown of the road and sniffed the air as it gazed in the general direction of the women. Suddenly, a much larger, gray birdlike shape sprang out of a nearby earthen mound and—fast as a camera shutter—snatched the unwise kangaroo rat from its spot. The shadowy apparition flapped its big wings a few times, than circled back around, only to disappear back into the mound from which it had come.

"What was that?" Carrie's question came breathy with surprise.

"Burrowing owl. They live in holes all through the brush." Ruth waved her hand toward where the rat had been. "Open road's their dinner table."

Carrie shivered a little, took a deep breath. "Well, I murder chickens almost every day. This really shouldn't bother me." She paused. "I suppose it was the suddenness of the thing that caught me off-guard."

Ruth nodded. "Predators are like that. They don't give fair warning; they just strike. The best thing that less aggressive creatures can do is *not* to put themselves into a position to be easy prey."

Carrie faced her friend. "You're talking about these jealous ranch wives, aren't you? You think I'm wrong in going through all this trouble to use my car for the business. You think I should just use the truck and shut up about it. Don't you?"

"That's up to you, Gal."

"Ruth, do you think I'd be hurting our business going through with the trailer idea?"

"I don't know. I'm not a businesswoman. *I'm* just one of the ranch wives." Ruth scratched at a gravy spot on her apron, then looked up. "I told ya. I think the whole thing's a hoot. Just you be aware that there are predators out in the brush that'll try to tear at you just because you're there and they've got nothing better to do. Some of em'll think you're a spoiled rich girl, and they'll want to teach you a lesson. Knock ya down to their level."

"What do *you* think?"

"I think the Lord wanted us to be friends, just like He wanted me and Hannah to be friends." The older woman looked off into the night for a moment. "The way I see it, a friend can know unflattering things about you, but still not mean you any harm." Ruth turned back around. "What do *you* think?"

Carrie chuckled. "I think I like what you think."

Ruth didn't comment but rather walked up onto a raised hump in the main road until her son's house came in sight. She indicated the house with a tilt of her head. "Sam's wife's been on my mind of late, and I believe the Lord's put her there. The life she and my son have carved out for themselves has got her down. She looks sad all the time." Ruth sighed. "And she hides from everybody. Needs friends, but it's so hard to talk to her."

Carrie came up beside her and looked toward the distant house. "Can I help somehow?"

Ruth shrugged. "Maybe...maybe, if both of us just keep waving and smiling at her whenever we see her, maybe someday she'll talk to one of us."

Carrie nodded. "Okay. What's her name?"

"Beatrice, but she likes to be called Bee. She used to talk to me, especially when Sam's drinking picked up after the war, but the last year or so, she's just closed herself off from everybody."

Carrie smiled. She liked the idea of returning Ruth's kindnesses in some way, even if it wasn't directly to Ruth herself. "Well, perhaps we can open her up again."

Ruth turned back down toward her driveway and started walking. "I'd like that. Bee was a pleasing young woman when I met her. I hate to see what a life of sorrow has done to her."

When the women got back to the barnyard, it was almost dark, and they heard the purr of the Stutz's engine from the shadows at the far corner. The headlights shown against the hillside, and Jack sat in the driver's seat, leaning on the closed door, talking to Ben, who stood with his foot on the running board. Carrie bristled and sucked in a sharp breath at the sight of all this male aggression perpetrated upon *her* sacred property.

Her shoulders and neck turned to steel, and she took in a second rush of air between clenched teeth. She decided she would not let this trespass go unchallenged and was on the verge of loosing a storm of verbal bolts into Jack's easy confidence when Ruth put a gentle but firm pair of hands on her shoulders. Carrie felt the hands holding her there with just a little bit of loving force for no more than two seconds, then she heard Ruth whisper "Amen". After that, Ruth released her grip with an easy pat.

That's when, to Carrie's complete surprise, something strange took place. The anger that boiled so hot within her just a moment before now seemed to slowly leech out through her pores as her upper body muscles went slack. In less than five seconds, she went from coiled spring to fluffy pillow, but the strangest thing yet took the form of a total reversal of her position concerning *her* car. All of a sudden, she found herself thinking what a good idea it would be if Jack had a chance to drive the Bearcat on rare occasions— like right now.

As she got to the car she noticed that her husband had indeed moved his grease tarp to the seat where he now reclined. For some reason, this soothed her even more. She didn't understand it, but she found herself powerless to resist the urge to be sweet and accepting. Strange feelings these, and ones with which she did not have a lot of experience. At the moment, it felt soothing while, at the same time, liberating not to be obligated to do battle over this small violation of her sovereignty. So, even though Carrie did not comprehend why, she settled submissively into the passenger's seat without comment. She looked back at Ruth with a question both in her mind and her expression, but the older woman only shrugged and smiled. Carrie then turned her attention back to the men and their conversation.

Ben was talking. "Yeah well, why don't ya come on down Sunday? Things get started about eight. You're used to being on the road earlier than that."

"What's that?" Ruth asked, as she, with arms folded, stepped up next to Carrie.

"Church," Ben said. "Askin' 'em to the church."

"Oh yeah!" Ruth beamed. "Ya oughtta come! We're gonna have a pot luck dinner after!"

Carrie liked the idea and almost accepted for the family but felt the inexplicable need to let Jack handle any responses.

And he did just that, but he looked and sounded uncomfortable in the extreme. "Well, maybe later on," he said. "Right now we're awful busy. Soon as we can get a little breathing space, we'll be down for sure though."

Carrie felt the weight of disappointment, but, at the same time, that mysterious air of calm acceptance continued to surround her. A few minutes before, she would have reacted with a vigorous protest, but right now whatever had taken hold of her urged her to do nothing more than offer a small, silent prayer. *Your will be done, Lord.* Then she relaxed again, and the oddness of her emotions made her giddy. She giggled and looked at Ruth again, but the older woman seemed to be occupied with the struggle to keep a straight face and made no verbal response. The term *drunk with the Spirit* passed through the younger woman's consciousness, but she couldn't recall the chapter and verse of its origin.

Attentions drawn by her out of character behavior, both men glanced over at Carrie. Jack looked ready to question her for a moment. But, in the end, he merely emitted a resigned sigh, rubbed his eyes and continued talking to Ben. "Thanks for the invitation. We *do* appreciate it and we *will* be down soon."

Ben smiled. "Well, we'll be glad to see ya then."

They all said their goodbyes and goodnights, as Jack eased the car into gear and started up the drive toward home. Darkness had almost prevailed by that time, but the moon remained ample, so Carrie could easily make out Bee and Seth Smith uphill in the distance, gathering up gardening tools in their front yard as the Stutz headed their way. Carrie remembered what Ruth had said, so she shot a hand into the air, whipped a vigorous wave in her neighbors' direction and hollered with all her might. "Evening, Bee...Seth!" She had second thoughts about using Mrs.Smith's first name without a proper introduction, but it had already left her mouth, and there was nothing to be done for it now.

Bee Smith made no response at all. She simply stood stock still with her hands at her side, half looking away. Seth, on the other hand, returned the hailing with an enthusiastic wave of his own. "Evenin', Mrs. MacGregor! The boys finished their chores, so I came home to help Ma."

Carrie started to thank him, but before Seth had even finished speaking, Bee grabbed his slack arm and tugged at his shirt while giving some inaudible orders to the boy. He seemed to argue, looking disappointed, for a moment, but she repeated the action, and he finally relented from whatever stance he had taken and retreated toward the house, head down, tools in hand. His mother turned away from the road and evacuated the yard just as Carrie and Jack passed by.

A mild sadness swept over Carrie after this stillborn encounter—not for being snubbed, but because of the unnamed painful difficulties that must have caused Ruth's daughter-in-law to react that way. At that moment, she determined to keep her word to Ruth, just the same, and not give up on this strange woman. *You've not seen the last of me, Bee Smith,* she vowed in stubborn silence, then she settled back into her seat as Jack turned down their own driveway. He went over a rut a shade too fast for her liking and she felt the old critical nature pull at her tongue, a good indication that the rosy I-don't-care mood was starting to wear off. Her last thought before Jack stopped in front of the house was, *I wonder how much longer this feeling will last?*

Chapter Twenty-Four

"Look out!" Ruth yelled just a moment before Carrie stepped off the raised end of the boardwalk and fell another three feet to the ground.

In the midst of her unexpected descent, out of pure reflex, Carrie jettisoned her two-pound package of bacon back over her shoulder in Ruth's general direction. In the blink of an eye, the older companion shot up a well-muscled right hand and snatched the butcher papered package from its flight with the same quick reactive ease of Shoeless Joe Jackson in the first inning of a Saturday double-header home game.

"There!" The older woman gasped with satisfaction. "I've saved your bacon!" She chuckled at the pun and extended her other hand down to help a dusty, rattled Caroline up from a little plot of adobe clay and gravel. "That was quite a circus act." Ruth leaned a little further over the edge of the boardwalk, grasped the younger woman's upraised hand with her own, and pulled her neighbor to her feet. "You all in one piece?"

"What happened?" Carrie shook and dusted off her blue and white floral-print dress, which was almost identical to Ruth's. She tried to focus her eyes, then checked for injuries.

"You forgot to take an alaman-right down them stairs." Ruth pointed to the set of forsaken steps that led to the right of the boardwalk down to a dirt alley. "You just walked off the end of the loadin' dock, gal!" Ruth shook her head and descended the afore mentioned steps to ground level. "You looked a hundred miles away. What was you thinkin' about?"

"What was I thinking about?" With an ample measure of humility, Carrie accepted her bacon back from its savior and swiveled her head around to make sure her neck was still in its proper place upon her shoulders. "Oh, something stupid!" She started walking toward the Sweet Springs Market twenty yards down the road. Ruth caught up, fell into pace beside her and waited for the rest of the answer. "You were right as you could be," Carrie said, "about most of the women around here. With the exception of those right on the outskirts of town, everyone calls up Henri at the inn to order chickens or eggs from me only once or twice. And they do that merely to see me drive up in the Stutz, pulling the trailer. Then I don't hear from them ever again."

"And taking orders for you doesn't bother Henri?"

"I pay him four cents an order. He says it's the easiest money he's ever made, so he doesn't mind." The petit chicken rancher shrugged. "And I guess he wants to help keep us going."

Carrie very carefully ascended the steps onto the next stretch of wooden sidewalk at the brick market's entrance, taking each creaking step as if it were part of a mine field. "I've dropped by at some of the women's houses later on to see if they wanted to order again, but no one ever does." They went into the store and walked past the counter where Mr. Henley stood, ringing up something for Sue Linn on his shiny, ornately cast, polished nickel cash register. Carrie exchanged a brief nod with the market owner but continued talking as she and Ruth headed back toward the spice shelves. "The ranch women say they've decided to keep raising their own chickens," she continued in a slightly lowered voice. "And the town women say they'll just get theirs here at the market, which really doesn't matter very much because I'm slowly becoming Mr. Henley's main supplier." She picked up a small can of sweet paprika, glanced at the little price sign attached to the shelf, then stuffed the container into her canvas shopping bag and turned toward Ruth. "The thing that puts me off, though, is that not one of them has invited me to anything. I hear of reading groups, taffy pulls, and quilting bugs all over both canyons, but do I get invited to one? No, not even one!" With the last word, she threw a can of black pepper into the bag with a little too much English, so that it clanked hard against the paprika tin.

"Quilting Bee," Ruth said.

Carrie snatched some cumin from the shelf. "What?"

"You want to go to a quilting bee, not a quilting bug." Ruth seemed to be trying to hide a smile.

"Oh." Carrie paused for an instant, then went on. "And I can't even get a couple of seconds of normal conversation from anyone in town, outside of a few big customers! Every time I start to talk about anything other than eggs, suddenly whoever I'm talking to has something important to do that just can't wait another minute!" She manhandled some dried mustard into the bag where it settled amongst the other containers. "I've never seen so many busy women in all my life."

Carrie stopped speaking long enough to take a deep breath and let it out slowly. Her shoulders drooped, and she thought, *how stupid I must sound complaining. This is exactly what Ruth warned me about. I should just admit it in full.* So she did. "You were right about my car causing me trouble, Ruth! Absolutely right!"

Ruth moved over to the soap flakes and slid a box into *her* booty bag. "Is it important to you...to be accepted like that?"

Carrie followed suit with the laundry soap and spent a moment in thought. "Yes," she said. "This is where we live now. I'd like to be part of what goes on here." She glanced down then back up to Ruth. "And I must admit it does hurt more than a little to be cast as the village leper."

"Well, you might just be in luck." Ruth moved to the produce bins and picked at the potatoes. "This weekend's got more things going on than should be lawful. Lodge suppers, a reading, a rug hook, at least two candy socials, and a potluck. With all those targets, you should be able to get a hit somewhere." She paper bagged a few spuds and put them into her poke. It was then that they heard the musical chatter of female voices coming from the canned foods isle.

Ruth stepped slowly around the end of the shelves, employing a gentle hand to draw Carrie with her. Then together they peeked at the group of four women who stood in a knot at the isle's center. "All right," Ruth whispered. "There, before your very eyes, stands a quarter of the Sweet Springs Ladies Literary Society whose monthly meeting is Friday afternoon. Do you know any of them?"

Carrie leaned around the corner again and searched the faces of the flock. "All of them. I've sold something at least once to each one."

Ruth kept her eyes fixed on the group. "Then why don't you just saunter up to Henrietta there and ask to attend their reading. I think you'll have her by the tail on this one; she's always whinin' they don't have enough new members. 'Not many serious readers in Sweet Springs,' she says."

Carrie gave the once over to the guardians of Sweet Springs' culture and assessed her chances. The one who stood out immediately was the well-known Henrietta Black, a retired elementary school teacher that Carrie guessed to be at least sixty years of age. Her silver-shot copper hair, that looked to have been bright red at one time, competed for attention with the ample bosoms that dominated her torso. She had clad herself in a conservative gray dress today, ankle length, with a white collar. And topped with a broad brim, flowered hat, she received much-needed foot support from a pair of black thick-heeled, orthopedic shoes. A sturdy-limbed woman who peered critically through wire rim glasses, she had yet to be caught exhibiting any sort of verifiable smile. It took only a glance from even the most casual observer, to realize that this woman had to be the undisputed leader of this gathering. And her shrill voice, audible at almost any distance, added trustworthy credence to that assumption.

The other three women boasted little importance compared to the old schoolmarm. Mere younger copies of her to one degree or another, their demeanor gave the impression they would follow almost any of her suggestions as if it were a God-given commandment. Carrie knew she would only need to gain the acceptance of the boss female to procure the confidence of the whole group. So with that in mind, she took a deep breath and nodded to Ruth. "Okay, I'll do it." Then she eased into the little isle and confronted the literary covey with as much confident sunshine as she could gather.

"Ladies, what a stroke of luck to meet you here," she said as four sets of eyes turned toward her and went wide, with Henrietta's being the widest.

The flock's shepherdess sputtered briefly then took command of the unexpected situation and responded with a tone of cool, controlled distance. "Oh, Mrs. MacGregor. What a pleasant surprise. Doing a little shopping, are you?"

Back at the far corner of the store where the cash register stood, Mr. Henley lowered his phonograph's needle onto a record, releasing a shower of undulating static through the machine's megaphone. The tinny, recorded strains of a ballroom orchestra and male tenor closely followed. The offering, popular for some time, had proven a particular irritant to Carrie, but, at the moment, it afforded her time to gather her faculties and think of what to say next. She appreciated the diversion and extended it by turning her head in the direction of the sound, pretending for a moment to be distracted by the tune.

Yes, We Have No Bananas was the song's title as explained by the recorded tenor, in time with several muted trumpets.

Carrie allowed two full seconds to lapse then returned to the veiled confrontation she'd begun. She considered exchanging polite, harmless chit-chat with Henrietta, but she'd tried that before, and all it ever won her was a few seconds of tolerant but meaningless conversation from the woman, soon followed by the brush off. Carrie decided it would not happen that way today. She would offer the main subject first this time and just let things take their course for better or worse. So she said, "I've heard you are in charge of the Literary Society here."

There was a slight, stifled giggle from one of the covey before Henrietta could respond. "Well, I wouldn't say 'in charge'," she answered, "but the ladies of the society have honored me with the responsibility of keeping track of the monthly business and helping to maintain a certain order." She squinted in an unsuccessful attempt to imitate a smile while she nodded with regal affectation to her three companions ... one at a time.

Carrie politely waited for the silent applause to die down before she pressed on with her mission. "Yes, *that's* more or less what I've heard." She took another small breath of resolve and internally chided herself for being affected so by the reverse snobbery of these small town hens. Carrie felt like simply telling them exactly how inconsequential they were and how silly they would look next to the truly important people with whom she'd grown up, but instead she said, "I have also heard that you are seeking additional members for your chapter. If that's true, I would be quite pleased to join. I've always enjoyed reading. It helps add color to the more ordinary parts of our lives. Don't you think?"

There was another awkward moment of silence while the four sets of eyes exchanged glances and counter glances. "Well, I wouldn't exactly characterize our lives as colorless or ordinary," Henrietta countered, "but I do agree that the reading of fine literature does tend to enrich one according to the degree to which one makes use of the opportunity for enlightenment."

The old duelist's rebuff threw Carrie off. Somehow Henrietta had taken the younger woman's innocent comment and turned it into a supposed slur. This was an unexpected tact, but the wily old predator was not done yet.

"Now, as to your participation in the proceedings of our literary society, I must warn you that we do not take membership lightly. There are certain standards to maintain." Henrietta paused a half beat before bringing her next gun to bear. "Are you familiar with the works of Byron, Keats, and Shelley, Mrs. MacGregor? They have been the mainstay of our readings, along with some of the more contemporary authors."

This time Carrie's return fire was quick and confident. "Yes." Her tone was low key and very matter-of-fact. "My elementary tutor considered them essential reading for *young girls*. She required me to memorize quite a bit of their texts and recite whole portions on demand. Usually, before I was allowed to eat dinner and especially when there were important guests at the table."

"Really?" Henrietta muttered as she looked from one of her followers' faces to the other. "And who might these guests have been?"

"I can't recall them all," Carrie was relaxed now and taking her shots as she pleased. "I do remember that the British consul thought my recitation of Shelley's *Ode to the West Wind* was charming, but Mr. Hearst said he was especially partial to my reading of Juliet's death scene as dining entertainment."

This time one of the coven reacted. "Who's Mr. Hearst?"

Carrie maintained her just-a-day-in-the-life-of-a-princess demeanor. "William Randolph Hearst." She paused. "He's in the newspaper business. Not a novelist or a poet, but still…involved with writing in his own way."

323

The underling realized her oversight in stepping into Carrie's snare and, as penance, quickly turned crimson. She lowered her head in silent apology to her captain, who retook the helm in a rush.

"Yes," Henrietta said. "Most of us have heard of the Hearst publications." She sighed. "Well, as I said, we take our membership in the society very seriously, but in view of your previous education and experience in the realm of the classics, perhaps you might like to give our little group the benefit of your expertise." She pulled a small, embroidered handkerchief from her beaded purse, dabbed at her nose and sniffed. "Our agenda for this month's meeting is already set, but maybe you could prepare a lecture about how you see literature adding color to our dreary lives." She replaced the hanky and willfully snapped the purse shut, holding it firmly just above waist height as if it were an ancient shield. "I'm sure that I can speak for the majority of the group when I say that we would be most interested to hear such a presentation…next month. It would be ever so much more convenient than the confusion of trying to rearrange seating and refreshments at the last minute for this month's meeting. A woman of your background, I'm sure you understand."

And there it was. Carrie knew the battle was over, and Henrietta had won. She had successfully put the ex-debutant in her place without actually issuing a straightforward insult. Carrie had lost in her attempt to be accepted into their little band, and, now, to add insult to injury, she was expected to make some sort of response to the older woman's offer to let Carrie give a presentation at a later date. And, since no *genuine* invitation had actually been issued, in order to avoid looking like the sinking ship she now in fact was, Carrie would have to think of a clever response without appearing overtly insulted. She knew she had to do this soon, but at the moment she was busy feeling foolish and could not come up with a workable exit line.

Almost a full second ticked away, and she knew she was beginning to look pathetic. Then Ruth's booming baritone broke the silence. "Ya can't do it, Carrie!"

Her neighbor's intrusion startled Carrie, as if she had been shaken from a deep sleep. "What?" She said. "I can't do what?"

Ruth barged her way past two of Henrietta's chicks, raising the volume and lowering the vocabulary level of the conversation. "You can't prepare a presentation for next month because you're helping me write my Sunday school lessons for the next few days. Don't you remember?"

Carrie came out of the dark pit of defeat and caught up with Ruth. "Yes. That's right! I did forget! Sorry, Ruth. And my apologies to you, Henrietta." She placed one theatrical hand over her heart and pretended to fan herself with the other. "This completely slipped my mind. But I'll probably contact you in a month or two about the presentation. And I do appreciate your invitation." Carrie began to smile again as she maneuvered into tactical retreat.

Ruth started off toward the door with Carrie at her elbow, but spoke over her shoulder to the chief hen as she went. "Oh, and I think you've been a little forgetful too, Henrietta. Wasn't you and your group supposed to take the train down to Los Angeles next month to hear young F. Scott Fitzgerald speak? Or at least that's what the invite you sent me said." Then Ruth ushered her friend out the door, winked at Mr. Henley and Sue Linn, who had long since turned down the phonograph so they could better hear the combat ensuing two isles away.

Carrie heard the spring bell ringing as they left and thought it a good punctuation to what had just taken place.

"I'll put those items on you accounts, ladies," came the voice of Henley through the screen door, followed by the scratch of the phonograph needle upon the record and the sound of the *bananas* song beginning again.

The two ranch wives had just started down the steps toward street level when Sue came bursting out of the market, wearing a mile-wide grin. "That was tops, Ruth! You should have seen old Henrietta's face just now! She was fit to be tied! I thought she was going to pop or something!" Sue filled her cheeks with air, plumped out her arms, and rotated her head first one way then the other, all the time alternately blinking and bugging out her eyes. Then she popped her cheeks with her hands and lapsed into laughter. "Mr. Henley tried so hard not to laugh, I thought he was going to choke." She tilted her head toward the store entrance. "You know, when I came out here," she giggled, "he went into the storeroom, so he could laugh out loud, I think." She giggled some more, then seemed to remember something. "Oh, Mrs. MacGregor, Ezzie said her uncle just went sappy over your Farmers' Soup. He told her mama he'd never had anything so good in his life. She says you're a real hit with her whole family now. I guess that Cordon Bleu place really knows what it's doing, huh?"

The three dismounted the steps and continued on up the road toward where Carrie had parked her car. "What's all this about an uncle?" Ruth pulled the drawstring at the top of her bag and slung it over her shoulder.

Carrie opened her mouth to respond, but Sue chimed in ahead of her. "Mrs. MacGregor gave Ezzie's mama a real snappy recipe to make for her uncle. She got it from her family cook, who went to this fancy French cooking school in Paris. And—" Sue nodded toward Carrie. "She learned all kinds of stuff from him, and she's got it all up here!" She pointed at her head.

"Is that a fact?" Ruth said, a small, subtle smile barely showing on her face.

"Well, I gotta get back to work." Sue peeled off from the pair as they came abeam of the Hunter's Inn. She waved a small brown paper bag in the air. "Haddie only sent me after some almonds and that was a half an hour

326

ago." The young woman grinned again. "She must be having a regular fit by now." She raised her eyebrows. "Again! Bye!" She waited for an approaching truck to pass, then strolled across the street, not too concerned, Carrie thought, about how quickly she got back to Haddie.

The trip back up the canyon from town passed without incident. Ruth seemed to like riding fast in the Bearcat with the hot summer air blowing her hair to tangles. She smiled almost all the way back, but said next to nothing as she surveyed the dry grass and yucca-covered hills. Ruth usually had some sort of comment or reaction to almost everything she saw, so this uncharacteristic silence made Carrie curious.

"Thanks for the rescue from Henrietta," she said.

"Welcome," came Ruth's sparse response as she focused her attention on one of the ranch houses just up hill from the road.

"I don't know why I let her get the better of me like that." Carrie downshifted for the plateau.

"You're just a little bit of a fish out of water up here. You'll fit in soon enough. Don't you worry." Ruth gave her a brief glance then went right back to watching the scenery slide by.

All right, Ruth. What's going on? Carrie wondered if she'd committed an unforgivable breach of some unspoken, unpublished code of rural living. Had she somehow unknowingly perpetrated some sin that even Ruth's charity-rich heart could not tolerate? She hoped not. "Ruth, are you all right?"

"Yep."

That did it for Carrie. A one-word answer from Ruth. For sure, something had gone amiss. But what? She culled her memory and finally came up with one possibility. She had done very little for Ruth in return for all the help and support the old Christian had sent in her direction. *That must be it,* she thought. *And I've probably not shown much in the way of verbal appreciation either. I suppose I have started to take her kindness and aid for granted. Well, I'll change that just as soon as we get to the house.*

They were already supposed to stop at the MacGregor ranch for a couple of dressed chickens Ruth had paid for. *And there's another possibility,* Carrie continued. *I shouldn't have taken her money! Even if I did only charge her cost. I should have simply given them to her! Oh, how could I have been so stupid? So selfish!*

So, she set to work trying to find some way to make up for her bumbling. And after a few seconds of near frantic mental searching, the image of a fur-lined, champagne-colored, satin robe came to mind. Carrie had bought it right after she had moved back to the Marner Bay compound, in a hopeless attempt to soothe her sorrows, and for some reason she could not explain even to herself, had brought it with her to the ranch. She did love it so— something frivolous, impractical, and *very* expensive. It made her feel pampered when she wore it, which, of late, did not occur often—one of her few possessions that had nothing to do with chickens. Just the fact that she owned it gave her a sense of importance. She could take it out of the closet and say to herself, *no one else around here can afford anything like this,* and she would for a few seconds feel a little better than her neighbors. She'd bought it oversized so that she could get lost in it, wrapping herself up in the thing like a baby in a blanket. *Good,* she decided. *Then it will have no trouble fitting Ruth. She can feel pampered for a change.* That course of action set, Carrie finished the drive up the hill with a much-lessened degree of anxiety.

Upon their arrival at her house, she leapt from the car ahead of her friend and raced inside to collect wrapped chickens from the ice box and an almost new, two-hundred dollar, satin robe from the closet. Unfortunately, she had already thrown away the sales box, but she decided, after she had shown the thing to Ruth, she could wrap it in the same white butcher paper she used for chickens.

Carrie heard Ruth enter the front room and groan as she seated herself, so she hurried out from the bedroom and presented the robe to her friend.

"This thing's just too fancy," Ruth said, wide-eyed as she stroked the fur collar across her face. Then she let out something that Carrie thought sounded halfway between a hiccup and a laugh. "But I love it!" She winked at Carrie. "Ben's gonna bust a gut when he sees this!" She looked up from the overstuffed couch and grinned. "Why are you giving me this beautiful and, I imagine, quite pricey piece of fluff?"

Carrie turned away from the question and walked slowly to the kitchen doorway, where she unconsciously traced her finger around a rebellious lump in the flowered wallpaper. "I don't know. I thought you'd like it, and I also wanted you to have it." She toyed with the fringe that hung from the inverted half-globe of a stand-up lamp, then settled semi-gracefully into the grasp of the couch's matching stuffed chair. Her eyes dropped down to the sanded plank floor and began an aimless inspection the large braided rug that covered the center two-thirds of the room. "Do you—" she asked with only one furtive glance up to her friend. "Do you really like it?"

Ruth rose from where she sat and went to Carrie's chair. "Ya know." She put a hand on the young woman's shoulder. "I'm your friend whether you give me anything or not." There was a moment of no response, then Carrie told her what she'd been thinking on the drive up. Ruth nodded once. "You've got some faults; that's true, but they're not so bad that you have to buy friends. Some might consider it an insult just that you thought that about me, but I know where you come from. I'll consider that and take no offense." She patted the younger woman again—but a little harder this time.

Carrie looked up at Ruth through her lashes. "Do you really like the robe?"

"It's of no conceivable use on a farm." Ruth paused as if considering something, then smiled. "Like I said, I love it!"

"Good." Carrie relaxed. Whatever the reason, giving this gift made her feel good. It was almost as if *she* was receiving the gift, rather than Ruth. "It's important that you have it." Caroline paused. "It expresses a little of how I've come to feel about the way you've befriended me." She shook her head. "Or something like that. I'm sorry, I'm not very good at...at—"

"Saying how you really feel?" Ruth finished for her.

Carrie turned to face her friend. "Yes. Sometimes...with people I care about." She started to turn away, then stopped. "I've been taught not to do that—reveal my feelings, that is. And I've spent much of my life hiding what's truly inside. In my old world, you don't speak out your thoughts unless you want them used against you."

Ruth nodded. "Kind of makes it hard to share. Don't it."

"Yes."

"It'll get easier the longer you're away from your old crowd." Ruth gave her two more heavy shoulder pats, walked to the mud hall door, then turned. "You are my friend and my sister in Christ, even if you haven't made it to church yet." She smiled slightly. "I'm gonna do you a favor. That's what I was thinking so hard on when we were in your car." She swiveled back around and walked toward the front door.

"What kind of favor?" Carrie was out of her chair and following now.

Ruth answered through the internal windows, that separated the front hall from the living room—but kept on walking as she spoke. "You'll see."

"What is it?" Carrie swung into the mud hall, but Ruth was already out the front door and starting down the footpath toward her farm.

"Don't fret," the older woman said without turning around. "You'll love it even better than this!" She waved a handful of satin and fur over her shoulder and disappeared beyond the pines, leaving Carrie alone with her guesses and apprehension.

A few minutes later, after all hope of an immediate answer from Ruth had waned, Carrie donned her steadily fading blue bibs and a big, light grey, broad-brimmed Stetson, Jack had bought her. She shucked her stylish town shoes in exchange for her work boots and started for the door to dive into her afternoon chicken chores.

Then she stopped short for a second as an annoying little loose-end recollection surfaced. *Ruth forgot her chickens.* She considered running them down to the Smith farm, but decided against it when she calculated all she had to do and how little time she had to catch up with the day after her trip to town. *I'll send Kenny down with them later,* she decided.

So she exited the house and threw herself into the afternoon's work. With practiced speed and efficiency she filled the mash troughs, scraped floorboards, and roughly transferred cockerels to Death Row for the next day's orders. She'd been working at the slaughtering duties for a little more than an hour and had just finished placing the last of the wrapped, dressed birds into the cold room, when she heard a loud knock at the front door.

"Carrie girl, you in there?" It was that border time between afternoon and evening when the breeze in Saber Canyon changes direction and the silence becomes so overwhelming that the flapping of a hawk's wing can be heard for a quarter mile. The most dominant sound at the moment, Ruth's voice, resounded off the hill behind the ranch house like distant thunder. "Carrie, come on out here;

I got something to tell ya!" The excitement in the older woman's voice could not be mistaken. It sounded as though some piece of life-or-death information had suddenly grown too big for its human vessel—Ruth—and the thing now waited, impatient and poised to burst out.

Carrie hurried to the door before her friend exploded. "What is it?" She ran out onto the porch as the new screen door slammed behind her. "What's the matter?"

Ruth stood beside Ben in the driveway, the two of them sharing a suspicious grin. Ruth glanced at Carrie's chicken-debris-covered overalls and blood-stained fingers then she emitted a mild laugh.

"Well," she said, "it's a good thing ya put on your Sunday best. 'Cause in just a little while, unless I'm mistaken, you're going to have a visit from several local ladies."

Ben stretched his neck, and surveyed the length of the canyon's main road. "Thought I'd just mosey up with Ruth," he said, glancing back at Carrie. "I truly do want to see this." His grin widened and he returned to his down-canyon vigil.

"See what?" Carrie came down off the porch. "Ruth, what are you talking about?"

Ruth took her by the arm and led her to a break in the pines for a better view of the road. She pointed to a tiny dust funnel that followed a dark speck—a car, starting off from one of the ranches far down canyon. "See that?" Ruth pointed at the moving vehicle.

Carrie strained forward and nodded. "Yes."

"That's the first of 'em."

"First of whom?" Frustration nibbled at the edge of Carrie's voice.

"There's another 'un!" Ben pointed at a second telltale dust trail a little farther away.

Carrie turned to Ruth with a questioning look. She hadn't any idea what this was all about. "Please, what's going on?"

"I'll answer ya with a little story," Ruth said, still maintaining her smile.

"Ruth!"

Carrie's neighbor continued to beam. "Now, just hold your horses. This'll only take a second." She took an instant to follow Ben's gaze to the rise on the other side of the draw where a woman driving a buckboard pulled by a chestnut horse Ruth recognized had just come into view. The Smiths traded a quick, knowing look. "All right, Carrie. Here it is. As you know, when Ben and me owned the Hunter's Inn, I was the chief cook there. Always cheaper to hire kin, ain't it, Ben," she said to his back.

"Yep," he answered without turning around.

Ruth winked at Carrie. "So, where was I? Oh yes, I was chief cook. Well anyway, during that time, the women around here got in the habit of asking me how to make this dish or that dessert. I learned from my ma, who used to cook at a hotel in Chicago, but these women never had such a stroke of luck. So, they'd come and ask me how I did this and that. After the word got around that I knew such things, I kinda became the cooking expert for Sweet Springs. Even after we sold the inn, they still kept on a' calling every time they needed help. I've never minded much. I figured that was the gift the Lord gave me to share, sort of like a little ministry. Ya know?"

"Has Haddie always been Henri's main cook?" Carrie was only two-thirds paying attention to Ruth for a moment; the other part of her concentration being lured away by the additional cars, trucks, and wagons that were beginning to show up on Saber Canyon Road. She found herself looking back and forth as her conversation with Ruth went on.

"Yep. Haddie's been in charge of the kitchen there ever since I left."

"Then, why don't the local women call *her* for advice?"

"Haddie don't want to be bothered. She's a little cantankerous most of the time, in case you haven't noticed. When she started working at the inn, she figured her skills, what there were of 'em, and her recipes were her own secret business, and if anyone wanted a sample of it, they could just go down there and buy a meal. She didn't give out free advice."

Carrie watched the first vehicles turn up the final stretch of road that led up the plateau to the ranch. She shook her head. "So what does all this have to do with me receiving visitors?"

"That's the best part," Ben contributed over his shoulder.

Ruth picked a dried up wildflower from the top of a small bush. "Like I told you before, this weekend, there's a lot going on, what with suppers, socials, and such. I usually spend this evening mostly on the phone just answering all the cries for help as to what to cook or what little tidbits to prepare." She shook her head and shrugged. "But not this time."

"Why not?"

Ben half turned around and laughed, "You should've heard her! Soon as these women start makin' their usual Thursday calls, Ruth up and tells them that she *ree-tired* from the recipe assistance business. She says you got trainin' from a chef that come all the way from Paris, France, and that beats her like a full house beats three of a kind!"

Carrie's eyes went wide. "You didn't!" She said with more than a little shock running up and down her spine. She unconsciously backed up a step and glanced quickly back and forth between Ruth and the rapidly filling dirt road.

Ruth's sunny grin turned to a closed-lipped smirk but retained every bit of its original width. "Yep, I did."

"And that ain't all!" Ben leaned one-handedly against a large pine as he continued his road vigil. "She told all of 'em that she ain't answerin' no more questions as of today, an' if they want any help for their cookin' and such, they'll just have to talk to you!"

"But we've got no telephone!" Carrie felt like one of her chickens tied down to the chopping block, squawking in protest against what she knew was about to happen anyway. "They *can't* call me!" She held up her hands as if to ward off a blow.

"Yep, I know," Ruth answered a little too calmly. "That's why I told 'em they'd have to stop in and ask for your help face to face." She paused, seemingly for effect, and extended her open palmed hand toward the approaching stream of motorized and horse drawn vehicles. "And here they come, gal." Her toothy grin returned. "I always wondered if I'd be so popular a person if these women didn't need me so darned much." She shrugged. "Looks like this is my year to find out."

"Say, Ruth," Ben piped up again while staring down the canyon. "Does Henrietta drive a green Maxwell?"

Ruth looked over at her husband. "She sure does."

The old farmer turned around and winked at the two women. "Well ladies, here she comes," he said and pointed at the last car down the hill.

"Oh, my God!" Carrie looked up and down the traffic-strewn road, then noticed she was still wearing her chicken dung coated bib-overalls, at which point she emitted a small high-pitched scream. "Oh, no!"

Ruth gave Carrie a side hug. "I don't think poor Haddie could fill the bill even if she wanted to. She's just an old railroad and ranch cook. She don't know what you know. Heck gal, I don't either." She turned her young friend around to face her. "I think this is where the Lord's put you for His own reasons. He's given you this gift. Guess someone must've been prayin' for ya." She patted her gently. "So tell them how to cook like Paris or one of those places and don't waste God's gift. I guarantee they're all gonna want to be your friend." Ruth shrugged. "So to speak."

Carrie found she could barely breath, while alternating fear and joy played havoc with her nervous system. The first truck had made it almost to the property, and it looked like there were at least six more soon-to-be *friends* behind it. She grabbed Ruth's hand. "Aside from a silly robe, I've never returned any of your kindness. Tell me what I can do! Please!"

"It's gonna get crowded here, Ruth," Ben said before disappearing down the path between the trees. "I'm going back to the house."

"All right," Ruth answered. "I'll just be a minute." Then she clasped both her hands around Carrie's. "Do you mean it?"

"Yes!" Carrie felt love and gratitude begin to overcome her fears.

"Come to church with Ben and me."

Carrie bit her lip to hold back the overflow of her feelings. She nodded. "I will. I promise I will!"

Ruth hugged her again, then let go and started after Ben just as the dust coated brakes of Carrie's first new *friend* came squealing down into the driveway. "You'll do well," Ruth called back. "Just remember that God gave you your knowledge for His reasons. So don't let these women worry ya none. You've got what they need. You got the reins of the buggy. Remember that."

With that, Ruth disappeared, and Carrie turned to face her first visitor of the afternoon, one of the ladies from down canyon she'd sold eggs to once.

"Mrs. MacGregor," she said. "I'm so glad I've found you at home. I do hate to impose on you at chore time, but I wonder if I might ask you a small question."

Carrie decided to delay her response for just a second. She didn't think it a truly unchristian thing to do. It gave her time to pick a feather or two out of the front bib-pouch of her overalls and to enjoy the helpless, uncertain expression on the approaching woman's face.

Then she remembered. *Oh dear. Ruth has forgotten her chickens again.*

Chapter Twenty-Five
May, 1924

"*E stupida*! Watch where you are going!"

Carrie struggled to keep her paper-wrapped chickens from falling out of her arms while the busboy she'd just collided with picked himself up off the floor of the kitchen hallway at the Hunter's Inn. "I'm sorry, Raul," she said. "I didn't see you coming. I'm having a devil of a time with these bundles. I just couldn't see around them."

Raul straightened his white jacket and focused on the person who had just sideswiped him. "Oh, Mrs. MacGregor! Excuse me! I did not know it was you. *Yo siento mucho*! I didn't mean to call you—"

Carrie cut him off. "That's all right. It was entirely my fault."

"Where are you going with all that?" He helped steady a bundle that was trying to slip out from under her elbow, then he stretched his wiry arms. He had brown skin, a hawk's nose, and looked to be about thirty, but no one around town had ever been interested enough to ask his age.

She eased by him in the narrow space. "Oh, Sue Linn called Mrs. Smith, who brought me the message that Henri needed chickens tonight."

"Henri?" Raul scratched his head. "Oh, you mean Hank!"

"He wishes to be called Henri," she said in a very proper but polite tone. "You know that."

"I know, but it's so much fun to call him Hank and watch his ears turn red." Raul grinned.

Carrie decided to tease. "He's going to give you the boot. You know that, don't you."

Raul shook his head. "Naw. Who else could he get to work so long for so little money?" He shined his fingernails on his lapel, then blew on them. "I'll still be here when my children are grown."

While they were talking, the sound of a heated argument drifted from the direction of the kitchen. Carrie listened for a second and made out the voices of Henri Reneau and Haddie Seals. Distance, however, distorted their words down to mere garbled echoes in the hallway.

"What's going on?" Carrie asked.

"Big trouble. You'll see." Raul ran a quick comb through his thick, black hair, smoothing it back until it all met at a point in the rear. "You want me to help you with *los pollos* before you drop them?"

"No, I wouldn't want to keep you from whatever you were on your way to do."

Raul smiled and took a few of the chickens. "Oh, Hank just sent me out to watch for you. He was worried you didn't get the message in time to be down here before it was too late. I wish he would've said you was bringing all this! I'd have brought the wheelbarrow out." Then he led the way toward the noise. "Come on. You don't want to miss this."

They emerged out of the hall into the kitchen just as short, portly Haddie sent a cast iron pot hurtling to the right of her employer's head. Both Carrie and Raul instinctively ducked, letting the thing pass over and ricochet off the walls behind them. Haddie, oblivious to the near disaster she had just caused, stood next to the time-worn kitchen counter, hands clenched, feet wide apart with Henri fixed in her glare.

She grabbed a round, long-handled griddle and banged it on one of the big, black, iron cook stoves in cadence to her words. "And that's another thing! How can you expect me to cook a fancy meal perfect on an old wood burner like this? I'll just bet them *la-de-da* places this guy's used to all have gas cookin', so that a body doesn't have to keep turnin' everything around so's it don't get burned on one

339

side and raw on the other!"

Henri held up his palms. "Haddie, he didn't complain about the way it was cooked. He merely said the dish was unimaginative."

Haddie banged the griddle again. "Well, what in tarnation does that mean?"

Henri shrugged. "It simply means he wants to taste something a little less ordinary," he replied, his Cajun accent thickening as his voice tensed.

Haddie's face went blank. "What do ya mean, less ordinary?"

Henri rolled his eyes. "He wants something different, something a little better, something unusual. No? Not just baked chicken."

"And what, may I ask, is wrong with *my* baked chicken? I've cooked it up for years, and everybody around here likes it just fine!"

Henri sat down on a stool by the chopping table. "You'll have to try something else. That's all there is to it."

Haddie tossed the griddle onto the top of the stove. "Oh, I do, do I! Well, we'll just see about that, Hank! She pulled the scarf from her head and shucked her apron.

"My name is Henri."

Haddie scooped up her purse from a corner counter. "As far as I'm concerned, your name is *good-bye!*" Carrie and Raul stepped aside as she rumbled through the doorway, echoing her last words down the hall. "So, you can just go find yourself another cook! One that cooks for dudes, 'cause I'm through!"

As the service door creaked back on its springs and slammed shut, Henri raised himself up from the stool and flicked his black tux tails out from under his buttocks. His middle-parted, dark brown hair was neatly slicked back, and his clean shaven, cherubic face appeared as impeccably unwrinkled as his penguin suit. Yet, as he sat back down and leaned upon his elbow, he exhibited the glummest of expressions. His face went vacant and he seemed to contemplate the chopping block for a moment. Carrie couldn't help but think the Hunter's Inn's proprietor looked more than just a little frazzled. He sat there semi-motionless for some time, then turned and looked, glassy-eyed, at the pair in the doorway, both of them still rooted to the floor, dumbfounded, with their arms full of wrapped chickens.

"*Mon Dieu*," Henri finally moaned. "What am I going to do now?"

Carrie managed to throw off the shock of what she had just witnessed and set her burden down next to the Cajun, followed by Raul.

"Henri", she said, "what's happened?"

He didn't respond right away, but stared in confusion at the pile of packages in front of him. "What's all this?" he asked.

At that moment Sue Linn and Ezmeralda came into the kitchen from the pantry. Both in aprons and headscarves, they had the reticent look of people just coming out of a storm shelter. "Is Haddie gone?" Sue Linn scanned the room, as if searching for a dangerous animal.

Henri waived a hand of dismissal but kept staring at the packages. "Yes...and for good, I think"

Sue Linn removed her scarf and shook her coarse, black hair so hard it fanned straight out. "If my mother would have talked to her boss like that, she'd have been in a locked basket and on her way back to Canton in an hour!"

Puzzlement reigned on Ezmeralda's face. "I thought your *father* was your mother's boss."

The little Chinese cook nonchalantly picked the battered griddle off the stovetop and put it back on its shelf. "He was."

"Oh." Ezmeralda nodded then went back to the original subject. "Boy, that's the worst I've ever seen Haddie!" She walked to the table and fingered one of the packages. "What are these?"

"Chickens." Carrie answered.

"Why'd you bring so many?" Henri unwrapped one bird and nodded his approval of its quality. "Looks good, but we don't need all these?"

"Really?" Carrie chuckled with surprise. "I just did what Sue asked, at least, according to Mrs. Smith."

Henri turned to Sue with raised eyebrows. "I just said to have you bring a *couple* of chickens."

Sue's responded with moderate agitation. "You didn't say a couple! You said *some* chickens, so I told Mrs. Smith, 'Tell Carrie to bring a bunch of chickens'!" She took a breath. "Some...bunch...it's the same thing!"

Henri waived his hand in surrender. "Okay, okay! We'll take the chickens! I have enough problems tonight without fighting over dead poultry!"

Carrie returned to her original question. "Hank...uh, sorry—" She fought a smile and momentarily won. "Henri, please tell me what happened."

Henri opened his mouth to speak, but Ezmeralda answered first. "Some big, muckedy-muck food critic from a newspaper in Los Angeles told Haddie he didn't like her chicken."

"A food critic? Here?" Carrie began to organize the pile of chickens into a flat-topped pyramid. "What's his name?"

"Garret Dennis," Henri said and slumped a little, as if he'd spoken an ominous curse.

"Garret Dennis has moved down from San Francisco?" Carrie finished her stacking with a pat to the last dearly-departed chick and finally gave Henri her full attention. "The last thing I heard him say was that he couldn't be blown out of the bay area with dynamite. They must've offered him half the newspaper to get him to Los Angeles."

The rest of the group froze into a dazed silence, until Henri finally voiced their thoughts. "You know Garret

Dennis?"

Carrie felt her face flush with embarrassment as if she'd been caught showing off at an ice skating rink. "Well, not really." She looked around the room at all the stunned faces and had the immediate urge to make an excuse, if not an apology. "I was still in finishing—uh, I mean high school, and he invited my father and the rest of the family for dinner."

"For dinner?" Henri repeated with an almost religious reverence.

Then it was Ezzie's turn. "In his *house*?"

Carrie's responded in a very subdued tone. "Well, there were a lot of other people there, too. It was his birthday."

Next Sue took up the banner of astonishment. "He invited your family to his *birthday party*?"

This is getting worse and worse, Carrie thought. She searched the faces around her for some sign of forgiveness, but when none appeared, she decided to modify the subject slightly. "Henri, did he say anything *after* he said the food was unimaginative?"

Henri blanched at the reminder. "Yes. He said he was still hungry, and it was a long drive back home. So he'd give us another chance and come back in an hour and a half." Hank turned a mortified rose color and looked down at the table. "He said that if we could come up with something edible and save him from a roadside hamburger stand, he would forget all about Haddie's chicken." His face lifted to meet Carrie's gaze. "Why do you ask?"

Carrie stroked her chin for several seconds, then clapped her hands and rubbed them together. "How important is his review to you, Henri?"

"I tell you the truth, Mrs. MacGregor."

Carrie interrupted. "Carrie."

"What?"

"Call me Carrie."

"Very well, Carrie." Henri smiled. "If we don't get a good enough review to draw some big spenders up from down below, I'm not sure how long I can keep the inn open. I'm sure you've noticed there are very few actual *hunters* that stop here anymore."

"Looks more like none to me," Raul piped up.

Henri rolled his eyes. "Thank you, Raul. You're fired."

"Okay, I'll leave then." Raul made a mock half turn.

"Never mind." Henri put a hand to his own temple and began to massage it. "I'll fire you tomorrow."

"Sure thing, boss." Raul walked to the chicken-bearing table. "You want I should put these in the ice house?"

"Might as well," Henri said.

"All but four," Carrie added.

"Why?" came Henri's only response.

"Because I'm going to *cook* them for Mr. Garret Dennis."

Henri put his fingers to his chin. "Go on," he said.

Carrie walked halfway around the table with a coy little expression. "Well, It just so happens that I know what Dennis's favorite chicken dish *is*."

"Do you?" A faint smile began to germinate on the inn owner's face.

"Yes, it's what he had served at his birthday dinner. *Garlic and Herb Chicken.*" Carrie leaned across the table toward the tuxedoed Cajun. "I heard him say that it was not only his favorite type of chicken, but his favorite dish of all time. He said he likes its subtlety."

"Did he, now?" Henri paused for a moment. "All right, but what makes you think you can prepare it well enough to impress the West Coast's most prestigious food critic?" Hank drummed his fingers, then added, "You are no chef...are you?"

"Neither was Haddie," Ezzie said.

Hank ignored the comment and kept his eyes on Carrie's face, then he seemed to recall something. "Oh, yes! That's right! I have heard something about you. You have learned things from your family cook. No?"

"I told you!" Ezzie's words squirted out, but Henri gave her a withering look and she closed back up.

Carrie hesitated for an instant. She was still a little self-conscious about her background, but she had already committed herself here. Consequently, she stalled just one more heartbeat, then took a breath and jumped in with the unlikely truth. "My father's household cook of twenty years was trained at Le Cordon Bleu School in Paris. He has been sharing his knowledge and skills with me almost that long. I can cook Mr. Dennis's chicken for you, but we'll have to hurry. We've burned precious time already."

Henri still looked a little skeptical. "Who is your father's cook?"

"Rodrigo De Leon."

Hank nodded. "Yes, the Spaniard. I know of him."

"Come on, boss!" Sue chided. "What've you got to lose?"

Hank slapped his fist on the chopping block. "Bien! We do it! All of you." He pointed around the room. "You do what she says! No?" Then he turned to Carrie and put his hand on her arm. "So, tell me what I can do."

Carrie smiled and returned the gesture. "Go choose your best white wine, then try to relax."

"I will try. *Bon chance, mon ami,*" he said, then left for the cellar.

For the next hour, the kitchen was a whirlwind of words and motion. Carrie looked as much like the captain of a warship, sailing into some epic sea battle, as she did a chef. She wasted few words, but left no doubt as to her directions. Her crew snapped to her orders, and within minutes after she had assumed command, "Operation Snobby Chicken" proceeded at flank speed.

"Raul." She pointed at the chopping table. "Take all but those four birds," she pointed to four packages she had just marked with a pencil 'X', " to the ice house then come back as soon as you can."

"*Si, senora*." He got them all up into one armful and disappeared.

Then Carrie turned to the rest of her international crew. "All right, ladies. We need soy sauce, twelve cloves of crushed garlic, parsley, paprika, basil, thyme, salt, and cayenne pepper. So get thee into the pantry now!" She smiled at her own theatrics as did Sue and Ezzie. Then the reality of the situation hit her. She'd been waiting her whole life for this; she'd just not realized it until now. All those years of apprentice cooking suddenly had meaning and purpose, making her the only one who could pull this miracle off at this time and place. She loved it.

Raul returned in minutes, and Carrie threw him into action, while she pulled a couple of baking pans from an overhead cupboard. "I need the big oven to be at least 350 degrees, so start restoking the stove right now and don't stop until I tell you."

He nodded and reached for an oven mitt with which to open the firebox.

She filled a pitcher with water at the sink and poured it into the pans just as her assistants returned with the seasonings.

"There's less than an hour left!" said Ezzie, checking the wall clock. "We better just cook these birds whole. No time to cut 'em up."

Carrie shook her head as she pulled open the package wrappers. "I've already cut up these four before I came here." She grabbed the soy sauce from Sue's hand and quickly doused the chicken parts with the brown liquid. "I didn't know how Henri needed them." The women dropped the remaining supplies onto the table, and the Captain-Chef issued her next order. "Ezzie, crush the garlic cloves."

Carrie heard, "Yes, ma'am", but didn't look up from her work.

"Raul!" she yelled. "How hot's the oven?"

The sinewy Mexican stopped stoking for a second and looked at the thermometer above the oven. "Three-twenty-five, she says."

"All right. Open the damper for a couple of minutes, and keep stoking."

"Got ya, boss." He mopped sweat off his face with his jacket sleeve, then put the hot-glove back on so he could grab the damper.

Carrie's hands moved so fast they almost seemed to blur as she tossed the chicken pieces in the pans and rained seasoning down on them. Ezzie returned with the annihilated garlic and offered it to her commanding officer, who threw it into the water around the poultry.

"Why do we need four chickens for only one snobby little man?" Ezzie asked as she wiped her garlic-soaked hands on the front of her apron.

"I'm not taking any chances with that wood burning dragon." Carrie fussed with the positioning of a couple of chicken thighs, then turned toward the oven, a pan in each hand. "Four chickens means a four times better chance that something will turn out right, especially with all the turning you have to do with these cast-iron monsters to make sure everything cooks evenly. I totally agree with Haddie on *that* point. Raul, is it ready yet?"

He leaned toward the thermometer and shook his head. "Three-forty, boss." He turned to Carrie. "Just a couple more minutes." He mopped his face again.

"We don't have two minutes anymore." She nodded toward the oven door. "Open it up now, and we'll just keep stoking it to bring the heat up and keep it there when I turn them."

"Sure thing," Raul swung down the big iron oven door.

"Here," Sue scooped up two of the four pans and helped Carrie feed the stove/dragon, which seemed to snap its jaws shut when Raul slammed its iron lips back into position.

"How come you know so much about woodstoves?" Ezzie asked. "I thought you used to be a rich gal! Rich people all have gas cookin', don't they?"

"Our house was so far from town that it took several years for the gas line to get out to us. So my father had the house built with a Franklin stove in every room and three wood burning cook stoves, very much like this one, in the kitchen. That's where I got my first lessons before we finally switched to gas." She smiled with a memory. "Our chef used to say that a wood cook stove is like a bear. You never turn your back on it." She snickered. "Unless you're trying to warm up the seat of your pants on a cold winter's morning."

That brought a laugh around the room and a little relief from the tension. After that Carrie just continued to baste, check, and turn at ten or fifteen minute intervals. Every time the oven door creaked opened a collective inhale froze until Carrie's voice came echoing off the oven walls that nothing had yet burned and all seemed to have progressed well. Then the room would exhale again, and everyone would return to their individual tasks. Raul kept the firebox gorged with small chunks of oak or eucalyptus, and Ezzie scrubbed clean everything that couldn't escape her grasp. Just before the last basting, Sue prepared the mixed vegetables and mashed potatoes, then made a small salad and bathed it in the house dressing that Henri always made himself.

The aroma of the dinner-to-be began to fill the little room. It soaked itself into everyone's senses and gave the group a small whisper of hope. *My goodness, that smells a lot like Rodrigo's birds*, Carrie thought. *This might just turn out right.*

"He's out there!" Hank stuck his head around the corner. "I've already given him his wine. How's everything going?"

"Tell you in a second." Carrie's bemittened hands laid two sizzling baking pans on the chopping table, then she whirled about on her heels and retrieved two more.

Everyone gathered around the results of the last hour's frantic labor to read their future in the steaming fare. No words emerged from anyone's lips for several seconds. None were needed. They could all plainly see what had taken place the last ten minutes in the heat of the oven.

Silence so completely dominated the inn that the creak of the single occupied dining room chair, as it shifted with its burden, could be plainly heard by the tense little kitchen crew. Carrie took a long cleansing breath. She knew that someone was going to have to say the obvious soon; they couldn't all just stand there forever.

Ezzie volunteered. "They're perfect. All four! They're beautiful!" She leaned over the pans for an instant and breathed in their aroma, then she straightened up, closed her eyes and crooned. "M-m-m-m-m-m!"

"Mrs. Mac...I mean...Carrie," Henri spoke in a reverent tone. "Uh, which one should we give him?"

Carrie shrugged. "Take your pick. They're all the same."

Henri's uncertain finger hovered over the pans for a moment, then pointed to the lucky one. "Those pieces there." He seemed to take heart with the decision, and began to sound more in charge. "Nardo," he called down the service hall, and, like magic, one of the waiters appeared in the doorway. "Serve the salad." The man took a small bowl from Ezzie and disappeared. "Sue?" He gave his head a small shake in the direction of the fortunate chicken and sighed. "Put that one on a plate with the side dishes and garnish it up for him."

A few minutes later, Nardo returned, accepted the prepared dinner plate from Sue, then ventured forth into the dining room, the hopes and fears of the Hunter's Inn resting tentatively in his hands.

349

Everything went as well as it could possibly have gone, and ten minutes later a pencil mustached Garret Dennis was chewing his first bite of a garlic and herb chicken thigh. The kitchen crew cloistered itself in a tense circle around the chopping table, except for Sue, who loitered in the hall halfway to the dining room entrance. All waited in silence for progress reports from Henri, who stood submissively just inside the dining room itself.

He leaned back around the dividing wall and whispered something to Sue.

"Mr. Dennis is chewing!" She relayed and crossed her fingers.

All the rest, except Carrie, mimicked the *good luck* gesture. She just stood there, with her hands flat on the table, her eyes closed. *Father,* she began internally. *Please, give these people this blessing. It would be such a small thing for you, but would mean so much to them. In the name of your son, Jesus. Amen.* Her prayer finished, she opened her eyes just in time for another relayed message from Sue.

"He made a face and took another bite!"

"What kind of a face?" Ezzie asked, a little too loud.

Sue shrugged and waived her crossed fingers in the air.

Carrie prayed again. *Father, please!*

"He's smiling!" Sue traced an upturned crescent in front of her mouth.

"*Madre de Dios....*" was part of a mumbled Spanish sentence that came from Ezzie.

When Carrie looked over at her, she saw the woman cross herself with her eyes closed as she recited something in her family's language.

"He's wolfing it down like a little piggy!" Sue giggled and made a pig snout by pushing the end of her nose up with an index finger. "He likes it! He likes it!"

"He most certainly does like it!" Carrie said. "Garret Dennis rarely takes more than three bites of anything before making up his mind. If he finishes it, he doesn't just like it. He loves it." But to her Heavenly Father she said, *Thank you, Lord!*

After he'd cleaned his plate of seconds, Garret Dennis asked to meet the staff that created such an enjoyable meal, so Captain/Chef Carrie and her loyal crew—Nardo, the waiter, included—assembled in front of the critic's table.

"I must confess," Henri said. "Mrs. MacGregor is not our regular chief cook, but she *is* mostly responsible for tonight's success."

"You don't work at the inn, Mrs. MacGregor?"

"You could say I was brought in during the intermission, Mr. Dennis."

Dennis eyed her for a moment, stroking his chin as if trying to recall a faint memory. "Do we know each other?"

Carrie was pleasant but cool. "We had a mutual acquaintance a few years back, but you and I never really got beyond a brief introduction." But her prayer was, *Oh Lord, please don't let him remember me!*

"Well, no matter." He dismissed the subject with a wave. "The fact is, Henri, I cannot in all truth publicly recommend this meal as being representative of your fare here at the—" He hesitated.

"Hunter's Inn." Henri filled in the blank.

"Yes, well be that as it may," Dennis continued. "If this meal is not typical... in other words, if Mrs. MacGregor is not going to be your regular cook after today, I cannot recommend your dining room."

"Then she will be our regular cook...uh, if she wishes to, that is." Henri turned to her and silently pleaded.

"Oh, I don't know, Henri." This had come too fast, too unexpected. She wanted it. The very thought excited her, and the timing seemed perfect. Something in her spirit made her uneasy, though. And she had an uncharacteristic urge to call the rail-yard and see what Jack thought she should do.

Henri's eyebrows rose. "I'll pay you double what Haddie made!"

"Was Haddie the one who prepared the first chicken?" Dennis asked.

"Yes," Henri said in a low tone.

"Well then," Dennis laughed, "I would pay this fine woman at least three times the wages of her boring predecessor."

Henri gulped. "Three times?"

"Well, man. How much is your future success worth to you?"

The Cajun jerked his head up and down in a very stiff nod. "Very well. Three times Haddie's wages. What do you say, Carrie? I need you. *We* need you."

Carrie was going to ask if she could briefly use Henri's phone. The words were on the tip of her tongue, but something started another line of reasoning within her. *What am I afraid of? Do I need Jack's permission to do every little thing? Am I so untrustworthy that I can't make decisions on my own? I did just fine before I married. Why should I suddenly go helpless just because I have a husband?* "I'll do it," she heard herself say. Then she added, "But only for late lunch and dinner. Just eight hours. I'm not going to be here for breakfast or early lunch."

Henri looked to Dennis, as if asking permission to agree. The dinner guest shrugged. "I don't review breakfast. I'm sure your staff could manage the ham and egg crowd without Mrs. MacGregor."

"Done then!" Henri sighed as he spoke. "Carrie, how's one o'clock tomorrow?"

"That'll be fine."

"Oh, and here's a little something for tonight, not to mention my gratitude." Henri handed her a twenty-dollar bill. "Consider that a first day bonus."

Carrie smiled. "Thank you, Henri."

"Carrie, hmm." Dennis mused. "What's your given

name? If you don't mind my asking."

"Not at all," Carrie responded. "It's Caroline."

"Caroline MacGregor, eh?" Dennis was silent for a few seconds, seemingly lost in thought. Then he shook his head. "No, that doesn't ring a bell. But, there is something...oh, well...I'll get it sometime. For now, thank you all for a surprisingly enjoyable evening."

Everyone smiled and seemed happy, Caroline most of all. *Now all I have to do,* she thought, *is figure out how to tell Jack I didn't need his permission or advice...again.*

Chapter Twenty-Six

W hen Jack arrived home from his twelve-hour shift at the freight-yard, he stopped in the mud-hall and yelled a distant "hello" to his wife. He shucked the grimy shirt and overalls from his body and tossed them into a separate hamper, labeled "Railroad Clothes", as was his nightly custom. From there he went through the boys bedroom into the family's small, indoor bathroom—one of the few in the canyon—and spent almost twenty minutes in the shower-tub scrubbing away as much coal soot and grease as he could. Then, came his migration to the main bedroom to don a "never-worn-to-the-rail-yards" shirt and a pair of bib-less denims. In the end, he completed the much-repeated ceremony by entering the living room, where he had intended to relax in his *waited-for-this-all-day,* overstuffed chair. There he would sit most nights to heal from the day, embrace his sons, and pass hopefully pleasant conversation with Carrie while she heated up his share of whatever she and the boys had eaten for supper. But this final step did not occur as Jack had anticipated.

He'd come within only a few feet of his much anticipated final destination when he stopped cold in the middle of the braided rug. There, between the Franklin stove and the kitchen wall, on the big round table where Carrie usually did her sewing, a red and white checked tablecloth, Jack had not seen in two years, had been spread. On it reposed two of Caroline's heretofore desperately guarded Bone China plates, "rarely seen by the eyes of man," as Jack sometimes put it. Each treasured plate enjoyed the company of a silver place setting, complete with linen napkin, and each boasted a lit, long, white candle in a crystal holder positioned directly in front of it.

She's plundered her hope chest, came Jack's primary reaction. And he didn't know what to do at first—settle into his regular chair or go back outside and start over. The proper procedure remained a mystery to him at this point, so he just stood in the middle of the room and ran a hand through his hair, as had become his default reaction to many things of late. *Why'd she drag all this finery out? It's not even Sunday.* But his contemplation bore no fruit. No answer revealed itself. "Where are the boys?" was all he could think up to throw out at this point.

"Having supper with Ruth and Ben," said the *little-too-nice* voice from the kitchen.

"What's all this for?" He offered the obvious question as Carrie came into the room and put two expertly-cut crystal tumblers in their appointed places. Something odd lurked in her manner, but what?

She repositioned one of two *stolen-from-the-kitchen* chairs. "It's just a little celebration." Carrie avoided his eyes by fussing with one of the forks. "I sold an extra batch of chickens to the inn this evening." Stumbling on the rug while leaving the room, she kept talking from the kitchen. "Some important food critic from a Los Angeles paper came up, and Henri was desperately trying to prepare a meal for him that would bring a good review." She came back in with two steaks on a serving platter. One looked like it consisted of most of the steer, while the other was so Lilliputian it appeared to be a wayward sliver off the first. Carrie set them down and disappeared again.

Jack chuckled. "Haddie's going to impress a food critic? That's a real laugh." He sidled over to the table and inspected his reflection in one of the silver spoons. Something was up—for certain.

She came in and deposited a dish of green beans and a small plate holding two baked potatoes. "A laugh. Yes, isn't it, though?" she said, registering a strained quaver.

Jack looked up, ready to say something like, *It sure is.* But Carrie had evaporated from the room again. He put the spoon down, scanned the table's fare and wondered how many chickens she'd sold to afford the steaks. "Isn't this spread a little too pricey for us?"

Carrie returned with a lemonade pitcher and filled the goblets. "Nothing to worry about. We're still within the budget." Then she set the pitcher down and, keeping her eyes lowered, pulled out one of the chairs. "Come sit down, Sweetheart. You must be tired."

Sweetheart? Now there's a name I haven't heard in a few years. Jack eased himself down as his wife slid the chair beneath him. *Much more than a little strange,* he thought, but decided he liked it just the same. He figured he'd go along with this mystery game as long as Carrie thought she needed to play it. He would let it wind out to its end, knowing the true reason for this maharajah's banquet wouldn't be forthcoming until then, anyway. So he stretched his feet out and exhaled the fatigue of the rail-yard. "How'd old Haddie *do* anyway?"

Carrie took her seat across the table, placing the pitcher of lemonade precisely in front of her face. "Do at what?" She looked up from her empty plate, her face a blank slate.

Jack sensed the evasion from his usually too-direct wife. Was she stalling, buying time to think of a way to tell him something he wasn't going to like? With only one way to find out, he let out a low groan and moved his verbal pawn one more square. "How did she do…cooking for this food critic?"

Carrie coughed a little and cleared her throat. Then her hand went out across the table. "Hand me your plate."

Jack muttered, "Oh, yeah," and complied but thought, *I wish you'd just spit out this whatever-it-is!*

"She didn't." With a slight tremble deviling her usually deft fork hand, Carrie slid the larger steak to a floppy landing then cured its loneliness with potato and green beans. She returned the plate to her husband and began to serve herself. Then her gaze returned to the tablecloth's level.

"What do you mean, she didn't?" Jack had already begun carving.

"Jack?" Carrie left her utensils on the table and sat facing him with folded hands. This time her gaze shot just a little over his head.

"What?" He had a piece of steak navigated almost to his mouth.

"You're forgetting grace." She lifted her interlaced fingers slightly off the table as if to demonstrate to her backsliding spouse how it should be done.

"Oh." Jack gave the almost-tasted morsel a sad glance before returning it to the plate. He wrapped one fist around the other and leaned his forehead against it. "Lord, bless this food to the nourishment of our bodies. Amen." He thrust the beef to where it had been originally headed and spoke while chewing. "What do you mean she didn't?" Jack relaxed a little. It was hard to really concentrate on marital chess with good beef satisfying one's taste-buds.

."Oh, Haddie?" She finally began to cut into her potato.

"No. Al Jolsen. Of course, Haddie!" *So much for relaxing.*

Carrie delivered a pat of butter into her split tuber and laid her knife down with a seeming air of surrender. She sighed, then spoke after a pause. "She cooked one meal for him, but he sent it back." Carrie shrugged. "So she quit."

Jack chuckled. "Walked out on old Henri?"

Carrie nodded. "Exactly." Then she hiccupped and held her hand to her throat.

Jack shook his head. "Well, what do ya know. So what did Hank do?"

Another hiccup erupted, followed by a third.

Jack snickered. "Maybe you ought to try that sugar-swallowing cure."

She waved off the suggestion. "I'll be all right. I simply have to stop thinking about them."

"You sure?" Jack hadn't had hiccups since childhood, but back when he did, he remembered the sugar-cure always worked.

"Yes, I'm sure." A hint of irritation now haunted her tone. "Just stop talking about them."

"Okay." Jack shrugged. *We're on edge about something, aren't we?* "So like I said, what did Hank do?"

"He hired another cook." A fourth hiccup. This one bounced her almost an inch out of her seat. She frowned.

Jack stifled a laugh. "Well, that's news. And on short notice, too? Who'd he get?"

Carrie hesitated, took a long gulp of lemonade, then hiccupped again and gasped for air. "Me."

Jack swallowed hard and almost choked. Then he too found need for lemonade. "You cooked for this critic?" He thought about it a moment. "No....wait a minute. That *does* make sense. Old Rodrigo's taught you much more than Haddie could ever learn cooking for ranch hands and railroaders." Jack went over the probable scene of Haddie leaving poor Henri in the lurch just as Carrie arrived with her chickens. Suddenly, things became clear to him. "I'll bet you volunteered your services before Hank could even ask, didn't you."

Carrie pushed her little sliver-stake around the plate with her fork. Then, while holding up a finger to indicate Jack should wait for her response, she took a deep breath and held it.

Jack suppressed his urge to laugh out loud. He remembered now. Carrie only got the hiccups when she became overwrought – either worried or angry. Sometimes they caused extreme pain or made her sick. He used to feel sorry for her when they'd showed up. "You're holding your breath to stop the hiccups?"

She nodded and kept her cheeks inflated for another few seconds. Then she released her air fast and made up for lost oxygen with several quick pants. "Henri… needs the business that critic can… bring in to keep the inn open." She took one more short deep breath. "And, since he's two-thirds of our business, if he closes down, so do we." She looked up. "I was helping *us* as much as Henri. Besides, he should have replaced Haddie long ago."

Jack nodded. "I'll go along with that; I've eaten her cooking more than once." He made a face. "Not even in the same universe as yours." He saluted his wife with a fork full of garlic green beans then happily consumed them. "So who's he getting as the regular cook to replace the old shrew?" Jack began carving off another piece of steak and thought he heard Carrie take yet another very exaggerated breath.

"That would also be me," she said in a low tone.

Jack stopped carving and put down his utensils. "What?" He leaned forward on his elbows and met her faltering gaze.

"He hired *me. I'm* the new chief cook …chef, if you will, at the Hunter's Inn."

Jack felt the back of his neck tighten. She couldn't have just said she'd made another major family decision without telling him first. There had to be more to it. *It's probably just until Henri can find someone else.* "So how long is this supposed to be *for*?"

Carrie put her plate to the side and folded her hands. "This isn't temporary, Jack. As of right now, *I'm* Henri's new chef…indefinitely." She sighed and waited for a response.

"You should have said something to me before you took the job." The legs of his chair squealed against the hardwood floor as he rose from the table with his plate and glass in hand.

Carrie did not turn to follow Jack as he shuffled into the kitchen like a wounded animal. "There wasn't time to discuss it with you," she droned.

This can't be a misunderstanding; she's got to know she's defying me. He put his mostly uneaten meal into the icebox. "You didn't have time to call me at work?"

She hesitated a moment. "No." Her voice was calmer now, devoid of its previous strain. "Besides, I didn't want to bother you on the job."

He finished his lemonade and put the glass in the sink. *Is she trying to tell me I'm not head of the family anymore? She's going to do whatever she pleases no matter what I say?* He washed his hands even though they were still clean from the shower. "Something like this...." He dried his hands and tossed the dishtowel onto the sink board. "It's important enough to call me."

She got up from the table and leaned on the door-jam as she faced Jack in the kitchen. "I told you; there wasn't time."

"You could have told him you had to talk to me about any permanent jobs." He folded his arms and leaned back against the sink. "Hank'd wait for that."

She shifted her weight to the other side of the doorway. "And show everyone I'm some kind of ninny who can't make decisions without my husband's permission?" She tilted her head at a sarcastic angle. "I did just fine without that while you were away flying."

There it is. Jack nodded unconsciously in response to his thoughts. *She's not going to forgive me for leaving her alone that six months. She doesn't trust me enough to let me have the steering wheel.* He shook his head before he spoke. "I can't picture *anyone* thinking you're a ninny. But it would've shown that we were a family, instead of roommates that happen to share a couple of kids." Jack pushed past her into the living room and finally settled into the big, overstuffed chair. "By the way, did you stop to think of who's going to do your share of the chores or watch the boys? This is still a working ranch, ya know." He felt even worse after his last comments. They were cheap, little vengeful swipes and had the ring of a man who believed himself powerless. He wondered how long his past mistakes would be held like a gun to his head.

Carrie swiveled around to face him. "I'll only be working afternoons and evenings. I can work here mornings. Kenny's at school until three. After that, both the boys are running around with Seth or their other friends until supper anyway, and by that time you'll be close to arriving home." She rolled her eyes once quickly. "Well, You'll make it home in time for a late supper anyway." Carrie glanced down at her hands. "Ruth said she'd be glad to watch them or give you any help you needed, and, if you don't feel like cooking, stop by the inn. I'll give you something to take home." She ventured a small, fleeting smile. "It's part of my deal with Henri."

Jack stared at the cold Franklin stove on its brick dais near the far wall. "You should have asked me."

She walked by him and stopped at the entrance to the mud hall. "It'll mean more money for us, Jack." She paused, fidgeting with a small ceramic dog from an end table. "And it's something I really wanted to do." She stroked the make-believe mut's muzzle then replaced it onto the table and looked up. "You still think I should have asked you, don't you."

"Yes."

Carrie laced a *tisk* and a sigh with a headshake.

Jack straightened up. "You've done this twice now." She didn't answer, so he went on. "Are we a family or not?" She said nothing. "Are we believers in the Word of God or not?" Silence. He waited a moment longer and spoke with slow deliberation. "Do you still want to be married to me?"

Carrie stood there quietly for a moment, her eyes fixed on Jack. "You know I–" She hesitated then whirled about and strode almost into the mud hall and had to lean around the corner to finish her exchange with him. "I'm not going to fight with you. So you do what you want. I'm just going for a walk." Her footsteps echoed on the hard floor. Jack heard the front door open. "I'll be back later," she called. Then, she slammed the thing shut.

Suddenly, an old memory came to Jack, something his grandfather said about a cow pony that kept jumping the corral gate. The little mare had been penned in for a long time, healing from an injury, and had apparently decided she'd been taken care of long enough, making this clear by jumping the fence. No matter how often Floyd and his wranglers put her back in the corral, the horse would always make a break for freedom as soon as possible. Finally, the old man gave up trying to restrain her and walked away saying, "Well, if she goes, she goes." Then he said. "If she stays, she stays. We'll know come morning. I ain't gonna fret none. The heck with her; I'm gonna eat supper."

Jack nodded in silent agreement with the recollection and made his way back to the icebox. He pulled his supper plate out and set it back onto the table. His appetite had returned with a vengeance now, so he sat down again and primed himself to begin his delayed feeding. That's when another small thought passed through his mind. *I wonder if she's still going to want her half of supper.*

Chapter Twenty-Seven

Carrie's angry pace got her down the dark road to the Smiths' house in half the usual time. She muttered to herself most of the way and barely noticed the skittering noises in the brush or the yellow reflections of a half-moon's light off a score of little eyes as they watched her pass. The buzz of a not too distant rattler did manage to catch her attention, but only for an instant as she neared Ruth's front porch and prepared to knock.

"Carrie!" Ruth pushed herself away from a supper that smelled awfully good from outside. Carrie remembered at that moment that she'd just officially skipped supper. When the Smith matriarch reached the front porch, she threw an ample arm around her young friend and drew her into the vestibule. "You're early, gal. We all just set down to eat."

"Who is it, Ruth?" came Ben's baritone from the table in the dining room, his hearing loss having kept him from catching his wife's first use of their visitor's name.

"It's Carrie," Mrs. Smith called back then half whispered to her friend, "Is everything all right?"

"Is everything all right?" Ben's voice seemed to almost vibrate the windows as he by coincidence repeated what he had *not* just heard his wife just say

It made Ruth roll her eyes. "Yes." Then she said in a much lower tone, next to her neighbor's ear, "Old man's gonna be deaf as a post someday."

"Hello, Mama," Eddie hailed.

Stepping forward a little to bring the table into view, Carrie waved at her sons. "Well, hello to you two ... too." She produced a brief smile for her children. "Everything's fine. You men can go back to your dining. I simply wanted to see Ruth for a moment."

"Oh," Ben gave out a good-natured grunt.

"She called us men," Eddie giggled to his brother.

Ben rumbled something low about eating before the food got cold, and the table conversation trailed off.

"Let's you and me go back out onto the porch." Ruth took her friend's hand and led her outside. "A site more private out here. Now, what's happening? Is anything wrong?"

Carrie shook some dust off her skirt and sat deftly on the porch rail. "That louse is what's wrong!" She pointed uphill toward her own home.

Ruth leaned against the wall. "You mean Jack."

"Who else!" She turned her head to hide the trembling on the right side of her lip. Her face sometimes reacted this way to tension, no matter the emotion—mad or sad, the ole half-lip-tremble would take hold, usually when she least expected it. She hated that; it gave her a weak feeling— weak and out of control. Why couldn't she just maintain a stone face like a man. And the hiccups! She prayed *they* didn't return.

Ruth shifted her weight slightly and folded her arms. "You told him about the job."

Carrie shook away a renegade tear and turned back to Ruth. "He said I *still* should have called him, even after I told him there wasn't time. He said Henri could have waited a little for our answer."

Ruth chuckled. "He could've."

Her friend's comment shocked Carrie, but she continued her story. "I told him it would mean more money and how much I wanted to do it." She wiped away more angry drops from her cheeks and sniffed, however, she fell prey to no actual sobs. "But he just gave me a bunch of baloney about it!"

"Baloney?"

"Yes, you know. Nonsense." Carrie sniffed again.

Ruth glanced up at the porch rafters for a second then back to Carrie. "What sort of baloney did he give you?"

Carrie slid off the railing and leaned against it. "Oh, same old caveman stuff." She scrunched up her face into an exaggerated stern expression and held her elbows away from her body to pantomime a man's bulky torso. "Listen, woman," she said in a guttural mockery of Jack's voice. "That's twice you done this!" She wagged her finger at a smiling Ruth. "Ain't I head of this here family?" She took a stiff-legged step toward the other woman. "Are we Christians or not?" She ended with her finger in the air like a Southern senator.

Ruth had to stifle her laughter in order to speak. "So, did he say anything else?"

"Yes." Carrie collapsed against the railing again. "He said, 'Do you still want to be married to me?'" She looked up at Ruth, all the mocking humor of a few seconds before gone from her face. "That sounds rather like a threat. Don't you think?" The thought of Jack's words put a knot in her stomach and stole the air from her lungs.

Ruth now wore a more sober face, too. "No," she said. "I think it's a question."

"What do you mean?"

"I think it's just something he wants to know." Ruth gave her head a half shake and raised one eyebrow.

Walking toward her friend, Carrie clasped her hands behind her. "What makes you say that?" What was Ruth getting at?

The older woman descended the front steps, strolled a short distance into the barnyard and turned around. "I'm not sure yet." She paused, looking off into the darkness of the high desert night. "Never mind." A sigh followed. "Well, what did you say to all this?"

Coming down from the porch, Carrie kept her hands clasped behind her and paced in front of the flowerbed that bordered the house's foundation. She felt a small flash of frustration that her friend was questioning her so. After all, she'd originally fled down the path seeking sympathy and comfort, and, so far, all Ruth seemed to be interested in were the details of the argument, like someone listening to a blow-by-blow description of a prizefight on the radio. Nevertheless, Carrie was curious enough to volunteer more information. "I didn't say anything, except that I was going for a walk. Why?"

Ruth crossed her arms again. "Because the questions he asked were good ones. You'll have to answer 'em sometime, either now or later, to Jack or maybe just to yourself."

Carrie flared a little. "I can't believe this, Ruth. You sound like you think I should have called him about my job, no matter what!"

After a moment of calm silence, Ruth turned toward the barn and began a slow walk in that direction. "I'm going to check the horses."

"Well, do you think that?" Carrie said, following alongside.

With Ruth gently shushing Carrie, they entered the barn. "Ya gotta' talk softly at night around Cain and Abel or ya might startle 'em awake and then they might kick something loose...like my teeth." Ruth walked around the big Belgians with practiced care until she was sure they were awake, then, after lighting a small hanging lantern, she spent several minutes feeding them extra oats and stroking their necks. She spoke softly to Carrie over Abel's back. "What's important is what *you* think."

"What?" The younger, angrier woman now stood in the empty stall between the two giant draft horses and took care to insure that her voice did not match her mood.

Abel lifted a heavy hoof and Ruth checked to see where her toes were in relationship to it. "It's important what *you* think about whether or not you should've called Jack first. I mean...it's only important what *you* think, not what *I* think. I 'spect that's *another* question you'll have to ask yourself." She made her way past the open stall and switched to Cain, causing Carrie to turn around. Finding a tumbleweed burr in the animal's mane, Ruth began to work it out with her fingers. "By the way—" She extracted the spiky ball and tossed it into a nearby coffee can full of discarded pebbles and nails. "Why *didn't* ya call Jack from Henri's?"

Carrie turned instantly indignant and fired up again. "I am not some—"

Ruth motioned for her to lower her voice while she ran a soothing palm over Cain's hide and spoke gently near his ear. She took the lantern from its hook and signaled her friend to follow her out of the barn, where they picked up their conversation again as they strolled toward Ruth's garden in the relative coolness of suppertime.

Carrie had not lost any of her frustration. "I am not some little farm wife that can be—" She realized her mistake and the insult she had just manufactured before she was halfway through her sentence. She put her hand to Ruth's arm. "Oh, Ruth! I didn't mean...I mean, I wasn't thinking—" She would have jumped off a cliff at that moment if she could have found one.

Ruth waved a relaxed hand of dismissal. "Don't pay it no mind." Then she winked and added, "I didn't."

Carrie rearranged the words in her head and started over. "What I meant to say is that I am a modern, educated woman. I don't need a husband to guide my every move as if I had no brain of my own!"

They stopped near a row of corn. Ruth stooped, set the lantern down, and pulled a few weeds. "So, is that why you didn't call Jack?"

"No. I mean, I don't know." Carrie knelt down and helped with the weeds. "I'm not sure. I just didn't think I should *have* to call." Her next words were spoken in a whisper. "I'm really not *sure* why I didn't call." She paused in the darkness, the only sounds being her breathing alternating with that of her friend. "I'm still a little confused about that, I think."

Ruth half raised up a little and duck-walked from the corn to the squash, where she began the distraction of weed-pulling anew. "Sounds like it was more something you *felt* you shouldn't have to do."

Carrie knelt down beside the older woman. Her self-righteous anger had begun to dissipate. Within seconds, uncertainty had taken its place. She didn't like *that* feeling either. Like the quivers and the hiccups, it felt like weakness, retaining for her little if any control.

Carrie remembered a time she felt uncertain about a course of action as a child and made the mistake of expressing that feeling to her father. "Don't stand there quibbling like some stupid fruit cart vendor!" he had said. "Act like someone worthy of the name Van Burean! Set your course of action and forge ahead with it! Let those pathetic souls who haven't the courage to make their own way in life worry about whether they're technically right or wrong!"

But that had been before she'd grown up, before she'd gotten married to a man with more heart than money. That had been before she had been saved. Since that time, Carrie had come to know another Father, one with even more power than Albert Van Burean, but possessing a different kind of wealth. Her new Father *valued* the heart over money and love over power. This last thing often brought confusion to Caroline; it was not the way she had been raised, not the philosophical ground floor she had been originally given to build her life upon. Since the day she had chosen to leave the well-to-do environment of her old Van Burean life, she had often found herself not knowing the right thing to say or do. This was one of those times, and, as usual when it occurred, she became unhappy with the situation. It put her in a position of having to be humble, something she still had a little trouble with. She had lived the first twenty years of her life surrounded by servants and her father's employees. How else should she be?

She took a moment beside Ruth to go over all this for the hundredth time, or was it the thousandth? Then she cleared her throat and spoke. "You think I was wrong. Don't you."

Ruth neither looked up nor answered.

Carrie swallowed to clear a sudden dryness. Still being a little unfamiliar with sincere humility, she wasn't quite sure how to express it without seeming sarcastic or condescending. Yet she valued Ruth's friendship, so this uncharted emotional territory made her nervous. Carrie tried again. "Ruth, please help me. What do *you* think I should do?"

The farmer's wife brushed some moist loam from her hands and turned to her young friend. She stood up and shook out her skirt. "You used to go to a little church down by Hannah's, didn't you."

"Yes." Carrie felt confused again. What did this have to do with anything?

"But you've not gone to church since you've moved here." Ruth sighed. "Not even after you promised me."

"No." Carrie gave the next garden row a quick glance. "We just haven't had the time." She winced inside as she spoke the little half-lie she'd heard so many backsliders recite back when she and Jack were faithfully filling their Sundays with hymns and sermons at the little Crossroads Church.

Ruth simply gave her a momentary smirk then began to weed around the carrots. "Do you and Jack read the Word together?"

Carrie shook her head.

Ruth tossed a thistle shoot over her shoulder. "Do you leastwise read it by yourself?"

369

Carrie hung her head and reverted to the truth. "No," she half whispered. "Not lately. Not for several weeks now, anyway."

"You mean, not since things have been a little easier for you." Ruth balled up one last handful of weeds and tossed it off into the darkness.

The younger woman nodded knowingly and replied through a throat constricted with the emotion of conviction. "You're right."

Standing up to stretch, Ruth put her hands on Carrie's shoulders. "You need to do that. You need the Word of God in your life every day like these vegetables need water and sunlight. Without it your life withers." She sighed. "You asked me, so I'm a tellin' ya. Read the Word and get yourself to church on Sunday. You do that and things'll probably start to turn around for ya. I'd bet Ben's suspenders on it."

Carrie backed up from Ruth's grasp. "I'm not going to become some Dumb Dora that does everything Hubby says!"

Ruth cleared her throat and moved on to the green beans.

Carrie toyed with a vine pole. "I always liked reading my Bible." She nipped off a sun-browned leaf with her fingernail. "But I don't know about church." She remembered the constant teaching from the Crossroads church pulpit about a wife's duty to submit. It seemed to be all about surrendering authority—surrender your authority to God...surrender it to your husband. How could she surrender authority to a man she wasn't even sure she trusted yet? All those wonderful times she and Jack had spent as the happy, church-going couple were before he abandoned his family. Before she knew he was even capable of doing such a thing. A lot had changed since then.

"I'll have to think about church," Carrie said in a freshly, hardened tone.

Turning toward the carrots, Ruth spoke over her shoulder in a tone of her own that was even harder. "You do that."

Chapter Twenty-Eight

Carrie heard the *fump* as a dark shape blocked her vision, and something feathery-soft brushed against her nose and forehead. She turned and saw the thing whoosh, whoosh, whooshing away into the growing shadows of evening. *An owl!* She glanced down at the now empty plate in her hand where a moment before a blueberry muffin had resided. Shaking her head in near disbelief, she stood next to her car in the dirt parking lot and waited a moment while the full realization took root. *I've just been robbed by a bird!* Then she wondered if the theft could have been prevented by not taking the checked kitchen towel off the baked treat before she got it into the church. *Too late for that now.* She tossed the empty plate onto the right seat of the Stutz. *Very well, then. I'll go in unarmed.*

Carrie had just parked the *Chickens by Caroline* trailer behind the Hunter's Inn, as was her habit of late, and jaunted up the hill in the Stutz to the Sweet Springs Community Church for the much anticipated, and partly dreaded visit to God's sanctuary—the very first since the MacGregor clan had arrived. The action made Carrie more than a little apprehensive, not only because of the length of her family's absence from formal worship, but also on account of the distance she, over the last few days, had begun to feel between herself and the all-powerful, loving God she had heretofore clung to so closely.

This estrangement initiated a growing tide of guilt within her, the same guilt she used to founder in when she hadn't studied for a test in school. She usually flunked those tests because she was not a good last-minute crammer. Confidence came only when she prepared herself well in advance by keeping up on her daily study. Carrie had not been doing that in her spiritual life; rather, she had been letting the cares of the world push the Lord out of her consciousness little by little. And now, she felt neither

372

prepared nor worthy to come back to God's house, and that old suspicion had arisen again that somehow she was going to flunk whatever well-deserved spiritual pop quiz the Lord might throw her direction today. *Maybe,* part of her mused, *I should try this another time, another day after I've had the chance to get back into reading the Bible again.*

No, another inner voice responded. *You're going in— no more excuses!*

So now Carrie forced herself along the brick walkway toward the front door of the little, white New England style structure. She stopped for a moment at the threshold to look back down the hill at the cluster of buildings and cottonwood trees that made up most of Sweet Springs proper. For some strange reason she had hoped that this pointless little ritual of looking out over the town would give her some sort of last minute encouragement or solace, as rural vistas viewed from hillsides sometimes can. But it didn't. She saw only an obscure, time-warn, almost miniature whistle-stop, hugging its one lone intersection, complimented by a single croaking raven circling a small, backyard corn patch. When she faced forward again, the church doorway still awaited her, as did the decision whether or not to enter. So she took a deep breath and let her conscience push her body forward.

With the exception of a paint splattered construction ladder, penetrating a small trap door in the ceiling, Carrie found the vestibule empty, as was the pantry-sized office connected to it. So she ventured on into the sanctuary, which looked like the inside of most small churches only a little smaller. Traffic-polished pine plank floors shown between modest, un-upholstered oaken pews, and a thick, hand-hewn pulpit of the same stubborn hard-wood stood dead center on a dais just in front of a large, dark, Mahogany cross. The place looked quite ordinary—quite traditional. But, odd as it seemed, it turned out to be that very commonness that first began to bring a little serenity to Carrie's troubled demeanor. An atmosphere of respectful neatness seemed to almost dominate the very air within the building, not at all like the decades-worn, slapped-together, bare-wood look of the old Crossroads Church. But, at the same time, this place still shared the same basic Godly feel, the same spirit she had enjoyed at Crossroads. *Spirit?* Yes, that word described what she sensed right now, *spirit*. Then all at once, conviction, mixed with a certain homesickness, set in and penetrated through her being all the way to the innermost chamber of her existence. And, at that instant, she knew, just as if someone had spoken it to her, that she'd been away from God's house much too long.

Carrie looked around again for the minister or at least a caretaker, but the main sanctuary appeared to be as empty as the front entrance. *Strange with the front door open. Someone must be coming back soon.* She strolled, with a slow deliberate pace, up the center aisle and stopped in front of the pulpit, folding her arms. Seconds passed as she stood with eyes closed, simply breathing in the soothing familiar *churchy* aroma she had only now identified as such. She breathed it in and waited as if some unnamed but expected supernatural thing would take place at any second. But nothing of the kind occurred. She sighed and let her shoulders droop.

The room had begun to grow dark with the failing of the day, but she could still see the stained glass rendition of Jesus, the good Shepard, in the big window above and behind the cross. Carrie stepped up onto the dais and gazed up into the face of the sectioned colored-glass Christ. *I feel your breath here but not you. It's like you've stepped back from me. I know you're there, but you won't touch me like you used to. You won't touch me; you won't talk to me. I've sensed you less every day this week!* For an instant, she forgot where she stood. In her mind there existed only her and the Father-in-Heaven she could no longer feel. *You're beginning to get too much like my earthly father!* Carrie fixed her attention upon the Lord's eyes and cried aloud, giving voice to all her frustration, "Where are you?"

"I'm up here," came an unexpected male voice from somewhere up high and distant.

"Oh!" she shrieked, then stumbled backward and sat down hard onto the floor. Shock shot through her chest, making it difficult for her to breath. She heard someone's weak, croaking voice whine, "Where?", then realized the voice had been her own, although she couldn't recall speaking.

"Up here." The masculine voice echoed again.

Carrie gathered her wits and rose from the floor. "Who...where...where are you?"

"I'm up in the belfry."

With newly regained composure, she started back for the vestibule just under the bell tower, but stopped short of going through the doorway from the sanctuary when she heard a loud yell from above. "Whoa, look out down there!" Crash! A large wooden toolbox impacted right-side-up onto floor, barely two feet in front of her just an instant after the warning call. A gray rain of dust shook from the tools that had, upon impact, danced once in their carriage. A length of prehistoric rope dropped next, coiling fast beside the tools and raising a gray particle cloud of its own. Carrie stood dazed in the doorway, coughing in the polluted cloud that had engulfed her.

"Hey!" A dirty man in faded bib-overalls and checked shirt scurried down the narrow belfry ladder to the floor of the little entrance room. "You all right?" He stopped in front of her, pushing a half wayward hammer back into its proper canvas overall-loop on his hip.

"Yes." Carrie brushed off her dress. "Just a little startled, I think."

The man looked to be in his late twenties with a shock of black hair half covering his eyebrows. He shook his head. "Well, I'm glad you didn't get all the way out here before it fell. When I turned around to answer you that last time, I must've accidentally pushed the toolbox through the trapdoor." He flashed her a humiliated grin. "Sorry."

"Well, no harm done." Carrie relaxed. "At least I don't think so." She glanced up. "What were you doing up there, anyway?"

"Stringing a new bell rope. The old one was starting to rot away. Plus, I think Kaiser Bill's been pulling strands out of it." He picked up the length of ragged hemp and tossed it off toward the far end of the room.

Carrie stamped the dust from her shoes and coughed again. "Kaiser Bill?"

The man seemed to suddenly notice how dusty he was and slapped his bibs a few times. It made *him* cough too. "Oh, he's the big barn owl that lives up there." He pointed up toward the steeple. "He conducts his own brand of unrestricted torpedo warfare on anything edible that gets within his range, so the congregation here dubbed him Kaiser Bill in honor of our late adversary." He momentarily snapped to a stiff attention and clicked his heels, Prussian style. Then he chuckled and retreated back into his earlier embarrassed smile as if he thought he'd overdone the humor.

"I thought all the owls around here were burrowing owls that lived in holes in the ground." She sneezed and unconsciously rubbed her nose.

The man took out a red handkerchief and mopped sweat-soaked mud from his face. "Generally, that's true, but Bill's the slightly larger exception to that rule, and it seems he's partial to our belfry." He took a moment to work the kinks out of his shoulders then glanced up toward the ceiling. "But nobody's said anything about getting rid of poor old Bill yet. Probably because he helps keep the place rodent free."

Carrie pulled a maverick curl from her eye. "Well, I agree with you about the warfare part. He torpedoed a blueberry muffin I was bringing for Reverend Fisher."

"You know, that's a tragedy." The man picked up the toolbox and put it into an open storage room near where he had thrown the rotted rope. "And, in consideration of the fact that I *am* that same Rev. Fisher who would have received that muffin, it's a particularly large tragedy." He picked up the rope, threw it in after the toolbox and shut the door with a slight theatrical flair.

Carrie's face flushed, and she tucked in her chin slightly as she tried to make amends for her assumption. "I'm…I'm so sorry. I—"

Rev. Fisher came closer to her and smiled. "You mistook me for the caretaker. Am I right?"

"Sadly, yes." Carrie looked up through sheep's eyes.

The reverend waved away her concern. "Pay it no mind. It's understandable." He indicated his attire. Then, noticing the dirt on his hands, he motioned for Carrie to follow him out of the room, which she did.

On the way, she took the opportunity to berate herself. *That was smart, Caroline! Mistake the pastor for a janitor! A good first impression!* She walked alongside the dirty man trying to think of what she was going to say next. Hopefully, it would be something she would not regret in five minutes.

"So tell me," the man said as they passed from the sanctuary into the kitchen. "What can I do for you, Mrs. MacGregor?"

"How did you know my name?'

He turned on the sink faucet and soaped up his hands. "You've been pointed out to me several times by church members." He smiled as he rinsed. "It's a small town."

Carrie nodded. "Yes, isn't it." She turned away and took a moment to muster a little formal distance as an antidote to the uncomfortable vulnerability that this visit had so far forced upon her. Then, when she felt ready, she faced him again. "I've come to talk to you about coming to your church."

Fisher finished drying his hands and hung the towel on its hook over the sink. "But you're already here."

Carrie rolled her eyes and, before she could stop herself, ventured a small laugh at the man's deadpan pun. And that was that. She had lost the armor of aloofness now—too late to get it back. Her mask had slipped, so she simply smiled and gave in to the pastor's open easy manner. "Yes, all right. I mean I'd like to come regularly with my family. Or at least my sons. I don't know if my husband will be coming or not. I haven't told him about this yet."

"If God has called you here, who am I to say no." He extended a polite hand of direction and showed Carrie, once again, through the doorway and back out into the main sanctuary, where they almost collided with a semi-plump apple cheeked woman, apparently participating in her latter middle years.

With her arms full of purse and overflowing manila folders, she successfully avoided contact with Fisher and Carrie then bustled her way toward the upright piano to the left of the pulpit. "Oh, excuse me, Reverend!" she sputtered without slowing or even breaking stride. "I have to go through the music for Sunday and get back home before the stew simmers too long." She successfully swung her ample torso down onto the piano bench without aid from her encumbered arms, a feat that should have won her a blue ribbon at any international gymnastics competition—even with two points taken off for the shrieking of the bench as it scraped two inches across the floor. "I promise not to disturb you." She balanced the music sheets upon their perch above the keyboard and began to thumb through them. "I'll be quiet as a mouse," she said, without looking up.

The good reverend smiled. "I'm sure you will, Mrs. Hocksey," he responded over his shoulder. "Do whatever you need." Then he returned his attention to Carrie.

"Good. We'll come this Sunday." Carrie glided past the man and stopped almost in the exact center of the church proper. Her eyes scanned the room, and she drank in the details like candy. That's the way she felt right now, like a child in a candy shop. The same way she had felt whenever she ate some of Rodrigo's walnut fudge. As a little girl, she called this sensation *happy on the inside.* The tense foreboding apprehension of a few minutes ago had gone—poof—just like that. And *now,* this is what she felt —happy inside— but there existed something else as well. *What is it?* For a moment, out of long-bred habit, she blocked the answer from her conscious mind, but then something, some strange irresistible unction, caused her to surrendered and let the new feelings float to the surface for confession. *I don't want to leave this place! I feel like I could just stay here forever!*

She recognized the truth in this simple statement the instant she told it to herself. But what made it true? That answer did not come in a quick or easy manner, so she stalled, hoping to stay until it surfaced. "Your church is beautiful," she said and ran her hand over the back of one of the Spartan pews. "It's so simple, so honest and uncluttered." Carrie strolled up the aisle and looked around just as she would, had she been at an art gallery or a museum. But there existed nothing of worldly value to see here—no paintings or statuary, no rare porcelain figurines. No, nothing graced the physical realm here save white-painted plank walls and rectangular windows of cheap, small-paned stained glass. And yet... "Just beautiful." she repeated, then folded her hands in front of her lap.

"Is there something you would like to talk about, Mrs. MacGregor?" Rev. Fisher had caught up to her and now leaned against a pew across the aisle.

"No," she lied and meant to turn away, but found herself caught in the current of an almost irresistible need to face him and speak the truth. So she did both. "Yes. You're right; there is something. It's about whether or not I deserve to be here." She sat down in the pew behind her and, for the next half hour poured out most of her doubtful and troublesome thoughts and feelings. She told her new confessor about how she'd not read the Bible or gone to church in a long while and about how she'd felt so distant from God lately.

"A little over a year ago, my husband and I separated. I found myself having to make all the family decisions. My father raised me to be independent, so I had no problem taking over. But, now that Jack and I are back together again, I still want to keep making those decisions. I don't think I trust him yet. He hurt me...us, and I sometimes feel like he has not yet earned the right to be head of our family. I keep thinking someday, if things get too boring for him or too tough, he'll just take off again and leave us to float on our own like he did before." She sniffed and cleared her throat. "I know that's not giving him a fair chance to make good, but I can't seem to help myself." She shook her head and looked down at the floor. "It's just the way I feel." A stray tasseled bookmark lay beside her. Its crimson fringe seemed to call her to distraction, so Carrie picked the thing up and played with it while she spoke.

"One of the reasons I married Jack was because he didn't worship wealth. I was sick of the way my family valued material possessions above people." She paused. "Or love." Her chest heaved with a massive inhale; she held the breath for an instant then released it into the atmosphere of the sanctuary. "But when Jack was gone, we had so little money to live on. And later the boys and I went back to live with my parents. They're fairly well off." She paused again. "That's when something changed in me. Once I was living back in my old childhood home again...I started to sort of slide back toward what I had been before Jack and I met. I began to crave the comfort that beautiful, expensive things can give, and I ended up having to fight all my old temptations...every day...just to keep hold of my faith."

Her gaze left the bookmark and sought the reverend. "My family can afford some *very* expensive things." Carrie abandoned the bookmark to its original resting place and turned to studying the floor planks. "As a matter of fact, I went a little overboard when we lived with them. Gorged myself on everything my parents' world had to offer. Well, almost everything." She glanced up at the reverend. "I know this is all sinful. Does it mean I'm evil?" She didn't know why she had said that last part. Not the most intelligent sounding statement she'd ever uttered, and she hated how childlike it must have made her sound. But it did have one simple virtue; that of being an honest confession of what she had wondered for weeks in the more secret chambers of her mind.

Rev. Fisher lowered himself down onto the pew bench across the aisle. He looked genuinely sympathetic. "I don't think you're any more evil than anyone else in my church, although there are a few who may *think* themselves a little above the rest." He stretched his arms and yawned, then seemed to remember his manners. "Excuse me. I've been working on the place since five this morning." Leaning back in the pew, he seemed to take time to gather his thoughts. "These are strenuous times for all believers – new challenges to faith, more carnal temptations than ever before. Yours is not the worst story I've listened to this year. There are several in our congregation who carry an even larger burden of guilt. Believe me." He paused. "I think much of what's happened in your life is a result of being hurt. Your husband should never have left you alone without proper support. But now he's come back and is again taking care of his family. I believe that God's hand is in this. The Lord's brought you all back together again, and, now—something just as important—he's brought you back to His house." The reverend indicated the sanctuary with half-raised arms.

Carrie had been listening with her mouth slightly ajar, almost mesmerized by the soothing tones of the man's voice. It made her think of hot chocolate or a warm quilt on a cold windy night – comfort from the storm. It also reminded her of what Jack's voice sounded like before the war. And he—the good reverend, with his soothing manner and God-inspired words—reminded her of someone else, as well. But who?

She shook herself. "So, does this mean we can still come to church?"

The man in the bib-overalls stood. "Fixing family rifts and healing broken hearts is never easy after trust has been shattered. You're going to need support and comfort from people who care for you. We are...." He stretched out his arms again. "We are your family in Christ." He smiled and shook his head. "Mrs. MacGregor, you not only *can* come; you *must* come." He placed his hand over hers and squeezed in a manner that spoke of no more than Christian reassurance.

Carrie grinned without reservation for the first time since she arrived at the church. That's when her memory kicked in, and, in an instant she knew who this man, who appeared even younger than herself, reminded her of so much—ancient Pastor Williamson back at Crossroads. How strange. Pastor Williamson had to have been at least eighty. And that was back during the war. But this very young man that now stood before her could not have seen his twenty-sixth birthday yet. So what made them so much alike in her mind? She did not even have time to wonder at this question because the answer came through too quick and too clear. *They both echo the words of God! Both of them forgo their own opinion in favor of the Lord's wisdom. And, as Pastor Williamson used to say, that always attracts the blessing of the Holy Spirit. That's the hot chocolate. That's the comforter, the Holy Spirit. No wonder this man's words are like a healing balm. They're drawn from the very mind of God! Well, I demanded that God show himself to me again. So he has given me his own words through the mouth of His servant.*

After learning the MacGregors' first names and the exact location of the ranch, Rev. Fisher walked Carrie out to her car as Mrs. Hocksey began to play the first strains of *Amazing Grace.* She slid into the seat and wrapped the empty plate in the checked towel that, had it not been discarded into the car, might have saved the coveted blueberry muffin from Kaiser Bill. "Ruth Smith tells me you're not married," she said. "I've never known a single pastor before."

"I was married," he replied after a slight hesitation. "She died in the influenza epidemic."

"I'm so sorry." Carrie flushed. Why had she asked such a personal question so soon. *He must think me a busybody.* "I didn't mean to be too personal."

"Quite all right. It's not the first time the subject has come up amongst the ladies here. I suspect in most women's minds a pastor without a wife is like an unmade bed. They just naturally have to remedy the situation. It seems everybody has a sister or daughter they want me to meet."

Carry couldn't get rid of her flush. "Well, you're safe with the MacGregors. Neither Jack nor I have sisters, and the boys are our only offspring."

He furrowed his brow and smiled. "That's a pleasant change. Not that I don't intend to get married again someday." He shoved his hands in his pockets and stood there for an awkward second before changing the subject. "So this is the infamous Stutz Bearcat."

They looked at each other and recited in unison, "Small town." Then they both laughed a tension-releasing laugh together.

"Thank you for everything," Carrie said as she started the car. Then she told him she'd be back Sunday with her family in tow.

The trip down the hill toward the Hunter's Inn was a short one, lasting only a minute or two. However, it gave Carrie time enough to remember that Ruth had indeed mentioned something about finding Rev. Fisher a good Christian wife.

Let me see. She drummed her nails on the steering wheel. *Who would be a good match?*

Chapter Twenty-Nine

The sound of a large squirrel skittering over the roof descended upon those assembled in the room below. Jack, goaded by instinct, looked up from where he and his family sat on time-loosened, folding wooden chairs behind the backmost row of pews in the Sweet Springs Community Church. Rev. Fisher finished the last few minutes of his sermon on the Prodigal Son, while Jack experimented with leaning back as far as his center of gravity and the construction of the prehistoric furniture would allow.

Earlier in the service, somewhere around the point where the ungrateful son confronted his father for his inheritance, Jack had discovered that if he rocked his chair to the rear, the outside world came into view through the only unstained window in the east wall. Leaning back a little farther, he found he could just barely see the cottonwood tree that squatted inside the white picket fence out by the road. So now the game was to see exactly how much of this outside world he could frame without falling backwards and thereby causing the collapsible-chair to actually collapse and eat him.

The standard Sweet Springs fifteen-mile-per-hour breeze rustled the old tree's pale green leaves and caused a thin, low branch and the small bird that sat on it to sway in rhythm with the gusts. The little winged creature had a brownish-gray top half and a yellow belly; not being an official bird watcher, that's all Jack knew about the critter, other than the fact that it managed to sit the bucking branch quite well. But then most birds had a good sense of balance...just like pilots.

Bees harmonized around some unseen hive up between the church's rafters, competing with the sound of the reverend's voice. These background distractions made it easy for Jack to drift rapidly into non-biblical musing. *If they* didn't *have a good sense of balance, they'd sure have a short career in the air.* His last thought referred to both birds and pilots. He smiled at the concept of a bird with bad balance, careening dizzily through the air, slamming into trees and rocks every few yards. He played the scene out in his mind like a moving picture, and eventually had himself almost laughing out loud.

That was all it took. His concentration being focused more on the internal movie than the teetering chair, Jack went back a little too far and rapidly arched toward the floor, all *his* balance gone. However, at that same moment, Carrie's hand shot out and grabbed the chair of her arm-flailing mate. Easing the front legs back down onto the floor as inconspicuously as possible, she gave her man a quick glare.

Understanding the obvious message of disapproval, Jack ceased all reckless activities. But he couldn't resist leaning his head back just a touch to see if the yellow-bellied bird still held its grip on the branch when the wind gusts increased a couple of minutes later. That's when a small drop of gladness pumped through his thoughts, grateful that the church had been full enough today to warrant the breaking out of extra chairs. There would have been no such acrobatic leaning in those pews that sat, like oaken monuments, firmly fixed to the floor in front of him. He unconsciously shook his head and risked one last peek at the tree. *Wouldn't have been able to see out from the middle rows. That would have been a pity.*

"As you arrived this morning, you probably noticed a quite large, cast iron cook stove setting on Orvil Griswald's wagon," Reverend Fisher's strong youthful baritone echoed off the room's exposed rafters. "It's the one we've been praying for to cook those big common meals on. It just came a little earlier than we expected." He paused. "I've been asked not to say their name, but someone in this room got nudged by the Lord and has given it to the church for just that purpose. I think we should all give a prayer of thanks today for this generous gift, but while you're at it, also pray that God's giver will be blessed as well."

Jack had already daydreamed through all of Rev. Fisher's teaching, and, now, the young preacher had almost finished with the announcements as well. For some reason Jack could not understand, that set well with him.

"Well now, we're going to need some volunteers to lift it off the wagon and get it into the back shed." The reverend leaned expectantly on the pulpit for a second while he calculated the show of charitable hands. He looked more than a little surprised as he took his elbows off the pulpit and straightened his back. "Praise the Lord! That's most certainly more than enough." He cleared his throat and shuffled his notes into a neater stack. "Yes, it must go into the shed for now. Unfortunately, there's not sufficient room yet in our little kitchen for such a grand cook stove as this. Our building program has not yet caught up with our new kitchen equipment." The reverend leaned forward onto the pulpit again and peered hawk-like down upon his congregation. "So, if anyone feels the Spirit's urging toward giving extra generously to the kitchen expansion fund so we can hasten the sharing of our bounty with the poor of Sweet Springs, be assured you have my blessing." A wry smile crept across his face as a very mild wave of laughter ran through the room.

Jack mixed a small sigh with a half groan. How had he gotten here, and why did he feel so out of place? The answer to the first question was, simply put—Carrie. She had returned from Ruth's the night of the fight over her job at the inn with an entirely different attitude than the one with which she had left. They had to go to church, she had said. No two ways about it! She sounded desperate and looked quite determined that they should do this.

"You asked if we were a Christian family," she had said. "Well, my answer to you is *yes*. And since we are a family supposedly governed by the word of God, then there's one place we need to be on Sunday, and that's in His house. Don't you think?"

And that was that. Trapped by his own challenge, there existed no way for Jack to justify staying away from church—not without destroying what little authority and credibility he had left. But there was still one hitch. He didn't really want to be here. He hadn't wanted to go when Carrie confronted him on the subject, and he felt the same way now.

He did not, however, know why.

Then a disquieting notion struck him. *Have I been away from church too long?* Had his faith suffered that much during his time of no fellowship? He had no answer for that yet. The fact that he *had* come seemed a promising possibility though. He had not argued about that. He knew his wife to be in the right the first time she spoke about coming. But still, he did not have the same excitement about worship as he'd once had when they used to attend down at the Crossroads Church. Maybe, that's why he agreed to come so quickly. Maybe, he subconsciously wanted to see if he could get a little of the old good feeling back. What his grandmother called *God's peace.* So far that hadn't even *begun* to happen, but there could still be time enough for that. And Jack thought it important that he give it a chance.

"All right. Apparently, my original count was wrong. We still seem to be one man shy for the stove crew." Rev. Fisher had been speaking all through Jack's musing. "Who'll be the brave soul to volunteer his brawn in the Lord's service?"

Jack yawned and turned his head toward Carrie as he stretched his arm behind her. That's when he noticed her giving him *the look*—not the adoring look he sometimes saw during rare tender moments between the two of them, nor the unfocused, looking-right-through-you expression of faraway thoughts. No, this could not be mistaken for anything other than the look a husband gets when he's not doing something his wife thinks he ought to be doing *without her even having to mention it!* It was the *you-should-be-raising-your-hand-and-volunteering-to-help-with-the-woodstove* look. There existed no question in Jack's mind as to any of this. But submission to wifely pressure had no place on his list of things to do this morning. He had come at Carrie's insistence without the slightest argument. He thought that quite magnanimous by anyone's standards. Plus, it was too darned early on his only day off, and, if the good folks of this church wanted their stove moved, they would have to do so without him.

So Jack did not raise his hand, but neither did he protest his wife's obvious silent rebuke. He merely met her stare with an innocent smile. By now the service had officially ended with a final prayer by the good reverend (Something about traveling mercies and continued Christian behavior throughout the week), so Jack sought long awaited relief by rising from his chair and walking to the vestibule doorway. By this time, however, search as he might, he couldn't find the yellow-bellied bird.

Carrie finally showed up beside him. She had, at this point, given up the look. Instead, she led Jack outside to shake hands with the reverend and mingle with the congregation.

Everyone outside appeared friendly, almost too friendly for Jack's liking, descending on Carrie and him like dogs on a soup bone. Their faces beamed as they pumped his hand. Even old Henrietta Black slid her dead eel of a hand through the grasp of both MacGregors and did her best to give a waxy impersonation of a smile. Jack knew her only through Carrie and Ruth's descriptions, but she gave him the shudders, just the same. She reminded him of every witch he'd ever imagined in every fairy tale he'd ever heard.

Glad I didn't meet that one on a dark stormy night!

Then there remained more people to meet and more hands to shake. He saw Ben, Ruth, and Seth coming and felt a little relief. *Finally, someone I know.* Out of habit he thrust his hand out in Ben's direction, but the old man waved it away and simply clapped his young friend on the back.

"I figure you've already pumped a gallon with that arm; I wouldn't want to wear it out." He laughed at his own joke. "I seen a whole passel of new folks show up here." He shook his head and laughed again. "I do swear, this is the most hand-shakingest church I've ever been in. Must take new arrivals most of a week to get the feeling back in their fingers after their first Sunday here."

Jack looked at his hand and flexed his fingers. "Do you think they're all really this friendly?"

Ben looked pensive for a moment, then nodded. "Yep. I think they are for the most part. Folks up this way tend to be more on the honest side than not."

"I see." Jack remained not quite convinced of that. "Aren't these the same women who wouldn't invite Carrie to any of their little get-togethers?"

Ben shook his head. "Your wife swept in here all full of new ways, lookin' like a Gibson girl, and driving the fastest car by far in these parts. Women were all afraid of her." He winked. "Or maybe a little jealous. Just took 'em a little while to lose the fear and warm up to her. They didn't really know her before. And now that they see her at church with everybody else—" He shrugged. "I think they just had to see she wasn't on a high horse or somethin'."

Jack glanced down at a small stone he'd been toeing in the grass. "Maybe so. Just looked a little hypocritical to me."

Ben's face turned calmly serious. "I know it probably looked that way, but mostly it's not. You know, these here common meals the reverend's a talkin' about are gonna be mostly for them what can't afford their own food. Lot of those kinda' folk come into town from the rail-yard nowadays, but then I suppose you already know that." Ben tilted his head to one side. "Now, it's true some people don't like the idea of feeding the poor, especially if the poor happen to be hobos, but most in the church think it's a fine idea. I might be wrong, but my guess is that there are more that aren't hypocrites here than them what are."

Jack didn't comment any more for a while. He believed Ben to be sincere, but, as yet, he didn't know whether or not he agreed with him.

"Ben, if you and Seth are going to help with that stove, you'd both better get over there." Ruth gave her husband a loving shove.

"Yep." The old man flexed his muscles as if to impress his wife. She made a mock face of revulsion and waved him away. "Come on, boy." Ben winked at Seth. "Let's go show 'em how it's done." He put his arm around his grandson and led him toward the stove-laden wagon.

"Can we go watch, Mom?" Kenny rested his hand on his brother's shoulder while he waited for the answer to his plea, which sounded so desperate one would have thought the fate of civilization rested in the balance.

Carrie looked to Jack who shrugged that he had no objection. "Will you two stay out of the way?" she said. "I do not want you squashed like a pancake because you got under foot." Both boys responded with energetic nods, so Carrie shooed them off.

Ruth strode up to Jack and put a friendly hand on his arm. "You did the right thing bringing your wife here today. She needs the Lord right now…and some more friends." She gently patted him. "I think God's herded your family into the right pasture."

"Maybe." Jack tried to sound skeptical as he answered, but something about Ruth's last statement caught him off guard. A brief image of Jesus as a Shepherd, firmly nudging his sheep along flashed across his mind's eye. Then suddenly, without warning, he felt something like an electrical shock run through him and he had trouble catching his breath. That lasted only a few seconds but seemed like days to Jack. Then it ended, and a wave of calm flooded through his being. And all at once, most of the doubt and distrust of the people at the church left him. At the same time, he felt a desperate need to pray, a thing that he'd not done for a long while. *Lord, what have you done to me? What do you want from me?*

Serve me, came the answer in his head.

Yes, Lord. His breathing still came only with effort. Then conviction, born from months of spiritual selfishness and irresponsibility began to settle in his heart. And the weight of it made his breathing even more labored. *I'm sorry it's been so long, Lord, since—*

Never mind. Serve me now.

Jack knew now he had to obey the words of that still small internal voice before he went insane or his chest exploded, which ever happen first. He swallowed hard to remedy the dryness that had invaded his throat, then he tapped Carrie on the shoulder, causing her to turn from her conversation with Ruth. "I think I'll go help with the stove," he said. He paid little attention to his wife's shocked expression and the small gasp that escaped her open mouth. He just turned away and took off at a fast walk that would soon catch him up with Ben and the other men. *What the heck am I doing* ran through his thoughts for an instant, but in the end he decided to just go along for the ride, let God drive, and see where the journey ended up. *This must have been what Carrie was talking about when she said the Holy Spirit was yelling in her ear.*

Chapter Thirty
August, 1924

C arrie closed her car door and walked to where Ruth, Ben, and Seth stood cloistered around one end of the Smith garden.

"What are you doing?" She said as she tried to rubberneck around Ruth, who stood beside her male workforce with her back to her approaching friend.

"Plantin' pine trees for windbreak," she answered without turning around.

Carrie moved around them where she could see. Seth shoveled dirt around a two-foot tall tree that Ben held in place about fifteen feet from the vegetable rows. It was the last in a line of eight trees that ran east to west.

Ruth watched until Ben and Seth stopped their work, then she elbowed her way closer. "Seth, put some more dirt down; I don't want those roots showing after the first rain. And be sure you make a good berm to hold the water."

Carrie watched with idle fascination as Seth molded a circular earthen wall around the little tree to form the crater shaped berm with a trough on two sides connecting it to the irrigation furrow. "What's a windbreak?" she asked.

Ben looked up. "That's a line of trees that blocks the wind from the garden so's it can't do harm to what grows there."

Carrie knelt down beside the baby pine, fingered one of its boughs, then looked up and down the row. "They look awfully small to do much about the wind." She held down her skirt and wrinkled her nose as a rogue gust blew up from the draw. "Especially up here."

Ruth nodded. "It's true, they do have to grow some before they're much good, but you have to plant 'em some time. We sunk another well this last fall, so now we've got water enough for a garden windbreak."

Ben rubbed the dirt from his hands. "In truth, it's a bit late in the season for plantin', but it took an age and a half to get these here two year old pines from Zachary." He worked a kink out of his shoulder. "Have to *buy* 'em now. I can't march around the mountains a' lookin' for seedlings anymore, like I used to." He half looked around and winked. "Too old and useless."

Ruth lightly slapped the top of the old man's head and backed out of the tree-planting huddle. She wiped her hands on her apron and walked toward the house. "You could stand to plant some more trees around your place too, Neighbor."

Carrie instinctively got to her feet and caught up with her country mentor. "I don't think so. At least not now. Jack's either gone or too tired, and I wouldn't know how to plant one with a gun to my head." She giggled a little.

Ruth turned toward her. "Oh, that's hogwash. All you do is dig the hole deep enough for the roots to be amply covered, mindin' to make that hole twice as wide as the saplings reach. Then you throw in a little season-old horse manure, mixed with vegetable scraps and topsoil." She snapped her fingers. "And there you are. Ya planted a tree."

The *waf, waf, waf* of a hawk's wing sounded low over their heads and caused them to look up and track the predator as he rose back up to his circling height over Ben's rodent-rich oat field. Some dust swirled off the road on its way downhill and temporarily engulfed the parked yellow Bearcat. Carrie gasped a little at first, then surrendered to the inevitability of dirt coating her car and sighed.

The two women finally reached the hitching rail in front of the porch. Carrie leaned back against it. "Where does one acquire these trees?"

Ruth stepped up onto the stoop. She removed her shoe and spanked it upside-down. A minute pebble fell out and clattered down the steps. Then she lowered herself carefully into one of two red-painted porch chairs. "Old man Zachary has a greenhouse full of them."

A smile crept across Carrie's lips. "You don't mean that crazy little old man who eats lunch at the inn every Saturday." She relocated to the porch and sat down in the vacant chair next to Ruth. "He looks like he's a hundred years old!"

Ruth snorted. "Ninety-seven. Claims he came to California during the first gold rush. Don't rightly know if that's the Gospel or not, but he knows how to coddle a seedling into a healthy tree." She slipped her shoe back on and tied the laces. "By the way, why'd ya stop by?"

"I need some more sisterly advice." Carrie pulled a foxtail out from between two porch planks and toyed with its whiskers.

Having finished their tasks, Seth and his grandfather sauntered up to the porch and stopped to listen to the conversation in progress.

Ruth got up from her chair and leaned back against a porch pillar. "Go ahead. Shoot."

"School will be in session in less than a month, and, what with both my business and my job, I don't see how I can take Kenny to school like I used to." She tossed the foxtail away and looked at Ruth. "I saw Seth riding an old gray horse to school last term. I was wondering if, uh…."

"If Kenny could ride to school with me?" Seth grinned. "That'd be the berries!"

"Be the what?" Ruth's face wore an uncomprehending expression.

Carrie translated. "That means he would like it very much."

"Oh." Ruth seemed to contemplate Seth's words a moment. "The berries. Hmmm. I like it. The berries." She let out a husky giggle.

Seth excused himself into the house to wash up, but Ben stopped and leaned over close to his wife's ear as he arrived at the top step. "You're the cherries."

"Berries," Ruth corrected.

Ben remained undaunted. "All righty then. You're the berries."

Ruth started to smile, but then turned and feigned disgust. "I'll berries you, you half-deaf old buzzard!"

Ben mimed exaggerated surprise. "Ya will, huh!" Then he kissed her cheek with the speed of a Mojave rattlesnake. She swatted at him with a well-practiced tardy swing. He straightened up and grinned as broad as a watermelon slice. "She's a corker, ain't she?" He rumbled a deep laugh as he stomped his way into the house and disappeared into its shadows.

"That man!" Ruth turned her face away for an instant.

"You're blessed, Ruth." Carrie said.

"I know." Ruth touched her fingertip to her reddening cheeks. "Always get so sunburned in the garden."

Carrie indulged a momentary yearning for Ruth and Ben's relationship, knowing that the one she and Jack had paled in comparison. Everything else seemed to be going so well. Half the valley either was or wanted to be her friend. Chickens by Caroline boasted a very good business, and her position as chief cook—she did not know why Henri didn't just break down and call her a chef—seemed to be fast turning into a dream come true, especially with the not infrequent compliments she received from the dining room's new upscale patrons. That restaurant review from Garret Dennis had done the trick as per bringing new business to the inn. Patrons for the dining room had almost doubled since the critic had made his praise of the place public—more than enough business increase to justify Carrie's unprecedented triple salary. Even though Henri had not yet admitted that.

Sometimes, Carrie would stand behind the louvered blinds in the waiters' alcove and sneak peeks at customers as they ate. Sometimes she recognized old friends or acquaintances and would secretly take amusement from thoughts of "if they only knew."

Lately, everything had turned out to be simply the bee's knees, so why had Jack become such a sour puss? *First he gives me a stern Bible Belt lecture about being a Christian family, then he snubs most of the people at the new church, most of whom are some of the sweetest folk I've ever met.* Jack had been the one who insinuated that Carrie had pulled away from God. Now he seemed to be doing that very thing himself. Why had he turned into such a flat tire? *Oh, Lord. Please, tell me what's going on. He seemed to open up when he helped with the stove at church. But later he went right back to being his same old brooding self. I don't understand.*

The wind rose again, only this time quartering more from the northwest, carrying the usual sweet, pungent smell of desert sage up from the bottom end of the draw. It whispered past Carrie's nose, and she drew it in. *That always smells like serenity. Okay, Father. I get it. Stay calm and listen for your voice. Thank you, Lord.* "Amen."

"Caroline? Are you there?" Ruth waved a hand into Carrie's line of vision, looking like this was not the first time the older woman had tried to get her attention.

Carrie realized she must have been inside herself longer than she thought. Sputtering a little, she said, "Oh! I'm sorry. I was just thinking."

"And praying." Ruth smiled with her soft sympathetic tone.

"How did you know?" Carrie's question held no embarrassment.

"Folks don't usually say 'Amen' when they're just thinking." Ruth's smile broadened. "You've been doing a lot more of that lately, haven't you."

That caught Carrie by surprise. "Now, just how did you know *that*?"

"A little bird said so."

Carrie stood up. "Knowing you, it was probably more like an angel than a bird." Now she smiled too, only not quite as wide. "It seems like praying comes easier since we've started back to church. I don't know why. It shouldn't make any difference, but it does. I mean, if we're believers, we should want to pray whether we go to church or not."

Ruth laughed out loud. "Carrie, sometimes I think you think too much!" She straightened up and enveloped her friend in her work-hardened arms. "Honey, don't take it apart to try to find out why. The Lord's just rewarded you with the desire to seek him more, that's all. He wanted you back in the body—His church. You went. So, like any good parent when his child obeys, he's given you a reward. Nothing simpler or more natural than that." Ruth raised an eyebrow.

Carrie laughed a giddy laugh. "It's hard for me, Ruth. I was raised to question everything."

Ruth gave her friend a squeeze. "That's what I figured, but just try letting go of the steering wheel as often as you can. God knows how to drive." She paused a half a heartbeat. "By the way, that's spiritually speaking about the steering wheel." She pulled back to arms' length and winked. "Not on the road in your car."

He does indeed know how to drive, Carrie thought. *But I wish He'd tell me what's wrong with Jack.*

Chapter Thirty-One

" Cracked." Carrie said the word with an assertive nod as she walked down the hall beside her employer.

Henri stormed ahead of her into the kitchen, an area he had not frequented much since Haddie left. His voice betrayed more than a little agitation. "What do you mean, cracked?"

Carrie caught up with the steaming Cajun. "I mean, the third stove is cracked." She had made the mistake of disturbing him in the midst of an attempt to impress some of the inn's newer, more affluent dinner guests by use of his little-used but still smooth New Orleans wit. She had waited until she and Henri were safely in the access hall to reveal the nature of the problem, but that did not seem to help much. His salesmanship had been brought to a stop by bad news, and that did not seem to be the best thing Carrie could have done for the man's disposition. She could sympathize without much effort. *The poor man gets a little ahead of the game after years of struggle, and I calmly tell him a third of his kitchen's just taken a powder. Were I him, I'd want to kill the messenger, too.*

"It happened while we were baking the rolls for tonight," she said. "I'm no blacksmith, but it looks like it just got hot once too often."

"What are you talking about? Too often." Henri rubbed the back of his neck.

"It's just an *old* stove; that's all." Carrie faced him with authoritative hands on hips. "It must be at least forty years old, if it's a day."

Henri sat on the tall stool and surrendered to the truth with a sigh. "Actually, it's more than sixty. It was originally a railroad stove from the Civil War. I had hoped it would last... a little longer." He paused and seemed to study the quarter inch wide crack that ran from the oven all the way to the middle of the firebox, then he nodded twice as if he were answering some internal question. "I do not think this can be repaired easily." He repeated the nod once more. "*Bien. C'est la vie.*" With shoulders slumped, Henri continued to sit and stare at the dead, cast iron traitor. "It is going to take me six months to put aside the money for a new stove." He massaged his temples. "And maybe another month or two to have it shipped up here. This is not good for us. And it is the second problem that has come to face me this week." He looked up at his chief cook and the two assistants that had gathered behind her. "I am probably going to have to let someone go until the new stove gets here."

Carrie heard Ezzie inhale and hold her breath. The junior kitchen assistant's expression said there was no mystery as to who would be haunting the employment agencies in Palmdale this week. Carrie felt the onset of frustration, but before the shadow of that had a chance to take over, a small light flickered in her mind. She knew this to be the time for a quick prayer, like the one she'd prayed back in Hannah's pasture. *Father, help us here, please.*

"I do not like it, either," Henri said as he gave Ezzie a quick glance, "but, I have not the money to keep three cooks on and solve the stove problem too. *N'est pas?*" He cleared his throat. "I have four waiters who work various shifts out in the dining room." He waved a hand in that general direction. "I shall have to let at least one if not two of them go, as well. But it must be, and there is no help for it."

In an instant, a powerful idea materialized in Carrie's mind and burst out as words before she realized. "May I cook the food for my church's common meals here Sunday nights?" Immediately after she said it, she felt like putting her hand over her mouth.

Henri's expression was like that of a man in the throes of a heart attack. He opened *his* mouth in an attempt to speak, despite his apparent shock, but Carrie merely held up her hands and continued. "I know that sounds like a very poorly timed request, but listen just a moment." She paused to take a deep breath. "My church has a much newer stove in working condition. The problem is as yet we have no room for it in our little kitchen." She stopped to see if her boss had anything to say. His countenance seemed a little more at peace, and he said nothing, so she went on. "What would you say to a year's loan of that stove to the Hunter's Inn in return for the privilege of the church being able to cook the Sunday common meal down here? That would give you more time to save for a new stove, and the church would not have to be in so much of a hurry to expand our kitchen. And you wouldn't have to let anyone go," she looked at Ezzie, "because you'd still have the profit you usually make from the third stove."

The slender tip of Henri's right index finger ran down one side of his mustache.

He eased himself back against the preparation table. "And this common meal would not be served here?"

A tightness in Carrie's chest, that she had only noticed in part the last few seconds, relaxed. . "All serving would take place at the church. The only thing we'd do here is cook."

"Who is *we*?" The stroking finger switched to the other side of the Cajun's mustache.

Carrie risked a small half smile. "My girls here." She put her arms around both Sue Linn and Ezzie. "If you allow them to help, that is."

"*Your* girls?" Henri seemed to be fighting a smile. "I thought they worked for *me*."

A little streak of crimson shot across Carrie's cheeks as she momentarily averted her eyes. "Yes, they do. But I've come to think of them as mine, too." She still had her arms around her assistants, so she gave them a small squeeze, and all three passed around a little smile of admiration.

The tuxedoed Cajun gazed off into space for a moment, then looked back to Carrie and slowly nodded his head. "I agree as long as we can use the stove the way we see fit the rest of the time."

The chief cook shrugged. "I'm sure Rev. Fisher will agree to that."

Henri's right eyebrow went up. "What? He does not know about this yet?"

"No." Carrie quickly glanced around the room. "But, that doesn't matter; he'll agree."

"How can you be sure."

Leaning back against the warm but dead, cracked stove, she stretched her back. "He needs the time to raise money for the new kitchen. Plus, he'll be getting three professional cooks to do the common meals…instead of the usual potluck fare."

Henri shrugged and got up from the stool. "*Tres bien.*" Wrapped in the look of one lost in thought again, he took a couple of steps. "But I am still not sure how long we can keep everyone working here." He turned around and revealed a look that depicted surrender to some inevitable sadness. "As I said, losing one of you is not what I want."

Carrie let go of her friends and took Henri's place on the stool. "You said the stove was the second problem this week; what was the first?"

Henri took a deep breath and answered in a tone that once again smacked of surrender. "Our business has been better since our little food review coup."

Sue Linn piped up. "I'll say! I've never seen so many people coming to eat here!"

Henri waved her off and continued. "*Oui.* That is so. But it only looks that way because we compare it to before when almost nobody came here." He stopped a moment and straightened his coat sleeve. He continued the process with the rest of his attire while he finished his explanation. "The truth is we still aren't bringing in enough money to really make a profit. I haven't drawn a salary in over two years, except for room and board. The inn's rooms are still mostly vacant much of the time, and, even with the new customers, the dining room business is not enough to pay the bills." He spread his arms. "This is the truth, my friends. I swear it by the blessed Virgin."

Carrie raised her finger tips to her lower lip. "Henri, you say the dining business has leveled off?"

"Yes."

She tapped the lip with her pinkie as she considered the problem. The Hunter's Inn had gotten a great review; what had gone wrong? *Lord, what is it? I know recently I've been praying for almost everything. I'm not sure. Is that wrong? I know things seem to go better when I do. Can one pray too much?* She didn't know the answer to that, but, considering the results of her new prayer habits, barring a direct intervention from The Almighty, she had no intention of stopping. *Father, why has this happened, and what should we do?* Then it happened again...in a flash, just like with the stove idea, she had the answer. "We need a big cheese!"

Henri shrugged. "Cheese?"

Carrie shook her head. "You know. Someone with a really important name that everyone knows."

"*Oui*, go on." Henri folded his arms and leaned back against the wall.

Carrie stood up and began to pace between Henri and the girls. "You see, so far we've been catering to locals, who mostly eat at home, and a small group of the upper class, who are basically out on a one time weekend lark."

She paused and waited for comments, but none came. "In other words," she continued, "they come to our little inn just to experience the place and say they've been here, but very few come back for a second or third visit. We've just been a passing fashion, and, now that fashion's almost passed. So, what we need is someone important whose opinion will mean something to more people than simply a small adventurous portion of the upper crust. More like the upper middle class or at least the lower upper." She looked around and saw that everyone, including Henri, wore a confused expression.

Carrie held up her hands again. "All right." She stopped to rephrase. "Someone other than one newspaper food snob. Someone famous who just likes the place and will influence lots of other people to like it, too—and for more than just one or two visits. We want to be their new favorite restaurant." She paused. "And their favorite place to spend the night as they travel to Fresno or Los Angeles either by car or train. We need someone who is important enough to make that happen."

"Ah!" Henri held up a finger. "The cheese!"

"Yes, the big cheese. Someone who is loved and listened to by the rich and the not so rich, as well."

Henri nodded. "Bon. So, how do we get such a big cheese?"

"I don't know yet." Carrie stopped pacing. "But I know how to find out."

Henri adjusted his angle of lean for a more comfortable posture against the wall. "Tell me."

Ezzie chimed in again. "She's going to pray." She took a step forward, hands clasped in front of her. "She's gonna pray real hard. She's been doing it for days, ever since she's been going to that church." She stopped and looked around at the others as if she'd embarrassed herself, but then continued. "I thought she was crazy at first, but sometimes when she prays like she does...sometimes...good things happen. So now I pray, too. Not as much, but I do it." She looked Henri in the eye. "It works...I think." She turned to Carrie. "I do." She grinned.

Henri did not seem impressed. "I see." He unfolded his arms and cast himself off from the wall. "Well, Ladies." He straightened his tuxedo. "If you wish to pray for our financial salvation, than please be my guests. I thank you for the kind thoughts. Just don't get too angry if I don't join in." He started for the dining room again. "It's not that I don't believe; I just think God has better things to do than to worry about one little hotel. But don't let that stop you. Feel free to pray away." Then he disappeared down the hall and the ladies of the kitchen crew, once again, *found* themselves *by* themselves.

Ezzie patted Carrie on the arm. "God, he will tell you something. I know."

Smiles materialized between the two as the young Hispanic girl went back to mixing dough for the supper biscuits. Carrie turned to fetch her recipes for the night, but stopped when she saw Sue Linn staring at her like an animal caught in a headlight.

"You really believe all this stuff." The forehead of the first generation Chinese-American girl furrowed in a seeming effort to understand. "You do, don't you."

"Yes." Thumbing through her cooking notes, Carrie spoke without looking up. "Do you?"

Sue Linn turned away toward a baking sheet that sat waiting to be greased. "I don't know. I just hope you're not all wet with all this praying." She looked over her shoulder at Ezzie who had begun to whistle as she mixed the dough. "And I hope Ezmiralda's not believing a bunch of applesauce when she should be looking for another job." She shook her head. "I just don't know." She glopped a spoonful of butter onto the pan and began to coat the surface of the sheet.

Carrie stared at the page concerning wine sauces but did not actually see much of the print. Too busy speaking through her heart, she paid little attention to what appeared before her eyes on the page. *Father, please help me to show Sue and Henri you're real. Show them your power.* She paused to collect a thought. *Please, bring the inn the big cheese it needs. In Jesus' name. Amen.*

Chapter Thirty-Two
Thanksgiving Day, 1924

"**M**om! Mom! Babe Ruth played ball with us at the sandlot!" Kenny pelted down the boardwalk of downtown Sweet Springs toward his mother. "And he signed a new ball. And he gave it to me." The boy shoved the holy object supposedly blessed by St. Babe close to his mother's face. "See."

Eddie came stumbling a couple of seconds behind his brother. He pointed at the ball Carrie now held. "Baby Ruth, Mama! Baby Ruth!"

Smiling at the boys' make believe game, their mother ruffled both their heads at once. "You mean Babe Ruth, the baseball player?"

"Yeah!" Kenny lowered his ball, still unapprised by Carrie.

"Baby Ruth!" Eddie nodded once.

"Not Baby Ruth." Kenny flashed a sour expression to his little brother. "It's just Babe...or *the* Babe."

"Oh, yeah." Eddie's nod appeared more scholarly this time.

"I see," Carrie said. Her boys never ceased to amaze her, and that included now. What imaginations they had!

Looking for them had made her late for work, but she wasn't concerned about that. The inn could get along without her a little longer. She knelt down to kiss Eddie on the forehead but stopped short and straightened up when she noticed Jack leaving the Lakeview Café. For a moment, she watched him shuffle across the lake road, his shoulders stooped, hands in the pockets of his rail-yard stained overalls. Then he pulled the bill of his cap low over his eyes and headed toward the airfield. Why was he going that way? Thanksgiving dinner at the church was tonight, and there remained barely enough time left for him to get cleaned up.

Switching her attention back to her sons, Carrie put an arm around Kenny. "So is this Babe a good ball player?" She decided to play along with the pretense. "I mean I know he's a famous man, but is he *really* that good?"

"The best they is, ma'am," intruded the ancient miner lounging on the wooden bench in front of the bank. He scratched his petrified overalls in a rude way and spit tobacco juice into a rusty can set just within range. "I been readin' about him in the paper. They call him the Sultan of Swat!"

"He's a New York Yankee, Mom!" Kenny turned to the man on the bench. "Isn't he, Orville?"

"Yep. He surely is." Orville repeated his scratch, intensifying its explicitness and extending its duration.

Carrie momentarily diverted her attention to Orville. "You mean he was really here?" She had assumed the whole thing to be only her sons' boyish exaggeration. "Babe Ruth was actually at the sandlot when the boys were playing?"

Orville smiled and nodded. "Not only was there, but played a whole game with them kids." The old man sat up a little straighter and folded his arms over his chest. "Paper said The Babe does this sorta' thing all the time. Gets bored rubbing elbows with all them upper crust types that wanta' say they know him. So sometimes he just grabs the first train out of whatever big city he's in and gets off at any one-horse little town what's got a baseball diamond of any sort...even a sandlot like your boys play on. Paper says the man drives the team managers wacky a'tryin' to keep track of his whereabouts."

"Look at the ball, Mom!" Kenny waved the trophy back into his mother's field of vision.

Pulling the clean new baseball away from her nose, Carrie carefully read its sacred inscription out loud for the world to hear. "To Kenny. Good game. Your pal, Babe Ruth."

"Eddie got one, too. But it don't say 'good game' 'cause he didn't play." Kenny patted the side of his overalls. "I got it in my pocket, so he don't lose it. All the guys got one!" The boy took the ball back and remained silent for a moment as he stared at the inscription on the cowhide artifact. Then he spoke with more awe than Carrie thought might be in him. "He played a whole game with us, Mom." Kenny looked up with glistening eyes. "He really did. He just showed up with his bat and glove and a whole big box of balls." He let his gaze settle back onto the unbelievable autograph. "And he played with us." The boy's last words came out as a reverent whisper.

And that reverence caught Carrie's attention. The look in Kenny's eyes told her that this day would remain in his memory for as long as he lived. He would tell and retell the story long after his children had children of their own. She knew she could not treat the event lightly. She should say something befitting such a momentous occasion.

That's what she should have done, but the appropriate words eluded her. And in the seconds that passed while Carrie searched for the right comment, mother habit took over. Something else, something much less respectful automatically slipped out and made her sorry the moment she spoke it.

"But why were you playing baseball?" Carrie heard herself say. "Isn't it football season now? I remember in college they always played football at Thanksgiving."

And there it was, a minor thought that had passed almost unnoticed through her mind. Although not indicative of her feelings about her sons' good fortune, it still managed to escape her brain, dash over her tongue, and shoot all the way out of her mouth before she could stop it.

Kenny rolled his eyes. Carrie didn't blame him. She wanted to do the same. Who cared why they weren't playing football? Her sons had spent an afternoon with

Babe Ruth! Even a *mother* should know how much that meant.

"Nobody in town's got a football right now," Kenny explained, using his most patient tone. "Frankie Cabot had one from last Christmas, but one of their horses stepped on it and flattened it." He shrugged. "So, since then, we always play baseball. Nothing much can hurt a baseball. 'Cept maybe a hay harvester."

"Oh." Grateful for her son's mercy, she let the subject drop.

Toward the tail end of this conversation, Carrie became distracted by a sort of low, rumbling cacophony that seemed to originate from behind the bank. Soon after, around the corner came a tide of townspeople—mostly young boys with a few girls of marrying age tagging along on the group's outer fringes. Some waved slips of paper at a full-girthed man with a wide, turned up nose. His dark, neatly clipped hair clung sweat-plastered to his broad head while his shirt-sleeved arms worked feverishly to satisfy the crowd with handshakes and signatures. Carrie nodded. This *had* to be Babe Ruth.

She instantly felt sympathy for this bear-size man now surrounded by admiring hounds. Despite his ear-to-ear smile, he appeared hassled and harried, as he attempted to work his way down the sidewalk toward the railway station. But the crowd, seeking autographs and bearing offers of everything from dinner to marriage, limited his progress. They had no intention of letting such a genie as this out of the bottle until he had blessed each and every one of them in some memorable way. Carrie wished they would all just get out of the poor man's way.

"Sorry, folks," she heard him say. "I have to catch my train."

With practiced skill, the Babe plowed a path for himself through the human sea. He maintained a sort of gentle politeness, but kept moving, nonetheless, and never showed an ounce of frustration—not even when the westbound four-fifteen for Los Angeles blasted its whistle for the third time. As she watched the man's struggle, Carrie felt her sympathy for him grow…right up to the time the idea hit her.

She pulled a scrap of notepaper from her purse and rapidly scrawled, *Good any time for lunch or dinner for Babe Ruth and guests at The Hunter's Inn, Sweet Springs, California. No charge. Caroline Van Burean MacGregor.* She didn't exactly have Henri's permission to carry out this little piece of promotion, but Carrie felt certain he would not disagree considering the once-in-a-lifetime opportunity here. Besides, there remained no time to ask him. With the speed of a bolt of human lightning, she folded the note and hurried off without explanation to her sons. No time to lose: she had to catch The Babe.

"Mr. Ruth!" Carrie kept her hands firmly clasped around the paper forming a sort of double fist and used that fist to force her way through the throng. "Mr. Ruth, I have something for you!" Despite her enthusiasm, her calls merely blended in with the noise of the small country crowd. Two more attempts to get the man's attention failed. Then it hit her. *You're calling him like you would a tennis partner at the country club. That's not going to get* this man's *attention.* So, she took a deep breath, imagined herself as Kenny, and hollered as loud as she could, "Hey, Babe!"

Instantly, the big man stopped dead and jerked his head around as if a tire squealing traffic accident had just occurred behind him. He scanned the boardwalk for the source of the voice. Finally, after swiveling his head around two or three times, Ruth let out a frustrated bellow. "Yeah, who's askin'?"

Surprised at herself, Carrie fought her way through the sea of hands and arms. But when she and the Babe met face to face, all she could think of to say, in a tone much

411

subdued by embarrassment, was, "It was me." She'd gotten his attention all right, but now she did not know what to do with it. After an uncomfortable split-second of silence, Carrie added, "I yelled at you."

"And who are you?" His tone still carried the gruffness of a thousand plays, disputed with sour-faced umpires.

Carrie took a calming breath which only half worked. "I'm Caroline Van Burean-MacGregor." She caught herself off guard again by including her maiden name, but something told her it would not be bad for business to drop a hint of her upper class past.

"Who is that?" someone asked.

"Who is who?" said someone else, and the general rumble of the crowd began to swell as the verbal virus spread person to person.

"Say, pipe down!" The Babe roared then softened his tone for Carrie. "You were saying?"

"I'm the…." She wanted just the right word here. "I'm the *chef* at The Hunter's Inn, finest hotel and dining room north of Los Angeles."

The Babe simmered down from gruff to slightly impatient. "The hotel chef, huh?" He chuckled and rubbed a finger on the side of his nose. "Well, that's just swell, Doll!" Ruth winked and took her outstretched hand in his then patted it. "And I'd really love to stop and gab with you about that sometime, but it's late and I've really gotta scram." He caressed Carrie a little too far down the small of her back. "So how 'bout you and I get together the next time I hit this berg." He leaned close enough for her to be engulfed by his invisible cloud of whiskey breath. "We could have a belt or two and discuss…cooking." He pinched her around the ribs.

She pushed his hands away. "I'm also Kenny's mother." She pointed back to her mop-haired ball player standing a few yards away on the wooden sidewalk. The Babe followed her gesture, and young Kenny waved his baseball back at Sweet Springs' hero of the day. "He thinks you're quite a guy...as far as baseball goes." Carrie raised an eyebrow. "And I'm sure my husband would agree."

Ruth sheepishly returned the wave and cleared his throat. "Yes, well I saw him play today. Quite a kid. Good arm. Good eye for the ball." He grimaced. "Look, Mrs. MacGregor." He hesitated for a moment as if he thought he recognized the name. "I didn't mean nothing by...uh...what I—"

"Mr. Ruth, I can see you're a very busy man." She paused to give him a knowing look. "And I'm sure you get all kinds of offers on various subjects. You merely mistook my intentions." Carrie allowed herself a restrained smile, as she pressed the handwritten meal ticket into Ruth's paw.

"What's this?" he said as he unfolded the paper.

"An invitation to the best meal you'll ever have." Carrie relaxed as control of the situation came her way. She allowed her small smile to broaden a bit. "You can take advantage of it...." She raised both eyebrows so he couldn't possibly miss the small irony she was about to deliver. "The next time you hit this berg."

Babe stood transfixed for a second, repeating her full name in a low whisper. Then his eyes brightened. "Caroline Van Burean-MacGregor! Say, you're that society dame, ain't ya? The one that Hollywood food critic's going on and on about."

Carrie grinned. The plan was working. "That's who I used to be." She winked and felt a tiny twinge of guilt, uncomfortable with the insincerity but excited by what seemed to be a successful pitch. "Now, I prepare meals fit for a king...or a sultan." She nodded toward Ruth.

As the Babe examined the paper in his hand, a cagey smile crept across his face. "You're also an okay salesman," he said.

"Saleswoman." Carrie's satisfaction spread through her like warm chocolate. *This* had been a good idea.

"Yeah." He nodded. "Well, no matter what you're called, whatever your boss is payin' you, it ain't enough. He's gonna make a gold mine off of you." The Babe took another glance at the meal ticket and nodded. "I'll be back, Mrs. MacGregor. You can count on it. After all this, I've just gotta see what all the hubbub's about." He shook her hand, tipped an invisible hat, and resumed his journey to the train station, hollering back over his shoulder as he went, "And I'll bring a few friends with me, too. So make sure it's a bang-up supper, Doll. I've been known to make or break restaurants with a single belch."

Carrie stood still as the tide of the crowd flowed around her in the swat sultan's wake. Then she leaned against the board fence that stood between the bank and the general store. Her breathing came a little slower now that the excitement had drained away. It was one thing to converse with the famous on an equal basis at a Marner Bay dinner party. But it was quite different, however, to approach someone like Babe Ruth as the representative of a small town hotel. It had almost made Carrie feel like a door-to-door salesman—at first. Then the excitement had set in...and she discovered she liked it. She had, in reality, been selling her talent as a chef as much as she had been selling the hotel. Just as the Babe sold his talent as a baseball player.

They were both celebrities of a sort. And, for once, her fame had not depended upon her father's name, but upon what she could do on her own. Carrie liked this, too. So she continued her fence-lean a little longer and beamed at the mental picture of Babe Ruth and friends unexpectedly showing up at the inn's dining room. Henri would be speechless.

But even as the satisfaction from this new victory began to sink in as a reality to be accepted, a slightly older question reared its head and demanded consideration. Where had Jack gone off to when she saw him leaving the

414

café? The thought shot out from the shadowy back of her mind and muscled its way to the front. The church Thanksgiving supper would be starting soon, and he should be there with the boys since Carrie had to work the first part of the evening. He hadn't looked happy…as usual. For weeks now, the man seemed to sulk and pout over almost everything. He would say nothing about what ailed him— no hint as to what all-consuming thing caused him to always look so downcast. Carrie's reputation as the inn's chef was growing beyond expectation, and Jack's job at the rail-yard seemed steady and secure. Everything seemed to be humming along just fine, so why all this insufferable unhappiness?

"What'd he say, Mom?" Kenny, who had magically appeared beside her, tugged at Carrie's dress, and pulled her back from her thoughts. "What'd you and the Babe talk about?"

Eddie too now materialized and demanded her attention. "Mama, you talked to Baby Ruth."

Kenny winced at the improper title.

She gave them both a quick squeeze, then patted Kenny's shoulder. "He said you were a good ball player."

"Really?" The boy's mouth dropped open and he clutched the autographed ball close to himself.

"Absolutely."

Eddie jerked on her finger. "And what'd he say 'bout me?"

Carrie smirked at the tiny male ego pleading for equal attention. "He said to give you to the Gypsies." She tickled him around the navel and was rewarded with the usual squeals as the boy squirmed away.

"I'm hungry," was Kenny's next contribution. His little brother nodded agreement and it became plain that the time to drop them at the church for supper had come, Jack or no Jack. Where had he gotten off to?

She herded the boys down the boardwalk and crossed Saber Canyon Road toward the church. No time to worry about a moody husband now. There were turkeys to finish and rolls to bake. Jack's problems would just have to wait.

Chapter Thirty-Three

The sound of an iron pan hitting the floor echoed from the kitchen to the front of the café. A muttered oath soon followed. One toothless, old ranch-hand raised his head and smiled; none of the other customers seemed to notice.

Lost in a mixture of tobacco smoke and guttural male voices, Jack sat unseeing behind a raised dinner menu. His head rested in one hand, elbows braced against a checkered tablecloth. He'd tried three times now to pick a supper for himself, but with each attempt his mind merely slipped off its intended track and skidded into thoughts of how much he hated his present life.

He considered ordering the steak and bemoaned the fact that he went to work in black smudged bib-overalls instead of a flying suit. For a moment the pot roast sounded good, but that subject faded into the background as Jack remembered how some of the other rail-yard switchmen called him high-handed because he used an occasional three-syllable word. Chicken with mashed potatoes, okay. Unfortunately, that led his thinking to how, after a twelve-hour shift switching boxcars, he never had enough time or energy left to help Carrie and the boys with either ranch chores or deliveries. And *that* dark tidbit made Jack's present gloom double in density. He hated his job more than a rat hates the trap. And to top that off, he often found himself plagued with feelings of failure, not to mention a recurring conviction that he couldn't take care of his responsibilities at home. He had been raised to never leave women and children to do the heavy work. That made present circumstances a bitter pill. All considered, the term *failure* did not sound anywhere near strong enough to describe Jack's current opinion of himself as he sat boring an imaginary hole in his menu. *Worthless* sounded more accurate…worthless and trapped.

"Say Handsome, think you've studied that long enough?" The voice of the waitress penetrated the mood with an unexpected abruptness.

His mind snapping back to the surrounding current reality like an overstretched rubber band, Jack dropped the menu flat onto the table. Then he jerked his gaze up to the blond woman clad in an apron that almost matched the tablecloth. After waiting a heartbeat, he cleared his throat. "I… uh…I haven't made up my mind yet", he said.

The woman responded with a wide smile. "Well, if you can't decide, Hon, just close your baby blues and point at something." She gave her head an attractive feminine shake. "Whatever it is, we'll cook it up for you." She winked.

A little, involuntary spark ran along Jack's nerves, the kind of intimate spark that, upon the rare occasions he experienced it, almost always occurred only when he found himself in close proximity to his wife. He recognized the minor electric sensation as the embryonic appearance of temptation. So he immediately began the well-practiced drill of shutting off the current of this sensual invasion before his mind wandered into places it should not go. On most such occasions, thinking of ice water did the trick. Or, if that didn't work, the image of the scowling, wrinkled face of his first grade teacher often proved more than adequate. However, this time neither treatment proved successful. The buzz caused by the attractive, blond bait holding the order pad remained unabated within. "Actually." Jack risked a furtive upward glance and got smacked in the consciousness by the poutiest pair of cherry-red lips he'd ever seen. The very sight of them caused his mind to freeze up for a moment before he could regain the power of speech. "I'm not really sure I'm hungry yet." Jack frantically created a mental image of Caroline on their honeymoon and quickly pumped it into his mind's eye. Then he looked back to the menu. "Nothing looks good," he lied.

Except for its corn silk color, her hair appeared to be coiffured the same style as that of the wife in his mental picture, but the presence felt different. This woman wanted to know what Jack needed. *Lately, Carrie's only concerned herself with Carrie.* She seldom even *looked* at Jack when she spoke. *This* woman gave Jack her total attention. *Well, what do you think she's going to do, Stupid? She's a waitress. You want her to take the order with her back turned?*

"Well, how about some coffee, Sugar?" She giggled and hid behind the order pad for a moment. "I mean coffee *with* sugar." She tapped the pencil next to her pout. "Then you can decide if you want anything more after that."

Someone came through the café door, causing a few moments of the mild breeze from outside to waft the waitress' floral scented perfume past Jack's defenseless nose. What did it smell like? He couldn't think. What kind of flowers? A sigh that sounded almost a groan escaped from deep within him. *Why is this angel here...now...when I feel the need for someone just like her... way too much?*

The little bit of common sense he had left told him he was too weak to stay here right now. So, in one tidal decision, he consolidated all his available marital resolve and acted in opposition to his gut desires. He stood with a sudden abruptness, and almost tipped over his chair in the process. "I'm sorry. I think I've made a mistake." He took his striped cap from his overall pocket and pulled it down onto his head. "I mean I'll just leave now and eat later." He touched the cap's bill. "Sorry to take up your time."

This apron-clad woman, with the huge turquoise eyes—and he only just now noticed their color—emitted an almost mystical, hypnotic effect when he finally looked her full in the face. And those eyes possessed such a wide-open appearance that Jack could see the reflection of the café' lights in them. But she lost her pouty smile as Jack turned toward the door.

"Well, maybe you can come back again when you're hungrier." She revived the smile. "What's your name, Hon?"

"Crusher calls him Birdie," came a voice from the counter.

Jack recognized the man as one of Crusher's caboose poker bunch.

The waitress never turned toward the rude, intruding commentator behind her, but kept her attention riveted on Jack. "Birdie? You don't look like a Birdie to me." She slid her pad into its big, apron pouch.

She took a step closer, and her delicious scent assaulted Jack again. His common sense hollered to simply turn and leave without responding, but his aversion to rudeness bade him otherwise—or could it have been the flower scent? "I, uh...I used to be a flyer."

"Flyer?" She looked blank.

"A pilot. You know. Aeroplanes."

She gave him a slow nod, still looking a little blank. "Aeroplanes." Then she smiled a slightly warmer smile. "I see." Her tone softened. "So what do descent folks call you?" A round of laughter erupted from the counter as the back-handed insult found its mark in Crusher's stooge.

"My name's Jack," he said, leaving off his last name. He wasn't sure why he did that, except that, at the moment, he just felt the need to avoid unnecessary disclosures. It left him with, at least, a little control of the situation, but the small act of distrust also left him a mild feeling of uneasiness.

"I'm Alma," she said and held out a slender, work-worn hand.

He barely touched the tips of her fingers with a grimy paw and nodded. Then the tingle started down his spine again and ran out to the ends of his fingers and toes. He couldn't stop it this time even if he wanted to. And, contrary to the efforts of the reasoning man within him, his other mental resident, the sensual man wasn't quite sure he *did* want it stopped. At this point, his throat tightened so he had to force his words out. "Pleased to meet you." Already backing toward the door by the time he finished that statement, Jack reached behind himself and fumbled with the knob. "I'm sorry. I have to go."

"Please, come again," he thought he heard Alma say.

After almost falling backward through the doorway, Jack thought the little spring-loaded bell would never stop ringing. Somehow, though, a little good fortune befell him, and he got himself turned back around to face forward again. That's when he took off down the lake road toward the airfield, walking faster than he ever had in his life. He'd made a fool of himself, and he knew it. But he also knew, if he had stayed, somehow things would have, sooner of later, gotten worse. Thinking on that, he quickened his pace.

Jack didn't remember much about his escape to the airfield. One moment he was stalking along beside the pavement, the next he found himself holding onto a fence post, his vision resting on a neat row of biplanes nestled birdlike in the yellow grass that grew on the town end of the taxiway. He could remember no deep or involved thoughts taking place during the trek, except the random surfacing memory of the demise of Copper, Smith's Irish Setter, who had fallen victim to the bite of a Mojave Green rattlesnake just a few months before. But following his arrival at the airfield, he let his attention rest upon the fallow flying machines, and, as he did so, he could feel the fibers of his body begin to loosen and give way to a strange sort of quick-spreading fatigue. His heart slowed soon after. He knew the airfield to be a safe place …safe from the café siren…safe from the semi-desperate sexual desires born of emotional starvation.

Jack felt comfort here, too—the kind of comfort one feels in a place of worship like a church or a temple, with the dormant flying machines before him taking the roll of holy idols, glistening in the subsiding sun, and the unpaved runway that stood before the temple/hangars becoming the alter upon which men and machines would be offered up for both divine errands and sacrifice. He sighed. *Peace.* That's what he sensed. He sagged against the fence post. More peace abided here than he had felt anywhere else for quite a while—including Carrie's new church. Blessed order existed at this airfield. All was as and where it should be. How long had it been since he'd felt like this? *Hard to say.* Jack let the twilight's growing shadows massage his memory back into a mode of recollection.

Not barnstorming! That time in his life had been too loaded down with the need to make a profit and the shame at not being able to do so. No. This kind of peace, for Jack, had existed only once in his life in a very unlikely place.

France! Flying over no-man's-land and German-occupied territory on the Western Front.

The war had, in an odd way, *brought* him this very peace that he had sought with such hunger ever since. Flying daily bombing missions over a hostile foe had whittled life down to just friendship and flying. No overdue bills. No gasoline to buy. No chickens to worry over. No working in the rail-yard. There had been only Jack, a war-worn De Havilland DH4 bomber, and the respect of the other pilots…and Dutch, the best gunner and most unlikely friend in the squadron. Jack had named the plane Caroline, like he'd done with all his planes since. He never could quite explain that habit to strangers when asked. He just knew it somehow made him feel more complete in the air.

Decisions came easier back then, made so by the very nature of open-cockpit aerial combat. Like on that last day, the early morning sortie to bomb the munitions depot at Saint Marie-Blanc when their old De Havilland had suffered her worst damage ever from anti-aircraft fire. Jack shifted his weight against the fence post and let his memory play out the old scene in the theater behind his eyes.

Two nights before that last flight, he had allowed his thoughts to sink into a dark place where they should never have gone. His squadron had lost a full fifth of their aircraft that week...five planes in as many days...five pilots...five gunners...ten friends he considered brothers. All the other times when something like this happened, he had succeeded in keeping the feelings of loss at arm's length, shielding his mind from the mental mangling this kind of sadness produced. But death had always snatched comrades piecemeal before, taking only one or two at a time, allowing one to bolster intellectual defenses like an emotional raincoat, so the pending pain could wash over the outside of the heart without much consequence. This last time, however, it had all happened at once and left no time or method to keep the damage out of Jack's inner being. So it soaked through and hit him square on the fifth night and dragged him down to the entrance of a dark, hopeless abyss he had never known before.

And he could not find a way out of this despairing place for almost a day. Praise God that happened to be a day he did not have to fly. He would have been of little use as a flyer for a while, and he knew it. So he used that opportunity to drink and wallow in self-pity at the officers' club.

"Oh, God," he had moaned after stumbling back to his quarters and rolling, almost helpless onto his cot. It was not just the memory of his dead friends from that week that attacked him now. No, the bottle of cognac, awash within him, had also opened the door to a prison cell in which he had incarcerated all his unwanted thoughts and feelings for the last several months—all the fear, all the trauma and recollections of all the *other* dead comrades. The totality of the things he had kept locked away, now bounded loose and proceeded to wrap an ever-tightening chain around his chest. They injected liquid fire into his bowels, and, in general, put a black shroud of deepest melancholy over his heart. This all made short work of Jack's emotional control. Soon he found himself praying for the first time in weeks. "I can't take this anymore," he muttered, keeping his eyes fixed on a large ceiling crack to avoid the dreaded bed-spins. "I can't see my way out of this darkness, Lord. Please, either make me stronger, so I can stand up to this, or get me out of here!" Then he passed out.

The next day he awoke with the worst headache of his life, nausea that would have killed an elephant, and the inability to make a fist until supper, which he almost forewent until he heard the officers' mess was serving onion soup and bread that night—the same fare that had helped rescue him from his last hangover during a leave in Paris. So he partook of the remedy with halting caution, braved one more small glass of the demon cognac—*hair of the dog*—and fell asleep again in his room like someone had hit him with a mallet. He had not done much thinking that day. It only made the headache pound all the more, so he decided to keep his mind in blessed neutral and put off any and all considerations requiring the use of his brain, until some future time when physical pain was no longer the major issue.

When he awoke the second day, not only had all evidence of alcohol toxicity left him, but he now possessed an unfamiliar sensation of well-being and a strange inward assurance that, somehow, everything would turn out all right...no matter what might lay ahead over the next few hours. It felt as if some wonderful, unanticipated treasure lay just beyond the temporal horizon, and it would not be long before Jack would, in some undecipherable way, reap its benefit. He could not explain these feelings, but neither could he shake them. So he took off on the morning mission in that state of mind, wrapped in optimism's warm, but inexplicable, blanket-like embrace. And he continued to feel this way when the German anti-aircraft shells began bursting beneath the bombers' formation. He knew he *should* be worried, but he just could not make the fear come. No matter what, the feeling that somehow all would be well would not leave—even when fragments from an almost direct hit tore through his aircraft.

Wafting smoke accompanied gaping holes, but no matter. The only true question remained whether or not his De Havilland could make it the twenty kilometers to the target. The lower half of Jack's flight suit had begun to soak red with blood from several shrapnel wounds, but they didn't seem too bad…yet. So he ran through a quick aircraft damage survey, a habit bred from training and experience.

The holes in the Caroline were ugly and drafty, but none of her vital flight controls had been disabled. However, the smoke…raised another issue. With no flame visible, that had to be caused by oil leaking over hot metal. So the unknown factor was…how fast was the oil leaking? Jack took his estimate from the thickness of the greasy fumes being forced up his nose by the prop-wash. *No. Not too bad a leak.* His best guess told him they could still make it to the target and then, with God's help, maybe back to the aerodrome.

He looked behind to see if any of the other bombers in the formation had been hit, but saw instead, to his complete amazement, the last of his formation turning back toward friendly lines…taking it upon themselves to abandon Jack and the mission altogether. *What's wrong with you guys?* Jack saw telltale battle-damage smoke streaming behind about half of his fleeing comrades. But what about the other half, the ones not in immediate danger of fire. Had they forgotten what the briefing officer had said this morning? This target had been confirmed as the Germans' main artillery supply point in this sector—thousands of shells in storage, all destined to rain down on Allied troops. *Each round kills ten or maybe twenty young doughboys or tommies who only want to make it home alive—just like me. This one's worth taking a little risk for.* Jack could hardly believe his friends would give up on something this important without good cause.

They must have control damage, or maybe most of them are hurt worse than I am. This flak's a lot more ferocious than anyone expected. He decided to satisfy himself with that explanation, for now.

So today, we're the whole stinking squadron, Dutch and me. For a split second Jack thought of how his father had rebuked him when he refused to attend law school. He remembered the man's even greater rage when he discovered his only son wanted to become first a race car driver, then later a pilot. That had been a bad time for the old father-and-son relationship. When he enlisted, his father had accused him of harboring childish fantasies about leading a heroic attack in some faraway, glorious battle. Jack had, of course, denied any such musing, even though he could not have sworn in court that the indictment was 100 percent false. For the most part, though, truth be known, he simply enjoyed the feeling of freedom that flying gave him. And as per why he had become an Army pilot with the guarantee of going into harm's way…he had just wanted to see if he could do it with competence and, perhaps, even some measure of honor; nothing more.

The ascending sun jumped out from behind a cloudbank and threw its blinding radiance through the propeller's spinning disc. Jack squinted against the glare, trying to make out any landmark in the French countryside below that would match those on the bloodstained map strapped to his knee. *Mostly open fields. But…yes, there's the canal. So, there should be a motor-bridge crossing it just to the East.* He craned his neck forward, almost lifting up from his wicker seat. He felt more weight shift to his injured legs, but there still seemed to be very little pain. Jack waited. *Ah! There it is, the motor-bridge. Target's almost dead ahead. Maybe another five minutes or so. Why did those idiots turn back? This is going to be duck soup.*

A thumping vibration traveled from the joystick through Jack's gloved hand. A split-second later, fabric exploded from both right wings as two neatly stitched lines of holes appeared there. The underside of another airplane over-flew the lumbering bomber then climbed almost straight up into the clouds. *German fighter! Looks like a Fokker Triplane. Must've surprised Dutch. I didn't hear the Lewis gun.* Jack felt his spine tense. Well, so much for duck soup. He swiveled his head once, looking for the enemy's hunting hound, but saw nothing save clouds and his gunner shrugging sheepishly. *I'll bet that Heinie was low on fuel. Just took a last potshot at us before heading home.* Jack vented some tension out through his nostrils.

Okay, how far to target? Jack switched his gaze back and forth between the map and the horizon. *Right. So, like I said, there's the motor-bridge.* He gave the map another quick look. *And the rail-yard should be just past that.* He waited again, straining his eyes, trying to make out shapes in the light haze ahead. *Is that it?* The battered De Havilland seemed to crawl along at a slug's pace.

Are those locomotives or just factory boilers. Is that steam or smoke? The landmark edged closer, and Jack raised up against the barrier of his safety belt, bringing the first truly sharp pains to his lower legs. *I think that's it.* He settled back down into the seat and blinked his eyes against the morning light. *Those big square things, what are they?* He hunched against the instrument panel. A second passed…then another, the only sound being the Liberty engine and the wind tugging at the sides of his leather helmet. *Boxcars! Those are boxcars! And likely all filled with artillery shells. That's the place, all right! It's going to be duck soup, after all.*

Jack crouched down out of the slipstream to make sure the bomb release lever remained undamaged. It looked serviceable, but then he felt another unfamiliar vibration through the joystick, this time followed by the jolting rata-tat-tat of Dutch's barking Lewis machinegun. Jack raised himself back up to eyelevel with the windscreen, or, at least where the windscreen *used* to be. It was gone now, completely shot away along with some of the engine cowling. *Good thing I wasn't sitting up straight.*

The same German fighter spiraled away. But this time, instead of climbing, it raced toward the ground, disappearing beneath the De Havilland's airframe. Was he gone for good or coming back? Did he have enough fuel for a third pass? The thought of his own death tugged like an annoying little demon at the outer borders of Jack's mind. So he pushed it away out of habit, formed through so many other such near-mortal encounters. That subject always drug fear with it. No time for that now. Later. I'll think about it later when we're back safe. Like I said, he probably doesn't have enough fuel to finish the fight.

Strangely, the word fuel stuck in Jack's mind, puzzling him for a moment until he realized the reason for his obsession. He could smell it. The stench of gasoline was all around him. He searched for damage and found a ragged bullet hole in the forward fuel tank, allowing aviation gas to splatter out onto the fuselage. He wiped several large drops of the stuff from his goggles. Fuel leaking from an airplane meant fire. Fire to a crew without parachutes meant land somewhere quick or be burned alive.

Cancel the duck soup again. Jack looked at his watch then to the rail-yards just ahead. They would be there in a few seconds now. He wiped his goggles once more. *Can we make that?*

Dutch's Lewis gun cut loose...once...then once more...and a third time in short expert bursts. *Aw, no. Not again.* The fighter had returned. Jack glanced back at their foe over Dutch's shoulder, then slumped a little at the controls, not wounded, but disheartened. *Will you go away, you dumb sausage stuffer! I'm trying to concentrate here!*

Then the three-winged camouflage-speckled mass of the fighter appeared off to Jack's left, a blackish-gray ribbon of oily smoke streaming from the engine cowling as it flew by. *Dutch got him!* There was barely time to see the German pilot salute before the craft gracefully rolled onto its back and dived for earth.

"Praise God!" Jack uttered and not totally in vain. For a brief moment, he did think of God…with gratitude that the Lord had spared he and Dutch one more time.

He mopped gasoline from his chin with the end of his flying scarf and looked down at the falling fighter, desperately trying to reach the ground before a now quick-spreading fire, licking its way back from around the engine, engulfed the German's cockpit. The Fokker looked to be already starting to pull out of its dive. Jack nodded. *I think you're going to make it this time, Fritz.* He twisted around in his seat so he could make eye contact with Dutch across the short length of fuselage that separated them. The gunner also watched the burning enemy's wild descent. Jack gave Dutch a grinning thumbs up. Then he leaned close to the rubber speaking tube and yelled against the slipstream that pulled at his lips, "I think we might be doing that very same thing real soon," he said to his gunner, "if this stinking gas decides to ignite."

"Whatchya hollerin'for, mister? What gas are ya talkin' about?" The man standing behind Jack looked familiar, but no name came to mind. He usually rode to town in an old buckboard pulled by a bay mare that looked even older than the man. But that didn't matter right now. No, today, this man had only one purpose, to signal to Jack that he was no longer on his reoccurring last bombing mission to Saint Marie-Blanc. He was once again back home in the present, standing on the side of a dusty country road, staring at a row of aging open-cockpit biplanes, his hands locked in a death-grip around the old, dry-rotted wooden post of a barbed wire fence.

The weathered rancher stood statue-still as if stubbornly awaiting an explanation for the strange outburst he had just witnessed. But Jack had no answer for him. At least not one he wanted to share right now. So he opted not to attempt any more conversation and simply turned away from the man and walk toward Saber Canyon Road, where he'd left the truck parked that morning.

He cursed himself for going by the airfield again—the third time in as many weeks. He'd have to stop doing this. It did no good. The sight of the old De Havillands parked in a row always ended in one thing. *Feeling sorry for myself.* He made a long-stride over an insolent lizard that had the audacity to block his path. *I need to face the music.* He fought back the lump in his throat. *The war is through, and so am I.* Jack sidestepped a migrating tumbleweed and leaped over a big dry-wash gully. Making the other side by a hair's breadth, he just missed falling into the miniature canyon. Once he had restored his balance, a sensible distance from the edge, he stopped to collect himself. *My flying days,* he swallowed hard, *my good days are over.* He looked down at his blackened clothes and moaned aloud, "I'm going to die working in the stinking rail-yard."

"You look pretty good for a dying man to me," came a very feminine voice.

Jack whirled around but could see no one. "Who are you?" It was more of a plea than a challenge.

"Alma...your waitress from the café," replied the disembodied voice, sounding breathy and a little closer.

Scanning his surroundings again, Jack fought back the near panic that comes when one is caught with his bare innermost thoughts sticking out in public. "Where *are* you?" He swiveled his head around once more.

"Down here, Sugar." She clambered up the near side of the gully with her arm extended, dirt falling onto her sensible shoes. "Give a girl a hand, will ya?"

Jack shook off his stunned-animal feeling and pulled the dusty blond up to where he stood. Then he said the obligatory stupid thing. "Hello." He rubbed his hands together while Alma dusted off her clothes. "Uh, what were you doing down there?"

"Trying to catch up with you, silly." She swung a playful blow at his arm but pulled it short when she saw the coal soot smeared there. She reined in her grin a little and glanced down at her clothes. "You're a regular wild man, jumping over gullies like they were cracks in a sidewalk." She took hold of her dress and held out its skirt. "I couldn't do that kind of hopping dressed like this." She let go of the fabric. "So, I had to just run after you the best I could." The grin broadened again as long, dark lashes fanned in front of eyes that Jack thought were almost too beautiful to be legal. "You're a hard man to chase." Her eyes lowered for just an instant.

Puzzlement overpowered Jack's embarrassment at having his self-pity overheard. He took a relaxing breath. "Why were you chasing me?"

Alma reached into her apron pocket and pulled out a twenty-dollar bill. "You dropped your money." She held it out.

Jack grunted, a signal that curiosity had fled, and the dark mood had returned. "Listen. Alma is it?" He shook his head. "I haven't had twenty dollars in my pocket for a very long time. As a matter of fact, right now I think I'm carrying about five or so." He pumped up a brief but polite half-smile. "I think that twenty belongs to someone else."

"Oh." Her shoulders sagged as she dropped the bill back into her apron. She clasped her hands in front of her and swiveled back and forth on her heels, causing her dress to swirl slightly as if she were dancing. She took a loud breath. "So…what makes you think you're gonna die in the rail-yard."

Jack felt his face burn and his ears tingle. "You heard that, huh?"

"Yeah." Alma stopped swirling and began rocking.

"I'm sorry." Jack turned away. I can't believe she heard that! "I don't want to talk about it," he said over his shoulder and took off in his original direction.

Alma kept pace beside him with her hands behind her back. "Well, that's okay with me, Jack. It's Jack, right?"

"Yeah, it's Jack." He caught a whiff of that floral perfume again, just like in the café. He picked up his pace, intending to tire her out or completely leave her behind. Why won't she leave me alone?

"Mind if I tag along?" She skipped to catch up, almost stumbling over a small yucca plant in the failing light, so she opted for a wiser course of action and slowed down.

"If you want." Too tired for a race so soon after work, he slacked off his pace also and fell prey to his other weak spot. He'd always had trouble being rude to women…no matter what they did. He'd experienced some of this polite reluctance at the café earlier —something to do with his upbringing. "But won't they miss you back at work?"

Alma took a second to catch her breath. "I'm on my break. Besides, my boss knows I'm the best thing that's happened to that old grease pit of a place."

Jack gave his walking companion a side-glance. "I can believe that," he said. And he considered it true, but he didn't know why he'd told her.

The two shuffled their way across the town's sandlot baseball diamond toward Saber Canyon Road. Jack's rattled nerves kept him silent most of the way. It didn't feel right, this walking alone with a woman other than his wife—and a very beautiful woman, at that. He guessed her to be available from her forward manner. And that did not help his nerves either.

"Do I make you nervous?" Alma said, just like that, and there it was...out in the open.

Jack stumbled. Boy, this one's not shy! He choked out, "No." But two seconds later he said, "Uh, yes, you do...a little."

"Why? Because you're married, or because you think I'm flirting, or because your wife doesn't know we're walking together?" She smiled an impish smile.

Jack's chest tightened, and his throat suddenly went dry. "How did you know I was married?"

She giggled. "Don't be silly. No man as good looking as you runs away from Alma like that," she poked a thumb back against her chest, "unless there's something wrong with him, or he's married." She looked up into his face for a silent moment then said, "Besides, you wearing your husband ring." She took a deep breath. "But I didn't notice that 'till after I caught up with you." She bit her lip and looked at the ground for a few seconds before returning her attention to him.

He nodded. "I see. Well, you got me. I'm married."

"Are ya happy with her?"

Jack almost tripped over himself. "What a question!"

"If ya don't ask questions, ya never find out anything."

He slowed up a little more and glanced at this woman who seemed to know he needed to talk. "Well, it's not really any of your business, but yes, Carrie and I are probably as happy as most people who have been married a while."

Alma tapped her button nose. "Carrie, huh?"

"Yes."

"The cook at the inn?"

"Right again."

The wayward waitress appeared to be lost in thought for a moment. Then she abruptly ended her semi-meditation with a *humph*. "Reason I asked is because ya don't look very happy."

Jack hopped down off the roadside berm and onto the pavement of Saber Canyon where his truck waited. When he reached the little black beast, he cranked it into a shivering idle. Then he slid into the driver's seat and sighed as Alma walked up to the open driver-side door. "Going to let it run a minute," he said and averted his eyes from her. "Give it time to warm up. Besides, I'm not really ready to drive home just yet." Jack ran his hand around the polished wood of the steering wheel, scanned the evening's darkening sky once, then swung his attention to the woman standing beside him. "You know, just because a guy doesn't grin like an idiot doesn't mean he's unhappy at home."

"No." Her tone was soft.

He played with a loose thread hanging down from a canvas patch in the rag-top roof. "I mean, an unhappy expression could come from any one of a hundred things."

"True." She added a sympathetic tone to the softness.

Jack wrapped the thread around his finger. "It might be an ailment, the weather." He paused. "Finances, a job. But it doesn't necessarily mean that a man's wife does not make him happy."

"Maybe." Alma clasped her hands in front again. "Or maybe, if his wife was keepin' him happy, that fella' wouldn't look so glum no matter what else was happenin'."

He slouched in the seat. "You think you got all the answers, don't you?"

"A few." She moved closer to Jack's door.

His dark thoughts began to hover close to his tongue. "As a matter of fact, we've already had one minor squabble this week." He grimaced.

The Ford's engine shuddered slightly. Jack leaned forward and adjusted the hand throttle, transforming the rattle that assaulted his ears to a more tolerable mutter. Because of the engine noise, he couldn't hear the wind whispering through the eucalyptus trees that hung over the road, but he could see the leaves move in hypnotic rhythm with each dry wind-gust. The hard, metallic clanking of the rail-yard had become almost inaudible at this distance, allowing a sort of respite to exist in Jack's mind, if only for a moment. That's when he relaxed some, and let a little of his dark mood dissipate into the open air. Next, his shoulders dropped, and he leaned farther back into the seat. *Better.* Then he took a breath. *And better.*

Alma remained quiet, watching Jack, her hands still folded in front. And a stronger evening breeze rose out of the south and gusted through the truck's cab. The tired man in the sooty railroad overalls inhaled it as if he'd been holding his breath all day. "You smell that?" he said.

"What?" She shifted her weight a bit.

"The wind. Can't you smell it? The scents. Dry grass, desert sage, high desert earth, and," he sniffed like an animal checking for predators, "of course, eucalyptus. Just what the doctor ordered." *Not to mention that darn man-trap perfume of yours.*

Alma eased closer and patted Jack's arm, despite the coal smears. "You sound like some kind of poet or something."

He chuckled. "I write short stories. I mean, I used to write them. Not much time for that lately." It was a small lie, since he *had* actually finished one just the day before. But he still considered that, at least, to be his own business.

She rested her hand back on his arm. "A writer *and* a flyer. Sugar...Jack, you being in that rail-yard is a gosh-awful waste." She stepped back and put her hands on her hips. "Why aren't you teaching in some college somewhere or flying one of them aeroplanes parked at the airfield?"

"That's a long story."

Her tone softened again. "I'd like to hear it sometime."

Jack gave her a weak smile, but the corners of his mouth lifted more as the aroma of someone's nearly-done supper hit him square in the nose. "Boy, that smells good. What do you think it is?"

Alma shook her head. "I don't know. I've been smelling food at the café all day. Can't tell the difference anymore."

He leaned toward the window and sniffed a good lungful. "Chicken? No. Too mellow for that." His stomach growled and he realized he may have been hasty in leaving the Café. "Not beef." Another intake of the evening's scent, then a grin. "Turkey! Turkey with...." Sniff. He waited. "With candied yams. Ohhhhhhh." He almost smiled for a second. "Brother, does that smell good." His mouth watered so much he had to swallow. Then something rang a small memory bell inside. He straightened up in the seat. "Oh, no!"

Startled, Alma jerked her hands to her throat. "What? What's the matter?"

"I think I'm supposed to be somewhere." Jack searched his memory. "But where?" he said more to himself than to the woman. He ran through the clues. Airplanes? *No.* Eucalyptus? *Don't be ridiculous.* Café? *No...wait. Café...diner...dinner. Dinner!* He physically jerked with the realization. "I'm supposed to be at the church for Thanksgiving dinner! But what time?" He fished out his pocket watch. "Holy Smokes! I'm already late!"

A sad little half-smile crept across Alma's face and she folded her arms across her chest. "Well, you'd better go then. But if ever you're hungry and there's no supper waitin' at home," she paused and changed her disheartened smile to a sultry one, "you just remember little old Alma. I'm always at the Lakeview Café, ten to ten."

"Been nice talking to you." A stupid reply, but all he could think of. "Be careful walking back." That one sounded even worse.

She nodded, blew him a kiss, then walked off toward the Lakeveiw, her hips seeming to sway from one side of the road to the other.

Turning away from the desert siren's call, Jack shoved the little truck into gear and released the handbrake. He didn't know what he was going to do about Alma's obvious attraction to him. He didn't even know what to think about her in general. But he did not have the time to mull that over now. It would have to be dealt with later. At the moment, he had something else to contend with...being late.

So much for avoiding a fight with Carrie. He turned the truck uphill toward the church as he went into second gear. *All right. What was it she'd told me this morning? Clean clothes are at Rev. Fisher's house behind the church. He'll let me clean up there.* He laughed out loud at the thought. *Well, preacher. I hope you don't mind a carload of coal grime all over your washroom. I'm sure Jesus doesn't care since He's the one that put me in the rail-yard to begin with!*

That last musing stopped Jack's laughing, as he remembered that he was really in no rush to celebrate this holiday at the church. All the rest of the folks there could afford to be as thankful as they pleased. They didn't have Jack's life. They didn't have to work with trained gorillas all day long and come home looking like a walking soot rag. Most of the people at church worked at the job they, at least, liked—the one they were trained for. Nobody made them give it up. *I bet they're happy at what they do. They don't hate every second they spend at work.* He thought of Carrie saying what a blessing the railroad job had been, and a short angry flash ran across his chest.

Jack slowed and turned into the dirt lot beside the church. His indignation suddenly turned to guilt. *Yes, Lord. I know we still needed the money. But why couldn't the ranch have panned out without help from the railroad?*

Why couldn't I make the extra money flying somehow? That would have been nice.

He parked the truck and trudged toward the back entrance of the church. Clearly visible through the large, unstained rear window, the spirit of celebration reigned in the open space behind the church's pews—happy ranchers and merchants bringing the bounty of their labors into the gathering and setting it all onto one of three long wooden folding tables. Jack felt a slight wave of jealous irritation and tried to ignore the scene as he headed for the service porch.

Why can't I do what makes me happy like these people? I was obedient to your will! I did what you wanted! I sold the plane and came home! But it's been a long time now, Lord. He stumbled over something unseen in the darkness, making him feel almost as if he'd been tripped by the Almighty. *When is it going to be my turn to be happy?*

The back door hung open. Rev. Fisher stood inside giving directions to a slightly rotund, cherry-cheeked woman holding a glass bowl filled with mashed potatoes. Out of unthinking habit, Jack uselessly wiped his hands on grimy hips and waved for the man's attention. Fisher smiled and nodded recognition, then sent the woman off to wherever the potatoes were supposed to reside.

"Hello, Jack," came the warm greeting. "Really glad you could make it." Fisher gave an index-finger-pointing signal to another church member, then strode, still smiling, toward Jack. "Good to see you. It's been a while," he said and shook MacGregor's hand. Then he peered through the doorway at the festivities just now getting under way. "What a wonderful night." He sighed with an accompanying nod. "I love Thanksgiving."

Jack responded with an almost imperceptible nod of his own. *Well, what the hey, Lord. I like turkey as well as the next man. Besides, I hear the preacher here's got an indoor bathtub that's even bigger than ours.*

Chapter Thirty-Four

"Aw, Dad! It's early!" Eddie, now five, squirmed away from his father as Jack tried in vain to direct him toward the bedroom.

"It's late." Jack folded his arms and took his best *brick wall* stance. Turkey supper at church had been even better than it had smelled, and his sons had both proudly clung to him during the meal. All and all, it turned out to be one of the best nights of the year, despite the trauma and temptation of early evening.

"How late?" was eight-year-old Kenny's contribution while peeling off his sweater.

"It's after ten o'clock." Jack put hands on hips and leaned toward his protesting sons. "What about school tomorrow?"

"It's Thanksgiving, Dad." Kenny matched his father's pose, tilting his head all the way back to look up. "There's no school 'til Monday. And Eddie don't go to school yet."

Eddie's face assumed an indignant expression, and he stepped forward into the fray. "I'll go to school next year!"

"Maybe," Kenny countered. "Mom said, 'Maybe.'"

"Yeah, maybe." Eddie looked at his shoes then back to his brother.

Jack gave up manning the brick wall and knelt down between his boys. "Well, school or not, gentlemen, you're going to have to start getting ready for bed." He winked at them. "Shows your mom I'm on the job." His hand shot out and tickled Eddy under the ribs. The boy squealed as he backed away, his cherubic face beaming at his father's roughhouse.

"Can't we stay up just a little longer, Dad?" Kenny screwed up his face into a pathetic mask. "Please?"

Jack gave them an exaggerated shrug. "And what would we do if we stayed up?" The idea had started to sound good to him, too. There were precious few chances to be with his sons of late.

Eddy leapt forward. "Read us a story, Daddy!"

Kenny grimaced. "Don't be a baby, Eddy."

"Oh, yeah." Eddy straightened up into a posture of practiced dignity. "Read us a story, Dad."

"Well—" Jack stifled a smile.

"Dad's too busy to write stories anymore, aren't you Dad?"

Jack cleared his throat. "As a matter of fact, wise guy…" He ruffled his older son's hair, "I just happened to have finished one at beans yesterday."

Kenny burst into a grin. "Hot Dog!" Then, in a flash, reverted back to a more mature subdued demeaner. "Uh, that's swell, Dad."

Eddy blinked. "What's beans?"

"That's what they call lunch on the railroad."

"Oh."

"What's the story about, Dad?" Kenny stuck his hands in his Sunday-best pockets and averted his eyes from his father.

Jack smiled. "No, you don't. You're not getting me started that easy." He pointed in the direction of the bathroom. "Teeth and pajamas first, then the story."

Scrambling and horseplay immediately ensued as the boys stampeded for their toothbrushes. Their father smiled as he watched the bathroom fracas, and an inward glow overtook him. Nothing lifted his spirits more than the sight of his boys when they were happy…except maybe with Carrie back in the early days. He shook the latter thought off right away. *No good to think much on those times. Only make you more discontent than you already are. Just concentrate on this moment and your sons. Squeeze all the smiles out you can before* these *moments are gone, too.*

Jack figured this last thought had to be the wisest advice he'd ever given himself. And he decided, this time, to follow his own council. After lighting the evening fire in the woodstove, Jack retrieved a small notebook from his lunch bucket. A clearly audible bump followed by a muffled bang resonated through the bathroom wall. "There better be more tooth brushing than fooling around in there, or there'll be no story." He waited a moment, and the general ruckus subsided. He had no real concerns about the pre-bed chaos. In truth, he'd be more worried if the boys didn't cut up a little. A certain amount of chaos just meant they were normal. *Normal boys despite all the discord that's existed around them. Thank you, Lord.*

His own prayer caught him a little off guard and made him feel funny inside. *Thanking the Lord. That's been a while coming.* Then he let that subject go, too. *Nothing too serious tonight. I need...we need some smiles.*

Drawers scraped and slammed and their sounds mixed with laughter in the little bunk-bedroom at the front of the house. Clearly, the struggle had moved on from teeth to bedtime clothing. Jack thumbed through the note pages until he came to the longhand story in question. "You gents'd best hurry up or I'm going to be too sleepy to read." The volume of merriment and commotion doubled instantly. He loved doing that to them almost as much as he suspected they loved him doing it. *Gives 'em an excuse to act a little crazier.*

Jack eased himself into the hand-me-down rocker and scooted it closer to the low-rumbling woodstove. Within a few seconds, pajama-clad Kenny slid to a stop, home-plate style, on the braided rug in front of his father. Likewise-dressed Eddy followed right behind and simply folded his legs up beneath himself, ending up beside his brother in sort of a rough squat.

"Ready, Dad!" Kenny sat at modified attention and elbowed his sibling.

"Yeah." Eddy smiled a gummy grin.

A chuckle slipped from Jack before he could catch it. "All right, then." He leaned back and opened the notebook. "This one takes place on the planet Neptune. It's about a band of sky-ship pirates, and it's called *The Raiders' Revenge.*"

Both children let out an involuntary "O-o-o-o" and settled into more comfortable rug positions. Jack felt his heart warm up several degrees. If nowhere else, for the next few minutes in this living room, life would be just a little better. *At least as far as my sons and I are concerned.* Then a small shadow that had hounded his thoughts the last week or so returned. *But who the heck knows what makes their mother happy these days?*

Chapter Thirty-Five

Saber Canyon's oppressive quarter-to-midnight darkness posed no problem for Carrie. She had driven it so many times now after sunset she could almost count the potholes and ruts from the inn to her front door. It made the run a much faster affair than for an outsider.

Thanksgiving dinner at the inn had run long and the clean-up even longer still. So now she had a bad case of the *tired-but-not-quite-cranky-yet* chef disease. Ben and Ruth had dropped by the busy kitchen on their way home from the church and given her some good news while she worked. Jack had made it to the Church's common meal. He'd spent most of the time with the boys and seemed to have actually *enjoyed* himself. The thought of this kept Carrie warm on the cold, windblown trip home; even warmer than the seldom-used soft plastic snap-on side windows and the Stutz's very expensive, special-order, knee-height heater put together could make it. The mental picture of her family seated together at the Lord's table; now that was something to defrost one's spirit. It made her smile against the night's fatigue and, in a way, lighted her path up the dark dirt road.

Her headlights swept past the ranch's water tank just as the November high desert cold began to overpower the little car heater. She pulled her knitted scarf from around her throat and, for the first time on the drive, felt the gentle bite of frigid air seeping through the seams of the plastic side windows. Braking to a stop beside Jack's truck, she smiled at the tiny *Chickens by Caroline* trailer residing by itself near the trees. Carrie released a sigh. No deliveries today. *Thanksgiving belongs to turkeys. Chickens just have to wait a day or two...or at least until the leftovers run out.*

She shut off the engine and headlights, unsnapped the snap-on window and popped open the door. Then she slid from the seat, stopping to lean against the car for a precious second despite the cold. The exhaustion of the long day had just caught up, ordering her body to stop right where it was. She obeyed and decided to feast for a few moments on the bright clusters of fall stars that awaited a tardy moon. *Lord, that's beautiful.* She took a deep cold breath and exhaled a short-lived cloud of steam. The big rectangular beam of defused light thrown through the kitchen window could not reach her where she stood, and the illumination from the rest of the house proved to be only an indirect soft glow, at best.

Carrie put a leather-gloved hand up to shade her eyes from the kitchen's distracting glare and sought out the Big Dipper. For some reason, this moment of star-gazing soothed her like a mental massage, and she considered simply staying right where she was for another few minutes. *Why not? What's the harm? There's nothing inside that won't wait.* That's when she heard what sounded like the boys screaming.

Carrie straightened up from leaning against the Stutz, ready to run to the rescue of her children. But the next volley of young voices stopped her. *No, they're not screaming...they're...cheering. Cheering?* She moved a little closer to the house. Then another kind of noise reached her ears. *Jack's laughing.* Carrie let out a breath she didn't know she'd been holding. *What's going on?*

She went to the kitchen window and peered through the glass, but couldn't see anything save the opposite side of the living room through the connecting doorway. Then another round of laughter emanated through the walls. *All right, what's so funny?*

Adapting the catlike tread of a burglar, Carrie crept around the rear of the little ranch house and entered through the back kitchen door. She tiptoed across the plank floor, grateful that this room, unlike most of the house, was set on a cement slab, preventing the usual telltale creaking.

444

She could hear the buzzing of conversation from around the corner, Kenny's alto asking a question and Jack's unmistakable answer in bass. *But what are they saying?* She leaned close to the doorway and peeked, one-eyed, around the jam.

Jack rhythmically worked the rocking chair near the fire, a worn notebook in one hand and Eddie, on his lap, leaning back against his father's opposite arm. Kenny lay prone on the thick oval rug, chin resting in hands, sock-clad feet aimed ceiling-ward behind him. Jack read from a dog-eared, lined page, while his sons listened, suspended in mesmerized silence.

"It had been the fiercest, close-quarters battle Gabar had ever fought as captain, and he'd never seen a sky ship take the punishment the Windstalker had and remain aloft, still able to navigate. But *they* had done it—the Windstalker and her crew—had stood up to an entire Kalvati squadron, and beaten them." Jack held the notebook close to Eddie. "Turn the page for us, Son."

Eddy beamed and awkwardly peeled the next page back.

Jack matched his smile. "But the greatest satisfaction came at the end of the day, after the maiden, Hasnah, had been returned to his side and Lord Bahlkor put into chains. Gabar called to the Windstalker's old chief rigger and ordered that, in place of the traditional victory pennant, the evil warlord's pantaloons be strung from the aftmast for all to see, a sign that the time of darkness had come to an end."

Jack closed the notebook, and the boys once again erupted into cheers, provoking their father to a round of hair tousling that melted their hidden mother's heart. *Oh, God.* Carrie's eyelid squeezed shut too late to seize a pair of escaping tears. *That's too sweet.* She wiped her cheeks and stifled a sniff. Weeping was so undignified, putting one's emotions out in front for the world to see. *Like being naked at the king's court, as Father would say.* The urge to sniff rose again, and Carrie gave in before she realized. Alerted by the sound, the story-time trio immediately turned heads toward the kitchen doorway.

"Mom!" The boys abandoned their father and swarmed toward their mother who still leaned against the door-jam, wiping her face with the back of her driving gloves.

She scooped up Eddie and hugged Kenny close to her. "Ooooh, hello." She let a caught-in-the-act smile go Jack's direction. "I was spying." Giving her sons each another squeeze, Carrie furrowed her brow. "Good story, Jack." She lowered Eddie to the floor. "At least the part that I heard."

Jack toyed with the notebook. "It needs some work yet." He got up from the rocker, half stretched, and tossed the story onto the table. "I'll rewrite it this week if I find the time."

Carrie knelt down face to face with the boys. "Did you and your father have a good dinner at church?"

"I'll say!" Kenny blurted as his grinning brother bobbed agreement. "They had a big old table." His arms spread wide in fish-story style. "And there was a whole bunch of turkey, and mashed potatoes, and cranberries, and candied yams!"

"And turkey!" Eddie thrust out his chest.

Kenny rolled his eyes. "I already *said* turkey."

"Oh, yeah."

"And there wasn't no chicken." Kenny wrinkled his nose.

"Wasn't *any* chicken," Carrie held up a correcting finger, then removed her gloves.

Kenny nodded. "*Any* chicken."

She feigned a hurt expression. "You mean my very own sons don't like chicken?"

They both lowered their eyes. Then Kenny responded with brief upward glances. "Well…we like chicken …sort of. It's just that…we…eat it all the time, Mom."

Eddie threw up his hands. "Yeah, all the time."

Kenny elbowed him. "Eddie!" Then he shrugged in surrender. "Chicken's just fine, Mom. 'Specially yours. Just fine."

Carrie held her hand over a struggling smile until it was subdued. "But you had a good time for Thanksgiving."

Both children nodded.

"Well, if that's true, and you still like my chicken...." She kissed their foreheads. "I suppose I'll just have to keep you around for a while."

Carrie threw out her best *witch's cackle*. "Yes, I'll keep you little boys around and have you for supper! Mmmmmmmm!" She raised both hands, mimed as claws, and wrinkled her face as best she could. This sent both boys escaping toward their father. Jack caught them like a predator-bear and administered the appropriate growling hug. The scene sent an unfamiliar feeling of affection through Carrie—unfamiliar because of how long it had been since she had felt it. All of a sudden, without fair warning, she wanted her husband, wanted him as she had when they were first married. It made her feel cozy and uneasy all at the same time, a two-edged sword. Like the tears she'd fought a few minutes before, it made her feel out of control.

Jack finished wrestling with the boys and gave a final growl of triumph. "Time for bed, gentlemen."

"Aw, Dad!" was the unison response. "Can't we just—"

"No." Jack shook his head.

"Mom." They turned to plead their case. "You just—"

"No." Carrie crossed her arms, then pointed toward the small bedroom in the front of the house. "You heard your father. I want to hear those bunk-beds squeak in short order." She waved them on their way. "Go on. Chop-chop."

Groans and *gee-whizzes* erupted all along the torturous fifteen-foot march across the house, but eventually, bunk

447

squeaking mixed with voices and last minute laughter prevailed.

"Chop-suey." Giggle.

"That's chop-chop."

"Yeah, chop-chop."

"Be quiet, Eddie."

"Chop-chop." Giggle.

After good-night kisses and head pats had been administered, after the noise from the far bedroom had subsided and only the low rumble of oak burning in the big cast-iron Franklin remained, Carrie put her arms around her husband and kissed him with a warm passion she had not shown or felt for several years.

At first, Jack's eyes grew into large ovals of surprise. However, after three seconds of uninterrupted kissing, the lids of said eyes slid down to the same half-closed position as Carrie's, and he returned her warmth with his own message of love and desire. It went like that for quite a while, before, by mutual consent, they eased their embrace and their lips parted.

"Well," Jack said after taking a long, deep breath.

"Yes. Well indeed." Carrie's breathing sounded shallow and came in rapid succession.

"What brought this on?" Jack caressed the small of her back.

Still a little short of breath, she said. "I don't know; I simply thought—"

"Mom, can we have a glass of water?" came Kenny's cry from behind an almost closed door.

Carrie felt the rush of blood to her face, causing her ears to tingle. She patted Jack's chest. "One moment." She lowered her eyes. "Don't go away."

After delivering the water and a short lecture about going right to sleep, Carrie returned to the living room. She caught Jack crouched before the now open woodstove and ran her slim fingers through his hair. "Now, where were we?"

Jack fed a piece of split oak into the iron dragon's mouth and prodded the coals beneath the grate with a poker. "You were saying you didn't know why you kissed me." He smiled and latched the stove's doors.

"I only meant it came over me all of a sudden."

Jack stood and turned with Carrie's hands still around the back of his neck. He reached around her waist and laced his fingers behind her. "Well, it was a nice surprise." His head leaned down and his lips sought hers.

"Oh, you forgot to put the screen back." She bobbed her head, looking around him to the Franklin.

"What?"

"The stove screen. You forgot to put it back."

Jack looked behind him but kept his arms in place around his wife. "I'll get it later." He smiled a tolerant smile and leaned down to kiss her again.

Carrie retreated just enough to maintain a technical embrace and spoke to his top button. "Please, do it now. A spark could hop out through the open vent and set the rug on fire."

Jack was silent for a long second. His arms remained around Carrie's waist, but she could feel them go slack. Then came the sigh, a long, slow, tortured one that spoke more than he could say in an hour. Finally, after more silence, he did speak. "All right, I'll get it." He released her and turned away, dropping the wayward screen into its place with an annoying thud.

After that, Carrie tried to rejoin the kiss. She resumed her original embrace position and successfully rekindled much of her tender feeling, despite Jack's exaggerated demonstration with the screen. But he merely replaced his earlier passion with an obligatory peck and an expression that looked more like heartburn than love.

Jack let his hands drop to his side. After a moment of confusion, Carrie did the same. Then *he* turned and shuffled into the kitchen without a word.

What's wrong with him? Is he mad now? What happened? I just didn't want the rug to catch fire. Is that such a terrible thing? She decided to confront him directly.

Carrie followed him as far as the kitchen doorway. "Where are you going?"

He stood by the sink looking out the window. "Like a glass of cold water."

"What?"

Jack turned and opened his mouth to speak but seemed to change his mind about something. After a brief silence he said, "I said I'd like a glass of cold water." Then he turned back to the faucet, filled a blue porcelain cup, took one small sip and poured the rest out. "Wasn't as thirsty as I thought."

More confused than before and feeling a fight waiting behind the next unfortunate comment, Carrie searched for an everyday subject. "Did you get a chance to check the feeders?"

Jack stood silent, leaning back against the sink-board. Then, remaining still as a stone slab, he stared into Carrie's eyes. He held his soundless pose just an instant past common courtesy. Then he sighed another long, put-upon-husband sigh and said in a slow deliberate manner, "I usually do check the feeders." He paused. "But this time I forgot." His eyes narrowed a little. "I'm sorry." He did not sound repentant. "I was distracted by having too much fun with my sons."

"That's fine, Jack." She could almost smell his anger now. "I just want to make sure the brooders get a little extra while it's cold."

One eyebrow shot to his hairline. "I know what to do, Carrie. I just forgot."

"It's *all right*, Jack."

"I know it's all right." The other eyebrow rose to join its twin. "I'd just come off a nine hour holiday shift before supper."

"I know." She also knew something bad was brewing. Jack's voice was becoming louder and more strained with each word. "I mean no offense. I'm simply trying to look after my chickens." As soon as Carrie spoke her last two words, she knew they were the wrong ones.

"*Your* chickens!" Jack took his weight off the sink and folded his arms. "When did they become *your* chickens?" He took a long step forward.

Carrie let her shoulders slump. "I didn't mean they're just mine. I've simply come to think that way because I've been the one that takes care of them most of the time."

She knew that sounded wrong, too—the moment it was out—but just now, she didn't seem to be able to say anything that would not sound provocative...or at least in a way not to upset her husband. Carrie felt as though she'd accidentally lit the sputtering fuse to a dynamite charge and didn't know how to snuff it out.

Jack strode to the kitchen table where his flying jacket hung on the back of a chair. "I know you think you're the head of this family by virtue of my absence and because Henri's appointed you kitchen straw-boss at that pipsqueak little inn!" His voice rose again to a point just short of hollering. "But let me tell you something! I contribute more than my fair share to the support of this family!"

Carrie clung to the door-frame. It felt like she'd collapse if she let go. *What's happening?* "I've never said you didn't," she responded, almost in a whisper.

Jack snatched up the jacket and slid into it. "And I'll tell you something else." He bulled his way past her and spoke as he headed through the house toward the front door. "*I'm* still the head of this family!" He stopped when he got to the door. "*At least* for now."

451

"Where are you going?" Carrie meant to follow him but found, suddenly, she no longer possessed the physical strength or mental clarity to do so. Her long hard day had finally delivered its *coup de grace* upon her body and mind. And that, she discovered, was that.

"A walk." Jack pulled the leather collar up around his neck and began to fumble with the front buttons. "I'm taking a walk. Not down to Ben's. Just down the road a ways." He swung open the door. "Gotta be near freezing out there. It's a perfect night to cool off."

Chapter Thirty-Six

Without thinking much about it, Jack kicked a chunk of granite while walking along the Lake Road a week after his last confrontation with Carrie. But he kicked it with so much force that it ricocheted off a speed limit sign, flushing a crow that had been perched on top. This had turned out to be a very unusual evening. A rail had turned over in the yard, derailing a cut of three fully loaded coal gondolas, all of which had rolled over onto their sides, spilling tons of hard black fuel lumps all over the place. Laborers had been brought in to clean up the mess and repair the rails, along with a steam crane and a crew of car knockers to repair the damaged gons. In the meantime, there could be no switching of cars as three of the most often used tracks were now blocked. As a result, all switchmen had been sent home two hours early. Yard master Mahoney had decided there was no use to pay men to stand around watching other men work.

So, with it being earlier and therefore not dark yet, Jack could easily see that the rest of the roadside between the rail-yard and the airfield appeared strewn with more such potential weapons like the one with which he'd just assaulted the sign. But he decided to leave them alone. He knew he should be happy getting off two hours early. But he wasn't—too much on his mind that a measly couple of hours off would not cure. He'd walked this same stretch of pavement out of necessity for sixteen months now and had long since grown contemptuous of the familiar pilgrimage. The tons of soot and coal smoke the S.P.'s steam locomotives threw into the air every hour, raining down upon everything unfortunate enough to be a little too nearby, had forced Jack to park almost a mile from the tracks. Otherwise, his poor old truck would have had a fresh coating of black filth each and every evening. *Good thing somebody scrubs down the passenger station every morning.*

And Sweet Springs seemed to hold a unique and distinctive position as per production of soot, at least on the Southern Pacific Railroad. It seemed to be the only terminal that boasted all coal burning locomotives. Jack had heard from other railroaders, who had passed through or transferred up from Taylor Yard down near Los Angeles, that all the other terminals had long since begun their transition from coal to oil burning steam engines. Most of the yards from New Orleans to Oakland had begun their change-over not long after 1900 and were now passing the halfway mark with reference to oil burners verses coal stoked Locomotives. Those men Jack had spoken to who had worked in Los Angeles, Indio, or even Mojave all said that the exhaust thrown into the local atmosphere by oil burners was about half as destructive as that emitted by those that ate coal. To be sure, without exception, they all had to admit that oil fired engines still did not make for a clean rail-yard (and the oil exhaust was, in fact, a little greaser that coal suet). But the use of oil over coal did make life for railroaders a little easier, if for no other reason than that oil residue washed out of clothing much more readily than coal. And Sweet Springs was the very last place to use coal exclusively—to the point where many other yards were sending the last of their coal burning engines up here to work out the last of their days and eventually die. *Bottom of the barrel,* Jack thought. *That's where I'm working...bottom of the gosh darn barrel!*

He glanced back down the grade at the low darkened haze that blanketed the track area where the railroad kept its rolling stock. *This is no life,* he thought, and groaned inwardly until it became audible in his throat. *That place looks almost as oppressive as it is.* He'd been an apprentice switchman for only sixteen months, and he'd already felt like he'd been at that job a lifetime. Sometimes, after one of those really horrific days—that came too often for his liking—he'd feel like he wanted to run off into the bushes, yelling like a crazed savage. But he never did. The MacGregors needed the money, and that's all there was to it.

Crusher, who was supposed to show Jack the ropes of working in the yard, had spent more time spitting insults and profanity than teaching anything useful. However, as fortune would have it, the job had proved to be uncomplicated and almost self-explanatory. Learn a few hand and lantern signals. Throw a switch or two to line the cars and engines into one track or another, or sometimes uncouple one of the cars already there, so the little switch engine from the hump could come down, hook onto it, and haul it away.

Working the yard did not require a college education or an army commission. However, ever since Jack had made the mistake of confessing to Crusher that he held both those honors, the man's abuse had never ended. And neither, Jack noticed, did his drinking. As a matter of fact, he could not remember ever seeing the foreman completely sober. But Crusher wasn't the only on-the-job drinker.

Work shifts in the yards often proved interesting, with a good half of Jack's co-workers maintaining a rosy glow, much lubricated by the bootlegged gin Crusher sold. Life threatening near-misses caused by stupid mistakes often proved more common than not. At times, it almost seemed to Jack that everyone but himself showed up for work intoxicated to one degree or another.

Today had been a prime example of what made the job almost intolerable for a sober man. The other switchman on duty with Jack just happened to be Homer, Jack's old rail-yard teacher (and second soberest employee on the property). The switch-engine up on the hump had already released an empty freight car to coast down to the lower yard. However, before it had gone even halfway to Homer's switch, Crusher showed up and began arguing with the old man over something Jack could not make out from where he stood by his own switch, three tracks away. The foreman looked to be growing more agitated by the second, grabbing the older switchman by the jacket and jerking him around in what could only be described as a violent manner. Homer seemed to be trying to explain something, his arms outstretched in a pantomime of surrender, but that appeared to only make Crusher angrier. He pushed the underling away from his post by the switch and onto the track, then he began shaking him even harder. And all during this conflagration, the downhill-bound freight car continued to pick up speed and draw closer to the main switches. That's when Jack realized that the vehicle was lined not only into Homer's switch, but onto the very track where Crusher held him. The rest took place so fast that Jack could hardly remember it all. He somehow made it across the three tracks between himself and the two men. Then he threw the vital switch before the approaching car arrived. This sent the great silent danger clacking, harmlessly, down a safe track to collide and couple with a cut of ore gondolas sitting in repose almost a quarter of a mile away.

Crusher had stopped his abuse of Jack's fellow worker as soon as the noise of the cars' meeting reached him. He dropped Homer onto the rails and just stood there, hands on hips, staring at the now motionless freight car. Jack, almost ten feet away, still found himself enveloped by the familiar invisible alcohol cloud that always surrounded the foreman. The man did not appear to be staggering drunk, but, at the very least, did not have full control of his faculties. The younger apprentice railroader fully expected the larger man to direct his violent demeanor upon him at any moment. Instead, however, Crusher, without the slightest mention of his recent semi-insane outburst, turned to Jack and said in a calm, matter-of-fact tone, "Now we'll have to get the switch-engine down here to fish that car out of there. You know it belongs over on track six for the morning hauler to Mojave."

This episode and many others of equal or even more extreme ferocity, could, in truth, be described as not unusual or even commonplace in the Sweet Springs freight-yard. Of course, other less deadly side events made up a good portion of the daily routine as well, acting as a sort of mortar to bind together the more lethal main-event semi-disasters. One time, some unseen mystery person had lined a stray, fast-moving flatcar onto a track where Jack stood, balanced atop a freight car, tying off its handbrake. The resulting collision, of course, threw him twelve feet to the ground. No bones being broken, the ex-pilot simply finished his shift and went home to put an ice bag on a bruised arm. No one ever confessed to changing the direction of Jack's switch, and he knew without doubt that he himself had lined it so no traffic would come his way.

On another occasion, he had just walked the top of an entire ten-car cut to release all handbrakes before the mainline locomotive hauled the cars away. But before he could descend the ladder, he saw someone—too far away to recognize—resetting the brake on the head-end car. Had he not gone back to release it again, just seconds before the big freight engine coupled-on to leave the yard, the unreleased brake would have, in time, overheated and most likely caused a fire that might have, after a few miles, derailed the car and the rest of the train with it. Had that happened, blame for the accident would have fallen upon Jack, since the release of the handbrakes was his responsibility.

Finally, the week before, just after dark, a hobo had come out from between two tank cars Jack had just walked past. He hollered at the switchman from behind, and when Jack turned around, the hobo hit him in the stomach with a brake-club. That not only doubled MacGregor over but dropped him to his knees. This was when the *strangest* part of this *strange* event took place. Instead of robbing Jack or just running away, the raggedy transient threw the club away into the darkness and said, in a truly remorseful tone, "I'm sorry, Mister. That there Crusher guy...he said he'd kill me if'n I didn't do this. I never done nothin' like this to nobody." Then he sniffed and wiped his nose on a well-worn coat sleeve. "I'm just sorry. That's all. No offense meant."

Jack had a question or two in mind to ask this unfortunate soul. He even considered taking a Godly tact and tell the hobo that he forgave him. But by the time Jack caught his breath, the man had disappeared.

So I'm creeping up on a year and a half on the old Southern Pacific, Jack thought as he continued his trek. He tilted his billed cap back off his forehead and felt warm rivulets of sweat run down his temple. *I wonder how much longer I can last on this job.* Some days, like this one, he didn't think he could handle more than another five minutes. He often felt trapped by the foul cloud that surrounded the yards, and sometimes he thought he could feel the crude hopelessness of the place soaking all the way into the very center of his being. It gave him a sense of darkness when he worked there—dark as the grease and cinder that settled on his clothes. *I've got to get out of there.* It always took a while after his shift ended for Jack's spark of life to re-ignite. Today though, with sixteen months on the job, it took a little longer than usual.

After walking a few more minutes, he came to the barbed wire fence that marked the boundary of the Sweet Springs Airfield. This had become his usual marker for resurrection. Something about the place—he didn't know what—somehow seemed to cleanse enough of the rail-yard depression away for Jack to feel almost alive again. But this time something wasn't working. The rebirth, the process that led to an escape from darkness hadn't even begun yet. The smell of heavy lubrication oil and coal remained in his nostrils; the sounds of hissing steam and clanking coupler knuckles still rang in his ears. *I've not yet laid the railroad ghosties,* he remarked to his internal self, and he sensed he'd have to walk a bit farther today to get out from under the Southern Pacific's shadow.

Jack continued his trudge toward the truck and tried to steer his thoughts away from trains, but the darkness fought back and hung on even tighter. Fatigue and hopelessness clung to him like fresh paint and he could still feel it soaking in. This time the intensity of the darkness proved worse than anything he had experienced since he'd signed on as a switchman. As a matter of fact, this particular dark shroud turned out to be something he hadn't experienced since that time before the last mission with Dutch.

I can't do this by myself. I'm too weak. He raised his mind to Heaven and silently prayed as he walked. *Oh, Lord God, You know what's going on. You know what a worthless bum I am.* He swallowed hard to soothe the dryness of his throat. *Well, we both know about that. I know I haven't been to your house much lately...even after making my Christian family wisecrack to Carrie".* He took a couple of needed breaths while giving a thought to his next silent words. *"But I need your help again..... Please, either build me up so I can stand this life or get me out of here. This is the same prayer I made to you in France, I know, but that was just after a few weeks of rough times. This has been going on for over a year now, and it doesn't seem like it's ever going to end. It just goes on and on. Please, help me, Father. Please forgive my sins and my weakness, but please help me... again..... Amen.*

The sun had descended close to the valley's rim and would soon disappear altogether. The day's breeze began its usual afternoon lull, causing sounds and smells to become more potent. The distant steamy sighing of

459

locomotives could still barely be heard, but Jack's internal ear blocked that out in an instant. The crow that had earlier fled the road sign had found a fence post to take its place and now gave the inconsiderate human a piece of his mind. Then came a strong *whoosh, whoosh, whoosh* from above. "Ah," Jack said to nobody at all, then looked up into a sky now far enough removed from the engine yard to be clear of coal smoke. A big brown hawk flapped hard for altitude as it cleared a cottonwood tree and headed for the closest hill. Jack closed his eyes for just a second as he walked. *These are the sounds to soothe a battered mind.* Then somewhere a distant internal combustion engine started up, drowning out all subtler noises, as a warm, gentle breeze blew from the foothills of the Angeles Mountains and massaged the escaped switchman's face. Smells that ministered to his spirit soon followed. Buckwheat, sagebrush, and chaparral came through strong, wrapped in a mixture of high desert heat and a faint suggestion of distant pine from the upper ridgelines. All of it a balm that always helped, but he could smell something else in the mix today, something different, yet familiar at the same time. *What is that?*

He took a lungful and waited for recognition. *Something different.* Two seconds passed...three...then he knew. *It's airplane exhaust! That was no car engine!* He jerked his eyes off the ground and searched for the source of his stimulation, soon finding what he wanted.

Off a little way across the airfield's bare dirt taxiway, staggered the most beautiful thing he'd seen in a long time, a De Havilland D.H.4, engine at low growl, prop spinning like a wooden dervish. Its wings teetered for balance as wire wheels of the main landing gear rolled over small rocks and the holes of burrowing wildlife. *They always did look like a duck on a hot griddle—at least whenever they taxied.* Jack smiled. *Lord, I miss 'em.* This one had been painted red with *U.S. Airmail* in big, white letters on its side. The front cockpit had been completely sealed, leaving the pilot to fly from the rear. *They must put the mail where I used to sit; I wonder how it feels to fly from the back.* He'd seen these planes here before, but always just sitting idle—engines off—like they were sleeping between flights. He'd even noticed the change in cockpit design once while walking past; he had purposed not to consider much about it—not anxious to get his thinking started on flying again, not wanting to think about last missions in France...again. But this was different. This airplane was alive, ready to go, and headed straight for him.

His musings were cut short by the cloud of dust thrown his way from the plane's prop wash when it arrived at the near end of the runway. It swung around to face the wind, putting its tail and a wealth of flying debris in the direction of the road. Jack turned away and squinted against the grit that harried his eyelashes. Then he returned his gaze to the biplane in anticipation of its imminent take-off.

But instead of the expected engine rev, the plane's occupant brought his machine down to a low idle, hoisted himself out of the cockpit, and dropped to the ground. He appeared a relatively short man with thick, gray wool pants, held up by bright red suspenders, topped with a white dress shirt, unbuttoned at the collar, sleeves rolled to elbow length. A fat unlit cigar dominated his clean-shaven face, and his thin, brown hair lay plastered slick to his square head. He had a thick muscle-bound frame, almost no neck, and a too-serious expression that promised to scare dogs and small children. Jack recognized him immediately—Sam Smith, Ben's son, the drunk he'd carried indoors months ago. The man chewed his cigar and walked around the tail of the plane to glare up the road. Jack deduced two things from this snapshot in time. Sam had been forced to wait for someone, and that did not make him happy.

The De Havilland sat perched on its haunches, also waiting, but with more patience than Sam. Its cylinders clattered a sweet song at low RPM in a rhythm that seemed to beckon Jack. *Come and see me. Come and see. Come and see me.* Jack could almost hear the words as he leaned on a fence post and watched Sam pace in front of a small gateway that connected the airfield to the road. *Come and see me. Come and see me,* the fabric-clad siren muttered. Jack inhaled a waft of the craft's warm carbon monoxide breath and negotiated a compromise between his heart, that said, *Jump the fence and steal this plane,* and his mind, that countered, *Ignore everything about this place, and just keep on walking!* Finally, as a result, he walked over near the fuming cigar-chewer and gave Sam a lame but friendly wave.

"How ya doing?" Jack put on his best *I don't really know you, but I'm going to talk to you* grin. Grinning wasn't hard just then. All he had to do was keep glancing at the plane.

"How's it look like I'm doing?" The cigar answered. Sam continued to pace the fence and search the road.

"Uh, I was just admiring your plane there." Jack felt stupid the minute his words emerged. How many times when he was barnstorming had some barefoot, hayseed said the exact same phrase. He gave himself a quick survey. *Yep, striped overalls, stupid little striped hat, all covered with coal soot. I really look like a pilot!*

The cigar talked over Sam's shoulder out of the corner of his mouth without taking his eyes off the road. "Yeah, ya wouldn't think so much of airplanes if you knew more about 'em." His head turned quickly in the direction of the distant hangers. A thin rooster tail of dust spread from the back tires of a stake-bed truck that had just careened off the dry grass stubble and onto the dirt taxiway. "This one..." he indicated the red plane with a toss of his head, "can be an unforgiving, merciless witch when she wants." Sam finally turned his attention to Jack, who still smiled at the De Havilland. The cigar looked from Jack to the D.H.4, then back again. "You haven't got any idea what I'm talking about, do you, Clem."

Jack kept looking at the plane as if in a dream. "I used to fly 'em," he said and didn't break his gaze.

"Oh, yeah?" came the skeptical tone. "Where and when was that?" Sam put his hands on his hips and stood with his feet wide apart as if challenging someone to a duel.

"France," Jack sighed. "Nineteen-eighteen." He turned to face the cigar. "Long time ago."

"Is that so." He chewed a little more of the stogie and looked at his pocket watch. "Ya fly any since then?"

"Yep."

"Ever fly the mail?"

"Naw, just barnstorming. I had a Jenny for awhile."

"So you was a dump truck driver in France."

"What?"

"Bomber pilot."

"Oh...yeah."

"Well, if you could do that, this'd be a cinch." Short Sam nodded for emphasis and stuck out his right hand. "Sam Smith." They shook hands. "I'm the supervisor of this pathetic excuse for an airfield. I own this crate." He indicated the red plane and cocked his head again. "And those over by the hangars." He pointed over his shoulder with his thumb. "I contract with and am the official headache of the Post Office Department." Just as he finished speaking, the speeding truck came to an abrupt stop a few yards away. The wind blew the dust out onto the road, missing the two conversing pilots altogether. Sam glanced quickly back at the truck and shook his head. "I'm also this idiot's boss."

A tall, clumsy looking man in gray, grease-stained overalls leapt from the doorless cab of the truck. He had a large nose and even larger elephant-like ears that almost seemed to flap as he galloped with long clown-like feet over to his employer. He tripped to a stop in a small cloud of his own dust and touched his right finger to the top of his snap-brim cap, as if to hold it onto his head. "Sam," he panted, "I just called Susie, and she ain't seen Andy since day before yesterday."

"Was he sober when she saw him?

The clown-man looked at the ground and shuffled a huge shoe in the sand. "Uh—"

"Never mind." Sam threw his dead cigar stub on the ground and compulsively crushed it with his foot. "I know the answer."

"Who's *this* guy?"

"Jack MacGregor." Jack stuck out his hand, but the clown pulled back from the black coal coating. Jack noticed the problem and automatically wiped the darkened paw on his shirt, only to apply a fresh coating of grime. It was then that he also noticed he'd already blackened Sam's palm. "Uh, sorry."

"No sweat, brother." Sam smirked in a cagey manner and wiped his colored hand on Clowney's overalls. The tall man flinched a little at the insult but held his ground. "Say." Sam looked thoughtful for a moment. "MacGregor...MacGregor. Doesn't your wife cook at the Hunter's Inn? Her name's Katherine or Karen."

"Caroline."

"Right." Sam appeared to put his memory to work again. "We're neighbors, aren't we? You know my folks."

"And your wife and son. Great kid."

"Yeah, yeah." More thoughtful expression. "Then you're the one who...." He paused as he bit the end off a fresh Havana.

"The one who what?" The clown leaned toward Sam.

"Never mind, Cal." Sam struck a match on the heel of his shoe and offered a Havana to Jack who shook his head.

Clowney hovered close for a moment. "How 'bout one for me, Sam?"

Sam gently, but firmly pushed him aside. "I'll let you know when you've earned one, Cal."

Cal's face dropped. "But I—"

Sam's right eyebrow shot up as he eased the unbitten end of the cigar into the flame of the match. He took several quick draws, then shook out the fire and turned to Cal. He spoke slowly in an ominous tone. "I *said* I'll let you know."

Cal glanced at his shoes and stepped back.

Sam sucked diligently at the tobacco and looked off toward the sun that had just touched down behind the western ridgeline. "So Andy's taken a powder on us again, huh?" He rocked on his heels a little.

"He'll be here, Sam." Cal sounded apologetic even though it was not *his* offense. "You know he will. He always makes it. Don't he?"

Sam stuck the stogie between his teeth and began to pace again. He stretched his suspenders with his thumbs as he walked. "Yeah, he makes it all right. Just sometimes two hours late, that's all!" He puffed up a big cloud of smoke, then blew it away. "Last time it was *three* hours."

Cal hung his head and looked at Sam through thin, gray eyebrows. "He'll be here, Sam. You *know* that." His voice was almost a whimper.

Sam flicked ashes on the ground and stepped on them. "No, I don't *know* that, Cal." He turned to face his employee. "But I do know that you're an ace mechanic and that your nephew, Andy, is a drunken bum!"

Cal looked at his shoes again.

Sam shook his head. "He's fired, Cal. And that's that. You can tell him that when he shows up. I'm not going to listen to anymore postmaster complaints, and your nephew's not losing this mail contract for me. The evening mail's going to be on time from now on! Do you understand?"

465

Cal shuffled his shoes some more. "Sure, Sam. Sure. But who's going to fly it tonight?"

"Well, either me..." Sam turned toward Jack with a shrewd smile. "...or good old Jack here. What do ya say neighbor? Think you can still wrestle one of these beasts off the ground?"

"Sam," Cal whined, "you just can't give Andy's job to the first yahoo that comes along!"

"What do you say, Jack? You'd be a full-time employee—regular paycheck." Sam unplugged his cigar to spit. "You want it?"

"Sam!" Cal pleaded.

Jack hesitated just long enough for another look at the plane and sighed. "I'll take it!"

Cal groaned.

"Okay, Neighbor. You got it." Sam nodded at Jack but looked past him as if seeing something behind his new pilot.

A rough, grimy, hand clapped Jack hard on the shoulder. "*What* ya got, Birdie?" It was the rail-yard foreman, grinning as if he enjoyed making Jack jump.

"Nothing." Jack answered the familiar voice but kept turned toward Sam.

"That's what I thought," Crusher growled. "Be at the Bull Moose in twenty minutes." The foreman kept a tight, painful clench on Jack's shoulder, pulling it back and forth as he spoke. "You and me got some talkin' to do." He released his grip when Jack finally turned around. "I've decided your poor little family needs a fuller pay bucket, so I'm gonna let you run some of my hooch to the thirsty folks up your way." A low rumbling laugh emanated from deep within Crusher's bulk. "It's right on your way home, Sweet Pea. Won't be no trouble for ya t'all." He wheeled about without another word and walked toward town apparently unconcerned about a reply.

Suddenly, Jack knew what he had to do. "No."

Crusher stopped and turned back around. "What'd you say...Birdie?"

"I said I'm not doing any bootlegging." Jack took an extra breath. "As a matter of fact, I'm not doing any *other* kind of work for you either."

The foreman took a slow step in Jack's direction. "Watch yourself, Birdie. You puttin' yer foot in a hole you might not get it out of."

"I don't think so." Jack added a little more wind to his voice, spurred on to courage by the fact that he was still alive. "I'm quitting the railroad as of right now." He paused to let the weight of his words take their full effect on himself as well as Crusher. "I'll contact Mr. Mahoney tomorrow."

"I'll call him *for* you." Sam inspected the hot end of his cigar.

"Thank you," Jack said to Sam then turned back to Crusher. "That's done then."

"More like *done for*, I'd say." Crusher stroked his right knuckles for a moment before he let out a short sigh. "I'll give you one more chance, little man." He resumed his strut toward town and spoke over his shoulder. "Be at the Bull Moose like I said and maybe I'll only hit ya once for contradictin' me." Then he merged into the twilight shadows of a large blackened oak, and tension dropped from the air around Jack.

"Likeable son of a gun, ain't he?" Sam had replugged his Havanna and began talking around it again. "Well, where you going to be in twenty minutes, brother? At the Bullmoose or—"

"I'm going to be on my way to...where am I going?"

"Bakersfield." Sam spit a small fleck of tobacco from his tongue.

Jack glanced at the foreman's grubby frame crossing the road toward the Bullmoose, then he said to Sam. "That's where I'll be—on my way to Bakersfield."

Sam looked Jack up and down. "You'll have to clean up some." He chugged at the cigar until the tip glowed red in the advancing twilight, and a thick smoky fog surrounded his head. He noticed the fog with a touch of irritation and took a step that brought him out of it. "I don't want the cockpit looking like a coal bin. I think we got some cleaner overalls in the hangar somewhere." He gave a questioning look to Cal, who shrugged.

"I got my own flying gear."

"What, back at your ranch?"

"No, in my truck...just up the road there." He pointed to the Model-T. "Was gonna throw it all away a while back...but never quite got around to it."

"Good." Sam turned to his clown. "Cal, you drive him. I'll wait here with the ship in case Andy shows."

Cal looked dejected. "You mean, if he showed up, ya wouldn't let him—"

Sam turned to face Cal, putting the cigar right under the mechanic's nose. "No, I wouldn't let him, and that's the end of it, Cal. Do you understand?"

Cal slumped. "Whatever you say, Sam."

"Then get going!"

"Okay. Come on, mister."

Jack pushed through the fence gate and followed Cal, as the latter shuffled back toward the big black truck that had almost run Jack off the road sixteen months before.

"Like I said, the name's Jack."

"Yeah, I heard."

They got into the stake-bed and rumbled off. Jack retrieved his canvas-wrapped flying gear from under the driver's seat of the Model-T truck where he'd hidden it over a year before. He took a sink-bath and changed clothes at the hangar, leaving one white towel black with railroad residue. Then he tried to scribble two small pencil notes on a piece of scrounged brown-bag paper while riding in the mail truck next to Cal, who sulked as he drove back to the runway. They stopped back near the same gate that faced the road, and Jack hopped out of the truck. He thought he heard the mechanic mutter, "Idiot," under his breath, but Jack decided to ignore the slight. This Andy fellow was Cal's nephew, after all.

Sam leaned on the gatepost as twilight neared the end of its snail-like journey to darkness. The biplane's engine was still running, singing a slightly different tune to Jack's innermost ear. *Come and fly me, come and fly me, come and fly me.*

Sam nodded at a cleaner, better-dressed Jack. Then he said, "Ya know, neighbor, I almost didn't recognize ya without the outer coating."

"That's all behind me, if this is a permanent job." Jack hesitated a second. "Say, I flat forgot to ask in all the hubbub. Is it? Permanent, I mean? Or is it just for a while?"

Sam used his Havana as a punctuator. "Brother, if you can stay sober long enough to get the mail to point 'B' and back without colliding with anything important, you can have this job until your whiskers reach your knees!"

Jack thought it ironically funny, Sam being the champion of sobriety in this case. But he smiled and said, "That's all I wanted to know." Then he handed Sam the two scraps of paper.

"What's this?" Sam held them a little away from his face and read.

"The long one's for my wife. She's—"

"I know," Sam cut in. "She's cooking supper over at the Hunter's Inn right now. I've eaten there a lot lately." He patted his slightly bulging belly. "Good food. She might be a keeper."

Jack smiled. "Yeah, she might. Could you give that to her after I take off?"

"Sure, no sweat." Sam had already started to skim the second note, but the last of daylight failed before he could finish. He walked to the truck, switched on the headlights and completed the reading. Then he walked back to Jack, shaking his head and let out a whistle of astonishment. "Who's this to?"

"The yard foreman...waiting at the Bull Moose. The one you saw here."

Sam looked at the paper again, as if he were reading, even though it had turned too dark to do so. "You're gonna turn him in to the district attorney if he bothers you again? You *sure* you want me to give him this?"

"Yep. Will you?"

Sam hesitated a moment, then a malicious grin spread across his face. "Why sure, brother. I'll make sure the greasy rat gets it. Matter of fact, it'll be a pleasure." He winked. "I'll try not to mix 'em up." Then he put both notes into his shirt pocket. "Say, you gotta get going." They walked to the plane, and Jack strapped into the harness and parachute. He pulled his leather helmet on and began a quick refamiliarization check of the cockpit. Sam leaned in and put his finger on a switch, then yelled over the engine. "Something new since you flew these." He flicked the switch, and two large beamlights, one under each lower wing, lit up. "Landing lights." He turned them off again. "If you fly over the Bakersfield Airport, the postal folks'll light gasoline drums for you, but there's nothing like landing lights on short final." He fished into a leather pouch screwed onto the airframe. "Your maps and flashlight are here. I got a red glass taped to the light so you don't go night blind after you read the map or your instruments. It'll take a little getting used to, though." He looked cross-eyed at the stogie in his mouth as if he just remembered he had it. He plucked it, threw it to the ground, and crushed it. "That reminds me. I taxied over to the fuel truck and threw in some more gas. You're all topped off again."

Jack adjusted his safety belt and moved the stick and rudder pedals while he looked around at all the control surfaces. "Thanks," Jack yelled back. "I thought she'd been idling a bit long." He aimed the red light on the temp gauge for an instant. "She's not hot, though. I guess your mechanic's on the job. Coolant plumbing was always the first thing to go on a DH4."

"Yeah, plumbing's always the demon with these liquid-cooled Liberties. Cal's a good man with a wrench though. That's for sure." Sam pulled out another cigar, then rolled his eyes, shook his head, and slid the Havana back into his pocket. "You just put one out, idiot!" he barked at himself.

"What?" Jack lifted the earflap on his helmet. That was the second time he thought he'd heard the word idiot tonight, and he wanted to know who Sam meant and why.

"Nothing," Sam responded. "Just talkin' to myself." He held up an index finger. "Okay, listen. Get your altitude as soon as ya can. You go straight up the valley and over those hills." He pointed to the Northeast. "And you'll be over Palmdale. Use the Palmdale lights for your bearing and head out three-three-zero degrees from there. Keep Lancaster, then Mojave on your right. Tehachapi too, but it'll be closer and you gotta be above eight thousand feet before you get that far. Then turn to two-eight-zero, but don't let down until you actually see Bakersfield, and you'll be all right. Got that?"

Jack nodded the exaggerated pilots' nod, bred from years of communicating over engine noise. "I got it."

"Oh yeah, I almost forgot." Sam reached into his pants pocket and withdrew a revolver. He handed it to Jack. "Here. You won't need this, but postal regulations require it."

Jack zipped it into the leg pouch of his flying suit. "A thirty-eight. Carried one in France."

"Just you make sure you get it back to me when you come in." Sam looked over his shoulder as headlights swept the plane. Jack glanced back and saw an expensive-looking touring car stop at the gate. It was full of women with the exception of one man who seemed to be struggling to get into a leather flying jacket.

"Andy," Sam said.

A large figure, someone other than Andy, crossed in front of the car's lights. He had a menacing stride and headed quick for the opening in the fence. *Crusher*. Jack and Sam saw him at the same time. They looked at each other and nodded.

Sam said, "Boy, good things come in bunches, don't they?"

Jack adjusted his feet on the peddles. "I think it's time for me to go."

Sam smiled. "I think you're right. This is going to be fun." He slapped Jack on the shoulder. "Kick her in the slats, neighbor!" He gave his new pilot a slight backhanded wave, then turned toward the gate.

Jack scanned his instruments once more, replaced the flashlight, and pushed the throttle full forward. Dust rose from behind the De Havilland as prop wash blew over Jack's face, and the plane began to move—slow at first, giving Jack time to remember to pull his goggles over his eyes. He put an ever-so-slight bit of forward pressure on the joystick. Then as the prop bit deeper into the dry air, the speed picked up and continued to build until the tail lifted off the runway. Soon, as he approached flying speed, Jack felt the hurtling sensation he loved. Then after another second, with a little back-pressure on the stick, came the smooth lift of the main wheels from the earth. *Thank you, Lord,* he thought. *I'd almost forgotten how this felt.* He added a little more back-pressure and waited a second for the big 400 horsepower Liberty engine to pull him a little faster and give him just the right feel of power and control over the forces of flight. And when that moment came, he pulled the nose up and began a smooth ascent, which soon became a climbing right turn as Jack circled back over the airfield.

It felt even better than he remembered, and he could have easily lost himself in revelry, but he recalled how critical the climb-out was here with nothing but hills in every direction—how easy it would be to kill oneself with inattention. That sobered him. *Save your joy for later, boy. Right now, watch what you're doing. It's been a long time.*

He maintained a climb rate of five hundred feet per minute, having already reached half that height above the ground. His speed remained at over ninety miles per hour, but from the aircraft's altitude, things seemed to pass beneath in the familiar slow motion Jack knew so well. Remembering the old illusion, he absorbed the sensation of comfort it brought him—like hot chocolate on a chilly day. He smiled and craned his neck a little to enjoy the darkening view below.

Traveling back over the runway in the opposite direction of his take-off, he saw Sam in the touring car's headlights involved in an animated, arm-waving discussion with the man in the leather jacket. *Sorry, Andy, whoever you are.* Jack tried not to smile but couldn't help himself.

He could also make out another figure some distance behind Sam and almost out of the headlights' range. It looked like a man in striped overalls stumbling away from the lingering cloud of dust left by Jack's take-off. Jack smiled. *Goodbye, Crusher.* The fellow on the ground stopped as Jack flew over. He looked up at the plane, and seemed to go into some sort of a dance. The man jumped up and down, waving his fists in the air and, at one point, picked something off the ground and threw it toward the plane. Jack realized that the man must have tried to catch up with him during the initial part of take-off, getting a face full of dirt for his effort. The figure on the ground soon crouched and grabbed his head. Jack wondered if he was protecting himself from whatever he'd just thrown, or if the missile had already returned earthward and struck him. He hoped it was the latter. *That would be the cherry on top of all this.*

Jack saw Sam wave at him from between the two unhappy men, and he imagined that his feisty new employer was already halfway into a fresh Havana and enjoying two confrontations for the price of one. Jack shook his head and laughed as he swung the mail plane back again to the Northeast to climb over the hills that stood southwest of Palmdale.

At five thousand feet, he leveled off, eased the throttle back to cruise RPM, and settled into a pace of just over one hundred miles per hour. The deafening complaint of the engine climbing to altitude now settled down into a low, contented grumble, and the resurrected pilot loosened his grip on the controls. He took in a calming lungful of cold, clean, mile-high air and let his shoulders drop from the "scarecow on a stick" position his knotted nerves had hoisted them to for takeoff and climb-out.

Well, what do ya know. He patted the De Havilland's fuselage with a gloved hand. *We made it. I don't know whose mount you were in France, Old Paint, but your tired, old wings are a dream come true to me! Praise God, I'm back!* He caressed the stretched fabric of the plane's flank as the truth of his good fortune finally hit him. *Yes, indeed!* He looked up at the clearest sky and brightest stars he'd seen in months. *Praise you, Lord, for bringing me back from the dead.* He glanced down at the tiny pinpricks of light that marked homes and ranches, and he sighed. *Thanks for getting me into the air again.* It was then that he remembered his almost unconscious prayer on the walk from the rail-yard and the desperation he'd felt less than an hour ago.

Wait a minute. Something's not right. Something's missing. He scanned the length of the plane. *Oh, yeah. There's no little blue flame coming from the exhaust stack.* Then his peripheral vision picked up the faint robins-egg glow flickering from behind his right shoulder. He turned and looked down. *Well, I'll be darned, a single exhaust pipe coming all the way past the cockpit from the engine. Not as cozy, but it'll save on night blindness...especially on landings. I suppose I can get used to my night-light burning behind me.*

Jack pulled his goggles up onto his forehead so he could drink in the night without distortion. He leaned his head out into the slip-stream and took a whiff of the engine fumes that rushed by the cockpit. Then, almost overcome by the happiness from his blessing, he began to laugh again. Not as if he heard a joke or saw his kids playing in the mud, but the kind of laugh that comes when a man makes it to a filling station just before he runs out of gas. Soon, intermixed with his laughter, he began to shout into the oncoming wind, "Thank you, Lord! Thank you, Jesus! Thank you! Ahhhh-ha-ha! Thank you." Then he laughed some more.

Then, during Jack's last round of madhouse laughter, a maverick glop of oil from the De Havilland's engine escaped through an errant valve and shot directly into Jack's open mouth. It smeared his teeth and coated his tongue as it slid back toward his throat. He shut his mouth instinctively and got ready to spit, but then thought better of it. Instead, he swallowed the dark elixir and imagined he could feel it spreading through his body like a healing balm. "Thank you for that, too, Lord." He cleared his throat and swallowed again. Then he repeated, "Thank you for that, too."

All right, back to business. The plane crested the last hill, and the lights of Palmdale burst forth from the darkness beneath him. Jack pulled his goggles back down over his eyes, lit the red-lensed flashlight, aimed it at the instrument panel and swung the De Havilland's nose toward a more westerly heading stopping the turn when his compass read three-three-zero degrees. Then he started a slow climb in preparation for the mountains of Tehachapi and settled back into his seat again, allowing himself to soak in the joy of the journey. *Lord, you've been good to me today.* Shortly he flashed the red light onto his altimeter to see how close he was to his new cruising altitude.

Chapter Thirty-Seven

"You said your brother was dead." Carrie wiped stubborn beads of rinse-water from the last two measuring spoons and placed said spoons into their assigned drawer, thus ending the oft-performed cleanup ceremony.

"No, I didn't. I didn't say he was dead…really." Ezzie scanned the kitchen of the Hunter's Inn until she found the pot she'd been looking for. "I said he was dead with our *dad*." She snatched the errant vessel from the sink-board and hung it on an overhead hook-rack. "He's just fired. That's all."

Carrie sighed and ran a washcloth over the preparation table one more time. "Fired is not dead, Ezzie. Fired is not good, but it's not dead." She lowered her forehead and gave her assistant a weak imitation of a suspicious look.

"No, but when our dad finds out Roberto got fired." Ezzie rolled her eyes. "Boy, is my brother ever gonna be dead." She whistled. "Or he'll wish he was—especially when our dad finds out *why* Berto got fired."

"And why *did* he get the sack, prey tell?"

"What sack?"

"Why did he get fired?"

"He wouldn't work Sundays."

"What?"

"He wouldn't work Sundays because he thought that was a sin." Ezzie untied the apron behind her back and let it hang by its neck loop. "He even told his boss out at that turkey ranch where he works that he'd work Sunday if it was an emergency or something. But that guy just wouldn't listen. He told poor Berto, if he wanted his Sundays free, he could have *all* his days free. That's when he fired him. But see, you're a Christian. You know about not wanting to sin against God. And that's why I thought Roberto should work for you." She took a deep breath, replenishing some

477

of the oxygen she'd been burning as she spoke. "And he knows all about turkeys. They're like chickens," she held a flattened hand, palm down, about waist high," only bigger." She raised the hand to shoulder height. "He should work for you."

"*Who's* gonna work for you?" Ruth bulled into the kitchen and let a canvas shopping bag drop onto the preparation table.

Carrie winced and moved the trespassing bag onto the counter. "Nobody. Roberto's simply lost his job."

"No, but he should *work* for you." Ezzie wadded her apron and stuffed it into the laundry hamper by the south doorway. "You're always saying that you're so busy you can't think straight, and you wished Jack didn't have to work so long with the railroad and come home so tired so he could—"

All three women finished Ezzie's sentence in unison, "Help more with the chickens."

"Yes," Ezzie went on. "See. You *do* need Roberto to help because Jack can't. *Que no?*"

"Jack!" Ruth blurted and fumbled first in the pocket of her skirt, then through both high-pockets of her woolen blouse. "I swear, I'm getting more feeble-minded by the day." She rolled her eyes to the ceiling and emitted a small growl. "I've got something for you." Ruth stomped a booted foot then shoved her hand into another pocket, this time the one on her heavy-knit sweater where she finally found the misplaced *something* for Carrie. "Ah-ha! Got ya!" She pulled out a folded scrap of brown-bag paper. "Sam gave me this…from Jack…for you…just 'afore I got to the door here." Ruth held the note out to her friend.

Carrie automatically dried her hands on her own apron and took the brown scrap. "Why would Jack be sending me a …" She unfolded it and read with moving lips until she got midway through it. Then Carrie's hands jerked and she almost screamed, "What?" She took half a backward step.

478

"Oh, Jack!" Her left hand reached out for the support of preparation table. "You big stupid—" Carrie bit off the sentence and her gaze shot up to the other two women. "He's ... he's quit his job on the railroad."

Ruth's brow furrowed. "Z'at a fact?"

"Yes." Carrie finished the note for the second time to insure she'd made no mistake. "And he's taken another job as a pilot for Sam, flying airmail."

"See," Ezzie said, "You still need Roberto."

"Flyin' for Sam, huh?" Ruth folded her arms. "Well, if that don't beat all. I didn't know Sam had any openings for new pilots. Otherwise, we'd have steered Jack there a long time ago."

Carrie continued to stare at the brown-paper omen of doom. "He won't be home until late tonight." She crumpled the note into a tiny deformed roll and dropped it into the hot-ash bucket beside the number one cook-stove. In less than a second, the offending message had turned dark, curled up, and ignited into an angry flame. "He's taking the night-mail to Bakersfield and back." Carrie found a stool and sat, still braced by the preparation table.

She remained silent for a long time, content to focus on a crust of dinner roll wedged half into the seam between one of the kitchen cabinets and the floor. *How could he?* She thought back to his promise to be more responsible when it came to his family. *'All I want is to take care of you and the boys.' Isn't that what he said...or at least something like that? And he's been doing so well, never missing a day's work. What happened? What was it this time?*

"Carrie?" Ruth's voice intruded.

Carrie stared at the breadcrumb for almost another full minute before she became aware of the passage of time or Ruth's hand on her shoulder. *Every time he tries to live out these aviation dreams, the boys and I suffer for it.* Memories of the months of poverty and humiliation caused by her husband's barnstorming adventures rushed upon her, drowning out most of the wifely trust she'd built up over the last year. *How could you, Jack?*

"Carrie?" Carrie felt the presence of Ruth again, behind her now, holding both the young chef's shoulders.

"What?" Carrie looked up still internally focused on a scene in which Jack took off from a dry grass field in his patched up, old Jenny. Kenny and Eddie waved their hero/father off with wild enthusiasm, as if Jack were leaving for war again. That time he didn't call or come back for six months, and, by the end of the year, Carrie had decided her husband loved flying more than his family.

"Anybody home in there?" Ruth gave the muscles between Carrie's neck and shoulder blades a gentle squeeze.

"Oh." Carrie shook her head slightly. "I'm sorry." She re-hung her in-control demeanor and produced a small manufactured laugh. "I suppose I took a little trip to the moon just then." She smiled her best formal Van Burean smile. "I'm perfectly all right now, though." Carrie cocked her head back toward Ruth. "Sorry again."

Ruth shrugged but did not release her friend. "Ain't no never-mind to me. Maybe you can tell me about it sometime soon."

"Yes." Carrie's smile faded. "Real soon."

"The moon, huh?" Ruth patted Carrie and returned to her previous leaning location against the service entrance door-jam.

"Yes." Carrie released the captive preparation table and stood to her full height, pulling the dishtowel scarf from around her hair.

"Well, you sure wasn't here." Ezzie doffed her own head towel and launched it, balled up, into the hamper. "You ok? You not sick or something?"

Carrie walked to the hamper as if in a trance and left her towel to keep Ezzie's company. "Sick?" She paused.

"Merely at heart." Another pause as she returned to her tall stool and settled there. "But not the way you mean." She smiled a sweet smile at Ezzie. "I was thinking, however, that you've been right all along."

"Huh?" Ezzie stopped in the middle of taking her long blue wool coat from the coat-rack near the pantry door. "Right about what?"

Carrie clasped her hands, wrung them a bit, and leaned one elbow on the table. "About Roberto working the ranch for me." She took one quick, gaspy gulp of air then got her breathing under control again. "I think I'm going to need him after all." She looked at Ruth then down at the floor. "As a matter of fact, I'm going to need him to start as soon as possible."

"*Si?*" Ezzie thrust both hands through the arms of her coat at the same time by raising her hands in a pantomimed surrender.

"Yes." Carrie looked up and nodded. "So have him at the house by eight tomorrow morning." She stopped her hand wringing and glanced at her wedding ring. "I'll discuss the details of the arrangement with Roberto then." She paused. "By the way." She looked down for a long second and considered her next words. "Can he drive?"

"Yes, he can drive. He drives real good."

"Good, because I'm going to buy a new Model-T truck in Palmdale tomorrow." Carrie met Ruth's raised eyebrows with a determined nod. "And I'll want Roberto to drive it back to the ranch. Also I'm going to have him do all the deliveries from now on." She fixed a scrutinizing stare upon the young Latina. "It'll be a big part of the job. Can he handle that?"

"He can handle that and anything else you need."

"That's good. Then I'll see him tomorrow."

"Bueno," Ezzie said. Then she giggled, turned, and marched triumphantly down the narrow hall to the service door. "*Adios!*" came the echo just before the door slammed shut.

Ruth cleared her throat before speaking. "A new truck, huh? For Jack or Roberto?"

"Jack can drive the old one. It's simply going sit at the airfield all day. I'll not waste a new truck on that."

"He doesn't know about this new truck yet, does he?"

Carrie shook her head slowly. "No, he doesn't."

Ruth stood silent for a few seconds, arms once again folded. Then, after one powerful sigh, she said, "You're wrong, you know."

"Wrong?" Carrie's eyebrows rose. "Nonsense. I think Roberto will make an excellent hired man."

"Not Roberto." Ruth shifted on her feet. "About Jack."

"No, I'm not." She bit her lip. "Besides, I didn't really say anything. Did I?"

"You didn't have to." Ruth cleared her throat. "You've always talked about his time flying like he was playin' hooky from school." She drifted closer to the table but kept her arms crossed. "Flyin's just a job, Carrie, just like any other."

"No, it's not." Carrie half whispered, half squeaked. *You don't know.*

Ruth sat on another, seldom-used tall stool Henri had recently purchased for his own use during menu conferences with Carrie. She laid her elbows on the table. "People can make a decent living with aeroplanes and support their families."

"Not Jack." Carrie pulled a handkerchief from her dress pocket and intercepted a traitorous tear that raced down her cheek. "He won't. He'll be the one in a hundred that won't be able to do that. You don't know him when he commits to something he really loves." She stopped two more runaway droplets then twisted the handkerchief into an elongated knot. "He loses all common sense and forgets

482

to do what needs be. He did it with auto racing. He did it with flying before, and he'll do it again."

"Carrie, you don't know that."

"Yes, I do." Her voice broke. "He'll do something wrong. He'll start acting like a big child and do something that keeps him from taking care of us." She sniffed. "Or he'll start working as far away from us as he can get...or maybe he'll start drinking and end up like...."

"Like Sam." Ruth straightened up. "A drunkard like Sam."

Oh, my gosh! Carrie's stomach tightened. *Take it back, Carrie! Quick! Take it back!* "No, Ruth! I didn't mean..." She held out a hand half way to her friend, but didn't dare touch her. "I'm so sorry. Please—"

"No." Ruth's voice was even, but with a slight quaver. "Sam is a drunkard, plain and simple. I wish he weren't, but he is." She took a deep breath. "He doesn't drink when he has to fly though. And he has pilots working for him that are sober. Those men make a good wage. Matter of fact, they make a bit more than a railroad switchman." Her arms refolded. "Quite a *bit* more."

"Really," Carrie said, but did not sound convinced.

Ruth got up from the stool. "He didn't leave you, Gal. He just got another job. Your marriage ain't over yet."

"Maybe." Carrie sniffed again. "We'll see." Then she remembered the insult to Ruth. "But please, I hope you don't think I would ever...I mean, you've been such a good friend since I...Oh, I —"

Ruth stuck out her chin as she waved Carrie's worries away with a dismissive hand. "'Nough said. I know you was just carryin' on. Sometimes women don't exactly say what they mean." She raised a finger to her lips and shushed the young wife. "But don't *tell* that to anybody," Ruth cackled. "It's a secret."

"None the less, it was a horrid thing to say, and I apologize." Carrie made a last dab at her face and put away her hanky. Then she took a breath as deep as Ruth's had been and stood. "So did you come over simply to give me that awful note or was there something else?"

Ruth picked up her bag from the counter. "Well, there was more, but I don't think it's a good idea now."

"Dear Ruth, it cannot possibly be worse than the news you've just given me." Carrie thought a moment. "Could it?"

The older woman emitted a small groan, then scanned the room before allowing her gaze to rest back upon Carrie. "Haven't seen Bee in several days. Been meaning to stop there, but I just got too dern busy doin' one thing or another." She glanced away. "So Seth catches up with me at the Market and says his ma hasn't been out of her room since yesterday. Got the door locked. Sam's been sleepin' down at the hangar last couple of days, and all I can get out of him is that Bee's in *some* kind of mood. But he says he ain't about to go back up to the house to find out *what* kind." Ruth put her bag on the floor. "She does get powerful moody on occasion, but I think it's mostly Sam's drinkin' what does it to her...that and the fact that she's alone in that house with the children most of the time." She shook her head. "A body's got to talk to someone what's growed up once in a while." Ruth chanced a quick smile. "Nothin' but children all the time; now that would drive anybody dark an' moody."

"I think Seth is a wonderful boy, but I don't know much about Sam and Bee's other child." Carrie stepped to the coat rack and pulled her long, checked woolen coat from its hook.

"Well, that would be my granddaughter, Elizabeth Bee. Five years old. Bee calls her Liddy-Beth. Ben and I call her Little Bee." Ruth beamed momentarily.

Ruth's smile spread to Carrie as the younger woman slipped into her coat and said, "Your grandmother badge is showing."

Ruth shored up her smile a little longer. "Oh, that can't be helped. That little girl's cute as a chipmunk. Talks your ears off. Smart as a tack." Her countenance fell. "But her mother's so high-strung, she won't let her daughter say nary a word, all the time shushing her or telling her to be still. Sometimes I get to where I can't take no more of it and I say right out I want to hear what the girl's got all stored up to say." Ruth let out a small low moan. "Then it's like a dam a'breakin'. You just can't get that girl shut off again." She shook her head. "Poor Little Bee. So much inside, and her ma's tied a knot in her spigot."

"That's very sad, Ruth." Carrie retrieved her gray cloche hat from its peg on the wall and settled it expertly onto her head, checking its cant in the reflection from a glass-doored china cupboard. "But I don't understand why you thought it important to tell *me*."

"Because I want you to go with me and see if'n we can pry Bee out of that bedroom."

Carrie froze in mid-hat adjustment and turned slowly to face Ruth. "You're joking."

"Not one smidge."

"But what could I possibly do? I don't even know the woman, and, so far, every time I've waved or made an attempt to speak to her, she's gathered up Seth and run into the house." Carrie performed a quick swivel and found her own canvas shopping bag, which was almost identical to Ruth's. "I doubt very seriously if Bee would even let me into her house to begin with, let alone allow me to help her in any way whatsoever." She paused, hoping that, somewhere in the wall of words she had just erected, Ruth would find some reason to decide Carrie was not a good partner for Bee's rescue.

But Ruth remained undaunted. "Of course she won't let you in. She's holed up in the bedroom." Ruth hoisted her bag again. "Seth'll let us in."

"But why me?" A drop of fear leaked out with Carrie's voice.

"Well, for one thing, you make two or more."

"I beg your pardon?"

Ruth held her bag two-handedly in front of her lap and swung it a little from side to side. "Wherever two or more are gathered together...there...I ...will...be...also."

Carrie's heart sank just a little. *Using God. That's not fair!* "That's not fair, Ruth." She snatched her bag from the open shelf where it sat. "You know this is going to make me extremely uncomfortable." Carrie lowered her gaze for an instant. "Privacy is something I was raised to respect. It's very important where I come from."

Ruth nodded. "It is here, too. But, if someone falls into a mineshaft, we don't just let them stay there." She shrugged. "Right now, I think Bee's at the bottom of a deep, dark shaft." Ruth was quiet for a moment, seeming to inspect everything in the room except Carrie. "She's family, Carrie. And she's a city girl. Sometimes I don't know what to say to her." She stopped her gaze from its rounds and let it settle onto her friend. "Will you help me?"

As her knees sagged and her heart caved in, something occurred to Carrie, and she said, "Ben didn't bring you down in the wagon, did he?"

"He did, but I sent him home a couple of hours ago." Ruth grinned. "I want a ride in that scooty little automobile of yours!"

♪

The wind whipped Ruth's hair into her eyes. She held her dark gray Stetson onto her head with one hand, but the gale beating against the speeding little Stutz folded the hat's broad brim up around the old woman's knuckles, causing both sides to flap like a bird.

"Yeee-haaa!" Ruth's Rodeo yip died just beyond her lips, half stolen by the onrushing air. "Go faster!" She bounced in the passenger seat like she was kicking a horse in the slats. "Faster!"

"I can't go any faster," Carrie laughed. "Too many potholes."

"There's a smooth patch just ahead." Ruth pointed at the last stretch of dirt road just short of Sam and Bee's house. "Ben graded it with the drag this morning. You can put the spurs to her there."

"Very well." Carrie smiled and glanced sideways at her exuberant friend. "But after that, I'm slowing for the turn." She dropped the Bearcat down into second gear and pushed the gas pedal to the floorboard as Ruth nodded. The acceleration pushed them both back into their seats as the car surged forward over the freshly leveled adobe and decomposed granite.

Ruth grinned and slapped the leather of Carrie's seatback. "This little car's a real barn burner, Gal!" Her grin widened. "It truly is."

Decelerating as promised, Carrie swung into Sam's driveway and stopped in front of a small white-picket-fence-bordered lawn that stood just in front of the also-white, banister-bound front porch. "End of the line, Ruth." She set the brake and shut off the engine. "That's all you get for five cents." Carrie got out of the Stutz and stretched. Her neighbor had worked her hard on the trip up from town, all the way insisting on more and more speed.

Ruth winked as she shut her door. "I'd pay a *dollar* to do *that* again."

Carrie shook her head. "Well, maybe we'll do it again, but next time it'll be all on the pavement." She massaged the back of her own neck. "My teeth are still rattling."

"Grandma, Mrs. MacGregor!" Seth, suspendered workpants partly hiding his long-johns, burst out of the front door to take both women by the hand and tow them into the house. "Ma's crying. I can hear her through the door." His breaths came fast, but he seemed in control of himself, if not the circumstances. "I been trying to talk to her all day, but all she'll say is 'It's no good' over and over again." He peered at Ruth as he stopped in front of Bee's bedroom door. "Then she just keeps cryin'. I've never seen her this bad, Grandma. I don't know what to do!" The boy took a deep breath and dropped his hands to his sides. "You gotta do something!"

Ruth gave her grandson a side-hug. "Don't fret now. We'll see to it."

Seth turned to Carrie. "Please, help her, Mrs. MacGregor. Before Pa gets back. He gets mad when he catches her cryin'."

Carrie could stand only a moment of the boy's searching gaze before she looked to Ruth.

"Seth, go on and mind your sister now." The old woman guided her grandson out of the hallway. "We'll see to your ma."

When they were alone, Ruth leaned close to the bedroom door and gently rapped on the jam. "Bee? This is Ruth." She glanced up at Carrie then back to the door as if she could see her daughter-in-law through it. "I know you think all the milk's a'way past spilt, but I need for ya to talk to me anyhow."

"Go away," the door said.

"Yeah, that's what I thought you'd say." Ruth studied the low hall ceiling as if her next words were written there. "Look gal, I know a good piece of what's wrong, so you might as well open this here door and talk about it."

A moment passed while the door sobbed and sniffled, then it replied, "You *couldn't* know."

"I couldn't, huh. Well, how about this?" Ruth took a deep breath. "I know most of your troubles have something to do with Sam's drinkin'. How's that for knowing something?" She glanced at Carrie. "You want to talk to me now?"

"How can I do that? He's your son."

"Yes, he is, and I love him." Ruth swallowed hard. "But I love my grandbabies, too." She drummed her fingers once on the wall. "And I love my daughter-in-law." She waited a second. "That's you, in case you weren't sure."

"Wait a minute." The voice through the door sounded pensive.

A sigh's-worth of tension escaped Ruth's lungs, and she gave Carrie a premature smile and a nod. "I got Carrie MacGregor out here. A real big city girl. She came over just to chat with ya."

The tone of the voice in the bedroom turned to panic. "Oh no! Ruth how could you?"

A cloud passed across Ruth's face. Then she waved Carrie to the door with an impatient hand. The younger woman complied as her friend stepped back.

"Bee, it's Caroli—It's Carrie MacGregor." *Oh, Lord. Now what do I say?* "Please, don't feel embarrassed." *As I do right now.* "I know it's hard to talk to someone you don't really know." *And won't even wave back to.* "But I do know what it's like to feel out of place here." *Or something like that, I guess.* Carrie rolled her eyes, but Ruth motioned her on. "So if you do ever wish to talk, town-girl to town-girl, I'm willing." *Why did I say that? Please, don't say 'yes'. Oh please, don't! Please, don't!*

A full five seconds passed before any sound came from the bedroom. "I heard my Sam almost ran you over." Bee's voice came out almost as a whimper. "Aren't you mad at all?"

Carrie remained silent as she searched for a wise response.

"She's a good Christian woman, Bee." Ruth smiled and patted Carrie's shoulder. "She don't carry no grudges like that."

"I didn't hear *her* say it."

Carrie felt a strange tightness in her chest. *All right, Lord. I'll say it!* "I bear neither you nor your husband any ill will, Bee. And neither does my husband. As a matter of fact, Jack's working for Sam now at the airfield." *Why did I tell her that?*

"Who's Jack?"

"My husband."

"And he's working for Sam?"

"Yes."

"Is that a fact?" Suddenly the lock turned, and the door creaked open, revealing an extremely disheveled Bee in an equally rumpled flannel robe, with slightly too-long sleeves that covered her hands. Her dark-rimmed eyes were reddened and sunk deep into pale puffy cheeks. For a moment, she simply stood in the doorway, then she swung her hands behind her back and surveyed her saviors. Finally, shaking back a clump of unruly bangs, she said, "So how long's your husband...Jack...how long's he been working for Sam?"

Carrie's instincts pushed her back a step. "He started tonight. Or so I've been told."

Suddenly, the door slammed shut, cutting the universe in two once more.

"I think it's a good thing, Bee." Ruth nodded at Carrie. "Jack's a good man."

"You think so?"

"Yes." Ruth waited a moment. "Bee, honey. Why don't you open the door."

"It's not locked anymore."

Ruth gently pushed the door open and led the way into Bee's little gingham wallpaper and lace world. The woman sat in uncharacteristic calm repose on a white-painted wooden stool, rubbing bandaged wrists. She exuded a self-conscious air and stared into an oval vanity mirror as if she

490

were waiting for something other than her reflection to appear upon the glass.

Carrie had to stifle a gasp when she spotted the bandages. Ruth knotted her hands firmly in front of her but said nothing.

"I wasn't really trying to do away with myself, you know." Bee looked up and grimaced at her company. "I was just trying to scare Sam a little. But he was too drunk to notice, and then I was afraid to let the children see me like this." She turned back to the mirror. "Ruth?"

"Yes"

"Does this Jack drink? I mean does he get drunk? Some of Sam's pilots do, you know."

"Not so's I've noticed."

"Do you think he might be a good influence on Sam?" She continued to talk into the mirror. "If he stays, I mean."

"I do."

Bee nodded to herself than swiveled on the stool to face Carrie, who mentally braced herself for whatever was to come. *I don't think I've ever seen anyone look so alone.*

Bee said, "Your name is Carrie?"

"Yes, it is."

"You said we could talk?" Bee stood and shoved the stool out of the way with her heel.

"Yes, I did." *Uh oh.*

"Could we do that now?"

Oh, Lord! "Yes, we could."

"Mama, Mama!" The little bolt of tanned skin, brown-eyed lightning raced around Ruth and headed straight for Bee, who, quick as a gunshot, thrust her wrists behind her back and buried them into the folds of her robe. "You all well now, Mama? All better? Seth said you were sick." She wrapped herself around her mother—arms encircling hips, cheek pushed deep against abdomen—like a starfish surrounding a tidal pool rock. "I'm glad you're all better now!" She looked up into her parent's face and took two deep breaths. "Mama, did you see the car Grandma and Mrs.MacGregor come up in? It went fast, Mama! Real fast like…like…the Fourth of July…like…woooosh!" She took another breath to replace the fuel she'd just expended on her firework imitation. "That's what I want when I grow up, a fast car just like that. And I want to be a pilot just like Daddy. Seth says he wants to be a farmer like Grandpa, but I want to be a pilot and fly all around the world and see mountains and jungles and castles where kings and queens live." Another breath. "Then I want to come home and ride in my fast little car and go faster than anyone—"

Just then Seth burst through the doorway; he too appeared to be trying to regain his wind. He glanced at Ruth. "Sorry, Grandma. She come around the corner from behind the house and ran right past me before I could get a hold of her!"

Bee remained silent and had yet to return her daughter's embrace. But her expression bespoke pain, and her eyes had begun to brim. That's when Ruth stepped in, prying the child loose from her wounded mother.

"Little Bee." She picked her up into her arms and allowed the child's limbs to encircle her neck. "Why don't I tell you what it was like to ride in Mrs. MacGregor's Bearcat."

"Bearcat?"

"Yep." Ruth spoke softly but with an excited tone as she looked the lightning-girl in the eyes and walked slowly toward the front door. "That's what she calls her fast little car—a Bearcat. And was that ride ever fun."

Chapter Thirty-Eight
July, 1928

"You know what you want yet, Good-lookin'?" Alma leaned down and let her hand rest on Jack's forearm.

He looked up from the weather section of his newspaper and said to nobody in particular, "Says here July's going to be way hotter than June was." Then Jack pretended to have just noticed Alma. "Oh, just coffee today, thanks." He smiled a little too long before tilting his head in Sam's direction. "Give him a bucketful."

"Humph." Jack's boss cocked his stubby frame at a different angle in the booth so he would have a better vantage point through the window.

"I'm ready for ya." Alma swung the speckled blue porcelain coffee pot expertly over Jack's cup and poured a measure of the deep brown stimulant.

"So it seems." Jack allowed his smile to grow. This low-key flirtation had become a regular ceremony since Thanksgiving of twenty-four, more than four years now. He told himself it meant nothing, but he also knew he looked forward to it. The ritual warmed him more than anything else the café served.

Sam put a down-turned palm over his cup when the pot came his direction. "I'm fine, thanks," he said and patted the rim.

Jack slid the cup out from under its owner's hand. "Fill him up."

"Awh!" Sam turned his attention toward the window.

Alma half-filled the cup just the same.

"Hey, Alma!" A voice rang from several booths down. "Do we get to eat this morning?"

She shrugged. "I better see if old Raymond wants hash and eggs this time or just eggs and hash." She placed a kiss onto two of her slender fingers and transferred it to Jack's cheek. He did not dodge it. "I'll be back," she murmured as she swayed away toward complaining Raymond's table.

Sam surveyed the room like a thief looking for cops. Then he slid a shiny flask from his back pocket. "I've got my own vitamins, thank you very much." He pulled the cup close and fortified the brew within. "One hairy dog, I'm tellin' you." Sam scrutinized the pour with a scientific air until it reached some ratio known only to himself. "There." Leaning forward he capped the flask and replaced it to its nest. "That's the proper cure." Then he sipped, shuddered, and smiled. "Mother's milk. Yes indeed."

Jack sighed.

Sam frowned. "Oh, stop it. You sigh like my wife."

"Do I have to say it?"

"What, that I'm drinking too much?"

"Yes."

"No, you don't have to say it."

"Then you agree?"

"No, but you don't have to say it." He abandoned sipping for a full-blown slurp and winked at Jack. "I'm not paying attention anyway. Besides, you're my chief pilot, not my mother...*or* my wife."

"You're saying you're not drinking more than last year...or even last month?"

"No." Sam took another hearty gulp. "I'm just enjoying life more than last year." He gave Jack a hard look. "How 'bout you? Are you against a man's enjoyment or have you joined the temperance league this week?"

Jack held up his hands. "Okay, okay. I get it. Not my business." He drank a little alcohol-free coffee. "Unless you try to fly that way. Then, as your chief pilot, it *is* my business." He put his cup down and returned his boss's stare.

Sam ignored him and scanned the dirt alley outside. "Well, there goes Crusher headed for the Bull Moose." He nodded toward the rail foreman as he swaggered his way

494

between the café and the speakeasy next door. "Ya know, he's the big wheel bootlegger in this town since Snuffy Franks died so mysteriously." The last word of Sam's statement fairly dripped with the sound of irony.

"Mysteriously?" Jack leaned toward the window as Crusher rounded the corner of the Bull Moose, as if doing so would help explain Sam's statement.

Sam smiled as Jack rose to the lure. "Oh yes. Very mysterious indeed."

"I thought he was just thrown from a horse and rolled down a cliff."

"That's what it said in the paper; thrown from a horse."

"Then what's the mystery?"

The telltale quiver of an almost-smile peeked out from the corners of Sam's mouth. "Well, from what I hear." He held up an emphasizing finger. "From very reliable sources."

"Stub Mahoney?"

"The very same."

Jack nodded. "Go on."

Sam's infant-smile grew a little. "From what I hear, Snuffy lost a leg in the war against Spain. He's been walking around on a wooden one ever since ninety-eight." Sam paused for effect. "He hasn't sat a horse of any kind in all that time. He walked, rode in wagons, and even autos, but he could not be gotten onto a horse. Said, even though the missing part was from his right leg and was not needed to mount himself into the saddle, just having his right boot in a stirrup aggravated his stump." Sam took a sip of the cure. "Mysterious, like I said. Especially if you consider that Snuffy's wife, Pet, has suddenly started sellin' Crusher's brand of cleaning-fluid gin at the Bull Moose. That's a real shame. They must've scared her something awful. Snuffy always said Petunia was afraid of neither man nor beast."

At that moment, Crusher reappeared in the alley, heading back toward the rail-yard, counting a small roll of currency as he strode.

Sam said, "I guess Snuffy didn't figure on his wife being cornered by something like Crusher. I asked her if she wanted my help a couple days ago." He let out a chuckle. "She told me to tend to my own business. Tough old woman, Pet is."

Jack shook his head. "I suppose she is at that."

Sam stared down the alley for a few seconds after Crusher had gone out of sight. Then he finished his fortified coffee and got up from the booth. "That was the last of Snuffy's moonshine." He patted the flask in his back pocket. "I'll have to start on Crusher's turpentine next. What's this world comin' to?"

Jack rose to his feet. "You ready to go to work?" He inspected his boss for steadiness, but wasn't sure of a decision yet.

"Like an old fire-horse."

"Good." Jack clapped Sam on the shoulder as they headed for the door. *Let's see if you can remain fairly stable under a light blow.*

Sam wobbled just a little and waved at Alma, who stood three tables away, serving Raymond but watching Jack.

Sam mumbled, "Now there's a sweet morsel to rekindle a man's spirit." He laughed a little, then stumbled a lot. "So how's your home life, Jack old boy? Does the toast of Sweet Springs still bring ya yer pipe and slippers?"

Jack scowled. "Like I've already told you…she's like an iceberg viewed from a mile away, cool and distant. You know all this. We've only discussed it for four years."

"Yeah well, I think it's catching—that iceberg disease. My old lady's had it for *at least* ten years. Probably gave it to your wife." Sam stumbled again.

496

Jack said, "I'll drive." Then he paused in the doorway and glanced expectantly back to Alma. She grinned and waved. Slightly uncomfortable yet warmed by the familiar attention, Jack followed Sam out the door and away from the Lakeview Café.

♪

The hangars weren't much, just three dented barn-like affairs of rusting corrugated steel plating, bolted onto large wooden beams. The ends of the steel sections on the two oldest buildings curled up slightly at the bottom, allowing sand, rattlers, and kangaroo rats to enter and rest within, undeterred by doors and windows that might be shut tight and locked. However, this micro-invasion seemed to eventually balance itself out, since the rat nests had begun to helped block out the wind and sand, and the snakes eventually ate most of the rats.

This morning, the big sliding hanger doors had already been pulled all the way back, and Sam stood inside just across the threshold staring at the small egg-shaped muddy pond that lay well within range of the naked eye. "Dang lake's almost completely dry now. Sure smells a lot better this summer, though, than last." He shaded his eyes against the conquering sun. "I guess all those dead fish have finally had a chance to dry out now."

"Funny." Jack navigated around Sam's bulk to stand in the hanger's shade. At eight o'clock, the mid-July heat could already be felt reflecting off the taxiway's oil-soaked, hard-packed dirt. "Before we came up here five years ago, we thought that lake would help bring us a new life."

"We?" Sam sauntered over to the hangar's long, infinitely-stained wooden shop bench and settled, with a groan, onto a tall stool.

"Carrie and me."

"Good. I'm glad you weren't including me in that *we* because the only time I ever thought about that stinking little puddle was when I wished it would do exactly what it's doing now. Drying up and blowing away so's I can buy the property and extend my runways. I could probably get it for a song from Snuffy's wife; she could use the money just now, and that's a fact. I've already talked to her about it. So far, she's still praying for the rainstorm of the century and hoping for a miracle." He shook his head. "But I don't think she'll hold onto it much longer, what with her still havin' to pay taxes on it and nobody paying dock or tie-up fees anymore." He took a fresh Havana from his shirt pocket, bit the end from the cigar and spit it off into the sunlight. "This airfield could become a real airport that would draw more business to this town than that so-called fishing lake ever did." He lit a match with his thumbnail and rolled the stogy to life over the flame. "You mark me." The usual gray plume began to gather around his head until he rousted it with his second puff. "It'll happen and we'll…I mean I'll be in on the ground floor."

Jack smiled. "Maybe you're right."

"Maybe?" Sam puffed. "You bet I'm right! This place sits just about as far as light planes can get on their way north from Los Angeles or San Fernando, if they don't use up their emergency fuel reserve. Sweet Springs'll become just like Banning Airfield is for planes going between Palm Springs and the coast. Most of those fellows have to land there for fuel or to wait out extreme winds and weather. It'll be just like that here, what with the way the winds get between Palmdale and Mojave and the winter rains and snow that comes off the San Bernardino Mountains. And all those good pilgrims headed for Bakersfield or Fresno will have to land right here at old Sam's airfield, buy our fuel, pay our tie-down fees, and—your wife and Henri'll like this part—eat and spend the night at the Hunter's Inn. That's the future of this sleepy little town, neighbor. And it'll be nothing but gravy from then on." He took a breath. "If I can just get Pet to sell me that worthless lakebed."

"Mr. Smith?" The voice surprising both Sam and Jack came from a tall mustachioed, bespectacled man who seemed to appear from nowhere. He held a tweed jacket and straw skimmer under one arm and slumped as if fatigued.

Sam gave Jack a lightning glance. "Who wants to know?"

"I'm Aaron Shontz." He wiped his pale forehead with the back of his hand, then stepped into the shade and finished rolling up the sleeves of his pinstriped shirt. "We've corresponded about renting a hangar?"

"Yeah. I remember." Sam flicked a new ash onto the concrete floor. "You're the fellow with the racer."

"Well." The man seemed uncomfortable with Sam's comment. He looked around as if he feared eavesdroppers. "We'll be attempting to set a new world speed record. Our aircraft won't be entered in an actual race." He glanced over his shoulder. "Our only competitor is the clock."

"The clock and whoever else is trying to set that record, too." Jack pulled off his flying jacket and slung it over his shoulder.

Shontz turned suspicious eyes upon Jack as if he'd just now noticed his presence.

"It's okay, Mr. Shontz." Sam disconnected himself from his stool and waved a hand toward Jack. "This is Jack MacGregor, my chief pilot." Sam chewed on his cigar as he smiled and clapped Jack on the back. "He handles things here a good part of the time. I assure you he's a man to be trusted."

"I hope you forgive my caution, Mr. MacGregor." Shontz put his hand out to Jack and the two shook. "You see," he said, "competition is fierce in this quest for speed records. The ownership of the fastest plane has been known to turn common men into manufacturers overnight."

"You must have a pretty hot ship if you're worried about the wrong person getting a peek." Jack's eyebrows arched, emphasizing the statement.

At that moment, the dull rumble of a big Ford double-T flatbed in low gear intruded upon the conversation. All three men stepped out of the hangar and watched as the big truck pulled around the corner. Behind it followed a long double-axle wooden trailer bearing a strange-looking, elongated mass, cocooned in thick tarps and heavy rope.

The rig squealed to a stop beside the group, and an unshaven man in a flannel shirt and watch-cap leaned out of the cab. "Is this the place, Professor?"

Shontz nodded in response.

"Professor?" Sam's smoldering Havana Corona rose slightly at the tip in coordination with his eyebrows.

Shontz shook his head. "Actually, I'm an engineer. Professor's just something he calls me."

The truck-driver gave the airfield a quick survey. "You want I should park this down at that second hangar?" He pointed at the next building to the north.

Shontz held up his hand. "A moment, Mr. Gilhooley."

Gilhooley leaned back against his seat and pulled the watch-cap over his eyes. "You're the boss."

Shontz turned back to Jack. "'We must have a hot ship,' you said."

A little puzzled by this curious man's manner, Jack hesitated but finally answered, "Uh, yes."

"And you say you trust this man," Shontz said to Sam.

"With my wife." Sam punctuated his last word with an exaggerated nod.

The odd Mr. Shontz seemed to contemplate something for a moment, then appeared to make some kind of internal determination. "We have several vehicles still parked out on the road." He paused again. "Give us an hour to get set up … then come take a look and judge for yourself how hot our ship is." At that point a fleeting smile sprinted across his lips, then evaporated. Shontz walked backward toward the double-T's cab. "The second hangar *is* the one we're renting, correct?"

"Yeah, that's the one." Sam seemed as curious about the mystery of the *hot ship* as Jack.

And Jack found himself to be very curious, indeed.

"Well, then." Shontz hopped up onto the truck's running board with surprising agility and took a firm grip on the door with his unburdened arm. "In an hour, gentlemen." He tapped the door with his foot. "Shall we go, Mr. Gilhooley?"

Gilhooley sat up and pulled the cap from his eyes. "Sure thing, Professor."

Jack stood in the sun looking after the tarped trailer and wondered if all aeronautical engineers were as strange as Shontz. "*Where* did you *meet* this fellow?" he said as he turned his face Sam.

"He wired me a couple of months ago about renting the hangar and using the airfield facilities, whatever that means. Fuel I suppose." Sam inspected the end of his cigar. "He said he wouldn't need anything else from us. They've got their own mechanics… tools, and parts, to boot. Or at least, that's what Shontz said in the telegram."

Six more vehicles, mixed cars and small trucks, rolled by and stopped beside the big double-T in front of the middle hangar. Shontz and Gilhooley tugged determinedly at the first sliding hangar door while others emerged from their vehicles to help.

Almost exactly one hour later, Jack and Sam filed through the small access door inset in one of the now closed large hangar doors. Inside, organized confusion reigned. Men rushed from one end of the main hangar bay to the other, stowing tools on or under long wooden benches. They hung massive, clanking chain-falls from the huge oak center-beam and searched for missing boxes they swore they had set down on the gasoline-stained concrete floor "just a second ago." The scene looked like an anthill, disturbed by some careless boot, with intense workers scurrying in random direction but each knowing exactly what he was about.

In the center of it all sat the tarp-covered trailer with Shontz bustling around it deviling his minions as they untied ropes and released turnbuckles. First one rope slid off, then another and another until the tarp itself remained the only thing keeping the secret that lay beneath. Shontz seemed oblivious to the presence of his landlord until one of the workers tapped him on the shoulder and directed his attention to the visitor/intruders. The engineer glanced over his shoulder and motioned Jack and Sam closer.

The almost paranoid caution he had exhibited outside earlier had now been replaced by a confident, authoritative air. "Gentlemen, I'm so glad you could come. We're still a little disorganized, but I think we're going to settle in just fine." He raised his arms in a waving gesture that indicated space. "More room here than I anticipated. Yes." He looked around like a lord surveying his estate. "This will do nicely."

"So, Mr. Shontz." Sam pulled out a fresh Corona, but, after seeing Shontz's eyes widen to saucer size, he held up his hand and let it remain unlit. "Will ya show us this secret weapon of yours."

Shontz looked to Jack. "Are you also still interested, Mr. MacGregor?"

Inwardly, Jack could hardly stand to wait a second longer. He wanted to rip the covering off the trailer himself, but instead of betraying that attitude, he took the subtlety cue from his boss. "Yeah, I wouldn't mind taking a look." Jack forced a yawn. "But I'll have to make it a quick one. I've got to get home. We're supposed to have gotten our new telephone today." He winked at Shontz. "I want to try it out."

A Mona Lisa smile flashed across Shontz's lips. "Well, I don't want to keep you gentlemen from anything important." He started to turn away.

Jack responded like lightning. "No!" He shoved his hands deep into his pockets to keep from grabbing the gaunt looking man and spinning him around. "Uh, as long as we're here…." He took a half step forward.

Shontz faced him again. "Yes?"

Jack deliberately brought his breathing and tone back to normal. "Well, as long as we're here, I *would* like to see what you're working on."

Shontz's smile grew and his eyes twinkled. "Then you shall." He gestured to several men standing around the trailer. "Let's get the tarp off now, shall we?"

The group fell to their work. Then, slowly, carefully, more like surgeons than mechanics, they began to slide the heavy canvas from off the mystery treasure until at last the far edge of the covering slipped past the mid-point and fell to the floor all at once.

Jack stood transfixed, almost unaware of anything else in the hangar. *Lord, she's beautiful!* Even with its wings detached and folded beside it, the single-seat, open-cockpit, bi-plane appeared to be exactly as anticipated. *One hot baby!* Bright orange laminated fabric skin, stretched tight as metal and gleaming like the dawn, drew Jack's attention to the most aerodynamically perfect airplane he had ever seen. The semi-enclosed liquid-cooled engine was a monster, taking up almost a full quarter of the craft's length. The cockpit was deep-set into the fuselage, low behind the firewall, keeping the pilot comfortably out of the slipstream's blast, which, at record speeds, would be considerable. The headrest stood high and transitioned into a sort of dorsal ridge that melded into the tail's vertical stabilizer.

Jack gave Sam a side-glance. "I think I'm in love."

Sam chewed the cold Havana until it bobbed like a band-leader's baton. Then he growled, "I seen her first."

♪

Carrie hovered close to the mouthpiece of the telephone like a moonstruck lover before a kiss. One hand pressed the earpiece against her hair while the other caressed the wall-mounted wooden box almost too tenderly. "Oh yes, I can hear you just fine, Bess. So what did the doctor say?" She looked up when she noticed Jack in the living room. Carrie winked and put her hand over the receiver. "It may be old," she said, patting the phone's polished cherry case, "but it's ours...finally." She pantomimed wiping her brow and mouthed "phew." "Yes, I can still hear you, Bess. He likes the dumplings. Go on. What? Wait a minute, Bess." Carrie shook her head at Jack as she half produced a silly smirk and crossed her eyes. "Mrs. Markham?" She raised her voice. "Mrs. Markham! Please, hold your call off for a few minutes. I can't hear Bess." Carrie turned back to Jack, guarding the receiver again. "Party-line." She made the face a second time. "Thank you, Mrs. Markham. I'll be off in an instant. Bess, are you still there? Oh, good. Tell me quick. Jack just came home. Yes." She nodded. "Yes." Another nod. "All right, then. Listen, I have your answer. Try a little more salt. Yes, in the broth." She listened. "Yes...yes, I will, but I have to go now. Do what I told you and they'll love it. I guarantee. Good-bye, Bess." Carrie sighed and said, "Yes, Mrs. Markham, it's definitely your turn now." Another pause. "Thank you. You, too."

"So I guess the phone works all right." Jack unslung his suspenders and let them dangle over his jodhpurs. "That's funny." He pulled his pocket watch from his pants and checked the time. "I thought Bell wasn't going to be here for another hour or so."

Carrie hung the earpiece respectfully back up on its cradle. "Yes. Well, the truck came to the inn this morning to make some repair or other, and I talked the man into coming here next, provided I drive home to show him the way." Carrie beamed as if she'd delivered some *coup de grás* in a chess match. "I was hoping for one of the newer free-standing metal ones like you have at your office or Henri at the inn. But this is all they had right now—old relics people down in Los Angeles have traded in. We're on the list for a new one, but it might be a while."

Jack glanced at the timepiece once more as if it held some relevant wisdom, then he snapped its cover shut and sighed. He knew, more or less, the argument about to take place but still could not avoid it without losing all self-respect. Jack shoved the watch back into his pocket, next to the loose change and walked slowly to the new electric wonder on the living-room wall. He ran his hand gently over the smooth dark box. "Cherry wood." His disappointment flavored his tone.

She said matter-of-factly, "Do you like the color?"

"No."

"No?" Her concern still seemed mild, at best.

"No, I would have rather had walnut. I told you, if we had to settle for an old wooden one, make it walnut." There it was. He *knew* she hadn't listened to him before.

"Oh." Carrie turned away from the phone and Jack to bounce down onto the nearby couch. She'd already changed into a fresh print dress, a far cry from the stained overalls she used to wear before Roberto and his cousins had taken over most of the ranch chores. "I could have sworn you said cherry." She stretched both arms and legs. "You want me to have it changed?"

Jack continued to face the phone. "I would have liked to have been in on the choosing."

Carrie stared at the cold July woodstove and recited her next words as if she had rehearsed them. "Yes, well, you weren't around and the opportunity presented itself." She glanced his direction. "It really doesn't matter, you know."

Jack turned around and leaned back against the wall. "Apparently not. You paid for it, right?"

"Right."

"So, you picked the box out."

"That's only fair, don't you think?"

Jack shook his head. "Sure, why not?" More audible sarcasm.

Carrie sat up. "Look, you're making too much out of this. It's just a telephone."

"That's right. Just a telephone."

She squirmed around on the couch to face him, sitting on one leg. "Is this about me making more money again, or is it the old *Who's-In-Charge-of-the-Finances* game." She sported her impatient frown now. "Because, if it's either, I really don't care to hear it."

"Yes, I know." Jack wanted to let it all go. It didn't seem that important. *It is only a telephone.* But, just the same, he knew he couldn't allow what had happened to pass without comment.

"I'm not ashamed Henri's given me a percentage of the dining-room's profits. I worked darn hard to earn it. Am I supposed to apologize for making more money than the airmail?"

"No."

"Is this about being head of the house?" She raised her hands in mock worship. "Very well. I hereby declare you grand-high-imperial head of the house in perpetuity." Carrie raised her eyebrows as she bobbed her head. "Is that satisfactory?"

The tightness in his throat and confusion as to why he felt so strongly about a walnut case prevented Jack from answering for a moment.

"If not," Carrie continued, "Simply tell me your wish, oh my master, and it will be granted thee." She bowed both head and outstretched arms.

Jack cleared the strange lump from his throat, suddenly realizing why it was there. "I just wish you'd have...." He studied the walls and ceiling.

"Called you?"

"No. I wish you'd have, at least, wanted to." He finally focused on her face. "Like you did when we were first married." He tightened from chest to stomach as he felt the last semblance of his relevance wash down the drain.

Chapter Thirty-Nine

"Bˮut before the blue horde could force Weber over the railing and into the canyon below, he laid hold of the lanyard that was connected to the detonator. Consequently, when he finally fell to his death two seconds later, the screaming savages, who had brought about the good captain's demise, had only a moment before the cosmic bomb went off and sent them, too, into the next world." Jack pushed the rocker backward in time with the rhythm he'd kept all through the story. "And that, gentlemen...." he said as he flashed a smile in anticipation of what was to come, "Is the end."

Then it came.

"No, Dad!" Eddie swung at the air like a prizefighter.

"Well, I'm sorry." Jack gently ruffled the nine-year-old's hair. "But that's the end of the story."

"Aw, come on, Dad." A twelve-year-old Kenny leaned comfortably against the overstuffed chair next to his brother. He was no longer wide-eyed, as in younger days, but he still reclined upon the floor without shame. "Read Eddie some more."

Jack furrowed his forehead. "Read *Eddie* some more, huh?"

Kenny nodded authoritatively. "Yeah, it helps make him get sleepy. You know, he forgets about the m-o-n-s-t ... o-r-s-s." Kenny gave his dad a clandestine wink, clothed with obvious pride at having (he thought) spelled out the word. Then a smile broke across his face.

"I see." Jack's left eye returned the signal.

Eddie rolled his eyes up, his mouth silently repeating the mantra of what his older brother had just encoded. Then, after much cerebral wrestling, the heretofore random letters formed a word...and Eddie exploded. "*I* can spell monsters!"

Kenny shook his head. "Well, how am I 'spose to know that? You can't spell anything else!"

Jack cleared his throat. "Actually, it's spelled e-r with one s."

But Eddie didn't hear. He remained occupied with the defense of his reputation. "I can too spell anything!

Kenny fired another volley. "That's not what Miss Elsbeth says." His wry smile broadened.

"I *can too* spell *anything*!" Taunted by the unfair reference to his new teacher, Eddie threw out his chest, punctuating the act with both thumbs aimed back at himself.

"Kenny," Jack warned.

Apparently, Kenny had also gone temporarily deaf. "Okay, you little wise-guy."

"Kenny!"

"Then spell *anything*,." Kenny said.

"Huh?" Eddie remained oblivious to the snare that had just tightened around him.

"I said, 'spell *anything*'. Come on. I'll even start it for you." He took on an air of mock instruction. "A-n-y...now you finish it."

At this point Eddie saw there was no way out of the trap. He rolled his eyes up again, in an apparent return to his skull depository of knowledge, but lowered them quickly and allowed them to dart side to side before they drooped down almost to his cheeks. There was, indeed, no escape for the victim. "Uh...a-n-y...."

On the verge of losing his fatherly straight face, Jack put his son out of his misery. "All right, you two. That's enough. And, by the way, there *is* no more story to read...unless you count the rejection slip."

Eddie remained in the land of mysteries. "What's a subjection slip?"

"RE-jection slip." Jack sighed and stretched with a mild groan. "It's the note the people who buy stories write to you when they don't like your story."

Kenny sat up a little straighter. "What'd they say, Dad?"

Now you've done it, Ace. You've sunk to a new low, seeking solace from your children. So much for mature professionalism. "Well," Jack said. "Let's see." He pulled the short letter from his pocket and unfolded it with a flare. "Dear Mr. MacGregor, Thank you for submitting your story, *Blue Horde of Kalot*. The plot and setting were most intriguing. However, your characters were, in all honesty, a little clichéd and one-dimensional. They lack the proper depth to make them interesting to the reader. Please feel free to submit other manuscripts in the future if you feel that your work has improved. Sincerely, blah-blah-blah-blah-blah." He looked up and raised his eyebrows. "And that's a rejection slip."

"They didn't like *this* story?" Kenny blinked in disbelief.

Jack shook his head. "Well, they didn't like the characters, anyway."

Kenny's brow furrowed. "They didn't like Commander Falkner?"

"No."

Eddie seemed almost dazed. "Didn't they like the blue king?"

"Nope, not him either."

Kenny waved off the notion. "They're crazy!"

"Now, That's a little on the rude side, don't you think?"

Kenny considered that for a moment. "Okay, then they're stupid!"

Jack stifled a smile. "Uh, I'd have to say 'stupid' qualifies as rude, too."

That stopped Kenny. He had run out of appropriate descriptions for the unappreciative story buyers.

"But," Jack said, "being honest, I do agree." He let his smile loose now. "They *are* crazy and stupid."

So the three shared a laugh and a few more *rude* comments at the publisher's expense. Then Jack sent his sons to bed with attitudes of avenged family honor still fresh upon their minds.

Later, when all noise from the boys' room had subsided, Jack pulled a fresh notebook from his flight bag and set to work on a new story. This act constituted a minor miracle. Unbeknownst to Kenny and Eddie, their father had been on the verge of putting all writing aside indefinitely— too much responsibility as the airmail's chief pilot, too many rejection slips, and the atmosphere of what used to be Carrie's appreciation of his writing skills and imagination had long since turned into a frozen vacuum, much like the dark lifeless *outer space* that existed between Earth and Jack's fictional planets.

By the time Carrie arrived home from work, Jack had almost completed the rough draft of *Falkner on Saturn's Moons.* It consisted of twenty pages of penciled longhand with multiple smudges, but lacked only two lines for completion. Or, at least, Jack felt fairly sure that was the case.

"I thought you'd sworn off writing after that last turn-down." Carrie dropped her canvas bag and purse by the couch and threw her unused sweater down on the arm of the easy chair.

"The boys talked me out of it." Jack closed the notebook and laid the pencil beside it with an air of accomplishment. "They decided the editors of *Future Voyage* magazine are all crazy and stupid to a man."

Carrie almost came close to displaying a pleasant expression. "You read to the boys again?"

"Yes"

511

Her look then changed from its end-of-the-day tightness to something softer. "That's nice."

"What?"

"Nothing." She seemed to muse on something for a moment. "You read them the whole story?"

He rose and stretched his arms. "Including the editor's letter."

She nodded recognition. "So that's where the *crazy and stupid* came from. You have strong allies in your sons, Jack. They'll probably despise that poor editor for the rest of their lives. The very idea, insulting their father's story." Carrie raised a sarcastic finger toward the ceiling.

"And rightfully so." Jack checked his watch. "Say, it's a little warm in here still. I'm going to take a short walk. Get some air."

"Are you going to be long?" Carrie rummaged in the canvas bag but pulled nothing out.

"Don't know." Jack crossed the living room as if to leave, but then casually loitered near the front hall doorway. "Never know when you're going to get jumped by a band of blood-thirsty editors."

Carrie turned her face away for an instant. Jack thought he saw the beginnings of a pre-smile expression, but he wasn't sure. He said, "Want to come along?"

"No, thank you." She continued to rummage. "I've got some things to see to yet."

"Right." *Of course you do. Keep busy, love of my life, or you might have to actually look at me.* "Be back in a while." Then he walked through the front door and out into the high-desert night.

The smell of chaparral and desert sage, still cooling from the heat of the mid-July day, engulfed him again, all at once, the way it always did when he had been indoors a little too long. Decomposed granite crunched beneath his boots, and the coolness of the dry mountain breeze eddied about his ears and played with the open front of his shirt.

Soon, he felt as if he could breathe again, like he had been under water and had just now breached the surface. This tight-chestedness had become a familiar feeling of late. He got it whenever Carrie would seem to draw close to him then back-paddle the way she did just now. *I wish she'd make up her mind about us. At least, as to whether she wants to call it quits or not, so we can get on with the divorce or a regular marriage—one or the other—and get this slow-torture game over with.* Jack felt anything would be better than the pretentious dance they had been doing for the last four years.

It appeared obvious she did not know what she wanted, first seeming to desire him as a husband, then changing her tact without warning and treating him like an unwanted roommate. If he ignored her, she eventually sweetened up a little, but, at the first sign of affection on his part, she would turn instantly into the ice-house queen. Jack disliked this game more than anything. It was tiresome and needless, and he felt pretty sure he'd almost had enough of it.

A burrowing owl swooped silently down over the driveway toward the road, banking from side to side in its search for a kangaroo rat or ground squirrel supper. Jack stopped walking and craned his head back to look straight up at the black backdrop of the sky, spattered with milky galaxies. He filled his lungs with cool, sweet-smelling air and allowed its dry serenity to loosen the knot that still lurked in his chest. *Lord, please. Pry her hands from the steering wheel and melt the coldness in her heart. Or, if not, break us apart clean. I know I haven't talked to you much, but I'm asking you to give me a hand anyway.* He lowered his gaze from the stars and began walking again, past the Stutz and the trucks, and out onto the road, where he promptly stumbled into a squirrel mound hidden by the windmill's shadow that cast itself broad and dark in the faint quarter-moonlight. It sometimes felt like he stumbled over a lot of burrowing animal mounds after dark. *Never knew how truly clumsy I was 'til I moved to the high desert.* He paused, cleared his throat and took a breath, even though he had no intention of speaking out loud. *Father, please help me. I know I think of leaving sometimes, but I love Carrie more than my life, and I don't want to go.* He found the center of the road where the holes were scarcer and less of a threat to his downhill shuffle. As he walked, his boots raised a little cloud of dust that gathered about his ankles.

A coyote yelped somewhere up the canyon, and Jack felt the familiar pang of loneliness he often experienced when at home with the woman he still loved. *Lord, I need something from you. I can't stand this much longer with nothing to go on!* Sometimes it went better, dealing with Carrie's swinging moods. Sometimes he could fix his mind on something, like work or writing, and halfway ignore what the woman was or was not doing to demonstrate her apathy toward him. But then would come the times, like right now, when he felt tortured. And when these spells came, he would think he could not endure her ambivalence much longer. More often than not, as things played out, Jack would decide Carrie did not love him at all anymore, and he would think a little too much on Alma.

"Mind if I tag along, or is this rut taken?"

Jack's nerves tingled just a little as Carrie materialized out of the darkness and fell into step beside him on the dirt road. He took an extra breath. "Guess I had my head more in the clouds than I thought. I didn't even hear you coming."

"You must have. I don't think there's anyway to sneak up on a body on this gravely ground." She exaggerated a march for a few steps. "Nothing but crunch, crunch, crunch all the way from the house."

"Wasn't expecting you."

"What were you thinking so hard on that the world went away?" Her voice sounded softer now than it had been in the house; her tone not so matter-of-fact. Instead she seemed like she actually wanted to hear her husband's answer.

"Oh, I don't know." He looked off toward a clump of deer-weed. "Just soaking up the sights, I guess." The light of the starving moon barely showed his hand as he gestured down the gentle slope of the plateau. Knee-high, dry foxtails shimmered in the breath of a warm Santana wind, once again evoking the poor-man's proxy image of a Kansas sea of wheat, complete with a gentle hiss, that sounded as if God had run his hand through the earth's hair. "Thought I'd come out and knock on the door to see if God's home." Jack smiled. "He is."

Carrie's voice came out even softer yet. "You haven't mentioned God in a long time."

"I know."

Silence reigned for several minutes as they strolled downhill. Rabbits darted across their path and one kangaroo rat finally *did* jumped from its hole to run in a confused circle until it regained its wits and dove back into its borough again. Then the two humans reached the turnoff for the Smith farm, and Jack heard Carrie's long sigh. It carried with it the tiniest hint of a moan as if a very small part of her was in pain.

"I haven't been very loving to you of late." She paused and took a very deep breath. "I'm sorry."

Jack waited for her to say more, but he heard only the *shush* of the night winds in his ear. Finally, after a very awkward gap, he resisted the temptation to say *It's about time* and offered, "That's all right; don't worry about it."

She took his hand, and again he waited for more words from her, but none came. Then he knew. This was all she was going to give right now...or maybe ever. And he would have to be satisfied with this gift, small as it was, with no explanations or elaboration. Carrie had gone as far as she intended to go.

Relief and disappointment all at the same time—Jack felt them crash headlong into each other on the path between his heart and mind. It all wrestled inside for a moment, threatening to bring back the tightening chest band and stomach knots again. Then, all in an instant, he tired of the whole thing and simply gave up. He decided it was useless to want something someone else was not willing to give. *What the heck. This is better than fighting.*

He pulled her close and placed a gentle kiss on her slightly parted lips. Surprise filled her face.

"You want to walk up to the spring?" he said. "You can see almost every light in town from there."

Jack felt Carrie's hand drop away. "No," she said. "I think what I want right now is a nice cool bath. It's been a long hot day." She patted him on the arm. "But you can go ahead if you want. I'll walk myself back."

That was the last thing she said before disappearing into the shadows of the upper road. Jack wanted her to say that she loved him or at least that the evening walk together had been nice, but that did not take place. He thought about calling out into the night and saying that *he* loved *her*. But then she might make the matter worse with some non-reciprocating answer or, even worse yet, no answer at all. Jack was not about to set himself up for that again. She had done that many times in the last five years. He was not going to give her that opportunity yet again.

Jack looked up at the stars. *Well Lord, I refer you back to my original prayer. I leave it all to you…because I have no idea what she's going to pull next.*

⚘

Back in the house, Carrie searched her canvas bag for the third time and finally found a folded note Ruth had left for her at the inn. *Carrie*, it said. *Today Bee told me she's almost ready to leave Sam on account of his drinking.* A small moan resonated from Carrie's throat. *I tried to tell her about what a help the Lord can be in bad times, but she would have none of it. I just don't know what to say next. Can you think of anything? Your old biddy neighbor, Ruth.*

Carrie sighed and gazed through the mud-hall windows at the lights of the Smith house over a half-mile away. "Oh, Ruth," she whispered to her absent friend. "How can I help Bee when my own fire's flickering so low."

Chapter Forty

Alma planted a quick kiss on the lips of a very off-guard Jack and had already started on her way to the kitchen before the man even realized what had happened.

She had given no warning, not a word or expression that would betray what she in mind. The woman had simply swooped in like a hawk as she passed by the table and made contact with her prey. Jack's eyelids shot up and bounced off his brows. The spoonful of sugar he held balanced between his thumb and first finger slid from its perch and plopped straight into his coffee as surprise engulfed him. Surprise...but not shock or regret. It had the singular honor of being the only kiss he had received in months—almost a year, in fact. And he could not deny that he had enjoyed it.

"That got you when you weren't lookin'," she said as her hips swung around a stray chair. "Didn't it, Sweetie?"

Not being able to think of anything appropriate to say, Jack remained silent. *Do nothing, Jack old boy. Don't let her get to you. Don't let her in. You're married!* He recaptured the runaway spoon and concentrated too much on the act of stirring. *She shouldn't have done that, almost empty café or no.* But try as he might, he could not work up a negative reaction to her boldness. It was what he had been wanting in the secret vault of his desires ever since the gutsy little waitress had followed him to the truck on a very memorable Thanksgiving. That had been almost four years ago. Since then, his supposed loving wife, Carrie, had grown more distant with each day. Alma, on the other hand, had circled ever closer as time passed. *It's not fair.*

She blew him another kiss, wrapped in a candy-apple smile. "Be back, Sweetie," she said, then passed into the kitchen between two half-length swinging doors.

518

"Well, *that* was a little more than howdy-do. You two are sure comin' along there." Sam practiced his standard lustful leer over the top of his cup and inclined his head toward the kitchen doors. "Yep. Comin' along indeed." He winked and went back to sipping what smelled to Jack like more gin than coffee.

"Nothing of the kind." Jack's insides twinged, not all from embarrassment. He flipped through the pages of a two-month-old magazine someone had left on the table. "Says here they had a big ceremony in both New York and Paris to celebrate the first anniversary of Lindberg's Atlantic crossing. Lindy says he expects regular trans-Atlantic flights to begin before the end of 1928. This article was back in May. Huh. Regular flights before the end of this year. I don't know. Hardly seems like a year's gone by since he made that Atlantic hop. Now he's saying regular flights." Jack tried a sip of super-sweet coffee. *How does Alma always know when to take another step toward me? How does she know when Carrie's backed away again? Is there a sign on my forehead that says 'Lonely and confused?'* Jack shook his head. "Alma's just used to acting wacky, that's all," he said out loud. "I'll have a talk with her."

"Yes, that's right. You have a talk with her." Sam took another sip from *his* cup and snickered into his coffee-gin.

Seeing that neither explanation nor verbal tap-dancing would get him anywhere this morning, Jack gave the new-subject-wheel a spin. "So, what was the very important thing you had to discuss with me?"

Sam lifted his face from behind the cup as if from a dream. "Ah yes, that's right, the very important thing." Another sip. "That very important thing is…adapting for the future."

"The future."

"Yes."

"What's important about the future?"

Sam raised his finger and his eyebrows at the same time. "Only this. If we don't adapt we're not going to have one."

Jack sat up straighter. "You're talking about the mail revenues going down." *Back at our old house near the coast, Carrie used to surprise me kind of like Alma with a wet-kiss ambush at the door when I got home.*

"That's right. I am most definitely talking about the mail revenues." Sam toasted his chief pilot with his cup and rewarded himself from its contents.

Jack nodded. They had nibbled around the edges of this subject before but never really chewed on the whole thing, even though both men knew the problem well. Ever since Sam had been awarded the Sweet Springs airmail franchise from the government, each new contract saw the Post Office Department pay the independent airmail carriers a little less per pound for mail delivered. So far, they had always managed to make up the difference by simply carrying more mail.

Jack tapped a contemplative finger against the side of his cheek. "We can't just add a plane and bid on another contract this time. It wouldn't bring in enough money to make the trip worthwhile." *Back in those days, Carrie'd smooch me two or three times before I could even set all my gear down.*

"Well, you're half right." Sam drained his morning cup, but did not refill it. This discussion involved business, and he usually stopped drinking at least long enough to finish the conversation whenever business took center stage. He slid a treasured Havana Corona from his shirt, bit off one end and lit the other. "It won't help to bid another contract, but adding a plane just might be the answer." He tipped up his chin and emitted a smoky gray cloud above the table. "All the smart carriers are buying ships that can carry both mail and passengers. Double cargo." He pulled three ample puffs from the powerful cigar. "That's the ticket, Jack, my lad. Double cargo, double cash."

"Passengers, huh? You know the boys aren't going to care much for putting up with cargo that throws up and talks back." Jack finally remembered to take another sip of his own coffee – that actually *was* coffee. It had cooled down to almost lukewarm now, but he indulged a second swallow just the same. *When was all that smooching with Carrie? Must've been twelve...no, fourteen years ago. Before the war, when I was auto-racing on the dirt tracks.*

"Oh, I don't know that passengers would be that much of a bother." Sam took his thumb and forefinger and picked a drowned gnat from just inside the rim of his cup, then flicked it onto the floor. "*I'm* either talking back or throwing up a good part of the time, and the boys don't seem to mind *me* much."

Good grief! Have we really been married fourteen years? Jack emitted a grimacing snicker. "So, what are we going to do about revenue?"

Sam leaned back against the booth's windowsill. "We're gonna buy a different kind of plane, one that'll carry mail and passengers both...in style—one with a closed cabin."

Jack stiffened. "Oh, no. I hate those things!"

"You ever flown one?"

"Yes, as a matter of fact. A guy brought a single engine Fokker to one of the county fairs when I was working for a flying circus; thought he'd save on gas giving five dollar rides four at a time. But the customers didn't like it, and you know why?"

Sam didn't respond, so Jack went on. "They said they couldn't feel the ride, the sensation of flight." Jack waved a dismissing hand. "He took me up and even let me have the controls for a while. Those folks were right. Even with the windows open, it felt like driving a tin lizzy around the sky. No wind on your cheeks, no visibility—like looking through holes cut in a box." He took another sip of his now almost-cold coffee and made a sour face. "Didn't seem like flying at all."

Sam shook his head. "You done?"

"More or less."

"All right, here it is." He nodded for emphasis. "Passengers who are traveling to a specific place on the map aren't joy riders. They're gonna be in the air for a lot longer than fifteen minutes, so they want to be comfortable. They don't want the gosh darn wind in their face, making them wear helmets and goggles so their hair don't blow off and their eyeballs don't dry up." He puffed his dying cigar back into glowing existence. "Get it? They want to be front-parlor, comfy-cozy. That's the way to survive the revenue reductions, and that's the way we're gonna make a by-gosh profit." He leaned forward to punctuate his words with the Havana. "And as far as you needing the open-cockpit feel of the aircraft...well, you can just get used to flying another way. You're chief pilot. You shouldn't let little changes scare ya like this."

Jack's cup slammed down on the table hard enough to spill half its remaining contents. "I'm not afraid of any airplane, and who do you think you are—"

"Hold your horses, Jack." Sam raised opened-palmed hands. "I'm not saying you're a coward. I just mean, don't let new things throw you. Like closed cabins. Ya gotta stay up with the times. Closed cabins are the future. And we're gonna be part of the future. Heck, the big regular airlines with their tri-motor Fords have been making this kind of money for two or three years now. So why shouldn't *we* get in on a little of that cash?"

Jack let the tension in his neck dissipate. "You already have a plane in mind, don't you?"

Sam smiled. "Not only in mind but picked out." He leaned forward in an almost clandestine manner. "It's the Ryan B-3 Brogham."

Jack's eyes widened. Of all the closed cockpit planes there were to hate, Sam had just named the only one that had ever captured Jack's imagination. "The type Lindberg flew." He muttered the phrase like a holy mantra.

"Actually, it's the next model after The Spirit of St. Luis. It's got a bigger cabin so it can seat six, including the pilot...or five and a mail sack." Sam's smile widened. "Some of the sales boys at Ryan still like to call her the *Paris Express* though." He puffed up another small cloud from the Corona. "What ya think, Jack? They're selling them with the Wright J-5 engine. It's just what we need. So, why don't we get ourselves one?"

Then something clicked in the back of Jack's consciousness, raising a question. "Sam, why are you hard-selling me like this? You own the company. If you think we need this plane so badly, why don't you just buy it?"

"Because they want 9,700 dollars for 'em." Sam's smile took on a slightly sheepish caste. "I only have half the money."

"So...."

"I was in hopes you could come in with the other half."

"You're offering me a partnership?" Jack held his breath.

"I am."

And there it was. The thing Jack wanted to hear most in the world and, at the same time, the thing he most feared—partnership, ownership, to be in business again. It was one thing to be flying once more, even to be Sam's chief pilot. But to be a partner—that resurrected all the old questions. Could Jack shoulder the responsibilities of a business? Could he be successful at handling affairs in that very competitive realm? He had been wrestling with these demons from his past for a long time now, and had yet to come up with an answer that satisfied. He gave himself another two seconds of internal debate before answering.

"I'd have to find outside investors to back me. I haven't any money of my own."

"What about your in-laws? I hear they're loaded."

Jack felt his neck muscles tighten again. "I wouldn't take money from them with a gun to my head."

"They look at you like the hired help, do they?"

"Something like that." Jack gazed down at his long-dead coffee.

"Well, how about your wife? She seems to be doing well." Sam looked up hopefully, then noticed something in Jack's expression that changed his mind. "Ah, that also appears to be a dog that won't hunt."

Jack sighed. "I have another source, *my* family" He massaged the back of his neck. "They might invest if I can present the idea to them in just the right way."

Sam almost smiled. "Your family has money?"

"More than enough for a Ryan." Jack contemplated the table for a while, turning his desires and fears over in his mind once more. If he failed in another business venture, he did not know if he could face anyone in the family again, especially Carrie. But if he could somehow make a go of things this time, he would regain all the respect he had lost in the last few years. "All right, Sam. I'll do it. I'll fly down today and see what I can put together." Jack drank the last of his coffee and set the cup down.

"'Done!" Sam grabbed Jack's hand and pumped it. "Good decision. With a new Ryan in our stable, we'll be graduating from mail carriers to airline before you know it." Sam stretched a getting-up-soon stretch. "Say, why don't you give your family a call before you take off. You know, long distance on the company phone. Nothing's too good for my partner." He winked.

"That's a good idea. Make sure they're going to be home."

"How about Carrie? You want me to let her know where you went?"

Jack's mood darkened again as the specter of the ongoing power struggle between him and Carrie raised itself again.

"No," he said with more apparent confidence than he felt. "I'll let her in on it myself...when I get back."

Floyd and Hannah kept stride with their grandson as he made his way to the pasture where the sun-faded De Havilland mail-plane swayed on its rubber claws in the onshore breeze.

"I think you're right on the money, Son." Floyd ran combing fingertips through his walrus-brush mustache. "If you're gonna make any money at all, you've gotta look to carrying more than just the mail. That's why the stage lines and railroads made a go of it years ago, and the Pony Express didn't." He straightened his crushed fedora and slapped Jack on the shoulder. "Sounds like you've thought things through."

"Thanks, Grandpa." Jack stopped when he reached the plane's tail, bent down, and began to unravel the knotted rope that secured the tailskid to a large, gnarled scrub-oak limb. He fooled with the exaggerated Granny knot much longer than the chore required. The termites of partial defeat still gnawed at his gut, and he needed a couple seconds to formulate some semi-dignified way to express himself. "I don't know if my father agrees with you, though." Jack pulled the loosened tie-down rope free of its fetters and coiled it automatically around his forearm between his elbow and hand. "He just sat in that chair like some giant stuffed bullfrog."

"Jackie." Hannah gave her head a slight, slow-motion shake. "He's your father."

Jack twisted the hemp line into a half-bow and tossed it into the De Haviland's mail compartment. Then he snapped the sheet metal lid shut and backed away four paces. He stood there in silence for several seconds leaning this way and that, inspecting the craft for nothing in particular. Then he took in and exhaled a cleansing breath before he spoke. "The only comment he had the whole time was, 'Why should I trust my money to you?' That's all. No questions about cost or profit potential. No, not him. Just why should he trust me?" He felt the termites bite again as he glanced back at his grandmother's face. "Nothing's changed between him and me."

Hannah patted her grandson's arm. "I don't believe that, Jackie. He came out to see you, and he listened. Didn't he?"

"My guess is that Grandpa put some pressure on him to show up."

A hand-in-the-cookie-jar look passed across Floyd's face for an instant before he stiffened his jaw and sniffed. Then he announced, "All I said was that he'd be a danged starched-collared idiot if he didn't give his only son a fair hearing. Then I told him how darn stupid he'd look if he refused to come here and you struck pay dirt later on." He nodded affirmation to his own statement. "That's all I said to him. No pressure about it."

Jack resisted the temptation to roll his eyes. "Like I said, he wouldn't have come otherwise."

"He came because he loves you." Hannah rubbed the arm she had just patted in a way that, for a moment, reminded Jack of how she had done the same thing once when he was eight years old. He had fallen off a jittery gelding during a wind squall, and his grandmother had comforted him in just this way after she had helped him back into the saddle. Jack let the memory remain in the forefront of his mind for half an eye-blink.

Hannah walked around in front of her two men and faced them. "Besides, I have a feeling your father's going to invest in your airmail business, despite what you think right now." She leaned to one side, peering around Jack and Floyd who were still facing the plane. She smiled.

"Oh, I don't know about that, old woman." Floyd canted his head and squinted at his wife through one eye. "George's *no* seemed pretty final to me. I don't think he sees the profit in flyin' mail and passengers. Probably sees it all as some kind of flash-in-the-pan that's gonna be gone and forgotten in a few years."

Hannah stood on her tiptoes for an instant and glanced over Floyd's shoulder. "You may be right about his doubts, but I think he's going to invest in Jack just the same."

"I don't think so, Grandma." Jack appreciated Hannah's encouragement, but he'd seen the contempt in his father's face. *No* is what the man had said, and *no* is what he had meant. "What reason would he have for changing his mind?"

Hannah grinned a mischievous elf's grin. "I can't say as to the reason, but it seems to be enough to get your father raising dust to catch you." She pointed behind the men.

Jack glanced over his shoulder and saw his father's black Packard bouncing over the meadow. "What the—"

Jack and Floyd whirled about. Hannah's grin grew. The Packard plowed through wild flowers and meadow grass like an angry bull, kicking up dust from gopher mounds with its new whitewall Firestones.

"What's that boy in such a darn hurry for?" Floyd tilted back his fedora.

"He wants to catch Jackie before he takes off." Hannah gave Jack's back a brief rub.

"Why?" Jack winced as his father's dark sedan vaulted skyward almost a foot after hitting a grassy ditch. It bounced twice more off the damp meadow earth then swerved into a straight course again.

Floyd groaned and murmured, "Easy on them springs, Son."

The Packard rolled to a civilized stop two car-lengths from the De Havilland's wing tip. Sunlight played through the windshield upon the linen-covered bulk of George MacGregor as he leaned across the front seat to the open window on the passenger side. "Ma...I mean...Mother?" He beckoned to Hannah. "A moment, please."

Hannah stepped over to the Packard where her son engaged her in a brief conversation. At one point she reached in and tousled the hair of the well-to-do Marner Bay attorney, which provoked him to pull back a little. Then he shook his head, handed his mother something, and drove away. He waved out the window as he bounced along at a safer speed toward the barnyard. Hannah waved in return. Then she turned around and fairly danced back to Jack and Floyd.

"Here it is, Jackie." Her face shined like an apple in candlelight. "I told you." She gave him a check signed by George. "I told you he'd do it."

Joy and confusion swirled inside Jack as a flush to match a tomato rose from his neck to his forehead. "But why. I don't get it. He was a brick wall just a few minutes ago. What changed?"

Floyd eyed his wife. "So just what did *you* say to George before we left the house, old woman?"

Hannah put an arm around each man's neck as George's Packard disappeared around the house. "I reminded him of the faith *his* father placed in him when he wanted to go to college and even later when he wanted to go on to Harvard Law School."

"What faith are you talkin' about? I was never in favor of that fancy eastern dandy factory."

"But you paid for it. Didn't you?" She took her hand off his neck and poked him in the ribs. "Do you remember what you said when we decided to send him off to his dream?"

Floyd looked off toward the rolling meadow to the southeast where some white-faced cattle milled about in the yellow summer grass. "No. I don't recall."

She poked him again much harder. "Yes you do, you leathery old liar. You said that maybe the Lord had a special purpose for George to have kept his nose in a book all through his childhood."

A faint hint of a stillborn smile struggled at one corner of Floyd's mustache, but he kept his gaze fixed firmly on the cattle. "Like I said, I don't recall."

Hannah turned to Jack and nodded. "That's exactly what he said. Believe me. He still couldn't understand, though, why his son never wanted to help out with the ranch that we'd built for *his* future."

Floyd snorted, then said, "Cattle or chickens. Didn't matter. He wanted nothin' to do with any of it. Always made that pitiful face like someone'd stuck a hot poker in his ear."

"But Floyd sent him off to the most expensive university in the country and paid the bills with nary a peep for seven years." This time she elbowed the old rancher. "That's what I reminded your father of, Jackie. A father having faith in his son even if he doesn't understand what that son's doing." She hugged Jack, and he could feel the warmth between his stomach and his chest rise up to engulf the lump forming in his throat. "You go buy your plane, Jackie," she said. "And prove to all the doubters they're wrong."

Jack smiled and hugged Hannah back. He knew himself to be blessed to have a family that loved him so much. And his grandmother was one in a million—true enough. *Just wish she'd left out that part about proving myself.* A quick cold chill shot down Jack's nervous system and grabbed at his stomach. But he shook it off by concentrating on a mental picture of the new Ryan monoplane. That's when he found he could share a little of Hannah's optimism.

Chapter Forty-One

"Henri, if you want me to continue preparing masterpiece meals, you'll simply *have* to leave me alone to do it!"

Carrie slid a cast-iron roasting pan into the dark maw of the wood-burning oven and closed the screeching door with a double-quilted hot pad. She turned to face the penguin-clad Cajun and tossed the warm pad onto the preparation table. "Why don't you tell them I'll see them some other time. If they're truly friends of mine, they'll understand."

Henri pulled a sample bon-bon from a desert tray and chewed it until he smiled. "Well, I would not say they are exactly friends."

"I see. Well, in that case, tell them whatever you like." She watched him devour a sampler éclair next. "Well?" She folded her arms. "How is it?"

Henri smirked. "How do you think it is?" He swallowed and blinked at the same time. "It is perfect, as always." He held his peace until he had finished the creamy pastry, then smiled again, with a nod this time. "I really think you should, at least, go and have a coffee with these people."

"Oh, Henri!" She raised her hands, turned her face to the ceiling, and growled her frustration. Then she leveled her gaze back upon the man. "I'm busy!"

Henri's tone and expression remained even. "Carrie, you've trained these girls so well." He indicated Sue Linn and Ezzie with a sweeping hand. "I have no doubt they can keep the kitchen from exploding for a few precious minutes. No?" One eyebrow crept toward his hairline.

Carrie stood, arms still folded, for several seconds, weighing the comment. *What do we have cooking now?* She glanced at the stoves as if she could see through the thick black iron. *Pudding and custard in pots on top...and that last roast for tomorrow morning's hash. That one will take a good while yet. And that's it.* "All right." Her arms dropped. "I'll talk to them." She undid her apron and doffed her scarf-turban, leaving them both on the preparation table.

"*C'est bon.* This way, Madam Chef." He bowed slightly at the waist then proceeded to push her down the access hall with a subtle but eager pressure against the small of her back. "Time is wasting, as they say."

"Stop pushing. I'll get there in my *own* time."

Henri increased the imposed pace. "Uh, there is no *time* for you to take your time. I assure you, you will thank me in a moment."

"Henri, if you don't stop pushing—" Then all at once, they stumbled out into the dining room, and Carrie froze. At a table not five feet from her sat her brother, Roger, dressed in a white silk shirt and a suit of summer linen. Carrie took in a quick breath. "What...how?"

He toasted her with a demitasse. "Greetings form Civilization, Sister Mine." He took a ceremonial sip and placed the tiny cup on the table. "I come bearing gifts."

Carrie laughed through the fingers that had risen to cover her mouth. "Oh, no." She laughed some more before half composing herself and assuming a mock-serious demeanor. "And what gifts might these be, brave pilgrim?"

Roger stood and spread his arms with a grace befitting the Globe theater. "Why, myself, of course. The company of one Roger, the Wanderer. Ample gift for any woman...even a long lost sister."

He continued to hold his arms aloft while his Shakespearian expression turned to a sincere-looking smile. Carrie ran to him and embraced her sibling with more affection than she had felt for him in years...or perhaps ever.

"My gosh!" she said into his linen shoulder. "I never expected to see you here! Never!" A hot tear crept down

Carrie's cheek, making her suddenly conscious of her emotional leakage and the fact that she was probably squeezing Roger tight enough to crack a rib...or, at least, wrinkle his suit. She released him as far as arm's length. "Oh, my. It's been...."

"Five years." Roger held her shoulders in kind. "Or thereabouts." His fingers played with the wash-thinned cotton of Carrie's print dress. "And not a moment too soon." He backed away in pseudo-horror, spreading open hands toward the dress. "*Who* is the tailor who designed this stunning gown?"

Carrie sighed. It was Roger, all right. No imposter here. "Woolworth of Palmdale." She added a spoonful of the old Marner Bay sarcasm to her own response. "Their summer kitchen line."

"I'll leave you two alone now." Henri, whom Carrie had almost forgotten, left in the direction of the kitchen.

"Let's be seated, shall we?" Roger pulled out the chair next to his at the table.

Carrie seated herself with long practiced grace. "Thank you, sir."

Roger and his grin sat down and leaned forward on his elbows. "We'll have to talk fast, Old Girl. The train only makes a thirty minute stop, and I fear we've used up too much of that already." He took a hurried sip from his cup.

Carrie added more theatrical sternness to her expression. "Then we must jabber away as fast as we can." *This is wonderful. No criticism of Jack or my job, only silly small talk. Like when we were children.* But there was something else nibbling at the farthest back corner of her mind. *What is it? Oh, who cares? Roger's here!* She felt a tingle just above her stomach.

Roger winked as he nodded. "Right-y-oh. What shall we jabber about, then? Would you like to hear about what's going on in the outside world?" He took another sip and glanced at his wristwatch. "I have a two minute *everything-*

you've-been-missing presentation, tailor-made for sleepy town stopovers."

"Yes. Everything." Carrie took hold of her brother's non-coffee hand. *Separated for five years!* She took a deep breath. "Tell me…everything."

"Well, let me see." He rolled his eyes for a moment. "Everything. Yes." He pantomimed a deep breath. "Some of the more fashionable ladies are wearing a sort of cloched hat called a peek-a-boo that has a brim so low it partly covers the eyes. Last winter men began wearing turtleneck sweaters like Gloucester fishermen. College boys wear huge raccoon coats to football games. From a distance they look a great deal like bears wearing porkpie hats while playing ukuleles."

Carrie stifled a laugh, but it escaped out her nose as a very unladylike snort. Out of instinct, she covered the offending nostril with tardy but dainty fingers.

"Almost every male worth knowing carries gin in a hip flask…or in the back pocket." Roger patted the back of his chair. "Women have them, too."

"Women have hip flasks? Where do they hide them?"

"Oh, they have sort of a half-garter half-holster affair. You know." He pointed under the table. "Underneath everything." He winked.

"I see." Another smile tugged at Carrie's face. She decided not to give in to it. After all, hiding bootlegged gin in one's underwear seemed a little pathetic, somehow. *But Roger can have fun talking about almost anything.* She remembered him at sixteen reciting lyrics from Gilbert and Sullivan's *Pirates of Penzance* at parties using names and subjects from the daily news. He was so much fun to be around in those days. She struggled with the urge to laugh again. *He's still fun.*

Roger swallowed more coffee and dabbed at his small mouth with a napkin. "To continue. A language lesson." He held up an instructive finger. "When one agrees with a statement one hears, one should answer with either the statement, 'And how,' or 'I should *tell you*,' depending on which best fits the circumstances. Upon witnessing a particularly well executed musical or dance performance, one should exclaim at the top of one's lungs, 'Get hot,' and, if one hears or sees something one does not like or does not agree with, the proper response would be either, 'Go fly a kite,' or 'Go cook a radish'. No, wait. Is that right?" He looked to the ceiling and muttered, "Go fly a kite and go cook a radish. Or was it cook the kite and fly the radish?" He took a moment to continue the muttering at a whisper. Then the finger shot up once more. "Yes, I'm sure that's it. Fly a kite and cook a radish." He shrugged. "Or something to that effect."

Carrie sighed and looked down at the table. *I miss this kind of nonsense. My life is so serious now. I can't remember the last time I did something simply to be silly. And I can't remember the last time I saw Jack even smile.* "Fly a kite. Cook a radish. Got it."

"Good. Has it been two minutes yet?"

Carrie shook her head on cue, having no true idea as to the elapsed time.

"Drat. Well then, what else is there? Ah! I know. Everyone says they're *disenchanted*. Something to do with the late war or prohibition or the League of Nations. I'm not sure. Back on the subject of attire and language, a few of the more sophisticated young men wear very loose-fitting trousers known as Oxford Bags, usually with saddle shoes. Uh, exciting women are known as fast or hot numbers, and… about songs. I don't propose to sing them but I can tell you their names."

Carrie wrinkled her brow. "You know we do have a few radios in town now. The barbershop has one. And the local speakeasy…or so I'm told. And there are a lot of phonographs about."

Roger pursed his lips. "My, my. You're in the midst of a veritable Sweet Springs cultural boom, aren't you?" He clapped his hands and rubbed them together. "Good. Then we'll play a game. I'll tell you the name of one popular song—and I mean popular in the city, not Chicken Track Acres—and you fire another title back to me. The one to run out of songs first loses and owes the victor dinner at the restaurant of his choice."

"Or her choice."

"Or her choice. Of course."

"Agreed." She shook his hand with an exaggerated final pump.

Roger nodded. *"Where'd You Get Those Eyes?"*

Carrie toyed with a napkin for a second. She'd heard some newer songs in the background over the last five years, but she'd been so busy between the ranch and the inn, she didn't know if she could remember their names. "Uh, give me a second."

"Time's a wastin'."

"You're not helping."

"Come on, you said you knew these."

"All right...*If You Knew Susie.*"

"If you knew Susie what?"

"Isn't that the title?" Carrie swept out the corners of her memory.

"No. It's half a title."

"If You Knew Susie Like I Know Susie."

"Okay. I'll let you have that one because you've been deprived. Now take this. *There's yes yes in your eyes.*"

Carrie gnawed on her lower lip. *"Runnin' Wild.* And that's also a movie, so, by all rights, I should get double credit."

"No, we're just doing songs today. *Will Ya, Huh?"*

Why don't Ruth and I ever have fun like this? All she wants to do is work and ride in the Stutz. "The Sheik of

536

Araby." The uncomfortable itch in the back of Carrie's mind started again.

"*Yes, Sir! That's My Baby.*"

I used to know lots of interesting people. "*Barney Google.*" A mild heaviness crept across her chest, almost unnoticeable but there, just the same.

"*Baby Face.*" Roger looked around the dining room and smiled with what looked like satisfaction.

The heaviness in her chest moved to her stomach and sat there like hunger. But a hunger that food wouldn't help. Carrie knew that. She was starving. Yes. But not like when one hasn't eaten. *Life shouldn't be all work and serious talk. I miss not having to think about everything I do. Does that make me evil?* "*Betty Co-Ed.*"

"I'm out." Roger held up his hands. "Do you want extra credit?"

"Of course. What's victory without my foot upon my opponent's neck?" She allowed an impoverished smile for an instant.

"Done. Who sings *Betty Co-Ed*?"

A little more life coursed through the smile. She knew this one, too. "Rudy Vallee."

"And he performs on the radio every week with his orchestra, the Connecticut Yankees," said a voice from behind.

The long unheard but still familiar male baritone whirled Carrie around with a start.

"Arthur!" The sight of her long-ago-rejected college beau sent a massive jolt of nervous electricity up Carrie's spine. "Arthur!" *You've already said his name, Smarty-pants; say something else now!* She stood, facing him, staring for what seemed like much too long. Finally, after wrestling her breathing back down to normal, she spoke again—with a softer tone. "Arthur."

"Now, that's three 'Arthurs' in a row." He stood a muscular six-six, black-haired and tan with the chiseled face of a Greek statue. "I don't think you're allowed another 'Arthur' by law." His white cotton shirt, unbuttoned at the top, suspended itself from his shoulder muscles like a banner hung from a castle wall. The same baggy linen pants described by Roger seemed to grab Arthur tight about the waist just to demonstrate the sleekness of his mid-section. His broad smile appeared exactly as Carrie remembered it, like the modern rendering of a Roman god.

Roger cleared his throat. "Like I said." He pointed to Arthur's feet, peeking out from under the billowing Oxford bags. "Usually worn with saddle shoes." He leaned over a bit and peered at Arthur's footwear. "And of superior quality, I must say. I hadn't noticed before. Where the devil did you get those, old sport?"

Arthur diverted his attention for a moment to Roger. "At a little bootery called Smedely and Sons in Sussex. I'll give you their card." Then back to Carrie. "My apologies. My intent was not to startle you, but I simply couldn't resist the opportunity for a dramatic entrance. I fear the temptation of the Rudy Vallee straight line proved too much for my will-power." He grinned a grin that, in times past, had often induced Carrie to fantasize about this man being Zeus or Apollo, traveling in modern disguise. "How have you been?" he said.

What should I say? How did you get here? That's silly. He obviously came on the train with Roger. It's been a long time? Very true...since 1911, our freshman year of college, when I broke it off with him in favor of Jack! What I should ask is why *he's here. Thanks Roger. This is just peachy!* She shook her head. "It's good to see you again. I was simply taken a little aback." She whipped her head back to Roger like a cornered animal but kept her voice even. "Why didn't you tell me?"

"And ruin the surprise?" Her brother stood up with a smooth grace as if nothing unusual had happened. "Far be it from me." He leaned down and took an unconcerned sip of coffee.

"Actually, there was no surprise intended." Arthur maintained his relaxed smile and slid his hands into his baggy pockets as if he hadn't a care. "I had a long distance call to make, and it took some time to negotiate with the local operator." He raised his eyebrows and smiled wider.

"That was Thelma. The switch-board's in her house just up the road." Carrie tried to act nonchalant as her mind split, half of it focused upon the Arthur in front of her, the other half seeing only the college boy of the same name who had asked for her hand in marriage so long ago. *How did he ask me?* She couldn't remember. But she knew it had been elegant and had made her feel like a *femme fatale* until well into the next day. He'd known all the right words. *Which is probably why he became class president.*

Arthur kept his hands holstered in his pockets and glided a little closer to the table. "Thelma...ah. Well, for a while, I wasn't sure my call was going to go through at all. There was something that sounded almost like music in the background—some sort of banging noise. Made it extremely difficult to hear the woman. Very frustrating."

"Thelma's sister, Wilamina, gives piano lessons as of last month." Carrie chanced a meager smile but held her excitement close. *Lord, he looks even better than the last time I saw him.* "The piano's an ancient upright somebody recently rescued from some old miners' saloon that partly burned down before the war. I admit it does sound more like someone hitting pottery with a hammer than music of any kind." *I wonder what I look like to him.*

"Well, well." Roger settled back down into his chair again. "This appears to be not so unpleasant a surprise, after all." He crossed his arms over his chest and locked his ankles, one over the other, then deposited the latter out into the aisle between the tables. "If I didn't know better, I'd say old Roger—that's me—had done a good deed." He glanced at his watch. "But, as I've said, we're only here on a water stop, and, as my sister has said, we'd best jabber fast as we can." He allowed his face a smirk that could only have been reproduced by a monkey that had just eaten his fill of bananas.

"How much time, Roger?" Arthur pulled out a chair but remained standing.

Carrie also remained on her feet, drinking Arthur in like lemonade on a hot day. *My goodness, he's gorgeous. I'd forgotten how gorgeous he was. More mature now. Time's kneaded the boy away and left a man that's even better. Why is he just standing there, staring at me? Maybe he's shocked at how old and worn I've grown. He probably thinks I'm a hag. Why are you staring, Author? Waiting for me to die of old age before your very eyes?* Then the realization soaked its way through. *Calm yourself, you ninny! You're the only one staring! He's simply waiting for you to sit down. He's being a gentleman. You remember gentlemen, don't you?* She felt her entire body flush with a tide of embarrassment. *Don't let him notice!* She managed an impoverished laugh. "Oh, you're waiting for *me*." She shrank into her chair and put a hand on her brow. "It's been a long hard week. Lots of meals. I'm liable to do or say most anything, you know." *Can you be anymore the schoolgirl? Why don't you just shuffle your feet and say 'golly'?*

Arthur nodded as he seated himself without scraping the chair. "Yes, I've heard about your culinary success." He held out praiseful hands. "You're a chef." He shook his head and broadened his grin to an unbelievable width. "I'm amazed, Caroline. What will you think of next?" He lowered his hands and leaned forward. "I remember you used to enjoy playing in the kitchen with Rodrigo." He glanced down at the table. "I remember it made me laugh— always thought it was more than a little silly." He looked up and locked his gaze into hers. "But here you are, the talk of food columns from coast to coast. I'd say that's a joke on me, eh?" He nodded again.

"Yes." Carrie's laugh reached new depths of pathos as she allowed her hands to rest on the table…a little too close to his. "Quite a joke." She felt the electrical current increase as it traveled up and down the course of her nerves. He was still looking into her eyes. *I wish he'd look at something else. Roger, why don't you say something. Make one of those sarcastic comments you're so good at and break this spell.*

"Roger," the Roman god in Oxford bags said to Carrie's brother without looking at him. "How much time is left?"

The double blast of a steam whistle from the passenger platform at the end of the street answered that question. Roger waited until the locomotive of the number three to San Francisco had finished having its say, then he added, "There's not even enough time to ask how much time we have." He rose all at once, depositing a wad of twice-folded dollar bills onto the tablecloth. "I think I'll just run along and stand in front of the train to hold it for you." He leaned down and placed a light kiss on his sister's cheek. "*Adieu.* Until the morrow, sweet Caroline."

Carrie looked up at Roger's sincere expression and, for the first time in over a decade, regretted his going. "Sooner than five years, I hope."

"As do I." He winked then looked to Arthur. "Do be quick. I don't know if I have enough cash to bribe an entire train crew."

"I will." Arthur kept his gaze fixed on Carrie's face.

"Right you are," Roger said and exited the dining room through the lobby.

"I suppose I'll have to go with him." Arthur inclined his head in the general direction of the train station. "Unfortunately, it's *my* train, too."

541

Carrie's voice escaped as a low moan. "No." *Why did I say that?* She slipped timid fingers over his hand, then pulled them back as if from a hot stove. *Why did I do that?* She had no answer. She only knew she didn't want him to go. "I mean, I *know*. You don't want to miss it. The next one doesn't come until morning."

Arthur traded his grin for a more serious expression. He stood, moved his chair back, and took a step away from the table in one fluid almost ethereal movement. Carrie ascended with him as if by command.

He said, "I want you to know I remember everything." He took her hands in his, and this time she did not pull away. "Everything we did, everything we said. I've not forgotten a minute of it." He paused. "And I think of you most of the time. I don't want to cause you trouble, but if you ever feel you wish to talk for any reason whatsoever, call me." He pressed a card into her hand then cupped *his* hands around both. "I'm at your service."

Carrie tried to speak as she tucked the card into her top pocket, but her throat proved too tight, or too dry—she didn't know which. Finally she managed a half-whispered, "I...uh...." Her power of speech seemed to freeze just behind her tongue, and her mind fairly exploded. *Why did he have to say that? What does he want after seventeen years? Lord, make him leave! No! No, don't let him leave! We have to talk. But why? About what? I'm married! Where's Jack? Arthur, why are you here? Why am I holding his hands? Has anyone seen us? What am I doing? Stop! No, wait! Wait!*

Carrie's hands trembled, and the trembling traveled up her body until it reached her mouth. Her bottom lip quivered. She bit it hard to make it stop. Her breath came in little gasps. Finally the words, "All right," issued from somewhere within her. The voice did not feel like her own, but more like an answer spoken by someone else standing behind her in some unnoticed shadowy corner of the room.

But she knew she had said it. She knew it because the voice had expressed a feeling that had already been lurking in her mind. "All right" she said again as the locomotive's whistle repeated its wail.

Arthur let her hands slide from his grasp. He backed up a step and half turned toward the lobby. "I really have to go now." He sidestepped away from the table. "Get hold of Roger if you ever have need to find me," he said over one shoulder. "He usually knows my whereabouts."

Sometime after Arthur had left, Carrie came out of her emotional daze and looked around the dining room. She tried to refocus her thoughts and regain some degree of lost control. How long had she stayed there alone, hovering by the table? She could not answer that because she did not know. Long forgotten memories and feelings from the past had, for a time, enveloped her and taken command of her attention. However, there remained one saving grace amid the fog and embarrassment of the present circumstances. The duration of her little trip to the land of what-had-been-before didn't matter. The room appeared empty, save for herself. In all likelihood, no one had seen her there at all, meaning her brief departure from the here-and-now had probably gone unnoticed. However, that unexplained itch in the back of her consciousness had grown more pronounced. This was no pleasant urge. On the contrary, it felt more than a little uncomfortable. And in the end, she recognized it for what it was—her conscience—the evidence of the Holy Spirit's presence inside her. His continual attempts to guide her away from obvious trouble had risen in intensity from the time she first saw Roger until the last moment before Arthur's departure. And this particular communication from the Spirit had, over those last few critical minutes, gone from a subtle unction to kicking at the moral doors of her mind. There now remained a confession to be made here. Carrie had known what God had been trying to do, and she had resisted. For that she felt an uneasy conviction. But, at the same time, she resented this feeling of semi-shamefulness and blamed the Holy Spirit for her unease.

And then there were Arthur's words that had begun to replayed themselves in her mind. *"Call me. Call me."*

Chapter Forty-Two

"**H**ey!" Jack banked the new Ryan hard left to circle the Stutz as it approached the center of Sweet Springs. The roadster didn't slow, though—let alone pull over and stop.

She didn't hear me.

He cranked the high-wing monoplane back around for another pass over Saber Canyon Road and cut the engine just as he passed over the Hunters' Inn. With the propeller of the big Wright radial engine wind-milling at idle power, Jack leaned out the side window again and waited until Carrie was almost under him. Then he dropped the left wing for an instant.

"Hey! Hey, down there!"

This time his quarry looked up and returned his wave. *Good. She's seen me.* He pulled the silk-wrapped message pouch from inside his jacket and hurled it out into the slipstream. On its way to the ground, a white gossamer tail unfurled, drawing all eyes to its descent. The Stutz stopped where the pouch landed. Carrie would get the note to meet him at the airfield.

Good. Jack banked right to correct his approach path to the runway, then he goosed the engine back to flight rpm. That's when he saw Alma by the front door of the café, one hand shading her eyes. *Oh no! Carrie's right across the road! Don't wave, Alma. Please, don't wave.*

She waved like her life depended on it.

Jack did not. *Oh, for the love of.... Did Carrie see that?* He twisted his head backward out the left window. She stood by the roadster's front fender, rolling the white silk streamer up in her hands. She'd likely read the note but as to whether she'd looked up while Alma advertised her infatuation with Jack remained a mystery. Why did he ever mention the new plane to the waitress? Then the railroad tracks passed under the Ryan's tail and Jack cut the throttle in time to sink down for landing. *Lord, don't let Carrie see Alma.* He kicked right rudder and held the Ryan's nose down. The oversized wheels of the main landing gear bounced once onto the airport's sunbaked clay, then crow-hopped back into the air. *Please, let Carrie be in a good mood this time.* He held the stick steady while the plane settled back to earth, the main gears and tailskid almost touching down at the same time.

He finished the rollout and taxied back to the airmail hanger, where he cut the engine, shut off the fuel, and opened the door in anticipation of a smaller version of Lindbergh's *welcome home* reception. *They're probably hiding in the hangar. After all, this is the plane that's going to save us, so to speak.* But the tarmac parking area remained empty and the hangar doors stayed closed. No mob surged out of the building to jostle each other for a look at Jack, the hero, or even his new metal and fabric steed. Not even the scorpion that scurried across the thin, heat-cooked asphalt strip in front of the hangar paid the new arrival any mind at all. Rather the creature made its way to a large crack in the pavement and wriggled out of sight.

Jack smiled. "Where'd everybody go, friend?" But the scorpion did not return from his lair to answer. The pilot looked at his watch. *Ah. Exactly midway between mail flights. No one much'll be here for another hour.* He looked off toward the hazy outline of the Bull Moose across the road. *And the world knows where Sam is.* A deep sigh filled his lungs as he exited the cockpit and leaned back against the airframe. It had been a long flight from the Ryan factory at San Diego. And it had been what seemed like an even longer train ride just to get down there to take delivery on the new plane. And this was after he had flown the mail plane back up to Sweet Springs from his grandparents' ranch. So, right now, what he wanted most was to rest and eat. But, fatigue aside, the euphoric arms of accomplishment *still* held Jack tight. The Ryan flew like a champion racehorse. *And half of it's mine!* That felt darn good no matter how exhausted or starved you were!

Jack turned around and took several steps backward. Then he just stood there in the afternoon heat, drinking in the picture of the Ryan, resting after her maiden flight, accompanied by the sound of the engine's exposed cylinder heads tinkling as they cooled. Her buffed aluminum cowling caught the sun's rays and flung them out 180 degrees like some magic crystal in a fairy tale. The shoulder of the cabin clutched a single square wing, its solitary existence a silent challenge to the biplanes so many pilots preferred. *With her tail down and nose up like that, she looks like she's going to leap into the air any second. Lord, she's beautiful.* Suddenly, the lack of a cheering crowd didn't matter to Jack. *Alone or not, this is a great day.*

Daylight glinted off the Stutz's glossy yellow hood as it rounded the hangar's western end. Carrie stopped just in front of the massive main doors and set the handbrake. After tightening the knot on her head-scarf, she swung her feet to the ground. Her apron and housedress flapped with easy grace in the early afternoon breeze. She stood with the car door half open while leaning forward with one palm on the dashboard and the other on the seat back. "All right, you've got me here, Ace. What's so important it couldn't have waited until tonight?"

Well, maybe not a great day, but it's a good day, anyway.

"What do you think?" Jack presented the plane with the hand gesture of a magician who had just produced a rabbit from a silk hat.

Carrie blinked. "It's a very nice airplane, Jack." She allowed a pause. "Closed cabin. Looks big inside." The wind blew the tail of her scarf across her face. She wore powder and rouge to work these days. Not exactly good kitchen sense, but she spent most of her time mixing with the guests in the dining room of late—perspiring into her coal-shaded eye shadow was no longer a serious risk. Carrie pulled the scarf back with patrician grace, revealing bright red nails, something she'd forgone for most of the last five years. "So, is it for carrying mail?"

Jack nodded. "And passengers, in the bargain. It'll seat three or four with mail, depending on the load." He patted one of the struts. "This is the same kind that Lindy flew to Paris. Brand spankin' new, too." He ran his hand across the smooth resin coated fabric with the same tenderness he would have employed to caress his wife's shoulder seven years ago.

"It looks expensive." Carrie cocked her head as her clothing made subtle flapping noises in concert with a warm rush of air. "Whose is it? Sam's?" A tiny smirk peaked out from the dimple next to her lips. "He can barely keep ahead of his bills."

A little knot formed at the top of Jack's stomach. A familiar sensation these days. It seemed to manifest itself whenever Carrie's old, sarcastic, critical nature resurfaced. Usually, the knot clothed itself with feelings to match the pain; sometimes anger, sometimes disappointment—more often than not, both. This time it hovered somewhere between the two. He decided to ignore it and press on. "It's ours." He swallowed hard knowing he had now opened a can that could not be sealed again. "Sam's and mine." He hoisted a smile and summoned all the courage he could against what he knew had to come now…and against that afore mentioned, very familiar knot in his middle that had now grown to cantaloupe size. "We bought it together. We're partners now." He waved toward the hangars. "In the whole airmail business, not just the plane."

Carrie's cherry-hued lips parted and her mouth opened the widest Jack thought he had ever seen it. Then she made a low moaning sound that Jack, at first, thought was some kind of gasp, but soon proved to be his wife's attempts to talk. This strange and somehow sad little noise persisted for more than a full second before it ceased, and actual speech finally emerged. "Who...who....who?"

"Whose idea was it?"

She nodded, while her eyes opened to seen-a-ghost diameter.

"It was Sam's. He only had half the money."

"Where did you...." She seemed to have trouble swallowing or perhaps breathing.

Here it was, the first real rock in the river. But he had an answer for her, one that he hoped would, at least, fend off the first blow against his my-point-of-view boat, so to speak. "Don't worry. I didn't mortgage anything. My family put up the capital."

She took a few shallow breaths and seemed to gain back a certain amount of control. "You talked Floyd and Hannah into this?" The sound of helpless shock had left her voice, as a knifelike edge replaced it. "And who else?"

"My father, believe it or not." Jack hung onto his outer confident calm, determined not to give in to the termite of self-doubt that had begun to gnaw at his spirit. "Well, I didn't really convince him on my own. Grandpa had a hand in that."

Carrie let herself fall into the driver's seat. She stared deep down past the floorboards and shook her head with the sad resigned look of one who had witnessed a shipwreck. "Oh, Jack." She sat in silence for several seconds, not moving, other than the low heaving of her chest. "How are you ever going to pay them back?"

"With profit from the business."

"But Sam's been losing money for months."

"The new plane will change all that. The profit's in passengers these days, not just mail."

She looked up, but kept her gaze straight out the windshield. "And how do you know that? Did Sam tell you? Judas Priest, Jack! He'd tell you anything to get your money! Why didn't you...."

"Why didn't I what?"

Her neck muscles stood out. "Nothing."

I know. Why didn't I discuss it with you? Why don't you just say it? "It's a well-known fact, Carrie. All the aviation businesses that are turning a profit are carrying passengers on a regular basis." *And why would I want to discuss anything with you. All you've ever had for me are three answers. No, don't, and stop. It's a good thing the Wright brothers weren't married to you, or I'd be delivering the mail on a bicycle. Besides, sounds like you've already got your mind made up.* Jack snapped shut the Ryan's door. He doubted she wanted to look inside. She wouldn't even look at *him*. "This is the future." He indicated the monoplane. "We're going to be on the crest of the commercial aviation wave."

She finally looked his way. "That's what you said about barnstorming with that junkyard Jenny. You ended up giving rides at a cheap carnival."

"Flying circus."

"No difference." She sniffed. "Didn't you say you ended up wearing a clown costume?" She closed the Stutz's door and created a hideous grating noise when she hit the electric starter with the engine still muttering.

"It's already running, Carrie." He shrugged out of his flying jacket and slung it over his shoulder.

"I know!" Carrie banged her fist on the dash, then hid a renegade sob behind her hands. She heaved through two quick spasmodic breaths. "Sorry."

"Why are you mad?" *Yeah, why? I'm trying to protect our future here.* He shuffled with an easy gait to the passenger door. "And, by the way, that clown act was a one-time favor for a friend. Larry got himself stuck at Union Station and—"

"I don't care, you idiot! My Lord, are you a complete moron?" She whirled sideways in her seat and sat there for two very long seconds, eyes and mouth wide, her chest rising and falling like a bellows. She seemed to be stunned and stung almost as much as Jack at what she had just said. Finally, Carrie allowed her lips to come to rest in a strange sort of pout, but she kept her husband in her sights.

Jack felt the first slice into his heart, as the cantaloupe-sized stomach knot grew to watermelon stature. All of a sudden, his mouth seemed very dry, and the inside of his throat began to shrink. *Why did you say that? I'm trying to make money for us. Why did you have to say that?* He held his last breath a couple of extra seconds to insure a calm reply. "Don't talk to me that way, Carrie." Success! His words had come out with an even tone, despite the moment's tension.

"How else should I address someone who has just made the same witless mistake that very nearly destroyed us five years past? And now you have increased the intensity of the blunder to make absolutely sure our family is ground completely into the earth, never to rise again?" She drew a fierce breath in through her nose, causing her nostrils to half collapse. It gave her the appearance of an angry predatory bird. "I can't believe you've done this!" She bullied a betraying tear from her cheek. "Why? I want to know! Weren't you happy just flying? You were chief pilot. Why couldn't you leave well enough alone? Why did you have to put us into debt...and for an airplane? Another dirty, oily, noisy mess of wires and bed-sheets that will cost us twice what it's worth!" She took another breath. "I only have one word for someone like that, Jack. Moron. Not husband. Not father. Just bumbling moron!" Her breasts began to heave again, but her war-face remained set.

Carrie's verbal cleaver had now penetrated all the way through Jack's heart, and the watermelon in his gut had already exploded. But these were nothing compared to the dwarf elephant standing on his chest. "I...." *Is that what she really thinks of me? I'm building a future, and she thinks I'm a moron? Where's the faith? Where's the loyalty? Where's the encouragement? I'm a moron?* His hand slid down from his shoulder, allowing the flight jacket to rest against the oil-stained asphalt. *She's no wife! My friends...no, people on the street treat me better than this...and with a darn sight more respect. Who do you think you are, Princess? Never mind. I already know.* He noticed his jacket touching the ground and folded it under his arm. *Don't take this lying down, boy. Strike back.* As a wave of righteous anger spread through him, his throat loosened enough to allow speech. "Well said, Miss Van Burean." The words gushed out of his mouth like stored water through a dam spillway. He waited until a slight flinch of her eyelashes told him his return shot had found its mark. "We're sorry our miserable efforts to please you have failed. With your permission now, we'll remove our wretched carcasses to some far shadowy cave and slit our throats. All hail Princess Caroline."

Carrie showed no obvious agitation, but she did swallow hard before speaking again. "You know, Jack." She looked around and cleared her throat. "I've spoken the truth, and I've said all I'm going to say on the subject at this time." Ice fairly formed on her words as they met the hot desert air. "You've sacrificed the security of your family for another selfish fantasy, and it makes me wonder how a man like that could truly love me or my children, let alone be trusted any farther."

"Why is it you're the only one who feels this way about me, Carrie. I get common respect from everyone else in town. Everyone but you."

"That's because they don't know you for the untrustworthy creature that you are." She put the Stutz in gear and released the hand-break. "But don't fret, Jack. If I'm the only one in town who does not think you are the very keeper of Winged Pegasus, what care you? I'm sure you'll receive accolades enough this afternoon to easily make up for any truthful barbs your evil witch of a wife has sent your way. Perhaps the comely Alma will sooth your wounded ego." Carrie raised her eyebrows. "I'm sure she will." She shook her head. "It all makes me wonder, Jack, why I ever married you." She let out the clutch, and, as the roadster turned back toward the street, she gave Jack a less than sincere-looking smile over her shoulder. "What *could* have I been thinking that day?" Then she and the car disappeared behind the hangar.

Jack returned to the Ryan and settled his buttocks onto the main landing gear's big tire. Then he locked his attention onto a hawk that circled a mouse-rich field east of the railroad tracks. *Moron? Idiot? Is that what she's thought of me all this time? I gave up everything for her. But she can't stand it when I'm flying...when I hold some small position of importance in the universe. She's only happy when she's in charge.* Now it was Jack's turn to shake his head. *Just like her father...got to be the big wheel.* He threw a stone at the hangar doors but it fell short by more than half the distance. It made him laugh out loud. *That's me all right, always falling short of Princess Van Burean's minimum requirements.* He got up from the tire and began a slow stroll toward the hangar. *Just don't measure up. Well, you know something, Princess? You don't pass muster either. Not by a long shot. In every way a man values a wife, you've failed, and that's a fact! So maybe we'd both be better off by ourselves. Maybe the boys'd be all right, too. They're older now.* He considered that last thought again, but could not settle on an answer that satisfied him. *Maybe they would be...or maybe not.*

He heard Alma's voice calling from the taxiway. So he stopped and returned her wave. *What timing. Did my wife send you?*

"She's elegant." Alma stepped over a tumbleweed and hopped toward the Ryan while she pulled a sticker from her sock. "Like some big wonderful bird that could take you anywhere. Can I look inside?"

Jack nodded. "Sure." He turned around and strode back to the plane he'd just left, but this time it took him half the steps. "Just don't touch anything."

"I won't, Sweetie. I'll be good as can be." She winked as she drew close.

Well Carrie, you're right about one thing. This unsophisticated little waitress always seems to be around when I need somebody.

"Will you tell me a little about it? I'm a fool for airplanes."

"Absolutely. What do you want to know?"

❧

Jack and Sam stepped out of the mail truck's cab just as Mr. Shontz's experimental biplane leveled out from its dive and shot past the first yellow-flagged marker pole. At less than thirty feet above the ground, the noise from the huge Packard engine nearly deafened those close to the course. Jack covered his ears with the palms of his hands. Sam preferred to use his index fingers, like Buster Keaton in a movie scene, where he's waiting for the dynamite in his back pocket to go off. Even through his hands, Jack could still hear the potent snarl of the unmuffled exhaust stacks, as the plane ate up the distance to the second pole a mile away.

"Rats!" Jack snapped at nobody in particular. "We missed it!"

The speeding machine had dropped from the sky and roared by so fast, it gave no chance to get a good look at it. Ever since Shontz had pulled the speed challenger's tarp away in the hanger, both Sam and Jack had been more than anxious to see it all put together and flying. And since the best reward of any new aircraft's preparation is the first takeoff, *that* event had become the thing both mail pilots had awaited with near childish excitement for most of the past week.

But, this morning, Sam had been afflicted with a more venomous than usual hangover, and the man could not be hurried. A half hour delay resulted. And even though Jack had driven like a madman to make up the time, the pair still arrived well past the moment of the new plane's hallowed first leap into the air. They hadn't even gotten to see what name Shontz had painted on his world record contender. The engineer had refused to give his landlords any hint on the subject, and said he wouldn't even allow the plane's artwork to be painted onto the fuselage until the day before the first trial flight.

Several seconds after the biplane's guttural roar had subsided, Sam pulled his fingers from his ears. He blinked his eyes with an almost desperate squeeze and massaged his temples. "Lordamercy, that thing's louder than my wife's mother!" He stretched his neck in two directions, then looked up at Jack with wet, sorrowful eyes. "Boy, Crusher's poison gin don't mix with high performance engines, and that's a fact. Now, Snuffy's old white lightning was more friendly on a body the day after. A man could do engine run-ups all day long without even the hint of a headache. You *know* the world's become a cold, heartless place, partner, when your own bootlegger doesn't care about your health."

Jack shaded his eyes and peered in the direction of the plane pulling skyward at the other end of the dry lakebed. He noted the remaining Lilliputian puddle, some still called *the lake,* had now evaporated down to almost half the size it had been just two weeks before. Then he mused again for just a moment on how he and Carrie had once pinned their hopes for success on the tourists they thought the dying lake would draw. *Not one soul mentioned it was drying up until we got here.* He let out a sigh of acceptance. *Been three years since they tore down the docks. Most of the boats are probably daisy planters by now.* It had been Carrie's idea to stay. *She had no idea she'd become a bigger draw to the inn's business than any lake. She's quite a woman, this wife of mine. And now she thinks I'm a moron.*

The previous night had been a silent one for the couple. They had both eaten supper separately in town while the boys had stayed with the Smiths. By the time Carrie arrived home from work, Jack was already feigning sleep on the living room couch. And this morning, he could still hear her rhythmic breathing from their bedroom when he left to wake Sam before dawn. Not a word had passed between them since the fight over the new Ryan. *What could I say to her? She'd just insult me again.*

"I'm afraid she's a complete washout today, gentlemen."

The unexpected sound of Mr. Shontz's voice so close behind startled Jack back to the current reality. "What?"

Shontz stepped between Jack and Sam with a semi-preoccupied air. He watched the biplane level off and turn back toward the runway, then he produced a pencil and wrote something short on a notepad. "Our winged brainchild has clocked in ten miles per hour too slow for the second time this morning." He raised his pencil and tapped the stopwatch that hung around his neck as if to emphasize the point. "I was afraid this might happen. We'll need a bigger supercharger to break the record. Today's results have made that clear." He slid pencil and pad neatly into his inside coat pocket. "Fortunately, we brought one along. It will put more strain on the engine as a whole, though." He pushed his Homburg back on his head. "This entire week has been quite a trying experience. A lot of frantic activity having to do with getting our challenger ready." He stretched his arms. "What I wouldn't give for a simple card game to untwist my nerves."

"Say, where did you come from anyway?" Jack unbuttoned his flight jacket in response to the climbing summer sun. "I didn't see you when we drove up."

Shontz waved a hand back toward a row of cottonwood trees that lined what was left of the fast-evaporating Santa Clarita Creek. "Back in the shade there. I hope I didn't startle you."

Jack shook his head. "Not really. By the way, what did you decide to christen your airplane? We didn't get here in time to catch it."

"We haven't named it anything, yet." Shontz scanned around as if he was looking for an explanation. "No one could come up with anything of a truly inspirational nature. So, we've decided to postpone our artwork until an appropriate idea comes to mind."

Sam opened the top of his coat and lit a Havana, which he pointed at the descending biplane. "So your mare won't make the jump, huh? Too bad. Fine looking ship. I had high hopes for her."

A thin smile traversed Shontz's face. "Oh, she'll make the jump, all right, Mr. Smith. She'll make the jump." He squared the Homburg back along his brow. "Once we get that supercharger installed, she'll jump."

"Are you sure?" Sam left the cigar to hang from his between teeth, then he turned to watch the plane bank into its crosswind leg for landing.

"As sure as one can be." Shontz spoke without looking at Sam, preferring to also keep his gaze glued to the biplane. "If not, we'll have to use a bigger engine. There is *only one* more powerful than that which we have. It came onto the market just this month, but that would cost us time." Now he turned to face the two. "And, *in* that time, one of our many opponents might well set a new record in our stead. Perhaps a record that could not be broken for years." He went back to watching his brainchild land at the far end of the airfield.

Jack considered putting a supportive hand on Shontz's shoulder but thought better of it. It just didn't seem to fit with the man. Instead he said, "I'd like to see *your* ship set that record."

"Thank you, Mr. MacGregor. So would I."

Sam cleared his throat. "So you say you could use a relaxing game of cards."

Shontz closed his eyes for an instant. "As a matter of fact, the pressure's been so intense lately, I've half a mind to let my chief mechanic handle the supercharger while I play poker-hooky somewhere. That's how I used to relieve tension when I was but a youth at university. Just before final exams I'd find myself an all-nighter game somewhere and come away with a clear head, ready for study." He shrugged. "Never failed."

Sam took in an extravagant measure of smoke from his cigar and created two smoke rings, letting a satisfied expression spread over his face as he worked. "Well, it just so happens there *is* one regular game in town. Takes place in a caboose at the south end of the freight yard."

Jack couldn't believe his ears. "Crusher's game?"

Sam's smile broadened. "That's the man."

Shontz raised an eyebrow. "Crusher is it? Sounds interesting."

Sam nodded. "To say the least. If you're of a mind, I can introduce you."

Jack's astonishment grew. "Sam, you've been to that game?"

"Ever since I started buying Crusher's hooch."

A picture of Shontz's lifeless body sprawled inside an empty boxcar flashed across the screen of Jack's mental theater. "That's not the place for a man like Mr. Shontz. I wouldn't take my mother-in-law to that game!"

"Thank you for your concern, Mr. MacGregor, but I can take care of myself. And as I said, it sounds interesting."

Sam waved his smoldering Havana at Jack. "The trouble with you, partner, is you've never learned to appreciate poor Crusher. I refer to the integrity he shows as a businessman. Why, I've won at least two pots there myself and lived to tell about it. Mr. Shontz would be as safe as a babe in its mother's arms. Old Crusher wouldn't want word of foul play to get around. His game would dry up overnight. This isn't just a switchman's game anymore. There have been some big spenders pass through that little caboose in the last year or two. Crusher's harmless. He wouldn't risk the loss."

"Mr. Smith." Shontz tilted his Homburg forward so that it shaded his eyes. "I'm definitely in. Sometime after dinner, you may show me to your notorious caboose, if you will."

Chapter Forty-Three

"I said, that engineer friend of yours is dead. We found him in a gully a mile from town, and his money-belt was in the brush behind the feed store." Eli Culkin, the new town constable, stood feet wide apart, arms folded, his head tilted back so far that one might almost think he was looking through his ample shoe-polish-black mustache.

Jack had just walked through the hangar's office door, but Eli's statement to Sam had brought him to a halt. "Dead? Shontz is dead?"

"Cold as a mackerel." Eli furrowed a brow at Jack, then turned his attention back to Sam, who sat, clad only in his underwear, slumped on his cot with his legs slung over the side. The old pilot's head rested in his hands, his body heaving in cadence with his breath.

"Night foreman at the freight-yard said you was at Crusher's game," Eli said. "So what I'm asking is…do you know anything about the man's demise?"

"No," Sam moaned and raised his head to take in the two men standing before him. His eyes were sunken into his cheeks and the whites were so shot with red they gave the impression Sam would bleed to death if he did not cover them with the skin of his lids real soon. "I don't know anything about it. I got to feeling a little under the weather at the game so I came back here." He pointed to the cot. "And I've been sunk into this torturous contraption ever since." Sam rubbed the back of his neck and let his contorted face advertise his pain.

Eli stroked his mustache. "Under the weather, huh? More likely the bathtub gin flu."

Sam risked opening one eyelid near to its full travel, closing the other tight in the process. "Eli, your intelligence and skill at investigation is a constant source of amazement to me. Small wonder you have risen to your present position of prominence." Sam staggered to his feet and groaned with a more desperate tone than before. "Am I under suspicion, Constable?" He swayed slightly to one side, then steadied himself on the back of a chair. "I'd hold up my hands for you, but I fear I might lose my footing."

"No, I just have to question anybody that might know something. Everyone else who was at that game claims Shontz left right after you." Eli paused and let out a sigh. "He was worked over pretty good...like with a gun butt, or an axe handle—"

"Or a switchman's brake-club?" Jack sat on the corner of the desk.

Eli nodded. "Could be." He pulled a pocket watch from his vest, popped the cover, and examined the face of the timepiece with the concentration of a man dividing up time by how many chores remained for the morning. Another sigh erupted, longer and with more wind than his last one. "All right, Sam. I'll be on my way. I've already told Shontz's chief mechanic and wired his wife. I wouldn't be a bit surprised if she contacted you right soon." Eli shuffled to the outside door, opened it, and turned. "You're gonna tell me if you remember anything, aren't you?"

"Word of honor."

"Much obliged." Eli squared the campaign hat on his head, giving the brim a slight dip in front and to the right. He pointed a friendly finger at Sam. "You take care of that cold now," he said with a sympathetic smile. Then he was gone.

As soon as the latch clicked shut, Sam managed to hold up one hand while keeping a grip on the chair with his spare. "I know. I know. You don't have to say it. I shouldn't have taken him to the game." He lowered his upraised hand to resume its much-needed duty of holding onto the furniture. "The poor man's fate is on my head for sure." He took a few deep breaths and blinked his eyes with an easy motion. "I never dreamed old Crusher would go that far."

Jack pulled another chair out from the other side of the desk and sat with the semi-catastrophic force of a sack of flour dropped from a second floor window. "So what do we do now?"

One of Sam's eyebrows struggled upward. "Do? We don't do anything, Jack, old friend. Not unless we want to end up like Shontz. Murders aren't our department. That's Eli's job, and I've already told him everything I know. I'm sorry about Shontz. But, to tell the truth, I could *not* talk that man into leaving with me—which I did try to do— anymore than I could talk him out of digging into that money belt in front of Crusher and the boys, which I also whispered a warning in his ear about." He eased himself around to the front of the chair and descended as if there were eggs in his back pockets. "So my responsibility for the man's death ends with taking a fool to a serious game of cards. I'm not heartless, Jack, but I'm neither Shontz's mother nor his wife. He said he could handle himself, but that just wasn't the case."

Jack lifted one leg straight out and rested his boot-heel on the corner of the desk. Something Sam had just said rang a small mental bell. *What was it? Fool, heartless, mother—*

The phone on the desk rang. Sam lifted his melting face and stared at the clanging contraption as if he didn't comprehend what it was or why it was making that noise.

Jack did the same for an instant, then his memory gears engaged. *Wife!* The phone rang again. Jack let his boot slide from the desk and bang onto the floor. "Eli said Shontz's wife might call!"

Another ring.

Sam waved away the phone and its abrasive ringing. "You talk to her, neighbor. I'm not up to full RPM yet."

A fourth ring.

"Well, what am I going to say to her?"

"Anything except you think I got her husband killed."

Jack swallowed against the sudden dryness in his throat, leaned forward, and snatched up the phone's earpiece in the middle of the fifth ring. "Sweet Springs Air Service." He took as quiet a breath as possible.

"This is the long distance operator. You have a call from Detroit; go ahead, please."

The connection crackled before the caller spoke. "Yes, May I speak to Mr. Smith?"

The Male voice on the other end of the line provided Jack with justification to relax a little. *At least it's not Shontz's wife.* "I'm sorry. He's not able to come to the phone right now. I'm Jack MacGregor, his partner; is there something I can do for you?"

"Possibly so. I'm Nathaniel Shontz. I was informed earlier this morning that my brother was killed in your town." The voice sounded strained.

Jack's relative serenity evaporated as his midsection tightened. "Yes, Mr. Shontz.

"Mr. Shontz?" That put a charge through Sam. He raised his flushed face to Jack as one wary eye-lid opened.

Jack shook his head, scribbled *His Brother* on a notepad, and slid it across the desk. "Our constable told us just a few minutes ago," he said, "and I want to say that Sam and I are both very sorry for your loss."

Sam ran splayed fingers over his sweat-soaked face and whispered, "What's he want?"

Jack mouthed, "I don't know."

Shontz's tone somehow sounded solemn and businesslike at the same time. "Thank you, Mr. MacGregor." He paused. "Let me be frank. Our family is devastated by my brother's death, his wife most of all. She has requested that I, both as a relative and her attorney, handle all business matters connected with my brother. Or at least, I'll be doing so until she's better able to handle her affairs, so to speak." Shontz stopped speaking again, but Jack could hear him clearing his throat and sniffing. "My sister-in-law, despite her present grief, is mindful of the fact that her husband's project to set a new world airspeed record was the most important thing in his life...next to his family, of course. She remains insistent that his efforts up 'til now not be in vain. Therefore, in that spirit, and against my advice, I might add, she has requested that I offer your company fifty percent of the speed-challenger enterprise on condition that you and Mr. Smith continue the endeavor, exerting your best effort to establish said new record. Of course, Mrs. Shontz would retain her half of all holdings for eventual monetary consideration, but you and Mr. Smith would retain working control." Jack heard what sounded like Shontz drinking something, followed by a barely audible gasp. "So, what is your answer, Mr. MacGregor?"

Jack leaned the chair back on its hind legs and kept wide eyes glued onto Sam, who had just performed the miracle of raising from his seat and now edged toward the extension phone on a small table near the cot. "Let me see if I have this straight, Mr. Shontz." Jack swiveled his head to loosen the neck muscles. "You want to sell half the biplane to Sam and I and have *us* finish the speed record attempt?"

At that, Sam could wait no longer. He tucked his undershirt into his boxer shorts, wiped his mouth on the back of his hand, and lifted the phone's earpiece from its cradle. "Hello, Mr. Shontz. Sam Smith here. Did I hear correctly? You want to sell us your airplane?"

"Ah, Mr. Smith. Yes, in manner of speaking."

Jack considered hanging up. It was obvious Sam had taken over. But then he thought better of it. *Even a junior partner should know what's going on.*

"Well, sir." Sam backed up to the cot, the second phone's earpiece in one hand and its mouthpiece-pedestal in the other, extra-long cord stretched tight across the floor to the wall. Then he eased his bulk down onto the ancient stained canvas. "That's a very tempting offer, but the truth is we simply don't have that kind of money right now. You see, we've just finished buying a new monoplane and that, more or less, has drained our reserves for a while."

"No, no, Mr. Smith. I'm afraid I haven't explained myself very well here. You don't need to put up any money. Your contribution will be your piloting and management skills there at the airfield and wherever the airplane flies for exhibition purposes. That's the only purchase price, as it were. Yourselves. I'm talking about a one-year agreement, during which time fuel, parts, and mechanics' salaries will be paid by Mrs. Shontz. You and Mr. MacGregor will have no salaries, of course. But you will keep half of all that the plane earns from prize monies and exhibitions. This is the offer my sister-in-law has asked me to make. Does that sound reasonable to you?"

Jack almost dropped the phone. *They're giving us the plane and putting us in charge?* For the first time in his life, Jack wanted to go to Carrie and ask her what she thought. *Wait! This is too good ...and too fast to be true!*

"That sounds very reasonable, sir." A large toothy smile stretched across Sam's face from corner to corner as he looked over the desk at Jack. He waved an exuberant fist in the air. "And my partner agrees wholeheartedly."

Why are you answering for me? Jack shrugged and shook his head. *Is it a good deal? I don't know. No time to think on it.*

"He's nodding his approval to me as we speak."

Jack exaggerated his shrug and shook his head harder.

"Very good then, Mr. Smith," Shontz said, the metallic-electric facsimile of his voice echoing through the earpiece from over 2,000 miles away. "I'll have the papers drawn up and mailed to you day after tomorrow. In the meantime, I'll send a wire... today... addressed to you and

Mr. MacGregor that will explain to my late brother's associates that the two of you are in charge there…effective immediately. I hope this meets with your approval."

The image of Grandpa Floyd appeared in Jack's internal theater. The old man stood leaning on a rail fence at the Orange County Fair, shaking his head at a land developer who had just finished his sales pitch about reclaimed marshland near the beach. "Reclaimed my Aunt Irma's corset," the old man had said. "That's all salt marsh; it'll be under water again with the next winter storm." Then the cerebral image of Floyd turned to face in the direction of Jack's mind's eye. "I've said this before and I'll say it again, son. If it sounds too good to be true, it probably is."

"Yes, sir. That's *very* satisfactory." Sam waved his hand upward as if Jack were supposed to say something.

Jack remained outwardly silent. *I shouldn't just let Sam speak for me like this. Why aren't I saying anything.* But, as soon as he broached the question, he knew the answers. *Because you don't really know whether this is a wise thing to do or not. Because if you refuse to go along with Sam on this, you wouldn't be able to give him a good reason why not.* Jack filled his lungs and let it out as silently as he could.

"Good." Shontz cleared his throat. "Then I believe that concludes our business for the time being. Send all requests for money to my office until further notice. I'll include address and telephone numbers in my wire." He stopped to sniff again and blow his nose. "Sorry."

Sam and Jack could hear Shontz take a deep breath of his own, but *he* didn't bother to disguise the sigh that followed.

"Well, I have arrangements to make and a brother to bring home," he continued. "Gentlemen, I hope my sister-in-law is right in this matter. And I hope, for her sake, you are the men to set this record. You know, my brother had planned to manufacture military aircraft if all things went

566

his way. His widow is considering the same course of action. She thinks you may be the ones to help her, based on what her husband had to say about you...and, I suppose, a certain amount of her own intuition. As I've said, I hope she's right." He coughed then said, "Good day to you both."

Jack hung up a little behind Sam, then internally faced himself for a moment. *So you really* aren't *much of a businessman after all, are you, Jack old boy? And not very fast on your feet, brain-wise, either.*

"Where'd you go, Jack?" Sam got up and put the phone back on the table. "If I hadn't been *looking* at you, I'd have thought you'd died."

Jack pushed the phone away. "That all happened pretty fast. I didn't have time to think. *And I might be a moron, to boot.*

⚘

"You did what?" Carrie dropped her canvas shopping bag to the floor.

Jack swallowed against what seemed to have become his new chronic dry-throat condition. "We've got a new airplane."

"*Another* one?" She attempted to pick up the bag while keeping her gaze on Jack, but the straps eluded her grasp and the unmoving bag mocked her. She looked down at it, moaned, then grabbed it with both hands and threw it onto the sofa as if it had said something offensive.

"It's Shontz's speed record challenger."

"Where are you going to...how are...." Carrie whirled away and stomped off toward the bathroom. "Oh, L-O-O-O-R-D!"

Jack followed in her wake. "No, we didn't buy it. Mr. Shontz's widow made us partners." *Why are you following her like some kind of puppy?*

Carrie snatched a washcloth from its wall-mounted ring, spun on the faucet, and drowned the defenseless rag under the stream. "Why on earth would she do such a thing?" She grated the bar-soap across the surface of the cloth with the energetic moves of a shoeshine boy.

Jack leaned against the door-jam. *Here it comes.* "She wants us to set the new airspeed record in her husband's place. The regular pilot quit when he found out Shontz's brother might be involved in the project. Some long-standing personal grudge between the two of them, he said. Refuses to be connected with the attorney-brother in any way." Jack shrugged. "So Sam and I are going to fly the ship and manage business affairs as well."

A strange look spread over Carrie's face. Her eyes went wide and her lips puckered. Then she began something that looked to Jack almost like choking, except air came out her nose with a snarking sound. She threw the soapy cloth over her countenance and scrubbed her forehead like her life depended on it. But finally her facial muscles and willpower lost some unseen battle, and Carrie began emitting peals of laughter that resembled what one might hear coming from an asylum.

It sent a small momentary chill through Jack...and made him a little angry. "You think something's funny?"

Carrie regained control as she purged soap from the cloth under the running water. "Are you joking? Of course, it's funny." She rinsed her clenched eyelids and blinked them open. "You...and Sam...trying to break the world speed record...." She stifled another giggle and ended up blowing a large soap bubble through one nostril. Then, all at once, it popped and she erupted into a series of uncontrolled guffaws.

The knife began to slice its way through Jack's heart again, and that part of his brain assigned to lightning-fast, witty responses all but froze. "It's not funny."

Carrie finished removing the last of the soap, snickering as she worked. Then she turned to the doorway where demoralized Jack still hung against the jam. "Well, all I can say is, if you don't want to be laughed at, don't act like a clown."

How can she say that to me? I would never hurt her like that, no matter what she had done or said. These words crouched right on the tip of his tongue to say. But, when he opened his mouth to speak them out, the wall phone erupted with the MacGregors' four-ring signal.

Carrie threw the washcloth into the porcelain basin and pushed past Jack. "Pardon me," she said with an obvious upper crust frost. In the living room, she answered the phone still half chuckling. "Hello?" The usual pause played out while the caller spoke. Carrie broke into a wide grin and turned to Jack, who languished in the doorway. "Why yes, *Sam!* He's right here. One moment." She dangled the earpiece cord from her fingers like bacon for a dog. "It's for you." She winked a sarcastic wink. "Must be important business," she said, performing an exaggerated, serious-faced nod as she waited.

"Carrie—" Jack took the phone.

She held up her hand as she made her way toward the bathroom again. "In light of our other *new airplane-partnership* conversation, this all makes perfect sense. You've not surprised me tonight at all, Jack. You've only confirmed things I've recently come to believe about you."

Jack stared after her as she left the room. *Why don't you just call me a moron again?*

He turned toward the wall and leaned into the mouthpiece. "Yeah, Sam."

"You've got to get back down here, neighbor. I've stumbled into a veritable treasure trove with this new crew of ours!" Sam's voice fairly dripped with fresh excitement as if he were twenty years younger.

Still half paralyzed by Carrie's ridicule, Jack let the words wash around him like a wave at the beach. "Treasure trove?" he monotoned like a neophyte actor reading from a script. "What do you mean?"

"What I mean is...the man we thought was just a mechanic is an engineer himself...just like Shontz. And get this. He flies a little, as well. Not a lot of hours, but he's taken off in the challenger two or three times and flown it around the pattern here. Not too fast but enough to get the feel. You know."

"Yes?" A little more air, life force, or something filtered into Jack's constricted internal spaces. Strange how talking about flying always seemed to have that effect. He took a breath to replace the one Carrie had stolen. "Go on."

"Well, this engineer says he got a pretty good feel for most of the little quirks of our aircraft...all the little ways she might try to eat us. Ya know? So it's no loss at all that that self-important jackass of a pilot jumped ship on us. We don't need him. Earnie will fill us in on how she flies!"

"Earnie?"

"*Our* engineer." Sam paused. "I like the sound of that, partner. *Our* engineer. Ha!" Another pause. "*And* he's giving me the inside story on this record challenge business, the mechanical problems, how to fly the record attempts and all that. You need to be down here, if you're going to do most of the flying."

"I am?"

"Of course."

"Hey, *you* were the fighter pilot not me," Jack said. "*You* should fly it."

"Nothing doing. You've got faster reflexes. Heck-n-back, Jack. You're darn near ten years younger than I am, *and* you've done most of the recent flying. I want to win this record thing, not make fools of us all as I crack up trying."

A condor-size butterfly somehow found its way into Jack's stomach and began flapping its wings with violent strokes. *Fly the challenger during the official record attempt?* He'd never even considered that. *Someone* had to fly it then, for sure. *Guess I just figured Sam would do it. But me?* Jack had to swallow again. "You think I can fly that beast for the record?"

"Nothing to it, neighbor. Old Ernie says he'll talk you through it first. Easy as pie."

"Yeah. Easy." Jack paused for another breath as his internals began to constrict. "All right." He checked his wristwatch. "I'll be down in a little while. But I'm telling you, I want a few hours in this monster before I come streaking out of the sky aiming at a pylon. I'm not keen on cracking up, either."

"Don't worry, partner. You're gonna be great."

⚘

Carrie waited until she couldn't hear Jack's truck any longer before she placed the call.

"Thelma, this is Carrie MacGregor. I need to place a long distance call to San Francisco." *What am I doing?* But the answer came back quick as lightning. *Don't pretend! You haven't been able to get your mind off him for days!*

"Of course, dear. And what number would you like?"

Carrie pulled Arthur's embossed card from a little pocket inside the waistband of her skirt. Thelma didn't sound near as formal as she had when Carrie had called Roger about the Stutz years before. *Knowing people makes all the difference in a small town.* She held the card up to the light and squinted at the tiny lettering. "Hilltower 9-9724."

"All right, I've got it. Oh, by the way, that raisin cake you told me about turned out divine. I tried some on Calvin out at the airfield, and he just couldn't get enough of it. I think he's almost got the nerve to ask me out now, and I might just owe it all to you and your wonderful cake."

"Thelma?"

"Yes, dear."

"Could you connect me with my number, please?"

"Oh my! I *am* sorry. Yes, of course. I'll be off the line for just a bit. Hold on."

Carrie stuffed the card back into its hiding place, feeling like a bootlegger concealing her stash. *This is wrong; I hope he's not there. No, I hope he is. Why am I doing this—because Jack's going back to his old habits? Is he really, or is he just being naïve and showing poor business sense? He's not a businessman, that's for sure.* She wanted a glass of water but knew the second she left the phone the call would go through.

"It'll be just another minute now, dear." The operator's voice echoed just as sweetly as it did every Sunday in the choir. Deborah, the butcher's wife from Temple Beth Israel, would watch the switchboard that day—an amicable arrangement. The word was she had worked as an operator for Bell back in New York before coming to California.

"Thank you, Thelma." *How can you respect a man who has no common sense? Just because he's well liked doesn't make him responsible. Of course he's well liked. He's like a big boy scout...with emphasis on the boy part. Not like Arthur. Now there's a man to be respected...even if he* did *used to be on the arrogant side. And that was years ago. Just one look at him makes you...makes you—"*

"Long distance from Sweet Springs." It was Thelma's official voice now, reserved for outsiders and local people she didn't like—not Carrie. "Your party is ready. Go ahead, please."

Oh, no! Maybe I shouldn't—

"American Mining Company. May I help you?"

I can't do this! I'm not—

"American Mining. Hello. Is anyone there?"

Hang up! "Yes, hello. Uh, may I speak to Arthur Hampshire, please?" *I said hang up!*

"And whom shall I say is calling?"

Don't say another word. "Caroline Mac…Caroline Van Burean." *No!*

"Oh, yes. Just a moment, please."

Was he expecting me to call? Carrie leaned against the wall and fought the urge to hang up. The weight of the universe pressed against her; and breath came in quick gasps, just as before when she saw Arthur at the inn. She twisted the tail of her blouse into a knot, then untied it and smoothed it out again. Then she tried to freeze her mind into numb submission by recalling the lyrics to *Yes, Sir. That's my baby!*

"Hello, Carrie?   .

It felt like her vocal cords had petrified, and there wasn't enough air in her lungs to keep a mouse alive. *Darn you! Either speak or hang up!*

"Carrie, are you there?"

"Yes." She didn't think the nerve closing around her chest could tighten any more, but it did. "I'm here."

"Are you all right? Is anything wrong?" Arthur's voice spread out from the earpiece like whipped cream over a sundae.

"Oh, as well as can be expected." She took a second to catch her breath. "Kenny and Eddie are simply wonderful." *Why did you say that?*

"Your sons, I presume."

"Yes."

"But, other things aren't going so well?"

Don't do it. "Oh—"

"That's all right, Carrie. Roger told me a little about your life of late. You need not say anything just now."

"Thank you." Her whole body seemed to tighten.

"Look, would you like to meet somewhere and talk, say Santa Barbara or even Bakersfield, somewhere you might feel more comfortable?"

Don't take one more step! "Uh…no…not just yet."

"I understand. Maybe some other time?"

"Maybe."

"That's fine. You let me know. I'll be here."

Hang up! "Thank you, Arthur." A sharp pain wound around her neck. "I have to go now. Good-bye." Carrie slid the earpiece onto its cradle and let gravity break the connection. *What have you done?* She turned around until her back braced itself against the wall, then she slid down slow like melting butter, assuming a seated position on the floor. Her breath came a little easier now, but she discovered her arms and legs were made of lead. *And what are you going to do now?*

Chapter Forty-Four

Massive hands closed around Sam's throat from behind, causing him to drop his Havana onto the table in mid-draw. He coughed so hard Jack could swear smoke came out his ears.

"Don't move, you little troll, or I'll snap your neck like a breadstick." The very large, chisel-faced owner of the trespassing hands stooped down from his six-foot-ten altitude, bringing his mouth to a hover next to Sam's ear. Then he grumbled, "Getting slow there, you little devil-mouse. Getting slow and careless."

"Slappy?" Sam exhaled the word with the last of the smoke. He retrieved his wayward cigar as the invasive hands released their grip. Sam turned half around and grabbed the man's arm. "Slappy!" They clasped hands. "Where the deuce you been?"

The man delivered a series of slaps to Sam's shoulders, as if he were putting out a fire. "What? You didn't read my letter? *Told* ya. Been in China making my fortune." He continued slapping for several seconds.

Sam jerked his thumb back toward his friend. "That's half of why they call him Slappy." He furrowed his brow.

"The other half's 'cause I used to slap those Huns right out of the sky just as soon as I saw 'em." He winked at Jack and Ernie. "So, Sam old boy, are you going to introduce me to your friends, or do I have to cry myself to sleep again?" Slappy eased around the café booth and leaned his tower-like frame toward the table.

Sam released a small gray stream of Havana smoke and slumped back down in his seat. "This malformed giraffe is Slappy Royce, second best fighter pilot in the best squadron in France."

"Hey," Slappy growled and put a light punch into Sam's shoulder.

"All right, introductions you want." Sam stretched and emitted a hearty moan. "Introductions you'll get." He pointed first to Ernie. "This is our chief and only aeronautical engineer, Ernie Wall."

Ernie raised a wiry hand in greeting. "Pleased to meet you."

Then Sam aimed his finger at Jack. "And this fellow here is my brave and loyal partner, Jack MacGregor. Don't let that innocent face fool you. He's a natural born killer, he is. Used to drop bombs on defenseless, unsuspecting Germans. Must have blown up over a hundred barns and outhouses belonging to the dreaded Hun before the cease-fire."

Jack nodded after a quick coffee sip. "Morning." *Boy, this is the cheeriest I've seen Sam before noon.*

"What squadron were you in during the war, Mr. Royce?" Ernie smoothed back most of the prematurely thinning hair on top of his head and rubbed the bridge of his ample nose.

"The Twenty-Second Aero Squadron, flying French Spad 13's, same as Sam here. We both got our fifteen victories in the old Shooting Star Squadron."

"Sixteen." Sam took a swallow of his uncharacteristic non-fortified coffee and looked up at Slappy with a challenging glare.

"Aw, Sammy. You going to start that again?" Slappy let a small smirk escape. Then he pulled an empty chair from the nearest table, without a word to the three men sitting there, and settled for a landing at the aisle end of the booth. "Sam claims he got another kill the week before the cease-fire, but nobody saw it, and the wreckage was never found. So number sixteen couldn't be confirmed."

Sam looked off toward the far wall and rolled the Havana as he smoked it. "Would have been confirmed, if my wingmen hadn't high-tailed it back across no-man's-land."

"Here we go again. We all had hot Fokkers on our tails. And by the time me and Wooley got shed of ours, you were nowhere in sight, and the time to refuel had long passed."

Sam waved his non-smoking hand. "Enough said." He scanned his booth companions. "I got sixteen, witnesses or no."

Jack bit the sides of his mouth to prevent a fuse-lighting laugh.

"Who were *you* with, Jack?" Slappy drew a toothpick from a shot glass full of them and inserted the pine sliver between his teeth.

"Fiftieth Aero Squadron. The Dutch Cleansers." *And I don't want to talk about it.*

Slappy's chin extended as he nodded. "You boys flew the raid on the rail-yards at Saint Marie-Blanc. Well, you're no stranger to anti-aircraft fire, are you? How many aircraft actually made it to target that day?"

Jack looked down at his coffee cup and muttered, "One. One out of fourteen." *Don't ask me anymore.*

Slappy smiled. "Well, whoever that one fellow was, he did a bang-up job. All those big fat boxcars all stuffed with Kaiser Bill's munitions…just sitting there waiting for the next big offensive. We heard secondary explosions all the way back to our aerodrome. My hat's permanently off to that man, whoever he is."

Jack kept his eyes on the cup. "I'll tell him, if I see him." *But he's a moron as a businessman, and he's just discovered he's getting more nervous the closer he gets to flying his new plane.*

Sam unplugged the Havana and waved the moist end at Jack. "You didn't tell me you were in on that rail-yard meat grinder."

"Never came up." *Which was fine with me.*

"How about you, Ernie?" Slappy tossed his toothpick onto the table. "What were you up to in 1918?"

"I designed, modified, and repaired airplanes for Glenn Curtiss, which I continued to do until four years ago when I got involved in *this* project."

"Oh?" Slappy's eyebrows rose. "And what project is that?"

"World speed record." Sam flicked a fat ash off into the glass ashtray. "We're going to break it."

Slappy looked around the group through widened eyes. "You're serious?"

Sam tilted his head up and blew smoke at the ceiling. "Yep."

"You've got the plane, the financing and all?"

"We do."

"Well, I'll be a stripe-bottomed ape!" He slapped Sam three more times on the shoulder. "I didn't know you had it in ya, Sammy. That's the way to show 'em. And I was going to give you a last ditch sales pitch about China. Who needs China when you've got a sweet deal like this?"

"Exactly," Sam said through teeth clenched around his half smoked cigar.

Jack looked up from the table. "What's this about China?"

Slappy leaned back. "Nationalist government has sent me to hire pilots for their young air force. After noting the effects of aircraft during the Great War, they've decided they want to make use of warplanes in their quest to unify their country."

"Mercenary pilots." Jack took a sip from his cup. His words had been a mere statement of fact, bearing no judgment.

"I prefer to call them instructors to the new Chinese Air Force. And what's the best way to instruct, says you? Why, through practical experience, of course, says I. So in a word, yes, these instructors *will* see combat but only with the intention of showing Chinese aviators how it's done, so to speak. And for that simple task said instructors will be paid, not only a base rate five times what we made in the Army, but a bonus for every mission...I mean every *lesson* completed. They're to be given field grade officer status, but will remain civilians on a one year contract, renewable at the end. Not a bad bargain in my book. Of course," he said as he cracked his knuckles, "none of that can hold a candle to breaking a speed record." He threw a fish-eyed gaze upon Jack. "No, I'd stay here if I were you, boys. But that's just my opinion."

"We intend to." Sam chewed the Havana some more.

"Good. China's a place for men who only care about making money, not for old happily married men like Sam here." Slappy winked at Jack.

Sam growled.

Slappy reached into the inside pocket of his tweed coat and fumbled around. "Actually, Sam." More fumbling. "I'm on my way down to San Fernando to sign up another fellow. I just stopped in here to invite you to a little going away shindig some of the boys are holding over in Palmdale tonight. It's going to be at a little Mexican place called the *Arena Cantina*. I was hoping you'd have a bite and a belt with me before we catch the train for San Francisco. You'll like the pilots I've collected. Interesting crew, if I do say so myself." He finally pulled his hand from his pocket but kept his palm closed. "Bring your friends along, if you like. Eight o'clock. Love to have 'em."

Sam's smile returned. "I'll be there." He toyed with his stogie, twisting its smoldering end in the ash-tray. "But I'd better not wake up with a headache in the hold of a Shanghai-bound freighter."

Slappy raised his unoccupied hand. "My word as a gentleman." He cleared his throat and tossed three printed cards onto the table. "Oh, here's how to reach me in Frisco. Just in case any of you gentlemen get crazy and change your mind. We'll be there another month, waiting for the aircraft to arrive by rail and be loaded aboard ship."

Jack finished his coffee and put the cup down a little too hard. "What will you be flying?" He didn't know why he asked. He didn't know what to think of Slappy. Was he a salesman or a warrior? *Maybe, both.*

"DH-4's, your old bomber. Got an excellent deal from the National Guard disposal officer in Idaho. Good reliable airplanes."

Jack said, "They *can* be, if you maintain the plumbing properly." *Otherwise, they'll overheat before you're in the air five minutes. That's when the engine starts to melt.*

"We'll see to the plumbing, all right. We're hiring mechanics, too." Slappy pushed his chair back and stood. "So like I said, I'm due down in San Fernando shortly, and I don't want to miss that train." He waved in lieu of handshakes. "It's been a pleasure meeting you all. Hope to see you tonight. Food and liquid refreshment'll be on me." He turned and gave his friend a final nod. "Sam." Then he hurried out of the café and turned toward the train station.

"A very interesting man." Ernie tasted his coffee for the first time since Slappy had arrived. Then he made a face that told Jack the stuff had turned cold.

"Yeah? Well, what I'm interested in right now is the supercharger." Sam canted his body toward Ernie. "How's that going, and how soon will our little sweetheart be ready to fly?"

Ernie glanced at some papers on the table. "A week. We have to make some major modifications. This supercharger was not designed specifically for this engine, so we have to adapt one to the other. Hopefully, it will all work when we do engine run-ups." He looked back to the papers. "Yes. One week should do it. Oh, and by the way, the airplane has a name now. It's being painted onto the cowling and fuselage as we speak."

Sam put his hand up in mock terror. "Go ahead. Hit me with it. I can't stand the suspense."

"Caroline." Ernie rested one arm on the windowsill. "Jack decided on Caroline."

Sam dropped his chin and peered through his eyebrows at Jack. "Oh, you disappoint me neighbor."

"Well, nobody else had any suggestions." *I don't know why I did that.* "And it's just something I've always done. My DH4, my Jenny. That name's been lucky for me, I guess."

Sam almost choked on his smoke. "Well, *that's* debatable."

"At least, I've always survived, no matter what happens."

"All right." Sam coughed and picked a piece of tobacco from his tongue. "You're going to ride her. You name her. Only…."

"Only what?"

"Well, I'd have thought you'd want to name her Alma." Sam snickered as he tilted his head in the direction of the lady in question, who busied herself from table to table pouring hot coffee with her usual seductive grace.

"Paint Alma on the plane. No. Not likely." Jack pushed his cup far enough away to insure a safe filling should the subject of the conversation happen by. "And by the way, that's not funny anymore, Sam."

"Oh, on the contrary, Jack old man. It's getting funnier by the day." At this point in the conversation, Sam seemed to settle into a quiet repose, keeping a patient watch over his partner, apparently awaiting some entertaining reaction that might surface as a result of his last comment.

And within a very few seconds he was rewarded. All of a sudden, Jack felt closed in…by his life, his shortcomings, his marriage…and even the booth in which he sat. This did not all happen as a direct result of Sam's barb. But the older man's words had been the trigger that motivated the younger's loss of control, setting free feelings and actions he'd been trying so very hard keep corralled all morning. All at once, he felt too warm, and his legs told him they were on the edge of cramping. *Need some room.* Without a word, he slid off the booth's bench seat and took Slappy's chair at the end of the table. He stretched himself out to full length, leaning back until the chair's front legs lifted off the floor. *Better! Well, a little better, anyway.*

But still something felt amiss between his mind and his body, in the narrow abyss that separates thought from reality. For just a moment, Jack couldn't identify the ethereal culprit. *What is it? What's wrong?* Then the answer came like a fast telegram. *It's pain.* But it didn't resemble the kind of pain a misaimed hammer might bring to a man's thumb. No, this felt more like what comes when years of insult and injury pile up, one-day's-worth upon another until the pressure surpasses one's ability to keep it all properly bottled and hidden from others. It was the shameful pain that comes when the one who should love you more than anyone else holds you in complete contempt. And it started when Jack's wife began to pull away from him, and it went into high gear the day she told him he was a moron. It felt like a backache that could not be relieved unless one moved or shifted to another position. Likewise, Jack felt the need to speak to someone about these assaults upon his spirit so as to relieve some of that pressure. But, as usual, he fought that need. As usual, he'd try to remain silent.

His exit no longer blocked by Jack, Ernie slid easily out of the booth and stretched his arms toward the ceiling. "Well, I imagine the slaves have the new supercharger out of the box by now." He swiveled his neck in an attempt to loosen stiff muscles. "I think I'll drop over to the hangar and work up some specs for the modifications. See if we have a chance at this record-breaking falderal or not." He dispensed a two-finger salute and left.

After a few minutes of the familiar silent effort to regain a reasonable facsimile of internal calm, Jack found that his special pain persisted. This had a momentary demoralizing effect that weakened his grip on his built-in whining mechanism and loosened his tongue as he stared out the window across the alley toward the Bull Moose. Were it not for this pain, he would have kept everything to himself. But at this moment, he knew he would have to say something to somebody or explode where he sat. "When I showed Carrie the Ryan," he said in Sam's general direction without looking at him, "she said I was a moron. And when I told her about our new biplane and the speed record attempt, she couldn't stop laughing." He paused and pulled his coffee cup closer. "To say she thinks I'm generally incompetent is very much an understatement. She doesn't believe I can do anything without guaranteed disaster."

"That's the biggest load of hooey I've ever heard." The voice belonged to Alma as did the hand that came from over Jack's shoulder to fill his cup with steaming brown elixir. She put the pot down onto the table and slid into the booth's empty bench seat, two things Jack had never seen occur in all the time he'd been eating at the Lakeview. She took his right hand, sandwiched it between both of hers and began a gentle caress.

Jack had such a jumble of things to say—some suitable to speak out in public, some not—he couldn't get any one particular comment through the log jam that had formed between his brain and his teeth. So he just sat there, eyes wide, mouth open, staring at Alma.

"I've known a lot of men in my life," she said, meeting Jack's wide blue eyes with a pair of her own. "And I've got pretty good at separatin' the big talkers from the genuine article." She swallowed and took a gaspy little breath. "You're a member of the brotherhood of the real McCoys, and the best kind, at that. You're the fella' that won't give up. You may not ring the bell every time you swing the hammer. But, as soon as you get your wind back, you always come back for another crack at it." She paused and glanced out the window at a small barefoot boy leading an ancient but well-muscled horse down the alley. "You used to fly, then you had to work in the rail-yard for a while, but what happened? You came back...and flew again. You used to own a plane, I hear. But you lost it. Now you own a whole field full of 'em, and two of em brand new." She patted his hand so hard it felt more like a slap. "You're the *come-back kid*, Sweetie! They can slap you down, but you always bounce back in their face. You're that big old rock at the ocean that the waves crash onto. But all that water just runs off, and the rock stays right there, darin' them waves to try that again. I'll tell you what I think. I think you can do anything you set your mind to, 'cause I know you won't quit 'till you get it done. And don't you let no frustrated, snobby iceberg tell you otherwise!" She gave the hand two more sensuous caresses, then released it and slid out of the booth, once again taking possession, with ballet-like grace, of the blue-speckled coffee pot. She ruffled Jack's hair as she left, and added over her shoulder, "That's what *I* think, anyway."

Sam finally let his smile out of its pen. He leaned toward Jack and kept his tone low. "Rah, rah, rah!"

"Oh, shut up." Jack looked down into his cup as if there were prophetic tea leaves in it and sighed. *She did it again! The wrong person saying the right thing. Why can't anything like that ever come out of Carrie's mouth? Why, God?* He pushed the cup an arm's length away to signify he had no further business with it. "Let's go watch Ernie wrestle with that supercharger." He screeched his chair back and stood.

Sam followed suit. "Anything you say, Come Back Kid."

Jack let go with half a snicker then strode toward the door. "Are you going to bother me with that the rest of the day?"

Sam stayed in formation off Jack's right shoulder. "No. More likely the rest of your life...or the rest of mine, which ever ends first." As soon as he came within range, he finger-flicked the little bell that hung over the door. Then his full-blown grin crawled out of hiding and spread across his face. "And in this corner, wearing blue trunks and a stupid look...the Come Back Kid!"

"Oh, geeze! Give a guy a break, will ya?"

♨

By nine that night, Slappy Royce's party of China volunteers had finished several platefuls of the Arena Cantina's tacos and enchiladas. At this point, everyone—all twelve of them—decided to make their way to the storage room, the management's euphemism for the place where they operated a speakeasy. Before prohibition, the proprietor had said, bags of onions and bouquets of hanging peppers used to wait their turn for sacrifice there. Now, bottles of tequila, wine, and beer graced the shelves.

"A much wiser use of space." Sam waved an indicating hand at a row of glimmering glass containers. "I couldn't have decorated the room better myself." He sat down and scowled across the *serape*-covered table at Jack who had brought his glass of orange soda with him from the dining room. "Partner, you are embarrassing me in front of these noble warriors. Can I not talk you into refreshment more befitting a hero of *Saint Marie-Blanc*?"

"Cut it out, Sam." Jack set his glass down on the serape.

"And what would you like tonight?" A black-haired girl, looking to be in her late teens, dressed in traditional

585

Mexican peon's skirt and blouse, held a pencil and order pad in her hand and a tray under her arm.

"Well, except for Mister Sody-Pop here," Sam jerked a thumb at Jack, "I think it'll be *mescal* all around, am I right?"

The man with the pencil mustache and the very attractive woman with athletic musculature and Dutch-boy brunette hair nodded. The waitress added her own nod and left to take orders from the rest of the crowd.

"So who the heck are you folks, anyway?" Sam fished a cigar from his shirt pocket. "At dinner, we were at the other end of a very long table from you."

"Chester Biggs." The man thrust out his hand and shook first with Sam, then with Jack. "Most call me Chet. This is my second time going east with Slappy. Made a pile of cash before, enough to buy my own orange ranch down by Santa Ana."

Jack took a self-conscious sip of orange soda. "So why are you going again? You want to buy a bigger ranch?"

"Nope. Got myself divorced." He shook his head. "She ended up with the lion's share. So...it's time to make some more money. Time to go back to China."

Dutch-boy hair said, "I'm Faith Bailey. And no, I'm nobody's girlfriend. I'm a pilot, like everybody else here."

"How'd you get hooked up with this bunch?" Sam bit off the end of his Havana.

"Slappy met me while I was flying movie stunts, mostly war scenes. So he says I can fly a fighter as well as any man he's seen, better than some. So he hires me."

"Do the Chinese know about this?" Jack found himself spellbound by this story and its teller.

"Good grief, no! I'm shipping out under the name Richard Bailey, and I'll be wearing binders up top, you know, and cut my hair again before we leave Frisco. Slappy says, if I stick to loose clothes and let him do all the talking, it should all work well enough from a distance.

586

And I do plan to keep my distance from any Nationalist officials." She grinned, exposing large, sparkling white teeth with a slight overbite, which did not detract from her beauty.

And she was definitely beautiful, in Jack's opinion. *As a matter of fact, that huge smile sort of adds something, same as the muscles. Very different from my slender Carrie...or even Alma. Strange...and sort of mysterious. Makes you want to find out more about her.*

"I've got me a big floppy Fedora. Thing's about a size too large." She giggled, which almost seemed out of character. But it added just the right pinch of femininity to offset the men's clothing she wore. "You can hide a multitude of secrets under a big hat. Something I learned in Hollywood."

The drinks came soon. Slappy stood, raised his glass, and yelled across the room, "Drink up, gentlemen...you too, China." Slappy nodded toward Faith and bowed at the waist. "Courtesy of the Nationalist Chinese Government."

"China?" Jack decided he'd missed something.

Faith took a sip of mescal, bringing a quick pucker to her face. "Whoa. They must have strained this stuff through a dead burro."

"You need to use the salt and lime." Sam pointed to the appropriate shaker and plate, then he lit his Corona.

Faith nodded and followed instructions for the antidote. After a moment she sighed and said, "Ah, I think I'll live now." She turned back to Jack. "What were you saying?"

"Slappy called you China."

"Oh, that." She waived a dismissing hand. "I went to this finishing school back in Long Island, believe it or not. My parents sent me there because I had been getting most of my culture lessons from the American sailors and marines off the Yangtze River gunboats. They used to come up-river to check on our mission."

Sam downed the last of his *mescal* and raised his glass for another. "Your folks were missionaries?"

"Yep. Their station was up around the *headwaters* of the Yangtze. Anyway, the girls at the Long Island school found out where I came from and started calling me China. I liked that more than Faith, so I started answering to it."

Sam took a fresh glass from the waitress. "So, how'd you get into stunt flying?"

"Had a flying beau from Princeton my last couple of years at the finishing school. He had wealthy parents and his own plane."

Chet started snickering and tried to drown his noise with a quick swallow of his drink.

China squinted, "And what are you laughing at, Mr. Pinstriped-double-breasted?"

"I was just picturing you at a fancy eastern finishing school."

"Is that right?" China's eyes opened so wide her eyelashes fused with her bangs. "Well, let me tell you something, you pencil-lipped orange plucker! If I so choose to flick the appropriate switch, I can turn on English and airs that would make you think a duchess had just entered the stinkin' room! My horse would be so high you'd need oxygen to survive in the saddle. Do I make myself clear?"

"Yes, ma'am." Chet held up his hands in surrendered as he struggled to keep a smile at bay. Then he let one wayward snicker escape through his nose, but that was the end of it. He won the battle by locking his hand over his mouth."

China raised her chin. "Oh, shut up. And don't interrupt anymore."

"Not one peep. I promise." Another small snicker.

She cleared her throat. "Where was I? Oh, yeah. Stunt flying." She took a breath. "My beau with the plane taught me to fly, and we flitted around the east coast off and on for nearly two years. Then about the time I was supposed to graduate, he took off to barnstorm. Plus he wanted to make his family as mad as he could—don't ask me why—and he figured becoming a flying bum would do it. He was right." She cleared her throat. "So, after my graduation day, I followed him out to California where he eventually got a job flying for the movies. Then one day I came home to find him and some painted up little flapper passed out in *our* bed."

Jack suddenly felt sorry for China, although he wasn't sure why. Something to do with her obvious rejection of her missionary parents' morals, or maybe it was her need to try to shock people. *But who am I to talk. Haven't been to church or even read the Bible in months. I don't know the why of that either. So how come I'm so mindful of this woman's mistakes. Maybe because we've both drifted off the path. She's just drifted a little farther, that's all.*

China said, "I knew he had to fly that day—big air battle scene that had to be shot while the weather was right. So I put on his helmet and jacket and did the stunts in his place." She winked at Jack. "Except, when the gaffer—"

Jack put down the orange soda. "The what?"

"The gaffer. That's the stunt boss. When he found out who'd done the flying and why, I was in for the rest of the picture, and my EX-boyfriend got canned." She smiled and leaned back in her chair. "The flapper was the gaffer's wife." She took another sip from her glass with lime and salt this time. "But this all just got my foot in the door. After I'd flown a movie or two, pilots and directors alike had to admit I flew better than most of the men. Slappy said the same thing. That's why I'm here." She paused. "That and my family."

Jack leaned forward, elbows on the table. "You're going to visit your folks at the mission while you're in China?"

"They were killed just before I left school—by reds or war lords or maybe bandits; nobody seems to know for sure." She took a long swallow of *mescal*, forgetting the antidote. "But I'll find out who did it. I know just who and how to ask." She sank down into her chair after that, holding her glass in front of her eyes as she swizzled the semi-clear liquid around.

Jack turned to Chet after deciding China needed a moment or two to herself. "So you say the money's good."

Once again on center stage, Chet perked up. "The easiest money I ever made. There's bonuses for everything from finishing a student's instruction to bombing the walls of a fortified city. It's like a department store; everything has a price tag." He scooped a handful of peanuts from a dish on the table. "A good pilot would have to be stupid or just plain unlucky not to make a small fortune in China."

"That's good to know." Jack swallowed the last of his soda and looked around for the waitress. "Very good to know."

Chapter Forty-Five

The first munition boxcar exploded like a melon struck by a mallet. It ignited the next car in succession, which set off the next, and so on down the line like a row of dominos until the entire train of ancient wooden freight-cars had become a mass of smoldering lumber, and two other identical trains on adjacent tracks had started to burn.

Good grief! What a bulls-eye! Jack gripped the joystick with a little extra fervor as the De Havilland rode out the shock wave. Then he kicked the rudder peddle and pulled the plane into a sharp right bank, bringing the ailing bomber about 180 degrees. *Time to go home.* He checked the fuel gauge, mindful of the gasoline still spitting out the jagged hole in the main tank. *We can make it. Of course, we can make it.* A thickened trail of acrid smoke wafted past Jack's face, as if to remind him of the other problem. *If the oil doesn't all leak out, we can make it.*

A second later, the ground erupted with machinegun fire as anti-aircraft bursts also blossomed by the bunch beneath the bomber. Jack shaded his eyes and found he could barely make out the tangled wire boundary of no-man's-land. Then the phone rang, but he ignored it. *Got to concentrate now. How far is it back? Twenty kilometers, maybe thirty?* Several rude bullets ripped through the engine compartment, sending more oil into the slipstream and over the exhaust manifold. *More smoke. Great. That's what we needed, more smoke...and maybe fire soon.* The phone rang again just as the first hint of flame started its dance on the surface of an oil-coated exhaust pipe. *Not now! I'm busy! Is that fire? Oh, God! Please, no!* Jack stared at the orange glow to be sure it was flame and not reflected sunlight. *It's fire. We got to get down.* He swiveled around to Dutch, who was oddly calm. Jack pointed to the ground and mouthed, "Going down." Then

591

he jerked his thumb back toward the smoking pipe. "Fire", he hollered into the wind. Dutch nodded and began fumbling with something down inside his cockpit.

The phone rang a third time, and Jack flew into a rage. He shot up out of his wicker seat, mindless that he wore no safety strap, and snatched the earpiece from its cradle. The obnoxious ringing ceased and he leaned against the wall for support, his eyes just now fluttering open. "Hey!" he slurred into the mouthpiece. "You realize I got a fire here? What do you want?" Then his eyes transmitted rude reality to his brain like a slap from a wet towel. Bedding trailed across the floor from the couch three feet away, where he now remembered he'd spent the night after another of Carrie's tongue-attacks. The last fleeting image of his faltering De Havilland evaporated from his consciousness as his breathing slowed and his grip on the earpiece relaxed. He turned his back to the wall, as the living room became much more a part of his actual world. *Okay. Another last mission dream.*

"You got a fire?" Sam sounded as much annoyed as concerned. "You mean the house?"

"No, no. Forget it. You woke me up. I was just dreaming. There's no fire." Jack shook off the twisted corner of the sheet that had wrapped itself around his foot. "What going on?"

"Plenty. Some young squirts up around Cleveland are gonna try to break the record with a plane of their own day after tomorrow."

Jack yawned. "What time is it?"

"Three o'clock. Shontz just called us. He got the dope on these Cleveland guys at some party in Detroit. One of the bankers picking up the tab for these fellows apparently can't hold his gin. He started spilling their plans all over the place. Shontz said the information's less than an hour old, so we still got a chance."

"Still got a chance? What do you mean, Sam?"

"Jack, are you awake yet?"

"Yeah."

"Good, then listen. They've got the same engine and supercharger we have. So it's a good chance they may come up with around the same top speed as we will. But if we get that speed first, *we've* set the record and these boomers'll just have to go back to the drawing board and figure out a way to top it by at least seven miles per hour. But that could take months... or years. But whatever they do, *we've* got the record and *we'll* reap the rewards. You get it?"

"Yeah. I got it."

"But we've got to do this today. We're waking everybody in the crew so's we can get our beast ready before dawn. So wake up partner! You're going to make history this morning!"

"This morning? I haven't even taxied this thing yet, let alone fly it!"

Sam sighed. "Jack. This may be our only chance. What we do today, we'll live with the rest of our lives."

"You and Ernie'll talk me through it before takeoff?"

"You bet your life."

"I wish you'd find another way to say that."

"You're going to be great, neighbor! Now, take your time. Just be here in an hour and a half."

"Right." Jack rotated his shoulders, causing something to pop. "Good-bye."

He heard Carrie moan in the bedroom, then he noticed the knotted bedding stretched out across the floor. *Right. First things first. Coffee!*

*

Carrie thought she heard the phone ring earlier, but hadn't wanted to surface yet from sleep's soothing well. In her slumbering consciousness, she stood on the long strip of sandy beach just below the cliffs of her family's estate, and Arthur's arms were wrapped about her as protection against a mild Pacific breeze. Everything felt perfect, the sunset, the seagulls' mewing, and…a metallic clanking. *No, wait.* The sound of the surf, and…a metal-to-metal grating. *No! What is that?* Then came the muted bang, and everything she wanted so much to savor disappeared. *Oh, no! I'm waking up!* For an instant a surge of loss flooded through her. After all, she'd been dragged from *someplace* she did not want to leave to a time and *place* she wished she'd already left. But that thought soon transformed itself into a nagging itch of guilt with that often annoying small internal voice telling her she'd also been *someplace* she should *not* have.

She pulled the quilt from over her face and raised up on one elbow. Faltering fingers fumbled the nightstand lamp to life and raised the alarm clock to slotted eyes. *Three-thirty.* She turned her head toward the window. *Still dark.* A drawer scraped shut in the kitchen, and the faucet there released several seconds-worth of water-sound. She grimaced. *It's Jack.*

Carrie unraveled herself from her bedclothes and shuffled through the living room to the kitchen doorway. And there Jack stood, his flight jacket open in front, next to the cook-stove sipping coffee. She yawned herself into the room and slipped into the robe she'd grabbed from her dresser. "What are you doing?"

Jack topped his cup off from the coffee pot and gave Carrie a cursory glance. "Sam called. Somebody else is going to try to break the airspeed record day after tomorrow. So we have to get the Caroline ready for her record attempt today."

Carrie blinked at the ceiling where the kitchen light tormented her from its inverted perch. "You named *this* plane the Caroline, also? That makes three. Aren't you tired of that name yet?"

Jack emptied a teaspoon of sugar into his cup. "No. It's a lucky name for me, and, since I'm going to fly her, she's going to be Caroline."

She settled onto a chair. *It's too early for this.* "You didn't tell me you were going to fly this thing."

He opened the icebox and emptied a dash of milk into his coffee. "Yes, I did, but you were busy telling me you wanted to take a day trip by yourself to the coast to break the monotony." He closed the thick wooden door, returned to his spoon, and stirred. "I guess you forgot what I said,"

"I thought Sam was going to fly."

"No."

She frowned. "But you've never flown this kind of plane before. It's so loud, I can hear it all the way to the inn. It's too big, too powerful, and it goes too fast. I don't want you killing yourself." *Strange. I really don't.*

"Thanks for the vote of confidence." He drank half the cup without a breath.

"Jack." She set her elbows onto the kitchen table and rested her head in the palm of one hand. "You flew an old lumbering bomber. You told me all about it. You didn't even like fighters, let alone fly one."

"She's not a fighter." Jack finished the other half of his coffee and set the cup in the sink.

Oh, no. He's got me into my full-daytime, problem-solving personality. I'm waking up even more, and I'll never get back to sleep now. I don't like waking up like this! "You've always said you don't like aerobatics. You hate flying upside down."

He ran some water into the cup and ambled into the living room. "Hopefully, I won't be upside-down today. The idea is to stay right-side-up and fly very fast."

Carrie rose and followed. "You mean faster than anyone's ever flown before, don't you?"

"Yes." His arm slid through the strap of his flight bag and hoisted it to his shoulder.

"Darn it, Jack!" She snatched her slippers from the bedroom and slid into them. *Has he lost his mind?* "You're not that kind of man!" *There, I've finally said it.* "Sure, everyone likes you, but you're simply not the kind of man who breaks records. That takes someone with lightning reflexes, gallons of common sense, and absolute confidence in his own decisions." She leaned on the wall with her right hand and placed her other on her hip. "Does that sound like you? Be reasonable! I don't even think Sam can pull it off."

"No, he can't. He's been drinking too long, and, by his own admission, he's gotten too slow." Jack turned and trudged through the mud hall to the front door.

Carrie found herself being drawn into the hall after him. "You need to hire a qualified racing pilot, or, at least, someone who has flown fighters and isn't too old." *Or even better, give up this whole lunatic project.*

He opened the door, then sighed and turned around. "No." He let the bag slide off to the floor. "It has been offered to *me*. Maybe it was luck." He paused and glanced at the bag. "Maybe it was God. I don't know. But, whatever it was, it has come to me, and I'm not going to walk away from it this time. So because it's come to me, I'm going to fly the record attempt today."

Carrie came halfway to the door. "Then you're stupid." *I'm sorry, Jack. I never wanted to say that. Why did I say it? I don't really believe that. I'll just say I didn't mean it.* But the words got stubborn on their way from her mind to her mouth and wouldn't come out.

"Stupid? Maybe." He reshouldered the flight bag and went out into the dark yard.

Carrie hurried out onto the porch. "You're not the man to do this!"

The squeak of the truck's door and the sound of Jack's bag hitting the passenger seat echoed off the trees. "*Today, I am.*"

She heard him jerk the Model-T's crank, but the engine didn't catch. "If you're trying to impress the boys," she said, "don't bother. You're already their hero. They'll love you, no matter what you do."

Jack cranked the truck again. This time it chattered and came to life. After a minute, the headlights ignited, poking two holes into the dark shadows beyond the reach of the front doorway's dim beam. Then the pickup performed a two point turn-around, and Jack drove up the driveway's hump and down the road toward town.

Carrie stood watching for a while. *What are we doing, Jack? Are we both going crazy?*

♪

"It's almost dawn." Sam grimaced through a grimy number two hangar office window at the dark ridgeline, now silhouetted against an advancing orange glow. "We should get this contraption ready so you can take off at first light."

Jack leaned against the corrugated steel wall that separated the office from the hangar bay. He'd been taking peeks through the doorway, watching Ernie buzz around the Caroline in the dingy light of six bare electric bulbs. The whole show amazed him. A dozen or so mechanics and apprentices scurried about the plane like mad mice bent upon the ingestion of a wedge of cheddar, except this bunch's job went far beyond just consuming cheese. This morning, they had come to help change the aviation record books. Channel-lock pliers clinked and socket wrenches sang their metallic muttering song as bolts and screws surrendered themselves to be secured into their proper places in the universe.

Jack took a deep breath and held it a couple of seconds. *I can't believe this is all happening. All this*

597

preparation, all this expense...so that I can climb into the cockpit and try not to make a fool of myself.

Cal, the faithful airmail mechanic, poked his head out from under the lower left wing. He raised his hands in surrender. "I can't find anything sticking out anywhere."

Ernie looked up from an armful of half-rolled blueprints. "Well, then go over it all again. The slightest protrusion in the skin could cost us two miles per hour or more." He stared at some detail on one of the diagrams, drawing his face closer to the paper. Then, pulling on one side of his mustache, he pursed his lips. "Danny!" He swiveled his head until he found the man to fit the name. "Did you check the fuel for condensation?"

A large-boned fellow in overalls and a backward snap-brim cap raised his head from behind an open engine cowling. "Not yet, boss. I've been running the electrical checks."

"Are you almost finished?"

"Yeah."

"All right, then. As soon as you're done there, drain some fuel. We can't have water in the tanks today."

"Sure thing, boss." The hat disappeared behind the cowling again.

Jack felt a tingle run up his neck and into his cheeks. Circumstances alone had put him in the pilot's seat today, despite his complete lack of experience with high-performance aircraft. Yet, nonetheless, he felt the same as if all this effort were for him personally rather than for the enterprise of the speed record attempt in a generic sense. It almost seemed, at the moment, that all these men working at a desperate pace to finish their tasks before the night's end were akin to medieval squires, readying their knight's steed and armor for battle. Mild humiliation surfaced again as Jack dealt with the self-indulgence of that image.

Then the old internal argument began anew as Jack stepped over the threshold from the office into the hangar bay itself. He crossed his arms and leaned back against the wall. At this point, his inner debate began, like it always had, as a struggle between the two differing self-appraisals. *I'm not worthy of all this. I don't fit the requirements.* Then a current of indignation shot along the pathways of Jack's mind. *What are you talking about? You can do this as well as anyone...maybe better! You're not going to get me to swallow that old inferiority garbage. Don't give the arrogant snobs that have tried to feed you that lie the satisfaction of knowing they've caused you to doubt yourself! Not any of them, not the great Albert Van Burean, not your father...not even Carrie...especially not Carrie.* On the tail of this last expression, he felt the strong fingers of an iron will enclose the mad, beclawed bats that whizzed around inside his stomach, so that the bats and the iron existed together in a sort of standoff. Then a strange feeling of comfort settled onto Jack as a result of this odd *bats-and-iron* coexistence. It's what he always did when he had to deal with something that dragged him beyond what he thought he could accomplish. *Sniveling coward with a* very *temporary steel determination, that's me. If I'm lucky, I won't throw up my coffee before I finish all this.*

"We've got a reporter outside from Los Angeles. Another's on his way here from Palmdale, not to mention old Norman from the Sweet Springs Bugle." Sam hung up the office phone. "But none of them have time to run any advance stories. Everything just happened too fast. Sorry, neighbor. No cheering crowd today. Just three guys with cameras. And, in Norman's case, it'll probably be a little Kodak Box Camera. Say, cheese." Sam clicked an imaginary photograph. Then he glanced back out the window. "Getting lighter. Won't be long now." A smile flashed from one ear to the other as he winked.

The largest fanged bat in Jack's stomach bit down hard, causing its host to grimace as he faked a return smile to Sam. The preparations around the Caroline had become a blur of activities and echoes, a fitting backdrop upon which a condemned chief pilot could project his last ruminations. *My first dirt races were like this, all worry and stomach bats. The cars were unreliable, the engines were louder than thunder, and everything was just a little too real to allow a man's senses to settle down. Nerves were always up on the ceiling.*

Through the eyes of his memory, he saw the rough-graded dirt track flash by the sides of his old racer. He even felt the centrifugal tug of the curve for an instant and recalled his determination to win races against opponents who fought like savages to take the prize for themselves. Then came the first time he *did* take first place. *Nothing like it! Worth every risk, every moment of fear, and then some. But I can't see my competitors now like I could then. They're not all around me, pushing for the inside position...eyes on the finish line. I just know they're out there somewhere, trying to break the record before I do. It's easier when you can see them. Gives you something to strive against.*

"No condensation in any tank, boss." The mechanic stood, wiping gasoline stained hands with a red grease-rag.

Ernie nodded. "Good. Then take the pitot covers off, and, after that, make sure all controls have free travel." He rolled all the schematics up and pushed them into a metal tube. "Calvin, where are you?"

"Right here." Cal flopped up, a screwdriver in one hand a socket-wrench in the other..

"Oil topped off?"

"Check."

"Windscreen clean?"

"Like a whistle."

Ernie massaged his chin between his thumb and forefinger. "Magnetos?"

"Brand new, both of 'em."

The engineer sighed and closed the cap on the schematic tube. "All that's done. Good. Then go find something that isn't done and do it."

"Right."

Jack heard the hiss of a fresh-struck match in the office and smelled Sam firing up a new cigar behind him. For a split second he wished he smoked, too. *Always heard it calms the nerves. That sounds good right now.* He remembered many of the pilots in his old squadron smoked, especially when they huddled around the briefing shack's pot-bellied stove on cold, dark mornings as they waited for the final confirmation of the day's target. Some would consume two or three cigarettes in a row, lighting one off another, looking out the window toward the east much like Sam had been doing this morning, waiting for a sadistic sun to lift itself over the horizon.

"Somebody get some more air into those tires! They're half flat. For crying out loud, gentlemen, do I have to tell you everything?" Ernie glanced at the big wall clock that hung over the office door. "Am I the only one that notices anything around here?"

Someone pulled a chain-fall through its crossbeam pulley with an ear-shattering half-clank-half-screech, and at the far corner of the hangar, a man began tossing wrenches into a greasy wooden drawer with the abandon that comes around the twenty-third hour of sleep deprivation.

"Clean her up now." Ernie rolled his sleeves up another full roll past his elbows then straightened his glasses. "Dirt steals speed. We don't want to lose to the Cleveland boys because we have a filthy airplane."

As one man, the hangar army descended upon the gleaming orange biplane with clean rags and brushes. Each began washing, scrubbing, rubbing, or buffing according to his assigned area of responsibility. One sopped an oil drizzle from the engine cowling; another wiped a gasoline stain off the fuselage near the fuel tank. All busied themselves at a frantic pace like bees around a honeycomb.

Ernie seated himself on a tall stepladder and checked completed tasks off a clipboard list. It seemed to Jack the man virtually hovered above the center of the clanking, ratcheting din, pointing and waving his arms like a philharmonic conductor during the crescendo of some classical overture. "Calvin, pull those chalks out of the way. Mr. Jeremiah, have you accounted for all the hand tools? We don't want anything sliding around during Mr. MacGregor's run, now do we? By the way, Franklin, are all rotating bolts and fasteners safety-wired?"

Jack reached around the corner into the office and retrieved the last of a half-consumed cup of black coffee from the desk nearest the door. *I guess this is really going to happen...with one result or another. Just like the dirt track races... or like morning missions in France. I'll either win or lose. Either I'll come back or I won't. That's all there is to it.* He rolled the warm metal cup back and forth in his hands. *I could foul up, make a big fool of myself.* He almost laughed, but his throat had clenched too tight for that. *Make a fool out of myself...yeah, that could happen.*

He took a small sip and hoped the caffeine wouldn't anger the bats too much. He decided to give the creatures some air and took a deep breath. The offering worked and they slowed down the rate and ferocity of their gnawing. Then the recollection of Carrie's laughter rang in his ears as he surveyed the Caroline's massive liquid-cooled engine. "You're not the man for this, Jack." *Isn't that what she'd said? Not the man. Someone else. Another pilot. A real pilot she meant, right? Anyone else. Just not me.*

"Sun's up! Canyon's brighter n' my nose on Saturday night." Sam knocked the fire off his cigar, leaving both glowing cherry and stub laying in the ash tray. Then he made it across the office in three strides and leaned out the open doorway past Jack. "Hey, Ernie!"

The maestro looked up from his clipboard. "Yes?"

"Is that skyrocket ready to roll or not?"

The potentate on the stepladder gave his checklist a cursory glance then surveyed the scene around the Caroline. "Uh, yes." He paused and nodded. "Yes, she is ready."

Sam turned to Jack. "You got your spurs on, neighbor?"

"Yes." A bat's claw snagged Jack's stomach right behind the navel. "I'm ready."

"Then let's drag the dragon out of the cave." He raised both eyebrows and stepped out of the doorway into the hangar bay. "Push her outside. Day's a wastin'."

"All right, gentlemen." Ernie descended the ladder and tossed the clipboard onto a workbench. "You heard Mr. Smith." He took stock of the hangar one last time. "You all know what you can and can't push on. Be mindful of the control surfaces and any unbraced fabric. Let's get four of you on the hangar doors right now." Ernie's orchestra fell to the work at hand with practiced rhythm. The bespectacled conductor rubbed his hands together and walked toward Jack and Sam. He flashed a quick grin, then returned to his usual serious demeanor.

"Now listen to me," he said to Jack as he, without necessity, repositioned his glasses for the umpteenth time. "This X-type Packard has twenty-four cylinders, so it's going to be more nose heavy than you expect."

Six men took position at the wing struts and fuselage. Sam shut off the power to the inside lights, plunging the place into semi-darkness. "Pull those doors back," he yelled, and the metallic creak of rusty rollers traveling over sand-coated rail echoed off corrugated steel walls. A blade of blinding white light split the gloom, then widened at the pace of the men who pushed the doors back until the view of the sun-drenched taxiway filled a rectangle two-thirds the width of the building. Everyone stood still for a full three seconds, awed by the sight of orange wings seeming to burn with the rising sun.

Sam came out of the spell first. "Well, don't just stand there! Roll her out!"

The crew pushed the biplane from the semi-gloom out into an already lukewarm summer morning with a reverence that demanded such silence one could hear the sand particles crunch between the tires and the pavement. Jack, Sam, and Ernie followed close behind, adding to the feeling that this was a morning that required a little touch of sacred ceremony to mark its passing.

Jack found himself almost able to maintain a subdued outer demeanor, but inside his senses remained under intense assault by the tension of the moment. In the end, the best he could do was clench his teeth and keep his breathing at an even cadence. Then, against the unction of his fears, he fixed his gaze on the plane into which he would soon strap himself. *Geeze, she's beautiful...in a foreboding sort of way.*

Ernie cleared his throat. "Right. So you'll be nose heavy. That means you'll need more back pressure on the stick and more runway before you get off."

Jack rubbed the back of his neck. It had begun to stiffen again, as it often did at times like this. *Engine looks a lot bigger out here. And, just like the Ryan, this ship also looks like she's crouching... like she could just sort of leap into the air and take off without me.* The two most aggressive bats in Jack's stomach began a battle to the death. He crossed his arms over his chest as he walked to hide the minor trembling. "Nose heavy," he said. "More runway. Got it." *OK, Lord. I don't know why you let my life with Carrie go sour, and I know I've pushed you away when you threw me into the rail-yard. But I need you now. I don't think I can do this. I'm either going to end up looking stupid, or I'm going to crack this ship up. If you really care, help me. Please.*

The crew turned the Caroline toward the west end of the airfield which lay across the road from town. The windsock atop the airmail hangar told of a westbound wind. This morning's takeoff would be to the east. The first record run would be to the west, also because of the wind.

As the trio caught up with the plane, Sam leaned close to Jack and spoke in a barely audible tone. "You can do this, partner. You're the man for it. I swear by the hair on my mother-in-law's warts you are."

Jack felt Sam's elbow between his ribs and heard his chuckle. The evil bats remained, but a pinhole of light appeared at the far end of Jack's darkness.

"What's that?" Ernie had the look of a man thinking too many thoughts at once. "What'd you say?"

"I was just telling old Jack here that if he fouls up today we can always use what's left of the ship as a geranium planter."

"I see." Ernie looked anything but amused. "As I was saying, this engine has 1,250 horsepower at 2,750 RPM...exactly. It's going to exert a lot of torque. So get ready to feed in enough aileron to prevent a slow roll...especially right after you break ground on takeoff."

Jack's pinhole of light grew to peephole size, and the sensation of bat combat became mixed with a teaspoon of excited anticipation. *Can I pull this off? Maybe? But pay attention now.* "Torque, opposite aileron on takeoff. All right." Sunlight glinted off the Caroline's polished steel propeller. With the tail down and the nose tilted skyward it made Jack think of some sort of challenge to the sky or maybe even the laws of physics. *Faster than anyone's flown before.* His heart rate picked up a little.

"I was able to get off the ground at 100 miles per hour. But you'll be carrying more fuel, so your takeoff speed might be a bit faster." Ernie ran his hand along the top-left wing and studied its surface for a moment. "You know these wings are a lot shorter than what you're used to. It's going to feel oversensitive and prone to high-speed stalls, so watch her in the turns. Try to keep your banks as shallow as you can without drifting halfway to San Francisco. You don't want her to just quit flying all of a sudden. And that could happen if you turn her too tight. You could become a speeding, propeller-driven rock very quickly."

That's encouraging. Jack began his walk-around inspection, checking everything from oil line to rudder. *Am I missing something? What am I not checking that could kill me?*

Ernie poked at a patch in the drum-tight doped wing fabric. "Now, for the main event. Airspeed. We need you to try to get up to at least 326 or 327. That'll give us that seven mile-per-hour margin over the Italian record from earlier this year. I can't stress this enough. We need at least that seven miles-per-hour, or it won't be an official record." Ernie gave the sky one cursive glance. "There's a rumor that old Charles Kirkham has scrounged up enough money to put that racer of his through its paces and set an *unofficial* record of 322 or thereabouts. I don't know why he'd waste the money on an unofficial record, but there it is. And, like I said, it's only a rumor. But if you can get 326, Kirkham'll still need another seven miles per hour, and that'll send *him* back to the drawing board and the money-lenders, as well." He whipped out his handkerchief and rubbed at an oily thumbprint near the cockpit. "But remember, at full power, you've only got twenty-seven minutes to fly one pass each direction between the timer pylons. After that, the engine will start eating itself up from the inside. And I don't mean just metal filings in the oil. I'm talking about pistons departing through the engine block. Do you understand?"

"I understand very well." Jack put one booted foot onto the metal step inset into the left side of the fuselage and swung himself up into the cockpit. He looked to Sam who stood out by the wingtips, his arms folded. "You ever notice we mount up on the left? Same as the cavalry."

Sam cocked his head. "Just a different kind of horse, brother." He drew closer to the plane. "Sorry there's no adoring throng to see you off to your doom." He inserted a fresh Havana between his teeth, but left it unlit. "But if I'm not mistaken there may be…" Sam shaded his eyes and scanned the grass along the taxiway. "Aha. Just as I thought. Look straight down there, neighbor." He pointed around the biplane's skyward cocked nose. "There's a sight for your sore eyes."

Jack leaned around the massive Packard powerplant and squinted against the indirect morning light as he locked his safety belt into place. "What are you…" *Alma.* She stood next to the taxiway, facing Jack, her feet together, arms at her side. A gentle morning breeze ruffled her skirt and toyed with her golden bangs. *She's a vision. No denying it.* A vision that, at once, Jack did and did not need.

Sam leaned in. "The Lakeview supplied the sandwiches and coffee for our crew last night. Some of these guys haven't slept since yesterday." He winked. "Neither has Alma. She asked me about your takeoff time when she delivered the last batch." The cigar bobbed as he chewed the end. "Who am I to stand in Cupid's path?" He slapped Jack on the shoulder. "See you when you get back." Sam stepped away, clear of the wings.

"Let's hope so." Ernie followed Sam's example then fixed his usual worried stare upon the orange cowling around the giant Packard engine.

Jack pulled the leather helmet from inside his jacket and slid it over his head, leaving the attached goggles perched just above his forehead. No flying suit or parachute this morning—too much weight. Then he applied toe-pressure to both rudder-peddle brakes. "Calvin?" He leaned out on the right side of the cockpit.

"Right here." Cal peeked out from around the plane's big orange nose.

"Prop her for me, will you?" Jack pumped some priming fuel into the engine and set the throttle.

"Sure thing." Cal paused a moment. "Switch off?"

Jack pressed a finger against the red-painted switch on the dash, making sure it rested full against its off position stop. "Switch off."

Cal stepped up to the prop that stood almost two feet taller than he. He grasped the raised blade to his left and forced it down until it rocked to a stop on the opposite side of the engine. Then he did it again with the other blade and stepped back. "Clear."

Jack leaned around the cowling. "Clear." He flicked the red switch to its hot position and leaned out again. "Contact."

Cal stepped up to the prop. "Contact." He raised one leg straight out in front and took a firm two-handed grip on the uphill blade. A moment passed while Cal took a deep breath, then he pulled the blade down with as much force as could be mustered and backed away by swinging his foot to the rear, rocking back onto it and following it with his other leg. This brought his whole body to a standing stop a safe long step from the Caroline's nose.

The Packard sputtered once, emitted a small gasp of smoky exhaust then died.

"Could it be the mixture," Sam yelled.

"No, leave the mixture alone," Ernie countered. "I set it myself. Probably some settled oil. Just crank it again."

Jack leaned around to Cal's side again. "All right, Cal. Switch off."

They went through the ritual twice more; then, at last, on the third propping, fuel ignited inside the cylinders and the engine roared to life. Everyone standing nearby backed up, some covering their ears with their hands.

A mild shock ran up Jack's spine as he grasped the throttle and eased the beast on the other side of the firewall into idling submission. After lifting the flaps of his helmet and twisting a tuft of cotton into each ear, he slipped his fingers into calfskin gloves and started crosschecking the instruments. *RPM's steady. Manifold pressure's coming up. Everything's in the green.* He turned to Sam and Ernie and raised a leather-covered thumb next to his Cheshire Cat grin. They returned the gesture.

Everyone in the crew waved for Jack to start down the dirt taxiway. He scanned around the Caroline one last time, released pressure from the brakes, then pushed the throttle forward, loosening the leash of the beast just enough to start the airplane moving. Everything rattled violently until the engine reached the smooth level it sought. At that point, the tumultuous shaking replaced itself with more of a guttural purr synchronized by a sort of washing-machine rhythm. As he S-turned from one side of the sandy lane to the other, always looking around the raised nose and through the spinning disc of the prop, he marveled at how relatively subdued the engine noise seemed from inside the cockpit, compared to when one stands nearby outside. *More tolerable when you're in the dragon's belly.* Of course, it didn't hurt to have cotton in his ears, either.

Another careful swerve and he caught sight of faithful little Alma. *What are you doing here?* He stepped on the right rudder-peddle and lost her slender body in the early morning gleam of the orange airframe. *I'm not the hero you think I am. Good grief, lady, can't you tell when someone's barely holding on?* Jack let go a microscopic sigh. *Yeah, you probably see it. But you honor me anyway.* He shook his head as he reached the dry grass on the right and kicked left rudder to swing back. And there she was again, but closer now.

Her usual print dress blew to one side with the morning wind as did her wavy blond tresses. Her feet remained together as if she were reporting for the first day of school. Tall tufts of foxtails hid her shoes, but Jack knew without seeing them that they would be simple yet attractive, much like their owner. She hoisted a timid wave as the Caroline drew near, not characteristic of her at all. And her expression lacked its usual confident smile. In its place hung a subdued look that revealed a certain degree of joy yet almost approached reverence. *Geeze, Alma! I'm neither the pope nor the president.* He waved as she blew him two handfuls of kisses and wiped her face as the dust overtook her. Jack kicked opposite rudder as she passed behind him. *Was she crying? Oh boy. Like I said, little girl, I'm not what you think. I'm just a bum who's going to crash an expensive airplane.*

But, all the same, he liked her being there. True, he'd rather it were Carrie. But, if his wife did not care to see him off to whatever was about to happen, perhaps this woman was the one who should be waving a heartfelt *bon voyage.*

Jack mentally shook himself. *Not the time for this. Concentrate on this airplane, or it'll eat you for sure.* He went back to his crosscheck. *RPM, manifold pressure, cylinder head temperature. All still in the green.* Another S-turn. *Got to see where we're going. Whose idea was it to design airplanes that have their tail on the ground and their nose in the air, anyway? Why can't they put the tail-wheel under the nose so I can see where I'm going?* He swung around at the end of the taxiway so the nose of the plane faced the runway. *Tail-wheel under the nose. Huh. Naw, that wouldn't work. Prop's too big. Thing would prang into the ground if the nose was level.*

He took out his old silk scarf and wrapped it around his neck, tucking the loose ends inside his leather jacket. His hands pulled the waiting goggles down over eyes that now blinked with the oblique light from the rising sun to his left. *All right, Jack old boy, time for the run up. Let's see if this high-priced outboard motor wants to blow up on take-off.*

He slid the toes of his boots forward onto the pedal-brakes again and straightened his knees until his buttocks almost lifted from the seat. Then, pushing the throttle forward, Jack watched the tachometer needle move around its dial as the engine resumed another deafening rattle and strained to overcome the brakes. *So...there's 2,000 RPM's. 2,500. 2,700...and 2,750. Now we'll see how you do on right mag only.* He switched the magneto selector to 'R'. *Yep, old Mr. Tachometer seems fairly steady. Then how about a little left mag while we're at it?* He swung the selector to 'L'. *Okydoky. Same story, no significant drop in power. So maybe you won't pop a jug or throw a rod, after all.* He centered the selector onto 'Both' and settled the throttle back down to taxi power.

A quick visual check straight up, then left and right told Jack he had a clear runway. *No company coming. So, let's see what'cha got, big girl.* Jack released the brakes and taxied out onto the runway, applying first the left brake to turn tight-left, then slight pressure on both once more when he'd gotten his steed pointed straight down the center of the clear dirt path in front of him. Now he felt the annoying vibration again, just like when he'd increased power when he'd first started to taxi back by the hangers. *Well, that shouldn't be; we're just above idle now. Is something coming unglued?* His gaze swept the instruments again and checked the cockpit for anything loose. *Nothing.* Then he noticed his hand shaking on the throttle and realized that his whole body was doing the same. The mystery vibration had been the result of Jack and his piano-wire nerves. *Oh, Lord.* He shook out his hands in an attempt to curtail the tremors. *Lord. Uh....* He flexed both hands then laid them back on the controls. *Oh, you know. Please, help me to not crack this thing up. Amen.*

At that moment, Sam's words drifted back. "You're the man for this."

Jack glanced upward out of instinct. "Thanks, Father." He nodded to the sky and took the deepest breath of his life. *Time to put the spurs to her.* He let the breath out. Off to the left, Alma waved some sort of red dishtowel. Then *in* went the throttle all the way to the firewall, and *off* went the brakes. Frustrated at being earthbound too long, the beast with the power of 1,250 horses roared out into the dry desert dawn. "Let me go!" the Caroline screamed to Jack's imagination, then she began her long-awaited roll down the scraped granite runway of Sweet Springs Airfield.

Jack felt like a rock being pulled back in a slingshot, as the initial part of the takeoff roll pressed him lightly into the seat. Then speed seemed to double as the prop got a better bite on the dry atmosphere. Next, the tail rose from the ground as the air rushing past it increased its velocity and provided sufficient lift. Hangars flashed by Jack's left periphery. That's when the takeoff became something different.

By now, the pressure holding Jack against the seat had increased several fold, pushing him through the padding to where he could feel the rivets of the seat frame. *Oh-my-God!* Rudder control proved very touchy at this point. Jack found himself already working hard on the pedals, trying to keep Caroline heading straight down the imaginary centerline. The biplane bounced several times on its main landing gears but refused to fly, even though her airspeed indicator read 100 miles per hour. The parked fuel truck sped past on the right. Very little runway remained.

With the tail airborne, Caroline's nose aimed almost level to where Jack could see straight ahead. He had an excellent view of the advancing dry lake-bed and the rude rock-strewn hill that squatted just beyond, not to mention the cottonwood trees that waved, sixty feet tall, in front of it—all getting bigger and bigger in the windscreen as each micro-second passed. *You'd better lift your skirts soon, old girl, or this is going to be a very brief flight.* Just then

Jack's battling bats found themselves pulled to the bottom of his stomach as Caroline did indeed rise from the runway, with a good hundred feet remaining to the plane-hungry hill.

But as soon as the wheels became airborne, the left wings dipped sharply, forcing Jack to pull the joystick hard to the right to avoid hooking into the ground. *That was close!* His hand shook a little on the control. *And stupid, too. Ernie said keep right aileron!* He sighed. *All right. We survived my official big stupid mistake. It's got to get better from here.* He eased the stick back as far as he could but, this time, remembered to keep it slightly to the right. Caroline stood on her tail and shot up to 500 feet above ground level before Jack could react and level out.

It took a second before he caught his breath. "Oh, son of a gun! That's just...that's..." He swallowed. "Wow!" A peal of near-insane laughter leapt from Jack's throat. "Wow!" Another breath. "Carrie, that was some skirt lifting!" He reached out and patted the fuselage. "Yes, ma'am. Yes indeed!" He banked around back toward the airfield and spotted the crew just now running toward the row of parked vehicles near the taxiway. "Oh, this is too good to keep all to myself." He dropped the nose into a moderate dive, and aimed toward the near end of the taxiway. "Sorry, Ernie."

Staying at full throttle and still holding the stick off to the right, Jack leveled out of the dive less than a half wingspan from the ground. Then, with the exhaust stack thundering its challenge against the outside of the hangar walls, he spurred his craft just above the taxiway, waving at the crew and Alma. The waitress sprang up and down, clapping her hands before she disappeared from view.

Jack took stock of the airspeed indicator. *Better than 200 just from a shallow dive. I can't wait to see what she'll do if I come barreling down from say 6,000.* He pulled up just short of the Bull Moose, cranked the plane into a tight

180 degree turn, and checked the crew's progress. *Heading to the timer pylons. Good. They should be there by the time we climb up to six grand.* He pulled back on the joystick and aimed the prop at the pale daytime moon that hung about fifteen degrees short of straight up. The elusion that Caroline could actually make that destination settled onto Jack's imagination for a moment and made the morning even more electric than it had been a second before.

The altimeter wound past four thousand in less than thirty seconds, giving Jack 1,000 feet of clearance above the airfield's 3,000 foot elevation. The bats in his stomach decided to stop their commotion and a warm expectant feeling spread through his body. He caressed the padded rim of the cockpit. *Ah, sweet Carrie, if you could only cook.*

He broke through 6,000 feet above mean sea level about a minute later, leveled off, and pulled the throttle back to cruise RPM. Next he started a lazy circle south of the airfield. An antlike row of vehicles flanked each pylon. Jack smiled. *They're already waiting.* Then the bats started in again. *Lord, help me do this right.*

One final check on the wind over the airfield brought a last minute surprise. Although Jack couldn't quite make out the position of the windsock, he spied the telltale smoke trail from the potbelly stovepipe of the Lakeview Café. *Whoa. Winds done a complete 180 since takeoff. Now she's the exact opposite direction from what she was when I took off. Well, that's easy to fix.* A quick but cautious dip of the left wings brought the plane about and lined it up for the northbound run. A moment's hesitation and a few quick breaths followed. This would be it. He'd either foul up or he'd make it. Jack swallowed a little harder than normal. *Then, let's get it over with.*

Forward pressure on the stick dropped the nose so steep it almost had Jack standing on the pedals. Then he shoved the throttle full forward. Engine RPM's leaped to 2,750, just short of the tachometer's redline. Airspeed 240 miles per hour. The Altimeter had already unraveled to just over 4,000 feet. *Always quicker going down.*

At first, the struts simply whistled as air raced around them at 260 miles per hour. Jack could feel the slipstream tug at his goggles whenever he leaned around the dashboard to check his position. But when the airspeed reached 300, the wings literally screamed, tortured by the wind's savage assault. The atmosphere's mad rush threatened to tear the helmet from the pilot's head. At 310 and somewhere around 500 feet from the ground—the altimeter needle could not keep up with the descent—the Caroline began buffeting, first a little, then increasing until it reached a state of almost wild abandon. Jack pulled back on the joystick as the ground loomed larger and time grew short. But the stick resisted as if it were welded in place. *Too much air pressure over the elevators! God... help...now!*

He tried again with only a small budge for his effort. 315 miles per hour. Another backward strain, with Jack yelling this time and with some joint somewhere in his body popping. He didn't hear the pop but felt it like the dickens. The signal flare shed sitting at the end of the taxiway grew bigger. The nose began to lift away from the ground like an old man rising from his bed. *Come on, Carrie! This isn't good enough. We're going to hit. Lift your nose like the snob you are!* But there was no response to Jack's back-pressure on the joystick, and the red flare-shed looked much larger now. There remained only one thing to do, and Jack did it instinctively in the final moment when death was certain. "O-o-o-o-h, Je-e-e-e-su-u-u-u-s!"

Then, in a little less than a second—but what seemed like a year—the Caroline *did* pull out of her desperate dive to level flight a little more than fifty feet from the earth. While her pilot's vision tunneled to near blackout status, she hurtled on a near perfect course toward the south pylon. Her throttle remained full forward against the stops, and

615

she easily transferred all the kinetic energy from her high-altitude dive into even more speed. First, even before his vision cleared, Jack heard the noise of the engine echoing off the ground, then came the voice. "Feed in right stick again. Do it now, or you'll roll into the ground." Jack followed orders before his logic had a chance to remind him that he sat in a single place airplane. But he knew it had been the right thing to do, and decided he must have given himself a subconscious reminder.

The first pylon raced closer. Jack checked his airspeed, but the needle bounced with such erratic fervor that he could only be sure that it stayed somewhere over 300, give or take 100 miles per hour. *Great! Thing's useless right when I want it. Well, so what. We'll just race like a scalded cat and see what happens.*

Pylon number one, the start of the timed run, flashed beneath. Jack leaned around the engine and peered through the spinning prop disc at the far end of the lakebed. The sun glared off the glass panes of his goggles, obscuring his view of the course. He leaned out the other side of the cockpit into the shadow of the top wing, and the glare stopped. *There it is—pylon number two. We're headed right for it, Carrie. Now give it everything you've got. Ernie said we need 326 miles per hour to beat the Italians. So let's give him 327.*

The ground became a blur of brown, tan, and gray as the Caroline ate up the distance over the lakebed to the north pylon. The separation to the course's end diminished so fast, the pylon seemed to grow in height like some mythical beanstalk, reaching for the sky. *A little farther.* A crosswind struck the biplane full broadside and raised the right wings. Jack felt the chain reaction of instability run through the stubby control surfaces trying to push him off the course's centerline or throw him and the plane into the ground altogether. His grip tightened as he compensated.

Right rudder. More aileron. Ah, Got you under control. Steady now. Almost there.

Then finally, the north pylon streaked by underneath just like the southern one had done. Jack eased the stick aft—with less abruptness this time—and let the prop follow its instinct home to 6,000 feet again. It took less than three minutes to reach that altitude. No waiting for the ground crew this time. Jack turned his climb into a second power dive with one simple turn and some forward stick pressure.

One more time, Carrie.

He wanted to correct his first mistakes but didn't know if he could. He tried to solve the problem of stiff controls during the dive by hauling back on the stick sooner and shallowing out the dive angle. This did work with some degree of success, but at the point of leveling out, Jack once more became convinced that certain death loomed close at hand as the aircraft sank much too close to the ground before checking its descent. This again resulted in his calling out the Savior's name at the top of his lungs. The blackout effects proved less with the shallower dive, enabling him to remember to hold right stick and keep to the center of the course with less effort. Early morning thermal updrafts began midway, but proved not too difficult to handle. Now headed in the opposite direction from the first run, the Caroline stayed on course all the way past the south pylon, Jack guessing the second timed run to be the slower and less terrifying of the two. The airspeed indicator still sallied back and forth over the 300 line, but, since it stayed closer to 400 for most of the run, Jack had no doubt he'd brought Ernie home his 327 miles per hour record.

As he throttled back and pulled up gently over the airfield, he considered performing one of the victory rolls he'd seen the fighter pilots do so many times in France. He'd done rolls himself as a barnstormer. And even though aerobatics had never been something he liked much, he almost felt it would be expected after setting a new world record. Then he recalled Ernie's warning on how twitchy the biplane's controls could become during extreme maneuvers. Adding that to his own experience with the freezing joystick and having to keep in right aileron for torque compensation throughout most of the flight, Jack decided on the better part of valor and simply turned back toward the runway after passing over the town. He set himself up for a no-monkey-business southbound landing and dropped the nose for a shallow approach. The Caroline settled onto the dusty hard-baked strip without crow-hop or any other form of aerodynamic complaint. *Smooth as a baby's cheek.*

Jack let her roll out her speed without braking until he came to the north cutover to the taxiway. There he peddle-turned around a scrubby juniper that squatted as sentinel on the corner of the intersection, then he let the biplane waddle, not too far above idle RPM's toward the paved apron, brownish-gray dust taking to the breeze behind him. When he reached the hangar, he spun the plane around into the wind and killed the Packard's 1,250 horses by flicking the ignition switch to the *OFF* position. Finally, he strangled off the fuel to make sure said mechanical steeds would not revive by accident. He checked his watch. *Twenty-five minutes in the air. Two minutes short of engine blow-apart time. Not a bad day's work, little girl.* He patted the cockpit's rim again and smiled. *Not a bad day's work, at all.*

*

By the time Jack had cleaned up and stowed his gear, Alma had already gone on to work and the ground crew had become quite busy going over Caroline in the hangar. Sam, Ernie, and Cal slumped quietly in the office as Jack walked in from the washroom. No one looked at anyone else. Cal in stained overalls leaned against the wall tossing a large bolt into the air and catching it over and over. Sam blew on the tip of his cigar, watching the ashes fly off and spiral down, while Ernie stared at the ceiling, where he traced figures with his finger on some invisible tablet suspended in the air above him. His lips moved now and then as numbers and phrases flowed from brain to mouth, but he made no sound, except for an occasional *tisking* noise.

This looking-like-we're-at-a-funeral routine must be somebody's idea of a joke. Well, I'm not going to bite. "So was that fast enough for you, Ernie?"

Ernie stopped his aerial calculations but kept his gaze on the invisible tablet. "Actually, it wasn't."

"What are you talking about? That was 327 easy." *It had to be. We were going faster than Lucifer's fire brigade. I couldn't have fouled this up...could I?*

Ernie finally turned. "No. It was three-seventeen. You didn't even match the Italian record."

In the time it took to blink an eyelid, Jack went over every move, thought, instrument reading, and function he performed during the flight. Nothing stood out as an obvious cause for defeat. "All right, then. How did I foul up?"

Sam laid his stogie in the desk ashtray. "You didn't foul up. Wasn't you at all. It was the plane."

Ernie grabbed an actual pad and pencil and scribbled a few real figures. "We don't have enough power, plain and simple. The Italians set their record flying over a European lake. Very humid there...bad for engine efficiency. Shontz and I...Aaron Shontz, that is. We thought the dry air over an equally dry lake would help boost the effectiveness of our available horsepower, especially if we planned our attempt to take place in the relative coolness of early morning." He jotted something else down. "We were wrong. We simply need more power, and that's all there is to it. We need that larger engine."

Cal stopped tossing his bolt. "What kind of an engine?"

Ernie put down the pad and pencil. "Rolls-Royce makes it. It's a V-12, as opposed to our X-type twenty-four cylinder Packard, but it has a much larger super-charger. It produces 1,850 horsepower to our present 1,250. Oh, and, instead of twenty-seven minutes of flight time before it destroys itself, the Rolls-Royce engine can run at full throttle for over 100 minutes without internal damage. It's exactly the ticket we need." Ernie paused to wipe his glasses with a small cloth he produced from his shirt pocket. "I called the Shontz family with our bad news just a minute ago. They have informed me that our Cleveland competitors have now ordered an Italian eighteen cylinder, 1,800 horsepower engine. I didn't even know there was such a thing, but Shontz's brother said they were just announced this week. Apparently, they're cheaper than the Rolls, but the British engine still has fifty horsepower on the Italian. And Shontz says this new engine boasts about half the endurance time." Ernie refolded the cloth and slid it back into his pocket. "Anyway, if the Cleveland boys need a new engine, that says to me *their* recent speed trials haven't been up to snuff either. Plus, I don't think they have the financial support we do. That's why they're buying the cheaper power plant." He paused and seemed to spend a second in some other universe. "Now, they don't have that engine yet, but there's no way to know just how much time we have left."

Sam looked as if he were studying Ernie's invisible figures. "We might not need more power."

"What?" Ernie's forehead furrowed like a fresh-plowed field.

"Maybe what we need is less drag." He retrieved the Havana Corona from the ashtray and began puffing at its dying ember.

"There are no unnecessary drag surfaces on that plane." Ernie shook his head. "It's totally clean."

"Then we whack off something we thought *was* necessary." A little glow emerged from amidst the dead Cuban ash.

"Explain." Ernie folded his arms.

Ernie's confusion spread to Jack. *Yeah, what are you talking about?*

Sam's old mischievous smile peaked out at the corners of his mouth. "I've been contemplating this for a while, so don't fly off the handle. We could lop a foot off each wingtip. I'm pretty sure that would give us the break we need. Less drag, less weight, equals the same as more power." He shrugged. "Simple, don't you think?" He dispensed a quick bow of the head. "No need to weep in gratitude. Flowers thrown at my feet will do nicely, thank you."

Jack opened his mouth to protest, but Ernie beat him to it.

"This dangerous little bomb of ours is already unstable enough as it sits. It's so torque prone now, Jack has to hold constant right stick just to keep her from rolling." Ernie's eyes lost their normal placid neutrality as they opened wider than anyone could remember. "And now you want to saw off what little stability the aircraft has. What are you thinking? Jack'll roll over and meet the ground inverted as soon as he takes off."

The burst of almost excitement from the engineer left the other two men dumbfounded for almost two full seconds. Finally, Sam regrouped and found himself once more able to respond. "I was *thinking* he could hold a little more right stick. He only has to do two little passes. Then he's done." He puffed up a small cloud from the Havana. "I admit it will be difficult…maybe a tad bit dangerous to a more inexperienced pilot. But Jack's no novice. You can hold a little right stick for a few minutes, can't you, neighbor?" Sam looked at his watch and pulled a chromed flask out of the top desk drawer.

Jack cleared his throat. "I don't know, Sam." *I hate it when he tries to sell me on something dubious by putting my skills in question.* "She was trying awfully hard to turn over a good part of the time."

Sam unscrewed the flask cap and gave the container a rapid upending with its opening secured to a thirsty mouth, followed in short order by the traditional back-of-the-hand wipe. Then he leveled his gaze upon Jack but kept silent.

Jack found a chair and settled down onto it. He could see Sam wasn't going to give in easily, if at all. *I know that look. You've got your teeth into this hair-brained wing-shortening theory, and you've gone blind and deaf to anything else.* "I honestly don't know if I can keep the plane steady after takeoff with that much wing gone. Besides, we have no idea how much it'll lengthen the takeoff…if we can take off at all with that much wing surface missing."

"I think I can, with all certainty, guarantee disaster with less wing." Ernie nodded agreement with himself. "The plane was originally designed for a minimal wing. It already has the shortest airfoils possible for safe flight."

Jack summoned some courage. "I agree, Sam. I won't fly it with shorter wings. That would be asking for trouble."

Sam chuckled. "That's pure banana oil. I've flown Spads home with almost a third of the wing fabric gone."

"Not at over three hundred miles per hour. Plus, I'll wager you were already in the air when you lost that wing surface. You didn't have to try to take off that way. Did you?" Ernie shook his head. "I won't allow it, Sam. I'm sorry. We should go with the bigger Rolls-Royce engine.

Maybe we can get it here in less than two weeks. It's better than destroying the plane and killing Jack in the process."

Sam turned to Jack. "And you agree with that?"

"Yes."

"Well, that's it then." Sam aimed his palms to the ceiling. "I'm out voted. But you two don't mind if I put some figures and sketches together to try and change your minds, do you?"

Jack and Ernie shrugged.

"Of course not," Ernie hunched forward and studied the floor. "I'm going to drop down to Los Angeles for a day or two anyway. I need to be on the phone to Detroit talking to the Shontz family about the new engine, and I can't do that kind of negotiating over a party line."

Jack leaned back in his chair. *You're giving up too easily, Sam. What are you up to?* "And this is all right with you, Sam?"

Sam recapped his flask and put it back in the drawer. "Absolutely. Like I said, I'm going to try to talk you into my wing idea, but if, after all is said, you two don't see things my way…" He chugged his cigar to life again. "Far be it from me to gum up the works. If you still want a new engine after I'm done talking, we'll strap on a new engine." Sam clamped the Corona between his teeth as he beamed at his associates.

A tiny itch began at the back of Jack's scalp. *Something's wrong. He's not fighting back. He's not even arguing. What's going on, partner?*

♫

"Roberto, do you have everything done?" Carrie stepped down from the porch, straightening the sleeves of her blouse as she went.

"Yes, it's all done. Everything…like you said." The young man's long black hair dropped over one eye. He pushed it back and adjusted the button loop of his suspender where it had slipped away from his tan woolen trousers. "I do the feed, the shoveling, and the candling. All done now."

"And the cistern pump? Did you fix the leak?"

"No, but I need new leathers from the hardware. And they're already closed until tomorrow."

"Hello, the camp!" Ruth emerged from the path between the pines. "I bring good news."

"All right, Roberto. I guess you're done for today." Carrie placed hands on hips. "Are you sure, Guillermo will be here in the morning?"

"He will be here, or I'll beat him silly."

"And he can drive a truck as well as you?"

"He drives like *El Diablo* himself." Roberto wiped grimy hands on his trousers, then he winked. "Almost as good as me."

"Well, hopefully slower than the Devil." She sighed. "Very well. I'll see both of you at six sharp. And make sure your other cousins are here on time. Some of them have started dragging themselves in here around seven, throwing the whole day's schedule off."

"I am sorry. I'll take care of that. Thank you. Guillermo not disappoint you. And we won't scratch your new truck."

Ruth mopped her brow with a red polka dot bandana as she reached the two from across the driveway. "What truck are we talking about?"

Carrie displayed a subtle smile. "Roberto and I were discussing the new Model-A pickup I've ordered." She smiled. "Our second truck for the business. Roberto has been picking up a lot of new customers for us in Palmdale and Lancaster—most of them stores and restaurants." She gave the young man's shoulder two quick pats. "He's quite a salesman, it turns out."

Ruth matched Carrie's smile. "Oh. And *Guillermo's* gonna drive the new truck?"

Carrie did not answer for a moment. *Yes, I know. What about my husband, right?* "Either him or Roberto. Our first old Model-T's still good enough to take Jack back and forth to the airfield. Like I have always said, it stays parked most of the day. But our other Model-T and the *new* truck are going to be working from dawn to dark. There's no sense in wasting a new truck by just letting it sit."

"I see." Ruth stuffed her kerchief back into her blouse. "Well, that makes sense." She pointed to a newly finished plank building uphill from the last chicken coop. "That's some house you built for yourself, Roberto. Looks like you're a more than passable carpenter."

"It's better than driving from my father's house every day. Now, me and Guillermo, we'll wake up and we're already at work." Roberto shrugged. "What's better than that?" He nodded to Carrie and Ruth. "*Con sus permiso, Señoras.*" He strode up the path to the plank sided, tar-shingle-roofed house. His gait betrayed the attitude of a man who knew he'd accomplished something worthwhile.

"Hiring him was one of the smartest things you've done." Ruth glanced uphill, then back to Carrie.

"I know." Carrie surveyed her surroundings. "He practically runs this place by himself. He's brought in a small crew of his relatives to handle most of the manual labor. And Guillermo will be taking over a good part of the deliveries." Carrie stretched her arms up toward a soaring raven. "It was getting hard to keep up with everything considering all the time I'm spending at the inn this year. Our chicken and egg customers must have doubled in the last twelve months alone. We're even selling to stores in Quartz Hill and Littlerock now." She rubbed at a dry spot on the back of her hand. "I don't know what I'd do without Roberto."

"Yes, I can see that." Ruth clasped her hands behind her back. "And what would you do without Jack?"

Carrie's eyes widened as her control mechanism slipped a cog. *And just what is that supposed to mean?* Then she mentally shifted gears and nudged herself back into control again. "What do you mean, Ruth?" Her response played out in a tone sweet as warm sugar cane.

"Because it seems to me you're more interested in some character named Arthur than you are in Jack."

And there it was with no warning, all spilled out on the ground like pickles dumped from a barrel. Carrie felt an electric burning shoot from her toes to her face. *Arthur's...not a secret!* She flooded her lungs with soothing air and held it there for an instant. Then she released her words in a slow careful stream. "If you are referring to the man who came to see me at the inn, he's simply an old college friend." She swallowed away the dryness. "Truth be told, he's really more my brother's friend now than mine."

Ruth slapped some dust from her divided skirt and set her boots a little wider apart. "Guess you forgot you were on a party line."

Carrie's burning intensified. "Did you listen in?"

"You know better than that."

"Thelma called you!"

"No. But a couple of other women did."

"Who?"

"Not important who they are. All you need to know is they're friends of yours. They didn't spread it around town. They both called me and me alone. The only way word'll get around is if someone else was listenin'—someone who's not your friend." Ruth put her hands into her skirt pockets. "I don't see that happening though. I'd have heard something by now."

Carrie put fingertips to her cheek and staggered to the running board of the Stutz where she sat down. "I didn't do anything wrong."

"Maybe not in the flesh, but you were thinking about it."

An impotent sputter of anger ignited behind Carrie's pooling green eyes. "And what makes you so sure of that?"

"First of all, the conversation was repeated to me...word for word...twice. Second, I think I've got you fairly well figured by now."

"And what gives you the privilege of accosting me in such a manner?" Carrie squirmed.

The hard line of Ruth's jaw muscles softened along with the look of her eyes. She walked over to the Stutz and knelt beside her friend, letting one hand rest on the cornered woman's shoulder. "Because *I'm* your friend, too."

Carrie's head snapped sideways as if it were spring loaded. She glared at this intruding old woman and shrugged the weathered hand from her shoulder. "You have no business...you have no...." The protests stopped just behind her tongue. She just sat there breathing like a coyote in a snare, wishing fire would come out of her eyes and burn the ancient busybody before her to a cinder. She wanted to speak terrible oaths of condemnation. But it did not happen. Try as she might, no withering flames would emerge from her eyes between blinks. Carrie could only speak out more powerless words. "You have no right."

Ruth put her hand back onto Carrie's shoulder. "I have the right of a friend who loves you enough to holler when you're gonna fall down an open mineshaft. Was this man your sweetheart before Jack?"

"What difference does—"

"Was he?"

The fine, almost invisible hairs on Carrie's arms stood up. She wanted Ruth to go away, but she also wanted her to stay. She wanted her to leave her alone and yet still pull her back from that mineshaft edge she'd mentioned. And she wanted it all at the same time.

Ruth gave Carrie's shoulder a gentle pat. "Was he your sweetheart before Jack?"

"Yes, but I don't see what—"

"You have to drop him."

"I haven't done anything!"

"You have to drop him from your heart. He's not your husband." Ruth kept her words matter-of-fact, but her tone was that of a loving mother speaking to a little girl who's just fallen and skinned her knee. "I know what you're passing through, and it will stop as soon as you let it. I *know* how you feel."

Carrie shook her head, throwing tears off into the dry desert air. "How could you know what I feel? You've never—you couldn't know." She folded her hands between her legs and looked down at them.

Ruth smiled an amused but friendly smile. "I've never thought Ben had packed on too much lard? I've never been scratched by that old beard of his when he kisses me? I've never gotten tired of his unromantic way of making jokes about everything feminine? And I've never wanted to live in a city for even a little while and be pampered like Astor's pet pony?" She gave Carrie a spirited wink. "If you believe that, young lady, you're not the smarty I took you for."

Carrie looked up. "Sometimes lately, I wonder what I was thinking when I gave Arthur up. He's everything a girl could want. Then I look at Jack, and I don't know what I ever saw in him. Do you ever think like that?"

Ruth watched the raven circle a moment before she answered. "A long, long time ago I did. But that went away." She stroked Carrie's hair with an almost imperceptible hand. "Those feelings are like an old stray dog. They always go away if you don't feed them. And do you know why?"

Carrie shook her head and diverted tears with a delicate finger.

Ruth sighed. "Because they're liars. The other man we remember, the dandy, the prince, he hasn't got one thing wrong with him. And that's because we made him up. He's not really the man we knew before we met our husbands. That old beau, the real man, made mistakes, said the wrong things, and, in the end, did something to make us throw him out of our heart. This Arthur, he did something to make you choose Jack over him, didn't he?"

Carrie nodded and sniffed. "He could be awful to people, and he was the most spoiled, arrogant boy I knew."

Ruth stood up. "And in your memories, you've somehow strained out all that bad and saved only the good." She shrugged. "So Arthur comes out of that wash looking like a prince. And from that point on, you'll always see Arthur through pretty emerald colored glasses and Jack through dingy gray ones…unless you throw away colored glasses, altogether, and just look at them both with truthful eyes."

Carrie got up from the running board and mopped her face with her handkerchief. "Jack's starting to get this little stomach. You know." She pantomimed holding something just in front of her abdomen. "Arthur takes care of himself. Probably spends time at the gymnasium, plays golf and tennis. No belly to speak of."

"When does Jack have time for golf or tennis. He's up in an airplane most of the time. And I think the nearest gymnasium is in Newhall right around thirty miles away."

"Ruth." She blotted the last teary remnant and put the hanky away. *How can I explain this, so you'll understand?* "I'm so tired of having to worry about every little dime we spend. And that's all I've done since Jack came back. I'm tired of doing nothing but work all day long…day after day. Never enjoying any leisure…never having any fun. Do you know what I mean?"

Ruth's tone remained sympathetic, but she said, "The Lord has blessed me with two wonderful, loving families…the one related to me by blood and my church family. I draw my pleasures from both of them." She shrugged. "I guess that all takes up so much of my time that I just don't think much about what I *don't* have." She paused a moment. "Well, maybe some times I think about it. Just a smidge. But the longer I live the life God laid out before me, the less important all that is to me. As a matter of fact, I often feel sorry for folks that have a lot of money. Most of them don't seem very happy to me. They remind me of a child that gets to eat his favorite ice cream all the time. After a few weeks of that, he gets sick of it, and it's not his favorite anymore. Sometimes I think that's why the Lord gives us our blessings a little bit at a time. So's we won't get tired of it all and lose our joy."

"Ruth." Carrie looked around the yard as if searching for spies. "When I think of Arthur it's like someone turned on a bright light somewhere. When I think of Jack, it's like someone turned that light out."

"Those are just feelings. They come and go like the weather. If you don't like the feeling you're having right now, just wait a minute. You'll have another completely opposite one soon enough." Ruth tapped on her cheek then sighed. "Here's the hard part, Carrie girl. You know the truth. You know you're just choosing to believe in a fairy-tale Arthur because that's what you want him to be. But inside…where the Lord talks to our heart…you know *that* man doesn't really exist—anymore than the totally worthless picture of Jack you choose to see really exists. You have to make up your mind to pay attention to what's true. The Lord says to take your thoughts captive." She crossed her arms. "If *you* don't, the devil surely will. Love's something you choose to open yourself up to, not something you wait for like rain."

"But these feelings are so strong!"

"Well, that's because you've been feeding and exercising them when you knew you shouldn't have. You feed any critter, it'll get stronger. Same goes for exercising them."

Carrie watched the raven circle close overhead, croaking the familiar clicking call to its mate. The other bird leapt from the top of the nearest pine and flapped its way to its partner's altitude where both creatures swung into an age-old aerial ballet. "But it's all so strong inside me."

Ruth took hold of Carrie's shoulders. "It's up to you. If you want your marriage to grow, you have to water it…and pull up the weeds. Arthur's a weed."

"How do I water it?"

"With prayer, to start with. Ask God to help you see things the way they really are." She shook Carrie with a gentle but earnest grip. "But don't expect any blinding miracles. Don't expect everything to change all in ten minutes. But you pray; do you hear me?" Ruth released her friend, turned, and started off down the hill toward her house. She spoke over her shoulder as she went. "You pray!"

She sounds like my old philosophy professor, not a farmer's wife, Carrie thought. *I know she's a wise old bird, but how did she get so articulate all of a sudden?*

"Holy Spirit," Ruth said without turning around.

"What?" Carrie sputtered.

"That's what the Lord put on my heart to tell ya—I think." Still walking away, she shook her head and shrugged. "Don't know why, but that's what I think He said."

Carrie reflexively glanced at the sky. *All right, Father. I get it. No secrets from you.* Then another nasty little thought surfaced. "What about Alma?" she said, having to speak up now, so her voice would carry the distance. She knew it to be a foolish thing to say as soon as it came out of her mouth.

Ruth stopped and turned around with a deliberate air, but showing no malice. "Alma's chasing after Jack is no secret. The whole town knows about that. But they also know Jack shies away every time she moves in on him. Folks have seen the way she tries to bust up your marriage, but they've also seen the way Jack stands up for it. In spite of how he might *feel.*" She gave her head another small shake. "And I think you already know all that. Alma's not going to get anywhere with your husband...unless you help her." And with that Ruth resumed her homeward trek.

Carrie watched after her for a few seconds then leaned back against the Stutz's driver-side door. *Pray. What do I pray?* Her body sagged like a leaky inner tube. The confrontation had almost been more than she could bear, and, just now, for a moment, her mind flung itself into a whirlpool of alternating shame and desire. *Oh, Father. Help me! I'm so confused!*

That second she heard Ruth's voice echoing in her memory. "Pray."

All right. Just like she said. Father, help me to see things the way they really are. Help me water my marriage...my love. Please, help me!

She glanced up where the ravens had performed their aerial dance, but they had both gone now. *Mating dance.* The knowledge of what the birds were probably up to right now produced a small envious sigh. Then for no particular reason, she looked at the small watch pinned to her blouse. It read five-twenty. She tried to picture both the men who competed against each other in her mind, but couldn't. *Don't expect blinding miracles. Remember?*

She wandered a few feet out toward the end of the driveway closest to the road and watched Ruth's progress down the path that connected the two homesteads. The wind had stayed true to its usual evening game of *playing possum,* becalmed until five-thirty when it would, like clockwork, begin to blow again in a different direction.

Right now, the plateau stood church quiet, and Carrie could hear Ruth's boots crunching on the path's granite gravel. A small rogue cloud drifted in front of the sun then seemed to slow. Deprived of its full ration of light, the landscape turned gray as if it were in mourning for the luminous loss.

Instinctively, Carrie looked up toward the offending cumulous. But instead of continuing its snail-like pace, the tiny renegade caught a strong fresh breeze and scooted out of the way all at once, giving Carrie's eyes a full blast of sunlight before she could turn away. For what seemed like forever, all she could see was a large blue disc directly in the center of her vision. Then, after what seemed like an hour, the large spot faded and her normal eyesight returned. But something else had occurred as well.

When she returned to musing upon Arthur, the first scene to play in her memory proved to be that of the young mining heir as a college freshman, throwing a glass of orange juice in a waiter's face and demanding that a fresh batch be squeezed. Somehow he had managed to soothe Carrie's outrage at his unbearable behavior that day and thus kept her as his fiancé for another month. Carrie tried to recall the more recent image of a more sympathetic man, but no matter how hard she worked at it, *that* Arthur would not appear. Plus, something else now newly emerged into her memory theater—how the young prince apparent had cooled Carrie's anger. Right in front of her, as if by magic, Arthur's manner and countenance seemed to change, transforming the boy into a more reasonable, considerate, and remorseful creature than he had been just a few moments before. Then he apologized and told her a short but very sad story about how his father had been harassing him, pushing to him to become the most celebrated athlete and student their college had ever seen. With seeming heart-felt sincerity, he had portrayed himself as very much the victim, rather than the bully. And she had bought it…for another four weeks. That's when Arthur seemed to regain some measure of confidence in his ability to control their relationship. And that's when his brutal sadistic abuse of the less affluent began again. *It's the same Arthur*, said the small voice, Carrie had learned to think of as holy. *He couldn't be trusted then, and he can't be trusted now. He'll do or say anything to obtain what he wants.*

In the next moment, just like the snap of a finger, a vision of Jack took over the stage. He did not appear to be doing much, just reading in the rocking chair to Kenny and Eddie, who lay stretched out on the floor, mesmerized by the tale their father had created. Then suddenly the scene changed to the Crossroads Diner, near Floyd and Hannah's place. A nerve-flustered new waitress had just gotten Jack's dinner order completely wrong—fish sandwich instead of hamburger and salad instead of fries. It had been a crowded Saturday night and the MacGregors had already waited thirty minutes to be served. The girl, now on the verge of what Floyd would have called a *conniption fit,* had given Carrie and the boys *their correct* order. But Jack ended up being the odd man out that evening. However, instead of voicing a complaint which might have gotten the young woman in Dutch with her boss, the newly born-again head of the MacGregor family, just smiled and said he'd always wanted to try the fish.

"I'll eat it," he said.

Carrie emitted a small moan as that memory played through, and she recalled how much Jack disliked fish. At that moment, a warmth invaded Carrie's heart and would not go away. It spread to engulf her whole consciousness like a soft blanket, soothing all spiritual wounds, caressing all mental abrasions until she could no longer resist the comfort of its embrace. *I do still love Jack.* Something inside her relaxed. *I think I'm all right now, Father.*

She glanced at her watch again. But when she saw the time, she laughed out loud. "It's been exactly ten minutes."

She laughed again and cupped her hands around her mouth. "Ruth!" She waited. "Ruth!"

Ruth, now almost to her own barnyard, stopped and turned around just as the evening breeze began to blow in its new direction—downhill, from the MacGregor ranch to the Smith farm. The older woman put an expectant hand behind one ear.

"I just got a blinding miracle!" Carrie fairly bounced on her heels as she pointed to her watch. "And all in ten minutes!"

Ruth raised both arms to the sky. "Halleluiah!" The sound echoed off the west canyon wall and drifted downhill on the wind toward the main road.

Then a doubt glanced off Carrie's heart like a bolt from a crossbow. "Ruth, will I stay like this?" *Lord, don't let the blindness return.* And she wasn't talking about blue dots on her vision from the sun.

Ruth shrugged an exaggerated, arms-raised shrug, then resumed her journey back down the path, delivering a backhanded wave as she went.

Carrie looked down toward the town, where she could barely make out the southernmost hangar of the airfield. *I've got to let Jack know* somehow...*without telling him what's been happening with Arthur.* She felt her rekindled warmth leap from her heart, spread over the grassy plateau of Saber Canyon, and race all the way down to the hangar where she pictured Jack and Sam tinkering with one of the beat-up old De Havillands.

I've got to find a way to make him believe I still love him. Father. Please forgive me! I've been in the dark so long!

Chapter Forty-Six

*Y*ou've got to kiss him goodbye!

The notion had been running through Carrie's head all night. It had popped into her thoughts like an evening moth that had slipped into the house through a tear in the screen-door. And from that moment on, she could not get it out of her mind. She heard it in her dreams and again when she woke up in the middle of the night. Now, after arising once more at five AM, she discovered Jack had already abandoned the living room couch where he'd spent the night…again.

Carrie hurried through her tooth brushing, then searched the boys' room and the kitchen. No Jack. She threw on her Chinese robe and slid into a pair of chicken-splattered rubber boots as she flung open the front door and turned on the driveway spotlight.

She stood there motionless for an instant, a strange feeling creeping into her consciousness. Then it hit her like a storm-wave overwhelming a small boat. All the rudeness, each insult, every disrespectful word she'd said to her husband over the last five years now flooded her memory. And trailing along with this tide came another long ignored thought. *Could he be thinking of leaving me? Could all this I've put him through…has it finally become more than he can bear?*

Carrie spotted the light reflecting off the Model-T's windshield. "Jack!" She leapt three feet out from the top step and ran. The silken tail of an intricately sewn Cantonese dragon flew up behind her. "Jack, wait! Don't leave!"

"What's wrong?" The disembodied voice came from just beyond the reach of electric illumination.

"Don't leave. You forgot something." She slowed down, almost falling out of the rubber boots, just as Jack stepped into view.

636

"What is it?" He held his arms wide apart in a questioning gesture.

"This!" She rushed him like a lineman in a college football game, then, wrapping her arms around his neck, fused her ample lips to his—not like a lineman. When she finally pulled back for air, Jack stood wide-eyed and open-mouthed.

"I prayed for a way to show you I love you," she said. "And this was God's answer." She kissed him again. "So." She took a breath. "I love you. Do you believe me?"

"Uh, Carrie...I...."

Tell him you're sorry for everything. I can't! You've hurt him. Now tell him. I want to, but I can't say that! It's too weak. I'll tell him something else. "I really do love you. Please, believe me." She nuzzled her head against his chest and squeezed him hard.

Jack remained silent for a long time.

Carrie began to feel like she was sinking into the driveway, and an empty cavern seemed to form just below her heart. *What's wrong? Why doesn't he say something or, at least, squeeze me back a little. Is he made out of wood? Or have I waited too long to do this? Say something, Jack! Oh, God! Make him say something! Don't let it be too late!*

Finally, Carrie heard Jack sigh and felt the gentle force of his arms against her back as he embraced her. "I love you," he said, sounding a little hoarse. "Of course, I love you."

"Good." She swallowed around the lump in her throat and gave him another quick squeeze. "I'll let you go fly then. Good thing you said that. I was going to hang onto you until you gave up and admitted I was the world's best wife. No telling how long we'd have been here." She let a tear roll off her face onto his shirt. *Don't cry, you ninny. All the man did was say he loved you. Nothing to cry about.* She decided to simply wipe the next several tears right onto the shirt. The sinking sensation stopped. Then she felt his chest fill with air and heard him sigh again as he began to stroke her hair.

"You be careful today," she crooned. "And come home early, if you can."

🎵

Boy, that came out of nowhere!
Jack slurped some more coffee as he balanced on his elbows and stared at the far wall of the cafe. That's where the memory of driveway kissing with Carrie materialized in his mind's eye. His wife seemed to have decided she loved him…just when Jack had given up on her, the very morning he'd started thinking in a serious way about Alma.

He gazed down into his dark brew like an oracle seeking a vision. She had wanted to know if he loved her. After five years of pushing him away, *she wanted to know if he loved her*.

He swished the coffee into a cyclonic whirlpool and watched a rogue ground descend to its fate through the funnel. Of course, he loved her! But he almost wished he didn't. Why did she want him all of a sudden? Was this some mood she was in again that would change with the next turn of the tide? He didn't know for sure if he wanted to find out, love or no love.

He took another sip. It had cost him a lot of pain to love her. He continued the vigil over his coffee remnant, a simple act that excluded the outside world and, for some reason, also helped subdue the current tumult within.

"Hello, Jack." Reverend Fisher slid into the other side of the booth, jerking Jack's attention out of the coffee and into the rude real world of the cafe. The young minister looked well groomed for so early in the morning. Not only did his hair shine with new oil, but he sported his Sunday suit, complete with bow tie.

Jack focused on the smiling man across the table. "I don't remember seeing you here before, Reverend."

"Well, I had a couple of early errands to take care of. I usually have my coffee at the church, but this morning's different."

Jack took a double sip, then agitated the cup again until he got another small whirlpool of undissolved sugar and more wayward grounds rotating with wild abandon. Then he gulped half the contents all at once. "What errands are those?"

"Oh." Fisher leaned forward and folded his hands on the table. "You for one. You're first on my list."

"Me?"

"Yes." The Reverend's agreeable features took on a more hardened look as he cleared his throat. "Look, I know you haven't exactly been a regular at church." Jack opened his mouth to speak, but Fisher raised restraining palms. "And I'm pretty sure I know most if not all the reasons." He paused. "But, regardless of any of that, I still think of myself as your pastor." He shrugged. "Which, when the smoke clears, means I care what happens to you...as well as to Carrie." He shrugged again and added the hint of a momentary smile. "So." He seemed to loosen his shoulders and stretch his neck, first to one side then to the other. "I'm not one to start trouble, Jack," he said. "But neither do I flee from it. So here it is, plain and simple. I've watched Satan bat you and Carrie about for five years." He held up a restraining hand again. "Now, I know there's been right and wrong on both sides, but the hard truth of it is...you're the head of the family in the eyes of God. That means, no matter what your wife says or does, you're responsible to set the right example." He stopped speaking and sighed.

Jack remained silent, clutching his cup as if it were a life preserver. God had engineered this meeting. Jack knew that as well as he knew the name of the café in which he sat. He had allowed Alma to keep up the flirting game to perhaps help repair some of the damage Carrie had inflicted upon his heart. But he'd always known that was wrong. *Lord, forgive me.*

"And here's the particularly hard news," Fisher raised one righteous finger but kept it in front of his own face. "The cat and mouse game between you and Alma is no secret. I know *you've* done nothing wrong ... yet; but we both know the whole thing's got to go one way or the other soon." He reclasped his hands and bowed his head in an almost prayer-like pose. Then he raised his gaze to meet Jack's. "If you want your marriage to survive, you have to make it clear to Alma you're not available. You have to cut this game off, no matter what it takes." The Reverend leaned back against the booth's cushioned seat and finally produced a more lasting but still faint smile. "You can take a swing at me now, if you like."

Jack released his cup. "How could I get mad at God's messenger for saying what's true." He leaned farther forward on his elbows. "The Lord did something to Carrie this morning. She came running out into the yard just to kiss me and say she loved me." He chuckled. "She almost knocked me down. And right now, I'm feeling more guilt than John Wilkes Booth." Jack felt the regret climb from his chest, through his throat, and settle behind his eyes. "I know what I have to do, Reverend." He sniffed. "I'll take care of it right now." He swallowed the last of the sweetened Java. "But I'm going to need this booth for that. Would you mind waiting outside? I'd like to see you after."

With his sympathetic smile in tact, Reverend Fisher slid off the bench seat and stood. "No problem." He clapped Jack on the shoulder and disappeared through the front door, the sound of the dangling bell announcing his departure.

Jack finished the last of his cup. *Lord, help me with this one. I don't want to hurt her.* He waited for Alma to turn his way, which didn't take long since only two other people graced the café that morning. He raised his cup, and she came to him, pot in hand.

"Little more for you, Sweetie?" She swung the pot forward.

Jack put down the cup and held up his hand. "Actually, I wanted to talk to you."

"Well, that's a switch." In one motion she set down the pot and slid onto the booth's bench-seat opposite him. "Usually, I'm the one that has to start the conversations around here. What's on your mind, and I hope it's the same thing that's on mine." She winked.

"There's no future for you and me."

Alma stopped moving as if she were a snapshot of herself.

Jack grabbed for the security of the cup again and gripped it with the pressure of a bench vise. "Things are looking up for me and Carrie." He saw Alma's lower lip quiver. *I hate this.* "I'm not going to leave her."

Her eyes widened and brimmed with liquid pain.

" I'm sorry," he said as he tried to rub the kiln baked glazing off the cup. "I know you were hoping for something different." He found it hard to keep eye contact with her, not to look away. Somehow he did it. "I'm sorry."

Alma did not move or speak.

Jack couldn't take any more. He'd hurt her worse than he'd expected. *Could she really have been that much in love with me?* He got up from the booth. "Look, I'll just try to stay out of here as much as I can. So you won't have to look at my ugly mug every morning."

"No!" She shook her head so fast tears flung themselves from her face onto the table. Then, somehow from somewhere she produced a sad little smile that still dripped with fluid despair. "I don't want it said Alma drove a customer away." She sniffed, fortified the smile, and wiped her cheeks with the backs of her hands. "You don't want me to get fired, do ya?"

"Alma, nothing's going to happen between us."

"Maybe it will. Maybe it won't." She wiped her cheeks some more. "Just don't stay away because of me. The town's too small. The gossip will be meaner if you stop coming."

"All right." He reached into his pocket for coffee-cash.

Alma waved him off. "Not today. This one's on me." She stood then turned away from him. "But ya gotta get out of here right now. Just for today. Tomorrow you can come back, if you want."

Jack nodded to the back of her head, then he left to the sound of the insolent spring-bell.

Outside, Reverend Fisher stood, finishing a yawn. "How'd it go?"

Jack glanced at the ground. "It was hard."

Fisher nodded. "It's supposed to be. But I understand you didn't want to create pain. I think you're a good man, Jack...all in all. Perhaps we can talk about things sometime soon. Maybe even later today."

"Maybe."

"I'd do it now, but I want to get over to the airfield with everyone else to see Sam break that record this morning." He gave his head a single shake. "I missed it the day you tried. But this time they put it in the paper in time for folks to set their alarm clocks."

"Sam? The record? Reverend what the—" Jack cleared his throat as he captured the inappropriate next word on its way to his tongue. "What are you talking about? Sam's not making any record attempt today. Hel—heck, Ernie's still down in Los Angeles, for Chri—for crying out loud!"

Puzzlement spread like sundown across Fisher's face. "Well, I don't know about that, Jack. It was in last night's paper. You haven't read it?"

"No. I've been catching up on our airmail paperwork. I kind of let the pilots take care of themselves the last couple of days. There was a lot to tend to. Yesterday, I had my meals at home, hunched over a stack of government forms rather than the newspaper."

"Well, then the paper probably got the date wrong. Some sort of misprint. Too bad. I think half the town's over there. Some of them aren't going to be too happy they got up before dawn for nothing." Reverend Fisher looked off toward Jack's truck. "Mind if I ride over with you? If there's no flight, maybe we can find some place to talk."

Jack nodded. "Of course." He sighed and glanced at the trickle of headlights still pulling off the road toward the hangars. "Might be a good idea for you to come along. Help me break up the angry mob when they try to hang Sam."

᛭

"He socked me right in the eye!" Cal pulled his hand away from the shiner and massaged his temple.

"Sam did this?" Reverend Fisher leaned forward to examine the darkening eye-socket. He turned Cal's face to catch more of the dingy light from the bare-bulb lamp that hung over the hangar's small rear door. It did not help the examination much, though, since the light possessed no more intensity than the pre-dawn twilight that already surrounded them. "Doesn't look too bad."

Jack peered over the reverend's shoulder. "What brought this on, Cal?" Then he looked around at the growing tide of humanity and cars ebbing onto the airfield. "Holy Smokes! This is more people than live here in town, and that's for sure."

The Reverend released Cal's chin, and the injured mechanic swung his arm to indicate the crowd that stretched off into the darkness. "They're all here 'cause of the newspapers. Sam called every paper and magazine he could think of a couple days ago. I didn't know 'til one of these reporters told me this morning." He waved his long arms straight out from his side. "How was I supposed to know he was gonna pull something like this!" His breaths came in a cadence on the edge of hyperventilation. "This one reporter said we was gonna set the speed record this morning. Told me this when I drove up. Well, I says that weren't true, but this reporter guy says it's *so*." He pulled off his snap-brim cap and wiped his forehead with the sleeve of his overalls. "So I go to ask Sam what gives, and what do I find inside number two hangar? The whole place is buzzin' with guys either drying the fresh doped wingtips or gettin' somethin' else ready for a new speed run today." He stopped to take several breaths. "He did it, Jack. He called in the whole crew except you and me. And he had 'em here since nine o'clock last night, shortening, covering, and doping them wing tips. He lopped about a foot off the wingspan, then he brought in oil heaters and fans to quick-dry the dope and paint."

The sun broke over the eastern mountains as Jack shook his head. "He waited until Ernie was busy down in Los Angeles, and I was either dealing with the airmail or sleeping at home. That bum!"

Cal blinked. "I was just coming to find you when you got here. I told him he shouldn't do this without calling you. I even grabs him and tells him he can't fly cause he'd been drinkin' this morning already. So he says he needed to *pree-voke* some hairy spirit or something."

"*To drink the spirit elixir that evokes heroism.*" Jack glanced up at the brightening sky.

"Yeah." Cal stabbed at the invisible words with a recognizing finger. "That's what he said. He sounded drunk, but he didn't *walk* like he was yet."

Jack surveyed the cars and trucks that lined the part of the taxiway he could see from around the hangar. "It's from a poem written by a Canadian fighter pilot in France back during the war. It got passed around from one Allied squadron to another, but it never actually got published.

The fellow died just before the armistice." He paused. "It's about summoning courage from liquor to do something you don't think you're going to live through."

They all locked eyes for a moment.

Cal shifted his weight to one foot. "Well, I tried to stop him. I told him I wasn't gonna let him fly for at least an hour. 'Til the gin wore off, you know. I even grabs him when he tried to get around me." He felt his cheek again. "That's when he slugged me." He glanced at his gunboat-size shoes. "So when I got back up, I decided to go find you."

"All right. I've heard enough. Where is he now?" Jack opened the rear hangar door.

"Out on the apron with the plane." Cal pointed through the hangar to the yawning maw where the two big front doors had been pulled back. True to the mechanic's word, there stood the Caroline, her orange skin once again gleaming with the rays of dawn – all four wingtips short as a nightmare.

Sam sat in the cockpit leaning around the cowling. "Contact!" he yelled to a ground-crewman who held one side of the propeller, his left foot poised in the air.

"Contact!" The man gave the prop a grunting pull downward, and the Packard growled to life—on the first try this time.

Jack bolted through the doorway and sprinted down the center of the empty work bay. "Sam!" He stumbled over a mislaid step-ladder. "Sam, don't!"

The engine's rumble drowned out all other sound, but Jack's peripheral movement must have caught Sam's attention. The time-toughened little man turned his head. And when he saw Jack, he pulled his goggles down over his eyes. "Clear away!" he yelled and swiveled his head in a visual scan. The ground crew backed away, and the instant the last scrambling man had cleared the wingtips,

645

Sam gave the biplane full throttle, sending it and himself bouncing down the dirt taxiway at twice the normal speed.

Too late, Jack slid to an exasperated stop on the tarmac—helpless to prevent the disaster he feared would come. "Why do you have to be such a stubborn old goat!" he screamed into the prop-wash as a surge of impotent frustration washed through his chest. "Why couldn't you just wait for the new engine?"

As soon as the echoes of the Packard's metallic thunder subsided, the adulation of the crowd became audible. They cheered, and waved hats and handkerchiefs as Sam taxied by, half burying them in dust. He saluted them all from the top of his leather helmet as he neared the taxiway's end, then peddle-turned onto the runway without halting for the usual engine run-up.

Sam wheeled his grumbling monster around a full 180 degrees to face straight down the path of his intended takeoff. Then he stopped and brought the engine down to idle, as if gathering courage, Jack thought, for what must be done next.

"Don't do it, Sam," The younger partner muttered to himself, barely noticing that both Reverend Fisher and Cal now stood on either side of him. He held a breath then let it out. "Don't do it." But he knew Sam would. The man had been waiting for this moment all his life…just like Jack. Only this time reporters and a crowd stood nearby, all waiting for the heroic act of skill and courage they had come to witness. How could he *not* do it? *Sam, don't!*

For a heartbeat, all movement in the universe ceased. Then the Packard roared its full-throttled challenge to the morning sun, and the Caroline began her takeoff roll. She left the barbed wire fence behind her, making it disappear within a dusty cloud. The plane's momentum doubled with every few yards of her run, but, by the halfway mark, even with the tail raising, smooth above the ground, the two forward wheels of the main landing gear remained pressed hard against the earth.

Cal snatched the cap from his head again and twisted it into a knot. "It's them stubby wings. He can't get enough lift to get off. He's gonna run off the end of the runway."

Jack shoved his hands into his pockets to hide his clenched fists. *Set the tail down and shut her off now, Sam, or it'll be too late!*

Reverend Fisher kept his gaze firmly fixed on the hurtling aircraft as it ate up precious ground. "Lord, put your hand on Sam…or under him, as You will."

Then the Caroline passed the three-quarters mark, still clinging to the earth.

"Too late." Cal relaxed the knot in his cap.

Jack pulled his fists out of his pockets and waved them in the air like they were on fire. "Shut her down, you moron! Shut her down!" *You can't get her off now! Just ground loop her and live!*

But Sam neither heard nor obeyed. Like a shell already fired from the muzzle of its cannon, he stayed on the takeoff roll as the end of the runway drew near.

Jack remembered a gulley, that stood just in front of the tree-line and the hill at the far end of the lakebed. Then he pushed those images from his mind.

All three men on the apron took a deep breath and held it.

That's when Sam's wheels left the ground and skinned the tops off some dry Russian thistle beyond the airfield's threshold.

"He's off!" Call yelled, and everyone from one end of the airfield to the other cheered their approval and relief.

Jack discovered that sometime during the last two seconds he'd clutched the arms of his two companions. He let a captive breath escape and released his grip.

Reverend Fisher seconded the sigh and murmured, "Thank you, Lord."

647

Cal started to put his hat back on his head, but froze in the middle of the act. "Wait a minute."

Jack squinted at the biplane for an instant, then spotted what Cal had seen. "It's rolling to the left. That stinking torque is rolling her to the left! *Sam, get that stick all the way over to the right! All the way to the stops! Get it over! It might stop the roll!*

But the rolling *didn't* stop. The plane kept twisting slowly in the same lethal direction, even while she continued to gain altitude. The cheers of the crowd dwindled. Soon the left wing pointed straight at the ground. The cheers died, and several bold photographers ran onto the taxiway and headed for the dry lake.

Jack felt his stomach tighten.

The Caroline continued her drunken rotation until she was almost inverted. Then the nose dropped earthward, and, in less than a second, Sam had plowed upside-down into the dried mud just short of the gulley and the cottonwood trees. That's when the secondary fuel tank erupted into flames. The main tank exploded a moment later to engulf the plane in a complete fireball.

Jack guessed that it had hit doing better than 150 miles per hour. He didn't run out to the crash site with the crowd. He just clenched his hands behind his back and went into the office. Reverend Fisher followed him as far as the office door but said nothing. Jack heard later that someone called the volunteer fire department to come out and shovel sand onto the flames.

Chapter Forty-Seven

The brass handle slipped from Cal's hand and *his* corner of Sam's coffin fell with a crack against one of the two-by-fours that spanned the open grave. The hole had been dug to a dimension almost twice as expansive as its purpose required. Nobody seemed to know why. Right after the drop, a secondary thud from within the pine box sent an embarrassed grimace circulating among all six pallbearers.

One of them chided Cal, whose shiner, as of this morning, had almost faded away. "Careful, dummy! Now ya moved him around in there!"

The five who still had a secure grip lowered the remaining three corners of the box down onto the slats with exaggerated care.

Cal held a palm up to his co-bearers. "Was wrestling with an oil pump this morning. Guess I didn't get all of it off."

"Try soap." The man next to Cal shook his head. "What a jerk."

"Pipe down, you mugs! There's people here!" This last comment came from a scar-faced man at Sam's head end.

"Oh, sorry." Cal straightened up and wiped the offending hand on the back of his suit pants.

Jack stood nearby, taking in the vaudeville comedy. He bit his lip to keep from crying or laughing out loud; he didn't know which. *All I want to do right now is laugh myself silly. I don't get it. And all I can think of, having to do with Sam, is how stubborn and stupid he was to do himself in the way he did. What a waste! Why wouldn't he wait for the new engine.* He closed his eyes in an attempt to block out the thoughts that bothered him so, and he opened them just in time to see Cal almost lose his balance at the grave's edge. *Lord, take charge of these jokers. Straighten them up.* He heard subdued whines and muffled snorts from some of the men around him and saw mourners with their hands over their mouths trying to hold back full-blown laughter. Jack followed their example. *God, please don't let me laugh now!* Then Cal stumbled over a large dirt clod, and Jack amended his prayer. *And please don't let Cal fall in the hole.*

From then on, the funeral proceeded in a more normal manner. Reverend Fisher prayed and preached. Jack had written every good thing he could think of about Sam on a penny postcard. And when his turn came to speak, he expressed what a loss Sam's death had been and read his list plus a couple of extra compliments that came to him on the fly. But something still didn't line up with the occasion. *Doesn't feel like the old scrapper's dead. He's got to be back at the hangar, grumbling over the bank accounts, puffing up a monstrous cloud of Havana smoke, and flicking the ashes onto the desk two inches short of the ashtray. He's just so busy, he forgot what time the funeral was, so he'll be a little late.*

After Jack had returned to sit beside Carrie and the boys, a large calloused hand clasped Jack's shoulder. "Hard to believe that little demon-mouse's really gone this time." Slappy let a slack-faced smile leak down from his damp red eyes. "He was always one to push things, to kind of kick the dragon in the nose, if you know what I mean. I...aw heck, all of us in the old squadron told him someday he'd meet his end going up in a big red flash." Slappy blew into a folded white handkerchief then sawed it back and forth under his nose. "He surely tried to prove us right for years, but, somehow, he always walked away from each and every disaster. Was as if the man didn't believe in death, like some kids don't believe in Santa Clause or ghosts." Slappy allowed himself a short laugh. "I guess he sort of convinced me for a while. I know he's burned crisp like a piece of bacon inside that sealed box. But ya know, I still half expect to see smoke from a fine Cuban cigar come

650

rolling out from under the lid with him kicking and hollering for someone to let him out." He shuffled his great brown shoes in the sand. "I went to the undertaker's yesterday. And I paid them to open the box. I had to know, you see? Had to know that what was left of old Sam was in there." Slappy took a long deep breath and paused with his lips tight together before he finally sighed. He rotated the brim of the brown Fedora he held between his fingers. "He's in there." Some more heavy breaths. "He's in there, all right. Most fearless little goblin I ever knew."

Then the reverend prayed some more and wound up by asking if anyone wanted to assure their place in heaven. Did anyone want to be saved?

Cal's hand went up like a shot, but the pallbearer next to him grabbed the mechanic's wrist and pulled it down.

"You don't even know what he's talkin' about." The man, one of Jack's older airmail pilots, struggled, to keep Cal's arms under control. "Don't make a fool out of yourself. 'Least not 'til after we've planted poor old Sam."

"I do so know what he's talking about!" Cal jerked himself free and raised his arm again. "I want to get saved, Reverend!"

Another pallbearer leaned Cal's direction. "No, you don't!"

"Yes, I do!" Cal's insistence grew, but only provoked shushing from those near the casket. Cal now had everyone's attention. He surveyed the assemblage, then flushed crimson as he looked down at one of the sparse tufts of dry grass that clung like a stubborn tick to the cemetery's sandy soil. "I guess I'll have to get back to you later about that, Reverend," he said, then turned back to the coffin.

Reverend Fisher smiled a friendly smile. "Any time, Cal."

Thelma from the switchboard sang her best rendition of *What a Friend We Have in Jesus* while using one hand to keep possession of her straw summer hat against the hot gusts of the late summer wind.

After that, the Reverend finished with a prayer and dismissed the gathering. The undertaker's assistants came forward, removed the two-by-fours, and, with skilled manipulation of the pre-placed hemp ropes, lowered Sam's coffin down to its final rest. Then two regular customers from the Bull Moose earned their five dollars each by filling in the grave.

Jack moved toward Bee, who had remained seated on one of the folding wooden chairs next to the graveside. Alone and almost motionless she stared up at a passing cloud that cast a fleeting shadow on the cemetery. She didn't look at Jack as he walked up, but just started talking as if continuing an earlier conversation. "Clouds make it look so easy, don't they?"

"Flying?" Jack obliged her with the rhetorical question.

"Yes." She didn't take her eyes off the cloud until Jack sat down beside her, then she turned to him "So do you believe all that stuff you said about Sammy, Jack?"

He cleared his throat. "Well—"

"Because, if you do, you're a whole lot stupider than I took you for!" She pulled a multi-smeared handkerchief from her purse and began to blot the little streams of emotion that ran down her cheek. Then she swallowed and took a breath. "And I *don't* think you're stupid!" She blotted some more. "So why don't you level with me."

He ran an unconscious hand over the back of his neck. "Bee, I can't do this."

"Ya can't?" Her voice became strident as she jerked herself from the chair. She fished a cigarette from her purse, lit it, and began to pace between Jack and the slowly filling grave. "Well, let me start it off then. Because I *can* talk about him *just* this way!" She took a deep drag and let the smoke wait for her first word. "The truth is Sam was a grade-A snake. He chose the bottle over responsibility, and he always chose fun over family."

Jack stood up and took a step toward her. "We all knew Sam had his faults, Bee, but he ran a good airmail business. No one could've done it better."

"No one could have done it better? Are you kidding me?" She pulled hard on her smoke, but this time exhaled long before speaking. "He had no business buying that Ryan with you. No business at all!"

"We got a better mail contract because of that plane, Bee. And now we can carry more passengers. It was a good decision."

She paced a little faster. "He had no right to stick you with the bill for that plane!"

Jack scratched his head. "Bee, what are you talking about? The Ryan's paid off."

"No, it's not, Jack!" She stopped and squared off with him. "No, it's not!"

He shrugged and held up his hands. "I paid cash."

"But Sam didn't!" She began to tear up again, so she paused to blot. "Okay? Sam didn't have the cash. He borrowed the money to buy the Ryan!"

Jack felt a cloud of confusion form in his brain, but he persevered. "He borrowed on your house?"

Bee sighed and shook her head. "No, Jack. The house's not ours. Ben owns it." Suddenly, her voice took on a soft, sympathetic tone. "Sam borrowed from an L.A. Bank, using the Airmail business as collateral. He did it just before he made you a partner. So now you're stuck with that loan. That's why he wanted to break the speed record so bad. He needed the money it would bring to pay off the loan. And now, as the surviving partner, you're stuck with everything, and half the Ryan belongs to the bank. They're your new partner."

Jack froze inside as the venom from the sting of Bee's words found its way to his mind. How could he believe

653

her? *How could Sam do that? Why did he lie? What was he thinking? It's hard enough to make a profit without loan payments on your back. I won't believe it!* "Sam wouldn't do that."

"Oh, yes he would, Jack. He sure as shootin' would." She walked to the graveside and looked down into its half-filled depths. She looked to the men who were shoveling the dirt and held up her hand. "Hold on a minute, boys." They stopped their labor with a collective shrug. She tossed the remains of her cigarette into the hole, then turned back to the shovelers. "Okay. Fill her up." Then she turned her back on Sam and returned to Jack, finishing her speech as she approached. "Like I said, Jack. He was a low down snake and he bit us both hard. I'm through with this awful brown place. I'm taking my kids and moving up to my family's farm south of Portland. It's green there, and I could use some green right now."

By the time Jack had digested all Bee had said, she had already gone and the Bull Moose boys had filled in Sam's grave.

Then Cal tapped him on the shoulder. "Jack?"

Jack shook off enough of Bee's aftermath to respond. "What, Cal?"

"I heard what Bee said."

"Yeah?"

"I just wanted ya to know. I didn't know nothin' about no loans."

Jack nodded. "I know, Cal. Sam wouldn't have told you. He knew you'd be too honest to have kept that a secret."

Cal shrugged. "I'm gonna get back to the hangar and see to the evening mail. And you won't have to worry about tomorrow's, neither. I can take care of that, too."

"Thanks, Cal."

"S'all right." He turned and stumbled toward the big mail truck. "I like being boss for a while."

Jack watched him for a moment as he walked away. *Funny, the people who turn out to be your trustworthy friends in the end. Cal wouldn't have buried me in debt. He would have told me the truth about the loan ahead of time.* Jack's stomach tightened. *Oh, Lord! A mortgage on the business! How are we going to keep afloat with a mortgage? I should have questioned Sam as to where he got his money. I knew the company was barely making it on airmail revenues. Where did I think he got the money for a new plane? I didn't think! That's the problem! I just trusted him.* All at once, every bit of strength drained out of him like water through a colander. He backed away from the grave and collapsed onto one of the wooden folding chairs supplied by the undertaker. He found himself suddenly starved for air, so he opened his black suit-coat, loosened his tie and unbuttoned his collar. *Carrie was right. I'm a moron, no maybe's about it.*

"Bee told you about the loan?" Carrie sat down beside him. Her voice sounded softer than Jack had heard for a long time. "Ruth just told me. She got it from Bee this morning."

Jack leaned forward and put his head in his hands. "Yes, Bee told me." He took a deep breath. "And I wouldn't blame you if you threw me out right now."

"Jack, I don't think it would be right for—"

"Mr. MacGregor?" said a new voice.

Jack looked up.

A man wearing the uniform of a county sheriff stood facing him. He looked vaguely familiar, but Jack couldn't place him.

"Yes." Deciding the fellow must simply resemble someone else he'd actually known in the past, Jack straightened. "What can I do for you?"

"I'm Deputy Sheriff Comings, sir. I'm sorry to disturb you under these circumstances, but would you mind if I asked you a question or two? It'll only take a minute."

"What is this about?" Carrie beat Jack to that question by an instant.

"And you are?" The deputy fished a pen and leather-bound notepad from a front pocket.

"*Mrs.* MacGregor." She patted Jack's arm.

"Ah, yes ma'am." Deputy Comings flipped the notepad open. "It's about a murder that occurred here in Sweet Springs a while back. The victim was a...Mr. Shontz."

Why are you asking me? Jack's stomach tightened a little more. *And why does your name sound familiar when I don't know you?* "I've already told our constable everything I know," he said, and decided to stop searching his memory for any personal connection to the man in front of him, so he could concentrate on the business at hand. "I thought that was all over with."

"Well, sir. Not quite. The State Attorney General's office has charged *our* office in Lancaster to come down here and reopen the investigation. The case was filed by your constable as an unsolved murder; however, the state A.G.'s office isn't satisfied with that. Between you and me, the rumor is that someone with a lot of influence leaned on someone who leaned on someone who leaned on the state A.G. But that's just a rumor, mind you. Me, I've got other fish to fry, but duty calls." He shrugged.

"Shontz's Lawyer brother...and maybe the wife. That's probably who did all the leaning. The brother didn't want us flying the challenger right from the start." Jack stood up. So did Carrie.

Deputy Comings' brow furrowed. "I wouldn't know, sir. But if I may, I'd like to get these questions out of the way."

"All right." Jack folded his arms. "Shoot." Jack grimaced. "You know what I mean."

"Yes." Comings flipped his pad to the second page. "Were you at the poker game in the rail-yard?"

"No."

Comings scribbled on the pad. "Did you encourage Mr. Shontz to go there?"

"Actually, I tried to talk him out of it."

"I see." More scribbling. "And where were you when Mr. Shontz met his unhappy end?"

"At home."

"With me...and the children." Carrie put a hand on Jack's shoulder.

"Uh-huh. So you had nothing to do with Mr. Shontz going to the poker game."

"That's right. That was Sam's doing. He'd been a regular there."

"That's Sam Smith?"

"Yes."

"But this Sam is dead now." Comings nodded toward the fresh-mounded grave.

"Yes." Jack nodded also.

"How did he die and when?"

"Just Wednesday in a plane crash."

"And where were you when *that* death occurred?"

"Now, wait just a minute?" Carrie grasped Jack's arm and took a half step forward.

Comings stopped scribbling and glanced up from the pad, his face sympathetic. "I'm sorry, Mrs. MacGregor. I'm required to ask such questions. May we continue, please?"

Carrie flushed. "Yes, *I'm* sorry."

"Not at all." Comings almost smiled. "So, where were you when Mr. Smith lost his life?"

"At the airfield, watching him take off."

"Jack tried to stop *him*, too." With one hand still holding Jack's arm, Carrie wrapped her free arm around him.

Comings wrote some more. "All right."

"You don't think Jack had something to do with Sam's death, do you?" Carrie caressed her husband's shoulder. "Everyone knows it was an accident."

"I don't think anything, ma'am. I'm just here to ask the questions." He turned another page. "And you did not tamper with Mr. Smith's airplane in any way before his crash?"

"No. He took it upon himself to make some alterations to the wings the night before. He had discussed those changes with me and Ernie, our engineer, and we both decided it was too dangerous. Sam did it anyway though. Ernie was in Los Angeles, and I didn't find out until Sam was about to take off. Cal—that's our chief mechanic—he and I both tried to stop the flight, but Sam took off before we could reach him. He even slugged Cal earlier."

"And where is Cal?"

"At the hangar handling the airmail for today. You can ask him about all this, if you want."

"I intend to." The deputy wrote some more, then flipped the page again. "And you say you were nowhere near the rail-yard on the night of the murder."

"I've told you that."

"That's very strange." Comings tapped his pen against his chin.

"What?" Jack and Carrie shared the word.

"Well, one of the game's participants, a Mr. Fitzpatrick, claims he saw you standing near the caboose when he stepped outside for a smoke. As a matter of fact, he came into the sheriff's station specifically to tell us about it." He rubbed his chin with the blunt end of the pen. "I think I'll have a little chat with Mr. Fitzpatrick as long as I'm in the neighborhood."

"You don't really think Jack was involved in the murder, do you?" Carrie's voice rang cool and even.

Comings pushed his Stetson campaign hat back on his head. "Personally, I'm inclined to agree with your constable, ma'am, that Mr. MacGregor had no connection at all. But I'm not the state A.G., so I don't have final say. However, if I can find enough evidence to clearly indicate your husband was not involved in foul play, I think the folks up at the capitol will have to go along with me and admit his innocence." The pen and pad went back into his pocket. "Off the record, that's what I intend to do. With what I know so far, I smell at least two rats, a wealthy, powerful one and a murderous one. Your constable said the same. I don't think they're connected to *each other*, but one never knows."

Carrie's expression softened. "Thank you, Deputy Comings. We appreciate your help."

Comings touched the brim of his hat. "Pleasure, ma'am." He nodded to Jack. "Mr. MacGregor." Then he half turned. "I just hope my superiors see it my way. Good day to you both." Finishing his turn, he strode down the little hill toward where the cars stood parked.

Jack slid from Carrie's embrace and walked a few steps past Sam's grave to the little picket fence that surrounded the sandy cemetery. He clasped his hands behind his back and stared out at the town and the airfield below. *I am a gosh-darn menace to everyone who knows me. I've invested my family's money in a dream that won't come true. I let a fast talker put me in debt. And now I'm a suspect for murder. All because I thought I could be a businessman.* He took in a big gulp of air and let it out slow. *So now I'm a moron* and *a criminal. Good job, Jack! I've got to do something before all this hurts Carrie and the boys. I have to protect them somehow.* At that instant, Jack sensed a change, almost an audible click within himself. Things were suddenly different, and, if he'd had any doubts about what he had to do, they were gone now. He felt Carrie's hands taking hold of one of his. He turned to her.

"It's all going to turn out just fine, you know." She massaged his hand as if she were trying to keep it warm.

"You'll see. By tomorrow, everything will be well on its way to being set straight."

Her words rang true in Jack's mind, but in a way that Carrie couldn't know or understand. "Yes, I'm sure it will." He patted her arm, and at that moment a plan took shape and a determination became set. *Yes, I will set things straight. I'll fix all that's been broken, supply all that's needed, and I'll never cause you trouble again.* Jack scanned the cemetery's dwindling crowd and found Slappy. *And for once in my life, I know exactly what to do.*

He took Carrie into his arms and kissed her like he hadn't done since their trouble began. At first she resisted, but when he would not relent, she surrendered to his advance. When he was finished, she put her palms flat against his chest and looked around as if she had been discovered robbing a cookie jar.

"Jack, there are people here!" Her face and throat flushed almost strawberry red. "And poor Sam's just buried! We can't just...." She stopped to catch her breath. "One must—"

"I love you, Carrie." Jack stroked her hair then pulled her crimson cheek close. "I didn't want you to leave without hearing me say that."

"Well, I love you, too." She snuggled into his coat. "I do."

"I believe you." He looked past the ribbon of her broad-brimmed straw hat to make sure of Slappy's whereabouts. Then he pulled back from her enough to look into her face. "Listen, I've got something to take care of here...some business. Why don't you and the boys head home?

Carrie pulled away just a little more. "Jack, I have to work tonight. I'm sorry."

Jack smiled. "That's all right. Just let them run around here for a while, and I'll take them with me."

"That's what I hoped you'd say. Poor Ruth and Ben need time by themselves. With their last child dead and Bee moving to Oregon with their grandchildren, I can't even imagine how they must feel right now."

Jack glanced at the Smiths, who were talking to Reverend Fisher. "Well, I know how I'd feel if we lost the boys at any age."

Carrie rubbed her arms in the summer heat as if she were cold. "Terrible. I can't even contemplate it. I just talked to them, but I couldn't think of one thing to say that didn't sound like empty words. I'm afraid I was no help to her at all."

"Yeah." Jack gave his wife a few seconds to let her darker feelings dissipate. "Say, there is *one* thing you can do for me."

"Yes?"

"Let me take the boys for a genuine Stutz Bearcat ride."

She looked up, sporting her Mona Lisa smile. "The boys have had many such rides."

Jack matched her smile with one of his own concoction and raised an eyebrow to boot. "Not with their father. Come on, Carrie. I used to race dirt track, for Pete's sake.

She pulled a little farther away and made a sour-lemon face for several seconds. "You better not crash it or send my sons flying off into the bushes."

Jack held up his right hand. "Word of honor."

She pantomimed thoughtfulness, holding her chin and tapping a finger on her cheek. "Very well. *Mi* Bearcat *es su* Bearcat."

They hugged and kissed once more before Carrie left for the Hunter's Inn.

Five minutes later, Jack grabbed Slappy by the elbow. "Got a minute?"

"I've got several. What's on your mind?" Slappy parked himself onto one of the chairs.

Jack sat backwards on the seat of the chair in front of him and leaned over the chair-back. "I'd like to go to China. Fly those DH4's of yours."

"That so?"

"But there might be a problem."

"That so?"

Jack glanced down at his buttons. "I'm…uh…under suspicion here…concerning Shontz's murder."

"The man who owned your skyrocket?" Slappy unbuttoned his coat.

"Yes."

"That all?" He took out a handkerchief and mopped perspiration from his neck.

"No. The sheriffs are interested in what connection I might have with Sam's death."

Slappy laughed as he put his kerchief away. "You gotta be kiddin'. His own pig-headedness killed him. And he's been that way all his life. Anyone who knew him knows that." He stretched his legs. "None of that holds any water in China. What does matter is whether or not you can do the job. Sam said you're a hot pilot. That's good enough for me. You want the job? You got it." Slappy thrust out a massive paw.

Jack watched his own hand disappear inside Slappy's grasp as they shook. "Thanks. You won't be sorry."

"I'm sure you'll do fine." The larger man stood up and loosened his collar. "Old Sammy left you holding the bag somehow, didn't he?"

"How'd you know?" Jack rose as well.

"For one thing, I know Sammy. For another, he wired me about a year ago about a China contract. He seemed keen for the idea then, but that was before he found a less dangerous way to get the money he needed. I'm guessing it was *some* kind of loan."

"A loan and me."

"That's what I thought. Sammy never did have much of his own money." Slappy raised both eyebrows. "Well, you've got the card I left you. We'll be in Frisco a few more days." He winked. "But don't make it too long. Whoever misses the boat, misses the boat." Slappy gave Jack the traditional shoulder slap good-bye. "See ya around, Jack. And by the way...if you should, for any reason, change your mind. Wire me at that Frisco address, would ya? So I won't be tempted to wait for a man who ain't comin'." He turned his back and sauntered down the hill in the direction of the passenger station.

Jack wiped sweating hands on his trousers. *All right, we're committed now. And it should solve everyone's problems. I'll send money back, and I'll be out of everyone's hair. Won't cause any more trouble here. Everyone'll be better off. Except for one thing. I'll miss my kids like crazy. And I'll miss Carrie. She* would *have to decide she loves me* now.

He had been standing there in the cemetery for several minutes with unfocused eyes, seeing only inward. Then, with the end of his introspection, his vision once again took in the outside world. And the first thing he saw? Ruth's piercing dark stare looking straight at Jack over Reverend Fisher's shoulder. Fisher carried on a conversation with a red-eyed Ben, but Ruth seemed to be more interested in Jack, giving him the distinct impression she'd been listening to his conversation with Slappy.

How much did you hear, Ruth? Jack decided not to wait to find out. He forced his eyes away from the woman's glare and started down the path to where Kenny and Eddie played some running, dust-raising game with a small group of children amongst the parked cars.

♣

"I don't give a hang if he's busy! I don't care what he's doing! Get Cal on the phone now!" Jack felt the angry blood rise to his temples.

"Sure thing, boss. Sorry. Please, just give me a second to get him."

Aw, why am I yelling at this kid? Not one part of this is his fault. "Of course I'll wait." Jack took a calming breath. "But tell Cal it's important. All right?"

"You bet, boss!"

Jack heard the phone at the other end drop and bang against something. He glanced at his overstuffed flight bag on the ranch-house floor. *Do I have everything in there I want?* he thought. *No, but it's everything I need.* He leaned a shoulder against the wall and tried to calm himself. *Last time I lean against this wall. Do you know what you're doing, Jack?* A distant verbal commotion began and the familiar sound of metal tools hitting the hangar's concrete floor echoed in the earpiece. *Do I know what I'm doing? Lord, I hope so...this time.*

Cal's muttering began in the distance and grew closer until the hangar telephone earpiece scraped against something. "Yeah, what's the rush, Jack! I was trackin' a coolant leak on number five!"

"Cal, which ship's ready that's not loaded with mail?"

"Well, let me see. Number five's the one I got half apart. Number two's dropping oil. Uh—"

"Cal, I'm in a hurry here," Jack growled, almost without realizing he'd done so.

"Well, all right then. No need to bite my head off."

"I'm sorry. Which one's ready right now?"

"Number six is fueled and ready for the midnight mail to San Fernando, but the mail sacks haven't arrived yet. They have to come in from Bakersfield tonight, don't you know."

Jack switched to his reserve tank of patience. Cal couldn't help over-talking, of course. It's just the way he was. "Good. Then trot out number six for me, will you. I'm taking her up on business. I'll be there in just a few minutes; have her running, please."

"Then I'll have to get another one ready before midnight."

"Yes, you will. So you better get busy. I'll be right there. Good-bye."

Jack slapped the earpiece into its cradle. *I hope he does it.* He snatched his bag from the floor and strode out the front door into the driveway where the boys tickled and tortured each other in the Stutz as a surrendering sun hovered just above the western ridgeline of Saber Canyon. Jack's black Sunday suit had disappeared in favor of a new flight suit which, when zipped, hid plain brown trousers and a blue shirt. He patted his leg pocket for the company-issued thirty-eight revolver. *Probably get more use out of this thing in China than I ever got flying the mail.* He tossed the bag onto the space behind the seat with the careless air of a man who will never be back.

"You gentlemen ready?" He slid behind the wheel and shut the door. The electric starter whined and a smooth grumble emitted from under the hood. Jack smiled and shared that smile with the boys. "Isn't that nice. It just starts right up. No cranking."

Eddie snickered. "Mom does it all the time, Dad."

Kenny nodded. "Yeah, she says a real lady doesn't go through life cranking cars."

Jack shrugged. "Guess I'm just not use to doing things the easy way."

Kenny adjusted himself in the middle of the front seat. "But you were a racecar driver. Weren't you, Dad? Mom said."

Jack didn't answer, but merely started the car moving down the dirt road. They passed Sam's old house. Bee sat behind the wheel of a new Model-A sedan while Seth tied one last suitcase to the bundle of luggage that clung to the back rack. Seth waved; Bee didn't.

Jack waved back at Seth for the last time and wondered for a second where Sam's widow got the money for a new car. *I thought they were dead broke.* He mulled that over for almost *another* second before he cut it loose. *Who cares! None of that matters anymore anyway.* Then he turned his attention back to his kids. "Yes. I drove race cars." he said, remembering his son's question. Then he tried to slow his breathing as he rested his elbow on top of the door.

"Well, didn't the race cars have 'lectric starters?" Kenny's forehead furrowed as he awaited an answer.

"No." The Smith farmhouse passed on the right, dark and brooding in its loneliness. "They all had to be cranked, and it was hard to do because the engines were so big. Take a strong man two or three tries and sometimes a skinned knuckle to get one going before a race."

Eddie squirmed around. "Where'd you race, Dad?"

Jack caught a glimpse of the ditch that broke his trailer axle just five years before, and a small shot of adrenaline burrowed its way into his chest as he recalled being trapped under the trailer with the rattler. "We raced all over: Los Angeles, Chicago, Albany," he said. "You name it; we raced there."

Eddie scrunched his face. "No. I mean did they let you race right on the street or what?"

Jack turned onto the unpaved section of Saber Canyon Road. The Stutz hugged the clay and granite surface through the turn like a gate hinged to a post, very different from the Model-T's that had to be wrestled down a straight road like a drunken hippopotamus. *Oh, this is really nice.* "We drove on oval dirt tracks, just like a horse race."

Kenny jumped in. "You raced on dirt?"

"Yep. Just like this."

"What was it like?"

666

A little lightning bolt of thought ran through Jack's brain and burst out onto his face in the form of a sly smile. "You boys hold on to this." He leaned over and patted the chrome passenger grip bar that ran along the dashboard between the glove compartment and the windshield. "Now hold on tight. I mean it."

Both young MacGregors obeyed, each putting a vise-grip onto the chrome.

Jack winked at them. "It was kind of like this." He dropped the shifter into the next lower gear and pressed the accelerator hard against the floorboard, gluing Kenny and Eddie to the seatback. Rabbits scattered in the dying light of sunset and sagebrush became a blur as it disappeared rearward. The tires fairly leapt from one stretch of adobe washboards to another as the speedometer's needle passed forty and the boys squealed with fear and delight.

A side road rolled up, and Jack down-shifted to thirty and accelerated into a four wheel sliding turn. "And like that!" He grinned at his sons through a mass of blond hair the wind had spread across his eyes. "I liked that part the best." The boys' wide-eyed looks almost matched their grins' intensity. "The driving was fun and kept the blood moving." He took the next turn faster than the last, maintaining a watch on his passengers, whose small hands were still welded to the bar on the dashboard. "But the part I liked the best was passing all the other cars. That was satisfying, indeed."

Jack leaned into the next turn, as did his sons. The Bearcat made that turn as if it were on rails then straightened out with no loss of control back onto the main road again. Jack up-shifted and continued his one-car dirt road race toward town as fast as he dared. "You gents know your old dad loves you, don't you?" Jack yelled over the rushing air as the car passed the mailboxes and the speedometer's needle passed fifty.

"Yeah," both wind-whipped boys agreed together.

A ramp-like rise of clay lifted the car off the ground, leaving momentary daylight between the front seat and Eddie's rear pockets. Tires screamed as they contacted the first few feet of pavement on Saber Canyon Road. Jack cajoled the fishtailing Stutz into a straight course. Now he and the Bearcat negotiated a new understanding. *Okay you piece of high-priced junk, go faster than you've ever gone before, so I can show off for my kids... maybe for the last time.* Equal-and-opposite reaction to the car's acceleration flung the three occupants back into the seat again as Kenny and Eddie's father roared up through a gear that had not been used as yet. The speedometer displayed eighty with mechanical pride. Both boys screamed pure joy out into the rushing air; their faces fairly glowed as they sneaked peeks at their father, the racecar driver. The speedometer needle tickled ninety and vibrated there in cadence with the energy being transmitted from the front tires.

Releasing the wheel with his left hand long enough to pull wind-whipped hair from his face, Jack leaned toward his jack-o-lantern-faced passengers. "I want you to know something." He glanced up and down the Sierra Highway crossroad as the stop sign approached. No traffic. "No matter what anyone…anyone at all tells you, I love you two monsters and your mom more than anything…more than my life. Do you understand that?" They roared past the stop sign at ninety-five and headed downhill toward the center of Sweet Springs.

Kenny kept his gaze on the windshield. "Yeah, we understand."

Eddie nodded his silent agreement.

"And no matter where I go, even if it's for a long time, I want you to remember I love you. And that will never change. Can you remember all that?"

Kenny glanced sideways. "Sure, Dad."

Jack remained quiet for a second or two. Then a very small temptation began to stew in his mind and eventually became an idea. "You see that plaque at the bottom of the dashboard?"

Kenny looked down at the small brass plate facing his knees. "Yeah."

Jack's smile began to grow again. "It says that this car has been tested at 100 miles per hour before it left the factory."

"Wow!" Kenny's eyes widened again. Then he grimaced. "Can this car do a hundred?"

"Well, that's what the plaque says." A quiet chuckle erupted up from Jack's diaphragm. "And, since we're going downhill, it might." *If I don't blow the engine first.* "Is that what you want? Try to break the old century mark in Mom's car?"

The unanimous *yeah* overcame the engine noise.

"All right then, gentlemen. One hundred it is, or bust. *Or throw a rod or crack the block. Carrie, forgive me. Lord, please don't let my wife's nightmare come true tonight. Please, keep your hand on this poor engine.* Jack's boot eased down on the gas pedal.

The boys sat transfixed, their bodies riding with the rocking and undulating of the Bearcat's springs, their gaze targeting the vibrating speedometer needle. "Ninety-seven, Dad!" Kenny leaned his face closer to the gauge's glass face as if it held the secrets to life within.

"Are you going away, Dad?" Eddie turned out to be the unlikely first to catch the implications of his father's earlier words. He leaned around his brother's head.

"Ninety-eight!" Kenny announced.

Jack winced, spared his youngest a flash-glance, then brought his vision back to the road. "I have some work to do someplace that's too far to make it home at night. I'll have to stay there until I'm finished. Then I'll be back to see you as soon as I can. Don't worry."

Eddie nodded.

"Ninety-nine!" Kenny yelled and bounced with the next dip in the road. "Almost there!"

A mule pulling a hay-wagon turned onto the road from out of the shadows and began its snail crawl directly in front of the hurtling Stutz. Jack hit the horn, but that only elicited a disinterested turn of the head from both the driver and the mule.

"A hundred, Dad. It's a hundred!" Kenny beamed.

Eddie clapped his hands once, then grabbed the bar again.

"Great! Now hold on tight, both of you." Jack let off the accelerator to swerve around the wagon and its unconcerned man and mule. All four of the Stutz's tires complained like the howl of the dead for the brief duration of the maneuver. But then the miracle of traction between rubber and pavement restored itself, and the blessed Bearcat continued its maniacal late-night hurtle toward town. "Everyone still on board?" With Sweet Springs less than a mile away, the Bearcat wound down below eighty. After a few more seconds, Jack downshifted and applied a little brake.

Kenny and Eddie shared the look of finalists in a grin contest—Eddie the most. "Wow, Dad!"

Kenny released his grip on the chrome bar. "That was the best!"

"My pleasure, gentlemen." Jack eased down closer to a normal speed. *Well, nothing blew up or fell off. The precious Stutz has survived to drive another day.* "Now you boys know not to tell your mother about this, don't you."

Kenny said, "Yeah."

Eddie nodded.

After throttling down to a slow roll, Jack stopped and shut off the engine in front of the Hunter's Inn. He pulled his bag from the back, dropped it to the ground, and handed Kenny the car key. "That's for your mom. I've got to go now." He bent over and hugged one boy in each arm. "You remember what I told you."

Eddie looked up as his father relaxed his grip. "You mean about dirt racing?"

Kenny swatted his brother on the arm. "No, dummy. The love stuff, right Dad?"

Jack smiled. "Yeah, the love stuff."

Eddie shrugged. "Okay."

Jack's hand tousled both heads, then he held his breath to restrain a sudden surge of sorrow that threatened to embarrass him in front of his sons. A second later when he'd gained control, he said, "Tell you what. Go ahead and tell Mom about our dirt racing." He took another breath and smiled. "And make sure you mention the hundred-miles-an-hour part." One more double-hug, then he backed away, snatching up his bag. "You go on in to your mom, now. I'll see you when I get back."

He gave them a quick wave, followed by a shooing gesture. The boys just stood there for a moment, and Jack worried they wouldn't go, making the whole affair almost unbearable. But in the end, they simply returned his wave and disappeared behind the screened service door that lead to the inn's kitchen.

Jack sighed and shouldered the bag. *Thanks, Lord. I couldn't have lasted much longer.*

He started his walk to the airfield along the street that passed in front of the Lakeview Café. Alma peaked out the front door and stood there for a moment, looking like she was going to speak or step out. At last, though, she retreated back inside, closing the door to possibilities and announcing her decision with the latch's loud metallic click.

Jack almost laughed out loud. *I always knew I'd lose one of these women. Just never thought it'd be both at the same time.* He sighed his surrender to circumstances and took a tighter grip on his bag. His former life felt truly gone now. After one deep breath, he accepted that. The comfort and security of wife, children, and the airmail business seemed by all evidence to be behind him. The thought both excited and unnerved him at the same time, much like things had in 1918 when he'd shipped out for France. Both then and now he had a plan, but an uncertain future, as well.

As the sun submerged itself beneath the western horizon, Jack crossed over the Lake Road and instinctively kicked a large chunk of granite out of his way—once more for old time sake. The thing ricocheted off a fence post, causing the dusk-lit raven at its top to fly off in search of a more peaceful perch...just as another bird had done several years past. In an instant, the memory of his last day on the railroad and his first day flying airmail ignited. The feeling of freedom at escaping the rail-yard, the satisfaction when he bested Crusher, and the sense of exaltation when he left the ground again after his long exile from aviation, all these memories flooded his spirit like a soothing tide, lifting his heart from the darkness of fear and loss to a momentary celebration of that one day when things went *so* right.

"Lord, let it happen like that again for me sometime," he said out loud. Then he squared his shoulders and picked up the pace on his way through the gate that lead onto the west end of the runway. In the distance, he could see Cal sitting in the cockpit of an aging De Havilland, while one of his underlings swung the propeller in an abortive attempt to kindle the Liberty engine to life. Jack noticed his hand had begun to shake against the flight bag's strap. He clenched his fist to make it stop. "Lord, please stay with me on this venture. I'm getting those old *you-ain't-comin'-back-from-this-one* shakes.

꙼

"He's What?" Carrie dropped the new menu onto the preparation table.

"He signed up as a...wha'd ya call it." Ruth paused, apparently to seek out the proper needed word here. "Uh, a mercenary pilot..that's it...a mercenary pilot for the Chinese. That Slappy fellow, old friend of Sam's from the war, he hired him." A very care-worn, still red-eyed Ruth settled onto the stool across from Carrie. "I heard it myself."

"But...what would...why...." All words froze in Carrie's throat. Circumstances had *left* her with nothing *left* to say. She knew the reasons for Jack's decision. She knew it all—except for one thing. "When did he say he intended to leave?"

"They didn't say." Ruth toyed with the snap on her small black purse. "Or maybe I just didn't hear it. My mind's been a wanderin' today something fierce."

Carrie brought her right hand up to her chest. "Oh, Ruth. I'm so sorry. Of course you're distracted. You must be sick with grief over poor Sam...and your grandchildren!"

Ruth bowed her head for just a moment, then brought it up again with a look of granite determination locked in place. "It's a mixed bag. You know?" She took in a breath. "Of course I miss Sam. Miss him something terrible. But I started missing him almost as soon as he got back from France. He didn't come back the same man. At least, not the son I knew. It was like some drunken demon had stolen my boy and taken his place." She sniffed. "He's been missing now since 1919. So I've had a while to get used to my son being gone. But now...Bee taking my grandchildren away...that's going to be a harder pill to swallow. That'll be the worst of it." She gave her head a quick single-shake. "But the Lord'll be with me. I won't be alone."

Carrie engulfed Ruth's hand in hers. "No you won't. I promise. And I don't just mean the Lord." She caressed her friend's fingers for a few seconds, then laid the old saint's hands gently back down on the table as Ruth nodded her gratitude. "Well," Carrie said. "Maybe I'll just ask Jack about these plans of his when he brings my car back." She flipped through the menu without seeing, as uneasiness began to settle upon her like a heavy dew.

Ruth clutched her purse as if to go but didn't move. "I think that would be a very—"

"Mom!" Eddie yelled and clomped into the kitchen like a stampeding herd of *something*. Kenny chased after him at an older-brother pace. "Dad took us dirt racing, and then we went a hundred miles a hour," the younger boy said. "And he told us some love stuff."

"Eddie, what are you talking about?" Carrie put the menu down again.

Kenny sat on a low chair near the wall counter. "Dad said he'd love us even if he had to go way far away to work."

One vague feeling made a quick connection with another, and all of a sudden everything came clear. Carrie shot off the stool. "Kenny, where's Dad now?"

"He took his flight bag—the big one—over to the airfield. And he gave me this for you, Mom." He laid the Stutz key on the table. "And he said to tell you about the racing and going a hundred."

Carrie snatched up the key and ran for the door. "Ruth can you—"

"I sure as heck can." She had just pulled a red bandana from her purse and now began to mop at her eyes. "Go!"

"You two stay with Ruth until I come to get you," Carrie's voice echoed back to the kitchen as she raced down the service hall. "And be good! Ruth, I'm sorry I couldn't—"

"I know, gal. Go on now!"

☙

As soon as Dutch gave the double shoulder-slap signal for *I'm ready*, Jack rolled the reluctant bomber into a wing-over and headed for the ground so fast that long strips of fabric tore themselves loose from around bullet holes in the wings. The flying wires between the wing-struts sang their banshee's wailing song, a familiar tune to veteran air crews of the Western Front who spent too much of their short lives in desperate dives like this one. The engine seized about halfway to the ground, and the oil fire spread from the manifold to the wooden frame that held the main fuel tank just as Jack flared out into a level glide ten feet above the twisted barbed wire and water-filled shell holes of the German side of no-man's-land.

Jack held the De Havilland's nose high until he felt the first shudder of the wings as they slowed to their stall-speed. Then he tore off his goggles, covered his face with his left arm and braced his feet against the firewall in anticipation of the impact to come.

But it *didn't* come. He waited another second. Nothing. And all sensation of movement had ceased, as well. He pulled his arm down from his face. No-man's-land had vanished. No barbed wire. No mud. No background echo of machinegun fire. Nothing came to Jack's ears but the benign racket of a tired but functional Liberty engine at low throttle. However, just that change of realities proved startling enough to give Jack's body an involuntary jerk.

As realization of the present settled upon him, he surrendered to the evidence that he now sat alone in a De Havilland mail plane. No Dutch to worry about. No mission to complete. The reality of the war, once again, ten years in the past.

Boy, is this getting to be a habit. I wonder how many times I've done that one stupid mission. Fifty? A hundred? I wonder how many more times I'll still have to do it.

He let out his obligatory sigh of relief, then checked his watch and the oil temperature of the idling engine. *I've been sitting here a full fifteen minutes. I'm lucky this beast didn't start to overheat. De Havilland's like to be airborne where the relative wind can flow through the radiator.* He decided to double-check the controls and his gear before he left. *Then I need to get out of here before I lose my nerve on this deal.*

.♪.

Carrie set the Bearcat's handbrake with a two-handed jerk and swung her feet out onto the gravel by the west side of the number one hangar.

"Why, why, why?" Her muttering fell into cadence with the crunch of her shoes on the ground. Then she reached the large paved squares of the concrete apron and her crunches turned to wooden-healed clacks. A few yards away she saw Jack sitting in the cockpit of one of the mail planes. She could hear the engine's idling chant and saw the reflection of the hangar lights shimmering off the spinning propeller. *I thought we had things all worked out. What's he thinking? He doesn't tell me anything! No...no, that's not true. He does try sometimes...but my ears have been closed to it. I put up my Van Burean wall and peer down at Jack from the top. I have to find out what's going on inside that thick head of his, if it's not too late. Oh Lord, don't let him get away before I can ask him. I'll do whatever you want! Just don't let him leave, please!*

At that moment, the faded biplane throttled up, causing an onslaught of prop-wash that threw more than a little dust and sand to the rear. Then the machine-induced storm lessened as the engine noise dwindled down to half its former intensity and Jack's plane lumbered Carrie's direction, its wings rocking a little in the light evening breeze. Carrie stopped walking and broke into a run.

♪

Jack glanced over his shoulder into the half-circle of light, emitted from the large bare bulb attached to the outside wall of the hangar. *Any half-awake mail pilots wandering near the plane? Nobody? Good, clear to swing left.* All gear secured, all last minute double-checks made, a slight nudge to the throttle and a firm foot on the left brake turned the De Havilland around at a gradual pace toward the taxiway. He pulled in a calming draught of warm dry desert air as the yellowish-white disc of hangar two's outside light passed by his line of sight. *Finally time to get out of here. And probably the last time to see any of this.* The sun-faded black fuel truck came into momentary view, hunched in semi-shadow between the two hangars like a sleeping pig. *You almost made a go of it here, Jack old sport.* He filled his lungs with the smell of sage, then tried to exhale some of the regret that made his chest feel so heavy. *Almost made it this time.* The illuminated open maw of hangar one became visible once more. Cal stood between two disemboweled De Havillands, directing four lesser grease monkeys as to the mechanical surgery at hand. Jack felt a small twinge below his chest and knew he'd actually miss this comedic man.

Whoa, now. Don't get sappy already, or you'll still be sitting here bawling when the sheriffs come to get you tomorrow. Jack glanced to the right and aimed his wingtip at the center of the hangar bay, a little game he'd played for the last five years that had little technical value except that it added a boyish air to an otherwise serious business, and it always lined him up perfectly with the westbound taxiway. He braked to a stop and watched Cal for a few seconds as

677

the master mechanic tortured a disobedient Liberty engine with a long-handled wrench. *Time to go.* Then Jack did something he had never done before.

He released the brakes and coaxed the throttle forward while his gaze remained fixed on the hangar crew. That personal moment lasted almost a full second, immediately after which, he chastised himself for looking in one direction and moving in another, something he would have scolded any of his hired pilots for doing, had he caught them at it. Then he swung his head forward again to peer around the engine, which was, as usual, angled skyward like a coyote preparing to howl at the moon.

♩

Carrie slowed from her run to a walk as Jack's plane stopped abreast of the hangar. She decided to approach him on his left. She'd seen him climb in and out of enough airplanes over the years to remember he always mounted on the left as if his machine were a horse. She had almost made it to within waving distance when, without warning, the big De Havilland pivoted on its left wheel and swung straight for her.

He doesn't see me. That stupid great engine's in the way! She cupped her hands around her mouth as she tried to back away. "Jack! Jack, stop!" Instinct alone had caused her to shout. The engine's roar would drown out every word, and Carrie knew it. She also knew she should stop walking backwards, turn, and run, but by the time that thought finished sprinting through her mind, the blurring propeller had almost reached her.

♩

Jack's left foot tapped on the rudder peddle, and the biplane's nose began a quick swing to the left, starting the

678

first of a series of S-turns that would take him on a serpentine journey down the dark taxiway. All seemed well until a fleck of something appeared through the flashing disc of the propeller's rotating blades. It wasn't much, just a bright bit of color that seemed to move just beyond the realm of the hangar door light. *What the—* Then it moved again...and became an arm..attached to a body that stood underneath a wind-whipped crop of dark hair. And it was all about to be devoured by the massive spinning prop.

"Oh, Geeze! Carrie!" Jack yanked back on the throttle and stood on the peddle-brakes. The mail plane lurched its weight up onto the big wheels of its main landing gears as inertia and center of gravity shifted forward. The hungry propeller arched toward Carrie's face, but stopped a hand-breadth short, then subsided the same distance.

Jack cut the ignition and shut off the fuel, fearing his wife would lose her balance and fall forward. Knowing a split second could make the difference between life and death, he unstrapped and de-parachuted himself, and slid to the ground faster than he ever had in his life. He ripped off his helmet and ran around the left lower wing tip, but slowed almost to a stop when he saw his wife. She stood stone still, frozen, inches from the slowing prop, eyes wide as planets, mouth open, chest heaving.

Jack let his leather helmet drop to the ground. "Carrie, don't move." He kept his voice careful and even, as he placed his hands on her shoulders from behind and drew her back just before the blades made their last revolution and jerked to a stop. At that same moment, the Liberty starved to death, exuding one last gasp of gray smoke. Danger having passed, Jack turned her around. "What were you doing?" He shook her. "Are you trying to kill yourself? I didn't even see you until the last second!"

"Kill myself?" Her eyes seemed focused on something distant at first, then, after a second, the look of recognition returned. "No, I'm trying to stop *you*. Where were you going? Ruth said something about China. What's all this about? China? I can't believe it. China!"

Jack released his grip, and snatched his helmet from the pavement. "Ruth was giving me the evil eye at the cemetery. I was *afraid* she'd gotten wind of something." He stuffed his helmet into a thigh pocket and zipped it shut.

Carrie emitted a quick sigh. "I'm glad she *did* hear something, or you'd have left us without saying a word."

Jack leaned against the wing. "It's not like that, Carrie. I wasn't leaving you."

"Well, what would you call it?" She spread her feet wide apart and crossed her arms. "Were you going to tell me why? No. Were you going to tell me anything? No. You just drop some cryptic hint to a nine-year-old and take off for Asia! Is that love, Jack? Is that being responsible?"

"Yes, on both counts."

"Oh, my Lord!" She threw her hands in the air, turned away, and took a step. Then she turned around again. "I can't believe what I'm hearing! How could you say that?"

"I was going to leave *because* I love you, and it's probably the most responsible thing I've ever done." His hands slid into his side overall pockets, as was their habit. "If I'm not here, I can't hurt anybody, and, if I'm in China, I can make lots of money and send it home to fix the damage I've caused." He shook his head. "I've done nothing but create problems for you and the boys, Carrie. I just want to change that." *Don't you understand? I'm trying to do the honorable thing.*

♪

Carrie saw Jack slump against the wing's sun-faded fabric. Right then, for reasons she could not explain, she discovered a new sympathy she hadn't felt for him in a long time. Instead of a selfish slacker with little common sense, she perceived a wounded casualty of life's war, struggling against heavy odds to make something of his life and still keep his promises to his loved ones. This change in perception took place all in an instant as if someone had turned on a light, revealing more than could have been seen before. Next came another new realization. *Thank you, Father. I know I'm seeing through your eyes. Please, guide me. Speak through me, and, please, put your hand on Jack's heart, as well.*

"Jack, let's take a walk." She narrowed her stance.

"A walk? You mean right now?"

"Yes. On the taxiway."

"On the taxiway...out with the rattlesnakes?" His tone told her he wasn't concerned about night reptiles, but he thought she might be.

"Absolutely." She nodded her head in an exaggerated fashion. "Out with the snakes." She took his hand and pulled him beyond the comforting circle of the hangar light out into the uncertainty of taxiway shadows.

They walked a few paces in silence, then Jack stopped short and dropped his wife's hand. "What are we doing?" he said.

Carrie let her arms hang limp. The fatigue of the day and the stress of the present crisis nibbled at her small reserve of strength. She took a slow breath. "We're going to talk about us."

Jack's hands found their pocket-burrows again. "What for?"

"Because I want things to be different." *Please, Lord. Let him believe me.*

"Just like that." He sounded doubtful.

"Yes." She pulled his hand out from the overalls and clasped it into hers. "Just like that." *Don't try to control him. That's part of what got you here. Think gentle tones.* "Are you coming?" she said in just such a tone. Then she just stood there, holding his hand, waiting.

A long second passed.

"All right." He came alongside her. "Let's talk then."

They began a slow stroll down the dark unpaved taxiway toward the dim lights of town. Granite gravel crunched against the clay beneath the soles of their shoes, flushing a field mouse from the dry grass. The creature shot across the taxiway between Carrie's feet, evoking an involuntary gasp and a double-step from the human.

She let go of Jack and put a hand to her breast, as the adrenaline subsided. Then she smiled. "Silly little thing gave me a start. You'd think I'd be used to them after five years."

Jack raised an eyebrow. "Didn't know you were afraid of mice...or anything else, for that matter." He shook his head. "At least not anymore."

Good. He's talking. "It's not the mouse so much." She brushed off her clothes even though they weren't dirty. "But I don't like unexpected things coming out of the dark." She walked a couple of steps with her hands behind her back. "I don't suppose anyone does."

"Anyone does what?" Jack shuffled to a stop.

"Like things coming at them...from out of nowhere."

"Oh yeah." He rubbed the back of his neck. "I guess not."

Carrie stopped and turned to face Jack. "This little China trip of yours did that."

"Came at you out of nowhere?" He took a step closer.

"Very much so."

"Sorry." He rubbed his forehead now. "You don't look very steamed about it, though." Jack took a deep breath. "How come?"

Say it right. This could be a fork in the road for more than you know. She clasped her hands together in front, glanced down at them, then locked her gaze onto Jack's eyes. "Because I think God's been trying to tell me you have good cause to be angry with me...for more than just one thing...and for a long time now."

"What do you mean?" he said.

At this point the little voice residing somewhere near Carrie's heart piped up again. *He's playing dumb because he doesn't know whether or not to trust you. He thinks this new contriteness could be just another mood change that will swing back later. You've made him gun-shy that way.*

Then came her internal response. *Okay, Lord. Please, guide me...because I'm not sure what to say.* And she hesitated for just another instant until the words came from somewhere outside her consciousness and began to build up inside like water behind a dam. Then the dam broke and the words flowed out all at once, not too fast, but too strong and steady for Carrie to stop them, even if she had wanted to.

"I've sinned against you and God," she heard herself say.

Jack just stood there silhouetted against the hangar lights. He looked as if he were going to speak, but his jaws remained clamped. Carrie waited for a comment...any comment, but none came. So she returned to letting the words from within her flow.

"I haven't shown you the respect you deserved," she said. "And you *did* deserve it. I know now you were doing all you could to make a life for us. But when things went wrong I blamed you, and I think I tried to punish you by not showing respect." She looked at the ground for a moment and toed a patch of loose sand. "And I guess I've been rather a bit of a cliché from time to time. You know. Spoiled rich girl...always wanting her way." She looked up and linked her gaze to his again. "It's true I suppose. You can't grow up being taught that you're superior to most other people and not have some of that attitude soak in just a bit. Sometimes I did actually think that—being superior, I mean. I didn't want to, and I didn't *really* believe it deep down. But it was just sort of an old habit that I had to break." She stepped forward and touched his arm with a gentle hand. "I fell in love with you, Jack, that first year at college. And I've loved you ever since…even when I didn't show it. And I know I haven't shown it as much as I should have. It's just that sometimes that little rich brat shows up…sort of *pops* up, you know. And I have to take the time to get rid of her so I can go on being what the Lord has made me *now*, in my true and real adult Christian life." She gave his arm a squeeze. "I *do* love you, Jack. I love you more than my life, and I'd hate to think what my days on this earth would be like without you. I know this now. I think I've always known it. That's why I used to get so upset when you'd go away to fly. Whenever you weren't around, it was like a big part of my heart was missing…just a giant hole where Jack used to be. And it felt the same when I took the boys to go live with my parents. Somewhere in the back of my mind, I think I always knew it wasn't the end for you and me. I still had the spark of a belief that somehow we'd be together again. God said we are one inseparable flesh, and He's right. Because when you're gone, part of *me* is, too."

"Wow." Jack coupled his monosyllabic response with a dumbfounded expression.

Carrie resisted the urge to smile. *But what else can he say when I've probably just voiced some of what he's been thinking for* years?

Then Jack found his tongue again and said, "Where'd all *that* come from?"

Carrie waited for him to say more, but when he didn't, she cleared her throat. "Bet you never expected to hear all this from me." She shuffled her feet a little more and tried to add a nervous snicker to her words.

"I never expected to hear *any* of it…ever." He glanced up at the stars then back to his wife. "D'you mean it?"

She shook her head. "Which part?"

"Any of it."

Anger kindled itself within her for just a moment. *What! Does he think I'm lying?* But then, something warm and gentle wafted through her, touching her thoughts, and her countenance softened again. "I meant all of it, Jack. Every word."

All of a sudden, Jack wheeled away from her, and she thought he was going to leave. But he didn't. Instead he just rubbed his face with the sleeve of his overalls then turned to face her again. "I love you, Carrie," he said with gravel in his voice, a half octave higher than his norm. "And I don't really want to go away from you." He sniffed. "But I just don't see how..." His sentence choked itself off, unfinished, and he tried to clear his throat, but the effort turned into a sort of half growl—half horse's whinny.

He started to face away again, but she grabbed hold of his arm, and this time she felt, not only the now-familiar sweet spirit flood through her, but also a selfless sort of power and a determination that seemed to, at once, strengthen and electrify every part of her being. And she said, in a firm but soft tone, "Jack, there's nothing we can't face together. And with God's help, we can prevail."

Jack actually cracked a miserable excuse for a half-smile. "Prevail?"

Carrie rolled her eyes and returned his expression. "We can...come out on top." She moaned a bit. "You know what I mean."

"Yes," he said. "But I just don't know if we can come out on top of *this*." A herd of wrinkles invaded his forehead. "This thing with the sheriff...and Shontz's family. I don't know. It seems like the deck's already been stacked so I end up with the losing hand, no matter what I do."

There existed, way in the back of Carrie's mind, something that felt very important. As yet she didn't know what it might be. That is, she could not have written it down if she wanted, but, somehow, she knew it to be on its way, soon to surface.

"Jack, I've got something else to tell you," she said.

His brow furrowed again. "Oh, yeah. What?"

The *important thing* had been making its way to her pool of conscious thought, and it had picked up speed but had not quite, at that point in time, arrived at its destination. "I don't know yet." Now Carrie's *wrinkled-brow turn* had come. She touched her hand to the side of her head.

"What do you mean you don't know?"

She began to breath faster. "I mean I *don't know* what it is yet."

"Carrie, you're not making any sense."

"I know." She laid both palms on top of her hair. "Look, it's something that's begun happening to me lately. It's difficult to explain...except to say that I think the Holy Spirit sort of gets into my head, and he gives me new ideas, new thoughts. And sometimes even things to say...like tonight."

Jack seemed to chew that over for a moment, then he pointed at her. "You mean like before when you..."

"Yes." She gave him an exaggerated nod. "Like before when I said...everything that's led us here! I know that was a long time ago, but...yes, it's very much like that...only more so." She breathed a few more fast heaves, then caught her breath. "Only sometimes it doesn't come out right away. Sometimes I get sort of a feeling...kind of like when I'm going to sneeze, only stronger ...like when you're trying to hold your breath, but eventually you have to let it out. I know it's coming, like a sneeze, but I don't know what kind of a sneeze it's going to be yet. And then when it gets here...I have to let it out." She doubled her brow wrinkles. "Do you understand?"

He looked hopeful for an instant, but then lost some mental connection and shook his head. "No."

She sighed and, for a couple of seconds, just stood waiting and looking off into the night. Then, very quickly, a smile grew across her face and, in the end, turned into a full-blown grin. "It's here! I've got it!"

"What?"

"The thing I have to tell you!"

He nodded. "Okay, shoot."

"Well, wait a minute," she said.

"Wait for what?"

"I have to do something first."

"What do you have to do?" Jack's voice groaned with the strain of waning patience.

Carrie grimaced and grasped both of Jack's upper arms. "Father, please." Her tone sounded desperate, and she hesitated for several seconds before continuing. "Father, please...fix this mess." She took a deep breath. "I know things look a little hopeless right now for Jack and me...what with Mr. Shontz's death and his family looking for someone to blame, not to mention the mess Sam left us in. But you say you can fix anything if we ask according to your will and ask in Jesus' name. So I ask you now. Please, make all these terrible things come out right, according to your will." She stopped and rested in a sort of breathy manner, as if she had just run a great distance. Then what she had forgotten floated up from her memory. "Oh yes, in Jesus name. Amen."

Almost five full seconds of silence passed before Jack spoke.

"Is that what you were supposed to say?" He looked a little confused.

"No," she said. "Well, yes. But there's more."

"What then?"

"Just this." She pulled him a little closer, clasping her hands on his shoulders. And when she spoke she shook him gently in cadence with her words. "Ephesians 5:22."

"Ephesians?" he said and almost laughed.

Carrie pulled her hands from Jack's shoulders and moved back a little. "Now don't laugh. Just listen. It's something the pastor read at church not long ago. I've never liked it, but the Spirit's almost yelling it at me now. Ephesians 5:22. 'Wives, submit yourselves unto your husbands, as unto the Lord.'"

Jack shook his head again. "So what does all this mean?"

Genuine shock spread through Carrie's being. "You don't know what that scripture means?"

"Of course I do." He waved an indicative hand in front of her. "But, I mean all this, what you're doing out here with me tonight...reciting the scripture. All this. What does it mean?"

She moved close again and wrapped her arms around him. "Just this, Ace. From this night on you are the true and official head of our family, God's deputy here on earth as far as the boys and I are concerned. Deputy of the King and second only to Him. From this moment on, you have my love and my full allegiance. I hereby submit to you and your will, as if you were the Lord. And I will depend upon you to seek the Lord in all matters and you will have the final word. I will not fight you anymore, Jack. I will not argue out of selfish pride. From now on...I'm on your side. We will be as one flesh. Whatever happens to you happens to me."

"Good grief, Carrie." He paused and searched her face. "You're serious, aren't you?"

"Absolutely. And here's a good faith token. Whether you go or stay is up to you. If you go, I'll be here waiting when you get back. If you stay, I'll do whatever you say...to help us...to help us come out on top of this mess. You're in charge." She dropped her gaze for just an instant. "Next to the Lord, that is." She smiled. "Anyway, we're in this together."

"Wow!"

"You've already said that."

"I know, but it's all that comes to mind at the moment."

Carrie had spoken all that without letting go of the man. And now she continued to stand there on the darkened taxiway, holding him close, as she let her head come to rest on his shoulder. The moon had been and still remained absent from the night sky. So the stars asserted themselves with a rare intensity that created the illusion that they were, in their brilliance, all hanging from some huge invisible dome that arched its protective mass low over Sweet Springs alone, to the exclusion of all else in the universe.

Carrie raised her gaze to these heavenly bodies, and a soothing warmth crept through her consciousness. *Everything's so beautiful—so comforting. Is that your doing tonight, Lord? Is that more of your Spirit at work within me?* And, as she felt the rareness of the moment engulf her, she drank it in like a dry cloth dropped into a pond. It all seemed so wonderful in its flawless simplicity. And she believed without a doubt that God had provided both the stars and the caress of the Holy Spirit just for her—just for tonight. A divine intersection in reality where all things needed arrive together at the exact right place and time.

It seemed perfect...and would have remained complete in its perfection, had it not been for the automobile spotlight that first swept across them, then centered itself upon the couple. After that, came the loud abrasive voice, originating from somewhere back behind the light, toward the hangars. Its shrill pitch intruded upon the soft desert stillness, battering the peace that had existed right up to that moment.

"Are you Jack MacGregor?" Night shadows kept the voice disembodied at first. But, soon after, a silhouetted figure of a man, striding forward beneath a broad-brimmed campaign hat, materialized.

Not having quite recovered yet from the emotional roller-coaster of the previous few minutes, Jack lagged a little with his answer. So the approaching figure spoke again, employing a more impatient tone. "I said, are you Jack MacGregor?" The familiar granite crunch accompanied the figure's steps. And a little more detail of his general appearance became apparent in the distance-diffused spotlight illumination. He wore the uniform of a Los Angeles County Deputy Sheriff and the expression of a junkyard dog that had just found a juicy trespasser.

"Yes, that's me." Jack had jump-started his voice into action…almost too late.

The dog-deputy came to an immediate sliding halt, drew a .45 Colt Peacemaker from its holster and leveled it with a one-handed grip upon Carrie's dumbstruck husband. "Ma'am, please step back from that man."

Carrie's reaction came in an instant. "I most certainly will not!"

The Deputy pressed on with his endeavor. "Ma'am, if you don't step away from him right now, I will arrest you for obstruction of justice. MacGregor, put your hands over your head. I'm placing you under arrest for the murder of…"

"Deputy Adkins!" Another voice rang out from the direction of the light. "We are not arresting anyone right now!" The familiar face of Deputy Comings, the man who had questioned Jack at the cemetery that morning, came into recognition range. He strode over to Deputy Adkins, who seemed now to be the man of lesser authority, and reached out to gently pushed his more eager subordinate's gun-hand back down to a not so lethal angle. "So put your weapon back to bed." He paused briefly, keeping his attention on Adkins, who, with some reluctance, returned the Colt to its former resting place. Then the senior deputy turned to the MacGregors. "Evening, Folks. Beautiful night, don't you think?" He craned his head back to take an unhurried look at the celestial ceiling. "Don't think I've seen the stars looking that close in a long time." He shook his head a little. "Sure is pretty."

Jack half turned to face the two peace officers. "Deputy Comings, what's going on?"

"Yeah!" Adkins piped up. "What *is* going on? You told me to find MacGregor and hold him for the Shontz murder. So that's what I was doing! And now you…"

"I told you to *get a hold of* Mr. MacGregor, so I could share a little more information about the Shontz murder with him. Having known Mr. Shontz, *Mr. MacGregor* is an interested party." Comings took in a deep breath and sighed with a seeming deliberate slowness. "And that's all. He's not a suspect."

Adkins took on a look of confusion. "Not a suspect?"

Comings shook his head. "No."

"He's not involved?"

"I have found no evidence of that."

Adkins folded his arms across his chest and rubbed his chin with one hand. "Well, if that's so, why is he all ready to skip town? Look at him! He's all ready to go! Got his flyin' suit on and got an airplane just waiting for him back there!" Adkins pointed an accusing thumb back over his shoulder toward the hangars. "So where's he going, if he's not guilty of anything? What's he leaving for?"

"He's taking the night-mail pouch to San Fernando. That's what he's doing," said Cal, as he too arrived at the gathering. "I put it in your plane, Boss. Sorry I'm late with it. Darn postmaster drug his feet getting it over here." Cal blinked and displayed his most innocent face as he surveyed the group. "And you're gonna be late if you don't take off soon." He paused. "What's going on?"

"Well." Comings clasped his hands behind his back. "I was just going to give Mr. MacGregor a bit of news about the Shontz case." He paused in mid-answer, demonstrating the deliberate slowness of one who is certain of complete control over the present circumstances. "It seems the witness who claimed to have seen Mr. MacGregor in the rail-yard the night of the murder…has changed his mind. He says now that, upon further reflection, he was mistaken. He also admits to having had too much to drink that evening…and doesn't really know *who* he saw." The senior deputy cleared his throat and glanced at his subordinate. "In other words, Mr. MacGregor, you have absolutely no official connection with this case."

Jack looked dumbfounded and even shook his head a little. "I wonder what made the guy change his story?"

Comings raised an eyebrow. "Guilty conscience maybe?"

Jack shook his head again. "I doubt that. There's never been much love lost between me and Crusher's thugs."

"Well then…" Comings gave Jack a congenial slap on the shoulder. "Other than the fact that business apparently dropped off to nothing today at Crusher's caboose-casino… after word got out that his man had accused you…" He gave Carrie a leprechaun's wink. "We may never know." Then he turned his face back to Jack. "I hear a lot of folks didn't like what Crusher's stooge tried to do to you. And they stayed away from that game by the…" Comings glanced to the sky and waited just an instant for the perfect inspiration. "By the train-load. Yep, that's it. They stayed away by the train-load ever since this morning." He smiled, satisfied with his performance.

Jack, however, still sported a very obvious dissatisfied expression. "But what about the Shontz family's charge that I had something to do with Sam's death," he said. "That I sabotaged their plane somehow before the speed trial?"

Comings waved a dismissive hand. "I've found no evidence to support that theory. And, as far as I'm concerned that's all it is, a theory. To a man, everyone who worked in, on, or near that aircraft, right up to the time Sam

Smith taxied out to the runway, all say that you didn't *even arrive* at the airfield until it was too late to stop him. They also say that the one person who tried to prevent the crash got socked in the eye for his trouble, and that it was Sam who did the socking. And the person who got socked was your mechanic here." He nodded toward Cal, who cast a self-conscious-looking glance toward the small-town lights to the West. "From the look of that black eye of his, that information was correct. No one who was here and saw what went on before that crash thinks you had anything to do with it. And neither do I. That's what my report will say." He gave his head a slow shake. "Ya know, during the course of this investigation, I've discovered that quite a few of the people around here seem to care what happens to you." He stopped speaking again and held his gaze upon Jack's face, as if to emphasize his words with a post-script of silence. Then he broke the verbal fast with, "But see that *you* take care of yourself just the same. Flying the mail tonight, I mean. Been nice meeting you folks." Comings offered a polite nod to the MacGregors then took two steps toward the hangar. But that's where he stopped. "I'm sorry. I can't just leave it at that," he said, then swiveled back around and retraced his steps to face Jack. "You don't remember me. Do you, Captain?"

A shadow of confusion crossed Adkins' countenance. "Captain?"

"Hold your peace, Deputy." Comings spoke over his shoulder to his partner, without turning toward him. Then he paused, took a breath, and focused his attention back upon Jack. "How could you remember?" He shook his head just a little. "I'd only been in the squadron three weeks when you left."

Now it was Jack's turn to shake his head. "I'm sorry...I don't—"

"That's all right, sir." Comings rubbed the knuckles of his right hand with the palm of his left. "I was Lieutenant

Morisey's gunner. Like I said, we were fairly new…but we got in five missions with you as lead."

"Lead?" Carrie broke in.

"Yes, ma'am. The bomber squadron I served with during the war." Comings indicated Jack with an open palmed gesture. "Captain MacGregor would always lead the formation on missions. We'd fly in V's of three or five aircraft, all formed beside and behind the lead aircraft, with him out in front sort of like the tip of the arrowhead, as it were. They called that flying *lead*. The commanding officer always picks the best flyers for that position. That was your husband, the best we had. He never got lost like so many did. He never turned too quick for those of us in the rear to follow. With inexperienced leads, Tail-end-Charlies like Lieutenant Morisey and me…often got left behind because of lead's turning too abruptly and not thinking about the whole formation. Those guys just flew their own aircraft and didn't take anybody else into consideration. But Captain MacGregor always thought ahead. He was always thinking about what was best for everyone behind him." The deputy glanced at the sky. "Like I said, when he was lead, we never got lost…never got left."

Jack raised an oscillating finger in front of his nose. "Comings. Now that I think about it, I *do* remember a Comings. And your pilot, Morisey, too." Jack nodded. Then he smiled with apparent recognition. "You were both pretty nervous, now that I recall."

Comings responded with his own nod of confirmation. "Yes, sir. With me mostly because I'd only had a few days training as a gunner and didn't really know my job yet. You sent Dutch to help me out, show me a trick or two." The Deputy smiled. "It helped. I gained some confidence along with some skill. Not long after that, the nerves wound down." He paused. "But what I wanted to tell you was this. That last day you led us. When we were getting pasted by all that ground-fire…we all wanted to turn back. I'd never been so scared in my life. But no one left formation. And I know why. Because *you* were lead...and all the pilots were used to trusting you, no matter how scared they were." Comings took a breath, then sighed it out. "But when the anti-aircraft got worse and everyone started taking hits one after another...things changed. I saw most of the pilots sending what looked to me like some fairly panicky hand signals to each other. Some actually wanted to turn back. But you waved them all off and gave us your final word, so to speak." He pantomimed a sort of vertical flat-handed signal that looked like someone chopping meat with a cleaver. "We were going to continue on through all that flak and proceed to target." Comings shook his head once...almost in slow motion. "That's when Captain Dubchek pulled the rug on you."

Jack looked genuinely puzzled. "Pulled the rug?"

"Yeah. He did the old head-pat, signaling the rest of the pilots that he was taking command of the flight. The ship on the other side of you was Captain Howard. He signaled to everyone on his side of the formation to follow Dubchek, and the next thing I knew everyone had executed a climbing right, 180 degree turn." Another head shake. "I know Morisey was thinking about peeling off from the rest and staying with you because he kept looking back toward you and Dutch. And I saw it in his face. He knew the whole thing wasn't right—letting you go on that way by yourself. But he was as new as I was, and he just didn't want to buck the senior officers on a judgment call like that. I saw you turn around even before Dutch could pass the word." He shrugged. "You watched us run away for about a second. Then you just faced forward again...and continued on to the target. I've thought about that for years, Captain." Now Comings turned to Carrie. "He knew he'd been left alone to do a job that had been planned for no less than fourteen bombers...and he went ahead with it, by himself, anyway." He paused. "Ma'am, I stayed in that war until the end—

November of 1918. And during all that time, I not only never saw anything as courageous as what the Captain and Dutch did—I never even *heard* of another crew doing anything like that!" He glanced quickly back at Adkins, then returned his attention to Jack. "I promised myself then that if I ever met you again, I would shake your hand and thank you for finishing the job we were all supposed to do." He thrust out a sturdy-looking hand, which Jack grasped and shook after a moment of hesitation. "Gutsiest decision I've ever witnessed, sir. It was an honor just to be there to see it."

They stood silent for almost two seconds, hands clasped, looking at each other with almost imperceptible smiles. Then, as if on cue, each man released his grip at almost the same moment. Then something unusual took place, something three of the four people standing there were not ready for. Comings took a short step back, locked his body into a feet-together rigid position of attention, and presented his old flight lead with the tight palm-down salute common only to veteran American warriors of the Great War. As Comings kept his hand poised against his forehead in ceremonial anticipation of the traditional response from a superior officer, Jack seemed a little taken aback and hesitated for just an instant before he duplicated the deputy's stance and returned the salute with a rapid-fire precision to match that of the younger man. It was only then, after Comings had dropped his arm and the debt of long-deserved honor had been paid, that both men appeared to relax a little, each nodding to the other and taking a long deep breath.

Carrie wanted to say something. She didn't know what, but something. She felt almost dumbstruck by what the veteran ex-gunner had said. According to him, Jack was the bravest, most honorable man he'd ever known. She had always thought Jack honest and not an obvious coward. But a hero? *That's just—true…apparently.* She looked to her husband with even newer eyes than she'd had when she'd arrived at the airfield. She swallowed big to overcome the dry throat that had resulted from a mouth that had obviously been agape longer than she'd realized. "Jack, you never told me any of this," she said, instantly mourning the inadequate sound of the statement. *My gosh! He deserves a testimonial speech and a ticker-tape parade...like Lindberg had after he flew the Atlantic! Not just you never told me!*

Jack glanced over his shoulder, then searched the surrounding ground, as if looking for an appropriate response. Finally he said, "It's what the dreams were about. You know." He almost winced. "I thought it best not to bring it up."

Comings stepped back so as to take in both Jack and Carrie at the same time. "We all knew you'd made it to the rail-yard and were able to release your payload. We could hear those munition boxcars exploding all the way back at the aerodrome. The first official report said that you and Dutch had been shot down right after. But then later we heard you were both alive and in the hospital. I could hardly believe it!" He took a long breath. "If you ever need anything, either of you, just call me...and I'll do whatever I can," he said. "It's the least I can do."

"Thank you." Jack sent a self-conscious glance Carrie's direction. Then he returned his attention back to Comings. "Say, what *is* your first name?" he said. "I think it's time I found that out. Don't you?"

"Yes, sir. It's Daniel—Dan to those who know me."

"All right then. Thanks, Dan. For everything."

"My pleasure, sir."

"Jack," the pilot said.

"Right. Jack. Good, then." Comings looked to Carrie as he touched the brim of his hat then sidestepped back to Adkins. "Mrs. MacGregor."

"Carrie."

"Right. Carrie it is." Comings put a firm grip on Adkins's elbow and turned him around toward the light. "You see anything in the last few minutes that bothers you, son?" he said.

"No," Adkins answered without expression.

"Good. Then let's go. We're done here." Comings cleared his throat, then led the younger deputy away.

Cal and the MacGregors stood there in the darkness of the taxiway until the sheriffs had walked back to their patrol car. In a few minutes, the officers drove away, disappearing into shadows far beyond the airfield lights. Then, as if on cue, the wife, the pilot, and the mechanic joined together in a collective sigh.

"Sorry if I was late with the mail thing, Boss." Cal doffed his cap. "I didn't pick up on what that first sheriff-bird was after 'til he pulls his gun out." Cal replaced the cap back onto his sparse scalp and shook his head. "Whoa, Nellie! I thought everything was about to go wrong by that time."

"Me, too." Jack raised both eyebrows and nodded.

"I didn't," Carrie said and gave Jack a quick hug. "I didn't think any such thing. We prayed for God's intervention on our behalf, and He came through for us. That's all. The Word says to trust Him...and we did." She shrugged. "It's as simple as that."

Jack smiled. "I guess it is." Then he looked off toward the lights of town. "I guess it really is."

Carrie stroked the back of her husband's neck just a little. "O.K., I breathed the big sigh of relief, too, when the deputies left. But that's just a habit the Lord hasn't broken me of yet. A little lack of trust in Him, that still hangs around." She paused a moment. "Here's what matters," she said. "God loves you, Jack. And he just proved it. I mean, good grief! What are the odds of someone you barely knew, but who obviously admires you, showing up in the middle of the desert ten years later? And that man is in charge of the investigation, no less!" She raised a righteous index finger skyward. "That, my dear husband, does not happen but by the intervention of a loving heavenly father, who thinks you're the greatest thing since sliced bread." Carrie lowered the finger and patted Jack's cheek. "God loves you to pieces, you dear, rare man." She lowered her eyes for a moment then looked up into her husband's face through long, moistening lashes. "As do I." She nestled her cheek onto his chest and just remained there for a while before speaking again. "So, are you really going to take the night-mail to San Fernando?"

Now it was Jack's turn to shrug. "I don't really know." He looked toward the mechanic. "Cal?"

The second man nodded. "You gotta' go now, Boss. I already give Clyde the night off 'cause I didn't know how long them sheriffs was gonna be here...and I didn't want two mail pilots to be showin' up for the same run with *them* here." He tilted his head and gave Jack his most clandestine expression. "Wouldn't look right. You know."

Jack looked down at Carrie's face. "I guess I'm taking the night pouch to San Fernando."

"Not to China?"

"Nope. Not to China."

Carrie gave him another gentle hug. "Do you want me to wait for you in town? The boys and I can take a couple of rooms at the inn. Henri has always *said* I could do that, if I wanted. Cal can call me when you get in and we'll all drive home together in the Stutz. The boys can ride in the rumble seat. That'll be a little bit of a treat for them since we hardly ever use it." She smiled. "We can do that, if you like."

"No. You all go on home. Cal can drop me off in the big truck when I get back. You don't mind do you, Cal?"

"Naw." Cal had already begun to drift in the direction of the hangar. "Say, Boss. I'm gonna get back to that

699

radiator mount on number three, if that's okay with you. Gotta have that finished by dawn, don't you know."

"That's fine, Cal," Jack and Carrie answered together just before their lips met.

In a moment, Jack turned his face toward his retreating mechanic. "Hey, Cal?"

"Yeah, Boss."

"Would you take my big flight bag out of my ship and put it behind the seat of the Stutz?" He kissed Carrie again. "I'm not going to be needing it after all."

"Sure thing, Boss. Whatever you say," Cal said before he ambled off toward the office.

Carrie snuggled up against Jack once more as he began a slow caressing of her hair. A soft sliver of diffused silver-white light had broken over the low hills to the east, as the tardy promise of a full moon at last began to rise from its hiding place beyond the horizon. Its luminescent majesty began to flood the night, causing some distant stars to fade in their splendor, but, on the whole, adding an almost holy beauty to all it touched, including Jack and Carrie.

"Oh." Jack made an unpleasant face—almost a wince. "Almost forgot. There's still the small problem of Sam's mortgage on the business. Not sure what to do about it. It'll be plenty rough making a profit with a saddle like that on our backs."

Carrie waited a moment, then smiled. "I think if you stay in prayer about it, the Lord will give you good advice." She paused again. "Maybe He'll send you a lot of passengers for your new Ryan."

"Maybe."

"Whatever happens, I believe God is with us." She snuggled some more. "And I don't believe He brought us this far simply to abandon us in the desert." She glanced up toward his face. "The important thing is that we're all together...you, me, the boys...and the Lord. Things will turn out right somehow if we trust Him. I know it."

"Yeah, I think so, too." Jack swung his attention to the big rising Lunar disk. "But I also think, sometime soon, I'm going to have to actually go fly that mail pouch to San Fernando."

Carrie tightened her hold. "I don't want to let go. It feels like everything will be all right as long as I don't let go."

"Really?"

"Yes. And to be honest, I think either being awake since three A.M. or having no supper is catching up with me also... because I seem to be going a little weak in the knees right now."

"Well, I've got a remedy for that," Jack said; then he bent down and scooped her off the ground and up into his arms. That's when he hugged her closer and stronger than he ever had before. And that's when she turned her face into his and kissed him again with like abandon.

After she had caught her breath, she kept her gaze locked onto her husband's countenance for several seconds; then she rested her cheek against Jack's shoulder and said, "So, you think you can carry me all the way back to the car, Ace?"

He smiled at the edgy style of her question, then turned toward the hangar and began an easy walk along the taxiway. "No sweat, Toots," he said, and didn't even break stride for the coyote that darted across his path.

Carrie saw the creature but did not startle at its suddenness. She only settled herself more deeply into Jack's arms and focused her attention on the moonlit creature escaping out into the tall dry desert grass. It stopped about twenty feet away and turned its head back around for one last look at the humans who had trespassed upon its territory. And in that instant, as the reflection of the airfield lights turned its eyes into burning coals, the coyote seemed to nod its head, not once, not twice, but three times, so that there could be no mistake in Carrie's mind that what she had seen had actually taken place and was not just some optical illusion. Then, all at once, the slender canine trotted off into the darkness, and Carrie moaned a pleasant moan of satisfaction.

Good touch, Lord, she thought to the emperor of the universe. *I think I'm beginning to love coyotes now, too.*